The Olive Higgins Prouty Omnibus

Start Publishing PD LLC

Manufactured in the United States of America

Cover art: Shutterstock/Taisiya Kozorez

Cover design: Jennifer Do

10 9 8 7 6 5 4 3 2 1

ISBN 979-8-8809-1883-6

The Olive Higgins Prouty Omnibus

Bobbie: General Manager
The Fifth Wheel
Stella Dallas

Bobbie: General Manager

CHAPTER I

I AM a junior in the H.C.H.S., which stands for Hilton Classical High School, and am sixteen years old. I live in a big brown house at number 240 Main Street, and my father is a state senator in Boston. I am a member of the First Congregational Church, which I joined when I was thirteen, and am captain of the basket-ball team at the high school. I have travelled as far east as Revere Beach, as far west as the Hoosac Tunnel, on my way to Aunt Ella's funeral in Adams, and as far south as New London, Connecticut, where I watched my oldest brother Tom row in a perfectly stunning eight-oared boat-race on the Thames. I haven't been north at all. I have had six diseases, including scarlet fever and typhoid, with which I almost died last year, and as a result of which am now wearing my hair as short as a child with a Dutch-cut.

I am not pretty, nor a bit popular with the boys. I can't play the piano, and I never went to dancing-school in my life. Most of my clothes are as ugly as mud, for I haven't any mother; and my hair has always been as straight as a stick. They say that the kink that has appeared in it since the typhoid won't last but a little while, so it isn't much comfort. In fact, the only real consolation that I have is a secret conviction which I keep well concealed in the innermost compartment of my heart. No one knows of its existence except myself, and I wouldn't be the one to tell of it for anything in the world. It is on account of it, however, that I am writing the experiences of my early life. I often think how valuable it would have been if William Shakespeare had told us about his school-days or Julius Caesar had described his family and what they used to do when he was a boy of fifteen. Of course I may not be a genius; but facts point that way. I hate mathematics, my imagination is vivid, my life is difficult and full of obstacles, and my handwriting illegible. My Themes are generally read out loud in English, and my quarterly deportment mark is frightfully low. Moreover, if I am not a genius I shall be awfully disappointed. Why, I think I should rather be a genius than to go to a College Prom. It makes everything so bearable, from a flunk in geometry, to not being invited to Bessie Jaynes' birthday-party last week.

My life has not been an easy one. Ever since I can remember I have been the mother of five children—two of them older and three younger than myself. They all call me Bobbie for short, but my real name is Lucy Chenery Vars.

Our house is a big ugly brown affair which Father built when we were all babies and the business was prosperous. The house has twenty rooms in it, and on the top an octagon cupola, which I have fixed up with a fish-net and some old tennis rackets, and call my study. I have a plaster cast of a skull up here, and a "No Trespassing" sign which Juliet Adams and I stole out of old Silas Morton's blueberry-pasture. It looks exactly like a college man's room now and I intend to do all my writing up here. It is a perfectly lovely place for inspirations! From my eight little windows I can see all over New England, and at night every star that shines. It is simply glorious up here in a thunder-storm, and when I have the trap-door once closed behind me, with all my cares and troubles shut safely away down below, I feel as if I could fly with the birds. I ought to write something wonderful.

In the first place I had better state that I haven't anything distinguishing about me except my experience. I am middling tall—five feet five inches, to be precise; middling heavy—112 pounds; and am one of six children—four boys and two girls—without the honour of being either the oldest or youngest. With Father there are seven of us; with Nellie and the cook (when we have one) and poor little Dixie, the horse, there are ten.

Father is a big, quiet, solemn man and is sixty-eight years old. He is president of the Vars & Company Woollen Mills, has perfectly white hair, and wears grey and white seersucker coats in the summer. Tom is the oldest and is in business out West. We're all awfully proud of Tom. He was a perfect star in college, and is making money hand over fist with his lumber camps in Michigan. Alec, the next to oldest, is struggling along in business with Father. Then I come, and next to me the twins—Oliver and Malcolm, aged fifteen and perfect terrors. Last is Ruthie; and after her, mother died and so there weren't any more. *I* was the mother then, and I was only a little over five. Father says he used to put me on the dictionary in mother's chair at the table when I was so little that Nellie had to help lift the big silver pot while I poured the coffee. Well, I've sat there ever since, pushed the bell, scowled at the twins and performed a mother's duty generally, as well as I knew how.

It hasn't been easy. Ruthie isn't the kind of little sister who likes to be petted or cuddled. The twins scorn everything I do or say. The house is a perfect elephant to run (there are thirty-three steps between the refrigerator and the kitchen sink) and our washings are something frightful. Alec says we simply can*not* afford a laundress, and the result is that I spend most of my Saturday mornings in intelligence-offices hunting cooks. Intelligence-offices are dreadful on inspirations.

Ever since I can remember, the house has been out of repair—certain doors that won't close, certain windows that have no shades, certain ceilings that are stained and smoked. It's hard to give the rooms the proper look when there are paths worn all over the Brussels carpet, exactly like cow-paths in a pasture, and the stuffed arms of the furniture in the parlour are worn as bare as the back of a little baby's head I once saw.

When Tom wrote that he was going to bring Elise, his young bride, whom we had never laid eyes on, to Hilton on their wedding trip, I nearly had a Conniption Fit. I thought Tom must have lost his mind. Any one ought to know what a shock our house would be to the kind of girl Tom would choose to marry. The concrete walk that leads up to the front door was dreadfully cracked, and the crevices were filled with a healthy growth of green grass. The iron fountain in the centre of the walk was as dry as a desert, and the four iron urns on the square porch as empty as shells. The ninety feet of elaborate iron fence that runs in front of the house needed a new coat of paint, and the little filigree iron edging, standing up like stiffly starched Hamburg embroidery around the top of the cupola, had a piece knocked out in front. But Tom *would* come, so I buckled down and made preparations.

I must explain a little about Tom. It isn't simply because he is the oldest son that we all look up to him so much. Every one in Hilton admires Tom. The *Weekly Messenger* refers to his "brilliant career," and the minister at our church calls him "an exceptional young man." He isn't a genius—he's too successful and everybody likes him too much for a genius—but he's different from the other young men in Hilton. When Father picked out some little technical school or other for Tom to go to, Tom announced that he was awfully sorry but that he had made up his mind to graduate from the biggest university in the country. And once there, Tom had a perfectly elegant time! Every one adored him. I saw him carried off once on the shoulders of a lot of shouting young men, who were singing his name. Why, I was proud to be Tom Vars' sister! He was captain of the crew, president of his class, a member of a whole lot of societies, and when he graduated his name was printed under the *magna cum laude* list on the programme (I can show it to you in my Souvenir Book) which meant that he was a perfect wizard in his lessons.

Tom graduated the year that Father's business began to look a little wobbly. Just when Father was looking forward, with a good deal of hope, to his oldest son's help and coöperation, Tom ran up home for over Sunday one day in May, and broke the news that after Commencement he had decided to accept a position from his room-mate's rich uncle in some wild and woolly lumber camps in Michigan. It just about broke poor Father's heart. He couldn't enjoy the honours of Tom's Commencement. But Tom went out West just the same—for Tom always carries out his plans—he went, smiling and confident, with never a single reference to Father's silence, ignoring absolutely the sad look in Father's eyes. He went just as if he were carrying out Father's dearest hope; and the funny part is, that inside of three years Tom had made Father so proud of his hard work and steady success that the poor dear man's disappointment faded away like mist before the sun, as they say in Shakespeare or the Bible—I forget which. The whole scheme worked like a charm, as Tom's schemes always do. There was faithful Alec to help Father; and the rich uncle, who had no son of his own, was simply aching to get hold of a fine, smart, clean young man like Tom Chenery Vars to boost up to success.

Whenever Tom had a holiday, except Christmas when he came home, he spent it in Chicago with his room-mate or the uncle. That is how he happened to fall in with such a lot of fashionable people—not that Tom ever boasted that his friends were fashionable, for Tom never blows his own horn—but I knew they were, just the same. He used to send stunning monograms to Ruthie and me for our collections, torn off from the notes which his wealthy young-lady friends wrote to him; besides, when he came home for Christmas he always had a pocketful of kodak pictures to show us of his life in the West. They weren't *all* taken in the lumber camps. Some were snapshots of house-parties, which he'd been on, and I assure *you*, I always took in the expensive background of these pictures—carved stone doorways, perfectly elegant houses, lawns kept like a park, and automobiles with chauffeurs sitting up as stiff as ramrods. I hadn't much doubt, when Tom wrote that he was engaged to be married to Miss Elise Hildegarde Parmenter, but that she was an inmate of one of these millionaire mansions, and I was absolutely convinced of it when I laid eyes on her photograph—one of those brown carbons a foot square—and counted the six magnificent plumes on her big drooping picture-hat. I knew that 240 Main Street, Hilton, Mass., would look pretty worn and dingy alongside Sunny-lawn-by-the-Lake, which was engraved in gold letters and hyphens at the top of Miss Parmenter's heavy grey note-paper.

The minute Tom wrote that he was going to bring his elegant bride to Hilton I button-holed Father and Alec one day after dinner, and told those two men that the house had simply *got* to be done over. It was disgraceful as it was; it hadn't been painted since I could remember; it was unworthy of our name. Father reminded me that the reason none of us went to the wedding (Tom was married in California, on Elise's father's orange ranch) was to save expense, as I already knew, and merely to paint the house would cost the price of a ticket or two.

"Let us be ourselves, Lucy," said Father to me, "*ourselves*, child. If Tom's wife is the right kind of woman, she will look within, *within*, Lucy."

"Oh," I said, "but the inside is worse than the out, Father. The wall-paper in the guest-room—"

Father interrupted me gently.

"Within our hearts," he corrected, touching his heavy gold watch-chain across his chest. "Within our hearts, Lucy."

Father is a perfectly splendid man, but I knew that spotless hearts wouldn't excuse smoked ceilings; and when, the next day being Sunday, I saw Father drop his little white sealed envelope, which I knew contained five perfectly good dollars, into the contribution box, I didn't believe any heathen girl needed that money more than I.

I am going to tell about that first appearance of Elise's in detail. But it's got to be after dinner, for fifteen minutes ago the big whistle on Father's factory spurted out its puff of white steam (I could see it from my north window before I heard the blast) and Father and Alec will soon be driving up the hill in the phaeton, with the top down and the reins slack over faithful Dixie's back. I must be within calling-distance when Father strikes the Chinese gong at the foot of the stairs. It's the first thing he always does when he enters the house at noon. We all recognise his two strokes on each one of the three notes as surely as his voice or step. Why, that ring of Father's simply speaks! It is as full of impatience as a motorman ringing for a truck to get off the track.

Father hates to wait for dinner. By the time he has taken off his overcoat, and scrubbed up in the wash-room off the hall, he likes us all to be seated at the table when he comes into the dining-room. "Hello, chicken," he says to me. "Hello, baby," to Ruth. (He calls Dixie "baby" too.) "Hello, boys," to the twins. Then he sits down at the head of the table, opposite me, clears his throat as a signal, and asks the blessing.

Father's blessing is always the same except when we have company. I can tell how important the company is by the length of Father's prayer. When Juliet Adams, my best friend, drops in for supper, she is served the regular everyday family blessing, but when we have company important enough to put on the best dishes, or at the first meal that Tom is with us, Father keeps at it so long that the twins get to fooling with each other under cover of the tablecloth. I wished Father would omit the blessing entirely when Elise came, and family prayers too. They're so old-fashioned nowadays; but I knew better than to suggest such a preposterous thing. Father is a member of the Standing Committee at our church, and has a lot of principles.

There he is coming now! I wish he could afford a new carriage. I'm simply dying for one of those sporty little red-wheeled runabouts!

CHAPTER II

AMONG the first things I did in preparation for Elise's visit was to set the twins to work on the lawn, and Ruthie to clearing up a rubbishly-looking place back of the barn where there was a pile of old boxes and barrel hoops.

I myself harnessed up Dixie, made a trip to the country, and brought back three bushel-baskets full of rock ferns from the woods. Juliet Adams helped me fill the iron urns the next day. I know very well that red geraniums, hanging vines, and a little palm in the centre are the correct plants for urns (there's a painting of one on the garden scenery at our theatre here in Hilton) but as geraniums are a dollar and a quarter a dozen, and the urns are perfectly enormous, I knew that such luxuries could not be afforded. I also knew that it was out of the question to work the fountain. I cleared out its collection of leaves, soused it well with the hose, and was obliged to leave it in the middle of the walk, out of commission, but at least clean. The tennis-court, which hadn't been used for tennis for ten years, had now passed even the potato-patch era and was a perfect mass of weeds. I paid the twins five cents each for mowing it twice, and then set out the croquet set with a string. I put a fresh coat of white paint on the wickets, and though the ground was far too uneven for any practical use, the general effect at a distance was not bad at all.

I spent two solid afternoons in the stable sweeping and cleaning as if my life depended on it. We don't keep a man now. Dixie is the only horse we own, and Alec does all the feeding and rubbing-down that Dixie gets. Poor little Dixie, rattling around in one of the big box stalls, can't give the place the proper air. It's a stunning stable—stalls for eight horses and a big room filled with all sorts of carriages. They are dreadfully out of style now (I used to play house in them when I was ten and they had begun their dust gathering even then), but Father says they were the best that could be bought in their day. I pinned the white sheets that cover them down around their bodies as closely as I could, so that Miss Parmenter couldn't see how out-of-date the dear old arks were. I cleaned up all the harnesses and hung them up, black and shining, on the wooden pegs. In an old sleigh upstairs I discovered a girl's saddle, which I dusted and hung up in plain view by the whip-rack; there's something so sporty about horseback riding! I was bound to have Miss Parmenter know that at one time we were prosperous.

But most of my efforts of course went into the house. It was terribly discouraging. We own loads of black walnut, and though I begged and begged for a brass bed for the guest-room, Father was adamant. He had allowed me to have the room repapered and *that*, he said, was all that I must ask for. The new paper really was lovely. I picked it out myself, pink roses on a light blue ground and a plate-rail half-way up.

I spent a lot of pains on the guest-room, carrying out the pink and blue colour-scheme in every possible detail. I took the light blue rose bowl off the mantel in the sitting-room and put it on the bureau, for hatpins. I rehung my "Yard of Pink Roses" over the guest-room mantel. My blue kimono I had freshly laundered and hung it up in the closet. A pair of pink bedroom slippers were carefully placed beneath. I found a book in the library bound in pink, entitled "Baby Thoughts," and put it on the marble-topped guest-room table alongside a magazine and my work-basket on which I had sewed a huge blue bow and inside of which I had placed my solid gold thimble. I also tied a smashing pink and blue rosette on the waste-basket; and the half-dozen coat-hangers which I was able to scare up out of Alec's and Father's closets Ruthie wound with pink and blue ribbons. I didn't neglect the more necessary details either. I paid thirty-five cents for a cake of pink French soap; and the only embroidered towels we own I strung along in a showy row on the back of the commode. In the tooth-brush holder I placed a sealed Prophylactic tooth-brush, which I read in the *Perfect Housekeeper* should be found in every nicely appointed guest-room; nor did I overlook the Bible, and candle and matches by the bed. The *Perfect Housekeeper* says that it is the little touches in your home, such as a fresh bunch of flowers on the shelf in your guest-room, or in cold weather a hot-water bag between the sheets, that count with a guest. I was dreadfully sorry that it was too warm for hot-water bottles.

I was in perfect despair about Nellie. Nellie is our second-girl and has been with us for years. Nellie doesn't look a bit like a servant. She has grey hair and wears glasses. People are always mistaking her for an aunt. I wrote out a set of rules for Nellie, tacked them up over the sink in the butler's pantry, and told her to study them during the week before Tom and Elise were due to arrive. Here's a copy of them:

Rule 1 When a meal is ready don't stand at the foot of the stairs and holler "Dinner!" Come to me and say in a low, well modulated voice, "Dinner is served, Miss Lucy."

Rule 2 Be sure and call me *Miss* Lucy, and Tom, *Mister* Tom. Never plain Tom or plain Lucy. And so on through the family.

Rule 3 When I ring the bell during a meal, don't just stick your head in through the swinging-door but enter all-over and find out what is wanted.

Rule 4 Don't offer a last biscuit or piece of cake and say, "There's more in the kitchen."

Rule 5 If any member of the family asks for any other member of the family, don't say, "They're in the barn, or down-cellar, or upstairs," but go quietly and find them yourself.

Rule 6 Be sure and put ice-water every night into Mrs. Vars' bedroom when you turn down the bed.

Rule 7 If you get the hiccups when waiting on the table, withdraw to the kitchen immediately and take ten swallows of water.

Nellie is a good-natured old soul. I can manage her beautifully, but it took a head to do anything with Delia. Delia was the cook. I was in the butler's pantry the day before Tom and Elise arrived, putting away the family napkin-rings (for of course I know napkin-rings are tabooed) when it occurred to me that we had got to have clean napkins for every meal as long as Elise stayed. If she was with us a week that would make a hundred and sixty-eight napkins in all, counting three meals a day and eight people at the table. We owned just four dozen napkins and that meant—I figured it all out on a piece of paper—that the whole four dozen would have to be washed every other day. I went out into the kitchen and explained it to Delia just as nicely and sweetly as I could. She went off on a regular tangent. It was enough, she said, all the extra style I was planning on, without piling on a week's washing for every other day. She said she'd never heard of such tommyrot, and if a napkin was clean enough for Tom and Tom's family, she guessed it was clean enough for Tom's wife, whoever she was. I was simply incensed!

"We won't discuss it," I said with much dignity. "Not another word, please, Delia," and I left the kitchen.

I heard her slam a kettle into the iron sink, and mutter something about "another place," so I thought it better policy not to press my point. I hate being imposed upon—there isn't a teacher at the high school who can talk Lucy Vars into a hole—but I wasn't going to cut off my own nose. So I went straight to the telephone, called up a dry goods store and ordered ten dozen medium-priced napkins to be sent up special. All the rest of the afternoon I sat at the sewing-machine hemming like mad, and Nellie folded the things so that the machine stitches wouldn't show. I knew that napkins should be hemmed by hand.

Tom and Elise were due at eight o'clock on a Wednesday night. I had it planned that Father and Alec would meet them at the station and I would remain at the house to greet them as they came in. I wished awfully that we had a coachman and some decent horses, but I begged Father to hire a carriage and he promised that he would. The suspense while I waited for them to drive up over the hill was as awful as when I've been sent for by the principal at the high school—kind of thrilly inside and as nervous as a cat. I walked from room to room like a caged animal, trying to imagine how the old house would look to a person who hadn't lived in it forever. I lit the open fire in the hall, arranged the books on the sitting-room table for the hundredth time, and watched the piano-lamp like a hawk. It smokes the ceilings if you leave it alone.

The twins, Oliver and Malcolm, stationed themselves in the parlour to keep watch of the road. About half-past eight Oliver hollered out, "They're coming, Bobbie!" and I went out into the hall and opened the door. I saw the big bulky old depot carriage draw up to the curbing out beyond the iron fountain, and I whispered to the twins, "Go down and help with their bags!" They pushed by me; and a minute after, everybody was in a confused bunch in the vestibule—Oliver and Malcolm with the suitcases, Father and Alec, Ruthie hanging on to my skirt, and finally Tom, big and handsome and natural!

"Hello, Bobbie, old girl," he said. "Hello, little Ruthiemus!" And suddenly behind him Elise appeared—tall, pale as a lily, quiet, and very calm. "Well, here they all are, Elise," Tom went on lustily, "Malcolm and Oliver, and Bobbie who is the mother of us, and Ruthiemus the baby."

Elise came forward, shook hands with the boys, and when she came to me she kissed me. I'd never been so near such a perfectly gorgeous Irish-lace jabot in my life. After she had leaned down and kissed Ruth she said in the quietest, lowest voice I ever heard, while we all stared, "I know you all, already, for Chenery has told me all about you."

Chenery! How perfectly absurd! No one ever calls Tom anything but just plain Tom. We all have Chenery for a middle name—it was mother's before she was married—but it is only to sign. After that remark about Chenery the silence was simply deathly, but Alec, who always comes to the rescue, exclaimed, "Don't you people intend to stop with us to-night? Usher us in, Bobbie."

There was none of the Vars hail-fellow-well-met, slap-you-on-the-back spirit about that evening. We all distributed ourselves in a circle about the sitting-room, exactly like a Bible-class at church, and talked in the stiffest, most formal way imaginable. I don't know why we couldn't be natural; but Elise, sitting there so perfectly at ease, smiling and talking so gracefully made us feel like country bumpkins before a princess. I was furious at her for making us appear in such a light. Why couldn't Tom have married somebody like ourselves, some jolly good sport who wouldn't be afraid to hurt her clothes? I knew Elise Hildegarde Parmenter's style. She wore some of those high-heeled shoes, like undressed kid gloves, and her feet were regular pocket editions. If we had acted as we usually do when Tom comes home, all talking and laughing at once, we'd have shocked this delicate little piece of china into a thousand bits.

I was dreadfully surprised at Tom when he said, as if Elise was not there, "Come on, Bobbie, bring in the apples."

You see it is one of our customs, the first night that Tom comes home, to sit up awfully late and eat apples, Father paring them with an old kitchen knife. But of course I wasn't going to have apples to-night, of all times, passed around in quarters on the end of a knife. So I said to Tom as quietly as possible, for really I was catching Elise's manner, "Not apples to-night, Tom. I ordered a little chocolate. I'll speak to Nellie." I had gotten out our best hand-painted violet chocolate cups, told Delia to make some cocoa and whip some cream, and had opened a fresh package of champagne wafers. Everything was all ready on a tray in the dining-room, so I went out and told Nellie to bring it in. When she appeared holding the big tray out before her I had to bite my tongue to keep from laughing. Nellie had never worn a cap before and it didn't seem to go with her style. It was sticking straight up on the top of her grey pug of hair like a bird on the tip end of a flag pole. I saw Malcolm and Oliver begin to giggle. I squelched them with a look and began stirring my chocolate hard.

"Hello, Nellie," said Tom, when the tray reached him, and though I'd cautioned Nellie a hundred times to address Tom as *Mister* Tom, she got it mixed up in some stupid fashion, and replied, "How do you do, Mister Vars," and Father who heard her come out with his name asked, "Did you speak to me, Nellie?" Nellie replied, "No, I didn't. I was speaking to Tom."

Late that first night, as I was turning out my light, and after I had set my alarm-clock for quarter of six (for I thought I'd better get up early and see how things were running) Malcolm and Oliver pushed open my door and came in. Behind them was Alec on his way to bed.

"Hello, Bobbie," they said, grinning.

"Close the door," I whispered, and then I wrapped myself up in a down comforter and crawled up on the bed. My brothers came over and all sat down around me.

"Well," I said, "what do you think of her?"

"Did you see the diamond pendant?" Malcolm began. "It was a ripper!"

"Tom gave her that for a wedding-present," Oliver explained.

"He did!" I was amazed. "Plain Tom slinging around diamond pendants like that!"

"He'll have to, to live up to being called Chenery. Did you get on to that?"

"Did I? Isn't it too silly? I hate such airs! We stand for good plain things and why couldn't Tom get something plain?"

"Oh, she's a blue-blood," said Oliver. "We're regular Indians beside her."

"No, we're not, Oliver Vars," I flared back. "Don't you say that. I shan't eat humble-pie for any one. We're just as good as she is. It's brains that count."

"I bet a dollar she couldn't throw a ball straight; and she looks as if she'd be afraid of the dark," said Malcolm.

"Oh, come ahead, you young knockers," interrupted Alec, who hadn't said a word till now—Alec never says much and when he does it's always nice—"Come along to bed, and let the General-manager here get a little rest. Good-night, Bobbie," he said, coming up to me and giving me a little good-natured shove, so that I toppled over on the bed. Oliver and Malcolm each grabbed a pillow.

"Good-night, angel," they sang out as they lammed them at me hard. I heard them dash out of the room and slam the door with a bang. Nice old brothers! We Vars never waste much time in kissing, but we understand all right.

The next morning I was down in the kitchen before Delia had her fire made. About eight o'clock when we were all flaxing around as fast as we could there suddenly broke out upon us a very queer noise. It sounded like a cat trying to meow when it had a dreadful cold. It startled me awfully and Delia gave a terrible jump.

"For the love of Mike, what's that?" said she.

I investigated, and after a little, I discovered the cause. Years ago we had some sort of a bell system that connected with all the rooms, with an indicator in the kitchen. We hadn't used it for a long time and I supposed the whole system was as dilapidated as the stable. Whenever we wanted Nellie for anything we found it easier to go to the back stairs and holler. It occurred to me that the electrician who had put in some new batteries the week before, for the front door bell, which before Elise came was dreadfully unreliable, must have monkeyed with the other bells too.

"Elise has rung for you," I said to Nellie, thankful with all my heart that the old thing had worked. I knew that Tom was already downstairs, so of course wasn't there to tell her that the old push-button didn't mean a thing, and I was glad of that. Heaven knew there was enough else to apologise for.

When Nellie came back I asked, "What did she want?"

"She wanted me to button up her waist and also to give me her laundry."

"Laundry!" gasped Delia. I never could understand why cooks hate washing so.

"Yes," I said, turning to her, "laundry! I told Mrs. Vars," I went on with much authority, "to put any soiled clothing she might have in a pink and blue bag which I made to match the guest-room, for this express purpose—for her to put her laundry in. That's only hospitality." I crossed the room. "And now you may put breakfast on, Delia," I finished, and went out.

After breakfast Nellie came to me and said, "Delia wishes to speak to you in the kitchen."

My heart sank. I left Elise in the sitting-room talking in her lovely soft way to Father and Alec. Delia was in the laundry standing by a regular haystack of lacy lingerie. She was holding up the most superb lace skirt I ever saw, rows upon rows of insertion and if you'll believe me made every inch by hand.

"I just wanted to say," she began, "that I don't stay if I have to wash these. They aren't dirty, in the first place, and what's more I'm not hired to wash company's clothes, and what's more I won't. And what's more still, I think you better hunt for another girl."

I couldn't have received more depressing news. I hated being ruled by a cook, and I hated to let her go. I didn't have a soul to ask about it. I didn't know what to do. I flared right up.

"The washing must be done," I said sternly. "*That's* settled."

Delia dropped the skirt.

"All right. I'll do the washing to-day," she announced, "and I'll leave to-morrow."

I just wanted to sit down and cry and cry and say, "O please be nice about it and help us out. Please stay! O please, please, *please!*" But I did no such thing. I bit my lip hard and replied, "Very well," and when I joined the others in the sitting-room, I was apparently as undisturbed as a summer's breeze.

Things got no better as time went on. Elise didn't fit into our family a bit. None of us was natural. Father didn't ring the gong when he came in at noon and call up to me, "Slippers, chicken"; the twins didn't fool under the tablecloth and call me "Snodgrass," "Angel" or "Trolley" (because of my shape); Alec didn't tilt back on the hind legs of his chair after dessert, with his hands shoved down in his pockets; Ruthie didn't practice a note on the piano; even Tom was different. At first he tried to whoop things up in the old Vars fashion, but he gave it up after an attempt or two. We wouldn't respond. We balked like stubborn horses, while all the time Elise kept right on being very sweet and charming, but, oh my, cold and far away.

Her tact got on my nerves. I realised that she was trying to be nice, but her appreciation of everything made me tired. Of course she had seen grander houses than ours and yet she pretended to enthuse over our old-fashioned mantels. "What fine woodwork in them," she'd say to Father, "and what beautiful mahogany in those sliding-doors!" or, as she gazed at our ornate black walnut bookcase, she would remark, "Black walnut is becoming so popular!" Once she exclaimed, "How many books you have!" and her eyes were resting on a row of black-bound town records Father insists on keeping. When she and I attempted a miserable game of croquet she remarked, "I think it is more fun having the ground a little uneven." Heavens, I would have loved her if she had blurted out, "Say, this is rotten! Let's not play." I despise insincerity.

CHAPTER III

ONE day at dinner (I've forgotten whether it was the first or second day of Elise's visit, but anyhow it was before the ice was broken) Father suggested that Tom take the new member of our family for a drive in the afternoon with Dixie (he and Alec, could go out to the factory by electrics), so as soon as Elise went upstairs to rest, as she always did after dinner, I escaped to the barn, to hitch up. Alec doesn't have much time to devote to Dixie and I gave that poor little animal such a currying as he had never had before in his life.

Then I drew up the check two holes higher, dusted out the phaeton, and put in the best yellow plush robe and lash whip.

Elise and Tom got back about half-past six. I was in the sitting-room when Elise came into the house.

"Chenery has been showing me all the sights," she said. "I think Hilton is lovely. I told Chenery we were staying too long. I'm afraid we're late for dinner. But I'll hurry. It won't take me ten minutes to dress."

Dinner indeed! I wondered if she called the layout we had at noon just lunch. We've always had supper at night and I hadn't intended changing for Elise. But if she'd gone upstairs to dress for it, I'd got to prepare something besides tea, sliced meat and toast, for all the trouble she was taking. I flew to the kitchen. We had a can of beef-extract, and I told Delia to make soup out of that. Then I sent Ruth for some beefsteak, hauled down a can of peas for a vegetable, and the sliced oranges which were already prepared would have to do for dessert. I rushed to my room, put on my best light blue cashmere and laid out Ruth's white muslin.

It was, after all, on the first day of Elise's visit that she took that drive with Dixie, for *this*, I remember now, was the first evening meal that she had had with us. An awful catastrophe took place during the ordeal too. In the first place, having dinner at night added to the strain the family were all under, and it may have been due to the general atmosphere of uneasiness that made Nellie so stupid and careless. I don't know how it happened, but when she was passing the crackers to Elise, during the soup course, her cap got loose somehow and fell cafluke on Elise's bread-and-butter plate. There was an instant of dead quiet, and then Oliver, who just at that moment happened to have his mouth full of soup, exploded like a rubber ball with water in it. He shoved back his chair with a jerk, and coughing and choking into his napkin, got up and left the room. Of course that sent Malcolm off into a regular spasm, and little Ruth began to giggle too. I could feel myself growing as red as a beet, but I didn't laugh. No one laughed outright.

Elise was the first one to break the pause, and this is what she said:

"I've had the loveliest drive this afternoon," and then as no one replied she went on, "Chenery took me around the reservoir. How old are the ruins of that old mill at the upper end?"

Perhaps you think that that was a very graceful way of treating the situation, but I didn't. We were all simply dying to laugh. We couldn't think of old mills with that cap sticking on Elise's butter. However, I heard Father at the other end of the table making some sort of an answer to Elise, and all of us managed to control themselves somehow or other. Nellie, red in the face, carried the bread-and-butter plate away; Oliver sneaked back into his place; and I slowly began to cool off. But of course it spoiled the meal for me.

As soon after the horrible occurrence as possible, I escaped up here to my cupola, and Tom found me here before he went to bed. I knew he must be disappointed at the way I was running things. I hadn't been alone with him before, and when his head pushed up through the trap door and he asked, "You here?" I didn't answer. I was sitting in the pitch dark on the window-seat, but Tom must have seen my shadow for he came up and stood beside me. He remained perfectly silent for a minute then he said, "Aren't there a lot of stars out to-night!"

"Oh, Tom," I burst out, "I'm so sorry! Wasn't it awful? Everything's going all wrong."

He sat down.

"It's all right, Bobbie," he said quietly. "Only I wish Elise might see us as we really are. *Then*," he added, "you would see Elise as *she* really is."

Tom didn't ask me how I liked her (he knew better than to do that), and suddenly I felt sorry for my brother. I could have almost cried, not because of the accident at dinner, not because of my failure, but because Elise hadn't made us like her. I did so want Tom's wife to be the same bully sort of person Tom was.

The crisis came the next day. At eleven o'clock in the morning, I found Delia putting on her coat and hat, actually preparing to go.

"What does this mean?" I exclaimed.

"Can't you see?" she asked very saucily.

"But the washing. Have you—"

"No, I haven't, and what's more I'm not going to." She was spitting mad.

I stood there, just helpless before her.

"I have telephoned to all the intelligence offices," I said, "and I can't get anyone to come until Saturday night. I thought, to accommodate us, you might be willing—"

She cut me right off:

"Well, I'm not! No one accommodates me here, and I'm not used to being treated like this. Two dinners a day and up until all hours!"

It didn't seem to me as if she had half so much to stand as I did. I wished I could up and clear out too. I thought she was very disagreeable to leave me in the lurch that way. But I didn't have any words with her. I told her she might go as soon as she pleased. I hated the sight of her standing there in the kitchen, which she had left all spick and span, not as a kitchen should look at eleven in the morning with half a dozen full-grown mouths to be fed at one o'clock.

I was on my way upstairs to break the news to Nellie when Elise called to me from the sitting-room.

"Oh, Lucy," she said in her musical voice, "will there be time for me to run over to the postoffice with some letters before lunch?"

I stalked into the sitting-room. She was sitting at the desk in her graceful easy way, with a beautiful French hand-embroidered lingerie waist on, that I'd be glad to own for very best. There were gold beads about her neck, and her hair, even in the morning, was soft and fluffy and wavy. She had her feet crossed and I took in the silk stockings and the low dull-leather pumps.

I had a sudden desire to tear down all her beautiful appearance of ease and grace.

"We don't have lunch at noon," I said bluntly. "We have dinner, just dinner. We've always had dinner."

"Yes, I know," she began in her persistently pleasant way; "people do very often, in New England."

I couldn't bear her unruffled composure.

"Oh," I said, bound to shock her, "it isn't because we're New England. It's because we're plain, plain people. The rich families in New England as well as anywhere, have dinner at night. But *we*," I said, glorying in every word, "are *not* one of the rich families. We have doughnuts for breakfast, baked beans and brown bread Saturday nights, and Saturday noons a boiled dinner.

We love pie. We all just *love it*. Father came from a farm in Vermont. He didn't have any money at all when he started in. You see we're common people. And so's Tom. Tom comes from just a common, common, *common* family," I said, loving to repeat the word.

She was sitting with her arm thrown carelessly over the back of the chair, and her gaze way out of the west window. When I stopped to see what effect my words had had she just laughed—a quiet pleased laugh—and mixed up with it I heard her say, "Why, Chenery is the most uncommon man I ever met." And she blushed like eighteen.

I went right on.

"We don't call him Chenery, either," I said. "We cut off all such fringes. He's plain Tom to us. I know how the plain way we live must impress *you*. I know you've been used to French maids, and push-a-button for everything you want. I'm sorry for the shock you must have got coming here. But you might as well wake up to the truth. You see what a mess the house is in, and how Nellie won't call us Mister and Miss, and how if she is on the third floor and she wants me she just yells. And," I said, pointing out of the window, "there goes Delia now. And there isn't a sign of a cook left in the house."

Elise sat up straight.

"Is she leaving without notice?" she exclaimed.

"Naturally," I laughed.

"How dreadfully unkind of her!"

"That's what I think, but Delia doesn't care if I do."

"Haven't you some one to help you out? What will you do?" Elise was really excited.

"Do?" I replied grimly. "Oh, I'll duff in and cook myself, I suppose."

Elise put down her pen.

"I can make delicious desserts," she said. "Can't you telephone to the family not to come home this noon? We can be ready for them by to-night. I know how to make the best cake you ever tasted in your life."

That's the way it came about. I took her out into the kitchen and didn't try to cover up a thing. She could see everything exactly as it was—smoked kitchen ceiling, uneven kitchen floor, paintless pantry shelves. She could go to the bottom of the flour barrel if she wanted to; and she did. Covered with an old apron and her sleeves rolled up, she was first in the kitchen pantry looking into every cupboard, drawer or bucket for powdered sugar; next in the fruit-closet feeling all the paper bags, in search of a lemon; then calling to me in her musical voice to come here and taste some dough to see if it needed anything else; in the butler's pantry choosing just the plate she wanted for her cookies; and actually underneath the sink, pulling out a greasy spider for panouchie, which she was going to make out of some lumpy brown sugar she discovered in a wooden bucket. I took grim pleasure in having her see the worst there was. I wondered if she could stand the fact that we didn't own an ice-cream freezer, when she suggested ice-cream for dessert, nor possess a drop of olive oil for her mayonnaise. I didn't care. I liked telling her the things we didn't have. When I heard her burst into laughter in the butler's pantry, and pushing open the swinging-door, saw her gazing at my set of rules tacked up over the sink for Nellie, I made no explanation whatsoever. I was delighted to have her read them. At sight of me she went off into regular peals.

Finally she gasped, with her finger on Rule 6, "She put—the ice—in a hunk, in the big pitcher in the wash-bowl!" and the tears ran down her cheeks.

I laughed a little then in spite of myself.

"Nellie's an old fool," I said and went back to my work.

It happened that Father and Alec had gone to Boston for the day on business, and the last minute Tom had joined them, so the men wouldn't be home until night anyhow. I called up the twins, just before their fifth-hour period (I had cut school myself) and told them to get a bite to eat at the high school lunch-counter. "I'll pay for it," I assured them, for I knew the twins would jump at the chance of a free spread, and as they had manual-training that afternoon, Elise and I were safe from any interruption from the male section.

We had supper at half-past six as usual. It was very queer about that meal. The awful strain we had all felt the same day at breakfast had suddenly disappeared. Elise had suggested that we shouldn't tell any one of Delia's departure, and on the outside everything was just as it was in the morning, even to Nellie's ridiculous cap.

"These biscuits are good, Lucy," Father said suddenly, as he reached for the plate. Father usually speaks of the food, but he hadn't done so once since Elise had come.

"There's more in the kitchen," announced Nellie blandly.

"There's a whole panful," added Elise. "I'm awfully glad you like them!" she exclaimed and then stopped short.

"There," I said, "I knew you'd let the cat out. Elise made them!" I announced.

"Delia's left–" Elise hurried to say.

"And we–" I put in.

"We got supper!" she finished proudly.

"*You* and Bobbie?" exclaimed Alec.

"Bobbie and *you*?" gasped Tom.

"Of course!" she said. "Bobbie scallopped the oysters."

"Give me some more," said Malcolm.

"Fling over the last biscuit," sang out Oliver. And in a flash Elise picked up the little brown ball and tossed it across the fern-dish straight as an arrow.

"Good shot!" said Oliver, catching it in both hands.

"Oh," piped up Ruthie, "make Malcolm stop. He took a cookie and it isn't time for them."

Father just chuckled, and said, "Pretty good! pretty good!" And I tell you it was simply glorious to be natural again!

"Don't eat too much," said Elise, "for dessert's coming and it's awfully good."

"And chocolate layer-cake with it!" said I.

"Oh, bully!" shouted Malcolm and Oliver together.

"Say," asked Alec, "isn't this a good deal better than last night when Nellie's cap fell into your butter?"

We all burst into sudden laughter and Nellie, who was filling the glasses, had to set down the pitcher. She was shaking with mirth. We laughed until it hurt; we simply roared; and suddenly Elise gasped, when she was able to get her breath:

"Wasn't it funny? I was so frightened by you all then, I didn't know what to say about that old cap. But now–O dear!" and suddenly she turned to

Ruth who sat next to her, put her arms around her and kissed her. "Oh, Ruthie," she exclaimed, "isn't it *nice* to know them all!" And I couldn't tell whether the tears in her eyes were from laughing or crying.

We stayed up late that night.

"Run and get my slippers," said Father to Ruth after supper; and all the evening he lay back in his chair and watched us children while we sang college songs to Elise's ripping accompaniment; and poked fun at the twins because they'd just bought their first derbies. It was eleven-thirty when we went up to bed.

"Come here a minute, Bobbie," whispered Elise to me, and I went into the guest-room. "Do unhook the back of this dress." When I had finished she said, "I'll be down at six-thirty" (we were going to get breakfast too), "and don't you dare to be late! I'm going to make the omelet. You can make the johnny-cake. Bobbie, isn't it nice Delia left?" And she kissed *me* as well as Ruth.

That night the boys all gathered in my room again. I wrapped up in the down comforter, and we were just beginning to talk when Tom appeared.

"Hello," he said, smiling all over. He came in and closed the door. "Well," he asked, "what do you think of her?" And I knew he asked us because he so well knew what we did think. But just the same I wanted to tell him.

I shot out my bare skinny arm at him.

"Tom," I said, "I think she's a corker!"

He first took my hand and then suddenly, very unlike the Vars, he put both arms around me tight.

"Bobbie," he said in a kind of choked voice, "you're a little brick!"

And, my goodness, I just had to kiss Tom then!

CHAPTER IV

IT has been nearly a whole year since I have written in this book of mine. I've been too discouraged and heart-sick even to drag myself up here into my cupola. I've aged dreadfully. I've been disillusioned of all the hopes and dreams I ever had in my life. I've skipped that happy period called girlhood, skipped it entirely, and I had hoped *awfully* to go to at least one college football game before I was grey. I am sitting in my study. It is a lovely day in spring. There are white clouds in the sky, young robins in the wild cherry, but *my* youth, *my* schooldays, *my* aspirations are all over and gone.

Miss Wood said to me one day last winter—Miss Wood is my Sunday-school teacher and was trying to be kind—"You know, Lucy, it is a law of the universe for us all to have a certain amount of trouble before we die. Some have it early, some late. Now *you*, dear, are having your misfortunes when you are young. Just think, later they will all be out of your way." Miss Wood hasn't had a bit of her share of trouble yet. Why, she has a mother, a father, a fiancé, and a bunch of violets every Sunday. She has perfectly lovely clothes, a coachman to drive her around, and was president of her class her senior year in college. Such blessings won't be half as nice, and Miss Wood knows it, when I'm old and grey. I just simply hate having all my troubles dealt out to me before my skirts touch the ground.

Our minister said to me that misfortune is the greatest builder of character in the world. Well, it hasn't worked that way with me. I'm hot-tempered and have an unruly tongue; I don't love a soul except my brother Alec; and the only friend I have in the world is Juliet Adams. I'm not even a genius—I've discovered that—and my religious beliefs are dreadfully unsettled. Years ago I used to lie awake at night and imagine myself in deep sorrow. I was always calm and sweet and dignified then, beautiful and stately in my clinging black, and near me always was a young man, a strong, handsome, clean-shaven young man in riding clothes (I adore men in riding clothes) and I used to play that this man was the son of the governor of the state. Strange as it might seem, he was in love with me and when my entire family had suddenly been killed in a railroad accident—I always had them *all* die—this man came to me in my lonely house and told me of his devotion. It really made sorrow beautiful. But let me state right here that that was one of the many empty dreams of my youth. When misfortune *did* swoop down upon me, I was not sweet and lovely, there was no man within a hundred miles to understand and sympathise, there was nothing beautiful about it. It was just plain hard and bitter. It's only in books that trouble is romantic.

Elise visited us in the spring a year ago about this time (it seems like a century to me) and my misfortunes began to pour in the following fall, when

I was a senior, and seventeen years old. That last year of high school had started in to be a very happy one for me. Father had finally allowed me to go to dancing-school; mathematics was a bugbear of the past; and our basket-ball team was a perfect winner.

I loved dancing-school. It came every Saturday night from eight to ten, and Juliet Adams used to call for me in her closed carriage and drop me afterwards at my door. I remember that on that last Saturday night I was particularly full of good-feeling, for I kissed Juliet good-bye—a thing I seldom do—and called back to her as I ran up the steps, "Good-night. See you at Church." I was never so unsuspecting in my life as I opened the front door. But the instant I got inside the house and looked into the sitting-room, I knew something was wrong. The entire family was all sitting about the room doing absolutely nothing. Father was not at his roll-top desk; the twins were not drawn up to the centre table studying by the student-lamp; Alec was not out making his Saturday night call; and, strangest of all, Ruthie was not in bed.

"What's the matter?" I asked.

"Take your things off and come in, Lucy," said Father.

I didn't stir. My heart stood dead still for an instant. I grabbed hold of the portière.

"Something has happened to Tom," I gasped, so sure I didn't even have to ask.

I suppose I must have looked horribly frightened, for one of the twins blurted out, in the twins' frank brutal way, "Oh, say, don't get so everlastingly excited. Tom's all right, for all we know. So's every one else. Do cool off."

Ruthie giggled. She always giggles at the twins, and I knew then that my sudden fear had been for nothing. The angry colour rushed into my face.

"Smarties!" I flung back at the twins with all my might.

"Oh, Lucy!" I heard Father murmur, and I saw Alec drop his eyes as if he were ashamed of such an outburst from his seventeen-year-old sister.

"I don't care," I went on. "Why do you want to frighten me to death? What's the matter with you all, anyway? What are you all doing? Why isn't Ruthie in bed? Why are the twins—"

"It's all about *you*!" Malcolm interrupted in a sort of triumphant manner.

"Me!" I gasped. "What in thunder–"

"Oh, Lucy!" Father again murmured.

"Well, what," I continued, "have you all been saying about *me*?" And I sat down on the piano-stool.

Father cleared his throat the way he does before he asks the blessing, and every one else was quiet. I knew something important was coming.

"Lucy," Father said, "we think the time has come for you to go to boarding-school."

It hit me like a hard baseball and I couldn't have spoken if I were to have died.

Father went on in his sure, unfaltering way.

"I have been considering it for some little while, and now as I talk it over with the others–we always do that, you know–I am more convinced of the wisdom of such a step than ever. Alec has been doing some investigating, and Elise suggested in her last letter that Miss Brown's-on-the-Hudson is an excellent school. I have, therefore, communicated with Miss Brown and a telegram announces to me to-day that a vacancy allows her to accept you, late as it is. Before worrying you unnecessarily, I have made all arrangements. I have written to Aunt Sarah, and she is willing to come and take your place here. So, my dear child, I am only waiting now for your careful and womanly consideration." I think he must have seen the horror on my face, for he added gently, "You needn't decide to-night, Lucy. Think it over and in the morning your duty will seem clear to you."

I have heard of people whose hair grows grey in a single night. It's a wonder mine didn't turn snow-white during that single speech. Boarding-school had never been intimated to me before. I had been away from home for over night only twice in my life, and then stayed only a week. Both times I had almost died of homesickness. I would as soon be sentenced to prison or to death. Oh, I didn't want to go away! I didn't want to! The silence after Father finished was awful. One of the twins broke it.

"When Father told us about this to-night," Malcolm began importantly, "we thought he was dead right. You see," he went on, "we want our sister to be as nice as any other fellow's sister."

"Don't you 'sister' *me*," I managed to murmur, for I wasn't going to be patronised by the twins who are a year younger than I am.

"Well, anyhow," said Oliver, the crueller one of the twins, "you haven't got the right hang of fixing yourself up yet. You go round with tomboys like Juliet Adams, and some others I might mention, that fellows haven't any use for. High school is all right for *us*, but, no siree, not for *you*. Some girls get the knack all right at home; but look at yourself now! You wouldn't think a girl of seventeen would twist her feet around a piano-stool like that!" I twisted them tighter. "Even Toots" (that's Ruthie), he went on, "seems to carry herself more like a young lady."

Ruth giggled at Oliver's last remark and I came back to life.

"I may be plain and awkward and gawky," I began, "and as homely as a hedge fence, but let me tell you two children, if I spent my time primping before the glass, and mincing up and down the street Saturday afternoons before Brimmer's drug-store like your precious Elsie Barnard," I fired, looking straight at Malcolm and bringing the colour to his face, for he was awfully gone on Elsie, "or Doris Abbott, Mister Oliver," I added, and Oliver flushed brilliant red, "you two wouldn't have any stockings mended or any buttons on your coats or any lessons either, for you know without me to explain every little thing you are awful dunces!"

Father said, "Oh, come, Lucy, let us not quarrel;" Ruth went over and sat on the arm of Oliver's chair (she always sides with the twins); and my older brother Alec just looked hard at his magazine.

There was a long silence and then I got up and walked over to Alec. I took the magazine out of his hand. I was calm now.

"Alec, what do *you* think about my going away?" I said.

He looked up and smiled his kind, tired smile at me. Then he took my hand but I drew it away quickly, turned and sat down on the arm of the Morris-chair in which he was sitting, with my back square to him. His gentle voice came to me from over my shoulder.

"Well, Lucy," he said, "you see, you've been working so hard for us all here, for so many years, that I think, too, you've earned a little vacation. You've been such a splendid mother to us—such a perfect little housekeeper, that now I'd like to see you less hard-worked. We don't want to cheat you of your girlhood. We want you to have all the good times, and gaieties, and clothes, and things like that, that other girls have."

Ah, yes! I saw finally. They were ashamed of me. Even Alec was ashamed of me. I was not like other girls. I was plain and awkward and wore ugly clothes. I wasn't pretty. They wanted to send me away as if I were an old dented spoon to be straightened and polished at the jeweller's. When Alec paused he put his arm over in front of me so that it lay in my lap. At the touch of it the sobs seemed suddenly to rise up in my throat, pressing after each other as if they were anxious to get out into the air, and I rose quickly, pushed Alec's arm away and left the room. They mustn't see—oh, no, they mustn't see me cry! I meant to go to my bedroom and have it out by myself, but instead I rushed to the kitchen and buried my face for a minute in the roller-towel. Then before I let myself give way, I drew the dipper full of cold water and swallowed those sobs back, forcing them with the strength of Samson. You see I knew my sudden exit would leave an uncomfortable sensation in the room back there, and I wouldn't have had one of them think I was emotional for anything. So after a minute I went back. They could see for themselves that there wasn't a tear in sight. Standing in the doorway, facing them all, this is what I said, my voice as hard as metal.

"Father, I shall be packed, and ready to go on Monday morning."

When I closed the door to my room that night I did not cry, although my throat ached with wanting to. As I drew my curtain and looked out into the dark night I thought of Juliet Adams, sleeping peacefully like a child, and I realised how little she knew of sorrow. When the big clock in the hall struck twelve I was kneeling before my bureau, stacking my underclothes in neat little piles ready for my trunk. How little I knew that what I then thought my pretty ninety-eight-cent nightgowns, long-sleeved and high-necked, would about die of shame for their plainness, before the beautiful lace and French hand-embroidered lingerie represented at midnight spreads at school. I'm glad I didn't know then that I would come to despise my poor faithful clothes.

I was piling my gloves into a box when there came a soft knock at the door. Alec came in, in his red and grey bath-towel bath-robe.

"Not in bed yet?" he said gently, and came over and sat down near me on the floor with his back against the wall, his knees drawn up almost to his chin and his arms clasped about them. We sat there for a moment silently, and I grimly folded gloves. Then, "Good stuff, Bobbie," he said finally–and oh, so kindly–"Good nerve."

I turned and looked straight at him.

"No, Alec," I said, "there isn't anything good about it. It's horrid feelings and hate that make me go."

He looked away from me as he always does when he disapproves, but he put his hand on my shoulder and I was grateful for that touch.

I turned on him frantically and burst out, "Alec Vars, you are the only one in this whole house I love–you and Father," I amended, for we all adore Father. "You're the only one who is kind or thoughtful. I've tried to do my duty in this place by you and the others, but I guess I haven't succeeded. Now I'm going away and we'll see how the twins enjoy a dose of Aunt Sarah." I paused, then added, "Look here, Alec, don't let Ruth go out to the Country Club. She is pretty and the older men–why, your friends talk to her and make her vain and hold her on the arms of their chairs. Don't let *her* go. And the twins–I haven't told on them yet–but they're smoking! They're dead scared for fear I'll tell Father, and I said that I should if I caught them at it again."

"Good Bobbie, you'd keep us straight if you could, wouldn't you?"

"No, I wouldn't," I flared back. "It's hate I feel and–"

Alec put his hand over my mouth.

"What shall I do to you?" he laughed.

I rose abruptly, crossed the room and closed the window at my back. There was a big lump in my throat and I stopped at the marble wash-stand built into one corner of my room, and took a drink of water. Then I went back to my glove-sorting. Finally I was able to ask, "Alec, were you at the bottom of this?"

"Oh, I don't know," he smiled. "Possibly–I–or Will Maynard."

"Will Maynard!" I exclaimed. Dr. Maynard is a physician in our town, and was a classmate of Alec's years ago in college. He has nothing to do with *me*.

Alec picked up one of my gloves and began turning it right-side-out, as he explained.

"We dropped into Grand Army Hall one afternoon a week or so ago when you were playing a basket-ball game. I'd never seen you play before. We stayed for a half an hour or more. Going home Will said to me, 'Why don't you send that little wild-cat sister of yours away to school?' I began to mull it over. Of course, Bobbie, old girl," Alec went on, "I admire your pluck and spirit in basket-ball. I like to see you win whatever you set out to. You played a fine game—a bully fine game; but there are other things in life to acquire—other kinds of things, Bobbikins." He stopped. "Oh, you'll like boarding-school," he said.

"I'll like Dr. Maynard not to butt into my affairs," I replied under my breath; then I remarked, "I'm ready for that glove, please."

Alec passed it over and got up.

"Good-night," he said. "Oh, by the way," he added, "here is something you may find a use for. Your tuition and board, of course, will be paid for by Father, but I know there are a lot of extras—girl's things—that you'll need. Possibly this will help." He dropped a piece of paper into my lap and was gone before I could look up.

I unfolded the paper and saw a check dancing before my eyes for one hundred dollars! I knew very well that we were as poor as paupers in spite of our big house, and stable, as empty now as a shell. I knew Father's business was about as lifeless as the stable, and that Alec alone stood by him trying to give a little encouragement. Splendid Alec! I fled after him. He was just groping his way up the stairs to his third-floor room. I caught him and very unlike my even temperament put my arms around him tight.

"O Alec," I blubbered, "it isn't because of the money; it's because of *you*." Then I added, like a great idiot, "Oh, I *will* try not to be such a tomboy! I *will* try to be worth something when I'm away, and all the things you want me to be." And then because I hated to pose as any kind of an angel, I turned, fled back to my room and locked the door.

I made a great impression with my announcement the next day in Sunday-school. Juliet could hardly believe me. She stared at me as open-eyed and awestruck as if I had told her I was going to China. She wouldn't sing the hymns, and during the long prayer she whispered to me: "You'll be going to Spreads!" And later: "You'll have a Room-mate!" And again: "Perhaps you'll be invited to House-parties!"

If I were about to be hanged it would be little comfort to me to be told that in a few hours I would be playing on harps, walking streets of gold and wearing wings. I didn't want to go away—that was the plain truth. I preferred Intelligence-Offices to boarding-schools; I preferred our big brown ugly old house, empty stable, out-of-date carriages, cruel twins, and uncuddleble Ruth to spreads, room-mates and house-parties. I wanted to stay at home! But I was bound that no one should know that my heart was breaking; I was determined that no one should guess that I was being sent away, boosted out of my position, like the poor old minister in the South Baptist church. I would go with my head up, and tearless! Only once did I give way, and that was in poor little Dixie's furry neck when I threw my arms about him in his stall. Poor little dumb Dixie! Poor pitiful dumb carriages gazing silently at me. "*You'll* miss me. *You'll* be sorry," I said.

On that last grey Sunday afternoon I took my good-bye walk, through Buxton's woods back of our house. I gazed for the last time on the precious landmarks that I had grown to love—the two freak chestnut trees, soldered into one like the Siamese twins; the hollow oak where we used to dig the rich dark brown peet and find the big, slimy white worms; the huge fallen pine, struck once by lightning, along whose trunk and in among whose dead branches we used to play "ship" and "pirate-boat." I walked alone—all alone. There was no romantic lover in riding clothes, as in my dreams, to share my sad reflections. Only a scurrying chipmunk or red squirrel, now and then, gazed at me with frightened eyes, then scampered away; only the dead leaves under my feet kept rhythm with my dragging steps. I was awfully lonely and unhappy. It seemed to me that even the sombre sky and the dead quietness of Sunday connived to add to my dreariness.

When I reached our iron gate on my return, it was nearly dark. Dr. Maynard was just coming away from one of his frequent Sunday afternoons with Alec and I met him by the fountain.

"Hello, little Wild-cat," he sang out cheerily. He always has called me Wild-cat, though I never knew why. "Back from one of your walks 'all by your lone'?" I think he copied that from Kipling. "Ears been burning? Al and I have just been talking about you."

I had never as much as peeped in Dr. Maynard's presence before—he's fifteen years older than I—but I couldn't bear his interference in my affairs and I retorted, "I should advise you not to meddle with wild-cats, Dr. Maynard!"

"Whew!" he whistled in mock alarm; and though it was not a pretty thing for a girl of seventeen to say to a man whose hair was beginning to turn grey, I finished hotly, "Or you'll get scratched!" and turned and dashed into the house.

CHAPTER V

IN thinking over my career at boarding-school I always recall three remarks which were made to me in the smoky Hilton Station as I waited for my train. Father and Alec and Juliet who, the dear old trump, had actually cut school to see me off, were at the station.

Alec had said, "Go slowly, Bobbie, and know only the best girls," and I had replied, pop-full of confidence, "Of course, Alec."

"And whatever else you do," exclaimed Juliet, "don't you dare to get a swelled head, Lucy Vars." "I won't," I had assured her.

Father, dear kind Father, his hand on my shoulder, had commanded: "Dear child, discover some one less fortunate than yourself and be kind to her." And I had promised, tussling with the painful lump in my throat, "I will, dear Father."

Father had slipped a paper bag into my hand then—a bag of lemon-drops (Father always buys lemon-drops) and two sticks of colt's-foot. The poor dear man had forgotten that I didn't like colt's-foot, but when I opened the bag in the train and saw those two little brown sticks, somehow I loved dear Father harder than ever. I put them into my travelling bag very tenderly, and have kept them ever since.

I don't know how to explain my impressions of boarding-school. I realise now that in spite of the pain at leaving home I did have buried in the bottom of my heart dreams of the vague, unknown joys of room-mates and spreads. Every young girl has such dreams, I guess. Even as I sped along in the train, trying desperately to dissolve that lump in my throat with Father's lemon-drops, I was wondering about the new bosom friends I should make. Edith Campbell, an awfully popular older girl in our town and a friend of Alec's, had been to a fashionable boarding-school in New York ever since she was a child, and she was forever bringing home girls to visit her, or whisking off herself to ball-games and Proms with "a Room-mate's brother" or "a Best-friend's cousin." I could hardly realise that I, Lucy Vars, was about to step within the same fascinating circle. Fifty girls to eat and sleep and walk with; fifty girls to choose my friends from; fifty girls to bring home with me for over a holiday; fifty girls for me to visit; and fifty girls with brothers or cousins at Harvard and Yale and Princeton. Perhaps that very winter some college man would invite me to a Prom; I would dance till morning, and become such a dazzling belle that by Easter-time I would look upon the twins as mere *boys*. Probably by summer I would be dashing about to house-parties, and talking to real grown-up men over a cup of tea like Dolly in the "Dolly Dialogues." Perhaps I would be president of my class at school, like Tom at college. Perhaps—perhaps—oh, I am forced to smile at myself now as I look back and see the funny little short-skirted, pig-tailed creature that I was, sitting there in the train, gazing out of the window, building my absurd little air-castles by the score, on the very way to the destruction of every dream I ever had. I didn't make a single friend at boarding-school. I didn't meet a man. Here it is almost summer, and house-parties seem as remote from me as they did ten years ago. I must try to explain why I made such a flat failure of things. It isn't a pleasant story, but here goes:

The first instant that I stepped into that school I knew that I was a curiosity to everybody there. Never shall I forget that first evening when Miss Brown ushered me into the big school dining-room and seated me beside her. It looked like fairy-land to me—red candles on a dozen little round tables and all the girls in soft, light dresses with Dutch necks. When I finally dared look up from my plate and glance round, I thought I had never seen such beautiful creatures. I couldn't find a homely girl among them; and such lovely hair as they had, done soft and full and fluffy with large ribbon-bows tied at the back of their necks. The girls at our table had the whitest hands and the prettiest soft arms, with bracelets jingling on them.

After supper Miss Brown seated herself in a big armchair by a low lamp in the drawing-room and read aloud from "Pride and Prejudice." The girls all gathered about her and did fancy work on big hoops. I didn't have any work and tried to make myself comfortable on a little high silk-brocaded chair. I felt horribly embarrassed. Every time a girl looked up from her work and scrutinised me from top to toe, I felt like saying, "I know I'm a perfect mess. I see it. I know my hands are like sandpaper, and my shoes thick-soled, and my dress a sight. I know my hair is ridiculous braided and bobbed up with a black ribbon like a horse's tail. I know it." I couldn't listen to a word that Miss Brown was reading. I was awfully disturbed thinking about my trunk on its way to me, filled with its queer collection, and wondering what in the name of heaven I could put on the next night. My blue cashmere haunted me like a bad dream. I think that first evening at boarding-school was the first time I really missed having a mother. *She* would have known the blue cashmere was ugly; *she* would have known that little bronze slippers with stockings to match were the proper thing; *she* would have known that girls at boarding-school wore Dutch necks and wide ribbons tied low, at the back of their necks. I simply dreaded unpacking that pitiful little trunk of mine. I wished it could be lost.

My room-mate's name was Gabriella Atherton, but when I entered the room which I was supposed to share with her I wished she had been plain Mary Jane. The bureau was simply loaded with silver things—silver brushes and mirrors and powder-boxes, and at least three silver frames with the stunningest men's pictures in them you ever saw. The walls were covered with college flags, and the window-seat was banked with college sofa-cushions. Why, I didn't know a single man, except high school boys, great awkward creatures like the twins. I hoped Gabriella wouldn't find out that I had never been to a college football game in my life, nor been invited to one either. My one last hope for consolation lay in the possibility that Gabriella was older than I. I thought she must be at least twenty to know so many men. When we were finally alone, getting ready to go to bed I asked her. My heart sank when she announced that she was only sixteen. I know exactly how a mother feels now when another person's baby born a month before hers talks first and shows signs of greater intelligence. I remember I was standing before my chiffonier braiding my hair for the night, pulling it flat back as I always did and fixing it in one tight short little braid, when Gabriella announced she was sixteen. Why, she looked old enough to be married, and I—I gazed at my reflection—I looked like poor Sarah Carew in the garret. No wonder the family wanted to send the old spoon away to be polished. No wonder!

"One of the girls," Gabriella went on to say, "has had a Box from home. She's asked the whole school to a Kimono Spread in her room. Do you want to go?"

A Spread! My heart leaped! And then I got a glimpse of Gabriella in the glass before me. She was a vision in a flowing pink silk kimono with white birds on it. She had her hair fluffed up on top and tied with a wide pink taffeta ribbon—she actually slept in it—and little pink shoes on her feet.

"I guess I won't to-night, thanks," I said, not turning around, for I didn't want her to see what a peeled onion I looked like; "the train made me car-sick." And I snapped the elastic band around the end of my braid.

After Gabriella had gone I turned out the light and crawled into the little brass bed, which Miss Brown had said was mine; but I didn't go to sleep. I just lay there listening to the muffled laughter and chatter at the end of the hall. It was only nine o'clock and lights were not due to be out until ten. I hated lying there wide awake and I kept wondering how I could get dressed in the morning without letting my room-mate see all my plain ugly things. Then I remembered that I had left my common cheap little wooden brush, the shellac all washed off with weekly scrubbings, on top of my chiffonier. I jumped up quickly and hid it in the top drawer; then suddenly I turned on the light, sat down in my horrid red wool wrapper, and wrote something like this to Alec, blubbering and dabbing tears all through it:

> "*Dear Alec,*
>
> I'm here safely, I've met all the girls and they are perfectly lovely. I'm going to love it. My room-mate's name is Gabriella Atherton—isn't that a beautiful name?—and she is a perfect dear! I can't write long for I am due at a spread; so, so-long until I have more time. This place is full of corking girls. They would, however, consider the twins mere babes-in-

arms. Tell Aunt Sarah that Father will want his flannel nightshirts as soon as there is a frost. They are in the all-over leather trunk in the storeroom. The girls will be wondering where I am, so good-night.

"Your enthusiastic "BOBBIE."

Then I went back to bed and bawled like a baby, until I heard Gabriella at the door. Another girl was with her and I heard her say, "Good-night, dear," and Gabriella call back exactly as they do in books and as they did once in my dreams. "Good-night, sweetheart." Thereupon I ducked my head down underneath the covers and pretended to be asleep. A half-hour later, when I felt sure that Gabriella was dead to the world, I opened my eyes and lay awake until almost morning.

But no one needs to think that I was homesick. Wild horses couldn't have dragged me home. I was bound to stick it out or die and I tried not to be a little goose and cry my eyes out. That wouldn't help me to make the best girls my friends and I didn't mean to disappoint Alec if I could help it. I was there for business and I meant to accomplish it. Alec had said he admired that quality.

But Miss Brown's-on-the-Hudson was awfully different from the Hilton Classical High School. They played basket-ball as if it were drop-the-handkerchief: there was no regular team. We exercised by walking two by two for an hour every afternoon. There wasn't the slightest chance for me to shine in athletics.

I was robbed also of my hope of being a genius. There was a girl who could write ten times better than I. It was after one of her poems was read out loud in class, that I discovered I wasn't gifted in the least. She was the marvel of the school, and whenever there were guests she was asked to read her poems herself. They were the deepest things I ever listened to—about the soul, and sorrow, and "swift sweet death." She *looked* like a genius too. She had jet black hair and wore it in long curls tied loosely behind, big dreamy eyes, and pale transparent skin. She wasn't very healthy and always wore black. Her mother was an artist in Florence, and Lucia (think of it, *my* name, but pronounced so differently) Lucia had always lived in Italy until she came to school. I tell you, as soon as I saw her and listened to her poetry, I was terribly thankful that I had never let any one know that I had ever thought *I* could write. I got A on my compositions, and A in everything else, but no one imagined that I was a genius. They considered *me* just a plain everyday shark. But I tried not to be offensively smart. I flunked on purpose once in a while; I passed notes in class whenever I could find any one to pass them to; I got so I could turn off a "darn" as neatly as any of them, and pout and say "The devil!" when I pricked my finger pinning down my belt. For I was determined they shouldn't think me a "goody-goody" or a "teacher's pet." I even crocheted a man's tie and pretended it was for a friend of mine at a fashionable preparatory school in Massachusetts. I went so far in my frantic endeavours, as to cut out from old magazines all the pictures I could find of an actor, whom, by the way, I had never even seen, and stuck them in the corners of the glass over my chiffonier.

Oh, I tried to be like the other girls. I knew they hadn't liked their first impressions of me, but I tried to show them that I wasn't as queer as I looked. I tried to be pleasant and accommodating; I tried to be patient and bide my time; I tried—heaven knows I tried, Alec—but it was no use. From the start it was absolutely no go. I couldn't make even the *worst* of those girls my friends. I tell you I did my level best, but I hadn't the clothes, nor the silver bureau-sets, nor the frames, nor the men's pictures to put into them, nor the college banners, nor the mother to send me boxes of food from home. Those girls treated me as if I were the mud under their feet. If I was in the room, I might as well have been the bed-post for all the attention they paid to me. If I was told to walk with one of them during "Exercise," that one was pitied by the rest. They looked upon my clothes as if I were a Syrian or Turk in strange costume. I used to get hot all over whenever I had to appear in a dress they had never seen. And, O Juliet—good old loyal Juliet—you were afraid I would be spoiled by admiration! I simply have to chortle with glee when I think of your warning to your old chum. A swelled head! My *eyes* got swollen instead, old Jule, with tears! And Father—dear Father—there wasn't a single soul for me to be kind to. *I* was the most miserable one in the whole school, the most unpopular, the most forlorn. And there's the truth in black and white.

After about five weeks of an average of ten insults a day, I got tired. Too long a stretch on the diet of humble-pie doesn't agree with me. There's an end to every one's patience. One day in late November little Japan up and fought; and once started, there was no stopping her. You see the girls had gotten into the habit of asking me to help them with their lessons. At first I was pleased, for I naturally thought that if they would let me see their stupid minds, they would admit me into a few of their intimacies and secret affairs—and oh, I did long to be friends with them! But I discovered they had no such intention.

One night I went into Beatrix Fox's room, by appointment, at quarter of ten. She was waiting and ready for me, but I could see the remains of a spread on the table and desk—crumbs, nutshells, olive-stones, and a half-eaten bunch of Tokays.

"Oh, here you are!" said Beatrix, and with no attempt at concealment, she went on. "I've been having half a dozen girls to a spread," she said. "But I told them to leave one piece of cake for *you*, Lucy. Here it is. Now let's get at the Latin."

I was awfully insulted. Beatrix Fox nor any one else had ever seen the least fire or spunk in Lucy Vars before that night, but I couldn't hold in a minute longer. I took the delicious piece of chocolate layer-cake and went over to the waste-basket. I threw it in. "There's your cake!" Beatrix stared as if I had gone crazy. "There's your old cake, Beatrix Fox!" I repeated, and went out of the room.

After that night I was a changed person. I couldn't be touched with a ten-yard pole. I became a regular bunch of fire-crackers—spurting and going off in everybody's face and eyes at the least spark. And oh, to speak out my mind, and to spit out my feelings at last, was simply glorious! It was like getting the rubber-dam off your tooth after a three hours' sitting at the dentist's. After that experience with Beatrix, there was no more Cicero translated nor French sentences corrected by Lucy Vars for a single one of those stupid-minded, rattle-brained young ladies. I made a notice on pasteboard in black ink and hung it on my door. It read: "A PUBLIC TUTOR CAN BE OBTAINED FROM MISS BROWN. DON'T APPLY HERE! LUCY CHENERY VARS." The girls thought the sign was perfectly horrid and I was glad of it. I wanted to be horrid. I revelled in it. I wanted to be horrid to everybody who had been horrid to me.

Once during "Written Exercise," I wrote a whole page of Latin Composition wrong, so that little cheating snobbish Barbara Porter next to me might copy it off on her paper and pass it in. At the bottom of *my* sheet I wrote, "I've made these mistakes on purpose. You may give me zero." Miss Brown, in a long talk in her private office, told me it was not a kind thing for me to do. But I didn't care. I had let Barbara Porter copy my Latin Comp for five weeks without a murmur, and she had never put *herself* out to be kind to *me*. I wasn't going to be anybody's door-mat!

At Thanksgiving all the girls "double up," which means that the ones who live far away spend the holiday with the ones who live near. Of course no one wanted me. Gabriella, who at times tried to be nice to me, felt conscience-stricken, I suppose, for she said to me one day when we were dressing, "It's too bad you're going to be here alone, Lucy. Don't you suppose Miss Brown would let you to come down to East Orange" (Gabriella lived in East Orange, New Jersey) "and eat Thanksgiving dinner with us?"

I replied maliciously, "Why, I'm sure Miss Brown would let me spend the entire three days with you, Gabriella."

Gabriella hedged then, as I knew she would. "Oh, I'm so sorry. I'm taking Grace and Barbara home with me, and there's a dance I do want to go to—and—if you—"

"O Gabriella," I broke in, "don't be alarmed. I shan't burden you for one little tiny minute. I just wanted to frighten you. I wouldn't give your friends at home such a shock as the sight of me would be, for anything in the world. I shall enjoy, on the other hand, the quiet of this room after my charming room-mate has departed."

That's the way I talked but I wrote home: "Gabriella wants me awfully to spend Thanksgiving with her. There is a dance and all sorts of plans, but in spite of all her urging I've refused. There's quite a bunch of us staying here" (the bunch were teachers), "and jolly spreads and sprees in store."

I didn't want my family to know—kind Alec, the arrogant twins, pretty Ruth, and Father who used to be so proud of me—I didn't want them to know what a poor little Cinderella I was. When I went home I wanted every one to think I had had a glorious time at school, as all girls do. I wanted my family to open their eyes and say, "My, how you're changed!" and every one at church to whisper when I came in a little late, "There's Lucy Vars home! Hasn't she grown up?" I wanted Dr. Maynard to raise his hat to me when he met me on the street, and call me Miss Vars. I wanted Juliet to gaze at me with envy. If there was any real silver underneath the tarnish on me I was bound it should shine when I went home at Christmas. And so it happened that I made up my mind that if I couldn't make friends with my new schoolmates I could at least learn something from them. I used to observe them very carefully and jot down important points in my memory. Even the things that I derided to their faces, I meant to copy when I went home. My brain became a regular copybook of rules.

"My skirts," I recorded, "should be below my shoe-tops, not above.

"The way to keep a waist down, is to fasten it with a safety-pin behind and a long black steel pin in front.

"My nails should be as shining as a dinner-plate.

"A shining face is not supposed to be pretty.

"Powder is used to remove shine, and isn't wicked like rouge.

"Girls of seventeen use hairpins and rats, and keep their hats on with hatpins instead of elastics.

"Mohair and gingham underskirts and Ferris waists are not worn by girls of seventeen.

"Huge taffeta bows underneath the chin, on the hair, or anywhere in fact, is the rubber-stamp for a girl of my age.

"Automobiles, actors, college football, and allowances are popular subjects for conversation.

"Don't break crackers into your soup.

"Don't butter a whole slice of bread.

"Don't cut up all your meat before beginning to eat."

I used to watch Gabriella dress like a hawk. She had lots of clever little tricks, like pinning up her pompadour to the brim of her hat, or rubbing her cheeks with a hair-brush to make them rosy. She used to put a little cologne just back of her ears, which I thought very queer, and she was forever asking me if I could see light through her hair. Every week she gave her face what she called a cold-cream bath. She said her mother always did, after riding in the automobile.

I planned to spend every cent of Alec's one hundred dollars on clothes. I did all my shopping in New York. I adored New York! Saturday afternoons when the other girls went to the matinée, the chaperone allowed me to spend the time in the big department stores. I didn't buy anything—just looked and looked, priced and priced, and when I had a nice clerk, tried things on. Once I had my nails manicured, so I would know how; once I went to a Fifth Avenue hair dresser, who charged me a dollar and a half to make me look like a sight; and one day I bought Father a necktie for fifty cents and Alec a scarf-pin for seventy-five. That is all I spent until just before Christmas when I blew in the whole hundred. For, you understand, it was not to impress the girls at school, but the people at home, that I bought my new outfit. It was not until after I had made a great many estimates and carefully planned it all out on a piece of paper that I asked one of the younger teachers, who I thought had good taste, if she would help me buy a few trifling clothes on the following Saturday.

We started on the early train and reached New York at nine o'clock. I think that Saturday was the happiest day of my life! I bought a suit for thirty-five dollars at Kirby's; a hat marked down to ten dollars at Earl & Kittredge's; a silk dress for twenty-five dollars; a spotted veil for fifty cents; a barette for twenty cents; pumps for four dollars; one pair of silk stockings for one dollar, and so on. I had just seven dollars and sixty-seven cents left after I had bought my last purchase—a lovely red silk waist for travelling. My suit was dark blue, my boots tan with Cuban heels, and my blue velvet hat had two reddish quills in it. I was awfully pleased with my selections, and I confided to Miss Davis, the teacher, that I wasn't going to wear any of the things until the very day I started for home.

"And now," I said, "I'm going to take you to luncheon, Miss Davis, after which I want you to be my guest at a matinée."

It was simply grand to have money! It makes you feel like a queen to fling it around as if it were paper. After I had spent almost a hundred dollars Miss Davis thought I was an heiress in disguise, and to carry out the part I left the whole of fifty cents as a tip for our waiter at luncheon. I told Miss Davis to pick out the most popular play in New York for us to see. We bought the best seats in the house.

Never, never as long as I live shall I forget those two hours and a half of perfect happiness! I'd never seen anything but vaudeville in my life, and I almost cry now when I think of that play. It was perfectly grand. The hero kept looking right straight at me all the time and what do you think? What do you suppose? He was the very actor whose pictures I had cut out and stuck in my mirror! He was Robert K. Dwinnell, and I hadn't known until I was inside the theatre and looked at the program that he was in New York. It seemed to me too strange a coincidence to be true. I don't believe in omens, but Miss Davis told me afterward she hadn't the slightest idea that I had been collecting his pictures. After that play I could hardly speak. The queer grey light of day after the glow of the footlights, didn't seem real. Boarding-school and all the girls seemed trifling. I couldn't think of anything except Robert Dwinnell and that play all the way back in the train. I felt that I was the beautiful heroine instead of Lucy Vars. I felt her joy at meeting her lover instead of my anguish at going back to a lot of unfriendly girls. I lived and breathed in the action of the plot I had just seen. I couldn't get away from it. Before I boarded the train that night I dragged Miss Davis into a small shop which we passed on the way to the station, and with the last fifty cents of Alec's one hundred dollars I bought a real picture of Robert Dwinnell. The picture is here now in this very cupola, in the top drawer of my desk and is the only comfort that I have. Mr. Dwinnell is sitting on the edge of a table swinging one foot, just as he did in the play—I remember the place in the third act—and his eyes are looking right at me.

I wonder, oh, I wonder sometimes, if he and I will ever meet.

CHAPTER VI

IT was about a week before the Christmas vacation that my last outbreak at boarding-school occurred. It was one noon after lunch when I was passing through the hall on my way upstairs. I had to go by Sarah Platt's room, where the little clique of girls I had once longed to be one of, used often to congregate after luncheon before the two o'clock study-hour. They were gathered there to-day, talking and laughing together in their usual mysterious manner, and I wondered vaguely as I went by, what they were discussing now. I never allowed myself to listen intentionally, but the conversation of those girls, who were still strangers to me, always fascinated me, and I confess I used to overhear all that I could without being dishonourable. As I sauntered by the half-closed door of that room I recognised the voice of Sarah Platt herself, who of all the girls I had aspired to make my best friend. Sarah was a dashing kind of girl and would show off to awfully good advantage before my family if I had invited her to visit me.

"Well," I heard her say, "I think Miss Brown is taking her in on charity."

I knew Sarah must be referring to me and I stopped stock-still.

"Why, she hasn't *anything*, and this horrid place is probably a palace to her!"

I flushed with rage. Palace nothing!

"I think," said a little Jewess by the name of Elsie Weil, "it's too bad for Gabriella. I'd hate to have such a room-mate forced on *me*."

"I don't think Miss Brown ought to take such a girl in at all and make us who pay a thousand dollars a year be intimate with a person we never can know socially," drawled Sarah Platt. "It's hard on her too," she finished patronisingly.

"Oh, don't mind about *me*," I breathed, ready to explode.

"I'm just tired," another girl broke in, "of having all the teachers, and Miss Brown too, talking and lecturing to us about being nice to *Lucy, Lucy, Lucy* all the time."

"And the spite and scorn that the child puts on lately," added Sarah, "is perfectly absurd. As if she had anything to back it up!"

"I know," went on the little Jewess, "her family can't be much. You can see that. Did you ever notice the row of old-fashioned family pictures on the back of her chiffonier?"

At that I caught my breath. My dear good family! And without waiting to hear another word I flung open the door. There were six or seven girls before me crowded together in a bunch on a couch in the corner. I felt myself grow suddenly calm as I stood there before them not saying a word, and they staring back at me as if I were an apparition.

"I heard every single word you said," I began slowly, "every single word!" Then my thoughts collected themselves and filed by in the order of soldiers on parade. "I don't care a straw for your opinions. I feel above every one of you. It makes me smile to think I would be the least disturbed by common and uneducated westerners," for Sarah lived in Missouri, "or Jews!" I spat at Elsie Weil. "You needn't any of you trouble about being kind to me. I don't want your kindness. I'm perfectly indifferent to every one of you. I am *not* here on charity; and as for the pictures on my chiffonier, if you don't like them, lump them, or else keep your eyes at home." I knew I was acting unladylike but I was fired up and couldn't help going on. "My family may not have fashionable photographs, my clothes may be as ugly as mud, but if you *knew* who my older brother is, if you *knew* who my father is, if you *knew*! My father is president of the Vars & Company Woollen Mills; my father is a director in the Hilton County Savings Bank; my father is a state senator; my father–oh, I shan't tell you all he is, because you haven't got enough brains to appreciate it. It would be like telling monkies about Abraham Lincoln!" I stopped just a moment, but no one spoke. All those girls huddled together in a bunch just kept on staring as they would at a rearing horse in a parade, meekly from the sidewalk. "You don't know about anything but clothes and theatres. And let me tell you once for all I don't want anything of *any* of you." Sarah Platt opened her mouth to speak. I cut her off short. "Keep still, Sarah Platt," I said. "Don't you dare address one word to me!" Oh, I wanted to do something insulting, like sticking out my tongue, or making an ugly face. But instead I just said, "And don't one of you in this room ever assume to speak one word to me as long as you live!" And I turned, stalked out of the room, and went straight upstairs.

I don't know how I could have said anything so horrid as all that, and I seventeen years old, but somehow it is always easier for me to roll off spiteful things than anything sweet and kind. I am always less embarrassed about it. Poor Alec would have been awfully disappointed to have heard such an outburst from his sister. Father would have said, "Oh, Lucy!" The arrogant twins wouldn't have wanted to own me. Only my dear old chum Juliet Adams would have been proud. She would have exclaimed, "Bully for you, Bobs!"

When I reached my room on the next floor, I calmly opened the door and went in. Gabriella was standing by her desk. I never shall forget how she looked—perfectly white and staring at me horribly. I wondered what ailed her, for she couldn't have heard my tirade on the floor below.

"What's the matter, Gabriella?" I asked.

"Oh, Lucy," she began, then sank down in a chair by her desk, leaned forward with her head buried in her arms, and began to cry dreadfully.

I went over to her.

"Gabriella," I said, sorry for her somehow, for though she was one of Sarah Platt's clique she had not been talking about me; she was, after all, my room-mate, and at least she let me see her cry. "Please, Gabriella, tell me what it is."

"Miss Brown," she choked, "wants—" she stopped, then wailed, "*you!*"

"Me?" I groped blindly. Me? Had my awful words been telegraphed to Miss Brown's office? Did she know already? I couldn't follow. Things were happening too rapidly. "Me, Gabriella," I asked. "But what for? Please stop crying and tell me."

I could barely catch a few words amidst her violent sobs.

"My father," she said. (I knew Gabriella's father had died the winter before when she was away at school.) "A telegram," she stumbled on, and I waited, "*your* father—"

My father!

I went to Gabriella quickly, put my arm about her and leaned my head down close to hers.

"Listen, Gabriella. Be quiet for just one minute and answer me. Did you say *my* father?" and then in a fresh torrent of sobs I heard her "Yes."

I left her crying there and went down through the long corridors to Miss Brown's office. I passed Sarah Platt's room without knowing it. I even passed some one in the hall but I have no idea who it was. I kept thinking, "This is your first test. Be ready and don't break."

Miss Brown was at her desk. She started a little when she saw me, then smiled—how could she smile—and said, "Oh, Gabriella found you. Come here, dear," and she put out her hand. I closed the door and then backed up against it. I couldn't go near Miss Brown. I didn't want her tissue-paper sympathy.

"What's happened to my father, Miss Brown?" I asked. "You can tell me the very worst right off."

She didn't hedge any more.

"He is very, very ill," she replied, going straight to the point as I liked to have her.

"Does that mean," I said, "that he is–is–" I couldn't say it–"is worse than very ill?" I finished.

"No," she replied. "No, Lucy. Your father is still living. I have just called up your brother by long distance telephone and they want you to come home immediately. It is your father's heart." Then she added, looking at me firmly, as if she were upholding me by the hand: "It is a long trip. You must be prepared for the worst, Lucy." I didn't answer and she turned to her desk, picked up a piece of paper and passed it to me. "Read it," she said. "It is a telegram for you."

I looked down and these words greeted me like dear, comforting friends:

"*Stand up, Bobbie. Be brave. We need you to be strong. Alec.*"

It was just as if my dear brother Alec were suddenly there like a miracle in the room beside me, and *now*, at last, I would not disappoint him.

I looked up at Miss Brown.

"When is there a train?" I asked calmly; but to myself I was saying over and over again, "Stand up. Be brave. They need you to be strong."

Miss Brown came over to me, and I must say I've always liked her from that day to this. She didn't say anything silly or comforting to me. That would all have been so useless. She just took my hand in a man's sort of way and held it firmly a minute in hers, "Your brother will be proud of you," she said. That was all, but do you think then I would have failed?

"We will go upstairs and pack," she added immediately, and I followed her, bound now to control myself or die.

I don't know how I ever got started. I only know there was a confused half-hour of packing, with Miss Brown helping and Gabriella close by me all the time. Gabriella couldn't seem to do enough. I saw her slip her pink kimono into my suit-case; I saw her pin one of her beautiful pearl bars on my red silk waist. She got out my new blue suit and brushed it; my new hat with the red quills; and while I combed my hair, she laced my new tan shoes. I understood that it was her way of telling me how sorry she was, for every once in a while she'd have to stop and cry. Once she said, "Oh, I am so sorry I've been so mean. I hope—oh, I do *hope* you'll come back, Lucy." But I didn't care now. It was too late. All my thoughts were with my family who needed me. I gathered their dear pictures together in a pile and put them in my suitcase—Father's picture too, but I didn't trust myself to look at it. Dear Father—but I didn't dare let myself think, just at first.

I felt in the air that all the girls knew my news about as soon as I did. Of course they didn't come near me. Even if I had been popular I don't believe they would have come. Sorrow somehow builds up such a barrier, and the one or two girls I met in the corridors kept close to the other wall and tried to avoid meeting my eyes. Gabriella and Miss Brown and the English teacher, whom I had always hated, saw me off. I begged to take the trip alone and Miss Brown finally allowed it.

I thought of everything during that journey, and the more I thought the more I trusted myself to think, I don't know what made me so clear-headed and fearless, but I'd run my thoughts right up to any hard truth, and they wouldn't balk; they'd go right over. My mother had died when I was so little that I did not remember it and so this was the first test I had ever had. Perhaps—oh, perhaps,—I faced it clearly and squarely—perhaps when I was met at the station they would tell me that I had come too late. I knew now that I wouldn't give way. Some great wonderful strength was in me and I wasn't afraid of myself. My home-coming was very different from the one I had planned, but when we drew near to the familiar old station I just said, "Be strong," and I knew that I should.

Dr. Maynard was at the station to meet me. The minute he got hold of my hand he said, "It's all right. You're not too late."

"That's good," I replied, but somehow I couldn't feel any more joy than sorrow. I remember, in the carriage, I asked lots of straight-forward, businesslike questions and Dr. Maynard answered me in the same way. There was no hope. The end might come at any moment. When he stopped before our door and helped me out, he said, “Bobbie, you’re a brave girl.” But I wasn’t. I couldn’t have cried. I didn’t know how.

I went into the house while Dr. Maynard stopped to hitch and blanket his horse. I found the twins and Ruth and Aunt Sarah all in the sitting-room. It didn’t come to my mind then, but now, as I remember it, it was all very different from the triumphant entry I had planned. No one jumped up to greet me, and my new suit and tan shoes and hat with the quills were all unnoticed even by myself. The twins came forward and kissed me—not embarrassed as they usually are, but scarcely realising it. They didn’t say anything, just kissed me and turned away. Ruth lay prostrate on the couch. She didn’t stir at sight of me and I went up to her and kissed her on the temple. At that she buried her face deeper into the cushions and began to sob. Aunt Sarah looked as if she had been crying for weeks. She sat quietly rocking by the west window and her big, dyed-out, blue eyes were swimming in tears, brimming over, and running down her wrinkled face. It’s something awful to me, to see a grown person cry. It’s like an old wreck at sea, and I just couldn’t kiss her. Everybody so horrible and silent and dismal, was worse somehow than death, and just for a moment I stood kind of helpless in the middle of the room. Then the door into the library opened and I saw my dear tired, patient Alec, and suddenly his arms were around me tight, holding me close—close to him and I heard him murmur, “Good Bobbie, good, brave Bobbie,” and oh, if I can hate people awfully, I can love them too. When he let me go, he said calmly, “Don’t you want to come and see Father?” and I followed him upstairs.

Dr. Maynard led me to the side of Father’s bed and I took one of Father’s dear, familiar hands in mine. Alec sat down on the other side and for a while we three waited silently until Father should wake up. I wasn’t frightened. It all seemed very natural, and none of the heart-breaking thoughts that came to me all during the weeks after he left us came to me then. It really seemed almost beautiful to be waiting there until Father should wake up. When finally he opened his eyes and saw me, he smiled, and pressed my hand a very little. Then he spoke.

“Lucy!” he said; and after a long pause, “Do you like school?” he asked, just as naturally as if we were having a nice little talk downstairs.

"Oh, yes, dear Father, I do!" I answered, and he pressed my hand again. It didn't strike me so very deeply then that my last word to my father was a lie, but afterward I used to cry about it for hours and hours. After a moment my father turned to Alec, "Stand by the business, my son," he murmured.

And without a moment's hesitation my brother promised, "I will, Father."

I didn't think Father would say anything more, for he closed his eyes again, but after a while he opened them and I saw he was actually noticing my hat and red waist, and the pearl pin Gabriella had given me. He smiled and I heard him murmur, "Pretty!" That was all; and oh, since, I have been so glad that my new clothes did so much more than I had ever hoped. For that was the last word my father said. I felt his hand grow limp in mine, and just then Dr. Maynard touched my shoulder and led me quietly away. He told me to lie down on the bed in the guest-room. I obeyed him and when, a little later, he came to me I understood the message in his eyes. I didn't feel the awfulness of it then nor I didn't have the least inclination to cry. I lay there very quietly for half an hour, then of my own accord I got up and went downstairs.

I found Aunt Sarah by the window still crying without the grace of covering her tear-stained face. The twins were not there. Ruth jumped up when I came in and clung to me frantically.

"Aunt Sarah," I asked, annoyed, "*why* do you sit there and cry?"

"Unnatural girl," she answered, "have you no heart, no tears? Don't you know your father has died?"

At those awful words poor little Ruth clung to me still tighter and wailed, "Oh, send her away, make her go off!"

I replied to my aunt, "Aunt Sarah, don't you know you shouldn't speak like that before Ruth? I'm surprised."

A little later Alec came quietly into the room. Poor Ruthie flung herself upon him just as she had upon me, and as he held her and patted her shoulder, he said, looking at me in a way that made me stronger, "Lucy, you will find Oliver in the alcove under the stairs. Go to him and give him something to do."

Poor Oliver was crying as only a boy of sixteen who isn't used to it can, I guess—dreadfully uncontrolled. He was sitting on the leather couch, leaning forward with his face in his hands. I went straight over to him and sinking down beside him, put my arms right around him. Poor Oliver—poor big broken Oliver! All the hate in my heart for that cruel twin rolled right away when I felt his great big body leaning up against me. I loved him just as if he were my son come home. We sat there together a long while—just Oliver and I—and finally when he was a little quieter he managed to say, "Don't—don't tell Alec and Malcolm—that I—I—"

"Of course I won't, Oliver," I assured him, and then I added just as if nothing had happened, "My trunk is still at the station, Oliver. I need it awfully. Here's the check. It's dark out now. Will you go down and see about it?"

He looked away and replied in a voice that tried to sound natural, "Sure, I'll go," and stood up and blew his nose very hard. I saw him glance into the mirror over the fireplace. Then, "Will you get my overcoat and hat?" he asked shamefacedly. When he went out of the house he had the visor of his cap pulled well down over his eyes, and his hands shoved deep into his pockets. We hadn't said a word about Father.

As for myself, I don't know what was the matter. I honestly didn't seem to feel a thing. I was just like a soulless machine. During the three following days I wrote notes, sent telegrams, saw about a black dress for Ruth, Aunt Sarah and myself, planned good nourishing meals for the family, went on errands, and "picked up" every room in the house, for they certainly looked awful. I didn't sleep and I wasn't hungry. I was wound up pretty tight, I guess, for it took me a long while to run down. On the second afternoon Dr. Maynard took me out to drive and then shut me up in my bedroom with the curtains all drawn tight and a little white sleeping-powder to take in fifteen minutes if I didn't go to sleep. I took the powder and stayed awake all night besides. Once during those blind, confused three days Juliet came to see me, to tell me how sorry she was I suppose, but I wasn't glad to have her. I remember I just said, "Hello, Juliet, how's basket-ball and high school?" I wasn't glad to see even Tom and Elise. When Elise held me tight in her arms and whispered, "Poor little Bobbie!" I felt like a hypocrite, and pulled away. Every time the door-bell rang and I knew that it was some one else who had come to try and comfort us, I wanted to lock myself in my room. My head ached and my eyes felt like chunks of lead. But I didn't want sympathy. I didn't need it.

The end came the night after the funeral. It hadn't occurred to me but that I would go back to boarding-school after Christmas. We were all in the sitting-room—all but Aunt Sarah who finally had stopped crying and was recuperating in her bed upstairs. Tom and Alec were discussing all sorts of plans, and I remember that Dr. Maynard, who seemed to be one of the family now, was there too. I wasn't following the conversation very closely, and suddenly I heard Tom say, "Well certainly the sooner Aunt Sarah packs up, the better."

"Why, who then," I asked, "will take her place?"

Alec looked up.

"What do you mean, Bobbie," he asked. "You'll be here, won't you?"

"Why, no. I shall be at boarding-school," I replied.

At that Ruth suddenly flopped over on the couch and began her usual torrent of crying. "I hate Aunt Sarah! I hate Aunt Sarah! I hate Aunt Sarah!" she wailed.

"The whole fall was rotten!" put in Malcolm. "Do you mean to say, Lucy, that you're going back to that school?" he fired.

"I guess your duty is *here*, Bobbie, old girl," said Tom; and Elise got up and came over to my chair.

"I know how hard it is to give up school," she said sweetly, "but they do need you, don't they, dear? Later, perhaps—"

"Well, I must say," interrupted Oliver, who was master of himself without any doubt now, "if this isn't the greatest! Look here, Alec," he asked, "do you intend to allow Bobbie to neglect us in this fashion?"

And Alec, dear Alec, across the room just smiled and said, looking straight at me, "I am going to let her do as she thinks best," and his eyes were full of kindness.

I got up then. My knees were trembling. I thought at last I was going to break down and cry. They wanted—oh, finally my family wanted me! I didn't know whether to trust my voice or not.

"Well," I said a little wobbly, trying to smile back at Alec, "I'll think it over." And as soon as I could, I sneaked out of the room, on the pretense of getting a drink of water. I went into the little back hall off the kitchen, took an old golf cape that was hanging there, threw it over my shoulders, and went outdoors. It didn't seem as if I could get my breath inside the house. It was dark, the stars had come out, and I went out of the back gate, walking as hard and fast as I could. I knew I must do something, for as wicked as it seems I was almost crazy with happiness, and I was afraid that at any moment, now at the very last, I should give up entirely, lie down at the side of the road and cry and cry. I almost ran as I hurried along, and all the time I kept saying, "Hold on. Be strong. Don't let go." Yet I knew the storm was gathering and I was losing my grip. I didn't plan to go to Juliet's house, but suddenly I saw it looming up in front of me, and it occurred to me to stop and tell Juliet my beautiful good news. So I hurried to the back door and burst into the kitchen. The Adams's cook gave an awful start.

"Good Lord!" she exclaimed.

"Hannah," I asked, and my voice was strange and hoarse, "where's Juliet?"

"Why, at dinner," gasped Hannah, staring at me. "What is it, Miss Lucy?"

"Tell her to come up to her room," I managed to say, and in our usual informal way I dashed up the back stairs to Juliet's room, which I knew so well. I waited impatiently in the dark and in a minute I heard Juliet pounding up the stairs. Then I saw her coming through the hall, her white napkin in her hand. I grabbed her.

"Juliet," I cried, "Juliet, I'm not going back to boarding-school! They want me here! I'm so happy I don't know what to do. It's horrible to be happy but I am, I *am*!" And then it struck me so funny to be happy on such a day that I laughed! I laughed simply dreadfully. All my pent-up feelings burst forth then, and I laughed till I cried. I could hear myself laugh and that made me laugh more, and then Juliet looked so queer and thunderstruck that that added to it. Pretty soon Mrs. Adams was there and they were putting cold water on my face, which struck me as the hugest joke I ever heard of, for they must have thought I was hysterical. I laughed so hard that actually I hadn't enough will or strength left to stop if I tried—I, who am usually so controlled. I got down on the floor finally, and then I don't remember anything more.

When I woke up it must have been hours later, for I was all undressed lying quietly in Juliet's bed, and there was Mrs. Adams going out of the door, and there—yes—there was Dr. Maynard behind her. There was a low light on the table by the bed and beside it sat my dear stolid Juliet. I thought at first I would burst out laughing again to see her sitting there with her funny little tight pig-tails braided for the night, with me in her bed getting her sheets all hot. Just then she looked up.

"Hello, Bob," she said in her commonplace, natural way. "Want a drink of water?" and she came over and gave me a little sip out of a glass. I didn't remember anything then, only that it was good to have old Juliet around.

"There was no one as nice as you at school, Juliet," I said.

"I guess that's a merry jest," she replied in her usual way. She took the glass away and I heard her go out of the room. I lay there very quietly and watched the dim light flickering. There was a little clock somewhere that was ticking quietly.

Then—oh, then I came back to life, and suddenly the thought of my dear, dear father returned to me. I began to cry softly for the first time, and finally fell asleep.

As I sit here this soft spring day and listen for the noon-whistle on Father's factory to blow, I shall not wait for the sight of Dixie and the phaeton coming up the hill, for Alec will be alone and I hate to be reminded of too many places left empty by Father. Father had so many favourite chairs. In every room in the house it seems as if he had his special place. And his roll-top desk closed and locked, his various pairs of shoes and slippers which he used to keep underneath all put away, makes the dear spot look as if it were for rent. I hate the neat orderly air of the sitting-room. It seems to be reproaching me. Father used to love to fill the room with all kinds and descriptions of papers. Everything, from a folder left at the front door directed to "The Lady of the House" to year-old newspapers, Father wanted preserved. There were three piles of the *Scientific Machinist*, four feet high, stacked up in one corner. I used to beg Father to let me carry off those *Scientific Machinists* at least—they collected dust fearfully—but he wouldn't allow me even to suggest such an idea. So on my own responsibility one day, I stealthily took away some of the bottom ones and packed them in the storeroom. I knew he'd never miss them and the pile was growing. Every month I'd clear out the paper case, preferring to annoy the kindest father a girl ever had to having an untidy room. I cry when I think of the kind of daughter I was; I cry and cry in the middle of the night. I wasn't good! I wasn't good! I write it down for every one to see. Of course it's too late now, but I've taken down the muslin curtains from Father's room, and the lace ones from the sitting-room. Father never approved of hangings of any kind. I don't allow the cat in the front of the house. I haven't destroyed a single folder, pamphlet or catalogue. The pile of *Scientific Machinists* I wouldn't move from the corner for anything in the world.

Oh, Father, if you were only here to be pleased; if you were only here to scatter papers around; if you were only here to ring the gong for dinner, call Ruthie "baby," me "chicken," say "Hello, boys!" to the twins, and then sit down opposite me, clear your throat and ask the blessing; if you were here again I would be a better oldest daughter. I wouldn't tease for a rubber-tired runabout, for new wallpaper, nor for that brass bed for my room.

I don't know where you are, nor where my mother is, but somehow up here in this cupola on a starry night, when I sit on the window-seat, lie flat back with my head out of the open window, and look up into that great dome of a sky, I feel as if you two may be together somewhere, perhaps seeing me.

But I don't *know*. There are times when I'm dreadfully doubtful; there are times that I don't believe anything. I think I may be an atheist! I have never discussed the subject with anybody, but occasionally it comes to me, just as the fear used to come that I was adopted, that religion is all a lie. I know I'm a member of the church, and it may be horribly wicked of me, but once in a while right in the middle of my prayers at night, I'll stop and think, "Perhaps no one is hearing me at all."

Really, I wonder sometimes if any other girl ever had such awful thoughts.

CHAPTER VII

ONE day last fall I received an important letter from Oliver. The twins are in college now, perfectly great fellows and awfully prominent. I don't know what they don't belong to down there at that university; and good-looking—well, I just wish Gabriella or Sarah Platt or horrid little Elsie Weil could lay their eyes on Oliver's last photograph. He's stunning! The big loose baggy clothes that college men wear, suit those two boys perfectly, and though I refuse to put on the worshipful air that Ruth assumes in the twins' presence, I'm just exactly as proud of my brothers as any girl in this world. Oliver is the better-looking of the two and the more athletic. He's a member of the crew now, and it gave me an awfully funny feeling up and down my spine when I saw my younger brother's picture in one of the Boston papers. Malcolm is the more studious, wears glasses and sings in the Glee Club. He isn't "a greasy grind" at all—not that sort, but he never gets into scrapes or mix-ups, and doesn't seem to need so much money.

Money was what Oliver's important letter to me was about. Usually he wrote to Alec but this time he appealed to me. When I tore open his letter at the breakfast table and started to read it out-loud to Alec and Ruthie as usual, I was confronted with great printed notices at the top and on the margins—PRIVATE! PERSONAL! DO NOT READ OUT LOUD! SECRET! and so forth. I assure you I shuffled that letter back into its envelope as quickly as I could and waited for a quiet hour by myself. This is what the letter said:

"*Dear Bobbie,*

"This is *very* important. So shut the door and read it carefully. I'm writing to you because you have influence with Alec, and you've *got* to use it. Alec doesn't seem to realise the demands on a man down here. When he and Tom were at college they had all the money they wanted, and they don't in the least understand the mighty embarrassing position it puts a fellow in to have *no cash*. I get pretty sick of sponging. There are certain class and society dues, Athletic Association fees, etc., that any kind of a good fellow must ante up on. Alec doesn't in the least appreciate the situation. He's getting mighty close lately, it seems to me, and every time he sends me my measly monthly allowance, he seems to think it's a good chance to drool out a sermon on economy. Economy! Heavens, I've been known time and time again to walk out from town after the theatre, to save a five-cent car-fare. I've been to some of the swellest dances that are given in a hired dress-suit. *Of course* I had to have some evening clothes. *You* would know that.

Now look here, Bobbie, it so happens that I've got to have something that resembles a hundred dollars! Don't jump. I'll pay it all back—every cent. But it's serious, and I *must have it.* If you can't get it from Alec, can't you borrow it out of the Household Account which you have charge of? I'll make it right with you in a week or so, and be more than grateful.

"Your affectionate brother,"OLIVER."

"P. S.

"Don't let Malcolm know I need this money, nor tell Alec what you want it for. And by the way, I must have seventy-five of the hundred by December third at the latest *absolutely.* Understand this is no ordinary matter. If I don't get the money somehow it will mean public disgrace. Comprenez-vous?"

Now Oliver knew as well as I that we were dreadfully poor. Ever since Father died, Alec had made it very plain to us that we were on the ragged edge of financial disaster. We had never been what any one could call prosperous—at least not since I could remember—but when Alec took hold of the reins at Father's woollen mills he found things in a pretty bad condition, I guess. He explained to Malcolm and Oliver just exactly how uncertain our financial future was, before they even started in at college. He told them that they must let it be known, early in their college course, that they couldn't afford the luxuries of well-to-do men's sons. He said that college must mean to them a period of serious preparation. It was only due to Tom's generosity, he explained, that it was possible for the twins to go to college at all. Tom assumed the responsibility of the twins' tuition. "And sometime," announced Alec emphatically, "both you boys are to pay back that loan, every cent." "Sure. Certainly. Count on us!" were the replies they made. They were overwhelming in their assurances. There was no grumbling *then* when Alec preached to them about economy.

It was just before the twins went to college that we were all put on an allowance. Alec called us together one day in the sitting-room and we talked it over. Alec conducts those discussions of ours with a lot of ceremony. He sits in Father's big chair and allows each one of us to state his or her opinion, while the rest sit quietly and listen. Even little Ruth may say what she thinks and no one is allowed to break in or interrupt. Alec is the jury and the judge all in one, and when he has heard both sides and weighed the question carefully he makes the decision. Tom is the higher court, but I've never known Tom once to disagree with Alec's verdict, so it doesn't do much good to appeal your case. At that meeting in the sitting-room it was arranged that Ruth and I should receive each twelve dollars a month, and when it came to the twins we all agreed that they ought to have a great deal more than two girls living at home. Alec said that he would start them on twenty-five apiece, and out of that amount everything, except board and room and doctor's bills, should be paid. At the same time Alec also arranged a household allowance, and I was very proud when he appointed me keeper of the Household Account. I was glad he thought me old and able enough for such a position and was bound to prove myself worthy. Every month he made out a check to me for fifty dollars and put it in the bank under my name. I paid the grocery and provision bill on the tenth of every month, submitted a report of the different items to Alec on a long ruled sheet of paper, which he, when he had time, examined and O.K'd. He impressed upon me again and again the absolute necessity of keeping the Household Account separate from my own. He told me in a long talk how awfully dishonest it would be if I ever used a single cent of that deposit for anything but household expenses. He went so far as to give me examples of cashiers in banks who were put in prison because they borrowed a little money now and then from the bank for their own use, fully intending to pay it back as soon as they could. So you see that when Oliver suggested my borrowing from the Household Account it was entirely out of the range of possibility to consider such a thing.

I felt sorry for Oliver. I knew exactly how much he must have wanted a dress-suit. It seemed to me a perfect shame to have two corking fine fellows like the twins cheated out of friends and good times and popularity—like myself at boarding-school—because they couldn't afford the proper clothes or pay their shares on spreads and theatre parties. A hundred dollars was an awfully lot but I put Oliver's letter into my work-bag the evening of the day it came and went down into the sitting-room after supper to join Alec by the drop-light on Father's desk. Every evening I sewed while Alec worked on the factory books. Alec didn't talk much lately. He didn't seem to want to. He was usually too tired for anything but bed, when he finally closed the big ledgers, but I was always there beside him just the same. The twins sent their laundry home every two weeks in an extension-bag, and it's quite a job keeping two strapping college boys sewed up. To-night as I weaved in and out across a delicate little hole in a mauve-coloured sock of Oliver's it looked to me as if it were an expensive sock: it had silk clocks embroidered up the side. I was so busy, planning just how I would approach Alec for that hundred dollars, that he startled me when he turned around in Father's revolving desk-chair.

"Bobbie, I want to talk with you," he said.

"All right," I replied gladly. "Go on." Perhaps, I thought to myself, there will be a chance to introduce Oliver's letter.

Alec folded his hands on the slide of the desk drawn out between us.

"We're spending too much money," he said simply.

I had heard that same sentiment expressed so often that I wasn't deeply impressed. I had observed in spite of Alec's continued talk about economy that there was always enough to pay the bills. I continued sewing.

"Of course; I know," I said, trying to appear sympathetic.

"No, Bobbie," Alec replied; "I don't think you do. It is different this time. Will you stop sewing?"

"What do you mean?" I asked, dropping my work in my lap.

"Bobbie," Alec said, "perhaps you will understand the seriousness of the situation when I tell you that I do not think that we ought to live in such a big house."

"Not live here?" I exclaimed.

"I'm afraid not, Lucy. It's a big place to keep up for just you and me and Ruth. We can't afford it."

"Has the business failed, Alec?" I interrupted with kind of a sick feeling in my stomach.

"Certainly not," he said in an annoyed sort of manner as if he had not liked me to ask. "We're simply living way beyond what we can afford; that's all. We've got to cut down. I don't know how long it may take to make a favourable sale of this house, but in the meanwhile we can't afford to keep two servants. I'm sorry, Lucy; I'm sorry; but it's a matter of economy *to-day*, not economy *to-morrow*. I've thought it all out," my brother continued, beginning now to pace up and down the room. "I know Nellie has been with us twenty years. We shall miss her; but she's not strong, she can't cook or wash. We must have a good young Irish girl—five dollars a week—not more. It means a big change this time, you see. I had hoped to avoid such a course as this, but if we are to escape a worse catastrophe—"

I don't know what Alec went on talking about as he walked up and down that sitting-room floor; I don't know how long he continued explaining, and trying to make clear to me the seriousness of our situation; I don't know; I really *don't know*. I sat stunned and silent in my chair, not stirring a muscle. *Sell our home!* Why, Father had built it. I had been born in it. *Dismiss Nellie!* Why, Nellie had known my mother. Nellie was part of the foundation of our lives. I couldn't take in the succeeding facts because those two were stuck in my throat. I felt like crying out, "Don't, don't cram any more in. I'm choking!" But Alec kept right on.

"The stable, of course, I shall close immediately. We mustn't keep a horse. I shall have to get rid of Dixie."

It isn't a nice figure, but at that last announcement I gulped up all that I had tried to swallow before.

"O Alec," I interrupted, "poor little Dixie! Please, please, *please* don't sell Dixie!" I pleaded. "Please don't sell our home," I cried. "Why, where shall we live? Don't send Nellie away. Don't! Don't! I'll do anything! I won't buy a stitch for myself. And I'll work—I'll work my hands to the bones! I can earn something. But oh, don't sell dear, poor little Dixie." I leaned forward suddenly and burst into tears. "Oh, everything has always been hard in my life—hard, hard, hard!" I sobbed.

Alec came over and stood in front of me perfectly silent. He hadn't seen me go into a passion like this for years. I could feel his tired kind gaze burrowing through my two hands that covered my face. I wished he wouldn't look so troubled and sad, for though I didn't glance up, I knew exactly how disappointed in me he was—how shocked by my tears. For a full half-minute he said nothing. He waited until I was perfectly quiet, then he spoke very gently.

"Why, Bobbie," he said, "ever since the day that you came from boarding-school when Father was so ill, and I came into the room and found you strong and calm and self-possessed, ever since then I have thought of you as *my partner*." He stopped. "But perhaps this—*this* is too much. Perhaps—"

"No, Alec," I said, ashamed; "no, it isn't too much. Just wait a minute, please."

"I will," said Alec kindly, and walked over to the window.

I guess it might have been two minutes he waited. His back was toward me when I mopped my eyes, when I tucked my handkerchief into the front of my shirt-waist and stood up. I summoned all my strength. Alec is my commander-in-chief, and I tried to rally my forces before him. I must not be a coward before Alec. I took up my sewing.

"I won't be so foolish again," I remarked evenly. "You can tell me *anything* now."

And my general replied, "That's the sort," and smiled. "As to the twins," he went on, taking me at my word, "here's a letter stating the situation to them." He gave a short laugh with no joy in it. "The twins' allowances are going to be cut down almost half!"

"The twins!" I had completely forgotten Oliver's letter. "The twins! Can't you possibly—O Alec, college boys need so much and—Oliver, you know—"

"I'm tired of Oliver's extravagances," burst forth Alec impatiently. "I don't want to hear another word from Oliver about money. If he can't get along on the amount I am able to send, he can come home and go into the mill."

Just here the cheerful honk-honk of Dr. Maynard's automobile sounded outside the window. Alec went to the door and let him in. As Dr. Maynard entered the room he brought in a big breath of fall evening.

"Hello," he said. "What are you two up to? Come on, Al, put on an overcoat and come out for a run around the reservoir. I've got my engine working like a bird again."

"Thanks, Will, wish I could," said Alec with that tired smile of his, "but I've got a lot of work on hand to-night. I think I'll send Bobbie."

"All right! Fine!" said Dr. Maynard, and though I didn't have much heart for going, I knew that Alec didn't want to talk with even Will Maynard to-night, so without a word I went for my things that were hanging in what we called the "Black Closet."

I was glad to escape for a minute to the protecting dark. I stood pressing up against the old overcoats and ulsters, waiting for my eyes to appear less swollen, and wondering why Oliver needed seventy-five dollars by December third. The vision of Oliver in overalls at work in the mills, disgrace, no home, no Nellie, no Dixie, rags, poverty, wriggled before my eyes like moving pictures. I took hold of the nearest garment at hand and pressed it against my face. It happened to be Father's old overcoat. I recognised it by the feeling, for often I had groped for it when Father had been alive and brought it out to him waiting in the hall. I reached up to-night and touched the dear familiar, worn, velvet collar. "O Father," I whispered, "everything is tumbling down. What shall I do about Oliver?" Probably another girl would have breathed a little prayer to God but I make all *my* requests of Father. It seems to me that Father is more likely to take a personal interest in my affairs than any one else in heaven.

"What are you up to?" Dr. Maynard sang out; and I called back, "Coming," and hustled into my warm overshoes.

It was a beautiful dark starry night, and I wished Alec could have felt a little of the cold air on his hot head. I love an automobile! I'm never happier than when I'm sitting with my two hands on the wheel, one toe on the gas, the other on the brake, a heel on the little pedal that makes the old machine snort up a hill like a horse dug in the side with a spur. But to-night I didn't care to run the car. I suppose I wasn't a very entertaining companion, for on the way home, after we had been out about an hour, Dr. Maynard asked in his friendly manner:

"What is it, Bobbie? You're leaving it to me to have most of the fun to-night."

"Dr. Maynard," I exclaimed, "I'd give anything in the world if I were a man and could earn some money."

"What profession would you follow?" he laughed at me.

"I'm serious. Has Alec ever told you much about the business?"

"Not much, but I know he's been disturbed about something lately."

"Well," I said, "there's one of those pictures in that big Doré book with illustrations of the Old Testament, that reminds me of the Vars' affairs. It's a picture of Samson, and he's standing in a great huge kind of hall, pushing down two perfectly enormous stone pillars. The walls and the ceiling and the roof are all caving in—people headfirst, arms, legs, great blocks of granite, children, men,—oh, everything you can think of—tumbling down in horrible confusion. That picture used to give me the nightmare; and now it seems to me as if some old giant of a Samson had gotten down underneath us. All our underpinnings are giving way and we're all falling down—headfirst a thousand feet, smash, on to rock-bottom."

"Why, what do you mean, Bobbie?" laughed Dr. Maynard, amused.

"I mean," I replied—though perhaps I ought not to have told—"I mean, that Alec is going to sell the house and Dixie and we're going to keep only one girl. I mean that the business is on the ragged edge of nothing, and that we're as poor as paupers."

Dr. Maynard slowed down our speed to ten miles an hour.

"Al's a plucky fellow," he said. "I hadn't an idea!" Then he added, "*You* want to help?"

"Well," I replied, "I've got to have a lot of money right off, and I don't like to ask Alec. It's for an emergency," I added. "Can you think of any possible way for a girl who can't do a thing on earth but scrub and darn stockings, to earn a fortune?"

I think we ran about a mile before Dr. Maynard spoke. Then when he did, he seemed to be almost apologising for his scheme, which seemed to me perfectly lovely.

Dr. Maynard has stacks of money and since his mother died, lives all alone in the big, white-pillared house where he was born. Eliza, their old servant, takes care of him. "But," he explained to me, "cooking and cleaning are Eliza's strong points. Now there are lots of odds and ends she doesn't have time for. She never liked to sew, and I have a pretty hard time keeping socks mended, and linen, and towels, and such things in good condition. I hire a woman now by the day once in a while. But I'm sure I'm way behind now. If the scheme appeals to you at all, I'll have Eliza lay out a pile of stuff that needs a few stitches, and you can sew on it at odd moments. Just keep track of your time and I'll pay you—well, you seem to be a fairly busy person, I'll pay you double what I'm paying now which would be about fifty cents an hour."

"Dr. Maynard," I said, "I think you're the very kindest man I ever knew!"

"Oh, no," he broke in, "this is purely a business transaction."

"But," I went on, "fifty cents is a lot too much. That would be giving me money."

"Well, let it be understood," he said, "I'm not giving you anything. You're earning it in just as businesslike a manner as a stenographer—or Eliza. I'd like you to keep an accurate account of your time, please, and send me an itemised bill. I said fifty cents and I stick to it. Shall I come over to-morrow with your first relay?"

I thanked Dr. Maynard with my whole heart. I was so relieved I didn't know what to do.

"Would you mind," I said as he opened the front door for me, "waiting just a minute? I've a note upstairs that I wish you'd mail on your way home."

I dashed up to my room, directed an envelope in mad haste to Oliver, and on a half-sheet of note-paper I scratched:

> "In spite of Alec's news I may be able to scare up some of the money.
>
> "BOBBIE."

Alec had half a dozen letters for Dr. Maynard to mail also, and I had the satisfaction of laying my note to Oliver on top of the announcement which cut his allowance in half. After the door had closed and Alec and I were alone, I went and kissed my brother good-night.

"Good-girl," he said wearily; "the ride brightened you up."

"Yes," I replied; "and I know we're going to come out all right, Alec." And I felt that we should, now that I was going to put *my* shoulder to the wheel.

CHAPTER VIII

TWO days later I received a frenzied reply to my note to Oliver. The words were underscored, smeared, repeated, blotted and scratched out. I never read such a letter. I think Oliver swore in it. At any rate my heart almost stood still when the words "for God's sake" struck at me like swords from the white paper. I knew at least that Oliver was terribly in earnest. I read and re-read the letter, then locked it away in the cupola in the lowest drawer of my table-desk. No one shall ever see it; no one shall ever know what it contains—no one but Oliver and me. I shall never tell Alec, nor his own twin Malcolm, nor even his wife, if he should ever marry. This is between Oliver and me. He had chosen to tell his older sister about his trouble to the exclusion of every one else, and she would prove to him that he had rightly placed his faith.

I don't want to imply that Oliver had been really dishonest. I am sure he had not been that, but it seems that he was treasurer of something or other down there at college, and had boggled the accounts. He never could keep money straight. Perhaps he had borrowed a little of it—like the bank clerk Alec told me about—and now suddenly he discovered there was more of a shortage than he could make good. He wrote that on December third he must make a report, and if he couldn't account for seventy-five dollars short in the treasury—well—There followed six dashes with three exclamation points at the end.

I wrote back I'd get that seventy-five dollars for him or die.

I scraped money out of every hole and corner I could find. I sold my lavender liberty automobile veil to Juliet Adams for a dollar and a half, and Ruth bought my rhinestone horse-shoe pin, which I paid three-fifty for, for seventy-five cents. I didn't spend a single penny of my own allowance for November and begged Alec for five dollars which I told him, without a quiver, that I'd got to have for the purpose of buying some new stuff for the kitchen. But most of the money had to come from Dr. Maynard. I sewed like mad. Locked in my bedroom with the alarm-clock keeping track of my time I simply devoured holes. I was like a hungry animal. I couldn't get enough of them—and the bigger they were the better they satisfied me. Socks by the dozens; table-clothes gnawed by rats; napkins worn to shreds; blankets to be rebound; sheets to be hemmed; *anything* that required a needle, I welcomed with rejoicing.

But of course a man doesn't need more than three dozen socks on hand, five dozen perfectly whole towels and ten table-clothes. There is an end to a bachelor's equipment, and even after I had finished mending with gummed paper a whole music-rack full of old sheet-music Dr. Maynard used to sing, I had earned only twenty dollars.

I was very unhappy when Dr. Maynard passed me my last receipted bill. He was looking at me out of the corner of his eye.

"Well," he said, "does this close our business transactions? Are you all fixed up now?"

I shook my head and blushed, ashamed somehow to be in need of so much money.

"Oh, I know," I hastened to say, "that there's no more work you can give me, and I do thank you—I do really."

"Let's see," Dr. Maynard said. "Let's see. What kind of a hand do you write? If it's plain and legible, I don't know but what I'll engage you to copy some old letters of my mother's—written to me when I was a small boy at school. The ink is fading and I want them preserved."

"Dr. Maynard," I exclaimed, "I don't know what I'd do if it wasn't for you!" There were almost tears in my eyes I was so grateful.

"Nonsense," he laughed. "But what do you want so much money for?"

"A bill—for some dresses I had made, and I don't want to bother Alec."

Dr. Maynard gave a long low whistle.

"Oh, I see." Then quite seriously he added "Better tell him, Bobbie."

"Dr. Maynard," I said, "if you mention one single word of this to Alec, you don't know the harm you'll do. You don't know!" Why, if Alec had gotten wind of what Oliver had done, there wouldn't be a scrap of lenience shown that poor twin. It would mean clattering looms for Oliver, as surely as the electric chair for a murderer; and I was absolutely fierce in my determination that that brother of mine should graduate from college, as well as all the others. Before Dr. Maynard went home that afternoon he had promised he would not tell Alec a word about our business transactions.

I enjoyed the copying. Dr. Maynard's mother must have been a perfectly lovely woman. She used to write to her son every Sunday, and oh, such sweet companionable little notes–all about what was going on in the town, and always at the end just a sentence or two about honour and ideals, and how she believed in her son and missed him. If Oliver had had a mother to write to him like that–to tell him how she wanted him to grow up in the image of his honoured father who had died, who rejoiced at every success he had, who sympathised at every failure–if Oliver had had a mother to write him letters every Sunday evening by the firelight, I don't believe he would have ever gotten into such a difficulty. I wondered if mothers wrote letters like these to their daughters. Of course they must.

Every once in a while, I would run across a reference to my own mother (for Mrs. Maynard was her neighbour) and, really, it was a little like seeing her for just a minute.

I know I'm neglecting my story, but I must tell about one special letter of Mrs. Maynard's, because it referred to me. It didn't happen to be written to her son but to a woman friend whom I didn't know. It was a chatty letter, that related all the important events and happenings in the town, very long and full of the littlest details you can imagine. It was on the fourth thin sheet that I ran across this: "And our dear neighbour Mrs. Vars has a little daughter three weeks old," I deciphered. "She has named her Lucy for herself. I went in to see her last week and took her a jar of my quince jelly. She is a very happy woman. She has always wanted a little girl. When she took the little baby in her arms she said with tears in her eyes, 'My little daughter and I are going to be "best friends" all our lives.'"

I read that precious sentence over and over again. My mother and I 'best friends all our lives'–and oh, I couldn't remember her smile. 'Best friends all our lives'–and she had gone before we could share a single secret. I leaned right forward over my copying and cried, "If you'd lived I wouldn't care if we were poor. If you and I were 'best friends,' I wouldn't care if I never had a good time. Oh, if you were here! If you were here!"

And yet, although I cried so hard, I was strangely happy that evening. Of course I don't believe in miracles. They don't happen nowadays, and yet it seems almost as if my mother might have sent that message to me, to console me in my struggle, to tell me that I wasn't all alone. I gazed at her picture—the only one she had ever had taken—under its cold glass over my bed, before I went to sleep that night. It is a profile, clear-cut and a little sad. They tell me she was only nineteen in the picture—my age, just my age now.

"My best friend," I whispered, "my best friend all my life!"

As the dreary days wore on, all the sympathy that I possessed yearned over my patient brother Alec. But I couldn't help him any. Time and time again I tried to cheer him up, but my attempts fell flat. There was a time when Alec used to go out among the young people in Hilton quite a good deal, but I observed that lately he had nothing but business engagements to take him away.

Alec had never talked to me about a certain young lady named Edith Campbell—I don't know that he had ever mentioned her name to me—but I knew that he had always entertained a sneaking admiration for her. Since father died he hadn't seen her so much and I had been glad of it. I don't like Edith Campbell. There is so much show about her, and she always contrives to make Alec look so forlorn and pathetic. I remember one morning not long after Alec's serious talk with me, that he went out of the door gloomier than ever with his green felt bag filled with the ledgers that he'd been working over till midnight. Just as he was going down the front steps who should appear but Edith Campbell in a sporty little rig, driving a new cob of hers—round and plump and shiny. She had some little out-of-town whippersnapper of a man beside her, and as she drew her horse to a standstill right by Alec, she looked trig and sporty enough for the front cover of a magazine. She gave Alec a play salute from the brim of her perky little hat, and my poor tired brother took off his limp grey felt. He went over and leaned one hand on the horse's brilliant flank, and gazed up at Edith. His overcoat that used to be black looked greenish in the bright sunlight and the velvet collar was worn about the edges.

"Hello, Al Vars!" exclaimed Miss Campbell. I could hear her through the open door, hidden behind the lace. "I haven't seen you for *one age*. You ought to come out of that shell of yours. Al *used* to be a pal of mine," she laughed to the man beside her and introduced them. The stiffly-starched little out-of-town man gave Alec a hand gloved in yellow dog-skin and Alec turned and said something I couldn't hear to Miss Campbell. She called her reply back over her shoulder as she drove off. "Sorry, Al. Can't. Too bad. I'm going to Florida with Mother and Dad for the winter next week!"

Alec stood forlorn in the middle of the street, watching her descend the hill. The back of the highly-shellacked little waggonette flashed in the sunlight. Miss Campbell sat erect, sleek as her horse. My feelings grew savage against her, and when Alec finally shifted the heavy green bag to the other hand and moved slowly off down the street toward the factory I wanted to run after him and tell him she wasn't worth a single thought of his. I wished that my life-long devotion might make up for this single morning's sting of Edith Campbell's heartless exhibition of prosperity. But it couldn't. It couldn't break through my brother's brooding silence for even an interval.

Ruth took our change of circumstances very philosophically at first. Ruth is sixteen now, and awfully pretty. She has boy-callers about three times a week. She's very popular. She can sing like a little prima-donna, and can dance a cake-walk like a young vaudeville performer. The twins think Ruth is the cleverest little creature alive. She's a very independent sort of girl. No one can give any advice to Ruth on what is the proper thing for her to wear; no one can tell *her* what is the correct way for girls of sixteen to act; at least, *I* can't. Ruth loves fashion and style. She was glad to have Alec dispose of Dixie.

"Why," she said to me in her little sophisticated way, "Dixie is eating his *head* off, and he *limps*! I'd be ashamed to be seen at a funeral driving Dixie! You may have noticed *I* never use him." She was delighted to learn that Alec was going to sell the house. "For he says," she announced to me gleefully, "that perhaps *now* we can live in one of those darling little shingled houses on the south side. Those houses have the loveliest little dens in them with a stained-glass window, where I could have my callers. I just hate the parlour here. There's a big new crack over the marble mantel, and I have a dreadful time making people sit with their backs to it."

"And Nellie?" I questioned.

"Good riddance, I think. She's the bane of my life, and she hasn't a scrap of style. She's been here so long she thinks she can boss me as if she were my mother."

Ruth's chief source of sorrow was the announcement that she couldn't attend dancing-school. That brought the tears and for three days she'd hardly speak a word. When I told her that she ought to be cheerful for Alec's sake, she slammed the door in my face and told me not to preach.

I am afraid Ruth and I aren't very congenial sisters. I try very hard to be helpful and sympathetic, for Ruth, of course, is as motherless as I am. But she's a difficult younger sister. She never wanted me to take her to places when she was a little girl. She hates to be petted. It troubles me a little to think we aren't closer friends, because we each are the only sister in the world that the other has.

It was Ruth who stepped in and upset my whole scheme with Dr. Maynard. She can be dreadfully annoying, and cause as much trouble as any grown-up person I ever knew. It was when I was within ten dollars of the end of my struggle. I had finished the copying, and now I was working Dr. Maynard's initials on about everything that that man owned.

It was on a Saturday afternoon, and Juliet Adams, who had come down from college to spend Sunday with her family (Juliet goes to a girl's big college now), had dropped over to see me. I was sitting by the west window sewing on some things of my own, for of course all Dr. Maynard's work I was careful to do in private. Ruth was upstairs getting dressed to go out to a party with one of her numerous boy-friends. Suddenly, with her hair down her back, and dressed only in her white petticoat and dressing-sack, she appeared in the doorway.

"Got a thimble?" she asked. "I want to baste in a ruching," and without asking leave she grabbed my work-bag that was on the couch. It was open and she caught hold of it in such a way that the contents all went tumbling out on the floor. A dozen new socks done up in balls, on which I had been working initials, rolled out in all directions. The red monogram stared me in the face.

"I'll pick them up," I said hurriedly, but Ruth was too quick for me and she pounced upon them before I could stop her. Very little of importance escapes Ruth.

"W. F. M.!" she exclaimed. "Who's that? W. F. M.! As I live, on *every* one of them! Who's W. F. M.?" She unrolled one pair. "Men's socks too," she said, holding them up to plain view. "W. F. M.!" Then suddenly she broke into hilarious laughter. "I have it!" she burst out, waving the socks over her head and triumphantly dancing around the room. "William Ford Maynard! W. F. M. William Ford Maynard!"

"Stop, Ruth!" I cried, my old anger beginning to surge up in me. "*Stop*, I tell you!"

But Ruth was deaf to me. She simply kept on tearing around the room like a wild Indian. "How do you do, Mrs. Maynard," she shouted at me in silly school-girl fashion, and amidst her mad laughter sang out, full of derision, "Juliet, let me introduce Mrs. William Ford Maynard!"

I was standing up in a minute and was at Ruth with all my might and main. I was firing mad.

"Ruth Chenery Vars," I cried, "stop, *stop*, STOP!" and then suddenly there was Alec standing quietly in the doorway in his overcoat and hat.

Ruth and I went out like flames.

There was a dead silence for an instant, then Alec asked quietly:

"What does this mean?"

Ruth answered him.

"I tipped over Lucy's work-bag and all these men's socks fell out. Every one of them is marked with Dr. Maynard's initials, and Lucy got mad because I made fun of her."

"Will's initials, Lucy?" asked Alec perplexed.

"Yes, W. F. M.," went on Ruth delightedly. "See?" She gave the socks to Alec. "Nobody is W. F. M. in this town, but William Ford Maynard," she finished and sat down on the piano-stool in a satisfied way, as if she had cleared *herself* of any blame, and now was ready for some fun.

I think it was here that Juliet got up and slipped out of the room. Anyhow I know she wasn't there during the whole interview.

"Well, Lucy?" said Alec, looking at me.

"I was paid for it," I exclaimed. "I was paid for every single initial and every single stitch I ever took for him! Oh, there was nothing sentimental about it. Ruth makes me sick! I did it simply to earn money."

Alec looked down at the initials.

"How much were you paid?" he asked.

"I was paid," I went on, still on the defensive, "I was paid fifty cents an hour. It was all business from beginning to end. Oh, there was nothing silly in it!"

"Fifty cents an hour?" Alec repeated.

"Oh, yes," I said. "Ruth is absurd. I made out bills and receipts and everything. It was absolutely businesslike."

"And how much has Will already given you?"

The colour for some reason rose to my cheeks. Alec looked as if he wasn't pleased and I was suddenly ashamed.

"About–sixty dollars," I murmured.

"Sixty dollars!" Alec flashed. "Why did you need so much money?" he asked me sternly.

I saw my danger then. It was as if I had had my hands on the steering-wheel of Dr. Maynard's automobile, and suddenly saw an enormous limousine headed for me around a curve.

"Why," I stammered, trying to keep calm, "I thought the business was doing so–poorly, that I–I–"

"Why did you think it necessary not to tell me about this–enterprise of yours?" asked Alec.

The limousine kept coming straight for me, you see.

I hesitated just a moment. I had no idea of telling about Oliver. After you've worked for a cause, you'll protect it if it kills you. But I was at a loss to know which way to turn, and I had to act quickly. An inspiration came to me. It wasn't a good one, but I was excited.

"I borrowed seventy-five dollars from the Household Account. I had a dressmaker's bill of my own to pay that had stood a long while, and so—now I'm trying to make it up."

Alec dropped the socks as if they had been hot. He didn't say a single word. He just stood there and stared and stared. I glanced up for a fleeting second and Alec's eyes were terrible. The vision of them remained with me for days, just as the image of the sun will dance before your eyes after you have gazed at its piercing light for an instant. I turned and looked quickly out of the window. The clock in the hall struck five. I counted it to myself. The last stroke died away, and still Alec stood and stared. He seemed to be willing me to bow down in remorse and shame. I couldn't help it. I tried and I couldn't. I wasn't guilty—oh, no, Alec, I wasn't guilty—but suddenly a hot wave spread over me up to my temples and I hung my head before my brother's condemning gaze.

He turned away then, and without a word went out into the hall.

I didn't know a silence could be so eloquent; I didn't know a silence could hurt. It sobered even Ruth. She slunk quietly upstairs. And when I discovered I was quite alone, I drew a long breath. Then I got up, gathered the poor socks that had caused so much trouble together in a pile and put them back into my work-bag.

I didn't go down to supper that night. Alec knocked on my bedroom door about nine o'clock, and came in.

"Please put the household check-book on my desk," he said shortly; "I will take charge of it hereafter."

"Very well," I replied, perfectly calm; and a thick heavy curtain fell quietly down between Alec and me like the curtain after the last act at the theatre.

CHAPTER IX

HOW can I tell about the days that followed—black, blinding days with Alec's silent displeasure following me wherever I went, Ruth looking at me askance and avoiding an encounter, and I, firm, uncommunicative, and dismal as the grave?

To save Oliver from disgrace cost me a big price. I paid Alec's confidence and respect to buy Oliver's honour. Sisters ought not to have preferences among their brothers, but, Father, you know, *you*—before whom now there is no deceiving or pretending—you know that there is no one in the world to me like Alec. Why, Oliver and I used to fight like cats and dogs. Ruth is Oliver's favourite. I don't know why I was putting myself to so much trouble for Oliver, breaking my heart to save his reputation. Father would have put Oliver into the mills; Tom would have put him there; Alec also; but at night when I look at the sad profile over my bed, that face which only until lately had been simply an old-fashioned picture of my mother, I wonder what *she* would have done. I know Mrs. Maynard would have sold her soul to protect *her* son's reputation. Perhaps I was saving Oliver from disgrace for the sake of my "best friend." At any rate there was no going back now.

Meal-time of course was dreadful. There was no connected conversation. The clatter of the slumpy general-housework girl, as she piled up our plates and took them away, was more annoying than ever, when we all simply sat and listened. It's a difficult thing, too, to ask for the bread, and avoid glancing at the person who passes it. I didn't join Alec in the sitting-room any more by the drop-light; I didn't hurry downstairs to meet him at noon; I didn't ask him if he were tired.

"Please, Alec, say *something*!" I said, almost desperate, at the end of the third day.

I didn't know Alec could be so hard and unforgiving. His reply made me feel awfully sympathetic and kind toward Oliver, or any one else who might have made a mistake. It seems that, besides shattering my brother's entire confidence in my honesty, I had shocked his sense of propriety in accepting money from Dr. Maynard. To call it a business transaction appealed to Alec as absolutely absurd. He assured me that he was going to pay every cent of Will's money back to him. I started to reply, but Alec shrugged his shoulders and turned away.

"I don't want to talk about it, Lucy. Let us not argue about a matter in which your honesty and reliability is so involved. I had such faith in you! I could have forgiven you your lack of pride—your utter ignorance of the proprieties in spite of your nineteen years, in accepting sixty dollars from a friend! But you have been dishonest. You knew as well as I the seriousness of your offence when you borrowed from the Household Account placed in your name at the bank. No, please, do not answer me. For what is there for you to say?"

I didn't know. I went upstairs—not to cry, not to grieve, but to sit down in my black walnut rocker by the window and think bitter thoughts. I didn't care if I had been improper; I didn't care if Alec was unjust and willing to believe the worst of me; *I didn't care*! I had sixty good, crisp dollars tucked safely away in a little chamois bag in the bandbox where I keep my best Sunday-go-to-meeting hat, and when my allowance came due on December first I should have seventy-five. I didn't care if all the world turned against me. I had accomplished what I had set out to do, and no one could rob me of my victory anyhow.

I had it all planned that on December first I would deposit the seventy-five dollars in the bank and make out a check for Oliver immediately. But something happened which made quicker action necessary.

When December third, Oliver's fateful day, was about a week off I received another letter from him. In his haste, in directing it, he had omitted the state, and the letter had travelled to a Hilton, New York, which I never knew was on the map, before it found its way to me three days later.

> "The business meeting has been set forward to November twenty-sixth, so you better send the check on the twenty-fourth, at the latest. You've been a trump to get it for me, and if you're good, I'll have both you and Ruth down for a game sometime, with a spread in my room."

I didn't read any farther. I reached for my calendar. I found the twenty-sixth. I followed the column up to the days of the week. Yes—as sure as I was alive—Saturday! To-day was Saturday. To-day was November twenty-sixth! Oliver must have seventy-five dollars to-day!

It was nine o'clock. Alec was at the factory. Ruth was not in the house. I went down to the roll-top desk and found a timetable. There was a train at nine-fifty. It didn't take me an instant to decide that I would deliver that money to Oliver myself. I would go down to that college town, hunt that boy up, and place my little packet of seventy-five hard-earned dollars in his hands.

I put on my hat and coat—the same old black coat, by the way, that I had had dyed when Father left us—instructed the general-housework girl to tell Alec that I wouldn't be home for lunch, and hurried over to Dr. Maynard's. I buried all the pride I ever had (which Alec had said was a small amount) and pulled the big front bell. I was glad when Eliza said the doctor was in. I had never called there before, and I refused to enter even the hall. I had come to beg for money and it seemed more correct to stand on the doorstep. I had made up my mind after Alec's cutting speech that I would never take another cent from Dr. Maynard as long as I lived. But I had to, you see. My allowance wasn't due for five days. I simply had to have nineteen dollars immediately—four for my railroad fare and fifteen for Oliver. I wasn't going to have that twin even fifteen dollars dishonest. I wasn't going to fail now, at the eleventh hour, even if it cost my reputation.

"Hello," said Dr. Maynard in the doorway. "Good morning! It isn't often I have calls from young ladies so early. Come in!"

"No," I replied. "No, thanks." I stopped a minute then I said, "I know you'll be very much surprised. I know I'm going to do a very improper thing. I must seem to have no pride at all, but—but—can you lend me nineteen dollars?" My cheeks were burning red. Dr. Maynard folded his arms and leaned up against the casement of the door. I could see him smiling. "I'll pay you back," I went on bravely, "in four days—at least fifteen dollars of it. The rest I can give you on January first."

Dr. Maynard sat down on the doorstep and made a place for me.

"Sit down, Bobbie," he said.

"I can't," I replied; "I'm in a hurry."

Dr. Maynard stood up again—he's always very polite with me—and refolded his arms.

"Alec came over last night," he went on, "and it seems, Lucy, that Al didn't approve of our little game. He took it a little more seriously than we did, and perhaps it's better, after all, if you're in any sort of difficulty to go straight to your brother, if you've got as good a one as Alec."

"Aren't you going to lend it to me?" I asked point-blank.

"Well, now, you see," Dr. Maynard smiled, "Al didn't tell me the story, but he implied that you had explained the whole thing to *him*; and of course, Bobbie, if he, your brother, doesn't approve of your cause—"

"I told him a lie," I interrupted; "I told him I'd just the same as stolen seventy-five dollars from the Household Account, which he put me in charge of; and I haven't at all. I simply haven't! I shan't ever need any more money after to-day. I'll never ask another favour after this, but I've got to have it. *I've got to!* If it would do any good to get down on my knees and beg, I'd do it. But it seems to me when I debase myself by asking you for money right out of a clear sky, you must know it's awfully important. Alec tells me I've been improper even to earn money from a friend. It must be worse to beg it. But I don't care—I *don't care*—just so you give it to me, and quick, because I've got to take a train."

Dr. Maynard looked very sober and serious for him.

"Can't you tell me what you need it for?" he asked.

For a moment I was tempted, but men are so queer and severe with boys who make mistakes, so terribly correct about honesty, how did I know but perhaps Dr. Maynard, too, would think Oliver ought to go into the mills.

I shook my head.

"I can't," I said; "I wish I could,—but, I'm sorry, I can't."

"How much do you need for your railroad fare?" he inquired, irrelevantly, and when I had told him he asked, "And what time does your train leave?"

"At nine-fifty," I burst out impatiently; "and I shall lose it if you don't hurry. We are wasting time. Oh, please decide quickly."

He didn't answer for a minute. He was biting his under lip, beneath his moustache, and gazing far away beyond my head. His arms were still folded.

"Four dollars; the nine-fifty," he contemplated out loud, unmindful of my precious minutes.

The frown between his eyes looked dreadfully unfavourable to me. I stepped toward him, and looking up to him on the step above I said, "Dr. Maynard, I copied all those letters of your mother's, and it seems as if I almost knew her now. I just know *she* would think my cause was worthy."

Dr. Maynard simply adored his mother, and I suppose it was the sudden thought of her that brought a kind of mist into his eyes. He stepped down beside me, took out his leather bill-book, and passed me two ten-dollar bills. "Then, Bobbie, here it is!" he said gravely.

I thanked him quietly, opened my bag, and put them away.

I have always thought Dr. Maynard was a mind-reader. His next speech simply staggered me.

"I should go to the train immediately," he said; "the nine-fifty will be crowded this morning, with people going to the game. And by the way, if by any chance, you have a notion of passing through any college town on the day of a big football game, you'll find it very confusing. Why not let me go with you? I'll ask no questions. Or will the twins meet you?"

"How did you know? How did you guess?" was on the tip of my tongue; but I replied instead, "Oh, thank you. I *must* go alone. I shall be back by dark—and—and some one will meet me," I stammered.

All the way to the station I kept thinking, "Why couldn't Alec have believed me worthy of good motives too? Why couldn't Alec have surmised and understood? Why couldn't it have been my brother who trusted and had faith?"

Before I bought my ticket I sent a telegram to Oliver, so he wouldn't be passing away with anxiety. "*Coming to-day. Bobbie*" I said, and five minutes later sank into a seat in the train with a sigh of relief.

It was nearly twelve o'clock when the last friendly, blue-coated policeman left me with a pleasant nod near the end of my destination. I didn't have a bit of difficulty changing trains, crossing Boston and weaving my way in and out and up and down a labyrinth of subway passages and various street-car lines. Everybody was awfully helpful and as long as I have a tongue I could travel around the world, I believe, without the least bit of trouble. It wasn't until I neared the end of my journey that I felt any nervousness at all. Oliver roomed at number 204 Grey Street and as I reached the nineties my uneasiness became quite apparent. I could feel it in my chest, as if I were hungry. I did hope Oliver would be in. I did hope I was doing the right thing. Probably my growing excitement was a little due to the gala spirit of the football day. It pervaded everything. It thrilled me. Crowds of people with steamer-rugs and overcoats over their arms had thronged the trains and street-cars all along my route—a good-natured crowd, prosperous-looking young men and stunning girls wearing great bunches of flowers and carrying flags. Everybody was excited, even down to the small boys selling programmes and banners in the square I had just left; everybody glowed with enthusiasm and with the foretaste of a triumph. I had never been to a football game in my life, and I had always wanted to. Perhaps Oliver would take me; perhaps we would have lunch together somewhere! I should adore to see the college buildings! Possibly—oh, possibly, he would introduce me to some of his friends!! The thought of the thrilling things that might be in store for me made me swallow to keep myself calm. As I hurried along Grey Street I was so excited that I somehow wished that the wonderful time was all over, and that I was speeding safely and victoriously home again, wearing a faded bunch of chrysanthemums that Oliver would buy for me, and hoarding in my memory the brand-new acquisition of a real College Football Game.

I was rather disappointed in the appearance of number 204. It was a big brick building and not at all my idea of a College Dormitory. It was just as plain and ordinary as it could be, with the door opening right square on to the brick sidewalk, and a horrid little tailor-shop and drug-store opposite. I didn't know what I ought to do. The big front door was wide open, and I could see into the hall. It looked like a prison—all brick and masonry, and bare granolithic stairs with an iron railing. I didn't know whether to go in or not. If there had been a policeman in sight I would have asked his advice, or an old lady, or a girl, but there was only a very good-looking young man on the other side of the street, so I rang the bell and waited. No one came. I rang again; I rang that old bell—at least I pushed the button—six times! No one answered, so I finally started up the stairs. Perhaps I was waiting at the basement door (the interior certainly looked like a cellar) and the parlours or reception-rooms were possibly on the floor above. It was while I was standing, hesitating on the second landing, gazing up interminable flights of cement stairs and brick walls, wondering how in the world I could dig Oliver out of such a tomb, that a door opened somewhere up above and down those stairs—bump-bump, clappity-clap, pell-mell, like ten barrels falling down one over another, shouting, laughing, guffawing—I heard what I thought must be a regiment charging down upon me. I drew back a little into the corner and suddenly four men—four stunning young college men appeared before me.

They all stopped shouting as if I had been a vision, and though they didn't say a word I could feel they observed me with a start of surprise as if young ladies in their corridors were a great curiosity. I blushed for no particular reason; they passed on quietly down the stairs; and would have left me there without a word if I hadn't spoken.

"Excuse me," I said to the back of the last young man. "Could you tell me—I'm sorry to stop you—but does Oliver Vars room here?"

They all halted and looked up at me. I blushed worse than ever. I suddenly felt as if I ought not to have been there, and though the young men were just as courteous and polite as they could be I was awfully embarrassed.

"Why, yes, he does room here," said the young man nearest me, taking off his hat. "Did you want to see him?"

"Yes," I stammered. "It's—it's very important. I'm sorry but I—"

"That's all right," he assured me quickly, for I guess he heard my voice tremble; "I'll find him for you." And oh, he had the nicest, straightest, cleanest look. "You go on," he said to his friends; "I'll be with you in a minute." Then to me, "Vars rooms here, but I am about sure he's out now. If you'll come with me perhaps—Must you see him right off?" he inquired.

"Oh, yes, thank you. I must. I *must*! I've come on the train to see him. I've got to see him if I sit here and wait for him."

"Oh, I'll get him all right," the young man said. "We haven't much of a place here to wait, but if you'll come with me, we'll find him," he assured me.

He stepped back to let me pass out in front of him to the street, and once on the sidewalk, he fell behind me a moment so that he might walk next to the curbing. Oh, that young man had beautiful manners! I'll always remember them. It was just the noon hour and he met lots of men that he knew. To each one he raised his hat as if he'd had a princess with him. They returned his bow in the same manner, with a curious look at me.

"They think," he laughed pleasantly, "I'm taking you to the game this afternoon!"

I flushed. I wanted to say, "I wish you were." If I had been the pretty girl whom we had just passed, in the black lynx, with a little round fur hat with a red flower on it, it would have been easy to smile, glance sidewise, and say pretty things. But from under my black felt sailor, side glances wouldn't be attractive. I kept my eyes straight ahead. "You can explain to them afterward," I said.

He left me in a drug-store. "I'll get him!" were his last words as he raised his hat.

I waited three quarters of an hour. It was after one o'clock when I saw Oliver push open the big plate-glass door. He had been hurrying. His face was red, his eyes startled and frightened, his hair tossed a little under the cap he wore. At sight of me he stopped, then strode up to me, where I was sitting on a stool by the soda-fountain.

"You!" he gasped. "You! For heaven's sake, Bobbie, what are you here for?"

"I telegraphed," I explained. "Didn't you–"

"No," he broke in, "I've had no telegram. What's the trouble anyhow? Who's dead? Who–"

"Why, Oliver," I replied calmly, "nobody's dead." Then in a lower tone, "I've come with the money," I said.

"The money! Why didn't you mail it?" he fired.

"Your letter didn't come till this morning, and–isn't the meeting to-day?"

"Oh, yes," he said still annoyed; "but there was no such rush. I've managed to borrow enough to fix *that* up. Oh, I knew I better not rely on your getting it here, and so a friend of mine lent me enough to tide me over." We had moved away from the soda-fountain and were talking in low tones beside a display of fancy soap.

"Then why–?" I began.

"Oh, because," he took me up, "I've got to pay Holmes back. No man of any respect owes money to a friend for a longer time than he can help. But Holmes didn't expect it till next week. It was absolutely crazy, your coming way down here. You went to my room, didn't you? What do you suppose the men will think? Do you know who it was told me you were here? Blanchard! Blanchard! A Senior! One of the biggest men here! Heavens, when he told me a girl wanted to see me–You don't have any idea of propriety, Lucy!"

"Oliver Vars," I returned, "I've brought seventy-five dollars down here in this bag for you, and you had better stop talking like that to me. If it wasn't for me and my impropriety, you'd be working in the mills, let me tell you. And I don't know but what it would be better. If Alec knew what you'd done—if Tom knew—"

Oliver's attitude changed immediately.

"Oh, I know," he interrupted. "It's been bully of you, Bobbie. I tell you I appreciate it. I suppose you had a hard time squeezing even such an amount out of old Al, and just now too, when business is so rotten. But I'll pay you back some day, you'll see. You've helped me out of a devil of a scrape. I'm going to have you down to a game or a tea soon."

"There's a game this afternoon!" I exclaimed. "Oh, Oliver—I've never seen a football game."

My brother frowned. "I'm more than sorry, but I'm taking some one this afternoon. Malcolm and I, two other fellows and four girls, a party of eight of us, are all going together."

"Couldn't I sit alone somewhere, off in a corner? I wouldn't mind a bit. I want to see the crowds and be able to say that I have been. Oh, I'd love to hear the cheering. You could call for me afterward, and—"

"Oh, no, Lucy; oh, no. That's out of the question. Why even if I could get a ticket, which I can't, it wouldn't do. You don't understand in the least."

There was something about the way Oliver glanced at my old rusty laced boots that made me say fiercely, "I don't suppose I'm dressed well enough!"

"Oh, it isn't that—not at all," he assured me, and suddenly I felt that it was. "Of course it isn't, though the girls do put on the best things they have. It's simply that no girl ever goes alone to a game."

"Well, then, here's the money," I said in a hard voice.

"Say, Bobbie, I'm awfully sorry. If you only had let me know. If you only—"

"Oh, never mind," I interrupted.

A young man in a grey sweater entered the store. Oliver glanced around at him, then flushed and finally raised his cap. The young man returned the bow generously. If I had been less sensitive I wouldn't have noticed how Oliver stood so as to shield me from the young man's gaze. If I hadn't walked that three blocks and a half with that young god Blanchard, whoever he was, I wouldn't have minded Oliver's half-apologetic bow. Mr. Blanchard hadn't been ashamed of me; *he* hadn't hidden me; *he* hadn't flushed when he met his friends. I wanted to get away from Oliver as soon as I could. I wanted to go home.

"Well, I might as well be starting along," I said. "I found my way down here without any trouble, and I guess I'll get home all right."

"Say, Bobbie, I'm more than sorry. I wish I could put you safely on the Hilton train, but I've got to rush like mad as it is—change my clothes, get some food, and call for Miss Beresford, all before two o'clock. So if you're sure—"

"I am," I tucked in.

"I'll put you on the electric car. Say—" his face brightened, "don't you want some hot chocolate?"

"Oh, I couldn't, Oliver. No thanks. Please."

I was glad to be alone again. I was glad of the protection of the crowds and the stream of strange faces. I sat in the corner of the car, where Oliver had left me, with a hard look about my mouth—at least I felt as if it were hard. There is no such thing as reward. Everything in life is unfair. Who was Miss Beresford? Would she wear coon-skin and velvet? Would Oliver buy her a stunning bunch of flowers to wear at her waist? Perhaps one of the actual dollars that I had earned would purchase a little flag for her to wave. Why should I pay for Miss Beresford's good time? Why should I have to work so hard, and wear ugly black? Why should I be going home—hungry and faint, and ashamed—while every one else was thronging in the other direction?

It was while I was changing cars, standing alone on the edge of the sidewalk, taking in all I could see of the excitement, that my eyes fell on a stunning creature in a long luxurious fur coat. She wore a huge bunch of violets, as big as a cauliflower. A great big sweeping plume streamed out behind. She was bubbling with laughter, and the young man striding along beside her was laughing too. They were a lovely pair, both of them full of the joy of living. The girl (I looked twice to make sure) was some one I knew. The girl, as sure as I was alive, was no other than Sarah Platt—Sarah Platt, whom I had longed to know at boarding-school; Sarah Platt who had always scorned the very sight of Lucy Vars; Sarah Platt whom finally I had almost spat upon as contemptible and mean. A half an hour ago, Oliver had tried to hide me, and now I tried to hide myself. I slunk behind a telegraph-pole. Sarah swept by like a gilded chariot; I heard her voice; I smelled the odor of her violets. "She'll always be glorious and happy," I thought savagely. "She'll always have a good time. She'll marry that young man. I know she will. And I—I'll always be poor and miserable and forgotten."

It was half-past two when I re-entered the big station, inquired of a news-stand girl the way to the restaurant, and found my way to the lunch counter. Instead of luncheon with Oliver, at a small table in some darling little college-town restaurant, I hoisted myself up on a stool and ordered a ham sandwich and a cup of coffee. The girl who drew the steaming black liquid out of the shining metal tank looked sour and dissatisfied. She slopped some of it on the saucer as she shoved the thick crockery toward me. She slammed down my check and slung a towel up over her shoulder with a sort of vehemence that expressed my feelings exactly. I don't know why she was so miserable; I never knew; but I sympathised just the same. When she dropped a glass and it shattered and broke at her feet, she merely shrugged her shoulders, and kicked the pieces as if she didn't care a rap if the whole station fell down and broke. Oh, I just loved that girl, somehow. I knew she thought life was cruel, hard as iron, and terribly unjust. I wasn't the only one who at that moment was not cheering with the crowds at the football game. I wasn't the only wretched person in the world.

CHAPTER X

ABOUT a week after I had been down to see Oliver, I observed that something strange had come over Dr. Maynard. The first time I noticed it was the day I hailed him when he was passing the house one noon, and gave him an envelope with my December allowance sealed up inside. I explained it was in part payment of the loan he had made me the week before. He didn't laugh; he didn't even smile; he was as solemn as a judge, as he took that envelope and put it in his breast-pocket. Usually there is a joke on the tip of Dr. Maynard's tongue. He is always saving situations from becoming serious by a bit of fun. I never knew what it was to feel uncomfortable with Dr. Maynard. The next day when he passed me alone in his automobile, when I was coming home from downtown, it flashed upon me as very odd that he didn't stop and take me in as usual. Then it occurred to me that he hadn't taken me out for a ride, for days. I got to thinking! The next Sunday at church he and Alec seemed friendly enough, but I observed that Dr. Maynard didn't drop in on us in the afternoon. The grave look that had come into his eyes when he passed those two bills to me that morning on his front porch, the solemn tone in his voice when he said, "Then, here it is, Bobbie," seemed to be there every time he spoke to me. I was sorry. It made me uneasy. It didn't seem as if I could bear it if Dr. Maynard should go back on me—along with the business, and Alec, and everything and everybody I ever cared a cent about.

I wondered what was the cause of Dr. Maynard's coolness. Perhaps he felt that Alec was blaming him for allowing me to take so much of his money; perhaps he was nursing the idea that he was responsible for the strangeness between my older brother and myself; or else, possibly Dr. Maynard thought that since I had committed such an unheard-of act as to ask him for money I would naturally feel embarrassed and ill-at-ease in his presence. But that was all nonsense. I didn't regret a thing that I had done. In spite of what Alec might consider my shocking impropriety, I didn't feel ashamed. I adored Dr. Maynard's cheerfulness! It seemed as if I must go and tell him that the only fun I had left now was the fun I had with him. I used to love his jokes and merry-making. I believe Dr. Maynard could make the worst catastrophe in the world a lark, if he wanted to. Why, whenever we had a puncture in the automobile, Dr. Maynard was so good-natured about it that any one would have thought he enjoyed punctures. "You've got a flat tire, George," he'd sing out to me (he calls me George when I am running the car), or, "Sorry, Miss; sounds mighty like a blow-out," he'd say, if he happened to be at the wheel; and while he was jacking-up, I'd flax around and unlock the tools. Before he had the shoe off, I was ready with the new inner tube, and thirty minutes from the time we had stopped we were zinging along again as good as new. Most of the sunshine in my life—literal sunshine and the other kind too—came through Dr. Maynard.

As I became more and more convinced that he was acting queerly, I began to realise how kind he had been to me. I suppose Dr. Maynard is really a better friend of mine than Juliet Adams, to whom I write twice every week, and for whom I make a stunning Christmas present every year. He has surely done more to fill my heart with gratitude and everlasting appreciation. It flashed upon me, one day, that I had never done a thing in my life, without pay, for Dr. Maynard. I began thinking and thinking what a girl of nineteen could do anyhow, for a man of thirty-five, who lives all alone and has all the money he wants.

It was when I was working on Juliet's Christmas present that it occurred to me that possibly it might please an older man, who didn't have any family, if some one gave *him* a Christmas present. The more I thought about it the better I liked the idea. It seemed to me a delicate way of expressing my thanks to Dr. Maynard for all that he had done.

I had an awful time deciding on the present. First I wanted to buy a wind-shield for his automobile but the price of wind-shields is something terrific. Fur robes, automobile clocks, a Gabriel horn all were delightful possibilities, but beyond the limits of my purse. My oldest brother Tom likes books, I always give Alec socks or handkerchiefs. The twins adore sofa-pillows for their rooms. Sofa pillows! Would Dr. Maynard like a sofa-pillow for his room? For a week I hesitated between a sofa-pillow and a hand-embroidered picture frame, but finally decided on the pillow.

I knew exactly how I was going to make it. I had seen one of my friends, who attends a big boarding-school near Philadelphia, embroidering a perfectly stunning one at Thanksgiving for a college man she knew. I copied hers. Of course I realised that Dr. Maynard had been out of college for years, but he is very loyal to his Alma Mater. He told me all about the fifteenth reunion he attended last June as soon as he got home, and seemed awfully enthusiastic. So I bought and had charged to myself, two yards of the most expensive and shiniest satin in the Hilton stores, had it stamped on one side with the seal of Dr. Maynard's college, and on the other with his initials and the numerals of his class beneath. It wasn't very complimentary to Dr. Maynard I suppose, but as I worked, I wondered if I would ever embroider a sofa-pillow for a real college man. I wished this one was destined for some one who was in college now. I should have enjoyed the thought that a pillow made by my hands would be piled high on a couch in the corner of a college boy's room, beneath posters and signs and flags, and that college men would lean up against it and play banjos and guitars. I wished I had half an excuse for making a sofa-pillow for Mr. Blanchard. Dr. Maynard graduated perfect ages ago, in the class of '90—three years before the World's Fair in Chicago, which is one of my earliest recollections. The pillow that I copied mine from has on it a big '09, and Mr. Blanchard is a member of the class of '06. I had only to turn my pillow upside down and it would have been perfect for Mr. Blanchard.

After I had finished the embroidery, I bought the best down-pillow for the thing that I could find—for I wasn't going to skimp on Dr. Maynard's Christmas present, after all his generosity—and also a heavy black silk cord to go around the edge. I must confess when it was all done—the black letters standing up so that they cast a shadow on the red satin, and the surface as round and full as a raised biscuit—I must confess it was perfectly lovely. I think Mr. Blanchard would have liked it very much. I wrapped it up very carefully in tissue paper, over that a layer of brown paper held together by pins, and put it well out of sight on my closet shelf. I was determined that Ruth shouldn't see it.

Christmas used to be a great day with us. Tom always came home from the West; and we had fricasseed chicken for breakfast; turkey and pies for dinner; figs, nuts and Malaga grapes for supper. We never celebrated with a Christmas tree (we considered them childish) and the younger ones of us—Ruth and I and the twins—never hung our stockings. Since Mother died there was no one to keep up the fiction of Santa Claus, and I remember we used to feel awfully set-up and superior at the church supper on Christmas Eve when we, with grown-ups, knew that the person in the old red coat and white beard was just the Sunday-school superintendent dressed up. We always opened our presents in the sitting-room directly after breakfast. Each member of the family had a chair of his own, with his presents piled in it. When we all finally got started on the opening, I don't know whether we were more interested in seeing the presents we had given, opened, or opening the ones we had received. It was a wonderful hour anyhow, and I can't even remember it without getting a thrill.

It's different now; everything is different—Memorial Day, Fourth of July and Thanksgiving—with Father gone. We can't seem to fill up the rooms without Father. When we try to celebrate a holiday I think it must be something like acting or preaching to an empty house. Father was a beautiful audience, and his applause made the day worth while. Since Tom has been married he hasn't been here for Christmas either. Elise's family wants her with them. Besides, she has two little daughters now and can't possibly come East anyhow. You can imagine with only Ruth, the twins, heart-sick Alec, and me—no Dixie, no Nellie, no money for presents, and the "For Sale" sign still outside the parlour window—it wasn't a very merry Christmas for the Vars family. It just dragged, I can tell you. I had to cook the dinner myself because Bridget, the general-housework girl, had too soft a heart to disappoint her second cousin, who had invited her to spend the day with her. Ruth and the twins started off on a skating-party about three in the afternoon, after we'd done up the dishes together. As soon as I was sure they were all safely out of the way—Alec was sound asleep on the third floor—I stuck on my red tam and sweater, and took my present over to Dr. Maynard.

I was dreadfully afraid I'd meet some one I knew on the way, and they'd inquire what I had in the bundle. It was the awkwardest thing I ever attempted to carry in my life. Try it sometime. When I struggled up to Dr. Maynard's front door, I wondered if he had been watching me from the windows, and asking himself what in the name of heaven was coming now. But he wasn't at home. Eliza who came to the door explained that Dr. Maynard had gone out horseback riding, but wouldn't I come in and wait?

I thanked Eliza—I'd never been inside Dr. Maynard's house before—and entered the hall. She showed me into a big square room at the left, and told me to sit down.

"I won't stop, I think," I said. "I'll just leave this. It's a Christmas present for Dr. Maynard. Don't tell him who left it. There's a card inside."

"I'll lay it right here on his desk," said Eliza, grinning with pleasure.

She'd no sooner put my bundle down than I heard the clatter of horse's hoofs on the hard driveway outside.

"I believe he's coming," I exclaimed. "How lucky! I'll wait."

After Eliza had gone back to the kitchen and I was alone, I gazed about the room. It was a dark, dull room with bronze-coloured walls. Low, black walnut bookcases were built in around two sides, and over them hung two solitary pictures—steel engravings of battle scenes. There were several huge leather armchairs, and a bare leather couch in one corner. There wasn't a single sofa-pillow on it. I didn't believe Dr. Maynard liked sofa-pillows after all. Everything was so big and dark and stiff in that room, I was afraid a pillow would look out of place. I walked over to Dr. Maynard's desk. It was just like the room—nothing pretty on it—a book or two, a big bronze horse, a piece of black onyx for a paperweight. There was also a small, dark leather frame, and in it a kodak picture of Alec on horseback. The horse was poor dear little Dixie, who had gone away. I remembered when Dr. Maynard had taken that picture. It was in our back yard last summer. The smoke-bush had been in full plumage. Just before he snapped the picture, he had called to me, "You get into it, too, Bobbie. Stand up here, in front, by Dixie's head." And there I was, as sure as life, pinching the dear little horse's soft under lip, and smiling at Dr. Maynard.

As I stood looking at the picture, wondering where Dixie had gone—for Alec hadn't told me and I dreaded to ask—Dr. Maynard passed by the window by my side. He was coming in from the stable by way of the front door, and Eliza would have no opportunity for telling him that he had a caller. As I heard him fitting his key into the lock of the outside door, it occurred to me that it would be fun to hide. I glanced around the room. There wasn't a drapery in sight. There wasn't a hanging of any description that I could crawl behind. So finally I dashed into what proved to be a closet—dark as pitch.

Dr. Maynard didn't stop in the hall. He didn't call Eliza. He came directly toward the library door and entered the room. The sun was just setting, and a few last rays came slanting through the windows. They burnished the room like magic brass-polish. The bronze-coloured walls shone like dull copper; the brown leather armchairs, the black walnut woodwork, the old camel-shaded rugs were absolutely golden. As Dr. Maynard stood in the late sunshine in his khaki coloured riding things, his face all aglow and ruddy with the cold, he too glowed like everything else. He looked very handsome in his riding boots (I could see him through the crack in the door) and much sportier than in automobile goggles and a visored cap.

He tossed down his riding whip and soft felt hat in a chair, rubbed his bare hands together as if they were cold, blew through his fingers, then abruptly flung himself full length on the leather couch. He clasped his two hands underneath his head, and lay there with his eyes wide open, staring up at the ceiling. I hoped he wouldn't keep me waiting long. A small travelling clock on the desk struck four-thirty, and he turned toward it. It was then that he saw the big white bundle resting on his blotter. He frowned a moment, as his gaze fell upon it (I was shaking with laughter) then got up and walked over to it. He picked it up, turned it over, and laid it down again. He examined the outside closely—for an address, I suppose—gave it up, then shoving his hands into his pockets, stood looking down at the bundle, as if some stranger had left a baby at his door and he didn't know what to do with it. Finally, he decided to open the thing at least, and began taking out the pins. Beneath the brown paper was the layer of white tissue paper, tied with red Christmas ribbon. I didn't think Dr. Maynard would ever get beneath that tissue paper. You would have thought that there was something explosive inside. He lifted up the rustling package gingerly by the red ribbon and looked it all over. My card was hanging from the under side. Dr. Maynard took it off at last and read it.

It was a plain white card with simply the words: "Merry Christmas to W. F. M. from his discharged chauffeur, George." Dr. Maynard gazed at that card as if there had been volumes written on it. He turned it over, searched on the back, and examined again its face. Then he went to the window, put the shade up to the top, and came back to the desk. His back was toward me; I couldn't see the expression on his face as he folded back the tissue paper, and my pillow finally shone up at him. He didn't speak nor make a single sound as he stood looking down at the initials and his class numeral. He didn't stir—just looked until the silence grew uncomfortable. Suddenly he sat down in his desk-chair, leaned forward, picked up Alec's picture and began looking at that in the same awfully still, quiet way. I couldn't bear it a minute longer. The tensity was something like a shrill, long-drawn-out note on a violin. I can't explain it, but it made me want to scream.

Suddenly I burst out upon him.

"Well," I exclaimed, "do you like it?"

He wheeled about, as if he'd heard a shot.

"Lucy!" he said, "Where did you—?"

"In the closet," I interrupted, "watching."

He still had the picture in his hands. He glanced at it, then laid it down, and for the first time in my life I saw the dark colour come into Dr. Maynard's face. He came over to me.

"Did you make it?" he asked me quietly.

"Every stitch for you!" I said, laughing.

He didn't answer at first. He just kept looking at me, with that queer, new look of his. He didn't joke. His eyes didn't twinkle with fun. When he spoke his voice trembled. He took one of my hands very kindly and gently in both of his cold ones.

"You have made my Christmas the very happiest one in my life, Lucy," he said solemnly.

I glanced up surprised. I wish I could write down how his eyes looked. I can't. I only know I was suddenly afraid. I drew my hand away and laughed, for no reason. I was actually embarrassed before Dr. Maynard!

"I guess I must go," I said nervously. The sun had set and the glow had all gone out of the room.

Dr. Maynard didn't answer me. He just stood there like a stone man. Oh, I think that silences are the most awfully eloquent things in the world!

"It's getting dark," I added desperately.

Without a word Dr. Maynard went to the library door and opened it. I followed. Then to the front door and opened that. He stood holding it back, still not speaking (but I could feel his gaze burning into me) and I sped past him out into the dusk, like a wild bird out of a cage.

I don't know how I got home. I half ran, half stumbled along the frozen road. My heart was thumping, and though I wasn't a bit cold (my cheeks fairly burned) my teeth chattered as if I were chilled through. When I reached the house there was a funny, choking feeling in my throat, and I dashed up to my room and locked myself in.

*

All this last took place not eight hours ago and it is very late Christmas night.

When I write down what has happened it seems absurd to be excited. But when I think of it—when I close my eyes, see his gaze, hear his voice, I can't sleep. So I have climbed up into my cupola. I have been sitting looking up at the stars. They are very bright to-night. There are millions shining.

I can see most all the houses in Hilton from my eyrie. They are dark now. It is after twelve. But there are two windows aglow. I can see them shining, side by side like eyes, through the bare limbs of our apple orchard. They are western windows, in a white house, and eight hours ago the setting sun shone into them, upon Dr. Maynard in his riding clothes. I wonder what he is doing so late.

It's a lovely night—cold, clear and so still. I'd like to walk twenty miles before morning. I'd like to fly a thousand.

O Father, I don't know why it is—it doesn't seem right, for the awful shadow is still over our house and Alec hasn't smiled all day—but this—oh, this is *my* happiest Christmas too!

CHAPTER XI

ON a certain night in April I was in the sitting-room trying to keep awake until Alec came home. His train was not due until midnight. I was awfully anxious to wait up for him, but at ten o'clock I was so sleepy that I couldn't keep my eyes open another minute. So I went to Father's roll-top desk and scribbled this on a piece of paper: "*Dear Alec—Be sure and stop at my room when you come in. Bobbie,*" and fastened it with a wire hairpin on the light that I left burning.

Alec and I were on friendly terms again, and the whole world was smiling for me. I didn't care if the "For Sale" was still hitting me in the face every time I entered the yard, since Alec had put me back in charge of the Household Account. I might have known my cheque-book wouldn't have lied for me. Alec didn't get around to look into my bookkeeping until about the first of January, and then he was so delighted to discover that I hadn't failed in my trust, after all, that he couldn't reinstate me quickly enough. It was so good to be friends again, such a relief to have his faith in me restored and made whole, that I guess he didn't want to risk urging me to explain what I really wanted the seventy-five dollars for. "I know you'll explain all about it, sometime," he said. And I replied, "Sometime, Alec." That was the way our quarrel ended. The next morning I walked to the factory with my brother; the next evening I sat with him by the drop-light and when he went to bed I carried to his room some hot milk and crackers so that he would sleep. Since then we have been nearer to each other than ever before.

There is something beautiful about our relations. I'd die for Alec. I don't believe there ever has been a brother and sister more congenial than Alec and I. I know just how to please him, and he knows better than any one in this world how to manage me. There isn't a prouder girl alive than I, when Alec confides his business affairs to me. I do not understand them very well. Companies and Coöperations, Preferred and Common Stock, Bonds and Bank-notes are all a perfect jumble in my mind. But I've learned long ago, that nothing will shut a man up more quickly than a comment on a girl's part that shows him how ignorant she is. So now I keep still; listen as hard and closely as I can; sympathise with my whole heart when Alec is worried, and rejoice with him when he announces that some Boston bank or other has lent him twenty-five thousand dollars, although I *am* frightened to death of borrowing. I never give my brother a chance to scoff at a girl's comprehension of business transactions. The result is, he talks to me by the hour, and thinks I understand a great deal more than I do.

Ever since last Christmas Alec has been running down to New York about every two weeks. There was a big order that he was trying to secure, besides some sort of an arrangement he wanted to work up with some rich men down there to increase the capital stock of the business, I think he said. I have an idea, though I never asked, that if he could have worked that arrangement it would have saved the business from peril of failing. Alec used to stay in New York about three days usually, and always came home a little more worried, anxious, and discouraged than when he started.

This time he had been away almost two weeks. I had had only one short note from him written the day after he left home. Since then I had not heard from him until his telegram had arrived announcing he would reach Hilton on the midnight from New York.

It was a cold blustering night for April, and before I went to bed myself, I went up into Alec's third-floor room, turned on the heat, filled a hot-water bag and stuck it down between the cold sheets of his bed.

I must have been sleeping very soundly when Alec stole into my room at twelve-thirty. I didn't know he was in the house, until I felt his hand on my shoulder and his gentle, "Hello, Bobbie!" I woke up with a glad start and found him sitting on the side of my bed. "My, what a sleeper!" he said and leaned down and kissed my forehead.

I knew from the first whiff that Alec must have been sitting in the smoking-car (he doesn't smoke himself) and I drew in a fine, long breath before I spoke.

"Oh, Alec," I exclaimed, "how beautifully New Yorky you smell!"

"Do I, funny Bobbikins?" he laughed at me, and at the sound of that name which Alec had not called me by for six months, a thrill of new courage ran through me.

I sat up.

"Alec," I said, "you've brought good news. I *know* it! I *know* it! I knew we couldn't fail. I've felt it all along. I knew Father's dear old business wouldn't go back on us. I had a feeling that *this* trip to New York would be a lucky one."

"I've been farther than New York, Bobbie. I've been to Pinehurst, North Carolina," Alec announced.

"To Pinehurst! Mercy! Whatever in the world—do tell me *every* word. I'm simply crazy to hear all about it."

"Well—" he began. "Say, Bobbikins," he broke off, "would you be very much surprised to know that it is—all right between Edith and me?"

Alec might as well have struck off on a tangent about George Washington or Joan of Arc.

"Edith?" I gasped.

"Yes," went on Alec gently; "Edith Campbell. Of course you've known I've cared for no one else for the last ten years. The business and our large family have always made it seem rather hopeless. But when I was in New York I had a common little picture post-card from Edith, who was at Pinehurst, and your disgraceful old brother here dropped everything and went down there. I was there for six whole days, and she and her family and I all came home together to-night after two rather nice days in New York. She's actually got a ring in a little blue velvet box which she's going to wear for me a little later, Bobbie."

He tried to say it lightly but his whole voice was exulting. "You see, I had to come in and tell my partner, didn't I? She would have to know first of all about such a great piece of news."

He stopped and I sat perfectly silent, stunned for an instant, not knowing quite what had struck me and knocked me down with my breath all gone. Alec waited and I tried to jump up, as it were, and speak, so he would know I wasn't dead.

"Why, Alec Vars!" I managed to gasp, and then the horror of his news flashed over me. The man I loved best in the whole world had just told me that he was engaged to be married to a girl whom I abhorred! I wanted to scream; I wanted to bury my face in my pillow and cry; I wanted to say, "Oh, go away, go away, Alexander Vars. Leave me alone. I want to die." But instead I remarked quite calmly, "You engaged? To Edith Campbell? My goodness, but I'm surprised." And then warned by the choke in my voice, I switched off into something commonplace. "Say, would you mind," I said jovially enough, "just removing your hundred and seventy-five pounds off my left foot there? You're crushing the bones in it."

Alec leaned forward and kissed me hard.

"You little brick of a Bobbie! I knew you'd take it like a soldier."

I gulped down a disgusting sob.

"But wasn't I the goose," I hurried like mad to say, for I was afraid I'd break down and bawl like a baby before his very eyes, "wasn't I the little goose to think it was the business that made you so happy?"

"Oh, the business," Alec announced, "is bound to succeed *now*."

"Sure," I broke in hastily, "just bound to. It's awfully nice, all around, isn't it? And I—" I floundered on, "I am just—just *pleased*!"

The hall clock struck one. I grasped the blessed sound like a sinking man.

"Is that twelve-thirty, one, or one-thirty? I haven't the ghost of an idea," I said lightly. Then desperately, at the breaking point, I gasped, "Is it cold out?"

Alec patted my hand.

"Brave girl! I understand. But don't you worry. Everything will work out all right. Now I'll say good-night."

I think Alec must have seen I couldn't hold in much longer. I was, in fact, using every atom of strength that I possessed to fight that pushing, shoving, tumbling crowd of lumps and sobs in my throat. Just as Alec was closing my door I managed to call after him, so that he might know that I wasn't crying, "Be sure and turn out the lights."

"All right, General-manager."

"And say," I added, "you know I think it's perfectly fine."

"Surely! Good-night."

Then my door closed, and I sank down on my pillow, opened the gates wide, and let the torrent of sobs rush through.

Can any one realise the torture of my mind during the long dark hours of that night? I hardly can realise it now, myself. The fact, "ALEC IS ENGAGED TO EDITH CAMPBELL!" glared at me horribly as if it were printed in enormous white letters on a black ground, like a big sign on a factory, and I stared and stared, hypnotised, beyond power of thought. I was so stunned and overcome by the fact itself that at first I was unable to comprehend what it would mean to me. I hated Edith Campbell. All my life I had hated her. She had always treated Alec like the dirt under her feet—forever flaunting Palm Beach and Poland Springs in his face and eyes, parading to church every other Sunday with smart stylish-looking men and planting them down in the pew two rows in front of ours to show them off.

Of course I had guessed that Alec had liked Edith Campbell. As long ago as I can remember he used to call on her when she came home from her fashionable New York boarding-school. Alec invited her to be his special guest, at his Class-Day, when he graduated from college. But she elected to go with somebody else, and pranced down there with a millionaire's son. Poor Alec didn't invite any other girl. I was in knee skirts then, but I was old enough to hate her for it. Not that I wanted such a creature to be nice to Alec. I didn't. I knew my brother was miles too good for her, but I couldn't bear to have such a flashy, worldly, inferior girl show scorn toward a prince. I never understood why Alec had admired her. She's absolutely opposite from my brother in every possible way. She has the most confident, cock-surest manner I ever witnessed. Her clothes are dreadfully flashy and her father is a mere upstart who squeezes money out of everybody he knows. Hilton used to criticise Edith Campbell before it commenced bowing and scraping to her. When she came home from boarding-school, she let it be known that her intimate friends lived outside of Hilton. She advertised that she visited at some of the big places in the Berkshires. She merely tolerated Hilton and its people.

Oh, I hate her! I never saw why men ran after her so frantically. It used to make me absolutely sick when the younger girls in Hilton got the Edith Campbell craze. They used to try to copy everything she wore. But *I* didn't. I wouldn't as much as turn my head to look at her. I was delighted when Alec stopped going to see her. I had thought, when Alec announced his engagement to me, that that little romance of his had been dead and buried for five years. It hadn't even worried me.

When I awoke the morning after Alec told me his astonishing news, and saw the sun shining in a square on the wall opposite me, I lay very still for a moment. "You've had a horrible dream," I said. "Alec didn't come home last night. Just a minute, and things will get themselves fixed." I sat up, but the dream didn't fade. There was the tell-tale towel with which I had bathed my eyes; there the glass of water; there the dissipated-looking candle burned down to its very last; here the confused tossed bed-clothes, and when I staggered to the mirror, there were my swollen red eyes and awful tangled hair. I dressed slowly, with a very heavy heart, and unable to cry any more, smiled at myself once or twice in the glass out of grim spite.

I had not gone to sleep until it had begun to grow light. I remembered now. And it was nine o'clock when I went downstairs for an attempt at breakfast. Ruth was devouring eggs when I went into the dining-room. I had thought she would be at school, but I had forgotten that it was Saturday. Alec had already gone to the factory. His eggy plate and half-filled coffee-cup stood at his deserted place.

"My, but you're late," said Ruth, emptying the cream-pitcher into her coffee. "Say, isn't it corking about Alec? We've been sitting here hours talking about it. I think it's simply dandy. Just imagine—Edith Campbell!"

I became very busy fixing my cuff-link, for I was ashamed of my swollen eyes; but Ruth was sure to see them. She glanced up.

"I might have known you'd take it like that," she broke out, though I hadn't said a word; "always acting like a thunder-cloud, and throwing wet blankets on everything. Now why in the world shouldn't Alec get married?"

"I didn't say he shouldn't," I murmured.

"Well," went on Ruth, "Edith Campbell is *great*. I can't get over the fact, that with all the men she's known, she likes Alec better than any of them. She's dreadfully popular. I'll bet she's had a dozen proposals. Oh, I think Al's done awfully well. The Campbells have piles of money. I know her younger sister Millicent, and their house beats anything I ever saw. You ought to see it. And besides, Edith Campbell is the best-looking thing! She's stunning on a horse."

Ruth always antagonises me when she talks about people she admires.

"*I* think," I said in a low voice, "that Edith Campbell is common and loud and vulgar."

"Oh, nonsense!" retorted Ruth. "I'm simply wild about the whole thing. The Campbells are going to do this tumbledown old ark all over, for a wedding present, and Al says her father is going to insist on Edith's bringing her horses with her. I don't call that common or vulgar. I call it generous!"

"Is she going to live here?" I gasped.

"Of course she is. Where else? And Alec says that you and I will each have a perfectly lovely room, and divide our time between here and Tom's. I tell you what, I'm glad for one, that we won't have to live like pigs any more. Edith Campbell is used to piles of servants!"

I don't know why Ruth's words made me so terribly angry.

"Ruth Chenery Vars," I said, "I hate Edith Campbell, and I'll never live under the same roof with her. I never will. Do you hear me? I never will!"

Ruth glanced up and met my fiery eyes.

"Mercy," she said, simply disgusted, "why get so everlasting mad?"

I shoved back my chair and left the table quietly, hurried up the stairs straight to my disheveled room, and locked the door tight. My mind was clear now all right; I could comprehend the meaning of the awful black and white sign *now*, without any difficulty. I was no goose not to know perfectly well that Alec's engagement meant that Miss Lucy Vars would be requested to hand in her resignation as General-manager, Keeper-of-the-Household-Account, Bosser-of-the-meals, Mother-of-the-family, and oh, too, Partner-of-Alec. Why, I had poured the coffee at our table ever since the day Father had put me there in Mother's empty chair. I had always sat there, pushed the bell, and told the maid to take off the plates for dessert. My place had always been opposite Father, and after he had gone, Alec had sat there. Ever since, he and I had held the reins together. There wasn't a chair nor a rug, nor a table in the house that I hadn't put in position. There wasn't a pound of sugar, nor a half-dozen oranges in the pantry that I had not ordered. For five years there hadn't been a servant engaged by any one but me. Now, suddenly, all such an arrangement was to be at an end. Ruth was delighted; Alec was supremely happy; the twins, who worship anything that means more cash, would be transported with joy. Everybody, in fact, would delight in a change in administration—everybody but the poor old dethroned ruler, who was locked in her desolate room trying to find consolation in vigorously making her bed.

When Alec came home at noon I saw him scanning my impassive face, for I had not been crying since the night before, and the trace of tears was gone. After our regular Saturday boiled dinner he asked me to come into the sitting-room. He closed the doors carefully and sat down beside me on the couch. I wished he wouldn't take my hand for it was chapped and red, and of course he had held hers, for which he had bought the beautiful ring in the little blue velvet box, and hers would be soft and white. I drew mine away. Alec talked to me gently and told me about the arrangements. I heard him say with a dull shock, that they would be married in the early fall. I remember wondering how they had decided such details in the course of ten days. I soon discovered that they had managed to go over the whole ground. There seemed to be no question undecided, no points untouched. Ruth, he said, would start in at boarding-school in the fall; the twins of course would continue at college and their vacations would, as usual, be spent at home. He repeated what I already very well knew that after the twins graduated they would probably go out West and start into one of Tom's lumber camps.

"So there'll just be me left," I hurried to say, kind of to help him out.

"And, of course, *you'll* live right along here with us," he said, "except, once in a while, when Tom and Elise want you there with them."

"I'm worse to dispose of than a mother-in-law," I half laughed, sorry in a moment that I had spoken so, for Alec looked hurt, and exclaimed, "Oh, Bobbie dear!"

"Oh, I'll try, Alec, I really will," I reassured him, for Alec always brings out the best in me.

"And go and see Edith very soon?" he said, following me up cruelly. "She'll be expecting you."

"Oh, yes, I'll try," I murmured, biting my trembling under lip.

"Good girl! I knew I could count on you. You'll like Edith," he said. "And she wants to be awfully kind to you and Ruth. I know you'll try and make it easy for her, Bobbie," he added, and left me as cheerfully as a summer's breeze.

Late that afternoon, about five I think, I started out for a walk in Buxton's woods, a quarter of a mile back of our house. I hadn't been gone very long when I heard a step behind me, and turning around I saw, mounted on her stunning black Kentucky thoroughbred, Edith Campbell, coming toward me. I wanted to run away, to hide perhaps behind a tree and let her pass, but I couldn't for she had caught sight of me.

"Hold on," she called. "Wait a minute," and she drew up beside me. "Hello, Lucy," she said in her familiar, breezy way. "Now isn't this luck?" Her dark, crisp hair was neat and firm beneath the little black derby—an affectation in dress that no one wears riding in Hilton except Edith Campbell. She didn't have them on to-day, but usually she wears long green drop-earrings, screwed on, I think—too New Yorky for anything. "Wait a jiffy," she laughed, "and I'll walk along with you. Pierre here, can mosey along behind." She sprang down from her saddle like a sporty horse-woman, came up and thrust out a gauntlet-gloved hand to me. She gave me a Hercules grip. "Has Al told you?" she asked, plunging straight ahead, with no delicacy.

"Yes, he has," I stammered, "and—I congratulate you both," I finished desperately.

It did sound stiff and formal and schoolgirlish, but I was angry with Edith Campbell when she laughed at me and exclaimed, "You funny old-fashioned child!"

She arranged one pair of reins over her horse's neck and used the other pair for a lead, slipping her arm through the loop.

"Come on now, let's walk," she said and put her free arm through mine, a familiarity from the wonderful Edith Campbell for which even sensible

Juliet would envy me. *I* wanted to edge away from her. "Alec," she went on, "thinks the world and all of you, Bobbie," (as if she had to inform me!) "and I want you to know right off, you won't be losing a brother, simply gaining a sister." (Usual, meaningless words! As if Ruth wasn't more than enough anyhow.) "And another thing," she ploughed ahead, "there will always be a room in our house for Bobbie. One of the things I told Alec was that he must look out for his sisters."

"Alec would do that anyway," I said.

"Of course. Nice old Al! He's as good as gold."

I couldn't bear her patronising manner. She has always treated Alec like that, just because she had money and he had nothing but goodness. I turned to her seriously.

"Miss Campbell," I asked, "how did you come to want to marry Alec?"

"You amusing chicken!" she laughed, then pinching me disgustingly on the arm, she added in a sly way, "You wait, you'll know when the right one comes."

I flushed but held my peace.

"I was only wondering," I said. "Alec has so little money, and you—I mean our business—our success is so uncertain."

"Alec is bound to succeed *now*," she replied in her cock-sure way. "I told Al there was no such word in my vocabulary as failure. Besides *Father* is going to look into the business, and Father never touched a thing that wasn't successful."

"Your father!" I gasped with the colour again in my face. Her father used to collect junk-iron. "Our business!"

"Oh, come, come. Just like Al at first. This Vars pride! Don't you see, my dear, that, independent of weddings, a man can put a little life into a dead business if he wants to?"

"My father's business isn't dead," I exclaimed, now filled with indignation.

"Oh, come, Bobbikins!"

"Don't call me that, please," I said and drew away my arm.

"Tut, tut! Come now! You and I are going to be friends." She treated me as if I were aged five. "You know," she went on, "when I come, I think there'll be an extra saddle horse, in one of the stalls in your stable." She used that mysterious tone you do to children when talking about Santa Claus. "I think if you will look very hard you will find your initials on him somewhere, Bobbie."

"I wouldn't touch it, Miss Campbell. I wouldn't touch one hair of the horse; and please call me Lucy."

We were breaking out of the narrow wood-path, and coming to a travelled road. We walked in silence till we reached the highway. It was almost dark. Suddenly Edith Campbell spoke.

"I must be hustling homeward," she said glibly, and as if nothing unpleasant had occurred between us she asked, "Lend me your hand, will you, Bobbie, please?"

I helped her mount, in silence.

"That's the way," she said. "Thanks. Now look here, poor little childie," she broke off, looking down at me like a queen from her saddle, "whenever you're ready to be friends, remember, so am I. All right, Pierre!" and she cantered off in the dusk.

I stood quite still for a moment, and then right to that lonely, empty road, I said out loud, "I can't live with her. I can't—I can't! Dear Alec, I tried. Dear Father and Tom and Elise, I tried, but I can't, I can't!" And all the dark way home, all the long night through, I ran over and over the words like a squirrel in a revolving cage.

CHAPTER XII

FOR three days and nights I wandered over the ruins of my life, back and forth, helpless, almost driven mad by the horror of it; and then at last Dr. Maynard came. I had not realised that he had been out of town. I had been so stunned by Alec's announcement that I had not missed him. He had been down to Baltimore for three days attending some sort of a medical conference and I had not known that he had been outside of Hilton.

Dr. Maynard and I were as good friends as ever now. Three whole months had passed since that Christmas Day when he discovered my sofa-pillow on his desk, and I had come to the conclusion that he had been merely surprised into his queer behaviour that day. He had never shown a scrap of the same emotion since. I remember the very next time I saw him he had dropped that newly acquired gravity of his. Somehow I had been disappointed. When he referred to my pillow in his old natural, jovial way, I had been hurt. "I tell you what," he had said, "I feel like an undergraduate again. Nice girl like Lucy Vars making me a pillow for my room! Won't you come to my Class-Day?" he had laughed. It was I who had flushed then. I managed to throw back some sort of a careless rejoinder, but I tell you, I didn't waste any more madly happy moments on Dr. Maynard. Grey-haired old bachelor! He was old enough to be my uncle anyhow! We had resumed our automobile rides just as naturally as if he'd never acted queerly at all. We took up our jolly repartee, returned to our old plane of good-comradeship, exactly as if I had never seen him gaze at my picture, and heard his voice tremble when he told me I had made his Christmas the very happiest in his life. *I* didn't care. I was glad of it. I had never wanted Dr. Maynard for a lover! But I wanted him for a friend.

I don't believe I quite appreciated how much I wanted him, until he came back from Baltimore and discovered me wandering about my ruins like a maniac. When I found myself bundled up in Father's old ulster, again beside him in his automobile, flashing through the cool night air, a great wave of relief ran over me. Dr. Maynard has seen me through so much trouble, brought me safely over so many difficulties, that it was a comfort just to sit beside him in silence. When we had reached a good clear stretch of road, he settled down comfortably behind the wheel.

"Now go ahead," he said heartily; "the whole story, please," and I knew that Alec had broken his news to him.

"Well," I started in, "since you've been gone, there's been a dreadful earthquake around here." (Dr. Maynard and I adore to talk in similes.) "My house has been smashed up, and I'm a pitiful refugee. I am cold and hungry and without a home."

"I've come with supplies," laughed Dr. Maynard, taking it up delightfully. "I'm a little late, but I've brought bread and meat and a tent, and want you to crawl in and warm up."

"I can't live with her, Dr. Maynard. I can't!" I broke out, too heart-sick to play with similes any more. "I hate her and I can't help it. She's taken Alec away, she's pushed herself into my dear father's business, and there's no place for me, as I can see, anywhere."

"Tell me all about it," said Dr. Maynard, and I related every single word of my whole pitiful story, growing sorrier and sorrier for myself as I went along, and finally at the end breaking down completely, repeating my old time-worn phrase, "I can't live with her. I can't, can't!" I covered my face with both hands. There were tears trickling down my cheeks.

Without a word of advice or comfort, Dr. Maynard shut off the power and brought the car to a standstill by the side of the bleak country road. He took hold of my hands and gently drew them away from my face down into my lap. Then in a low voice with the play and banter all gone out of it he said, "Could you live with *me*, Lucy?"

"Oh, yes," I replied quickly enough, "fifty times easier!"

Perhaps he smiled, for he added half laughing and yet gravely, too, "I would like to have you, if you want to."

"I only wish I could," I said desperately.

And then very seriously and very solemnly he told me his story. I can't say that I was exactly surprised. I had half guessed it for the last two years; but then I had half guessed a lot of preposterous things that never came true. "I talked with Alec last night," I heard Dr. Maynard telling me gently, "and if you would like—that is if you want to come with me, Lucy, your brother would be glad to have you, I am certain. This isn't the only talk Alec and I have had about you. I wanted to speak to you about this last fall, but Al thought it better to wait. And I wanted to speak again after—the sofa-pillow, and again Al couldn't quite make up his mind that you had grown up, and wanted me to wait again. So I did. You see," he smiled, "it isn't a *new* idea with me."

I listened calmly as Dr. Maynard went on talking in his quiet, unexcited manner. I didn't interrupt his long, well-planned speech. I simply sat dumb with my hands clasped tightly in my lap. I don't remember that I felt a single sensation during the entire explanation except at the end a kind of shock as I thought to myself: "So after all it's going to be just Dr. Maynard!" For when he had finally finished, I said evenly, with the moon standing there like a clergyman before us, and all the watching stars like witnesses behind, "I will come, Dr. Maynard," and I added, "and I think you are the very kindest man I know." For you see he had offered me his home, his protection, and his love, he said, for all my life.

There was something awfully silent and ominous about the gentle still way he turned the machine around and started for home. It was entirely different from what I had guessed might take place. In the dreams that I had woven I had never accepted Dr. Maynard. I had been grateful for his devotion, honoured by his proposal, deeply sorry for his disappointment, but like the girl in an old play called "Rosemary," my heart belonged to one who possessed youth and passion. In those absurd imaginings of mine I used to frame letters which I should write to Juliet Adams about poor Will Maynard. I used to plan just how I should break the news to my brother Alec. But now—Oh, now, I couldn't write Juliet at all; I couldn't tell Alec; I couldn't tell any one about my first proposal. I had accepted it in the first half-hour. There was nothing thrilling about it. I sat like a stone image beside Dr. Maynard. I couldn't speak.

"It took you an awfully long while to grow up," he said at last, half laughing. "I've actually grown grey waiting for you. Alec said to me the first time, 'Wait till she's nineteen,' and then, 'Good heavens, Will, she's nothing but a child yet. Wait till she's twenty,' and so on, and so on. Awful hindrance, because for the last two years I've been wanting to do some important research work in Germany. But I couldn't leave you to the wolves. How did I know but that some good-looking young chap would come along and snatch you up? But now, we'll go to Germany together, and, Lucy," he said, "Lucy—" but I didn't want Dr. Maynard to grow serious. I think he must have seen me kind of cringe away for he broke off lightly enough, "and perhaps some fine day the refugee and I will be seeing Paris together."

I stole into the house that night very quietly, crept up to my room and closed the door without a sound. I wanted to be alone. I was suddenly filled with a kind of panic-stricken wonder, for there had been actual tears in Dr. Maynard's eyes when he took my hand at the door (I hadn't known how to say good-night to him), a tremble in his voice that awed and frightened me. He acted very much as he had about my Christmas present. It had made me happy then, but, you see *then* I hadn't just promised to marry him. Oh, I hated having him look so serious and solemn about it, and now as I stood a moment with my back against my closed door, my hat and coat still on, I pressed my two cool hands against my burning cheeks and tried to comprehend a little of what it all meant. Suddenly I crossed the room, pulled on the gas by my bureau, leaned forward and gazed grimly at my familiar old face in the glass before me. So this was what was to become of Lucy Chenery Vars, I thought calmly; this was her story; this was her end; and oh, to think that all the beautiful unknown future of the person in the glass before me was wiped out and decided in one fell swoop, made me want to throw my arms about her image and kiss her for pity. I turned away.

Of course I liked Dr. Maynard—I had always liked him. And his big, empty, white-pillared house was in the very town, on the very street of my dear beloved home. There was a place for me there. Alec had given Dr. Maynard to understand that there would be no objection from him. Probably it seemed to Alec a good way to dispose of me. Oh, there was everything in favour of the arrangement. I had always longed to go to Europe. Germany and Paris were sparkling ahead, and here—*here* nothing but the nightmare of Edith Campbell everywhere I turned. I drew a long breath—there was no other course for me to follow—looked once more sadly into the glass, pulled down my curtain and began to get ready for bed.

I never shall forget that night. I don't believe I slept at all. I don't know what time it was when I got up and, lighting my candle, sat down at my desk, shivering in my long white nightgown. I just sat and sat; and gazed and gazed; and thought and thought; and dropped, I remember, little drops of melted wax along my bare arm, as I turned over my problem in my mind. "If only I didn't actually have to marry him!" I said out loud and turned and sank again into troubled silence. I got up once and carried the candle close to the cold, glass-covered picture of my mother that hung over my bed. Why did she have to die so long ago? What would she say—she who was to have been my best friend—what would she say if she could turn that clear-cut profile around and let me look into her eyes? I didn't know. I hadn't been old enough to remember even her smile. Shouldn't a girl be glad on the night of her betrothal? Shouldn't there be ardent looks, passionate words, tender caresses for her to live through again in thought? Shouldn't she long for the sight of the man whom she had promised to marry? "What shall I do, Father?" I said out loud. "What shall I do?" But only my clock answered me with its steady, unintelligible tick. No one could help me—no one in the wide world. I asked them, and they couldn't. Even Edith Campbell had said, "you'll know"; but oh, I didn't, I didn't.

So that is why, near morning, I got up again, went to my desk, opened a little secret drawer, and took out a picture. The picture was the one I had bought in New York after I had seen Robert Dwinnell at the theatre in the afternoon. Of course it is silly and very absurd for a girl of my years to treasure a picture of an actor in a secret drawer in her desk. I can't help it. That picture had been my ideal for almost five years now. It wasn't the actor that I liked so much (for of course I have been told that actors aren't nice); it wasn't Robert Dwinnell himself I admired. It was simply the jolly look in his eyes and the way he had—I remembered it so well—of striding across the stage, sitting carelessly on the edge of a table and swinging one foot. It had just about torn the heart out of me to watch that man make love. He had a kind of lingering way with his hands, and with his eyes too, every time the heroine was in his presence. Even before he had proposed to her, I knew he adored her and afterward—oh, really I think Robert Dwinnell must have loved that actress off the stage as well as on. Dr. Maynard's hands had never lingered about my shoulders when he helped me on with a coat; he had never gazed at me eloquently across a crowded room; and even after I had promised to marry him he hadn't crushed me to him in any mad wave of joy. I gazed for a whole half-minute at Robert Dwinnell's picture. I forgot all my problems for a little while—I forgot everything in the memory of that man's image. Call it absurd if you want to, ridiculous and impossible, but when I raised my eyes at last and rose, clear as the day that was just breaking, bright as a new-born vision, I knew—I *knew* I couldn't marry just everyday, kind Dr. Maynard. It was just as if Robert Dwinnell had gotten up from out of that picture, walked over to me, taken my hand and said, "You must wait for some one like me." And I looked up and knew that I must. It was like a miracle, and I shall never forget the sudden trembling assurance in my heart, as I found my way to my desk and in the light of that lovely new morning, drew out a sheet of paper and wrote to Edith Campbell and told her I was ready to be friends. For suddenly, brought face to face with the thrilling image of the man of my dreams, I was ready to live with twenty Edith Campbells. Of course, *of course*, I couldn't marry Dr. Maynard, and with a little pang of regret or something like it in my heart, I finally wrote him this note:

"*Dear Dr. Maynard,*

The refugee has thought it all over very carefully and has decided to gather the pieces of her house together and rebuild on the same spot, like San Francisco."

Then I added, dropping all play and with something I knew to be pain:

"I can't do it, Dr. Maynard, I've tried and I can't. But you'll always be the very kindest man I know.

"LUCY CHENERY VARS."

"*Now* if you don't come!" I said to the picture, and leaned forward and buried my head in my arms.

So that is how it happened that Dr. Maynard went away to Germany alone and I remained at home to fight my battle. It was a dull, grey morning that he sailed, some three weeks after that wakeful night of mine, and I was sitting alone in my room at precisely eleven o'clock—the sailing hour—trying to imagine Dr. Maynard down there in New York on the big, white-decked liner, waving good-bye in his Oxford grey overcoat.

I was wondering if the nicest, cheerfullest steamer letter I could write had reached him when suddenly Mary, the general-housework girl, pushed open my door and shoved in a long white box that had come by express. I opened it wonderingly and gasped at the big mass of fresh red roses that met my gaze. I lifted them into my arms. It was exactly as if the kindest man I know had thrown them to poor me upon the shore, just at the moment that the big boat was pulling out, and I had caught them safely in my arms. There was a little limp card that came with them. The stick had all come off the envelope and it fell out on the bed like a loose rose petal. I leaned and picked it up.

The ink had begun to run a little as if the message had been written on blotting-paper, but I could make it out all right. The three little words brought burning tears to my eyes.

The card said: "For plucky San Francisco."

CHAPTER XIII

MANY months have passed since Dr. Maynard went to Europe. There have been two crops of chestnuts for me to gather alone in October since he sailed away—two dull, grey, unimportant Christmas nights since my ridiculous happiest one. Edith has been in command of my father's house for so long now that all the difficult adjustments have been made, the machinery is running without an audible squeak, and the house itself has developed into a plant as imposing and prosperous as a modern factory. As I write to-day I am sitting in my elaborate new bedroom, built on over the new porte-cochère—my old room was cut up into two baths and a shower—and am surrounded with rose cretonne hangings, lacy curtains, and delicately shaded electric lights.

Even the people in my life have changed so radically that I hardly recognise them as the ones that I once worked and cared for. Ruth has grown into a charming young lady; the twins have graduated from college and are earning their own way—Malcolm in New York and Oliver in a lumber camp out West; Tom is middle-aged; Elise, whom I visited last winter, is becoming a little stout and her hair is sprinkled through with grey; Alec has buried his personality in Edith; nothing is as it was. Even Hilton is different. The old Brooks Hotel on Main Street, where George Washington once stopped for over night, has been torn down; there's a new postoffice, a new City Hall; there's a double-tracked electric-car line to Boston. There are two taxicabs in the town now and a new theatre. Dr. Maynard's house looks like a tomb. The wisteria vine is the only live thing about it. Like hair it keeps on growing after death—winding, coiling, across the doors and window-panes with no hand to push it back. A young man just graduated from medical school has taken Dr. Maynard's practice; and as for kind, gentle Dr. Maynard himself I begin to doubt if such a person ever existed. When he went away he sold his automobile to Jake Pickens, a plumber down on Blondell Street, and to-day as I glided grandly by in Edith's limousine I observed Mr. Pickens wheezing up Main Street, chugging along with awful difficulty. The poor old machine looked about ready for the junk heap. A great wave of pity for it swept over me that brought tears to my eyes. Oh, I wish I could have kept right straight on with my old story. But I suppose everything has got to change, houses and towns and automobiles, as well as people and their histories.

I can hardly believe it was only two years ago that I used to climb into the cupola and lock myself away from everything below. There *is* no cupola now. It was cut off, like an offending wart. I was surprised to discover what a perfectly enormous thing it was as it stood upon the lawn waiting to be carried off. It reminded me of a horse that has fallen down on the pavement—symmetrical enough in its proper position, but dreadfully awkward and absolutely colossal sprawling about on the ground. Why, it took four horses to drag it up to old Silas Morton's. Silas Morton is a farmer up near Sag Hill and he bought my sacred temple for fifteen dollars. He uses it for a hen-house! It seemed to me like sacrilege, but the hens laid eggs in it, Mr. Morton said, as if they were possessed. The upper part of the window-panes in the cupola are made of yellow stained-glass, and he thinks—Silas Morton is kind of an inventor—that the hens have an idea it's sunshine and that spring is coming. I tell him the cupola is inspired. I saw a picture once of a common little farmhouse where Mrs. Eddy wrote her book, "Science and Health." If my book were to be published, and some photographer took a picture of the house in which I wrote it, I guess that old hen-coop would win the prize for an odd spot in which to have an inspiration.

With the cupola gone and the French roof entirely obliterated, the iron fence and the iron fountain sold to a junk man, a spreading porte-cochère at one side of the house, a billiard-room at the other, low verandas like a wide brim to a hat surrounding the entire structure, and everything painted a bright yellow trimmed with green, you never in this world would recognise 240 Main Street, once brown and square and ugly. There's a new stable a quarter of a mile back of the house; there are lawns where the vegetable garden used to be; the old apple orchard is now a sunken garden with a pool in the centre. As I write I can hear the trickle of a stream of water that spouts out of the little artificial pond, and catch the prosperous sound of the hum of a lawn-mower run by a motor. The name that Edith has chosen to give to all this grandeur is "The Homestead." It is engraved at the head of every sheet of note-paper in the establishment. The Homestead! You might as well call Windsor Castle the "Bide a Wee" or the "Dewdrop Inn" as this glaring, officious, stone-gated palace anything that suggests plainness and sweet homely comfort. The last time I wrote to Juliet I drew a big black ink line through the words "The Homestead" and wrote above "The Waldorf-Ritz-Plaza."

I've tried not to interfere with the changes Edith has made. I will confess I appealed to Alec about the apple orchard. But it was of no use. It seemed a shame to me, to go among that little company of old friends—twenty or thirty bent and bowing apple-trees grown up now side by side, touching branches and blooming together beautifully every spring just as if they were not far too old to bear anything to be called a harvest. I told Alec that I thought an apple orchard and a stone wall with poison ivy climbing over it was the loveliest garden for a New England homestead that any one could lay out. Alec must have told Edith, for the next day she asked me, in her laughing way, if I wouldn't like chickens scratching in the front yard, and yellow pumpkins piled on the back porch. New England homesteads even managed, she added, to keep pigs near enough the house so that the family could breathe the healthy odour in the parlour. "Dear child," she said, "of course we can't let the place be run over with poison ivy! How funny you are!" And the apple-trees came down. There are formal paths in the apple orchard now, the imported shrubs are tagged with labels, the pond is lined with cement. I simply have to escape to the woods, every once in a while, to make sure that nature is still having her way somewhere in the world.

You must think from this description that Edith Campbell is something of an heiress. Now that word to me has a kind of aristocratic sound, and so I prefer to say in regard to the Campbells, that they have simply oodles and oodles of money. I hate the word "oodles," but it just fits Edith Campbell. It describes her worldly possessions to a T. Her father, old Dave Campbell, is rolling up a fortune that is attracting attention. Why, the cost of all the improvements on old "two-forty" here didn't make a dent in his bank account they say. Alec tells me that if it wasn't for Mr. Campbell, Father's woollen business would not have endured another twelve months. Mr. Campbell has gone into the business heart and soul, and I don't know whether to be glad or sorry. Father never had any use at all for Mr. Campbell. He used to call him "scurvy." I remember the word because as a child I thought it a funny adjective to apply to a man who had a perfectly flawless complexion. I had to muster up all the control I had when I first saw David Campbell's big, fat, voluminous body occupying Father's revolving desk-chair in the private office down at the factory. I didn't think Father would like it. But Alec says that Father would much prefer to have Mr. Campbell elected as a president of the Vars & Company Woollen Mills than that any concern bearing his, Father's, name should fail to pay its creditors a hundred cents on the dollar. Perhaps he would; I don't know much about business. Anyhow I try to be nice to Mr. Campbell.

I try to be nice to Edith, too. It isn't easy. I don't like her, and I don't like her methods, but I don't tell her so. We don't quarrel, although we mix about like oil and water. Of course Edith has her good points. For instance she is the most generous person I ever knew, and she's good-nature itself. She'll take an insult from you, pay you back in your own coin and then exclaim: "Oh, come on, let's not fight. There's a dear! Let's go to the matinée this afternoon." She has a lot of practical ability too. She's a born manager, and as systematic as a machine. The trouble with Edith is her ambition. She wants to stand at the head of all society in the world, and to get there she is ready to work till she drops. Just as soon as she struggles up on top of one heap of people she begins on another, and so on. I don't know where she'll stop. Juliet Adams' mother told me that she could remember when people in Hilton didn't like to invite Mrs. Campbell to their houses. That was years ago, of course, for now they thank their lucky stars if they are invited to hers. There used to be, and are still, lots of beautiful country places sprinkled around Hilton. These summer people never mingled very much with Hiltonites, but as soon as Edith was able to walk she was bound to mingle with them. Well, she has realised that ambition. The summer colony, which is the set that gives social distinction to Hilton, includes Edith in all of its big functions now, in spite of the damning fact that she is a "native" and an "all-the-year-round."

Edith's social activities are simply marvellous to me. She has her plan of campaign—the various combinations of people to be invited to dinner-parties, bridges, or small teas, all mapped out and written down in a book at the beginning of each season. Then she manages to inveigle, by means of big fat cheques, I imagine, lions—pianists, and authors, and lecturers, whom everybody wants to see and hear—to act as her guest of honour. So her parties are always rather popular, you see. Oh, Edith is clever. She may not understand my nature very well, but to the likes and dislikes, pet ambitions and pleasures of human-nature generally she can cater to the queen's taste.

She has fairly hypnotised Ruth. My little sister thinks there is no one like her. As soon as Edith married Alec, she took complete possession of Ruth, provided her with a lot of lovely clothes and sent her off, for the first winter, to a fashionable boarding-school in New York. After eight dazzling months of that sort of life she ordained that Ruth should return to Hilton and "come out." Last fall she gave her a reception that fairly thrilled the town. Edith's word is sacred law to Ruth; Edith's opinion the ultimatum to any doubt on any question whatsoever. *I* am a mere speck on Ruth's outlook on life; *my* ideas don't count; I am so old-fashioned and so easily shocked; I don't know what style is; I don't possess a scrap of what Edith calls social-sense. Perhaps as much as anything else it is Edith's complete possession of Ruth that hurts me. It seems a shame that she couldn't have been satisfied with Alec. I don't see why she had to rob me of my only sister too. I don't cry about it (I won't let myself) but I think I've missed my own mother more since I was twenty than before I was ten. It may be a comfort to mothers whose little children have grown out of the helpless age to know this from a grown-up daughter.

I don't know what to say to you about my brother Alec. I wonder sometimes what has become of him. I see him, I hear him speak, I reply, but I might as well be gazing at his picture and talking with him over the long distance 'phone. I have no idea what he thinks about this new life of ours. He doesn't confide in me any more; we are almost strangers now. Of course I should expect him to be loyal to his wife—he's such a thoughtful man that he wouldn't hurt Edith's feelings for anything—but I wonder and wonder where all his old qualities have gone. Alec used to be so firm and determined, so frugal and economical. Are those qualities still smouldering away down deep in him somewhere, or when Edith took possession of his house, did she take possession of his soul too, and sweep out everything she didn't like, just as she cut off the cupola and sold the iron fence? Some men let women do that with them, especially if it's a woman they've wanted terribly for a dozen years, and never thought themselves good enough for her to accept. Why, Alec simply wants to please Edith and her family in every human way that he can. I have an idea that he feels so grateful to Edith for accepting him, and to Mr. Campbell for saving the business, that he doesn't dare disagree with a single solitary thing the Campbells ever do or think or suggest. I believe my brother is so overcome by living in such continual grandeur, sleeping in a bed with gold trimmings—Napoleonic, Edith says—bathing in a bathroom with Florentine tiles, entertaining all the big bugs within a hundred miles, and travelling to the office every morning in a limousine, that he feels that he must have been a mere worm when Edith picked him up. *I* think he's more of a worm *now*! Anyhow he doesn't show any backbone.

Sometimes at the table I glance at him across the flowers, and once in a long, long while there's a look in his eyes when they meet mine that I recognise as my dear brother's. Usually it's when Ruth and Edith are discussing society; and after one of these clandestine meetings of Alec's and mine across the flowers, I always come up here to my room wonderfully comforted, with a feeling that I am not absolutely deserted, after all.

Perhaps that sounds as if I were unhappy. Please do not think so, because I'm not. I'm *bound* not to be. I should be ashamed of myself, if just because I happened to be ousted from my job and didn't fancy my successor, I simply "went out into the back yard and ate worms." That isn't what I'm doing at all. Once Alec was married and I had made up my mind that I couldn't run away to New York and earn my way, or hire a house of my own and live by myself, I buckled down and did my level best to adjust my likes and habits to the conditions of Edith's reign. One can get used to anything, I believe. I accepted Edith as a person ought to accept any circumstance that can't be avoided. What if her ambitions do seem to me unworthy? What if she has crowded me out of my little niche? What if the customs and the things I liked are desecrated before my very eyes? All this will not cripple me, as a chance railroad accident might. I'm not enduring physical torture. I can still see, and hear, and use my two unhampered feet for long sweet walks in the country. What if, indeed, Edith has robbed me of Alec, and Ruth too? She cannot rob me of the joys of out-of-doors, the messages to me in books, the thrill I feel at the sound of distant music.

I can generally find several hours every day when I am able to steal away somewhere by myself with a book. I never had much time to read when I was younger and no one to suggest and guide as I grew up. I had never read *Vanity Fair* even, nor *Silas Marner*, nor *David Copperfield*. So after Alec was married, I made it my task to catch up with other girls of my age. I have my nose buried inside a novel most all of the time now. At first I used to drive myself to it, allot myself a certain number of chapters to read each day and accomplish it as if it were a stint. Now I simply devour a book in great hungry bites and wish there were more when I am finished. I don't know what I should do if I hadn't learned to love to read. I wonder if it would open up other sources of joy if I should learn to appreciate symphony or Italian Art. Perhaps Beethoven and Leonardo da Vinci, mere names to me now, would become as individual and inspire me with their messages as deeply as dear old Stevenson, whom I couldn't live without.

I think you must have surmised by this time that I haven't proved a great belle in society. You're exactly right. In the first place I hate bridge! Whenever I attempt to play, I get hot all over, and I wish I could unhook my tight collar and roll up my prickly sleeves. When it comes my turn to play, and I find myself desperately at a loss to know whether to trump or not—my partner looking daggers at me across the table and everybody waiting in dead silence—I simply give up all responsibility in the matter, repeat to myself: "Eenie, meenie, mynie moe, Catch a nigger by the toe," etc., and fling down the card that's "it," in utter abandon. Of course, that isn't good bridge, and Edith says I'll never make a player. She says I don't possess any more card-sense than social-sense. I wonder what kind of sense I do possess anyhow! It was a big consolation when I learned that the emptiest-headed women often make the best card players, simply because no superfluous ideas are at work in their brains to interrupt the train of concentrated card thought.

I'm not much more successful in conversation than I am in bridge. I seem to be always on the outside of women's intimacies somehow. Edith's set know one another so confidentially—keep tabs on the gowns, the hats, the jewellery, the number of servants each one has, and guess at one another's incomes. And then they use such a lot of mysterious signs! Sometimes raised eyebrows, a little nod toward a person's back, very tightly pursed lips, somebody abruptly twirling her two thumbs, will set off a whole roomful into peals of laughter, while I simply sit dazed and blank. It's just so with Ruth's younger crowd too. They're always giggling or making unintelligible remarks. You see I'm a kind of an in-between age, not old enough for Edith's set, nor young enough for Ruth's. The girls I used to know in the high school have not proved to be of the fashionable society here in Hilton, and Edith won't let me have them at the house. I've drifted away from most of them, except Juliet Adams, who is doing settlement work in New York, and I can't find any one to take their place.

I've come to the sad conclusion that I'm not popular with men either. At the little dances given here in Hilton occasionally, I'm not a wall-flower, possibly because I'm Edith Vars' sister-in-law, but I'm never "rushed." I can't be very brilliant in conversation at a dance when I'm anxiously watching for some kind, charitable soul to deliver my partner from the fear of two numbers in succession with me. And I have a sneaking conviction that I don't dance very well. You see all Ruth's set "Boston" to a waltz and two-step, and I don't know how. When a man is good enough to ask me to dance it seems too bad to make him exercise until he perspires. No one knows that I don't enjoy dances very much. It looks as if I were having a good time, I suppose, but down in my heart I'm worried and afraid.

At first I used to be eagerly on the lookout for my ideal—for a fleeting glimpse of a face that resembled the picture locked away in my secret desk-drawer. But such a quest is mere nonsense. I go to Boston to shop with Edith quite often; but never, in all the trains, railroad stations, restaurants, or elevators in law-office buildings (where one runs across so many good-looking men) have I seen even once the face of my desire. Why, I searched for that face throughout Oliver's and Malcolm's entire class when they graduated from college; I look for it among the new young men that come to call on

Ruth, but I can't find it. Yet if I ever do marry, the man must be born by this time, I suppose. Sometimes, especially when I listen to music, I wonder where he is, in just what city, what house, what room he is sitting at that particular moment. I smile to think how unconscious he is of me, who some day will fill his life completely, and how surprised he'd be if he knew that I was loving him even now.

I wonder what he's doing this very minute—three o'clock on a Saturday afternoon. Perhaps he's playing golf in a Norfolk Scotch tweed; perhaps he's oiling an engine in blue overalls; perhaps he's at the point of death with typhoid fever and is lying in bed with a thermometer in his mouth, and I am going to lose him! Oh, I hope he will be spared! I'll love him, overalls and all, and be proud too, to stand at the back-door and wave my apron when his train goes by, just as they do in magazine stories. I don't believe, after all, I'm a bit ambitious when it comes to marrying.

I suppose every reader of this résumé chapter of mine is simply skipping paragraphs by the dozen in the fond hope that he'll run across some exciting reference to Dr. Maynard. People are always so suspicious of an old love-affair. Let me relieve your mind. As much as you may be disappointed, I must announce that I am not reserving any sweet sentimental morsel, for a climactic finale. Far from it. I haven't got it to reserve. I only wish I had. A sweet memory is such a comforting possession, a thrilling romance of the past such a reassurance. But it is very evident that Dr. Maynard has no intention of providing me with sweet memories or thrilling romances. All the balm and comfort that his proposal may have given me in the beginning he has destroyed by being hopelessly commonplace ever since. I wish you could read his letters! Impersonal? Why, they might easily be addressed to a maiden aunt. Never once has he referred to that starry night, when he asked me to go to Germany with him; never intimated that he wished that I were there to see the castles on the Rhine, or hear the music in the gardens above Heidelberg; never asked, as any normal man would do, if I had changed my mind. Not that I have in the least. I haven't! Only it seems to me almost impolite not as much as to inquire.

Dr. William Ford Maynard is becoming quite well known here in America. There have been several articles already in the magazines about him and the remarkable results of his scientific research. I ought to be flattered to receive envelopes addressed to *me* from *him* at all, I suppose. We write about once a month. His letters are full of descriptions of pensions, and cafés, and queer people at his boarding-place. I know some of his guinea-pigs by name—the ones who have the typhoid, the scarlet-fever, and the spinal meningitis; the convalescents, the fatalities, and the triumphant recoveries are reported to me monthly. But as honoured as I ought to feel, I suppose, to share the results of this man's famous work, the truth is I don't enjoy his letters one bit! I am glad I was foresighted enough not to marry such a passionless man. I never would have been satisfied. I see it clearly now.

My letters to him are regular works of art. I'm bound not to let him pity me, at any rate, and if he can write cheerful and enthusiastic descriptions so can I. To Dr. Maynard I am simply delighted over our burst into prosperity and social splendour. Edith's improvements on the house I rave over. I describe bridge parties, teas and dances as if I gloried in them. I refer to various men—mostly Ruth's suitors, I must confess—frequently and with familiarity. I am simply "Living," with a big capital L, in my letters to Dr. Maynard, and my stub pen crosses its T's and ends its sentences with great broad, militant dashes that are bold with triumph.

Once only did Dr. Maynard condescend to refer to the past, and that was in a little insignificant postscript at the end of a long humorous description of a German family that he saw in a café. This is what he wrote, all cramped up in a little bit of space, after he had signed his name:

"How is San Francisco progressing in her reconstruction? Does she need any outside help in building up her beautiful city? Please let me know when she does!"

I tell you I wrote him the gayest, most flippant little note I could compose—all about how busy I was with engagements, etc., etc.; and then after I had signed my name, along the margin of the paper I said:

"About San Francisco—she is progressing wonderfully, she doesn't need any help from any one, unless possibly lead weights to keep her from soaring. The earthquake did her good. She's becoming very modernised and when you see her next I doubt if you recognise her on account of all the changes. Is Lizzie better? Or was it Nibbles who had the typhoid?"

If Dr. Maynard couldn't afford a fresh sheet of paper, go upstairs and shut himself in his room, and ask me seriously and quietly if I were unhappy or lonely, I would starve first before I'd ask bread of him.

I have it all planned just how I shall treat Dr. Maynard when he comes home—very distantly and as if so much society had made me a little blasé. When his name is sent up I shall keep him waiting in the little gold reception-room for about five minutes, and then glide into his presence, in a long clinging crêpe-de-chine dress. After I have shaken hands and said, "How pleasant it is to have you with us again," I'll ring for tea, then go back and sit down in the carved Italian armchair with the high back, dangle the ivory paper-cutter in one hand the way Ruth does, and inquire what sort of a passage he has had.

If he should come this year I've just the gown to wear. It's black, with a gold cord around the waist. I look about twenty-nine in it, and awfully sophisticated.

CHAPTER XIV

RUTH'S coming-out party cost over two thousand dollars, they say. Her dress alone was made by a dressmaker in Boston who won't "touch a thing" under a hundred and fifty; and Edith's—shimmering blue, draped with chiffon covered with green spangles, and here and there a crimson one (it looked just like the shining sides of a little wet brook trout)—simply spelled money.

I tell you the whole party lived up to the gorgeousness of Edith's gown too. There were orchids frozen in ice, for a punch bowl, in the dining-room; Killarney roses by the dozens in the reception-room; chrysanthemums in big round red bunches in the living-room; and the stairway was wound with smilax and asparagus fern, with real birch trees—silvery bark and all—at intervals of four or five feet. There were extra electric lights, extra maids, extra everything; and on the morning of Wednesday, the twenty-fifth of October, there arrived a whole squad of caterers from Boston with cases large as trunks filled with pattie shells, a thousand tiny brown pyramids of potato croquettes, tanksful of mushrooms, crab meat, and sweet-breads, cratesful of Malaga grapes and actual strawberries imported from somewhere which they dipped in white fondant and then set away to cool in little frilled paper holders, all over the butler's pantry.

It took Edith and Ruth two solid weeks of discussion and consultation to complete the invitation list. You see Edith was careful to give the party early in the fall before the summer colony had gone back home to its winter quarters. After the reception itself there was to be a small dance, and the elect were invited to remain. It was a source of satisfaction to Edith that only a dozen native Hilton men were invited to the dance, and but eight girls. Of course such partiality and ruthless slight and scorn of the people of her own native city caused a good deal of feeling in Hilton, but I observed that most every one who was invited to the reception came, in spite of the fact that they had been omitted from the dance to follow. Every living woman in Hilton was anxious, I suppose, to prove by her presence that she had the distinction of a portion of the engraved invitation at least.

I remember one name was under discussion for a week—a Mrs. Hugh Fullerton who was simply crazy "to get into things," Edith said—an officious, showy little bride from the West, she explained, who had married that young Yale graduate, Hugh Fullerton. Hugh Fullerton had been invited everywhere before he was married. He had been in Hilton only three years, but he had taken well. New young men usually do take well in Hilton. It's the women and the girls who have to climb and scramble. Mr. Fullerton was from Milwaukee, Wisconsin, and was learning the boiler business in the Hilton Boiler Works. He was a fine, tall, athletic, bronzed sort of fellow; Edith used to invite him to The Homestead very often; he'd ridden every one of her hunters; he was supposed to be one of her favourites. Then he married, and Edith's invitations came to an abrupt end. I had never seen Mrs. Fullerton, but I felt sorry for her.

"She has been married only since June," I said to Edith; "why not invite the poor thing to the dance? What harm would it do? She may be a little homesick way on here in the East, and it might cheer her up a lot to have a little distinction if she's so awfully anxious for it."

"Bobbie, dear child, I'm not running an institution for homesick girls," replied Edith. "I know what I'm about. I rather liked the girl at first, I confess. She's got a lot of style, but she simply isn't being taken up—that's all.

The Ogdens live in St. Louis in the winter and this Mrs. Fullerton lived there before she was married. The Ogdens know everybody in St. Louis of any importance, but they never even heard of Mrs. Fullerton. I'm not going to try to float a girl in society, whom I know nothing about. You may be sure of *that*."

"I should think your position would be secure enough after a while, for you to show a little independence," I murmured.

"Independence! Why, child, I'm inviting her to the reception, as it is. Anyhow what can *you* know about it? I'll settle the invitations, dearie." That was an example of the manner with which my ideas were usually treated.

There was a house-party planned at The Homestead in addition to the tea and dance. Edith always does a thing up good and brown. She wrote to about a dozen out-of-town people and invited them to become the guests of the house for over the twenty-fifth. These consisted of boarding-school friends of Ruth's, several of Edith's; and Oliver and Malcolm, who of course came home for the event, provided a generous supply of men from their crowd at college.

The three automobiles were kept busy meeting trains all the day before the tea, and the expressmen were tramping up and down the stairs with dozens of various trunks of all styles and sizes. The guest-rooms in The Homestead looked very festive, all decked out in real lace and silver, with Edith's best embroidered trousseau-spreads stretched out gorgeously upon the beds. It really grew quite exciting as the time for the tea drew near—even I felt a little of the pervading delight. Of course I hated meeting so many new people, but everybody's attention was centered upon Ruth, and I was perfectly free to withdraw to my room at any time I desired. I, thank goodness, was only Ruth's sister.

The tea was on a Wednesday, October twenty-fifth, from five until seven o'clock. Edith had bought a lovely dress for me—pink and soft and shining—and about three o'clock she sent the professional hair dresser, who had been spending the day at the house, to puff and marcel Bobbie, she said.

I hardly knew myself when I gazed into my mirror after I was all dressed. My hair was done up high like a queen's, and there were two little sparkling pink wings in it. My dress was cut into a V in front, and my neck looked so long and slender with my hair drawn away from its usual place in the back, and piled up in a soft puffy pyramid on top, that I seemed almost stately. I just wished Dr. Maynard could see San Francisco then!

As I walked out into the hall, my train made a lovely sound on the soft oriental rugs. I stood at the top of the stairs and gazed about me. Everything was in readiness—maids in black and white stationed at the bedroom doors, the musicians below already beginning to tune their instruments, the dark draperies drawn, a soft illumination of electricity everywhere, and the faint delicious odour of coffee mixed with the perfume of roses. I was overwhelmed with the spirit of prosperity that filled every corner and cranny of my father's house. I wondered what Father would think of it all—big, calm, quiet Father whose tastes were so plain, habits so simple, and whose words of advice to us his children always so eloquent with the wickedness of extravagance. I put him out of my mind just as quickly as I could. I didn't want to think of him just now. I wanted to have a good time for once in my life; I wanted everybody to see that I wasn't shy and quiet and plain; I wanted to be clever and admired; and I would be too! I caught a glimpse of myself, whole length, in the long hall-mirror. My cheeks were flushed and rosy, my eyes were dark and bright. I really believed I was pretty! I could have shouted, I felt so happy. I ran down the side stairway, that leads to the hall off the porte-cochère, through the chrysanthemum-laden living-room and hall, into the rose-perfumed reception-room, where I found Edith and Ruth ready for the first arrival. I felt suddenly generous-hearted toward all the prosperity and luxury that made such a palace of our old house and such a new creature of me. I wanted to tell Edith how lovely I thought it all was.

I had more reason than ever to feel grateful to Edith about an hour later. It was at the very height of the afternoon rush, about quarter past five. I happened to be standing just back of Edith, waiting for a chance to offer her some lemonade which one of the ladies assisting had been thoughtful enough to send to her by me. There was a long line of women that stretched way out into the hall, just like a line in front of a ticket window at the theatre, each waiting her turn for a chance to shake hands with Edith, though most of them she sees every time she goes out anyhow. Edith was very gracious and cordial this afternoon. I've heard very often that she makes a lovely hostess. I watched her closely, trying to see just where the charm lay.

"Ah, good afternoon! Mrs. Fullerton, I believe?" suddenly broke in on my reflections, and I glanced up quickly, curious to see the poor little neglected bride whom I championed. There really was nothing very poor nor very neglected about her appearance. I couldn't see her face beneath her plumed picture-hat, but her costume was very costly and elegant—a lot of Irish lace over something dark.

"Yes, Mrs. Hugh Fullerton," she replied effusively. "Hugh has told me so much about his good times here at The Homestead, Mrs. Vars, and how kind and cordial you've been to him, and I *do* want to thank you. Haven't you a gorgeous afternoon? I'm so glad to meet you, after all Hugh has said. Why, I know some of your horses by name even—Regal, for instance—the one that threw Hugh—do you remember?"

Edith's manner cooled, hostess though she was.

"Regal has thrown so many!" she remarked. "Ruth, Mrs. Fullerton," she finished.

"Oh," went on Mrs. Fullerton to Ruth, not at all abashed, "I've met Miss Vars already. A bride remembers everybody new she meets, you know, and then of course I couldn't help but remember *you*." There was something hauntingly familiar about Mrs. Fullerton's manner and voice. I put the lemonade on a table near by and drew nearer. "It was at Mrs. Jaynes' bridge-party last week," she went on; "don't you remember? We played at the same table, Miss Vars."

"Did we?" inquired Ruth in her sweet, icy, little way; "I don't remember."

"Of course," flushed Mrs. Fullerton. "Débutantes meet so many new people. I know just how it is—I was there once myself. I don't wonder one bit. I remember *I* couldn't keep even the men straight, to say nothing of the women."

"O Lucy," suddenly exclaimed Edith, catching sight of me, "this is Mrs. Fullerton. My other sister, Miss Vars, Mrs. Fullerton. She'll take you to the dining-room and serve you some tea or an ice."

I raised my eyes to Mrs. Fullerton's. No, I hadn't been mistaken. I should have recognised that voice in China. Mrs. Fullerton's mouth opened in amazement as she gazed at me.

"Lucy Vars," she finally ejaculated. "Lucy Vars! Why, Lucy, don't you remember Sarah Platt?"

"Yes, I remember," I nodded.

"How lovely! How perfectly lovely!" exploded Sarah. "Why, Mrs. Vars," she sparkled, "Lucy and I are old pals! Isn't it too nice for anything? We were at Miss Brown's-on-the-Hudson the same year, and I guess if you've ever been to boarding-school yourself, you know what that means. Why, Lucy, you old trump, how are you anyway? I'm simply pleased to pieces!" And the once much-envied Sarah Platt of years ago, the successful, the glorious Sarah Platt, enveloped me at last in a huge schoolgirl embrace!

"Hypocrite!" I thought.

"I'd lost track of Lucy completely," she went on to Edith and Ruth, linking her arm familiarly through mine. "I'd forgotten your home was in Hilton, though I certainly knew it was in Massachusetts somewhere. Wasn't it stupid? Here I've been living for three months in the same place with you, Lucy Vars, and never knew it! Here you were all the time a sister to Mrs. Alexander Vars, whom Hugh wrote me so much about that I almost grew jealous," she laughed. "Isn't this world just the smallest place you ever heard of, Mrs. Vars? You must come right over and see me, Lucy, and make up for lost time, and I hope you'll both come with her," smiled Sarah upon my sisters; "I'd simply love to have you."

We moved away toward the dining-room.

"Oh, Lucy," went on Sarah, "I am so glad to see you again! It's just like discovering somebody from home. I haven't any friend here my own age at all. You've grown so pretty! You're looking splendid; and aren't your sister and sister-in-law just stunning!"

I drew my arm away from Sarah's. I remembered what she had thought about my family once.

"Don't leave me," she exclaimed, "please, or I'll perish. Stay while I have my ice. I don't know one soul in that dining-room."

Life works out its patterns very cunningly, I think. Once I had hidden in shame behind a telegraph-pole from this majestic creature; once she had looked upon me as mean and insignificant, unworthy of even her pity; now she actually plead for my favour, toadied to my family, palavered me with flatteries. I drew in deep breaths of satisfaction.

"Dear, dear life, how kind and just you are after all!" I said half an hour later, gazing into my mirror, in my own closed room. "My day is dawning now—mine, mine, at last! And I'm so happy! I'm going to have a wonderful time at the dance to-night. I feel it. Oh, it's good after all to have money and prosperity; it's good to wear soft, pink shimmering dresses that are becoming and make people gaze and whisper; it's good to hold such a position in a community that even Sarah Platts bow and scrape and try to please; it's more than good—it's exhilarating!"

I went out into the hall and started to go down the main stairway. It was deserted now. The hour was seven-thirty, just before the men were due to arrive for the supper and the evening celebrations to follow.

Half-way down this stairway, on the landing, there is a large portrait of my father. Amid all the preparations going on in the house I had not known that Edith had had the electricians adjust a row of shielded electric lights at the top of the heavy frame of Father's picture. The portrait had always hung on the landing where the light is very dim. We had had it for years. It was painted when we were prosperous, but I had never examined it very closely. It was an awfully black sort of picture, and before Ruth's tea I could not have definitely said whether Father was standing or sitting in it. I didn't know that a row of lights could make such a difference. As I turned on the landing that night and came suddenly upon the painting I stopped stock-still. Why, it wasn't a picture! I didn't see the frame, nor the canvas, nor the paint. It was Father, dear Father himself, sitting at his roll-top desk down in the sitting-room. I could see every little wrinkle in his face, the crows-feet at the corners of his eyes, the fine, tired-looking lines along his forehead. He was sitting in his big leather armchair, and I remembered exactly how the leather had worn brown and velvety like that, along the edges. As usual he wore across his breast his heavy gold watch-chain, with the black onyx fob—the one he used to let me play with in church, when I was very little—and in one hand, which was resting easily along the arm of the chair, Father held his glasses just as he used to hold them when he took them off to glance up at me before I dashed off to dancing-school on Saturday nights. "Can't you keep that hair a little smoother?" he'd say to me, and "Isn't there a good deal of trimming on that dress? Your mother always wore plain things with a little white at her neck. Keep your tastes simple, my girl, and your clothes neat and nicely sewed." They were plain, homely words. Any man could say them, but as I remembered them that night, they seemed terribly sweet—almost sacred—and I backed up against the wall, and stared at Father there before me, with tears in my eyes. He would not have liked the sparkling wings I was wearing in my hair. The dress that Edith had given me—all shining satin, wasn't like my mother's with a little white at the neck. The silent, sad expression in my father's eyes smote me. He was gazing straight at me, down into my heart. I almost saw his lips move. The words of the verse that he used to repeat so often at our morning prayers after breakfast, I seemed to hear again: "Children, how hard it is for them that trust in riches to enter into the Kingdom of God." Father was always quoting things from the Bible about vanity and riches. His heroes were always big, simple, honest men like Abraham Lincoln and Benjamin Franklin. As I stood and stared at Father's picture the musicians began to play some soft, dreamy melody, and just then Alec from above caught sight of me leaning up against the wall.

"Hello," he called cheerfully; "how do you like the new lights on the picture?" And he came tripping down all dressed up in his evening clothes to join me. I don't believe Alec had seen the portrait lighted before either, for he stopped short beside me when he came in full view of it. He was speechless for a moment. Really those lights made Father look as if he could answer if we spoke to him. He seemed to be actually sitting there amid all the luxury and splendour he had so despised. Alec came over beside me. He took my hand in his and for a long sweet half-minute, my old partner and I stood there together on the landing and gazed up into Father's noble eyes.

"It's miraculous," breathed Alec, softly, at last.

I couldn't answer. It *was* miraculous. I wished I was in my ugly old blue cashmere and could crawl up into Father's lap.

I didn't know anybody was coming up the stairs till suddenly Alec dropped my hand and left me.

"Hello—hello there," he called out jovially. "Come right up, Mr. Campbell. Just gotten here, haven't you? Everything's gone in tip-top shape so far. We're looking pretty fine around here, aren't we? Bobbie and I were passing judgment on Edith's new lights. Here, let me take that coat. Edith discovered that this old portrait of Father was by an artist who has a reputation now, so she had it properly lighted. It is marvellous what a really excellent likeness it is. Come and tell us your opinion."

I slunk away to my room quietly.

All that evening amid the babble of voices and din of violins, pianos and cornets, while girls in gorgeous raiment sat beneath Father's picture between dances with their partners on the top stair of the landing, and just below men gathered around the punch-bowl; while Edith and Ruth shone in jewels, and old Dave Campbell blatantly exhibited the latest improvements in the house to all his friends, Father looked down upon it all from his lofty position silently, disapprovingly, a look of censure in his eyes that I couldn't seem to escape. My little hour of triumph was snuffed out by Father's gaze like a candle in a tempest; my sudden self-satisfaction, my burst of eager joy in prosperity and position, born to feel the throb of life but for an hour.

I didn't enjoy the dance. I couldn't. I tried once or twice to "enter in," but it was masquerade. There had been champagne served at the supper. Girls as well as men were full of the spirit of mad merry-making. Everybody was having a glorious time—everybody but me. I hated the hilarious laughter. I don't mean to imply that any one became intoxicated, I don't think they did exactly, but just the same the whole affair seemed to me like a debauch going on in my father's house beneath his very eyes. I stole up to the landing about eleven o'clock when the music was still shrieking, Ruth's cheeks burning with excitement, Oliver laughing so loudly that I could hear him above the music, and switched off the lights above Father's picture. He shouldn't look on at such festivities—mute, unable to speak his mind, tied there in his chair, helpless and forgotten—he shouldn't if I could help it!

Late that same night—or it must have been the next morning—anyway after every one was quiet, and the house was finally dark I stole out of my room and crept quietly down on the landing. The house was dead still. I heard the big clock with the chimes strike a half-hour, and a second after all the other clocks reply. I was in my nightgown wrapped around with an eiderdown bath-robe. I found my way stealthily to the little button behind the portrait. I pushed it. There was a little click and suddenly Father was before me! I went back and sat down on the lowest stair, close up to the railing, and looked up into his comforting eyes. No one had known that I had spent the last six dances shut up in my room. No one had missed me. I had had a horrid time, but no one cared.

There were the remains of the orgy of the night before scattered all about Father's feet—a discarded bunch of violets, a torn piece of chiffon, a half a macaroon, a girl's handkerchief. As I sat there and wondered how Ruth and the twins and Alec could all go peacefully to sleep, unmindful of their strict and rigid bringing-up, forgetful of Father left here in the midst of the confusion of the things he preached against, I heard from somewhere, way off, a queer long laugh. I listened intently, and in a moment I could catch the rumble of voices from behind closed doors. I wondered who could be awake at such an hour, when a door opened downstairs, and as plain and distinct as day, a man's voice exclaimed, "Come on, boys, we'll have to carry old Ol up. Lend a hand, one of you chaps who can walk straight, and don't make any noise. Wake up, Oliver, old pal. We're going to bed." I heard a horrid guttural sort of rejoinder from Oliver, and I shuddered. Some of the men must have been sitting up in the dining-room and drinking! I knew, oh, I knew now, that Oliver must be intoxicated! I was in my nightgown. There was no time to turn out the lights over Father's picture, to shield Father from the awful sight of his son, drunk—horridly, helplessly drunk, being carried upstairs to bed. I glanced up at Father shining there in his frame. He was looking straight down the long broad stairway. In another minute Oliver and Father would meet face to face. I turned and fled back to my room.

CHAPTER XV

FOUR months later. Twelve o'clock at night. Wrapped up in my eiderdown bath-robe. Sitting at my desk.

It is midnight. I cannot sleep. I have been lying wide awake, listening to a strong April wind, howling around the corner of the house, for two hours! I've repeated the twenty-third Psalm over and over again. I've imagined a flock of sheep going over a stile (though I never saw it done) for ten minutes solid. I've swallowed two Veronal tablets. It's useless. I surrender. I don't want to get up. I shall have an awful headache to-morrow, besides heavy lead weights behind my eyes; and to-morrow—to-morrow of all days—I want to be fresh and bright and as beautiful as nature can make me. Moreover, I'd rather not write. But I can't read. There has never been a book printed that could hold my thoughts to-night. My mind goes back to the events of the day like steel to a magnet. I've tried solitaire, and ended by pushing the silly cards on the floor. You see something has happened—something big and actual and real!

I have seen Dr. Maynard!

I have met him face to face, talked with him, laughed with him, walked with him from Charles Street to the sunken garden, sat with him by the fountain. I am beside myself with excitement. I had better tell how it all happened. If I get it out of my system I may be able to snatch a little sleep, and I *must* sleep. I have an important engagement to-morrow at three.

It occurred at four o'clock this afternoon. I had bought a bunch of primroses from a man on the street five minutes before. I was on my way home from a shopping tour, and with my pretty early-spring flowers tucked in at my waist, and my hands full of packages, I turned up Charles Street as unconcerned as you please. At the corner I bowed to our minister's wife, and the remains of the smile were still on my face, I suppose, when I saw Dr. Maynard. I didn't know that he was on this side of the ocean, and when I observed him coming down the steps of the postoffice—vigorous and strong and buoyant—I stood still in my tracks, and the remains of the smile turned into something startled and afraid. Dr. Maynard approached me all aglow, stretched out his hand and took mine in a warm, firm grasp. A thrill went through me like a knife. He was as natural as day, beautifully tanned, smiling, big, broad-shouldered as ever, and yet different—oh, awfully different.

"Hello, Bobbie," he said in his hearty old voice, and I looked back at him, perfectly white—I could feel that I was—and speechless. "Don't be a goose. It's just Dr. Maynard," I tried to reason with myself.

"Am I speaking to Miss Lucy Vars?" I heard asked of me. "Miss Lucy Chenery Vars, of 240 Main Street, Hilton, Mass.?"

I nodded, and somewhere down there in the chaos in my chest, I found my poor little voice. "Is it *you*?" I asked shakily.

"Well, I'm not quite sure. Nothing looks very natural around here. I'm beginning to think I'm somebody else."

"Well, I *am* surprised!" I exploded. "I certainly *am* surprised! Why, I never *was* so surprised!" I stopped a minute. Dr. Maynard was smiling right down into my eyes. "I never was so surprised in all my life!" I repeated, as if I hadn't another idea in my head.

He leaned down just here and picked up a half-dozen bundles, more or less, that I had dropped when we shook hands.

"I better help you carry some of these home, hadn't I?" he suggested.

"Oh, yes, *do*," I replied eagerly, and somehow we managed to walk back to the house together.

I don't know through what streets we went, past what houses. I can scarcely recall of what we talked. "He's come home! He's come home! He's come home!" kept ringing in my ears over and over again, like jubilant chimes. "Dr. Maynard has come home!" And whenever I looked up and saw him smiling down at me—so naturally, so beautifully—it seemed as if I should have to make a pirouette or two, right there on the sidewalk. Every time he laughed I wanted to shout; every time he remarked upon a new building or a new house, and especially when he exclaimed, "Good heavens! What have we here?" at the sight of one of the taxicabs, I wanted to turn a handspring. When he first came in view of 240 Main Street and stood stock-still in his tracks, and gasped, "Where's the cupola, and the French roof, and the iron fountain, and the barn, and the apple orchard?" I wanted to throw my arms around him for joy. I must have felt like a dog at the sight of his beloved master whom he hasn't seen for months. It was so intoxicating to have Dr. Maynard beside me again that it seemed as if I must express my joy by jumping up on him, and half knocking him down. Which, of course, I didn't do. My voice broke a dozen times, my underlip trembled, my cheeks burned with excitement, but otherwise I walked along as sedately as if it were an everyday occurrence to run across a man I believed was hopelessly buried in a laboratory in Europe.

It was in the sunken garden that the most important part of our conversation took place. You remember, don't you, that in my letters to Dr. Maynard I had always been enthusiastic over the improvements Edith has made on old 240. So now it was with apparent pride that I led my old friend down the granolithic steps into the one-time apple orchard. I showed him the cement-lined pool in the centre, the Italian garden-seat, the rare shrubbery now bound up in yellow straw, with something like delight. I was so full of exultation at the mere sight of dear, kind, understanding Dr. Maynard that I could have rejoiced about anything. When I exclaimed, "And there's a squash-court connected with the garage, and a tennis-court as *smooth* as *glass* beside the stable; and where the old potato-patch used to be, there's a pergola!" my eyes fairly sparkled. "That sun-dial over there," I boasted, "was designed especially for Edith; and oh, there's the dearest, slimmest little stream of water that spouts out of the centre of the pool, in the summer. You ought to see it!" I was all enthusiasm. Edith wouldn't have recognised me. Ruth would have thought I had lost my reason. Even Dr. Maynard looked at me curiously.

"It certainly is all very fine, I've no doubt," he remarked.

"Yes, isn't it?" I exclaimed.

"But I must confess," he went on. "*I* never objected to the old apple orchard. Just about where the pool is now, there used to grow the best old Baldwins I ever tasted."

"Oh, my," I scoffed, "you ought to see the bouncing big Oregon apples Edith buys by the crate."

Dr. Maynard shook his head and smiled. Then he came over and sat down beside me on the Italian seat.

"Well, well," he sighed, "I suppose old Rip must get used to the changes that have taken place since he's been asleep—squash-courts and pergolas, great sweeping estates with granolithic drives and sunken gardens; new hotels; new postoffices; instead of the roomy, old-fashioned livery-stable hacks, taxicabs; instead of good old snappy New England Baldwins, apples imported from Oregon; and instead of a girl in a red Tam-o-Shanter and her father's old weather-beaten ulster, sitting behind the wheel of a little one-lunger automobile, running it, in all sorts of weather, like a young breeze—instead of that girl," said Dr. Maynard, looking me up and down closely, "a very correct and up-to-date young lady in kid gloves and a veil, a smart black and white checked suit, a very fashionable hat (*I* should call it), with a bunch of primroses, to cap it all, pinned jauntily at her waist."

I blushed with triumph.

"I've just about come to the conclusion," added Dr. Maynard in a kind of wistful voice, "that I don't know San Francisco at all now."

"Well," I laughed waveringly, "I do hope you'll find it a little more civilised than it was before."

"*I* never thought it was uncivilised," said Dr. Maynard quietly; "*I* rather enjoyed it just as it was, to tell the truth. I shall be sorry to find many changes in it because I shall have to become acquainted with it all over again and my time is so short."

"Short?" I exclaimed. I don't know why I had drawn the sudden conclusion that Dr. Maynard had come back to stay. His very next words put an end to my little half-hour of jubilance like the announcement of a death.

"Yes," he said; "I'm sailing back to Germany in two weeks. I was appointed an executor of a distant relative's will, and it seemed necessary to come to New York and attend to it. Of course I couldn't be so near—San Francisco, without coming to see how it prospered after the earthquake. I'm glad to find you so happy, Bobbie. You've richly earned all this," he glanced around the display that surrounded us, "both you and Al, and it's really fine that the change in your circumstances came about, when *you*, Lucy, were still a young girl, and just ready to appreciate and enjoy good times, and pretty surroundings, and new young people. Sometimes the apparent catastrophes work out for our best happiness. You *are* happy, aren't you, Bobbie?"

"Oh, yes—perfectly happy," I flashed indignantly.

"I thought so. Your enthusiasm brims over in your letters. Well, well," twitted Dr. Maynard, "who ever would have thought Al's little sister, whom I used to call 'wild-cat,' would turn into a society girl—a mighty popular one too, if *I'm* any judge. Parties and engagements all the time, I suppose. Now I'm just curious enough to wonder," went on Dr. Maynard teasingly, while my feelings, hurt and enraged, were working up to one of their habitual explosions, "which one of all those admirers I hear mentioned in your letters sent you your pretty primroses *this* morning."

"No one sent them," I blurted out. "If you *must* know, I bought them myself five minutes before I saw you. Those men in my letters were Ruth's friends, not mine."

Dr. Maynard glanced at me sharply.

"Oh," I went on fiercely, "I'm glad to know if you think that I'm happy. It shows how well you understand me. Happy! I'm perfectly miserable, if you want to know the truth. I hate and loathe and despise all this display you say I've so richly earned. I hate parties, and splurge, and sunken gardens, and pergolas, and I haven't a single solitary admirer in the world. I thought you knew me, but I see you don't. I thought if you ever came back *you'd* understand, but you don't—not one little single bit. I thought *you—you—*"

I stopped abruptly. There's no use trying to hide tears that run shamelessly down your cheeks. It was absolutely necessary for me to ask for my bag which Dr. Maynard held, and produce a handkerchief. He didn't say anything as I mopped my eyes. I thought perhaps he was too shocked to speak. He didn't offer me a single word of comfort—just sat and waited. I didn't look at him; and still with my face turned away I said, subdued, apologetically, "I don't see what is the matter with me lately. You mustn't mind my being so silly. I'm always getting 'weepy' for no reason at all." I opened my bag, tucked away my handkerchief, as a sign that the storm was over, and stood up. "I hope you won't think that I usually act this way with—with all those admirers of mine," I added, smiling.

Dr. Maynard ignored my attempt at humour.

"Lucy," he said quietly, but in a voice and manner that made me start and catch my breath, "my real reason for coming to America wasn't the will. It was you." He stopped and I looked hard into the centre of the dry pool. "I mistrusted some of your letters lately, though I confess not at first—not until last fall. You've been overdoing your enthusiasm this winter, Bobbie. So I decided to come over and find out for myself if you had been trying to deceive me. The will offered a good excuse, so here I am. And you *have* been deceiving me—for two whole years. Why, Bobbie," he said very softly, "what shall I do to you?"

I glanced up and saw the old piercing tenderness in his eyes.

"Don't be kind to me," I warned hastily; "not *now*—not for anything. *Please*, or I shall cry again."

I heard Dr. Maynard laugh the tenderest, gentlest kind of laugh, and in a second both his arms were around me. Yes, both Dr. Maynard's arms were close around me! I didn't cry. I just stayed there quiet and still and safe; and I've been there in imagination about every moment since.

When he finally let me go he said simply, but in a queer trembling voice, "Will you go to drive with me to-morrow afternoon at three, way off into the country, away from pergolas and cement pools, and people?"

I nodded, unable to speak.

"All right. I'll be here. Good night," he said gently, and turned abruptly and left me there alone in the garden.

I watched him hurry up the garden-steps and out of the gateway. He turned once and waved his hand to the pitiful little wind-blown creature he left behind in the bleak unbeautiful garden. I felt as if he had torn me from my moorings and that I must toss and drift in strange unknown seas until to-morrow at three.

I managed to gather my bundles together somehow, and come up here to the house. My cheeks were flaming when I opened the door. I left my packages in a chair in the hall and hurried up here to my room as quickly as I could. Once here I locked my door tight and threw off my things. "Oh, don't be silly; don't be absurd," I said, and buried my face in the dark of my arms on my desk. "It's just Dr. Maynard," I went on later, "and you know how you felt two years ago. Oh, be reasonable. Be calm." But all the time that

I was talking sense to myself, I was feeling strong arms about my shoulders, and a kind of sinking, fainting, going-out feeling that people must experience when they lose consciousness, would steal over me so that I couldn't think.

Finally to put an end to my nonsense I opened a secret compartment and took out Robert Dwinnell's picture. *He* would cure me of my delusion; *he* would keep me true to my ideals. I gazed at Robert Dwinnell for a solid sixty seconds, then deliberately, straight across the forehead, down the nose, through the very smile that once had thrilled me, I tore that poor picture into a thousand bits, and dumped the remains into the waste-basket. It was a dreadful act. I felt like a murderess. I don't know what made me do it, but Robert Dwinnell had lost his charm. Dr. Maynard, glowing with health, his eyes fierce with a tenderness that actually hurt, made my poor old idol look flat and insipid.

Some time later—ten minutes perhaps—an hour—I don't know—a maid knocked and asked if I were coming down to dinner. I got up and followed her mechanically, and for the life of me I don't know whether there was roast-beef or lamb.

Now I am again locked in my room, and my soul is actually on fire. It is as dark as death outdoors. Every one in the house is asleep. But I am sitting here gazing at a little faded picture of an automobile which I finally discovered in an old souvenir-book of mine. That little speck there is Dr. Maynard and I am going to see him to-day at three!

CHAPTER XVI

EVER since I can remember having any ideas on the subject at all, I have always longed to be married in one of those dark, little tucked-away chapels in some cathedral or other, in France or England, like a girl I read about in a book. Perhaps a late afternoon service would be going on up near the big altar; candles would be burning; the priest would be chanting queer minor things; poor women would be stepping in, crossing themselves, to say a prayer; and, all unconscious of me, nearly hidden by the big stone pillars, tourists would be tip-toeing about, gazing at the rose-window and the towering arches. There would be footfalls and whispers in the nave. Echoes everywhere. I should have loved the echoes! "But then," Edith said, "you wouldn't have had a sign of a wedding present, and you can't furnish your house with echoes, crazy Bobbs."

If ever there was a wedding opposite to my ideal of one, it was mine. For of course I am married to Dr. Maynard.

You aren't surprised, I know. It was all decided that afternoon at three, and two weeks later when Will sailed back to Germany it wasn't in imagination that I stood on the dock and waved him good-bye. I was there soul and body this time, and I followed with my fluttering handkerchief every motion that he made with his hat and great spoke of an arm. I watched him till he faded out of sight, and then with Ruth and Edith, who went to New York with me, I returned to the shops to buy my trousseau.

Will had to be back in Germany on May first to deliver a lecture before a very learned assembly of scientists and doctors. They wanted him to tell them about a few of his experiments with his guinea-pigs. It was a great compliment for so young a man, and an American besides, to receive an invitation to address a body of old-world sages. Of course he couldn't disappoint them, but he told me that by the middle of August he would be sailing back again and after a simple little wedding in the dead quiet of midsummer, he would at last carry his refugee back with him to Europe. He was not going to begin work until October. We planned to travel till then.

"So, after all," said Will to me that afternoon at three o'clock, "after all, some day—oh, Lucy—perhaps some day—" and *this* time it was I who finished the sentence.

"Yes, perhaps some day," I said sparkling, "the refugee and you will be seeing Paris together."

Our plans would have been lovely if they had worked out; but they didn't. I haven't seen Paris yet, and there's no prospect that I shall until Will's Sabbatical year comes around. We're going across then, he says, if we have to work our way on a cattle ship. You see Will no sooner got back there to Germany and delivered his lectures to those old sages, than the medical department of one of the biggest universities here in America sent him an invitation to become a member of their faculty. The position was quite to his taste, he wrote me. He could keep right on with his experimenting and guinea-pigs to his heart's content—the university had wonderfully equipped laboratories, the best in America—and what did I say? What *should* I say to a person whose very picture that had been taken for just me to put on my bureau, had appeared in two magazines that month? Such an insignificant tail to the big lion as I, ought cheerfully to go wagging to the North Pole or the Sahara Desert. Of course I didn't say a word.

I never saw anything like the way the magazines burst forth in sudden praise of Will. His appointment to the faculty of the university was reported in every paper published. I didn't know whether my emotions were of pride or fear. After reading an account of what Dr. William Ford Maynard had accomplished and how high his position was in the scientific world, and then, immediately following, seeing the announcement of his engagement to Miss Lucy Chenery Vars, of Hilton, Mass., I was filled with a good deal of apprehension.

Edith was delighted with my engagement. To boast of William Ford Maynard as a future brother-in-law was a great feather in her cap. The plans for an elaborate wedding were formed and crystallised before I had gotten used to wearing my engagement ring. I didn't want a big wedding, but it seemed useless to remonstrate. You see I was under obligations to Edith. All my linen, stiff gorgeous stuff with heavy elaborate monograms, she had given me; bath towels two yards long which I despise, sets of underwear all ruffles, fol-de-rols and satin rosettes, she had bestowed upon me; also my solid silver service, Sheffield tray and flat silver were gifts from Edith. I didn't like my flat silver. The design is awfully elaborate, representing a horn of plenty overflowing with pears and grapes and apples. Edith, however, thought it was stunning. I didn't like my wedding invitations, thick as leather, engraved in enormous block letters, my name staring at me like a sign over a store and a whole pack of cards besides. But Edith did. I didn't want the ceremony to take place in the Episcopal church which Edith has been attending lately, with a boys' choir preceding me up the aisle, when I've always been a plain straight old-fashioned Congregationalist. I didn't want eight bridesmaids of Edith's choosing, selected from the most prominent families that she could find. I didn't want all society invited. But I soon discovered that my wedding was to be Edith's party, not mine.

On the morning of the fifth day before the great occasion I was in the Circassian walnut guest-chamber looking at the overwhelming display of wedding presents. The original furniture had been moved into the stable and a low wide shelf covered with heavy white damask ran around the entire room. Edith had put all the cut-glass together in the bay-window, and under the glare of a dozen extra electric lights it sparkled bright and hard. There were two enormous punch-bowls, a lamp, a vase big enough for an umbrella-stand, thirteen berry dishes, baskets and candlesticks, two ice-cream sets, two dozen finger-bowls and six dozen glasses. I hate cut-glass!

"Lucy, Lucy, you up there?" somebody called as I gazed.

"I suppose so," I sang back, and I heard Edith coming up the stairs. I hadn't a doubt but that she would be staggering under a fresh load of presents and I wasn't mistaken. She appeared with a regular Pisa Tower of them, extending up to her eyes.

"How's this for a haul?" she gasped. "Come on, my dear, hustle up and see what you draw." Then she added, "Gracious, Lucy, where in the world did you resurrect that old dress? Don't you know every one will be dropping in at all hours during these last days?" Edith herself was fairly dazzling in stiff crackling white linen.

"It was so comfortable," I murmured, "and it has no bones in the collar."

"I should say it hadn't! Your bridesmaids will be here any minute. Hurry up and look at these things, and then go and get yourself fixed up. *Do.*"

I began silently on the bottom box, cut the string, removed the cover, and from beneath the tissue-paper drew out a red flannelette bag.

"It's another plateau," I said wearily before I unpulled the draw-string. I had seven already.

"A plateau! From the Elmer Scotts!" She tossed the cards over to me contemptuously. "That girl visited me for two weeks before I was married. They have loads. A plateau! Only the six-fifty size at that, and—how disgusting—*marked!*"

I didn't know the Scotts from Adam. Half my presents were from Edith's friends. I didn't see why the Scotts should give me anything.

"Why, they were invited to the reception, my dear!" said Edith, scandalised. "Come, pass it over! Here goes for three hundred and seventy-two," and she tore off a little number from a sheet of others, touched it with the tip of her tongue and slapped it on to the face of the plateau. She listed it under S in a small book and placed it with my seven other plateaus on the silver table. I hadn't liked putting them all together. "But, nonsense," Edith had said. "Don't you see, little simpleton, if they are together, people can tell how many plateaus you have at a glance? My goodness, three hundred and seventy-two presents so far and three more days yet! I'll bet you get five hundred. Dear me, Lucy," she broke off, "there come your bridesmaids. Do go and change your dress. Put on the embroidered mulle; and hurry, child."

I suppose my blue checked gingham did look faded and plain, but I went to my room with a great swelling loyalty in my heart for every plain thing in the world. I hung my blue gingham in the closet almost tenderly. Already my wedding costume was there, staring at me from the corner—shining satin and expensive lace, little sachet bags sewed into the lining, and, on the belt inside, the name in gold letters of one of the most fashionable dressmakers in New York. I was gazing at it, wishing with all my heart that I hadn't got to take the place of the tissue-paper now stuffed into the waist and sleeves, when my sister-in-law suddenly appeared at the door.

"Hurry, Bobbie," she said. "Hurry, do. Your bridesmaids are all here and the Leonard Jacksons have brought over the John Percivals in their car. Don't forget the Jacksons gave you the dozen silver coquilholders, and the Percivals the Dresden service plates. Be nice to Mrs. Percival. She's going to be one of your neighbours next year. I must run along. They'll be wondering." She started to go, but turned back and added, "Why in the world aren't you more enthusiastic, Lucy? You ought to be the happiest girl in the world, *I* think. I never saw a more elaborate trousseau or a costlier layout of presents in my life. I can't imagine what else you want!"

A maid knocked outside the door and spoke to Edith. I didn't hear the message, but Edith gave a little exclamation and hurried away.

"The King Georges or the Kaiser Wilhelms in their aeroplane, no doubt," I muttered, and made a face at my wedding-gown as I yanked down my embroidered mulle.

I am going to skip the details of my wedding—the broiling condition of the thermometer, the sweltering bridesmaids, the crowds, the push, the funny grown-up feeling in my heart when Alec and Tom kissed me good-bye so gently, the joy when the train finally gave a snort and a jerk, and I knew that Edith in her pearls and satin couldn't possibly follow. I am so anxious to describe the funny old brown house that Will and I leased in the shadow of chemistry buildings, law-schools, and dormitories down here in this university town, and the life—the curious, happy, contented life that I drifted into—that I do not want to waste any time.

The week after my wedding Edith sailed with Ruth for four months in Europe. That is how it happened that she wasn't on the ground to superintend the choice of a residence for Will and me. I knew very well that Edith would never have countenanced for a minute the house that we finally decided to rent for the winter. It was a brown, square affair, a door in the middle with a window on each side, not colonial in the least, nondescript as it could be, with a slate French roof. Will and I thought it would answer the purpose, however—even though the bathtub was tin—and moved into it when the brick sidewalk was sprinkled with yellow maple-leaves, and the gutter was collecting dry ones.

I didn't know a soul in the town. I didn't know the name of a single street except our own. I didn't know where to go to buy even a spool of thread. But I wasn't homesick—oh, no, I wasn't homesick. You see I had forgotten the joy of my own kitchen and pantry; I had forgotten what a collander looked like; I had forgotten how sweet a row of cups are hanging by their handles, underneath a shelf edged with scalloped paper!

I enjoyed acting as my own mistress too; though I am sure if Edith had known what I was up to, she would have left all the pleasures of Paris to set me in the right path. For I didn't even unpack some of my wedding presents. They didn't fit in very well with Will's furniture which he had freighted down from the old white-pillared house in Hilton, and every sliver of which I simply adored. It wasn't colonial furniture, understand, which is so fashionable nowadays, but black walnut of the seventies—high-backed armchairs and sofas and marble-topped bedroom tables. There were funny old steel engravings of the United States Senate, battle scenes, and Abraham Lincoln, besides some big heavy bronzes that Will told me were very valuable. The sideboard was black walnut like everything else and Edith's elaborate silver service made it look so out-of-date that I put on it instead my own mother's old coffee-pot—the one that used to be so heavy for me—and our old-fashioned silver water pitcher with four high goblets to match. I didn't even unlock my enormous chest of silver. Alec had let me take from the safe at home the forks and darling thin spoons and knives that had always been in our family. It was like sheltering old friends under my roof to care for them again.

Edith would have hated the life I drifted into. She would have called it "a mere existence" or "worse than the frontier." From September to February, I didn't go to a single luncheon, tea, or bridge! People had called—members of the faculty, I suppose, I'm sure I don't know, for the cards were mere names to me and I was always out when they were left. You see one evening I had run across something in a pamphlet of Will's on our living-room table that set me to thinking. The pamphlet was a sort of bulletin of lectures given by different professors in the college. There was a star after several of the announcements and at the bottom of the page it said, "Open to the Public." I hadn't a notion whether it was the right thing for me to go to them or not, but one rainy afternoon I hunted up Tyler Hall and Room twenty-one on the second floor and slunk into one of the back chairs at five minutes to three, very much frightened and wondering if I would be turned out. The lecture was the second or third of a series given by a Dr. Van Breeze on something in philosophy. I didn't understand more than about two sentences, but no one seemed to question my right to sit there, and I felt ten times more comfortable than I ever had at bridge parties in Hilton.

You see I have never been to college. Although I hated boarding-school with all my heart and soul, I have always had a sneaking idea I might have done better at college. I always liked to study and when I became aware of the fact that Juliet—who, though the best and staunchest girl in the world, was never very brainy—was soaring above me in knowledge, I used to be a little envious. It may seem odd to you for a married woman to be trotting across a campus every other day to attend lectures in class-rooms, as if she were an undergraduate, but after my first plunge into that discourse on philosophy by Dr. Van Breeze I never missed a single lecture in the series. I went the next week and the next and the next; and also bolted bravely into a series of

French lectures every Monday afternoon. I liked just to sit and breathe the air of those class-rooms. I liked the long line of blackboards covered with unintelligible words that belonged to a previous lecture, the row of felt erasers, the smell of dry chalk-dust. I liked sitting in those studious-looking chairs with a big arm on one side. It was as strange and foreign as a new country in those class-rooms, with the bare maple-tree branches grazing the window-pane, and in my ears the music of the French language which I hadn't heard since I left high school. I was a thousand, thousand miles away from the atmosphere of limousines and Edith, five hundred and two wedding presents, and a wedding-dress that cost two hundred dollars. It was like a distant echo from another world when I received an invitation for a bridge one day from a Mrs. Percival. It had completely escaped my mind that she was one of the individuals who had given me a dozen Dresden plates. Even if I had recollected I shouldn't have accepted the invitation. Why should I put handcuffs on myself again, now I was once free from a bondage that I loathed? I sent a very proper note of regret to Mrs. Percival, pleading a previous engagement. It was true. An old white-haired gentleman whom I often met at Dr. Van Breeze's lectures had asked me to sit beside him that particular afternoon at three o'clock in Tyler Hall.

I didn't tell Will about the lectures. He was usually busy at the medical school daytimes, and I was always at home when he arrived at six. I was ashamed to confess to Will that I, who never studied a science in my life, was presuming to attend lectures on the Geology of Fuels and Fluxes (for I took in everything that was starred), the Influence of Science upon Religion, and something about the Law of Falling Spheres. I hated to have him laugh at me, so I kept absolutely quiet on the subject of my ridiculous search for knowledge. I didn't even tell him about my new acquaintances.

The white-haired old gentleman and I developed quite a friendship. Every Thursday we used to walk home together as far as the Library, and he would explain things in the lecture that I didn't understand. He called me Pandora in fun because I was so inquisitive and couldn't bear to let things unknown to me alone. Once in a while a queer little man in a frock coat and a soft artist's tie would join us, and a woman—a Miss Avery in an ugly brown suit and a stiff linen collar like a man's. They used to think that my questions were the drollest things they had ever heard in their lives; but I couldn't help but feel that the sweet old man took quite a fancy to me. He gave me a book once on philosophy, by a famous scholar, and another time he asked me to come to his house to meet his wife. Naturally I didn't go, for I wouldn't have let any one guess I was Mrs. William Ford Maynard for all the wives in creation. It was a funny existence to drift into, wasn't it—cake and snow-pudding in the morning (I loved to mess about in the kitchen); economics, geology, philosophy and French in the afternoon; and evenings our open fire and cribbage with dear old Will, by the light of our big bronze lamp? It was a happy existence too.

I found something in those lectures of Dr. Van Breeze's which I had lost a long time ago. It was a precious thing and at first I didn't recognise it. You see every once in a while Dr. Van Breeze would say something that was better than anything I had ever heard in any church. I wasn't sure that I quite understood him, so I asked the old gentleman. It was a great eye-opener to me when I learned that such a great thinker as Dr. Van Breeze had a religion.

"Why, even *I* don't believe anything," I told my white-haired friend.

His little eyes twinkled at that. "And proud of it too, I'll wager," he laughed.

I blushed, for I think I did feel rather superior, just as I had felt wise when I knew there was no Santa Claus. Juliet and I had talked quite a good deal about religion. She took a course in "Bible" at college, which seemed to knock all the inspiration and the miracles out of it for her; and when it came to her course in philosophy, well—she said that she thought that ministers were a very credulous lot of men. She said you couldn't argue with them because they always wanted to prove things by quoting the Bible, while there existed simply dozens of other worthy reference books. She said that she preferred to rely on great scholars and philosophers for truth, rather than on men who only looked in *one* book for information. Naturally I didn't want to keep on believing in a fallacy, simply because I had never been to college. Childish as it may seem at first, I used to feel awfully unanchored not to say my prayers at night; but of course such a custom was silly, if I really was an unbeliever. I told my white-haired old friend in defence of my shocking statement (which by the way didn't shock him at all) that he might laugh, but anyhow I was backed up by scholars and philosophers, who since the year one had all been busy trying to prove that there wasn't anything in religion to believe.

"Why, my dear mistaken Pandora," smiled my friend. "On the contrary, philosophers have all been trying to prove there *is* something to believe, of some nature or other."

"Really?" I exclaimed. "It would be a big relief to me—but are you sure?"

"Did you ever hear of Benedict Graham?" he replied. Of course I had—every one has. He's at the head of the philosophy department at this university. The next week my friend presented me with Benedict Graham's "Introduction to Philosophy." I thought such a book would be way beyond my understanding, but it wasn't. I used to read a chapter or two by myself and then talk it over with my friend afterward. He made everything very simple to me and seemed besides to be an awfully well-informed old gentleman. I didn't think even Juliet could scoff at him, though he did *believe* a lot of things. After a week or two I felt rather ashamed at having so loftily pronounced myself an Unbeliever. I am no such thing! I can't tell you exactly what I am. I really don't know. But so long as minds ten times bigger and greater than mine (like Dr. Van Breeze and Benedict Graham, and lots of those learned old Greeks and Germans) so long as such intellects entertain the idea that there is *something* of *some* nature to believe in, I tell you, I'm going to believe in it with all my might and main.

CHAPTER XVII

EDITH didn't remain in Europe as long as she expected. She dropped down upon us one night, with Ruth trailing on behind, as unexpectedly as a falling star. I had just had a letter that said that she and Ruth and Alec—my brother had since joined them—were all installed in a fashionable hotel in Paris for six weeks. You can imagine my surprise when Edith and Ruth appeared at my front door.

Will and I were playing cribbage. He had laid down his big book; I had put aside my sewing; and the four little pegs on the cribbage-board had already run the course twice. We always play five games of cribbage every night before we go upstairs to bed. We call it our sleeping-powder. Will had just dealt the cards—it was almost nine o'clock—when the door-bell rang. Old Delia had creaked up to bed ages ago, so Will went to the door himself. I didn't bother even to uncurl my feet—I was sitting Turkish fashion—for I thought it must be the expressman. I yawned and waited.

I heard Will say, "Hello! hello! Well, well, of all—When did you—Where—" and a moment later, resplendent in a long sealskin coat, a sealskin hat, a perfectly enormous muff and a gold chain purse, Edith pushed into our hall, eyes simply sparkling and cheeks aglow.

"Hello, Turtle-doves!" she exclaimed. "Hello, Brother Will! Hello, Mrs. Bobbikins!"

I started up.

"Of all things!" I ejaculated.

Edith kissed me through a prickly veil. Ruth kissed me too. Ruth was simply overwhelming in a huge blue hat with not less than six blue ostrich plumes. They both kissed Will. We all began to laugh.

"We *knew* you'd be surprised," said Ruth.

"But I thought—" I began.

"Where's Alec?" asked Will.

"Why in the world—" I tucked in.

"Listen! Wait!" commanded Edith. "*I'll* explain. We thought," she said, gurgling with mirth, "it would be great fun to surprise you, so—"

"Alec got a cable last week—" put in Ruth.

"From my dad," Edith went on. "Business! Wasn't it disgusting when we weren't planning to sail for six weeks? Al had to go right on to Chicago—and The Homestead—"

"We had the bridal suite on the *Mauretania!*" I heard Ruth exclaim to Will.

"—isn't open," finished Edith. "The servants are scattered to the four winds. I've written to them, but of course they haven't had a chance to open things up yet. So we thought it would be fun to—"

"To pop in on you!" giggled Ruth.

"Can you put us up?" snapped Edith.

"Of course! How nice!" I tried to say cordially, with the image of my cold, unused, north guest-room dancing before my eyes, the floor covered with newspapers, two cut-glass punch-bowls, thirteen berry dishes and seven vases. "*Of course* I can put you up. Take off your things."

Will produced two dining-room chairs and Edith and Ruth buried them in no time beneath a stack of coats, hats and muffs. Edith was gowned—slick as a black suede glove—in a tight-fitting, broadcloth, one-piece dress, Irish lace at neck and wrists. Ruth's new Parisian hair was simply glorious. They strutted into our comfortable living-room like two peacocks, Edith surveying the walls and ceilings as if she were examining the dome of the Boston State-house.

"So this is where you coo!" she said in her horrid patronising manner. Imagine Dr. William Maynard of the medical department of one of the biggest universities in the country cooing! I blushed for Will. He pushed up a chair. It chanced to be one of Father's old morocco leather armchairs I had found in the storeroom at home. Edith made opera-glasses of her two hands, and pretended to gaze intently at the poor old piece of furniture.

"Hello, old friend!" she said, and made a mock salute. "You look familiar. Back into service again, hey? 'Comfy' anyhow!" she finished and settled into it.

"What sort of a passage was it?" asked Will, and for the next half-hour we listened to an account of a perfectly disgusting customs officer in New York, who made Edith pay one hundred and ninety-five dollars on a half-dozen mere gowns that already were simply worn to shreds.

It was when Will had gone to the kitchen for some water that Edith leaned forward and said to me:

"How'd you happen to take *this* house, my dear? And don't you dress for dinner, Lucy?"

"Oh," I said, "this? It's short and I can hook it up myself."

"I just *knew*," chimed in my own sister Ruth, "that Lucy would be one of those to get slack after she was once married. Now I've always said that *I*—"

"I didn't know," broke in Edith in a sudden burst of laughter, "that there were any houses left nowadays that had those funny old-fashioned storm-doors that you hook on every winter."

"Trust Lucy to pick out the oldest shack in the town," tucked in Ruth, touching the surface of her perfect coiffure with light fingers, and glancing sideways at herself in an old gilt-framed mirror on the wall.

"By the way, Lucy," Edith added, piling it on, I thought, a bit too thick, "people aren't using doilies under ornaments any more. Where are all those stunning plateaus?"

"Dear me," I laughed, bound to be good-natured, "I'd completely forgotten the plateaus. They must be in one of the barrels we haven't opened."

"Haven't opened! I *never* saw any one like you. Haven't opened! It certainly is a good thing that I've come home."

It was with a sinking heart that I took Edith and Ruth up to the guest-room in which I had put one of Will's black walnut bedroom sets.

"If I'd only known you were coming!" I began going up the stairs trying to explain. "The bureau is chuck-full of silver things—we ought to have a safe. And the closet—all my good dresses are there. We have so little closet-room in this house. In the morning I'll clear it out. I know you'd like separate beds too, but when Will's things were all unpacked there wasn't room for much new furniture. And I'm sorry, Edith, that you haven't a bath connected. We have only one bathroom in the entire house and even that—"

Edith wouldn't let me finish. We were in the guest-room now. Her eyes were on the cut-glass in the corner.

"I ought never to have gone to Europe," she announced. "Never in this world!"

I wished she had never come home, and when I kissed her good-night, all the old rancour and rebellion, dormant for so long, was raging in my heart. I stole downstairs after I was undressed, pulled out Edith's silver service from underneath the stairs and put it on the sideboard; I unlocked Edith's chest of silver, and began laying the breakfast table with the horns-of-plenty; I dragged out some elaborate breakfast napkins; I hauled down from the top shelf of the pantry a Coalport breakfast-set. At one A. M., when I was crawling back stealthily to our room, I had to pass the guest-chamber door. I heard voices, and stopped a moment.

"It's human nature for a man, single or married, to prefer a woman in pretty clothes, whoever she is," said Edith.

"Of course," Ruth agreed. "When she came in to say good-night did you see the horrid old red worsted bedroom slippers she had on?"

"And moreover," Edith went on, "a man likes an attractive house—pretty pictures, pretty ornaments, a place where he is proud to bring his friends."

"Naturally."

"A man likes to be proud of his wife too," went on the sage, "proud of her friends, of her place in society. Now Lucy—absolutely *no* social-sense—not a spark. No doubt, if she's made any friends at all, they're the grocery-man and the seamstress, or the woman who washes her hair."

Ruth giggled.

"Now *you*, Ruth," Edith pursued, "are a girl after my own heart. *You* are the kind to be the wife of a famous man. *You* could be Mrs. William Maynard with the right sort of go."

I had to smile at the thought of Ruth and Will. Will hates false things—puffs and brilliantine; he hates fluffy negligees, and silly, high-heeled unwalkable shoes; he hates fuss and feathers. I passed on down the hall.

"It will take more than Edith Campbell and my young sister Ruth to disturb me, I guess," I said to myself as I turned out several flaring gas-jets in the hall and bathroom, left by those two extravagant creatures to burn all night.

Edith awoke the next morning armoured for battle. I could see it in her eyes and feel it in her manner. I knew it was to be no slight skirmish, but a well-thought-out and carefully-planned campaign. I knew it was to be a serious engagement because neither she nor Ruth criticised a single thing for the next two days. If they were shocked and surprised, I knew it only by raised eyebrows, critical smiles or covert glances. I hated their silence. I felt as if the entire foundation of my life was stealthily being honeycombed with tunnels, laid with bombs and dynamite, and I wondered a little uncomfortably when Edith would light the fuse. Edith is wonderful in some ways, as you know. At a hotel or on a steamer she catches on to the right people to know within the first twenty-four hours, and by the third day she's playing bridge with them. As soon as ever her half-dozen pieces of baggage had arrived, she donned a Paquin three-piece velvet suit and set out to call on Mrs. Percival. That night the explosion took place.

"I called on Mrs. Percival this afternoon," she began after dinner. "She says, Lucy, that you never returned her call."

Will had gone to a lecture that evening. Ruth was playing solitaire in front of the fire.

"Has Mrs. Percival called on me? I didn't realise it," I replied.

"Not only has Mrs. Percival called, but every one else who should. That impossible servant of yours said that all these people had called." Edith took down the brass jardinière where I deposit all my visiting-cards. "She said that you were never in afternoons and had not seen *one* of them. Where under the heavens were you, Lucy?"

I felt ashamed to tell Edith about the lectures, so I said instead:

"Oh, anywhere—walking, shopping—*anywhere*. I never stay in afternoons. I can't bear to."

"How many of those calls have you returned?" cross-examined my sister-in-law.

"Well—I am *going* to return them all," I began. "They're such strangers to me that I've been putting it off. You know how I hate making calls anyway. But of course—"

Edith interrupted me.

"*The* people in this town are the ones connected with the university. I have always heard that. You've had every opportunity to know them. They've all called on account of Will. You've simply thrown away chance upon chance. Here are the Philemon Omsteds' cards. Mrs. Percival says that Dr. Omsted is awfully queer—kind of a socialist—but that Mrs. Omsted's musicales are the selectest things given. Here are Mrs. Daniel Haynes McClellan's cards, the Bernkapps, Madame Gauthier. I found out from Mrs. Percival, indirectly of course, that all these people are *in* things. Mrs. Benedict Graham—even *she* has called on you. And Mrs. Percival says that *she* was a Granville—daughter of President Emeritus Granville. Dr. Graham is an awfully prominent man himself. Surely you've heard of Benedict Graham, Lucy. Surely—"

"Of course!" I interrupted. "Every one has, Edith, and I'm reading his book, but I'd be frightened to death to go up and pull the Benedict Grahams' bell. I couldn't!"

"You ought to be married to a clerk or a barber, and then you wouldn't need to. I should hate to think I had married a man whom I couldn't live up to. Every one has heard of Will. He has been talked about all over the country. But what about his wife? Who is she?" Edith's words were beginning to cut now and I bit my lip. "There was a tea this very afternoon to which Mrs. William Maynard ought to have been invited. Were you?"

I shook my head.

"Of course you weren't, nor last week to a musicale that Mrs. Omsted gave, and I'll bet you had nothing whatsoever to do with the Charity Bazaar that the younger women in the university set get up every Christmas. Do you think a man wants to be married to a person who is not received—absolutely ignored, as if something was the matter with her? Whom in the world do you know here, anyway? Any one at all?"

Pictures of the little man with the soft tie, the dear white-haired old gentleman whose name I did not even know, and Miss Avery, all impossible I knew to Edith, flashed before my eyes. So I shook my head and Edith went on.

"And the house—it's simply impossible! Such a location! Why, no one lives in this part of town. You would think that Will couldn't afford anything better, but he can. You ought to have two maids. And why under the heavens all this old furniture? People don't use black walnut any more, and that old narrow, square dining-room table is simply beyond words!"

"And you have no butler's pantry nor back stairs," put in Ruth.

"And you ought to make your maid wear black afternoons."

"And turn down the beds," added Ruth.

"It's *my* house," I began. "If you don't like it—" I got up quickly and started to leave the room.

"Oh, come, Bobbikins," Edith said in her persistently cheerful way. "Don't get cross. I was only trying to be helpful." Then she went on: "I found this on the floor, by your desk. I couldn't help but see it. It's an invitation for dinner from Mrs. Benedict Graham. I can't understand why she invites you if you've never returned her call, but of course it's on account of Will. I can't imagine your not accepting this invitation and yet I heard you say that next Thursday, the sixth, the very evening of this dinner, you and Will had tickets for the theatre."

"Yes, we've been planning to go on that particular night for three weeks. It's a little secret anniversary of ours," I said sullenly; "and we're going too. Why should you, Edith, come here and try to upset the whole universe? We're happy. Will is satisfied. He loves things simple. I wish you'd leave us alone. Will doesn't care a scrap about society, and I hate it, hate it, hate it!" I was on the verge of bursting into tears.

"Well, if there's going to be a scene, excuse *me*, please," said Ruth, and started to leave the room.

"If you're through with that card-table, please fold it up and put it in the closet," I said to Ruth with my eyes full of fire. "I haven't got six servants."

"Whew!" whistled Ruth and began gathering up her cards.

"I should think," calmly went on Edith like a repeating alarm-clock, "you'd like your husband to be *proud* of you."

"Oh, please—please—" I fired back, and then suddenly, too full to speak, I turned abruptly and fled up the stairs to my room.

The sweet darkness enveloped me. I drew a chair to the window. *Will* would ask her to mind her own affairs; *Will* would talk to her; *Will* would tell her how he hated her mean ambitions, how he abhorred her contemptible snobbishness; *Will* would defend and stand up for me; *Will* would fix her! "Just wait for *Will*!" I said, and listened for his step on the sidewalk outside and the sound of his key in the latch. I heard him come in about half past ten. It was almost twelve when he came up to me.

"Not in bed?" he asked gently and leaned down and kissed me. "Edith was downstairs when I came in and we've been talking. I don't know but what we ought to keep two maids, Bobbie dear," Will said, and I felt as if I had been struck. Will went over and lit the gas. "I guess we might as well postpone our theatre party for next Thursday," he went on. "I think, after all, we'd better go to the Grahams' dinner. By the way," he broke off, "didn't you get an invitation to the Omsteds' affair last week?"

"No, Will, I didn't," I said dully.

"Perhaps you'll find time to pay back a few of those calls some time pretty soon, Bobbie dear," he said to me. And that morning about four A. M. I cried myself to sleep.

Edith went to the dinner too. She had Will telephone and fix it up someway. I don't know how nor I didn't ask. I was very miserable, very unhappy. My heart was heavier than it had been for a whole year. "Will wasn't satisfied, Will wasn't proud, Will was ashamed of me," rang in my ears from morning till night. During the few days that still must be lived before Thursday the sixth at seven o'clock, Edith exhibited the usual kindness and gentle consideration of any victor over the vanquished. I didn't make another plea. I was as resigned as a fatalist, and as unmurmuring as a stoic. I wrote my acceptance at Edith's dictation without a word, and silently fought the tears that came to my eyes, as I sealed the envelope.

"O Bobbie," said Will gently, "don't worry so about it, dear. You weren't so frightened about your own wedding."

"Exactly," said Edith. "And I've had dinners at The Homestead just as grand as this. You're simply out of training. People won't notice you so much as you think anyhow. Just act slowly, and don't try to talk. That's all. *I'll* be there and you can 'lean on me, grandpa.' *You'll* be all right," she assured me grandly.

I couldn't explain to Will and Edith how I felt about that dinner at the Grahams'. They wouldn't understand. Of course I had been to Edith's parties at The Homestead, but then I was simply Lucy Vars; and now I was Mrs. William Ford Maynard. Everybody in Hilton had accepted Lucy Vars long ago as a queer, quiet sort of shy little mouse, and treated her as such. She was used to it. But here, no one had as yet discovered Mrs. William Ford Maynard. She had been living for six, beautiful, unmolested months in idyllic secretion. But she had been run down at last, she must give herself up like a hunted convict, and by Thursday at midnight all of Dr. Maynard's learned associates would know just what sort of insignificant little person he had married. Oh, if only for Will's sake I had been born clever and brilliant; if only I had possessed a little of Edith's style; Ruth's *savoir faire*. Do you wonder then, that I trembled in anticipation of this occasion? Ruth's coming-out party, my wedding, a dozen dinners of Edith's, were as doll's tea-parties as compared to this, when Mrs. William Ford Maynard must come forth from her hiding-place and meet this test of a searching inspection.

I shall never forget the faint, sickening feeling inside of me as we stood waiting for admittance before the big colonial house. We must have been the last ones to arrive. A babble of voices in the drawing-room at the left greeted us as we entered. We walked up the old colonial stairway, and into a big bedroom at the top with a black walnut bedroom set. I noticed that even in my fright.

"Mercy, child, don't take off your gloves," whispered Edith to me.

"I *hate* them," I said, and ripped my arms bare. I wore a light blue silk dress with a Dutch neck, in spite of Edith in her low-cut ball-gown plastered over with glittering black spangles. My hair was done in its usual everyday knot at the back of my neck, bobbed up in the last five minutes after Ruth's sixth attempt at dressing it in the "new way." Edith looked like a fashion-plate: she had a perfect figure; her neck is marvellous; she wore diamonds and a string of pearls.

I followed her down the stairs very carefully, lest I trip in my little French-heeled satin slippers or lose the silly things altogether. My heart was in my mouth. "What shall I say when I am introduced? What shall I say? What shall I say?" I kept thinking in a panic and watched Edith sweep across the hall in her most impressive manner. I waited an instant. A minute more and Will was announcing, "And this is my wife, Mrs. Graham." My heart fluttered as it used to at parties at home.

The grand lady smiled upon me. She took my hand.

"So this is *Mrs.* William Maynard," she said. "I'm glad you could come. We all know Dr. Maynard so well—we're so proud to have him one of us—that I am glad to meet *you*." Was she thinking how funny and young I looked? Was she saying "What a strange little insignificant bit of thing indeed for such a man as William Maynard!" I wished, after all, I had had my hair marcelled.

"I want Dr. Graham to meet you," my hostess continued and, leaning over, touched the great philosopher on the shoulder with her fan. He was talking to Edith. "Benedict, my dear." He turned. "Mrs. Maynard!"

I trembled in my shoes and raised my eyes.

"You!" I gasped and stepped back. Dr. Benedict Graham—*the* Dr. Benedict Graham—was no other than my dear sweet old white-haired gentleman of the philosophical lectures! His hands went out to me—both of them—and gathered my ten cold trembling fingers in his warm grasp.

"You?" he repeated with the sweet light of recognition in his eyes. "You! *Pandora!* Julia," he said to Mrs. Graham, "Mrs. Maynard is Pandora of whom I have told you, my little friend who takes a walk with me every week. Well—well," he chuckled. "Well—well." Then to astonished Will he exclaimed, "Your wife and I are old friends," and oh, I could have kissed him!

The colour rushed back into my cheeks. My hand was in Mrs. Graham's again, and when I looked around the room I found I stood in a little circle—every one's eyes, like the lights, upon me. It was like a surprise-party, or a fairy story, or some trick worked by a skilful magician. First my eyes fell upon Dr. Van Breeze; and then, in a flash, on Monsieur Gauthier, who gave the French lectures; and suddenly coming toward me was the funny little man with the soft wide tie. He wore it even to-night. He took my hand cordially and Will exclaimed, "Do you know her too, Mr. Omsted?"

It all happened in a minute. I can't tell it quickly enough. "She has read one of my books from cover to cover," I heard Dr. Graham laugh, eyes twinkling into mine; and I think it was just after that remark of Dr. Graham's that Monsieur Gauthier stepped forward and bowing before me in the dearest, Frenchiest manner in the world, said in his own language with every one listening, "I have never been presented to Mrs. Maynard, but if I am not mistaken I think I have observed her face at my Monday afternoon lectures. Is it not so? Always the same chair—third from the back, two removed from the aisle—always the same. It has been a pleasure to see you there each week."

I understood every word. I didn't lose a phrase. The warmth, the light, those words in French, everybody's eyes upon me acted like just enough champagne.

"*Merci, Monsieur,*" I dared to say and swept him a little bow. I can hear now my voice and those two little French words falling upon the silence of that room like a noise on a still night. I don't know how I ever presumed to speak in French. I would have thought it affected in any one else, but at that exultant moment I could have mimicked Chinese. Two words in a foreign language I know should not be very amazing (any one could do it) but I could feel a little murmur pass among the people after I had spoken that was something—a little—like the applause at the theatre. A moment later the talking began again; I was being introduced at left and right; my own voice and laughter mingled with the general babble. It was exactly as though I had taken my plunge, come safely to the surface and now was swimming along with long even strokes with the others for the shore. Edith looked at me astonished. Will observed me as though I were a stranger. Easy words came to my lips, my cheeks burned, and every one was so kind—so good to me, that I forgot my dress, my hair and my French-heeled shoes.

I don't mean to imply that I was the belle of the evening. Of course I wasn't. It would be absurd for a mere slip of a girl, married though she was, to come among learned men and sages and have them all turning their attention and thought upon her. Even if she had been pretty, and skilful in the art of smiles and glances, which I am not, such an event would be amazing. I only mean to say that I didn't feel awkward nor wonder where to put my hands between the courses. I was placed at the left of Dr. Graham and felt as easy as if I were sitting beside my own father. The dinner, it seemed, was in honour of Dr. Van Breeze on account of his book about to be published, consisting of the very lectures he had been delivering in Tyler Hall. The talk centred about the book a good deal and though I didn't contribute a single idea to the conversation I understood perfectly what was being discussed. But I do not think Edith enjoyed herself. She was over-jewelled, in the first place, and kept running on to Dr. Omsted, who, you know, is a kind of socialist, about the gorgeous bridal suite on the *Mauretania*, the one hundred and ninety-two dollars duty she had to pay, and of how she smuggled in a thousand-dollar pearl necklace, until I was embarrassed.

We went home about ten-thirty. Just at the door as we were going out Mrs. Philemon Omsted stopped me. Will had me by the arm. Edith was just in front.

"Mrs. Maynard," she said to me, "just a moment, please. I have been very glad to meet you. And, by the way, Easter Monday I am giving a small musicale. Mrs. Graham is to pour for me. I should be delighted if you will assist."

I thanked her quietly (but oh, in my heart I could have crowned her with flowers) and passed out to our hired carriage.

I sat in the middle between Edith and Will. We drove away in silence, my heart singing, and my cheeks warm with excitement. Will pressed my arm with his bare hand hidden underneath the folds of my party-coat. I could feel his joy. It was Edith who spoke first.

"What a miserable stuffy little carriage," she said; then after a moment, "Those people may have brains, but I don't think I ever saw such a lot of frumpily dressed women in my life."

Will leaned forward then, and said playfully, but with a queer little sure sound in his voice, "What was your impression of Mrs. William Maynard?"

"Of Bobbie?" Edith asked raising her eyebrows, disgusted with Will's little streak of fun.

"Of Mrs. William Maynard," he corrected; then in a low voice he added, "Of Mrs. William Maynard, of whom I am so proud!" and I had to draw away my hand to wipe away two silly tears.

CHAPTER XVIII

IT used to be a source of great anxiety to Father that none of his children was married. He had a notion that the only way to make a family name a strong one was by increase. When Tom and Alec were scarcely out of college and the twins were still in short trousers, Father announced that he was going to present to the first grandson bearing the name of Vars, a check for three thousand dollars. We treated it a good deal as a joke then and used to poke a lot of fun at the boys about it. That was a long time ago—before Father died—and when we found the same offer written out in plain black and white in Father's will we were a little surprised and a little touched too, realising how dreadfully in earnest the poor dear man must have been about it, and how disappointed. According to his instructions, however, the three thousand dollars was put away at interest to await the coming of the first Vars heir.

At the beginning of this chapter three of us were married—though of course I didn't count, being a girl—and still the three thousand dollars remained unclaimed. Poor unlucky Elise had had four girls, and Edith hadn't had a baby of any kind. However, we all knew if ever such an event should take place in Edith's career it would be the most important occasion in the entire annals of the family. And we weren't mistaken. Edith had been married several years when the wonderful preparations were begun. One would have thought she was the Queen of Holland. Everybody in Hilton seemed to vie one with another in embroidering tiny martingales, knitting worsted blankets, or scalloping flannel shawls for Edith Vars' baby. The nursery that she had had built on the sunny side of Father's house four years before fairly bloomed into pink and white equipment. You had only to spend a half-hour there to discover what a popular person Edith was and what a select place in society she had at last attained. She was more than accommodating about telling from whom each little gift had come. For instance the superb baby-dress with Irish insertion Mrs. Alfred Sturtevant brought over herself yesterday; the elaborate hand-embroidered bassinette sheets were from Mrs. Barlow—*the* Mrs. Barlow, you understand; the silk puffs, silk socks, silk caps from Beatrice, Phyllis and Bernice. A hand-made, finely-worked Christening dress of Alec's, proving the family's prosperity thirty-five years ago (Edith herself had risen from the sod, you know; you may be sure *her* Christening dress wasn't on exhibition) had been rooted out of an old trunk in the storeroom. The most expensive "Specialist" within reach had been engaged, and a nurse from Boston was to remain for four months at the rate of twenty-five a week. You could trust Edith to do the thing up in the proper style; you could trust her also to carry away that three thousand dollars premium in Father's will. She felt cock-sure of it herself. Things had always come her way, hadn't they? *She* never did the ignominious thing, did she? Poor Elise and her four little girls she had always held in the lowest esteem. Fate simply wouldn't allow Edith Vars' baby to be a girl. Every one said so. Even I was convinced.

Alec treated Edith as if she were the centre of the universe. When the shocking news about Oliver reached us, Alec's chief concern was in regard to the effect of the news upon poor Edith. It was two years after that first dinner of ours at Dr. Graham's that the knowledge of my brother Oliver's latest escapade reached me one morning in early April.

I was diligently dusting the black walnut bookcases in our sunny living-room. I sat down in the nearest chair at hand, perfectly stunned for a moment, my jaw hanging open, no doubt, and read through the letter containing the fatal news at least three times before I had the strength to get up. The first thing I did was to hang up the square piece of hem-stitched cheese-cloth at the head of the cellar stairs; then I went and hunted up a time-table. There was a train due to leave for Hilton at eleven-ten. Will had left early that morning, for he had a nine o'clock recitation, so he wasn't at home when Alec's letter came. But I knew that nothing less than a death in the family could drag him away from his precious clinic the next day, so I hurried off for the train alone. I stuck a note of explanation into the dish of ferns on the middle of the dining-room table:

> "*Dear Will,*
>
> "I've had a letter from Alec. Oliver was married to a Madge Tompkins in February! He's bringing her to Hilton to-night. This is all I know about it. Will try to be back before Sunday.
>
> "BOBBIE."

During the last half-year Oliver had been superintending a gang of granite workers in a little town in Vermont. City life hadn't seemed to agree with Oliver's purse very well, and the diversions of the several middle-western cities, in each of which Oliver had made a great hit with all the nicest girls and their mothers, had interfered with his business hours. It was after he had tried six or seven positions, starting with banking in Pittsburg, and ending up with shipping automobile tires in Akron, Ohio, that Tom and Alec deposited Oliver, with scarcely a cent to his name, in Glennings Falls, Vermont, where the possibilities for spending money were rather limited.

Poor Oliver! I felt awfully sorry for him. He's such a brilliant-appearing fellow! It seemed to me as if he had struck an awfully hard run of luck since he graduated from college. He really is a civil engineer, but fate has swerved him into other lines, which I think is the cause of his checkered career. He always loved to build bridges and dams and toy railroads even as a small boy. After he finally succeeded in squeezing through college he conceived a foolish notion—foolish according to Tom—to take a course in Civil Engineering at Cornell. Of course he didn't have anything else to study—no bugbears like English Composition, Latin or Greek, so perhaps that is why he did so well in the Engineering. Anyhow he passed the examinations with some kind of an honour—the only one, poor boy, that he had ever been able to boast of in his life. Tom, who had pooh-poohed the idea of Oliver's wasting a year at Cornell, finally gave up his plan of putting the boy to work in his lumber camps, and Oliver started forth, hopes high and spirits aglow, to accept an engineering job in Arizona. On the way out, at Pittsburg, he stopped off to visit an old college friend for a fortnight, and at the end of the first week he wrote that he had struck a "gold mine." His friend's father was prominently connected with half a dozen banks in Pittsburg and had offered him a position. I could have told the friend's father that Oliver would never make a banker, but he found it out himself in a little while.

After Oliver left Pittsburg everything went wrong with him. No civil engineering jobs presented themselves, no more friends' fathers, no more "gold mines" seemed to be available. After that Oliver became a regular rolling-stone. He couldn't seem to keep any of his positions, or he wouldn't, I don't know which. He tried everything. It was manufacturing automobile parts in Toledo; selling motorcycles in Buffalo; making out orders for plumbers' supplies in Cleveland. He fizzled miserably each time. He never had any money. He was forever sending to Tom or Alec for a check for fifty until his salary was due. He was forever running down to New York or over to Chicago for a class reunion or a dance. He was forever writing to me vivid descriptions of new "queens" he had met.

It was when Tom and Alec had to pay fourteen hundred and fifty dollars for a "swell" little last season's roadster that Oliver had secured at a wonderful bargain from a friend of his in Akron (this was when he was a shipping clerk in a tire factory) and in which he had been sporting about through the streets of the place at a speed of thirty an hour, that he was summoned to the court of his older brothers, and after due consultation was sent up to Glennings Falls, like a convict, to work in the mines. His roadster was sold at a terrible sacrifice, he said, and that fact seemed at the time to be his greatest regret.

I could have cried for Oliver. There would be no "queens" in Glennings Falls; there would be no Sunday-night Lobster-Newbergs over a chafing-dish; there would be no stunning "visiting girls" whom he met at Class-Day or in Pittsburg when he was there, or in Toledo, Cleveland or Buffalo, for him to call on until eleven P.M.

When I arrived in Hilton, Alec was at the station in the automobile to meet me (I had had just time to 'phone him that I was coming) and Tom who had come flying on from the West the minute Alec's shocking telegram had reached him was there too. Malcolm had caught the midnight from New York and was waiting on the veranda when we ran up under the porte-cochère. It was really a family reunion, but all the joy of seeing each other again was buried beneath the horror and consternation in our hearts. Oliver's act was astounding. We're not an erratic family. We never figure in accidents or tragedies of any kind. We hate notoriety.

"And besides all the horrid publicity of a secret marriage," said Ruth, "Edith says the creature is too *common* for anything." Ruth dangled a dainty velvet pump on the tip of her toe as she made this remark. We were gathered in the room that used to be the sitting-room, all of us—Tom, Malcolm, Edith, Alec, Ruth and I. We had been talking for an hour.

"Common!" took up Edith. "She's absolutely impossible, I tell you! We stopped off to see Oliver for an hour on our way to the Green Mountains," she explained to me, "last fall, in the automobile. He didn't know we were coming. It was Sunday and he had some dreadful little frowzy-headed creature in tow, I'm sure her name was Tompkins—silly, simpering little thing—perfectly enormous pompadour and a cheap Hamburg open-work lingerie waist, over bright pink—oh, horribly cheap! I can't begin to tell you!"

"Well—well—we must try to make the best of it," said Tom lightly.

"Best of it!" scoffed Edith. "Well, if Oliver thinks for one minute that I am going to throw open my house to his precious Madge Tompkins he's greatly mistaken. Ruth is having a large bridge party Thursday—ten tables. This affair has simply got to be kept quiet until after that. Breck Sewall is coming up from New York to spend Sunday. You all know he's paying marked attention to Ruth, and the Sewalls—Heavens!—they're particular to a degree! Oh, we mustn't let a single word of this miserable affair leak out—not a single word! Oh, when I think of it, I just want—"

"Come, come, Edith," interrupted Alec. "Gently, dear. Gently, you know."

"Well, if any of you expect *me*," Edith went on, "to have that common person here, I must tell you that I can't—I simply can't! I'm not in a condition to endure it. I—"

"Now look here, dear," Alec said soothingly, "no one expects you to. Everything will be exactly as you wish."

Oh, he would have stopped the sun from rising if Edith had requested it. I've never witnessed such dog-devotion as Alec shows to Edith. He can't be five minutes late to an appointment with her, without telephoning a plausible excuse, or sending a special messenger. She has him wonderfully trained. You ought to see him run around and put down windows, raise shades, carry chairs or rush upstairs for her work-bag which she forgot and left on her bureau just before dinner.

At about five o'clock that afternoon Malcolm, who had been haunting the station all day in the hope of meeting Oliver and his companion, and hurrying them quietly into a closed carriage as soon as possible, burst in upon us, all excitement.

"What in the world is the matter now?" exclaimed Ruth.

"Have they come?" asked Alec.

"Has any one heard of it?" gasped Edith.

"Heard of it! It's gotten into the papers!" Malcolm announced.

Tom and Alec both got up.

"Very bad?" asked one of them, and Edith sprang forward like a cat and snatched the paper out of Malcolm's hand.

"On the front page," said Malcolm. "Here! There it is. Oh, no one can miss it."

"Heavens!" Edith ejaculated as her eyes fell upon the headlines.

"Read it," commanded Tom.

> "Romantic Love Affair of Oliver Chenery Vars ends in an Elopement. Son of William T. Vars, former President of the Vars & Co. Woollen mills of this City Marries his Landlady's Daughter."

She stopped short.

"Go on," said Tom in a low voice.

"Hadn't *I* better?" suggested Alec.

But Edith continued:

> "The friends of Oliver Chenery Vars will be surprised to learn of his marriage to Miss Madge Tompkins of Glennings Falls, Vermont. For the past year young Vars has been connected with the Glennings Falls Granite Works, and the attachment between himself and Miss Tompkins, daughter of Mrs. Ebenezer Tompkins, a widow with whom he boarded, has been a matter of some concern to the Vars family. The news of his marriage, which is said to have taken place last February, comes as a total surprise and few particulars are known. However, it has been ascertained that the young lovers have been forgiven and that they will be the guests of the Alexander Vars at The Homestead for the remainder of the week. The new Mrs. Vars is but eighteen and carried off the blue ribbon in the Pretty Girl contest at the Glennings Falls Agricultural Fair last September."

"How perfectly disgusting!" broke in Ruth.

"Rotten!" muttered Malcolm.

Edith couldn't speak. The paper fluttered to the floor and Alec went over and put her gently in a chair. Tom scowled and looked hard out of the window. We sat in silence for a full half-minute, then Tom turned suddenly.

"Look here," he said, "here he comes! Here Oliver comes!"

I leaned forward quickly, picked up the discarded paper and thrust it under my elbow on the table.

Oliver was alone. I shall always remember how he looked on that spring evening as he swung along, overcoat open and flapping in the wind, head held high and brow smooth and cloudless. His step was as sure and firm as when he joined us all after he had received his diploma on his graduation day at college. My heart went out to him—poor Oliver always getting into trouble, gifted and talented in a way (he can sing like an angel) awfully good-looking and lovable (he has friends everywhere), poor Oliver—what would become of him? I heard his step on the veranda, and a minute later he was standing, six feet high, smiling and confident in the door of the library. There is something irresistible about Oliver's smile. If he had only looked at me I should have smiled back, but his eyes rested on Tom.

"Hello, everybody!" he said. "Hello, Tom! Mighty good of *you* to come way on East. Well, well," he glanced swiftly around the room, "all here, aren't you?" Then he added, "Well, what do you think?"

"Seen the paper?" inquired Tom.

"Is it in the paper?" asked Oliver, and Malcolm pulled the horrible thing from beneath my elbow and thrust it into Oliver's hands. I watched Oliver closely. I saw the slow, dark colour spread over his face and across that cloudless brow of his. I saw his eyes travel once through the article and then go back and retrace each painful word of it again. When he had satisfied himself he laid the paper down and looked up.

"Well, it's true," he said, and six pairs of eyes glowered upon him.

"What explanation have you for this—step of yours?" asked Tom.

Oliver's confidence fell away a little. He picked off a bit of lint from the sleeve of his coat.

"Oh, why hash the whole thing over?" he said. "I'm married all right. What's the use—of course I'm sorry it is in the paper."

"Sorry!" sniffed Ruth.

"But *I* didn't let it out. Hang it all," he broke off, "you bury me in a hole like that—she was the only girl worth looking at. *I* didn't want to go to Glennings Falls. It was *your* plan."

"You had had six other positions before we resorted to Glennings Falls," fired Alec.

Oliver flushed.

"Oh, well—if you've all made up your minds to be disagreeable! I left Madge at the station to come up in a carriage," he explained. "She'll be here in five minutes. I hope at least you'll be decent to *her*."

"Decent to *her*, Oliver Vars!" Edith had found her voice, "I guess you better begin and think how *you* can be decent to *us*. Do you know what you've done? You've simply ruined our reputations and just when Breck Sewall—oh, you've disgraced us all! I shall never want to hold up my head again, and Ruth has invitations out for a big bridge. Madge Tompkins! Don't ask *me* to be decent to *her*. She'll never spend a night under *this* roof as long as *I* live. Oh, I've seen her—common little—"

"Be careful," shot back Oliver, flushed and angry now. "Madge's father was a minister, an educated gentleman, when yours at that period of his career was collecting scrap iron and junk from people's back yards!"

Edith grew red. The early life of her iron-king father had always been a sore point with her. I don't know what she would have done; perhaps literally have scratched Oliver's eyes out, if Tom hadn't interrupted.

"Oh, come. None of this," he said. "Oliver, you were hasty in what you said; and, Edith, let us see the young lady before we pass judgment on her. I think she's coming. At least here is a carriage."

It was very touching to me when Oliver went down to the carriage at the curbing and helped out the girl whom of all the hundreds (for Oliver could have had almost any one: Women adored him) he had chosen to honour the most highly. She was short and a little shabby with a sort of cheap flashiness that you could see a hundred yards away. I knew particular, fastidious Oliver must feel a little ashamed of the wrinkled checked suit she wore, the big-figured gaudy lace veil over her hat, the dingy white ostrich plumes. I felt very sorry for Oliver when at the library door she stepped back to let him enter, and he said gently, "*You* first, Madge." She stumbled in smiling and confused. She really was rather impossible: pretty in a way, but oh, miles and miles away from everything that is essential to a good taste and good manners. She wore white kid gloves and patent-leather slippers that pinched her feet. There was a celluloid comb in the back of her hair with rhinestones in it.

"Well, here they are, Madge!" said Oliver heartily.

Her first words jarred us.

"I guess we surprised you some," she laughed.

"Well—it was unexpected," said Tom finally.

She giggled at that; then she asked, trying to appear at ease, "Well, aren't you going to introduce me around, Oliver?"

It was very painful. She gave her fingers to us in a ridiculous fashion. "Pleased to meet you!" she said like a machine after each name, and then after I, the last one, had dropped her hand, in a moment of deep confusion she remarked, glancing around the room, "Oh, my, I think your house is just grand!"

Malcolm coughed; Oliver flushed.

"Did you have a long trip?" I asked.

"Just dreadful," she replied eagerly. "The dirt was something awful. We came up in a parlour-car. I just love parlour-cars! We've been staying at an elegant hotel in New York."

"Sit down, won't you?" said Malcolm kindly. He pushed up a chair and she glanced at him archly.

"Thank you ever so much!" Then she added coyly, and my heart bled for her poor pitiful attempt, "I know *you*. *You're* Malcolm. I was awfully gone on your photo once." She giggled again. Alec took out a large white handkerchief and wiped his brow. Malcolm shifted uneasily to his other foot, and she added confidentially, "It was something awful the way it used to make Oliver jealous."

At that moment Edith swept up before her. "I think I met you once," she began loftily.

"I remember," said Madge. "You came through in a big auto. My, but I thought Oliver had some stylish folks!"

"I'm extremely sorry that our rooms are all filled to-night," went on Edith grandly, "and that it will be impossible for me to ask you to remain."

Madge reddened. "I wouldn't trouble you for anything," she apologised.

"No," said Oliver and his voice shook with scorn, "we wouldn't trouble you. Madge, please wait for me a moment on the veranda." She looked up frightened. "Yes," he said, and she rose and without a word walked out of the room. Oliver closed the door. He was red in the face with indignation.

"Thank you all for your kindness," he said very scathingly; "I'm sure I'm very grateful. If this is what it means to be a member of a family, let me be free of it."

Tom got up. "Well—" he drawled, "if you can get along without us, why we—"

"Very well," retorted Oliver. "Very well, if that's your answer. I've thrown up the charming job at Glennings Falls anyway. I'm not so everlasting dependent as you have an idea. I'm off, and thank heaven! It's too bad if I've interrupted Ruth's bridge party. It's really too bad. I'm through with the whole lot of you. I'm through!" He turned. The door slammed. The room trembled to the very ceiling and a gust of wind snatched a pile of loose papers on the table and whirled them on to the floor. We heard the angry bang of the outer door and Oliver had gone.

That evening I wired to Will: "*Three of us will arrive to-night. Bobbie.*"

CHAPTER XIX

THE minute I heard Oliver explode out of that house of ours, and swing down the street—proud, angry, indignant, with that ridiculous little creature running on behind—I felt that he was headed straight to unhappiness and disaster. I understand Oliver pretty well, and knew that he saw, as plainly as any of us, all the crude rough corners of the little country girl, to whom he had been attracted, and married in some mad impulsive moment. After listening for half an hour to a lot of plagiarisms from Tom and Alec such as, "He must paddle his own canoe," "Experience is the best teacher," etc., I slipped out of the house and down to the station.

I told Will about it late that night.

"I found them sitting on a bench in the waiting-room. They weren't speaking. She had been crying. Oliver was glum and very silent. I think he was feeling awfully sorry that he had married her—I do really—and I don't know whether I felt sorrier for him or for her. So right then and there I decided to bring them home with me. We *must* do something, Will. We *must.* I finally wormed it out of Oliver that he was down to his very last one hundred dollars and not a single thing in sight. I know as well as you that Madge is a difficult proposition, but we've got to have her for a sister-in-law whether we like it or not. I know that our reputations are all tangled up in this thing, but a snarl will never get untangled unless somebody begins to pick it apart. Will, I'm so glad that you have got a mind that is concerned with the ailments of guinea-pigs rather than society and what people think. For you see, dear, I've told Oliver that he and Madge shall stay right here with us until something turns up for Oliver to do."

"But, Bobbie, my dear girl," said Will, "have you forgotten that for Commencement week we have invited Dr. Merrill, who is to receive an honorary degree, and his wife to be our guests?"

"No, Will dear, I haven't forgotten it, nor that I was giving my first really-truly little dinner next Wednesday; but I know that Oliver is my own brother and that I've simply got to stand by him and see him through."

Three days later I received a scathing letter from Edith:

"I suppose that you are posing as the Good Samaritan. We all think you acted very unwisely and not at all for Oliver's best good. You may be interested to know that the doctor says he wouldn't have allowed me to keep the girl here for one minute. I am still in bed, as it is, from the bad effects of the shock of the whole affair. I made Alec write something for the paper yesterday, denying the report that we were entertaining the couple here. On the contrary I have let it be known that I do not intend to recognise the new Mrs. Vars at all. It is the only safe policy. If you want to know *my* opinion, *I* think you are extremely foolish to have taken that girl into your house for one night even. You'll simply kill yourself socially. Remember you're a new member in the circle in which you are moving and will be known and judged by the friends and connections you have. It's a shame when you've just got started on the right path to ruin your chances, and Will's too. However, it's your affair. Do as you please."

"Oh, thanks," I said and stuffed the charming epistle into the kitchen stove.

My real difficulty however lay with Madge herself. The poor deluded girl had been brought up to believe that she was irresistibly charming. There hadn't been a prettier girl than she in Glennings Falls. She could boast of more "best young men," as she called them, than any girl I ever knew. Four young aspirants, before Oliver had appeared, had proposed to her, and she was only nineteen. Her father, a man of enough education to be a minister, had died of consumption, when Madge was a baby. Since then, she and her mother had managed to make a living by boarding some of the foremen and superintendents at the quarries. They had always had the distinction of entertaining the owner of the granite works whenever he came to Glennings Falls for a yearly inspection. It was he who had procured a position for Madge "to wait on table" summertimes at one of the big mountain hotels. There she had picked up a great many ideas on style and fashion, and copied them now in cheap exaggerated imitation.

The first evening after her trunk arrived at our house, she appeared decked out in a fearful display of lace and flashy finery, redolent with cologne, and manners that matched her clothes. She talked incessantly. Her lace and perfumery seemed to give her confidence. She discoursed volubly on New York, and aired her newly-acquired knowledge of hotel life in a way that was pitiable. Even Will, quiet and dignified, failed to impress Madge. All the scientific knowledge in the world could not awe the little village coquette into silence. She even dangled her ear-rings at solemn old Will and tried to flirt with him. It was not Madge who appeared ill-at-ease; it was the rest of us who squirmed in our boots, blushed at her mistakes, coughed, gulped down desperate swallows of water to cover our confusion. She was quite unconscious of the horrible burlesque she was playing. As the days went on, the more silent the rest of us became, the more she prattled. The more we failed to appreciate her loveliness and wit, the more toggery she pulled out of her trunk and exhibited for our benefit, the crimpier grew her hair, the higher, if possible, became her pompadour, the noisier her laughter. Once I humbly suggested that she leave off her ear-rings on a certain occasion when we were going shopping. She treated my interference with utter scorn, and appeared half an hour later ready to accompany me to the market, with two large pearls screwed securely into the lobe of each ear. "Every one wears them in New York," she announced.

I didn't know what to do with the child. For two weeks I rose every morning and went downstairs to a painful ordeal at breakfast; for two weeks

I saw Oliver flush and try to keep his eyes from meeting mine when Madge opened her mouth to speak; for two weeks I saw a threatening frown hover about Oliver's brow. I began to despair. Then suddenly, one evening, I found my poor brother in the gloomy living-room, brooding over an open fire. His head was in his hand, his elbow on his knee. I hadn't spoken to Oliver directly about Madge. I didn't now. I simply said very gently, "Want me to read aloud to you?"

"She wasn't like this at Glennings Falls," he burst out miserably, not stirring. "I want you to know it, because, well—I suppose you wonder why I ever was attracted to her. I wonder sometimes myself now—" He stopped a moment, then went on, talking straight into the fire. "I used to see a lot of her, you see. Every night and every morning. She used to pack my lunch and bring it up to me to the grove near the works every noon. I used to look forward to having her come—a lot. Glennings Falls is the deadliest hole you ever struck, and well—Madge was bright and full of fun. She isn't herself now. She wasn't like this. She was just as natural and simple. Upon my word," he broke off, "I've seen a lot of girls, one time and another, winners too, but somehow they none of them took such a hold on me as Madge. I thought she'd learn quickly enough, as soon as I got her down into civilisation, and so—anyway, I married her. Since—Well, it's no go, that's all. It's been bully of you to take her in, but I see clearly enough it can't work. Of course I mean to stick to her," he went on. "*Of course.* I suppose I've simply got to find a job out West somewhere, a long way off from everything and every one I know or—care about, and clear out. I mean to do the right thing." Then raising his eyes to mine he said with a queer, forced smile, "I guess *my* fun's all over, Bobbie."

"Oh, no, no, *no*, it isn't." I said fiercely. "Don't say that." I put my hand on his shoulder. "No, it isn't, Oliver," and suddenly, because I couldn't bear to see Oliver unhappy and despairing, because my voice was trembling and there were tears in my eyes, I went quickly out of the room and upstairs.

I was surprised on passing the guest-room to hear muffled sobs. I stopped and listened, and then, quite sure, I abruptly knocked and immediately opened the door. I was amazed to discover Madge face downward on the bed in tears.

"Why, what's the matter?" I exclaimed. I had never seen anything but arch glances in her eyes before.

"I want to go home! I want to go home! They're not ashamed of me at home!" she wailed.

I closed the door and went over to her.

"I just hate it here, I just hate it!" she went on. "Oliver thought I was good enough at home." She was crying all the time and each sentence came brokenly. "Oh, I wish I'd never *heard* of Oliver Vars," she choked. "I've tried and tried to be like his folks but he finds fault with every single thing I do, or wear, or say, or think, and I'm going home. I think his people are all stuck-up, horrid old things anyway and I just hate it, hate it, *hate it here*. Oh, go away, go away!" she cried out at me in a torrent of sobs.

Instead I sat down beside her.

"Look here, Madge," I said sternly. "Stop talking like that. Stop it. You can't go home. Don't you know you're married? Why, it's perfectly absurd!"

The sobbing stopped suddenly and she lay still with her nose buried in the down comforter. I went on talking to the cheap rhinestone comb in the back of her head.

"I've got something to say to you," I said, "and I want you to listen. I've been wanting to talk to you ever since you came to this house, and now I'm going to do it. You say Oliver finds fault with you, and let me tell you I don't blame him a bit. He certainly has reason to. Why, I never have run across a young lady who knew so little about things as you do. You don't know how to do anything properly. Your clothes are atrocious, and your manners—your self-assured manners here in my house are inexcusable. You're only a young girl of nineteen years who never has had any experience nor seen anything of the world. I don't blame you, understand. It isn't your *fault* that everything you do or say or wear makes us all blush with shame; but it does—it does, Madge. Why, I had to give up inviting some people here to dinner because I was afraid of the breaks and the horrible remarks you might make before my friends. Edith wouldn't have you in her house. That's the bald truth of it, my dear. You might as well know how we feel. It may sound cruel and hard, and I wouldn't say these things to Oliver's wife if she had come here modest, unpretentious, and anxious to learn; but she didn't, I should say she didn't! The worst ignorance in the world is that which parades itself up and down thinking itself very grand and elegant while all the lookers-on are laughing up their sleeves. That's what you've been doing, Madge." I stopped a moment to give the poor girl a chance to say something.

"Go away—go away—*go away*!" she burst out at me, turning her head enough to let the words out into the room. "Oh, go away!"

I stood up.

"No, Madge," I replied calmly. "I shan't go away, and neither shall you. You don't seem to know what's best for yourself, so I will tell you. You're going to stay right here with me, and work and study and learn. You are married to Oliver Vars and you're to make a success of it if it kills you; and it won't kill you. You're going to make him and the rest of us all proud of you before you get through and I am going to help you. Do you hear me? We're going to work it out together. You've got it in you. I know you have. I *see* you have," I lied. "You're a fine girl underneath. Don't you remember up there in Glennings Falls how you used to bring Oliver his lunch at noon? He has told me all about it—how nice you were, I mean—and how sure he was that you would learn as soon as you came down here. Well—you're going to begin to-night. Hereafter you'll do exactly as I say."

"Go away!" came again from the depths of the down comforter.

I ignored it entirely.

"Get up now and bathe your eyes," I said cheerfully. "Dinner will be ready in half an hour. I want you to wear the white muslin you had on this morning and no ear-rings. Remember," I added distinctly, going to the door, "remember, absolutely no ear-rings to-night, please."

But Oliver and Will and I had dinner alone that evening. "She won't come down," Oliver had announced gloomily. "She's in an awful state. She's crying. She wants to go home," he said, and my heart sank for I knew I had played my last card and lost.

That night Will had brought home the long-looked-for good news of a position for Oliver. We discussed it quietly at dinner—the three of us with Madge crying upstairs. A friend of Will's, a civil engineer, had said that if Oliver cared to go down into South America to some God-forsaken spot in the Argentine Republic—no place for a woman, by the way—there was an engineering job down there waiting for somebody. The job would take some five or six months; there might or might not be any future—Will's friend couldn't say.

"I'll go. I'll go right off," said Oliver. "Madge is unhappy and wants to go home anyway. I'm sure it's best. It was all a mistake," he admitted sadly to Will, "my taking her away from Glennings Falls. I might have known it wouldn't work." I stared hard at a saltcellar. Will began carving the steak silently. "You can go ahead now and have your people here for Commencement," observed Oliver; "Madge and I will both be gone in a week. I'm relieved it's settled," he added gravely.

It was during our dessert, after Delia had taken up a tray to Madge, that I was told that Mrs. Vars wanted me in her bedroom. I excused myself and slipped upstairs quietly. Madge was in bed; her hair was parted, braided neatly down her back; her tears were dried; her plain little nightgown buttoned at her throat. I had never seen her look so pretty. Her dinner stood beside her bed untouched.

"You wanted me?" I asked.

"Yes," she replied. "I'm not going home. I'll do anything you tell me," she said.

And she didn't go home. We packed Oliver off alone for South America, the next week, and as I rode back from the station in the open car with his slip of a wife beside me, on my hands for the next half year, I drew my first long free breath. Oliver, I recognised, had been more of a responsibility on my mind than Madge. My way was clear now. Lessons could begin any day, and no one will ever know what earnestness and determination went into the task that I had undertaken. From the beginning I took it absolutely for granted that since our stormy talk that evening in the guest-room our relations thereafter would be those of scholar and teacher; my authority would be unquestioned.

I overhauled the child's entire wardrobe with the freedom and cruelty of a customs officer. The cheap lace things I sent to the Salvation Army. The rhinestone comb I dropped into the stove before her very eyes. Ear-rings, jingling bracelets, glass beads, enameled brooches, I put in a box in the storeroom. A much-treasured parasol made out of cheap Hamburg embroidery I presented to Delia. Even Madge's toilet accessories were somehow done away with. Her elaborate hand-mirror with decorated porcelain back and hair-brush to match were replaced by a set of plain white celluloid that could be scrubbed with safety every week. The perfumery was poured down the bathroom sink. As soon as I was able, I purchased for Madge a few plain white shirt-waists with tailored collars, and a "three-fifty" stiff sailor hat made of black straw. When the crimp had all been soaked out of her hair, a wire pompadour supporter, three side-combs, eighteen hairpins, a net, a switch that didn't match, two puffs and a velvet bow had been extracted from her coiffure, I parted the little hair that remained and rolled it into a bun about as big as a doughnut in the back of her neck. She looked as shorn as a young sheep that has just been clipped. Her eyes fairly stared out of her head. I discovered that they were large and blue, with long lashes. Her features, unframed by the dreadful halo of hair, were flawless—small and finely cut. After I had gotten all the dreadful veneer off of the child she reminded me of a lovely old piece of mahogany discovered in some old attic or other, after the several coats of common crude paint have been scraped off and the natural grain finally appears perfect and unharmed.

She looked on at her metamorphosis, and at the cruel ravage of her treasures, passive and apparently indifferent. After her surrender to me she had no spirit left. She accepted my rule with a meekness I couldn't understand. After that night in the guest-room she became a different creature. She dropped her little airs and affectations as abruptly as if they were a garment that she could hang up and leave behind her in the closet. She became dumb at our table, and with Will actually shy and frightened. I thought her sudden change was due to ill-temper, and I bullied the poor beaten little creature terribly. I domineered, tyrannised, scorned and mocked. I didn't dare be tender, for I was convinced that success lay only in complete submission. Poor little "alone" thing—I did feel sorry for her at times! Her eyes were often red from crying. She didn't eat very much and her cheeks grew pale before my sight. She used to sit sometimes for an hour at a time without saying a word, until I longed to put comforting arms about her. When she accompanied me to the market several weeks after Oliver had gone away—quiet, silent, subdued, Glennings Falls would never in the world have recognised their gay sparkling little village coquette who had had a word, a nod, and a smile ready for every one who passed.

Oliver had been gone about six weeks when Madge told me her astounding news. I didn't know what to say to her for a moment. I was awfully surprised. She seemed such a baby, and I suppose it always comes with a jolt when you first realise your younger brother is actually a man. I was amazed too that such an apparently weak little thing as Madge had so pluckily kept her big secret to herself for so many weeks. She had known of it before Oliver had gone away, but she hadn't liked to tell him, she confessed. He had left her without as much as a premonition of the truth, and it was because of what was waiting for her in the future that she had been frightened into staying with me. She hadn't known what else to do. I stared at her open-eyed. It was when I saw her under lip tremble like a little child's and two tears fall splash upon her wrist, that I put out my hand and drew her down beside me on the couch. She leaned against me and began to cry in earnest then.

"Oh, don't, don't cry, Madge," I pleaded quietly. "Please! I'm just as glad as I can be, dear," I said. "Everything will be all right. Don't be afraid." But still she sobbed. "Listen; I've been wanting to tell you for days how well you're doing—even Will remarks on it. Please, please don't cry, Madge. Why, I hadn't an idea of *this*. I didn't dream of it. But we'll see you safely through. Oh, Madge, don't cry so hard. Listen, my dear girl, you can go home to-morrow if you want to."

Suddenly she turned and buried her head on my shoulder. Her hand sought mine and held it tight. She clung to me as if she needed me very much.

"I don't want to go home. I'd rather stay right here with you," she sobbed.

My arms went around her. Remember I have never had many friendships with girls. Staunch, true, loyal Juliet would nurse me through the smallpox if necessary, but she doesn't like to be kissed. Years ago when we stayed all night at each other's houses we slept on the extreme opposite edges of the bed and if one of my elbows as much as grazed Juliet's shoulder-blade, I was vigorously poked in the ribs and told to get over to my side. My younger sister Ruth had not sought one of my hands since she was able to walk alone. She would rather cry into a pillow than on my shoulder. If there had ever been any doubt about my loving this little helpless creature, who turned to me now in her hour of fear and dread, it was entirely dispelled during that half-hour on the couch in our living-room.

It was after that day that our best work began. I continued stern and severe with Madge, but there was unmistakable affection underneath. I resorted to every device in the world for my little protegée's education. I laugh as I look back to some of the drills and tests I put her through. Fridays, for instance, were our shopping days in Boston. Department stores are regular educational institutions. It wasn't a month before Madge was able to detect machine embroidery from hand-work; imitation Irish crochet from real; coarse linen from fine. We spent hours at "window-gazing." In that old, popular childhood game of "Choosing," Madge became quite an adept. I used to make her pick out the suit, or the hat, or the piece of dress-goods in a window display which was the most conservative, and verify her choice by my selection. Conservatism I preached to her from morning till night, and she got so she could recognise it a block away. Homeward-bound from those Friday shopping days, I would indicate an individual opposite to us in the car, and that evening a vivisection of her toilet would take place in our library. I have often felt sorry for the poor mortals whose oversupply of imitation fillet, high-heeled ill-kept pumps, or spotted veil we so severely criticised; for the young girls—gay, unconscious creatures—who laughed too freely, talked too loudly for our fastidious requirements.

Madge's table-manners had been shocking. She mashed her food with the prongs of her fork and poured gravy over her bread; she ate enough butter for three men. We used to have written examinations on table-manners. After she had progressed so that she could eat a poached egg without daubing the entire plate, and a half-orange with a spoon without sprinkling the front of her waist with drops of yellow juice, I advanced her to my place at the table. For a month she sat opposite Will and played at hostess. She offered the bread; she inquired if any one would have more of the dessert; she learned to address Delia with consideration. I left it to my pupil to suggest that we adjourn to the living-room at the close of our meals. I made her pour the coffee into our tiny best china cups.

The effect of all this training upon myself was as miraculous as upon Madge. You don't know what confidence in a subject it gives you to teach it. I honestly believe Madge did Will and me about as much good as we did her. Our meal-times became regular little models of perfection—quiet voices, good conversation, and manners fit for a queen. I began to dress every evening for the ceremony, as an example for Madge, and it was then that Will who entered into the game beautifully began changing every night into a dinner coat. The fussy little frills—candlelight and coffee served in the living-room, which I had spurned after leaving Edith—I returned to for Madge's sake. For her (for I discovered that my pupil considered me as a model of all that is proper and correct) I dressed myself with greatest care—spotless white kid-gloves, carefully adjusted veil, neat and well-kept boots—and sallied forth to pay some calls. As an example to Madge I invariably inquired what time Will would return in the evening and made a point of arriving at the house at least a half-hour before him, so that he might find me calm, quiet and freshly attired, like a lady leisurely awaiting her lord, in an apartment as neat and well-kept as the library of his Club. I didn't allow myself to slump awkwardly into a comfortable chair in his presence, nor yawn and stretch my arms. I even tucked away the horrid, red worsted bedroom slippers and from my supply of unused negligees drew forth a blue china-silk kimono. There was a pink one like it which I gave to Madge. Her eyes sparkled as they fell upon it. "Save it till Oliver comes," I said, and I, who had scoffed in my heart at Ruth's and Edith's conversation which took place in that same guest-room of mine eight months before, repeated their very words, as if they had left them printed on the walls. "You mustn't be the kind to grow careless before your husband. A man likes a woman to be dainty whether he is married to her or not. A man likes to be proud of his wife," I repeated parrot-like. Oh, you see, there was more than one conversion taking place that spring in the ugly brown house in the unfashionable street, and the greater of these was not, in my estimation, that of the little country girl from Glennings Falls, Vermont.

CHAPTER XX

WILL and I used to run up to Hilton for over Sunday very often. But when Edith found out that Oliver had gone to South America and Madge had remained with us, she wrote to me immediately and warned me never to attempt "to cram the girl down her throat." She had no idea of *ever* recognising Oliver's wife as any connection of *hers*. If Will and I came up to Hilton she must ask us to leave our preposterous protegée behind.

I didn't see that it would hurt Edith any to be formally courteous to Madge. She needn't have become intimate. I didn't expect Madge to be invited everywhere I went. I didn't take her anywhere with me in my social life at the university. But I did think that Edith was neglecting her duty as a woman to ignore Alec's own brother's wife, whoever she was. It was almost inevitable to avoid the growth of a feeling of hostility between Edith and me; but I did want to escape an open break. I didn't want to quarrel about Madge, so whenever I saw Edith I tried to overlook the existence of any bone of contention between us. I made a point of running up to Hilton very often for the day, and tried to refer to Madge in a natural, open, frank sort of manner that made little of the seriousness of the situation. I didn't go to Hilton to court trouble, I assure you. I made my fortnightly trips for the express purpose of promoting family peace and harmony.

The arrival of Edith's baby was only about a month off when I went up to carry her a little afghan I had crocheted. I found her unpacking some baby scales and the most elaborate weighing basket I ever saw. It was all beruffled and trimmed with artificial rosebuds around the edge. It was when I stood off and admired it that I remarked with a sigh, and in the most offhand way in the world, that I guessed Madge's baby would have to be weighed on the kitchen scales if at all. I meant it as a kind of tribute to Edith's basket. Besides I thought it a good idea to refer to Madge's expectations. It seemed more friendly to the family to take them into my confidence in such a matter.

You would have thought a bomb had gone off in the room.

"That creature going to have a baby!" Edith exclaimed.

"Yes," I said. "Just think of it! Oliver with a little son or daughter!"

Edith turned suddenly upon me.

"Oh, I see!" she flashed. "I see! A son indeed! So that's the story! I suppose the girl has her eyes on that three thousand, without doubt. Designing little minx!"

"Why, your baby comes first, Edith," I replied. "Of course if you shouldn't get the prize, I think Madge could make pretty good use of three thousand dollars. She probably needs it more than you."

"Oh! So you hope I won't have a boy! That's it. Very well. We'll see. You hope—"

"Why, Edith," I interrupted, "I don't hope anything of the sort. I—"

"We'll see if this girl of Oliver's has any right to that money," Edith went on excitedly. "We'll see about that. When is her precious baby expected? Too soon for decency's sake, I suppose—horrid, common little—"

I flushed. "Edith Vars," I fired, "don't you imply anything like that about Madge. Don't you *dare*!"

I was angry now and Edith knew it. She seemed to glory in it, for she prodded me again with another false accusation against Madge, and before I could stop it we were quarrelling dreadfully. I don't remember all we said to each other that morning in Edith's room, but I know our words came thick and fast; I know our voices shook with our fury, and that we glared at each other across the expanse of the snowy bed with actual hatred in our eyes. It all ended by Edith's suddenly flinging herself face down upon the pillows, and bursting into awful sobs. Not until then did I realise that my sister-in-law was not well, nor quite herself these days—I had never seen her cry before in my life—and frightened I went out of the room to call for help.

That noon Alec sent for a doctor, and half an hour later it was announced that Edith had a temperature. A trained nurse appeared at four o'clock and Alec called me into the library.

He was dreadfully concerned about the consequences of my news in regard to Madge; I shouldn't have mentioned it, it seems; it might be the cause of the most dreadful results—he couldn't tell. Edith was very excitable just now. I ought to have known better. He blamed me wholly. I had been careless, inconsiderate and cruel. I had better leave for home as soon as possible. The thought of me in the house annoyed and disturbed Edith even now; she had inquired three times if I had gone. Alec had ordered the automobile; I could catch the five-thirty if I hurried. He wished I hadn't come to see Edith at all; she had been so well; everything had appeared very favourable before my arrival; Alec couldn't understand my attitude toward Edith anyway; she had done everything for Ruth and me (had I forgotten my wedding?) and I paid her back with gratitude like this!

I didn't reply to my brother. Alec and I had travelled too many miles in opposite directions to understand each other now. A bitter antagonism arose in my heart against Edith. I should have quarrelled with Alec too had I opened my mouth to speak. I went out and got into the automobile without a retort, and as I whisked out of the driveway and looked back at Edith's curtained windows, a wicked wish was born in my heart. I said to myself, "I hope it *will* be a girl. 'Twould serve her exactly right."

It was, however, a pretty discouraged ambassador of peace who crawled back to her little brown refuge that night about eight o'clock. Will was sitting by the fire reading a big book, his hair all ruffled up as it always is when he reads. Madge had gone upstairs to bed. The comfortable lamp-light, the dear, homely black walnut furniture, Will's quiet sympathy, never seemed more precious to me than that night.

"O Will," I said tearfully when he kissed me, "I've quarrelled with Edith and Alec. And, oh, dear, it was the last thing in the world I meant to do."

"Tell me about it," he said and laid aside his big book. I took its place on the arm of his chair, and told him my story. After he had rung up Edith's doctor by telephone and found that there wasn't cause for alarm, he came back to me and called me "young wildcat" which sweet words were music to my ears. I knew at the sound of them that Will didn't consider the quarrel serious. "It will all blow over in a week. You see!" he laughed, and I went to sleep comforted.

But it didn't blow over. That fateful visit of mine marked the beginning of an understood family war. Clouds of trouble grew thicker instead of blowing away. The very next evening I received a brief note from Alec asking that I postpone any more visits to Hilton until after Edith's illness. Ruth wrote she couldn't understand me in the least; she thought it was dreadful that Madge was going to have a child anyway, but if she got Father's three thousand dollars it would be the unjustest thing that ever happened! Tom—even fair-minded Tom from out West—told me to remember that Oliver's marriage had been rather out-of-order, and asked me if I was championing a cause I could call worthy. When Ruth ran across me one day in town a fortnight later she treated me like a bare acquaintance. Alec went so far as to cancel a Saturday golf engagement with Will. Long distance telephone calls between our houses came to an abrupt end. Malcolm from New York bluntly referred to the "family row."

I didn't tell Madge about the trouble brewing in our family. I never even imparted to her the knowledge of the premium to be paid for the first Vars grandson. Silently I sat with her sewing by the hour on her meagre little outfit of five nainsook slips, three flannel Gertrudes, two bands, two shirts, and three flannellette night-gowns, with never a word of my eager thoughts. I became very loyal to the cause I had chosen to defend. It didn't trouble me that our little baby-clothes were so much plainer than Edith's, for night and day, day and night, I was hoping against hope, wishing against chance, willing and frantically demanding that Madge's splendour might lie in her victory.

You can imagine the ecstatic state of excitement I was thrown into when the news of the arrival of Edith's nine-pound daughter reached me some six weeks after my last visit to Hilton.

I must have felt a good deal like the supporters of a weaker foot-ball team when their side makes the first touchdown. I could have thrown up my hat with joy; I could have shouted myself hoarse. Madge had an opportunity! Madge had a chance! It seemed too good to be true, and I longed to share with Madge the triumph so nearly hers. But Will was afraid she might worry and fret about it,—there was, of course, the possibility of disappointment,—so I followed his advice and kept on building my air-castles in secret.

It was on November twenty-first that Madge's little child was born. We had written to Oliver in June and he had started on his homeward journey as soon as Madge's belated letter reached him, some time in August. He had tramped a hundred miles down a tropical river, had lain sick for five weeks with a fever in a native camp, had dragged himself in a weakened condition twenty miles farther on to the coast, and finally had caught a slow-travelling freight-boat bound for Spain. Blown out of its course, becalmed, disabled by a terrific storm, Oliver never saw the coast of Europe until well into November. His mite of a child was two weeks old before he reached home.

Oliver had done well down there in South America. Reports of his ability had reached the Boston office months before Oliver himself appeared. It seems that Oliver's chief had written a long letter telling all about the ingenuity which young Vars had shown in working out some technical problem connected with a suspension bridge down there. I told you Oliver's line was civil engineering. The Boston office informed Will they had offered Vars a good position right here at home with a salary that he could live on. I was delighted, and as soon as we learned that he had started for God's country, I began to hunt up apartments.

I wanted Oliver to see for himself and *by* himself what a perfect little housekeeper—what a lovely little creature, simple as she was, he had chanced to pick out up there in the mountains of Vermont. I honestly began to fear Oliver wouldn't appreciate half of the delicate points that Madge had developed. I wished I could give my brother a course of training too. He is the kind to be rather impolite inside the walls of his own domain. I selected for Madge and Oliver a suburb where the rents were not high, about half an hour by trolley from Boston. I planned to have Madge well established in her own five sunny little rooms before the arrival of either her husband or child. From my safe-full of silver and attic-full of Will's furniture, which I couldn't use, I could easily have set up two brides at housekeeping. I sent over a whole load of things from our house to Madge's and we spent days afterward settling the darling little rooms. On November twenty-first I went over to the apartment alone. Madge had complained of not feeling very well and I didn't want her to get all tired out before she actually moved the following week. The kitchen utensils were waiting to be washed and set in rows on the cupboard shelves, so I started out straight after breakfast and spent the whole day "playing house" there alone. I didn't get back until after seven o'clock at night. Will must have been watching for me, for he met me at the door. The instant I entered the house I knew something unexpected had happened. There was a white pillow on the couch in the living-room. I smelled ether.

"Will," I said all weak in my knees, "where's Madge? What's happened?"

He closed the living-room door and turned up the gas.

"She's all right, dear. We didn't send for you, because there was nothing you could do. I was here all the time."

"You mean—" I began. "Will," I said, and then my mind leaped over a league of details to one question, and after I had asked it Will took my hands and replied gently:

"No, dear, a sweet little girl."

I couldn't answer at first. I crumpled down in a heap in Will's big chair.

"It was the only thing I ever really, really wanted," I said brokenly. "Oh, Will, I can't believe fate would be so unkind! Tell me again—did you say a girl—really a *girl?*"

"Yes, dear, a fine, perfect, lovely little girl."

I stared straight in front of me.

"Isn't it too bad, too bad, too bad," I said. "Oh, Will!" I broke out, and began to cry.

Will came over and put his arms around me.

"Why, Bobbie dear," he said sadly, "I should think the little kiddie was yours."

I couldn't have been more disappointed if it had been. All the victorious telegrams, all the confident, buoyant notes to the different members of the family were more than useless now. The poor little mite of humanity wrapped up in a piece of flannel upstairs in the sewing-room in the clothes-basket, which Madge and I had lined with muslin, had shattered all my plans—had frustrated its poor little mother's only chance for glory.

It was all I could do to muster up a smile for poor, broken, beaten Madge herself, when the nurse ushered me into her bedroom the next day. I was glad when I saw her smiling up at me from the pillows that I had not confided my eager hopes to her.

"Oh, Lucy," she said to me, "it's a girl! I knew you hoped it would be a little girl, because you were so happy when Edith's baby came. And I—"

"Are you glad?" I asked tremblingly, feeling like a hypocrite before an angel.

"I—oh, I *prayed* for a girl. I wouldn't know what to do with a boy. My dolls were always girls."

It wasn't until I ran across Edith, most unexpectedly, several days later in town, that I woke up to the fact that that little girl of Madge's was a blessing in disguise. Edith's daughter was then about three months old and she was flitting about again as gay as ever, feathered and furred, stepping like a horse who has just had a good rub-down. I had seen her several times in the last month. She does all her shopping in Boston and I am often there myself. Of course we had spoken, even chatted on impersonal subjects as we chanced to meet here and there. On this particular day we happened to find ourselves in the drapery department of a large department store both waiting for the elevator to take us to the street.

"Oh, how do you do?" she said to me loftily. "Gorgeous day, isn't it?"

"Fine," I replied.

And then she asked evasively, her curiosity getting the better of her. "How's everything at your establishment?"

"Oh, all right. I have a note already written to you. There's a new member in our family, you know."

I saw the colour rush to Edith's face.

"No!" she exclaimed. "Really?" Then arming herself against a dreaded blow she gasped, "Which is it?"

"A girl," I hated to announce; "born Thursday."

"A girl! Did you say a girl?" Edith's voice broke into a nervous laugh. "Lucy Vars, has Oliver's wife a little girl? Is she dreadfully disappointed? How is she? When was it? How much does it weigh? A girl! Well, well, is it *possible?*" Her eyes were fairly glowing now.

I followed her into the elevator.

"You mean it? You aren't fooling? This isn't a joke?" she exclaimed as we dropped a floor.

"No," I assured her.

"Poor thing! Poor thing!" she ejaculated with sparkling eyes. "A girl. A girl!" She found my hand and gave it an eager little squeeze. "Won't Oliver be just too cute with a daughter?" she bubbled.

By the time we reached the ground floor, she had slipped her arm through mine.

"You've got to come and have lunch with me, Bobbie Vars," she said. "Let's let bygones be bygones. I hate fights. I'm tired to death putting myself out to be disagreeable. Heavens! I can hardly wait to tell Alec. A little girl!" She led me out into the street. "I'm starved," she ran on. "We'll blow ourselves to the best luncheon in this town. I want to know *all* the details—every one. Do you know I felt in my bones she would have a daughter, and I simply never make a mistake; and by the way, way down in my boots, *I* wanted a girl myself. I *said* I preferred a boy, but that was talk. You can dress girls up in such darling clothes. That's what I'm telling people anyhow," she confided frankly. "Remember, should any one ask."

In spite of the many things about Edith I do not like, she has some splendid qualities. "Look here," she ejaculated abruptly, "I believe I'll send that poor little creature of Oliver's some flowers. I don't suppose she has many. Come on in here, Bobbie, and help me pick out something stunning!"

Next Wednesday Ruth 'phoned from town. Friday she came out for dinner, and not very long afterward, the expressman left a lovely embroidered baby's coat and cap "for the dear little daughter," it said on Edith's visiting-card in her bold unmistakable handwriting.

It was Oliver himself, who had been at home about two days, who opened the package. He and I were alone in the living-room. He flushed when his eyes fell upon the card.

"So Edith—" he began.

"Yes," I assured him; "and the roses on Madge's bureau are from Edith too."

He flung the card down on the table and came over and stood before me.

"Look here, Bobbie," he said. "I must have been completely run down or something, before I went away. I don't know what ailed me. Everything bothered me horribly and to think I took it out so on poor little Madge. Why, Madge—Say, Bobbie, isn't Madge—" He stopped. "Pshaw!" he went on, "I've known a lot of girls in my day but not one to come up to Madge. Did I ever tell you how she can cook? Like a streak! You ought to see her arrange flowers in the middle of the table. Looks as if they were growing! Madge is worth twenty society girls. Could Ruth run a vegetable garden, do you think? Could her boarding-school friends go into the village store and run the accounts when the regular girl's off on a vacation? Madge can! I knew she would learn city ways and manners quickly enough once she was here.

I *knew* it. And say—isn't she pretty? Isn't she simply—lovely with the kid? Humph—" he broke off, picking up Edith's card and tossing it down again. "I knew the family couldn't help but like Madge once they knew her, and I'm mighty glad!"

"So am I, Oliver. She's got the loveliest, sweetest disposition! Sometimes I've been afraid that *you* would be the one not to appreciate it. She's thinking a lot how to make you happy, Oliver. Her head is full of schemes and little devices to please and satisfy you; and I've been wondering if you've been thinking up little ways to please her. Sometimes married people take it for granted that schemes and methods and contrivances for happiness are superfluous, if they love each other; but *I* believe that new love needs just about as much care and tending as that little helpless baby in there. I hope you think so too, Oliver."

"I don't know as I'd thought much about it. I'm not much of a philosopher on such subjects. Things come to me in flashes, and they stick too. I remember the last time I ever had a real good old time with the college crowd was at Ruth's party, two or three years ago. I drank more than was good for me that night and when I came to go upstairs about four A. M., right there on the landing waiting for me was Father. Somebody had left his picture lighted up, you know, and it was absolutely gruesome how he stared down at me out of his frame—like a ghost or something. I never forgot it. I tried to get the fellows to put out the light, but they couldn't find the switch. It was horrible to struggle up in front of Father in my condition—I can't explain it; but from that day to this I've never been able to enjoy that sort of a time since. I've never taken more than I should since that night, and I never shall again. I'm sure of myself now."

"Isn't it splendid to live on in the way Father does?" I remarked quietly.

"Well," went on Oliver, "the first sight of Madge in there with the baby was like that lighted picture of Father. Do you know what I mean? It flashed over me, 'Heavens, I've got to amount to something now *anyhow*,' and those flashes stick, as I said. I *shall* amount to something. See if I don't!" He stopped a moment, embarrassed. "I don't know as you understand at all about that picture of Father, and Madge in bed in there, as if they had any connection. They haven't, only—"

"I do understand, Oliver," I said; "I do perfectly. And I'm so glad and happy and proud! I always felt you had it in you!"

About a week later Edith called me up from Boston.

"Hello," she said. "You, Bobbie? It's Edith. Ruth and I are in town. We've just had lunch. I've got to go to the tailor's at two, but we thought later we might come out and see the baby." ("It's Edith," I whispered excitedly to Will with my hand over the receiver.) "Will it be all right?"

"Surely," I called back. "Come right ahead."

"Is Madge able to see people yet?" ("She wants to see Madge," I told Will.)

"Oh, yes! She comes downstairs every afternoon now. We'll expect you—good-bye."

I hung up the receiver, and went into the butler's pantry to prepare my tea-tray. Ten minutes later I casually remarked to Madge:

"Oh, by the way, Edith and Ruth are coming out this afternoon. I think I shall ask you to pour tea, Madge."

"All right," she replied quietly, like a little stoic. "I understand. I'll do my very best, Lucy."

I felt something of the same tremulous pride of a mother listening to her daughter deliver a valedictory at a high school graduation, as I watched Madge at the tea-table that afternoon. Her parted hair, simply knotted behind, pale cheeks tinged with a little colour, her frail hands among the tea-cups, her shy timid manner, were all lovely to behold. Oliver, from the piano-stool, glowed with pride; Edith and Ruth, from the couch, could not fail to appreciate the careful, calm, and correct collection of napkin, plate, tea-cup and spoon. Edith has a great faculty for observation. I knew she was sizing up Madge out of the corner of her eye, even as she rattled on to me on the wonders of the little niece in Hilton whom I had never seen.

She and Ruth stayed until just time to connect with the six-thirty train for Hilton. It was closeted in my room that Edith said to me in her erratic way, "My dear, I never saw such a change in any living *mortal*. Do you realise that having that baby has simply made that girl over? It's wonderful—put refinement into her. Why, really, one wouldn't guess the child's origin *now*.

Listen to me. I've decided to invite the whole family bunch, as usual, for Christmas (one may as well be forgiving in this short life, I've concluded); so I came to have a look at Madge. She isn't half bad, you know. I had a nice little chat alone with her when you were showing Ruth the baby. She says she was simply crazy for a girl, and I think she means it. She isn't as impossible as I feared—not half. All she needs are some clothes and I've gotten it into my head to take her to my own dressmaker in town. One may as well be generous, Lucy. Besides, if the girl comes to the house at Christmas she must dress decently. I've a good mind to take the little thing in hand myself and polish her up a little. She's pretty enough. You see," Edith broke off, "Breck Sewall will probably be around Christmas-time—won't it be wonderful if he should marry Ruth?—and I simply had to have a look at Madge before inviting her. However, I really think she'll do."

The instant the door had closed on Edith I rushed back to Madge. I threw my arms about her.

"You've passed your preliminaries, dear child!" I said and kissed her hard.

CHAPTER XXI

DID you ever attempt to buy a lot of fifteen thousand feet at fifty cents a foot, and build a house on it of twelve rooms, three baths, a shower, a sleeping-porch and a small unpretentious garage for fourteen thousand dollars? This isn't an example in mental arithmetic, but it was a problem Will and I laboured over every March and April for three successive springs, before deciding each year to stay on for another twelve months in our old rented brown box, gas-lighted and tin-tubbed. I am not going to explain how such a problem can be solved, because frankly I don't know.

Will is a regular miracle-performer in some lines. He'll work for hours over some knotty proposition in his laboratory, and come home from the hospital simply glowing with enthusiasm over the successful onslaught of a squad of his well-trained microbes upon an unruly lot of beasts who were making life miserable for a poor man almost dying with carbuncles. The medical journals describe Dr. William Ford Maynard's accomplishments as miraculous. However, I can vouch that he is utterly unable to perform any feats with wood and plaster and plumbers' supplies. Two hours working over our house-plans used to exhaust Will more than four days solid in his laboratory. He said there was more hope in discovering the haunts of the wary meningitis microbe than in finding a contractor who would build us a house at our price.

Will and I adored our first little home, of course, but then there were disadvantages. Every time it rained I had to put a basin in the middle of my bed—in case the roof leaked—and the fireplaces did smoke when you first lit them, and the kitchen stove did need a new lining. The owner was awfully disagreeable about repairs, and after we had been vainly pleading for three months solid for a new brick or two in a disabled chimney, which threatened to burn down the house, we began to consider moving. We didn't intend to build. We thought it would cost too much. We didn't even intend to buy. We simply wanted to find something better to rent.

Rummaging about among second-hand houses is very depressing, I can tell you. Some of the same old arks that had been on the market when we were first married, were still without a master, like certain wrecks of servants who haunt intelligence-offices. Dilapidated run-down old things—I hate the very thought of them! They have a musty, dead-rat sort of odour that's far from welcoming when you enter their darkened halls. You always wonder if it's the plumbing and ask why the last people left. And oh, the closets in those houses—little, black horrid holes! I used to pull open their doors, and time and again find some sort of human paraphernalia left behind on one of the hooks—a man's battered straw hat, or once, I remember, a solitary pair of discarded corsets. Spattered places in the bedrooms, paths worn on the hardwood floors, ink spots, grease spots, and on the walls an accurate pattern of the arrangement of the last family's pictures, actually offended me. I've heard that robins will never take possession of a last year's birds' nest. I know exactly how they feel about them. Oh, it isn't inspiring to hunt for a home among other people's cast-offs. Will and I were awfully discouraged after we had inspected the fifteenth impossibility—a dreadful affair with high ceilings, elaborately stencilled, and in the corners of each room little arched plaster grooves designed for statuary. For six months Will and I searched in vain for the sweet, clean little ready-made cottage of our dreams, shining in a fresh coat of white paint, its perennial garden in full-bloom, waiting for two nice home-loving people like ourselves to open its gate, stroll up its flag-stoned walk, and claim it for our own.

On our way home from impossibility the fifteenth, we took a street that had just been cut through some new land where little brand new houses were springing up like mushrooms. There was one, a tiny plaster house trimmed with light green blinds with half-moons cut in them, that I thought was simply adorable. It wasn't completed; I could see the workmen through the open windows. The temporary pine door stood open.

"Let's go in, for fun," I suggested, and Will helped me up the inclined plank that led to the little front stoop.

We stayed for a whole hour in that house! It was like gazing on sweet sixteen; it was simply refreshing; we didn't know anything so lovely existed. There was a darling little bathroom with open plumbing, and a shining porcelain tub. There was a marble slab for mixing in the pantry. The bedrooms were painted white. The closets, tiny though they were, smelled of fresh plaster. Will got into conversation with the contractor while I amused myself by planning which room I would choose for ours. But the house wasn't for rent. A man who ran a fish-market was building it. I saw Will get out an old letter and begin figuring on the back of the envelope. That place, lot and all, wasn't going to cost that fish man but ten thousand dollars—Will told me that night that we could own a house that cost fourteen thousand and still save money on our rent. I was excited. We didn't look at another house to hire. We dropped them as if they were infected. The very next Saturday afternoon we set out to search for lots.

We weren't very particular at first. Any little square of ground that we looked at with the idea of possible ownership seemed perfectly lovely to me; anything with a tiny glimpse of horizon, and a place in the back for a garden, was like a little piece of heaven. We were both awfully easily pleased the first month. There were so many pretty places to build on, we simply didn't know which one to choose. Then one day the agent sent us up to look at some land that had just been put on the market at sixty cents a foot. Of course it was more than we could pay, and we went to inspect it simply out of idle curiosity. The result was that the next day among that whole townful of open spaces and green fields, there was only one solitary spot that Will and I wanted for our own. You see after we had once climbed up on to that expensive little hilltop and looked off and seen the view—a round bowl of a lake with a clump of pines beside it, and beyond, a hill with a long ribbon of road leading up to a real New England white farmhouse with a splash of red barn beside it, we couldn't think kindly of any other spot in town. After we had sat down on the stone wall that ran right square through the back of the lot, and watched a glorious sunset reflected in the lake below, Will said, "By Jove, we'll have this!" There were six old apple-trees on the lot, a wild cherry and a dear little waif of a pine-tree. Will and I made a solemn vow to each other that we would build a cheap house, and get along a while longer with one maid for the sake of that lovely sunset every night when we ate supper. I said I'd as soon live in a lean-to. Will said we'd live just where we were for another year until we could afford to put up even a lean-to. We bought the darling of our hearts seven days later. It used up over two-thirds of our fourteen-thousand-dollar house fund.

We ate picnic suppers on our stone wall, and winter-times drank hot coffee there boiled over a tiny bon-fire built in the rocks, for three solid years before we began to dig the cellar of our lean-to. I had hollyhocks and a whole row of Canterbury-bells flowering in our garden for two springs before there was a door and some steps to lead out to it. It's all very well to vow you'll build a cheap house, but it's another thing to do it. Of course we had to have plumbing and heat; electric light fixtures seemed a necessity too, as well as a few doors here and there.

Will and I literally laboured over those plans. They had to undergo a dreadful series of operations. Every spring when it seemed to us as if we couldn't endure another summer cooped up in our noisy, stone-paved, double-electric-car-tracked street, I'd haul down the architect's blue-prints and stretch them out on a card-table. We amputated so much from those plans I wondered they held together. Of course the shower-baths and the garage, oak floors, and a superfluous bathroom came off as easily as fingers; but when we began cutting out partitions here and there, a treasured fireplace or two, two closets, and even the back stairs, I tell you it was ticklish! Even when we'd shaved off two feet from the length of the living-room, four from the dining-room, and squeezed our hall so that it was only nine feet wide, even then we couldn't find a generous-hearted builder who would even try to be reasonable in his charges.

Our house wasn't, by the way, anything like the fish man's. It wasn't a plaster house with light green blinds, with half-moons cut in them. It seemed to our architect (and to me too, as soon as he suggested it) that the most New England type of house possible—flat-faced, clapboarded, painted white, a hall in the centre and a room on each side, would fit in with those apple-trees better than anything quaint or original. Oh, ours was just the housiest house possible, with nothing odd about it like oriel windows, or diamond trellises, or unexpected bays and swells.

The first day the plans arrived I did some measuring, and cut out of cardboard on the same scale as the plans, patterns of our furniture. That night Will and I moved into our paper house, shoving the furniture around the rooms with lightning speed, shifting hall-clocks, davenports, and grand pianos from parlour to bedroom with surprising little effort. Why, I rearranged my rooms time and time again before I ever stepped foot in them. If you'll believe me, I made a complete new bedroom set for the nursery, and a little crib which I placed between the windows, when the real room was only a square block of air above the apple-trees.

You can imagine how excited we were when at the end of three years we finally signed the contract with McManus & Mann, Contractors and Builders. We were simply house-crazy by that time. I wanted to celebrate the important occasion somehow, so I went down to Mr. McManus's office and ordered several bundles of six-foot-length laths, such as are used in plastering a room, to be sent up to our lot on Saturday morning. Will and I always spend Saturday afternoons together, and, provided with the roll of plans, a yard-stick, a hatchet and my lunch-basket packed with tea and sandwiches, we started out about two P. M. to lay out our house, life size, with the laths on the very spot where it was so soon now to stand. By five o'clock I was serving tea before the fireplace in the living-room, and apple-blossom petals were blowing through the kitchen and hall partitions into the very cream-pitcher by my side.

It was just when the water over my alcohol stove had begun to boil that our first guests arrived. Dr. Van Breeze is married now, and his wife, Alice, and

I are very good friends. For the three years that Will and I had been working on house-plans she had followed the changes in them as if they were hers. So I 'phoned her that I should be delighted if she and George (George is Dr. Van Breeze) would take tea with us Saturday afternoon at four-thirty in our new house. When they appeared in their touring-car at the foot of our hill, I saw that dear Dr. Graham and Mrs. Graham were in the back seat, and I dashed through the living-room wall and down to the road to meet them. Ten minutes later the Omsteds arrived strolling up the hill from their house which is the nearest one to ours. Will had already arranged boulders for chairs around the fireplace, and my dainty little sandwiches and tiny cream puffs were laid out neatly on plates covered with fresh napkins. The tea was hot and strong and fragrant; the decorations of six trees full of apple-blossoms, lovely to behold; the illumination of a pink and blue sunset, reflected in the lake below, more beautiful than a hundred electric lights.

After we had drank tea and eaten the last cream puff, I invited my guests to inspect the house. Every one entered into my little game. Dr. Omsted made us all respect the partitions as if they existed; George Van Breeze insisted on walking up the front stairs; and dear Dr. Graham found a grasshopper somewhere and exclaimed chuckling, "Oh, my dear Pandora" (he still calls me that silly name), "what of your housekeeping? I saw dozens of these in your pantry!"

Oh, it was just the nicest house-warming in the world. I like every one of Will's friends; they may be awfully learned, but they seem just plain natural and unpretentious to me. They stayed until nearly six o'clock. We waved them good-bye from our front door. When they all had disappeared over the brow of the hill, Will drew me into our hall and kissed me, just as if there had really been walls. Then he came into the living-room and helped me clear up.

I haven't mentioned yet the thorn I keep hidden in my heart and carry everywhere I go. I don't like to talk of it because Will doesn't like to have me, but it robs every joy I have of completeness. As Will and I strolled home that night perhaps we ought to have been very happy. We had the best and pleasantest friends in the world—I granted it; ground for our dream-house was to be broken on Monday morning; we had been married four years, and loved each other more than ever.

"Oh, Will, four years—four long years," I exclaimed, and sighed.

"Pshaw," he replied, and changed the subject.

Ever since Madge's little baby was born, I've wanted one of my own. I didn't care before that, but when I held the warm little thing in my arms for minutes at a time, dressed it, cared for it when the nurse was out, and listened to its poor pitiful little cry in the middle of the night, something seemed to spring open in me that I can't close.

I want a little daughter-companion of my very own! I want to wash her, and dress her and take her out with me. I want her to sit with me rainy afternoons in her little rocking-chair and play while I sew. I want her to tell me all her secrets, and I want to give her all the love, all the good times and pretty things a little girl wants. When Madge brings over her Marjorie, and I see her clinging to her mother's knee when I come into the room, I'd give anything in the world to have some little girl cling to *me* like that! Will has always loved children; he has wanted them even longer than I, though he never told me. Will affects indifference on the subject, but he doesn't deceive me in the least. I know the lurking hunger is always in his heart as it is in mine.

Why I was so especially down-hearted to-night as we walked home from our tea-party on the hilltop was on account of a remark of Alice Van Breeze's thrown off in her quick, careless fashion. I think Will kissed me in the hall to soothe a little of the hurt of Alice's unconscious words. People who have babies of their own don't guess how many times they stab those who haven't.

"What an ideal place this is for children!" Alice had exclaimed. "Such air! Such sunshine! If you don't mind, Lucy," she had caught herself up, "I shall bring Junior up here often to get some tan in your adorable garden."

"Do," I had said, looking away.

"How is the little chap?" Will had asked her kindly. Will can't even talk about a child without a little note of tenderness in his tone.

"Oh, he's perfect!" Alice had laughed. "The very world revolves about him. Why, we're prouder of that little bundle of bones and flesh than of his father's latest book!"

I didn't look at Will and Will didn't look at me. We're so filled with pity for each other at such moments (and there are many of them) that we can't bear to gaze upon the hurt look in the other's face.

Our whole sad little story can be traced in our house-plans. When we first decided to build, we talked bravely *then* about the nursery on the sunny side; it looked out towards the south and east; it was large and airy, with four big windows, and a fireplace for chilly nights. When the first sketches arrived the room was plainly labelled in printed letters, and I remember that the mere word gave me a queer thrill of joy. I had, as you know, immediately made patterns of the nursery furniture, placed the paper crib in position, and estimated the number of steps from my bed to the baby's. I had had it beautifully planned for contagious diseases: Will could move into the guest-room, and I and the sick children could be absolutely isolated from the rest of the house, in two lovely rooms with a bathroom of our own. But I needn't have planned on children's contagious diseases. There will never be any little children with measles, or chicken-pox, or whooping-cough in our house, to take care of. I am sure of it now. On the last roll of plans which our architect submitted to us the word printed across the face of the southeast room had been changed from Nursery to Chamber! I think Will must have requested it and I knew then with awful finality that even Will had given up hope. I never asked how or why the room's name had been changed. I simply understood without asking and cried it out by myself in my room. The next day I burned the nursery paper furniture—the crib, the folding yard, the toy-case like Edith's—in the kitchen stove, with a pang as big as if they had been real.

After that I called the southeast chamber, "Ruth's room." I had always secretly hoped that Ruth would live with me if ever I had a house of my own. I had hoped it ever since Alec had married Edith. It hadn't come to pass—it never would. Ruth is so fastidious. But she has spent a night with me very often so I decided to make over the room that no little child seemed to want to occupy, for my only sister. It really was easier to refer to the room as Ruth's. I was glad, after the first shock, that Will had made the change. The evident question and pity in people's eyes when we had called it by its old name had become unpleasant for both Will and me.

I grew very philosophical about my disappointment as time went on. I didn't mean to allow it to shadow my whole life. There was lots else to be thankful for. But that night after our little tea-party my philosophy seemed to leave me. It always does when I'm a little tired and need it most. I couldn't keep up any kind of conversation at dinner that night. I tried, but I couldn't. My thoughts got to travelling the wellworn path that they will stray away to every once in a while in spite of me, and it's always Will who comes to my rescue and pulls them back on to safe sure ground, before they lose themselves in utter dejection.

"Let's play some cribbage!" he suggested lightly after dinner.

I laid down my useless embroidery and listlessly drew up to the table. We played three games without an interruption. I won them all. Then just as Will was dealing for a fourth game I had to get out my handkerchief and wipe my eyes.

"Oh, my dear girl!" said Will accusingly.

"I know it, but I can't help it!" I replied. "It seems *too* cruel! I simply can't bear not to use the room we built the house around. I wish we could find a little child somewhere that we could—borrow. You see, Will, a woman, to be really happy, seems to require a family to take care of, unless she's a genius—an artist or a poet, or something like that, which I'm not. Why, Will," I broke out, "I'm getting so I don't like to hear about other people's children—or see them or want them around. When Alice spoke about bringing her baby into my garden it seemed as if I'd simply have to find *somewhere* a little creature of our own to play with the flowers I've planted. Don't I *know* it's a perfect place for children? Don't I know it? And does she think we also wouldn't be prouder of a little child than of your discoveries? Oh, Will, I know how disappointed you are. You won't say it but I know it's awfully hard for you too."

"Nonsense," Will scoffed. "What's hard about it? I've got you, haven't I? You and I are the two best children at playing games in a garden that *I* ever saw. *I'm* perfectly satisfied. Come ahead, cut the cards. I'm about to beat you now at five games of crib."

I shook my head and looked away.

"You're mistaken," Will went on, "if you think *I'm* envying anybody anything. I've yet to meet two people happier than we. Children are pleasant enough incidents in life," Will went on, "but don't you draw any wrong conclusions that happiness is dependent on them. It isn't. Look at Dr. and Mrs. Graham. They never had any, and two more congenial, more contented, happier people never existed—except perhaps ourselves. Dr. Graham has too much sound thought to allow the denial of any *one* of the supposed blessings of life to disturb his peace. And so have we, Bobbie, don't you think? Some of the very best people in the world, some of those who have accomplished the most effective work, never had children. It isn't the first question we ask about a great man or a good woman. I might have reason to complain if I didn't have my health or a good sound mind, or if after these few precious years together, I lost *you*. But as it is—well, please don't ever say again, young lady, that our present conditions are hard for me. Hard—Nonsense!"

Dear Will! I'd heard this same little speech of his dozens of times before. When he tries so hard to cheer me it seems too bad not to respond; so I smiled now.

"Will Maynard," I said, "you don't deceive me for one minute by all this talk! Don't think you do! *I* know—*I* understand. But I'll say this—and I've said it a hundred times before—you certainly *are* the kindest man I ever knew."

"Bosh!" he laughed.

"Yes, you are—yes, you are. And I guess if I've got you I'd better not complain." I put away my handkerchief. "It's all over now," I announced, "and I'm ready to beat you at those five games of crib."

He dealt the cards and for five minutes we played in earnest; then suddenly Will reached across and took my hand.

"Who says you and I aren't perfectly happy?" he asked.

CHAPTER XXII

IT wasn't a week after that Sunday afternoon of ours on our darling hilltop that I received a letter from Ruth announcing her intention of paying me a visit. I was amazed.

Ruth usually prefers to visit at houses where she can stay in bed until ten o'clock in the morning and sink luxuriously into an upholstered limousine fitted up with plum-coloured cushions and a bunch of fresh flowers, every time she goes out of doors. She isn't the type who likes making her own bed and helping with the dishes—not that I require such toll from a guest; but you know our house has only one bathroom and Ruth says a tin tub always looks greasy. She says that black walnut furniture has a depressing effect on her, and assures me that she doesn't dare turn over in my guest-room bed for fear the head of the thing—a big towering mass of black walnut blocks and turrets—will fall down on top of her in the night. Ruth suffered the hardships of my establishment only when it was necessary. Whenever a taxicab did draw up to my door and deposit my dressy sister for the night, I knew that it was because she had an early appointment with her tailor the next morning, or had missed the last Hilton Express. I didn't remember that Ruth had ever spent a single night under my roof for the mere friendliness or sisterly love of sleeping between my embroidered sheets. Ruth has a very sensitive temperament—so sensitive that certain combinations of colour will affect her spirits. My guest-room has mustard-coloured walls with reddish fleur-de-lis.

Ruth is an extraordinary girl. She doesn't seem a bit like a Vars. We're such a conventional and just-what-you-would-expect kind of family. Ruth contrives somehow to shroud herself in a veil of mystery and create an impression everywhere she goes. I guess she's the most discussed girl in all Hilton. She affects heliotrope shades in her clothes, combining several tones in one gown, and wears large, round, floppy hats. She always manages to select big stagy chairs to sit in, that set her off as if she were a portrait. I have to pinch myself every once in a while to make sure she isn't a foreign adventuress of some kind with an exciting past, instead of just my common ordinary little sister Ruthie. She has the queerest ideas on life and love that I ever heard talked outside of a book, and she preaches them too. I don't know how she dares; but somehow a little wickedness, a little cynicism, from so very pretty a girl seems simply to add to her piquancy and charm. Ruth dabbles in every artistic line that exists—sings with the finish of a prima-donna and loves to improvise by the hour on the big drawing-room piano at home, while some love-lorn suitor sits in silence in the half-dark and worships. She's clever at drawing—has designed book-plates for all her friends, besides having modelled in bas-relief several of their portraits in clay. She writes poetry too. She never read any of it to *me*; I suppose I'm not sympathetic enough for it; but I got hold of some of her papers once and spent a whole hour with them. I never knew till then what deep ideas Ruth really has! I copied several of the verses and Bob Jennings, who is an instructor in English at the university down here, said they were "full of promise."

When Ruth's letter arrived announcing her proposed visit, my only sorrow lay in the fact that her room in the new house wasn't ready. I was going to have it papered in lavender chambray and had already selected a wisteria design in cretonne for the hangings. It was going to be the most artistic room in the house. I wasn't going to hang a single picture on the walls (no pictures is Ruth's latest fad) and the furniture was going to be plain colonial mahogany. It's queer how all the family pay homage to Ruth. She's younger than I, by three years, but I've always longed for her approval. I used to criticise her extravagance, and tell her she was vain and selfish, but down in the bottom of my heart I've always thought Ruth was wonderful. Will makes fun of me for laying out my best linen every time Ruth comes to see us. It *is* foolish, but I don't want Ruth to think that I don't possess any of the fine points of the people she most admires. I began to plan to make her first real visit with me as much of a success as I knew how. Ruth likes to have parties planned ahead for her, so I decided to invite the Van Breezes to dinner one night, and Bob Jennings another.

Bob is a perfectly splendid young man and awfully good-looking. I was sorry that Ruth had to meet him for the first time in the unkind surroundings of our house. Setting, background, atmosphere, influence her so much. If she sees a man for the first time in company with black walnut and marble-topped tables, she is apt to think him as offensively old-fashioned as the furniture. And I did want to prove to Ruth that there existed a decent man with several degrees to his name, who knew how to dress properly for dinner and converse intelligently on the latest opera.

Will and I both met Ruth at the station when she arrived. She kissed me and gave both her hands to Will in her most engaging manner. She presented him later with three trunk checks. I was flattered. I was glad that there happened to be several teas on hand, and a musicale at the Omsted's that week. I would show Ruth that all our friends didn't live in ugly brown French-roofed houses, and that she hadn't brought all her pretty gowns to my house in vain.

But here I was disappointed. After dinner Ruth announced, "Oh, no; I couldn't. Don't make any engagements for me, please. My time won't be my own while I'm here. I didn't mention in my letter that Breck Sewall is coming up from New York to-morrow. He has invited me to several things in town. I thought it would be simpler for me to spend my nights here, than to go back so many times to Hilton."

I didn't say a word, but my heart skipped a beat, I think. I had thought the affair with Breck Sewall had blown over. The Sewalls haven't occupied their summer place near Hilton for three years. It hadn't occurred to me that Ruth's visit could have any possible connection with Breck Sewall. Ruth knew that Will and I disapprove of him; she knew the sound of his very name was unwelcome in our house. I felt like telling Ruth to go upstairs, lock up her precious trunks, and go home. Once I would have spat out something nasty to my sister about accepting attentions from a man she knew was not nice, but now I was too anxious to become her friend to quarrel with her on the first night she arrived. I had learned that the safest course for me to follow was simply not to oppose Ruth in anything.

It was Will, turning from fastening the windows, who blurted out bluntly, "Are you still keeping up your connections with that man?"

Ruth smiled, raising her eyebrows a little, and then folded her hands behind her head, her pretty arms bare to the elbows.

"Don't you approve of him, brother William?" she inquired archly as if she didn't care a straw whether he did or not.

"Do *you?*" asked Will.

Ruth laughed an amused, silvery laugh and replied lightly, "I am engaged to be married to Breck Sewall, I suppose, if that answers you."

Will didn't say a word for a minute. Then, "I am sorry to hear that," he replied shortly.

"Really?" smiled Ruth. "Breck and I shall certainly miss your blessing, William." She always calls him William when she's making fun of him. I don't see how she dares to mock a man so much wiser and older than she, but Ruth would deride the President of the United States if he interfered with her little schemes.

Will replied; "You're too fine a girl to make such a mistake, Ruth."

She rippled into another laugh and my cheeks grew warm with indignation. She leaned forward and selected a chocolate-cream from a box of candy on the table.

"That's a very prettily veiled compliment, William, and I thank you," she said. She nibbled a bit of her candy as she spoke.

She was awfully exasperating, sitting there so gay and unconcerned. Will stepped up to her chair and I could tell from his voice that he was angry.

"I know all about Breck Sewall," he said. "He's not the kind of man for any nice girl to associate with. He spent a year at this university. He was expelled, not only because he could not keep up in his courses, not only because he was brought home time and time again too disgustingly drunk to stand alone, not only because of these things, but because of another and more disreputable affair. I think you ought to know about it before this goes any further. It was an affair with a girl. There was no doubt about it. He acknowledged the whole thing. Why, Ruth, he isn't the kind of man for you even to speak to!" Will said. "Sometime I will tell you the whole story—sometime—if it's necessary."

Ruth took another bite of her chocolate-cream.

"Do *now*," she smiled, "if it amuses you. But it will be no news to *me*. I know all about that college affair of Breck's. He has told me the whole story himself. I know the girl's name and all the particulars. Breck isn't afraid to tell me the truth. Nothing in the world shocks me, you know," she announced with bravado. "Did you think I was so narrow-minded and hemmed in by prejudice not to overlook the follies a man may have committed when he was hardly more than a boy? I don't care what Breck did before he knew me. What other awful news have you to break to me, William?" Ruth inquired sweetly.

Will stared at Ruth as if she were something he never knew existed.

"Nothing else," he said shortly, "if that isn't sufficient."

There was an uncomfortable silence. My sister must have felt a little uneasy under the gaze of Will's astonished eyes; for when she had finished her candy, daintily touched her lips with her bit of a white handkerchief, tucked it away, and spoke again, her manner towards him had changed.

"Will," she said, "I'm so different from any one you ever knew that you can't understand me, can you? Now I know you told me just now about that little unfortunate affair of Breck's because you want me to be happy. And I do appreciate your interest in me—I do really. Of course I have no mother," she put in quite tragically; "I never had. Perhaps that is why I am so different from other girls. I'm not shocked at the things young girls are brought up to be shocked at. I don't tremble at the sound of unadulterated truth and bare facts. I am aware of it. I am not living under the false illusion that the man I am to marry is perfect. I know he isn't, and I am content. Why, the very qualities I require in a man preclude at least a few of the supposed virtues. Perhaps, Will," said Ruth patronisingly, "you do not understand a man of Breck's tempestuous nature. *You're* so scientific. It's easy for you to stay within the narrow path. But you shouldn't be severe on others."

"Do you love Breck Sewall?" asked Will point-blank.

"Oh, *love*!" Ruth shrugged her shoulders. "Love would be the last thing I would marry a man for. I'm not as short-sighted as that. Love may last a year, or two perhaps, but it is not enduring. I marry for sounder reasons than love. You must know that the Sewalls are immensely wealthy. Their position is as established as royalty in England. Oh, you see," laughed Ruth, standing up and walking over toward the bookcase, "how dreadfully worldly and wicked I am! Have you La Rochefoucauld? Let me read you a little saying of his."

"No, not dreadfully worldly—not dreadfully wicked, Ruth," said Will; "only dreadfully young, I think."

Ruth hates to be accused of youth.

"But old enough to marry whom I please, William, perhaps," she flashed.

"Oh," scoffed Will, "that doesn't require much age, nor much wisdom. You are young enough to think it rather clever and smart to scorn virtue, make fun of love, and pretend to marry a man for his wealth and position. It sounds so bookish and so sophisticated!"

Ruth would not have deigned to respond to such an insulting assault as that if I had made it, but to Will she replied, "You're mistaken there. I've thought and read on this subject. I'm not so young as you think." She walked over to the mantel and leaned her back against the white marble, then folding her arms across her chest, like a judging goddess, she continued: "I believe, and several people of reputation agree with me, that the most important thing to consult in considering marriage is one's temperament. Ask yourself what your tastes are and then see if the new life will gratify them. Temperament never changes. If you love music when you are twenty, you will love it when you are forty. Well, I have studied my nature very closely. I know what pleases it. I know what annoys and disturbs it. I'm different from the others in our family. I often wonder from whom I inherit my peculiarities. I love beautiful music, beautiful pictures, soft rugs, fine furniture, delicate lace at the windows. Low, artistic lamp-light, the comings and goings of soft-footed unobtrusive servants, a dinner perfectly served, exquisite china, old silver, exclusive people—all such things give me actual physical pleasure. I enjoy position and influence. My nature grows and expands under recognition. It dries up and dies under slight and disregard. The people I envy most in the world are those who are born in high positions. I can't alter my birth, but I have been invited to become a member of a prominent and influential family, and as one of that family I shall be invited and received everywhere, without any of the humiliating striving. I'm proud, you know. I despise toadying. I don't want to work for social position. I want it placed upon me, like a king his crown. Why, Will, Breck Sewall can supply my nature with everything it demands. Why shouldn't I marry him?"

"Can Breck supply your intellect with what it demands?" asked Will.

Ruth laughed good-naturedly.

"Poor Breck! Poor old maligned Breck! He isn't exactly intellectual, I agree, but don't you worry, Will, I shall find congenial minds enough in his circle. The Sewalls entertain all sorts of interesting professional people—the top-notchers, I mean. My intellect won't suffer. Where is the woman, anyhow, who discusses her soul with her husband? How can a woman read poetry with a man who has just been grumbling at the price of her prettiest gown?" Ruth shuddered. "No, no! Please! I prefer not. But I shan't be lonely. Never fear." She gave Will a meaning look from beneath her eyebrows and added in a sort of bold, daring way, "There will be some one."

I don't know why Ruth loves to preach such wickedness. She doesn't mean half she says. I waited for the walls to fall. Will abhors married women who attempt to flirt with other men. Ruth waited too for the clap of thunder she thought must follow her startling implication. But when Will spoke there wasn't a trace of anger in his voice—just disgust—just plain unflattering disgust. "Come, Lucy," he said to me; "I've had about enough of this. Let's go upstairs to bed."

The Sewalls are the high-muck-a-mucks of the Hilton summer colony. They're New York people and their place, just outside Hilton, reminds me of the castles that give distinction to so many otherwise nondescript little towns in Europe—not in age, for I can remember when the Sewalls' place was rough cow-pasture land, but in its relation to the town and the surrounding country. It's Hilton's show-place. We always point it out to strangers when we take them on their first drive. The wrought-iron gates cost five thousand dollars; the distance around the house and adjoining buildings added together measures half a mile; the big entrance hall, we state (and we're proud of our knowledge too) is hung with old tapestries and furnished in carved English oak.

After Mrs. F. Rockridge Sewall's advent, there was established among the Hilton summer colonists a new law of society. You were either of the elect or of the rejected; you were either entertained by Mrs. F. Rockridge Sewall or you were an ignominious nobody. There existed no self-respecting middle position in Hilton after Mrs. Sewall arrived in mid-July with her retinue of some twenty-odd servants, her four or five automobiles, and half-dozen hunters. Mrs. Sewall was for some time a very disturbing factor in Edith's life. The lights of a ballroom, the sound of dance-music, however lovely they may be, are absolutely irritating to my sister-in-law, if seen and heard from the outside. It took two long discouraging seasons of scheming, manipulating, and rather bold attacking, before Edith gained the proper kind of entrance to the hallowed ground inside those five-thousand-dollar wrought-iron gates. It was really due to Ruth that she was admitted then. Young Breckenridge Sewall had chanced to see a stunning young creature in lavender and grey at a garden-party at Mrs. Leonard Jackson's, one afternoon late in August, during his mother's second season at Grassmere, the name of their place in Hilton. He had only to see Ruth once to beg for an introduction. That is the way it is with every man across whose field of vision my sister steps. I think that Ruth is the loveliest production that Hilton, or Hilton's environs, ever produced; and Breckenridge Sewall thought so too. Three weeks after that introduction at Mrs. Leonard Jackson's Ruth rushed in upon Edith one Friday noon and announced, "I'm invited to a house-party at the Sewalls'! One of the out-of-town guests has disappointed Mrs. Sewall at the last moment and Breck wants me to fill in!" Before the Sewalls went back to New York that fall, Ruth was the most distinguished young lady in all Hilton. She was pointed out everywhere she went as the girl to whom Breck Sewall was paying such marked attention; she burst into notoriety; and Edith's position was at last made secure. Trust Edith to squeeze into the limelight along with Ruth. I don't know how my sister-in-law manages such things but it was clear sailing for her after Breck's discovery.

That man rushed Ruth for two years and a half before there was any word from my sister about an engagement. During the summer he used to call on Ruth about six evenings a week, and as Edith made us all go upstairs (this was before I was married) on the nights that Breck came, by nine o'clock, it got to be a nuisance. At first I remember we were all a little flattered by the young millionaire's attention to our pretty Ruth and even I used to feel a thrill of pride at the thought of such a brilliant match in our quiet midst.

Breck didn't propose to Ruth till after I was married. She came in from a long motor run one Sunday in July, when Will and I happened to be in Hilton, and told us the news before she even took off her hat. I remember it very well for there followed one of our dreadful family discussions. By that time Will and I, and Alec too, had begun to feel a little doubt as to Breck's desirability. We had always heard rumours about his habits, but Edith prized Breck's attentions to Ruth so highly, that Alec had neglected a thorough investigation. He thought that Breck didn't intend to marry Ruth anyway, called it a summer affair and trusted that time would cure them both of their fancy. So when Will came out with a few telling facts detrimental to Breck Sewall's character, Edith was simply furious. She told me that I shouldn't come back meddling after I was married. Ruth loved Breck Sewall—she was sure of it; we might be the cause of wrecking the child's happiness for life if we interfered. Alec looked awfully distressed as we talked but he didn't rise up in indignation, stampede as he should have, and swear that no sister of his should ever marry a man with Breck Sewall's reputation, so long as he lived. Alec is awfully ineffectual when Edith is around.

I don't know how it all would have come out, if Mrs. Sewall hadn't interrupted matters. Suddenly, right in the midst of the thickest of our discussion, three or four days after Ruth's announcement, Mrs. Sewall decided to go abroad. She closed up her summer mansion, mid-season though it was, barred the windows, locked the gates, and sailed away to Europe, Breck and all. She didn't come back for two years, and even then she didn't come back to Hilton. The excitement about Breck and Ruth died down like fire, and about as suddenly. He didn't even write to Ruth after three or four months, and just before Ruth came down to visit me and announced her startling piece of news, I had read that Breckenridge Sewall was reported engaged to his cousin, Miss Gale somebody or other, a débutante of last season.

Ruth's news was an awful shock to me. I knew without being told how jubilant Edith would be, how helpless Alec in the face of what seemed to both the women of his household such a brilliant victory. I didn't know what to do. It didn't seem as if I could stand by and watch my own sister marry the kind of man Will said that Breck Sewall was. I lay awake a long while that night after Ruth's arrival at our house, wondering what under heaven I, whose ideas on life my sister considered so provincial—what there was that *I* might do to swerve her from her purpose.

I could hope for no help from Will. Ruth had thrown him utterly out of sympathy with her. He washed his hands of the whole affair; he told me so that night when we came upstairs to bed, and I knew by his manner to my sister the next morning at breakfast, courteous enough though it was, in what contempt he held her. I told Will I couldn't send Ruth back to Hilton, and, as distasteful as I knew Breck Sewall's coming to our door would be to him, I hoped he would let me keep Ruth with me as long as she would stay. I didn't have any plan, any deep-laid scheme. It simply seemed to me that it must have been an act of heaven that Ruth had been sent to me during such a critical period in her history, and I didn't want to fly in the face of Providence.

I began by being just as nice and kind to her as I knew how. I didn't offer one word of opposition; I didn't advise; I didn't criticise; I appeared even to welcome her suitor when he first arrived to carry my sister in town to dinner and the theatre; I chatted with him pleasantly while she put on her party coat upstairs. I served Ruth breakfasts in bed at eleven A. M.; and admired and praised all her gowns and lovely fol-de-rols as she dressed every afternoon in preparation for her lover.

For five days Ruth blandly carried on her love-affair in our house, going and coming at her own sweet time, accepting our hospitality as a matter of course, while she bestowed her rarest smiles upon a man whom she knew Will considered disreputable and whom therefore I could not approve of. For five days she lunched, motored, and dined with Breck Sewall, and in between times talked with him over the 'phone for twenty-minute periods. I despaired. I didn't see any way out, and as the days went on and the house became more and more perfumed by Breck Sewall's roses and violets and valley-lilies, I began to give up hope.

On the sixth day I received a letter from Edith:

> "Ruth would go down to you. I told her that neither you nor Will liked Breck Sewall and it wouldn't be a bit pleasant. Alec and I are both very much pleased about the engagement, because Ruth really loves Breck Sewall with all her heart, and since his renewed attentions, the dear girl has been simply radiant. I write this because I'm afraid that you'll try to poison Ruth's mind against the man she loves. We all want her to be happy, I'm sure, and I think you would assume a lot of responsibility in trying to stop a girl from marrying the only man she ever has cared for or ever will. She likes to boast that she doesn't love Breck. It's pose. I, who have been with Ruth so intimately for so long, know she is *wild* about Breck Sewall, and loves him madly. Don't

meddle with it, Bobbie. I'd hate to be to blame for *my* sister's broken heart."

That letter of Edith's set me to thinking. It hadn't occurred to me that Ruth was simply *pretending* to marry for position. I didn't think that such a repulsive creature as Breck Sewall could inspire anything so divine as love in my sister's heart. And yet, perhaps—how did I know (I understand Ruth so little anyway)—how did I know—perhaps Edith was right. Perhaps, after all, Ruth was simply trying to conceal her love by contempt and scorn of it. It wouldn't have made any difference as to my opposition, but it would have cleared Ruth of unworthy motives, at any rate. I was determined to find out.

She had told me when she left the house at three that afternoon that she and Breck were going to motor to somebody's place on the north shore and would not be back until late in the evening. It was eleven-thirty when I finally heard Breck Sewall fumbling with the lock and a minute later I caught the odour of his cigarette, as I lay waiting for it in bed. I knew then that he and Ruth were established in the living-room for their usual half-hour alone before he bade her good-night. I don't suppose it was a very honourable thing to do, but after about five minutes I got up, put on a wrapper, and crawled quietly down to the landing, stepping over the third step which creaks awfully. It was pitch dark in the corner near the wall; there was no danger of being seen from below; and I stood perfectly still, eavesdropping for all I was worth. Ruth had lit one dim burner by the piano and from my balcony I could plainly see Breck Sewall, low as the light was, ensconced in a corner of our davenport-sofa.

CHAPTER XXIII

HE was making himself entirely at home. He had crossed his feet and had placed them square in the middle of the mahogany seat of my nice little Windsor chair, which he had drawn up in front of him. His toes pointed to the ceiling; his cigarette pointed there too; for he had comfortably pillowed his greasy old head (Breck's hair is jet black and always looks as if it was wet) on the top of the low back of the sofa. The smoke that he blew at times from his nose went straight up like smoke from a chimney on a windless day. I didn't think it was a very pretty attitude for a man to assume in the presence of a young lady. His hands were stuffed in his trousers pockets, and when he spoke the only trouble he went to was to roll his head in Ruth's direction. He's anything but good-looking. He has half-closed eyes like a Chinaman's, and a yellow, unpleasant complexion.

"Come on over here," I heard him say in that kind of guttural voice a man uses when he tries to talk with a cigarette in his mouth, and I saw him shift up one shoulder to motion Ruth to sit down beside him.

I couldn't see my sister but I heard her reply. "I don't feel like it to-night, Breck," she said.

Breck smoked in silence for half a minute, then he asked, removing his cigarette, "Say, what's the matter with you to-night? Are you back again on that old subject which your precious saint of a professor here raised up out of the past? Haven't I explained that to you a dozen times?"

"I wish you wouldn't refer to members of my family in such a way," replied Ruth. "It isn't respectful to me. You're not marrying beneath you, as your manner sometimes seems to imply. My brother-in-law whom you choose to call a saint is a noted man, if you only read enough to know it, Breck. Oh, no, I'm not thinking about that college affair of yours. I'm not a jealous kind of girl. You know that."

"Well, what is it then? It gets *me* what I've done to deserve such treatment. Weren't they the right kind of flowers?"

"Don't be absurd, Breck. As if ornaments or flowers were what I required! I'll tell you what's the matter, if you want to know," said Ruth. "It's simply this: I don't think you're treating your engagement with proper respect. It seems out-of-order to me that I should have told my family about our intentions before you have told yours. It isn't a bit as it should be. I hate even to speak about so delicate a thing—but, Breck, why hasn't your mother written to me? Why hasn't she set a day for me to come and see her? Here *my* family are all recognising *you* as a future member of their group, while your family haven't even as much as made a sign."

"Oh, now, now," replied Breck soothingly. "That's it, is it? Don't you worry, little one. The mater will come around, all right. Give her time. For my part, though, I'd rather step into the Little Church Around the Corner and get it over with in a swoop."

If Ruth was sitting down, I'll wager she stood up now. Her reply came like lightning.

"Breck Sewall," she exclaimed, "that's the third time in a week that you've suggested eloping to me! I wish you'd stop it. It is absolutely insulting!"

Breck looked up surprised.

"Insulting?" he repeated dazed.

"Exactly. Insulting," went on Ruth in hot haste. "I'm not a servant-girl. I require all the proprieties that exist, understand. Why," she added, "until your mother recognises me publicly as your fiancée, I'll never marry you as long as I live!" She stopped suddenly. I knew she was very angry, for Ruth.

Breck chuckled in a horrid insulting sort of way, and lay down his cigarette.

"Say," he broke out, putting his feet down on the floor, leaning forward with his elbows on his knees and rubbing his two hands together, "say, you're simply stunning when you're mad." He was looking at Ruth as if he'd like to gobble her up. "You're glorious! You're great! Most of 'em cry and make sights of themselves, but you—you—" He got up. He strode over to Ruth. I suppose she was simply too stunning, too glorious, too great to resist. I don't know. The portière hid her and I was glad of it. I shouldn't enjoy seeing Breck Sewall as much as lay a finger on my sister. I closed my eyes and waited. I should have been afraid of a man like that, myself, but I suppose Ruth suffered herself to be kissed by him with the indifference that she offers her cheek for the same caress to a girl. When she spoke again her anger seemed to have spent itself.

"You're very silly, Breck," she said.

"And you—you're as cold as a little fish," he replied as tenderly as he knew how. I really think he loved Ruth, though I was convinced that she didn't have an emotion of any kind for him. "But I'll wake you up, you little marble statue," he went on. "I'll make you care for me. Women are all alike. See if I don't."

"It's more important," I heard Ruth reply, "to make your mother care for me. You see, Breck, if we hope to get married in October you had better tell her your news as soon as possible. Why not to-night when you go back to the hotel? She has been here now three days with you and if she wants me to call I can go to-morrow, or the next day, before I go home. You say she came on so as to make arrangements to open Grassmere this year. Certainly the engagement must be announced immediately, so that I shall be received by your mother properly this summer."

"You seem to care more about my mother than about me," objected Ruth's lover.

Ruth laughed prettily.

"Poor abused creature!" she mocked. "Poor sulky boy! If I showed my feelings for you, Breck, all the time, you wouldn't care for me half so much. I understand men. You call me a little fish and that's what I am—always slipping out of your fingers, always evading capture, for I know that once a man gets his fish and puts it in his little basket, the cat can eat it then for all he cares."

"You're a clever little piece," said Breck admiringly. "Half the time I don't know what you're driving at."

Just here I saw Ruth walk over to the table and pick up Breck's gold cigarette box. I don't remember that I have ever been so shocked in my life as when, staring like a cat out of my dark corner, I saw my sister—my own little sister Ruth, over whose bed hung the pure, clean-cut profile of my mother, in whose heart must dwell the memory of the best, the noblest, the finest father a girl ever had—select a cigarette, light it, and actually place it between her lovely lips! I wanted to call out, "Ruth Chenery Vars, what are you doing? Have you lost your mind? Are you crazy?" I saw her sit down on the corner of the sofa that Breck had left empty and lean her head back in much the same luxurious fashion. I saw her blow a fine little ribbon of smoke up to the ceiling. I waited until I saw Breck cross the room to her side, and then, too sick to endure the awful spectacle another instant, I turned and groped my way upstairs to bed.

I couldn't sleep for hours and hours. I turned over at intervals of four to eight minutes, until it began to grow light. I may have dropped off into semi-consciousness. I don't know. Anyhow my dreams were one continuous nightmare of my waking vision. Had it been Ruth whom I had seen with my own eyes smoking a cigarette in my living-room? Had it been my own little sister? Had she done it before? Did she do it often? If I had been anxious to save Ruth from Breck before my horrible discovery, now I was determined. She shouldn't share such a life as his. She shouldn't! She shouldn't! I waited impatiently for the morning light. I was eager to be about my undertaking. I had a disagreeable task before me, and haunted by the dread of it, very much as we are visited by the fear of an operation that must be undergone, I wanted to get it over with and out of the way as soon as possible.

After Will had left for the university and I, as usual, had carried the breakfast-tray to Ruth (lying as sweet and fresh as a carnation in her white sheets—you would never have dreamed she had ever tasted a cigarette) I went upstairs to my room, put on my best eighty-five-dollar Boston tailor-made suit, and grimly set out for town.

It was ten-thirty when I sent up my name to Mrs. F. Rockridge Sewall at the Hotel St. Mary, where I knew Breck had been stopping since his arrival in town. The clerk behind the yellow onyx counter that enclosed the office of this exclusive hotel, had informed me that Mrs. Sewall had just breakfasted and therefore could assure me that she was in. He asked for my card and summoned a bell-boy. I withdrew to the rose-brocade writing-room at the left, and five minutes later into the envelope in which I placed my card I slipped a note that read something like this:

> "*My dear Mrs. Sewall,*
>
> "It occurs to me that you may not remember who I am from my card, or if so, be quite at a loss to know what prompts this call. I have come to consult with you on a matter that concerns your son, and would be greatly obliged if you will see me.
>
> "LUCY MAYNARD."

I must confess my heart acted like a trip-hammer, as I waited for my answer. I experienced a moment of misgiving and apprehension, as I gazed at the pattern of the rose brocade on the walls. I had not confided to Will my intention of a consultation with Mrs. Sewall, and just for a moment as I sat there on the edge of a formal little gilt-trimmed chair, I wondered if my intuitions were leading me into a dreadful social blunder.

"She will see you; suite thirty-three. The boy will show you up," suddenly broke in on my reflections, and in another moment I was silently shooting up the elevator shaft, gazing at a row of brass buttons on the bell-boy's coat and estimating their number, to keep myself calm.

The room into which I was conducted was empty when I entered it—a typical hotel-suite drawing-room, furnished with elaborate and very puffy looking stuffed furniture. I chose the only straight chair in the room, and sat down and waited again. I had met Mrs. Sewall only once in my life, quite formally at a party of some sort at Edith's. We may have exchanged a half dozen words, not more. I had never been invited to her grand house, and most of my knowledge of the lady had come through hearsay, and the social columns in the papers. It was necessary to keep my mind pretty closely fastened on the cigarette spectacle, or else I might have lost courage, and quietly withdrawn before Mrs. Sewall appeared. She kept me waiting in torture for at least fifteen minutes (I can tell you the subject of every one of the engravings on the wall, I am sure) but the queer thing is, that when she finally joined me and I rose to speak, I forgot to be afraid. Will says that such an experience is very common with him in making an after-dinner speech.

"You don't know me, Mrs. Sewall," I began.

"I fear I do not," she replied, smiling formally. She was dressed very plainly, but elegantly too. Her iron-grey hair looked as if it were cut out of marble not a wisp astray; and you simply felt, so perfect was everything about her, that the nail of her little finger was as nicely pointed, polished, and pinked as all the rest.

"But your card," she went on, "your name sounds familiar."

Of course it did—she probably had seen it signed after Will's articles in the magazines, I thought—but I replied simply, "You met me before I was Mrs. William Ford Maynard—in Hilton—several years ago. My name was Lucy Vars."

I was quite prepared for the expression of hostility that crossed Mrs. Sewall's face at this remark.

"Vars," she repeated a little vaguely. "Oh, yes, I remember. There was, I believe, a Ruth Vars. Are you related?" Then as if she had forgotten it up to this time, she suddenly asked, "Won't you sit down?"

I thanked her and did so, she herself sinking into a voluminous tufted armchair opposite.

"I am Ruth Vars' sister," I explained, "and it is about Ruth and your son that I have come to talk with you."

Mrs. Sewall raised her brows.

"Your sister? My son? Really? How extraordinary!"

"Why, yes. You must know," I went on, "that your son is seeing a great deal of Ruth lately."

Mrs. Sewall smiled in a very patronising manner and replied, "It is very difficult for a mother to keep track of all a young man's fancies."

"This is more than a fancy, Mrs. Sewall. Ruth and your son are engaged to be married," I announced calmly.

A slight flush spread over Mrs. Sewall's face to the very roots of her marcel wave, but her voice showed no emotion when she spoke.

"Would it not have been more delicate to have allowed my son to have told me this piece of news," she asked me cuttingly.

"I was not thinking much about the delicacy of my call, I'm afraid."

"Evidently," she agreed.

"I have come simply to find out if you approve of this engagement and, if not, what we can do about it."

Mrs. Sewall looked me up and down deliberately, then:

"You seem to be a very courageous young person," she said, "but I fear this interview cannot alter my opinion. Your sister is no doubt a very charming young girl, but I have other ambitions for my son, Mrs. Maynard."

"I thought so. I guessed it from a conversation I overheard, and that is why I have come this morning. I thought we could work better together than alone."

"I plainly see," said Mrs. Sewall, gazing pityingly upon me, "that it will be necessary to be quite blunt with you. Did you never suspect that I closed Grassmere three years ago, simply to separate my son from your sister? As soon as I learned that my son actually intended to marry Miss Vars I was forced to take him to a different environment. When you consider that I have fought against this attachment for so long, you will see how absurd it is for you to hope to win my approval now, however bold your attempt."

"Oh," I flushed, "it isn't to win your approval that I am here. You have misunderstood me. It is to win, or rather to assure myself of your disapproval. You see I'm not in favour of the marriage either."

"You're not in favour of it?" Mrs. Sewall ejaculated.

"I'm not in favour of it," I repeated. "Ruth doesn't love your son. She's marrying for position—and I want to save her from such unhappiness. I don't want her to marry any one she doesn't love," I hastened to add.

"Well, well," Mrs. Sewall interrupted, "this is a novel experience for me. I wonder," she broke off in a sudden burst of friendliness, sarcasm and patronage gone from her voice, "I wonder I never discovered you in Hilton, Mrs. Maynard." Then she added with an amused twinkle in her eyes, "You are rather unlike your very enterprising sister-in-law, Mrs. Alexander Vars."

"Yes," I smiled, "perhaps a little. I have rather old-fashioned ideas on marriage, I suppose."

"I trust," Mrs. Sewall went on, "that you are sincere in saying you are opposed to this affair between your sister and my son."

"Sincere? Oh, yes, truly. Perfectly sincere." I blushed in spite of myself.

"I believe you—oh, I believe you," Mrs. Sewall reassured me quickly. "I know without your saying so that there may be other grounds why you object to your sister's engagement. You know," she smiled, "there is a different code of morals for every class of society that exists."

"I know," I murmured.

"But we won't go into that. It is sufficient that you *do* object. And now that we discover ourselves to be, instead of enemies, fellow soldiers, fighting together on the same side for the same cause, I am going to be very frank and tell you how low my ammunition is. I am powerless to do anything to influence this affair, I fear. A mother's wishes are of little account these days—my advice, my desires, not worth consideration. There are some things, I am learning, that I cannot control. A determined and hot-tempered young man in love with an ambitious girl, who sees wealth and position in her lover's proposals, is a combination beyond hope of breaking up."

"Oh, no, it isn't," I interrupted.

She shook her head.

"I have opposed and opposed. My son knows my hostile and bitter attitude toward the whole affair. It does not make the slightest dent upon his intentions. I have talked by the hour; I have cajoled; I have threatened; but to no avail. Mrs. Maynard, my son ought to marry a girl with money. His fortune is greatly overestimated, and until he ran across your sister again—oh, by the merest chance three months ago on Fifth Avenue—he was devoted to his cousin, Miss Gale Oliphant, whom you may have read about when she made her brilliant début last season. I heartily approve of such a match—appropriate in every way."

"Of course," I tucked in. "Why, Ruth has barely enough to buy her necessary clothes."

"Exactly," Mrs. Sewall sighed. "Oh, I don't know how it all will work out; I really don't know. At least your sister is a nice girl. My son might have chosen some one who wasn't educated or cultured—he has had so many fancies—and I shall have the satisfaction also, I suppose, of having avoided the notoriety of an elopement. My consent was forced from me, but it seemed the only way."

"Have you consented?" I asked alarmed.

"Reluctantly. Why, I could do nothing else. Breckenridge threatened a month ago that if I didn't consent he would elope with Miss Vars. At least, if the marriage *must* take place, it had better be decently. When he disappeared from home a week ago, I thought the worst had happened. I was so relieved when I placed my son at this hotel and found he was still single, that I decided to accept the inevitable with as much grace as possible now that I had been given a second opportunity. Breckenridge says your sister will marry him at any time if he but says the word, and he assures me he *will* say it unless my note of welcome reaches Miss Vars—to-morrow. So—" She shrugged her shoulders.

"That isn't true!" I replied. "Not a word of it! Ruth wouldn't elope for anything in the world. She's awfully proud, Mrs. Sewall. I ought not to have done it, but I listened to a private conversation between Ruth and your son. I heard Ruth say, when your son suggested a secret marriage, that the idea was absolutely insulting to her. She was awfully angry, and that was only last night at eleven o'clock."

"You heard her say that? Last night? You are sure?"

"Yes," I went on quickly, "and what is more I heard her say she would never marry Breck in this world till you accepted her publicly as his fiancée. It was when I heard that, that I decided to come and talk with you."

"Breckenridge has been misrepresenting the situation," Mrs. Sewall remarked.

"Ruth *is* ambitious," I went on. "Ruth *is* fond of wealth and position, but she's the proudest girl I ever knew. I thought if you understood how important a part *you* and your attitude played in the engagement, you could act accordingly. Ruth would break it off herself, if—it sounds awfully disloyal to her—but if you made the situation uncomfortable enough for her. I'm sure of it."

Mrs. Sewall got up and walked over to the little mahogany desk.

"I was afraid the maid had already mailed it," she exclaimed, holding up the little square envelope with Ruth's name and my address upon it. "It was a note of—" she smiled wryly—"of welcome to your sister. How fortunate," she added, "that you called just when you did. It throws a different light on the matter."

I remained with Mrs. Sewall until nearly twelve o'clock. We talked the situation threadbare before I left. I told her all I knew of Ruth's hopes and visions of the future. I repeated my sister's speech to Will of the peculiar demands of her temperament. I discussed her as freely as if she were a patient with important symptoms, and Mrs. Sewall the physician. I explained the situation in Hilton, Edith's influence upon Ruth, at what a high value my sister-in-law placed Mrs. Sewall's recognition, how persistently she preached the advantage of a connection by marriage. In the face of the force of Edith's influence, I pointed out Ruth's saving traits of pride and self-esteem. Ruth was as haughty as the highest. I enlarged on the absolute impossibility of an elopement as far as my high-spirited sister was concerned. Oh, I urged Ruth's humiliation as the only hope for success!

Before I left I had the satisfaction of seeing Mrs. Sewall tear up my sister's card of introduction to the Sewall family, and deposit the remains in the waste-basket. As I rose to go Mrs. Sewall took my hand in both of hers. Edith, I am sure, would have been surprised if she could have witnessed such intimacy between grand Mrs. F. Rockridge Sewall and Bobbikins.

"I am so glad you came," she said. "I owe you so much. I haven't entirely decided on my exact course, but if you later hear of my opening Grassmere, do not be surprised. There may be method in my madness."

"I'll leave it all with you," I reassured her. "Only I hope you won't make it any worse for Ruth than necessary."

"I won't, my dear; and by the way, sometime when you are in Hilton, will you let me know? Or by any chance in New York? After this we surely must be friends."

"Instead of connections?" I asked.

"You would be delightful as both," she laughed, and I bade her good-bye.

I felt like a traitor that night at dinner. Ruth never seemed sweeter. She had explained as she sat down to our evening meal that she was going to visit with Will and me alone that night. She was returning to Hilton in two days and she had told Breck that one evening at least, she intended to devote to her sister. I felt dreadfully guilty. But for me, her long-looked-for, much-coveted note of welcome from Mrs. Sewall would now be on its way to her; but for me, her bright visions of a social position being placed upon her head like a crown would have become a reality. I wished she wouldn't keep on piling coals of fire upon my head. She started in on her appreciation of my hospitality right after dinner. She said she would always remember her nice little breakfasts that I had served her in bed, whatever her future life might be (and she implied that it promised to be rather grand); she remarked she hoped I didn't believe all that she said to Will the first night she was with us; she assured me that my quiet and gracious acceptance of Breck had made an impression that she would never forget. She kissed me good-night of her own accord.

I told Will about my call on Mrs. Sewall as soon as we were safely in our room. I wanted to get the secret knowledge of it off my mind. I was beginning to feel a little apprehensive and doubtful. I really don't know what right I have to snatch Ruth's life away from her and treat it as if it were mine. But Will always reassures me.

"Well," he said, "if you do succeed in breaking off this disreputable affair, Lucy, I'll take off my hat to you, and so will Ruth—some day."

"Oh, do you think she will?" I asked relieved.

"Know it. My, but what a girl I did marry! You *do* take the bull by the horns. If you had had a son what a staver he would have been."

I forgot Ruth and her affairs in a twinkling.

I wilted like a flower plucked from its stem.

"You used to say that in the simple future, and now it's past subjunctive," I trembled.

Will laughed at me. "Don't like my tenses! What a particular person! Well, how's this? Here's a sentence in the simple present. It always has been present tense, always will be present." He leaned and whispered something in my ear.

"Pooh!" I scoffed, smiling for his sake. "That's too easy. It's the first tense of the first verb given in every grammar of every language in the world!"

CHAPTER XXIV

IT was five months later, sometime during the last of September, that I again heard directly from Ruth and her love-affair with Breckenridge Sewall.

Miss Kavenaugh, the dollar-and-a-half-a-day university seamstress, had come to help me with my muslin curtains. Miss Kavenaugh is a very much-sought-after lady, and when I am able to secure her for a day, I give up everything else, sit down and sew with her. She plans, cuts and bastes, and I run the chain-stitch machine like mad. We had been working since eight A. M. in my darling new bedroom that looks out on my row of late dahlias. I could hardly keep my eyes on the machine-needle because of the distracting flame of several maple-trees against some dark green cedars across the lake. Will and I had been in our new house about two weeks and we adored it! I was perched on the step-ladder at the particular moment the telephone bell rang, hanging the last muslin curtain in the room we called Ruth's. Miss Kavenaugh was puttering with the cretonne overhangings, pulling and patting them as tenderly as if they had been dainty dresses hung up on forms.

It was Ruth on the telephone calling me from town.

"I'm in here shopping," she said. "Can you possibly come in and have lunch? Do, if you can. I want to see you."

Now whenever Ruth did honour me with an invitation to luncheon it was in quite a different manner. To-day she actually asked me to set the hour and seemed inclined to adapt her plans to mine. I didn't want to leave Miss Kavenaugh in the least (she couldn't give me another day for a week), but if Ruth was as anxious to see me as all that, I decided I had better meet her if it broke a bone. I told her I would be at the appointed place at one-thirty.

Since June, Will and I had been buried in a little out-of-the-way spot in Newfoundland. The few letters that I had received had scarcely mentioned Ruth's affairs. Only one from my sister herself early in July had given me any inkling that Mrs. Sewall was acting on my suggestion. In that letter Ruth had briefly said that her engagement to Breck would probably not be announced till fall, and asked me to say nothing about the matter to any one. I was delighted not to.

Ruth was looking as pretty as ever, when I finally found myself sitting opposite to her at one of the side tables in the dining-room of the only hotel in town where she will condescend to eat. If she had anything of importance on her mind she certainly exhibited no outward agitation. She was dressed in a scant, tailor-made white serge suit, and had on a big, floppy, soft, fur-felt hat, which no other woman I know would have attempted to wear. It was lavender in shade and the brim drooped as if it had lost all its stiffening. Around the crushed crown was tied a piece of hemp rope. I never saw a hat like it in any shop. Ruth is always discovering odd, outlandish "shapes" in the millinery line and trimming them up with things no one ever thought of putting on a hat before. This particular creation looked as if it had been blown on to Ruth's head, but I must say it had landed at just the right angle to reveal a bit of her pretty hair, and to frame her face in a halo of soft mauve.

"What shall we eat?" asked Ruth in a bored little way, and tossed me a menu. After we had decided on mock-turtle soup, sweet-breads a-la-something, little peas, and Waldorf salad (Ruth isn't the kind to pick up a ham-sandwich and cup of coffee at a lunch-counter, I can tell you) and the superior-looking waiter had departed, Ruth opened her shopping bag and tossed two dress samples down upon the white cloth.

"What do you think of these?" she asked nonchalantly.

I wondered if Ruth had dragged me all the way in town, occupied and busy as I had been at home, to show me dress samples. Always the psychological moment to share a confidence, or to announce a startling piece of news, is after the waiter has departed with your order. But Ruth took her own time.

"I'm trying a new tailor," she went on. "I've ordered the black-and-white stripe. It's very good in the piece. By the way, don't you prefer butter without salt? Waiter!" Ruth is very imperious when she is in a hotel. Clerks and maids and bell-boys simply fly to obey when Ruth gives an order. We were supplied with crescents, corn-muffins and slim brown-bread sandwiches, fresh butter, ice-water and two napkins apiece, before a man lunching alone at the next table could get his glass refilled.

It wasn't until we were well started on our elaborate menu, that Ruth thought best to gratify my curiosity. It was while she was pouring the tea, and after I had given up hope that she had anything thrilling to announce to me after all, that she asked, "Sugar, I believe?" and then as she dropped one little crystal cube into the cup added, "Oh, by the way, I've broken my engagement to Breck Sewall."

I didn't show a trace of wonder or surprise.

"Is that so?" I said, as if I didn't much care if she had, and then after I had taken a swallow of tea I asked, "How did that happen?"

"Oh, I simply decided to," Ruth replied shortly; and as if the subject were closed, she inquired, "How's the new house?"

I was simply aching to ask a few questions, but I didn't allow myself even one.

"Oh, it's very nice," I replied; "we've been in it two weeks now."

"How did the lavender room turn out?" asked Ruth, travelling away as fast as possible from the subject of her engagement.

"*Your* room, Ruth, you mean," I replied patiently. "Very well, I think."

"Is it finished yet? I mean could any one sleep in it—to-night?"

"Will you come home with me, Ruth?" I asked eagerly.

"I thought I might—possibly, if you'd like to have me, and if you have an empty bed. At least," she added, "I'm not going back to The Homestead."

"Oh, you're not!" I replied, vaguely wondering if it were the tailor who was keeping her or the manicurist. "Well, I can lend you a nightgown and you can buy a tooth-brush."

"Oh, my trunk is at the station," said Ruth. "I was determined to go somewhere. You see things are not very pleasant for me just now in Hilton. Besides, Edith and I have quarrelled."

It wasn't very charitable to rejoice at such an announcement; it wasn't very noble of me, I suppose, to delight that conditions at Hilton were too disagreeable for Ruth to remain there; but remember I had always wanted to shelter my sister—remember I had always been jealous of her loyalty and devotion to Edith, and remember, also, ever since the plans of our house had been put on paper, I had hoped and almost prayed that *some one* would wish to sleep in the southeast chamber.

I reached for a biscuit to help conceal my feelings.

"Well," I said steadily, "your room is ready, and you're free to use it or not, as you wish."

"It won't be for very long," apologised Ruth, "and perhaps I can help you settle. You mustn't let me be the least bother. I haven't forgotten, you know," she said smiling, "how to wipe dishes."

"Didn't there used to be a lot of them in the old days at home," I remarked.

"And wasn't I horrid?" she followed up in a sudden burst of generosity. "Wasn't I horrid about helping? I was never very nice to you, I'm afraid, Lucy."

"Of course you were!" I scoffed.

"Oh, I know I wasn't, but you used to be awfully rabid. It seems to me you've improved a great deal in that respect since you were married. I noticed it when I visited you last spring." She stopped a moment. Then, "I want to tell you," she went on, "that I think you were awfully decent about Breck Sewall. You may not have liked him, but I appreciated your not trying to urge and influence me, the way Will did. If you had mixed yourself up in the affair too much I wouldn't feel like coming to you now."

I lowered my eyes as a hypocrite should.

"Of course not," I murmured ashamed.

Suddenly Ruth shoved her tea-cup to one side, her plate to the other, and folding her hands on the table in front, abruptly launched out into the midst of the details of her broken engagement.

"Edith," she began, "is willing to humiliate herself to any degree for the sake of a promotion in the social world. Now I'm too proud to stoop to some things. Edith actually advised me to marry Breck without Mrs. Sewall's approval. She said Mrs. Sewall would be sure to come around once the affair was settled. Could you imagine me in such a position?"

"Oh," I said, "didn't Mrs. Sewall approve?"

"Haven't you heard?" asked Ruth. "Every one else has. It has been anything but pleasant. When I wrote you that my engagement wouldn't be announced till fall it was simply because I hadn't heard from Mrs. Sewall. Breck said he hadn't told his mother and I believed him. She was ill or something, and I was willing to wait until it seemed wise to break the news to her. I was willing to meet her half-way, you see. I meant to be patient with Mrs. Sewall. Of course I realise I have no money nor position; but I won't be insulted by any one! She opened Grassmere in August, and brought along with her a young niece of hers, a Miss Oliphant—a silly creature, I thought; and she set in entertaining for her as she's never entertained before. Hilton has never been so gay, and everyone who was within the range of possibility was invited to Grassmere—everybody except Edith and me. Think of it! Think of the insult! It was the most pointed thing you ever saw. Edith is simply furious. Mrs. Sewall avoids her everywhere she sees her, and me too for that matter. *I* don't mind so much. It is Edith whom it stings so. *I* simply long for a chance to cut Mrs. Sewall. That's *my* attitude. However I don't enjoy being gossiped about, and all Hilton is buzzing. Oh, it's horrid!"

"I should say so," I murmured, stunned by the disaster I had caused.

"Well, during it all Breck has kept right on coming to see me—late every night after his social engagements at Grassmere. That was the feature I hated most, and the one that Edith, on the other hand, clung to as our only hope of salvation. But I'm not the kind to become the secret fancy of any man, even if he is the King of England. If I'm not good enough for his mother to recognise, then I don't want anything of him. Anyhow I consider myself, from the point of view of culture and education, superior to the Sewalls!"

"Of course," I agreed.

"The whole thing has made me sick and tired of the social game," ejaculated Ruth. "I don't believe there's any such thing as pure, unadulterated friendship between people who are socially ambitious. Why, some of the girls, who I thought were my best friends, have been acting very cool and offish since they've observed Mrs. Sewall's attitude towards me. And both Edith and I are omitted from lots of other people's parties besides the Sewalls, simply because Mrs. Sewall and Miss Oliphant are often the guests of honour. Oh, I think that all women are vain and selfish and insincere, and, if sometimes they *appear* thoughtful or sacrificing, it's simply because such an attitude toward someone will help them up another rung on the ladder. I'd like to get away from society for a while. It almost seems," Ruth added vehemently, "as if I'd like to enter a convent!"

"Oh, I'm awfully sorry, Ruth," I began.

"There's nothing for *you* to be sorry about. You couldn't help it. If I only had more money," Ruth went on, "I'd travel. I'd escape this sort of life. But what can any one do on my income? Eight hundred dollars! And I won't take any more from Edith."

"Did you quarrel very badly?" I dared to ask.

"Oh, quite. She went into an awful passion when I told her that I'd broken the engagement. She called me a short-sighted little fool! Breck, you see, wanted me to marry him in spite of his mother. Imagine me eloping! I wouldn't do such a vulgar thing. Edith said that her mother had run off with her father (imagine comparing me to that impossible Mrs. Campbell!) and that if I didn't marry Breck everybody would think *he* had gotten tired of *me*—cast me off, and all that sort of thing. I don't get angry often, but I gave Edith a piece of my mind that I guess she'll remember for a long time, and Alec didn't like it a bit. So this morning I just decided to decamp."

"But of course Breck will follow you," I suggested cheerfully.

"Oh, no, he won't. I've quarrelled with him too." Ruth smiled. "I seem to have quarrelled with everybody. But Breck threatened, and threats never have the least effect on me. He really did want to marry me, in spite of what people said about his marked attentions to this Oliphant girl. He was crazy to marry me. Things got to an awful pitch of excitement and one night three days ago, he said that if I wouldn't run off with him in the dark like some common girl in a newspaper story, and get married by a country parson along the road somewhere, he wasn't going to spend any more of his time waiting around. He said that Gale—that's Miss Oliphant—would marry him, mother or no mother; she had some heart and feeling in her. I told him that *I* on the other hand wouldn't lower my self-respect one iota, for love, or position, or any other reason. And so ... well, here I am, with all my bridges burned. By the way," Ruth broke off, "please don't ask me to discuss this matter with Will. He was too intolerant last spring for me to care to talk it over with him now."

"You needn't mention it to him," I assured her.

"You can imagine," said Ruth, "that I'm not feeling very much like talking about it to any one."

"I understand, and we won't refer to it at all. I know how hard it is, Ruth,—but time—"

"Oh, time!" replied my sophisticated sister. "There's no scar on my heart for time to heal. You see now, don't you, how safe it is to keep such affairs strictly in the region of one's head."

Two or three weeks later I received a letter from Mrs. Sewall. I didn't know her writing but I saw Grassmere engraved on the envelope, so I suspected before I broke the seal.

> "*My dear Mrs. Maynard,*
>
> "You will be interested to know that the engagement of Miss Gale Oliphant to my son is to be publicly announced on Wednesday next. But for you I am afraid this very happy alliance might not have been arranged. Relying absolutely on what you told me I could expect from your sister I have acted on your suggestion, with these results. I was sorry to treat so lovely a girl as your sister seems to be in so cruel a manner, but such an object-lesson seemed to me the most effectual way of showing what a future relation with me might prove to be. Let me say I think she is a very fine-principled and

high-minded girl, and another season when I shall return to Grassmere with my son and his bride I trust I may see a great deal of her. Another season I hope I may set everything right with Mrs. Alexander Vars also, whom it seemed necessary to sacrifice for a little while to our cause, if, in fact, I cannot do something toward reparation this year in the few weeks left before I return to New York. Let me add with all heartiness that I am particularly anticipating the pleasure of entertaining, sometime soon, an old fellow-soldier of mine.

"Sincerely,"FRANCES ROCKRIDGE SEWALL."

"Take off your hat," I said to my husband late that night. "You promised you would. The engagement is broken. Breck Sewall is going to marry his cousin, and Ruth is in bed in the southeast chamber."

During the weeks immediately following Ruth's decision in regard to Breck Sewall, she became an absorbingly interesting proposition, to herself. For the first month she wouldn't show any interest in anything outside her own problem. Ruth has admirers where-ever she goes and under any circumstances; and as soon as it was learned that she was staying with me the telephone began to ring every day—the door-bell every night or so with would-be suitors. But Ruth wouldn't see any of her callers or accept any invitations. She assumed such a blasé and indifferent attitude toward life that it worried me. She used to take long walks alone over the hills and improvise by the hour by firelight in our living-room. Evenings after dinner she spent in her own room reading Marcus Aurelius, Omar Khayyam, Oscar Wilde and Marie Bashkirtseff. I used to find the books missing from the book-shelves, and discover them on the couch in Ruth's room later. A drop-light arranged on a small table by the head of the couch, a soft down quilt wrapped around a china-silk negligee, and Ruth nestled down inside of all that, was the picture to which Will and I always sang out good-night when we closed our door at ten P.M. She used to devote several hours a day to writing, but whether it was a novel or an epic poem that she was so busy about, I didn't know. She kept her papers safely locked away in her trunk and I didn't like to intrude on her intimacy. I think Ruth rather enjoyed herself during these first days after the settlement of her affair with Breck. Her newly-won independence, her freedom, brought about entirely by her own will and volition, filled her with a little self-admiration. She appealed to herself as rather an unique and remarkable young person, bearing the interesting distinction of a broken engagement. She was young and fresh and lovely, and belonged to no one; her future lay in her own hands; she didn't know what she should do with it, but it was hers—hers alone, and full of all sorts of exciting possibilities.

"I don't want to see anything more of men for a long time," she would say. "I haven't decided yet what I'm going to go into, but I want to *do* something. I want to see all sides of life. I have had enough of society and bridge and silly girls who only want to get married. I'm seriously considering settlement work in New York. Sometime I'd like to go to Paris and study sculpture."

At the end of Ruth's third week with us—one Saturday night, I believe it was—the door-bell rang about eight o'clock. The maid answered it and when she came upstairs and passed by the door of Will's study (which is a little room over the front door and where we sit evenings) I said with a sigh of relief, "Thank goodness, it's for Ruth. I did want to finish this ruffle." And a moment later I added, "I wonder what excuse she'll send down to-night."

I was surprised five minutes later by Ruth's appearance in the doorway. She had put on a favourite gown of hers—crow-black meteor satin, so plain it had kind of a naked appearance, with a V-shaped neck that showed a bit of Ruth's throat. There wasn't a scrap of any kind of trimming on it.

"Will you hook this up please?" she asked, and when I had finished, "Thanks," she said, and with no explanation went downstairs.

"I wonder who it can be!" I exclaimed after she had departed. "It's the first one she has seen."

Will looked up and smiled.

"Oh, it's just a *man*. Rest assured that this pose of Ruth's can't last much longer. Three weeks of a diet that excludes all forms of masculine admiration is a long fast for Ruth. They'll be calling here thick and fast now."

But it wasn't just a man! About nine-thirty I stole down the back stairs to get two pieces of chocolate cake and two glasses of milk for Will and me. I peeked into the front hall before crawling back again.

"Will," I said two minutes later, "leaning up against the Chippendale chair in the hall is a man's walking-stick and it has got a plain silver top like Bob Jennings'. I introduced Bob to Ruth last week at a Faculty Tea and he walked home with her, before I was ready to leave. It does seem odd that he didn't send cards up to us too, doesn't it?"

It was almost eleven o'clock before I heard the front door close and Ruth snapping off the lights in the living-room. Will was staying up late to-night, and I had put on a soft wrapper and curled up in the Morris-chair with a magazine. The door was slightly ajar, and as Ruth passed it on her way to bed she stopped just outside, and asked softly:

"Are you both still up?"

"Surely," I replied. "Come in."

She came over and stood by the table where Will was working.

"Can you be torn away from your precious books for a while, Will?" she asked sweetly.

"Of course I can," he replied.

"Because," Ruth went on, "I want to tell you something." She paused.

"Yes?" encouraged Will. "Fire away."

"I suppose," Ruth continued, "you two are wondering when I am going home. I've been here nearly a month now and I ought to decide what I am going to do. I'd like your advice if you're not too busy."

"Certainly I'm not," Will responded heartily.

Ruth can be very complimentary and deferential when she chooses. She chose so to be now. Will closed his books. Ruth was standing by the table; her tapering finger-tips just reached the mahogany surface, she leaned lightly on them; her face was in the shadow, for the only light was Will's low reading-lamp, and her arms suddenly appearing out of the dark were startlingly white and pretty.

"It was Mr. Jennings who called to-night," she went on. "I saw him because he rather interested me last week when I met him at one of your Faculty Teas. I was talking with him to-night a little about my life. It came in after I had read him a few of my verses, which he said he would be kind enough to give me his opinion about, when I told him last week that I wrote a little. He suggested a plan that rather appealed to me. I don't know what you think of it, but he says that there are a lot of girls who take special courses here at Shirley (Shirley is the girls' college connected with the university) and that, even though I'm not a college girl, he thinks he could arrange for me to take a course or two in poetry and literature. He wants me to develop my talent. Oh, I'd love to do it!" Ruth exclaimed, suddenly enthusiastic. "Mr. Jennings is *so* encouraging! He thinks I really might write something worth while some day. I've always thought that poetry was the very highest form of expression. Mr. Jennings thinks so too. He says, Lucy, that you attend certain courses connected with the university that would be excellent for me. He says that I could go to some of those afternoons with you perhaps. He's going to get the Shirley catalogue and lay out a course of study for me. Do you suppose, Will, that you could find a place for me to room somewhere around here?"

"To room, Ruth? Why, we should want you to stay right here with us," I exploded.

"Oh, of course," Ruth scoffed, "I couldn't break in on you and Will that way."

"But, Ruth," I began.

"Oh, no, Lucy, I wouldn't do that. I've been fifth wheel at The Homestead for years, but I don't intend to be here."

"Nonsense," said Will; "we'd like to have you. Lucy spent a lot of time preparing that room you're in and—"

"No. Please. I shan't listen. Why, you haven't even talked it over. Wait till morning anyway. I simply came in to ask your advice on my turning into a 'blue-stocking.' Do you think it absolutely ridiculous?"

We thought it was splendid—both Will and I. We talked and planned and built air-castles with Ruth till after midnight. She even read us some of her pretty verses and before she went to bed at one A. M. she had already become a poetess of renown with contributions appearing frequently in the most exclusive magazines.

A new-found genius slept in the southeast chamber that night, and at seven A. M. when the sun and I crawled into her room together we found her fast asleep with one hand tucked cosily under her cheek. Her hair, which is neither blonde nor brown but kind of a dull mouse-colour and almost mauve when she wears the right shade, was braided and flung up back over the pillow. Upon the pillow beside her lay her left hand upturned and free from jewellery of any kind. That upturned hand had kind of an appealing, wistful expression about it that made me want to cry. Somehow the sight of Ruth's bare unpromised hand making the only dent on the surface of the pillow by her side filled me with a wave of thanksgiving. She breathed softly, regularly, her violet-tinted eyelids quivering a little, a half-smile lingering in the corners of her mouth. A fly lit on Ruth's chin and, unmolested, walked audaciously up along the flushed, velvety surface of her cheek. It stopped just beneath her long-curved eyelashes. She didn't stir—just kept on with her even, measured breathing and her steady sleep. I frightened that bold creature away with a wave of my hand. I honestly believe that Breck Sewall hadn't disturbed my sister any more than the fly on her cheek. She seemed to me the most superbly virginal creature I had ever gazed upon.

I sat down and touched her shoulder softly.

"It's morning," I said, and when she was entirely awake I continued, "It's morning, and you wanted us to wait till morning. We've talked it all over together alone and we both still want you to stay with us as long as you possibly can. Why, Ruth, we built this room for *you*—especially for *you*—and I do hope you'll like it well enough to stay."

"It's prettier than my room at Edith's," replied Ruth. Then suddenly she put out her hand and touched my knee. "Lucy," she said, "I'm *crazy* to stay. I'd *hate* a stuffy boarding-house."

"Of course you would!"

"This is so adorably fresh and clean and simple. Have you and Will really talked it all over? I think I ought not to stay, but I'll promise not to be the least bother in the world."

"Bother!" I exclaimed.

"I'll be busy with my studies daytimes and keep out of the way evenings. Really," she asked, "do you want me?"

"We really do," I said solemnly.

She turned and suddenly sat up beside me on the edge of the bed. She was a lovely creature with her long thick hair, her white arms, and her pretty, soft, beribboned nightgown falling off one shoulder. She seemed too lovely to be my sister. She flung one arm around my shoulders.

"Lucy," she exclaimed, "from this time on, I'm going to be nice to you."

I don't remember that Ruth had ever before put her arm around me of her own accord. A lump came in my throat. Tears blinded me. I got up hastily and began putting down the windows.

CHAPTER XXV

IF you want to know what became of Ruth I'll tell you—I'll tell you right off. She fell in love with Bob Jennings. She fell awfully in love with him—absorbingly, overwhelmingly in love. Ruth, the lofty, the high, the pedestalled! Ruth who prided herself on her coolness and her circumspection, Ruth who boasted that fate had foreordained a brilliant marriage, lost her head over a young college instructor who taught English composition to freshmen and sophomores, at a salary something less than three thousand a year. It simply proves that the eternal feminine will crop out, however much it has been choked and blighted, just like a dry bulb that's been kept in a damp dark cellar all winter. Once you put it in the sun and warmth, and give it a little water, it just can't help but grow up bright and green—brilliant rank green, full of juicy stalks and buds. Why, Ruth got to be such a normal sort of girl that she blushed every time Bob's name was mentioned. Ruth the invulnerable! She even lost her appetite—of all ordinary things—and great circles appeared under her eyes. The most astounding feature to me was that Ruth fell in love before she was asked to. Imagine that if you can. Ruth the haughty! The bulb began to send out shoots like a common onion or potato, before invited by the sun. Things came to such a pass that Will finally touched on the delicate subject with Bob. We thought the man must be blind, crazy or heartless, not to have seen the tell-tale symptoms in Ruth's manner long before circles began to appear. But Will found that Bob was simply penniless. This university pays salaries about large enough to keep two canaries alive, and Bob told Will that though he had loved Ruth ever since the day he first saw her, he couldn't say a word to her about it, because he already had a mother quite alone and dependent living with him, besides a sister he was trying to put through college, and he knew Ruth was a girl who had been used to luxuries.

Bob is a kind of dreamy sort of man. He says the simplest things in a way that thrills you. His letters, even his notes accepting dinner invitations (and such are the only kind I have ever received) have a kind of "way" with them—exclamation points here and there, single words, capitalised and perioded, to express a whole sentence. Oh, Bob is awfully individual; but he'll never be rich. He's a teacher, in the first place; and in the second, he hasn't a father with a fortune. When I realised that Ruth loved Bob Jennings, I was worried about those demands of that temperament of hers—the soft-footed, unobtrusive servants, the exquisite china, the fine lace, the dinners perfectly served, all those expensive things that Bob couldn't supply in a lifetime. If only Bob had had Breck's fortune, or Breck had had Bob's poetic soul, everything would have been all right; for I am sure Ruth would have eloped with Bob Jennings the first time he asked her.

I realised that Ruth was thinking seriously about Bob Jennings when she began inquiring of Will about the salaries of instructors at the university. Later she asked me how much rents were, in this section of the country. She was perfectly aware from the very beginning that Bob earned just about enough to afford an apartment the size of Oliver's and Madge's, which she had formerly pronounced "cunning" but "impossible." If Ruth, as she boasted, confined matrimonial questions to the region of her head she ought to have sent Bob on his way the very instant that she learned these salient facts about him. But she didn't. She kept right on seeing him, night after night, as if he were a millionaire who could supply her every desire by merely dashing off his signature. She kept on reading her poetry with him, discussing art and literature by the hour, and quoting him to me all the next day as if he were an authority. Ruth simply lost her equilibrium over Bob. I don't believe she had ever seen a man like him before. He certainly is different from Breck Sewall, packed with sentiment, full impressions and delicate sensibilities. I overheard him talking with Ruth about women smoking once. He said you might as well deface a beautiful picture by painting cigarettes in the angels' mouths. I suppose it might have been the fact of being classed with the angels that "took" Ruth so. Anyhow she wanted Bob for her own, salary or no salary; she wanted him so badly that we couldn't even joke on the subject in her presence. By Christmas-time the situation was tragic.

The quarrel with Edith, as all quarrels with Edith are sure to be, had been of short duration. The fact that Mrs. Sewall had invited her to assist at a tea before her final departure from Hilton had assuaged her grievances somewhat in that quarter. Moreover a startling piece of news in the New York papers in early December, ten days before the Oliphant-Sewall wedding was to take place, had vindicated Ruth's course of action even in Edith's eyes, beyond a shadow of doubt. It seems that there was already a Mrs. Breckenridge Sewall. Breck had, after all, been more decent than Will thought. He had married the girl whom he had known in college, and it was she who was now bringing suit against the groom-to-be. So as there existed nothing but kindly feelings between Edith and Ruth now, there was no reason why Ruth should not have spent the holidays in Hilton, but she simply wouldn't give up a single hour with Bob Jennings. He always came Tuesdays, Thursdays, Saturdays and Sundays. Our electric-light bill, dim as Ruth prefers the room to be, was a dollar extra a month, after Bob began to call.

I was glad to have Ruth with me during the Christmas vacation. Otherwise I should have been all alone. Early in December Will had gone to a medical conference of some kind in Chicago, and just as he was about to start for home, some big physician out there called him in, in consultation, on the case of a little boy, who had some awful thing the matter with his spine. He was the son of a millionaire, and experts and specialists from all over the country had given up hope of recovery. The father was just about crazy and when Will suggested some radical treatment of his own which he had tried out successfully on one of our little guinea-pigs, he wrote that that father simply clung to him bodily, got hold of him with his hands and told him he could have every cent of money that he possessed in the world if he'd only give him back his son. So Will stayed. He would have stayed if the man had been a pauper, if he'd loved his little boy like that. You see it is just the way Will would feel about *his* son. He understood. I wanted him to stay too. I was only sorry that, after all the long nights he had to sit up by the little chap's bed (for first there was an operation before Will began his treatment; and

Will wouldn't leave much to the nurses), after the weary nights, the doubtful dawns, the long uncertain journey to the day of the crisis, I was only sorry that Will couldn't bring the little boy he saved home with him (if he saved him) for ours to keep and love. He fought for the life of that child. He wanted it to live awfully; and I, hundreds of miles away, would wake often in the night during the long struggle—at three, at four, at seven when it grows light—and wonder, and hope, and, I suppose you'd call it, pray.

It was just before Christmas that my dread and fear about that little boy's life in Chicago became intermingled with a thrilling hope that was very much nearer home. My startling realisation came so unexpectedly to me after all the waiting, so undreamed, so miraculously a gift of heaven, that I couldn't believe at first that there was any real substantial fact about it. I couldn't, or I wouldn't, I don't know which. I dreaded disappointment. But oh, the mere possibility of such a joy being mine at last, made me so happy that I couldn't help but show a jubilant spirit in my letters. I wrote to Will that somehow, suddenly, I felt that that little boy out there was going to get well; I'd been as doubtful as he last week, but now, unaccountably, I was sure that the dear little fellow was going to live to grow up. I didn't tell Will *why* I felt so (it was such a silly woman's reason) but I kept on writing it over and over again, every day, as I woke each morning with the reassurance that the thing I wanted more than anything in the world was coming true.

I never thought I was superstitious, but you know how over-particular and over-careful you are about anything that's awfully important. Your anxiety borders on superstition before you know it, and when somebody accuses you, you simply don't care, you're so eager to have everything propitious. Well, I somehow got to believing that that child's life in Chicago that Will was striving so hard to save and the life of my hidden joy had something to do with each other. The idea obsessed me; I couldn't get it out of my head, fanatical and ridiculous as I knew a sensible person would call it, and I kept writing to Will as if that millionaire's son were mine. Will said it was a good thing that he wasn't a practising physician if I took his cases so much to heart as all that; but, just the same, he told me that my letters did fill him with hope and courage.

All during this period, while Ruth was eating out her soul for Bob, and Will was eating out his soul for the little sick boy, and I was eating out my soul for a gift I'd have died to possess for a day, no one would have guessed from Ruth's and my pleasant good-mornings, our casual calm and undisturbed conversations at meal-time, and Will's cheerful paragraphs, that we were all living through crises. Ruth and I with our anxieties grew very near to each other at this time. She was a lot of comfort to me and I tried to appreciate the feelings of a proud girl in love with a man who has not spoken. During the evenings that Bob called I sat up alone in Will's study, embroidering a centrepiece for the dining-room table. Evening after evening my fingers fairly ached to get out the rustling tissue paper patterns that Madge had left. But I wouldn't let myself—I wasn't going to be heart-broken—I wouldn't let myself put a needle to a single bit of nainsook.

It was on Saturday, January fifteenth, at ten o'clock at night, that Will's special delivery letter came. My fingers trembled as they tore at the envelope. I closed the study door to be alone. "If the little boy has died," I said out loud, "I mustn't be superstitious. I simply mustn't." But oh, he hadn't died! He hadn't died! Will's letter was one triumphant song from beginning to end. The little boy had passed the crisis; he was going to live; and live strong and well and normal. The miracle had been performed; the serum had done its magic part; there had been just the response that Will had dared to rely on; everything had been gloriously successful; and he was coming home in five days!

I let myself be just as superstitious then as I wanted. I had said if that little sick boy lived, so would my hopes, and I believed it. I lit a candle and went up into the unfinished part of our attic where there is a lot of old furniture packed away. It's rather a spooky place in the dark, and cold too, but I didn't notice it to-night. 'Way over in the corner stood the little old-fashioned cradle that belonged to Will's mother—one of those low, wooden-hooded ones with rockers, that you can rock with one foot. I had always planned to use that. It's so quaint and dear and old-fashioned. In the cradle in a green pasteboard box was a whole bundle of Will's baby-clothes—the queerest, finest little hand-made muslin shirts, and dresses with a lot of stiff embroidery and ruffles.

I had no idea what time it was when later I heard Ruth calling me from below.

"Lucy, Lucy! Are you up there?"

"Yes," I answered. "What time is it?"

"Why, it's after midnight! *What* are you doing?"

"Oh, looking up some old stuff. I'll be right down."

I met her on the stairs. I felt guilty. I was afraid that joy was written all over my face. I might as well have just left the arms of a lover.

"Oh, Ruth," I exclaimed, "isn't it *fine*? That little boy in Chicago is going to live! I've had a special delivery from Will. Isn't it *great*? He's going to get well!"

"That's splendid," said Ruth, and then, eyes sparkling, voice trembling, she exploded, "Oh, Lucy, Bob has just gone! We're engaged!"

I blew out the candle for safety's sake, and put my arms about my sister.

"Really, Ruth?" I exclaimed, and we sat down side by side on the dark stairs.

"He's cared for me all along, *all* the fall—*all this time*! Of course we both couldn't help but know it! But Bob—he's just that honourable he wouldn't say a word till he told me all about his circumstances and—everything. Circumstances! Oh, dear, I—What do you think of Bob, Lucy?" she broke off.

"I've always said that, next to Will, I'd rather marry Bob than any man I've known," I replied heartily.

"And does Will like him?" quivered Ruth.

"Will calls Bob the salt of the earth. *Everybody* likes Bob Jennings, Ruth!"

"I know they do. I know it. I don't see how I ever got him. You know all the men in his classes simply adore him! His courses are awfully popular. He's going to have juniors and seniors next year. The President stopped Bob the other day in the street and complimented him on his work. Oh, Bob is going to go right to the top! And he isn't a bit spoiled. His dear old silver-haired mother worships him just like everybody else. Do you know, Bob was afraid I wouldn't want her to live with us—she's the loveliest old lady—of course I do! And he thought, besides, I'd hate an apartment and one maid. But he didn't know me. My nature isn't the kind that requires 'Things.' If it didn't have sympathy and understanding and inspiration, it's the kind that would simply shrivel up and die. But Bob, he responds in just the right way, to every side of my temperament. It's wonderful!"

"Isn't it?" I agreed. "Why, we're all happy to-night! Will because of the little boy, and you because of Bob, and I because—" I hesitated just a moment, and then in the pitch-dark of the back stairs I confided to Ruth, "because the southeast chamber has a waiting-list."

"A waiting-list?" queried Ruth.

"Yes, I was upstairs when you called, seeing if Will's little old-fashioned mahogany cradle would do."

"Oh, really!" said Ruth not very much impressed after all. "Of course. My room *was* meant to be the nursery. I remember now. Well, I suppose you're glad, and there'll be a vacancy all right for some one to fill in June. We're going to be married right after Commencement. We've got it all planned. Isn't it exciting?" she exclaimed, eager on the trail of her own happiness. "We're not going to Europe, or anything grand like that. We're going to begin by saving. With my eight hundred a year and Bob's salary, and a little he has besides, our income will be about four thousand. We're going to have a lovely honeymoon! Bob likes the word 'honeymoon' though no one uses it now. Bob's so funny! We're going to camp out all alone for a whole month on a little lake we know about in the Adirondacks and I'm going to cook while he cuts wood. Bob didn't know I could cook. Why, he was awfully surprised when he discovered how practical I am, and that I trim all my own hats even now. Lucy, don't you think that Bob's *awfully* nice-looking?" she asked and pressed my hand.

"Yes I do. I've always told Will that Bob was the best-looking man on the faculty," I replied and pressed back.

An hour later we groped down the stairs together. It was two o'clock in the morning. The light in the study was still going and I went in and turned it off.

At my door Ruth begged, "Come on into my bed, Lucy. I shall never be able to get to sleep to-night."

"All right. In five minutes," I agreed.

When I went into Ruth's room she was sitting by the window ready for bed, her long hair braided, and a knitted worsted shawl wrapped around her white shoulders.

"Well, Ruth, it's half-past two," I said.

"Bob's coming at nine o'clock, before his first recitation," remarked Ruth dreamily. "That's six hours, isn't it?"

"And a half," I smiled.

"Oh, Lucy," suddenly exclaimed Ruth, standing up before me, "I'm terribly happy!"

"Are you? Well, so am I!" I replied.

"It just seems as if I'd have to open a window and let off steam somehow!" said Ruth.

"Well, let's!" said I.

The Fifth Wheel

Ruth Vars Comes Out

I SPEND my afternoons walking alone in the country. It is sweet and clean out-of-doors, and I need purifying. My wanderings disturb Lucy. She is always on the lookout for me, in the hall or living-room or on the porch, especially if I do not come back until after dark.

She needn't worry. I am simply trying to fit together again the puzzle-picture of my life, dumped out in terrible confusion in Edith's sunken garden, underneath a full September moon one midnight three weeks ago.

Lucy looks suspiciously upon the portfolio of theme paper I carry underneath my arm. But in this corner of the world a portfolio of theme paper and a pile of books are as common a part of a girl's paraphernalia as a muff and a shopping-bag on a winter's day on Fifth Avenue. Lucy lives in a university town. The university is devoted principally to the education of men, but there is a girls' college connected with it, so if I am caught scribbling no one except Lucy needs to wonder why.

I have discovered a pretty bit of woods a mile west of Lucy's house, and an unexpected rustic seat built among a company of murmurous young pines beside a lake. Opposite the seat is an ecstatic little maple tree, at this season of the year flaunting all the pinks and reds and yellows of a fiery opal. There, sheltered by the pines, undisturbed except by a scurrying chipmunk or two or an inquisitive, gray-tailed squirrel, I sit and write.

I heard Lucy tell Will the other day (Will is my intellectual brother-in-law) that she was really anxious about me. She believed I was writing poetry! "And whenever a healthy, normal girl like Ruth begins to write poetry," she added, "after a catastrophe like hers, look out for her. Sanitariums are filled with such."

Poetry! I wish it were. Poetry indeed! Good heavens! I am writing a defense.

I am the youngest member of a large grown-up family, all married now except myself and a confirmed bachelor brother in New York. We are the Vars of Hilton, Massachusetts, cotton mill owners originally, but now a little of everything and scattered from Wisconsin to the Atlantic Ocean. I am a New England girl, not the timid, resigned type one usually thinks of when the term is used, but the kind that goes away to a fashionable boarding-school when she is sixteen, has an elaborate coming-out party two years later, and then proves herself either a success or a failure according to the number of invitations she receives and the frequency with which her dances are cut into at the balls. She is supposed to feel grateful for the sacrifices that are made for her début, and the best way to show it is by becoming engaged when the time is right to a man one rung higher up on the social ladder than she.

I had no mother to guide me through these intricacies. My pilot was my ambitious sister-in-law, Edith, who married Alec when I was fifteen, remodeled our old 240 Main Street, Hilton, Mass., into a very grand and elegant mansion and christened it The Homestead. Hilton used to be just a nice, typical New England city. It had its social ambitions and discontents, I suppose, but no more pronounced than in any community of fifty or sixty thousand people. It was the Summer Colony with its liveried servants, expensive automobiles, and elaborate entertaining that caused such discontent in Hilton.

I've seen perfectly happy and good-natured babies made cross and irritable by putting them into a four-foot-square nursery yard. The wall of wealth and aristocracy around Hilton has had somewhat the same effect upon the people that it confines. If a social barrier of any sort appears upon the horizon of my sister-in-law Edith, she is never happy until she has climbed over it. She was in the very midst of scaling that high and difficult barrier built up about Hilton by the Summer Colonists, when she married Alec.

It didn't seem to me a mean or contemptible object. To endeavor to place our name—sunk into unjust oblivion since the reverses of our fortune—in the front ranks of social distinction, where it belonged, impressed me as a worthy ambition. I was glad to be used in Edith's operations. Even as a little girl something had rankled in my heart, too, when our once unrestricted fields and hills gradually became posted with signs such as, "Idlewold, Private Grounds," "Cedarcrest, No Picnickers Allowed," "Grassmere, No Trespassing."

I wasn't eighteen when I had my coming-out party. It was decided, and fully discussed in my presence, that, as young as I was, chance for social success would be greater this fall than a year hence, when the list of débutantes among our summer friends promised to be less distinguished. It happened that many of these débutantes lived in Boston in the winter, which isn't very far from Hilton, and Edith had already laid out before me her plan of campaign in that city, where she was going to give me a few luncheons and dinners during the month of December, and possibly a Ball if I proved a success.

If I proved a success! No young man ever started out in business with more exalted determination to make good than I. I used to lie awake nights and worry for fear the next morning's mail would not contain some cherished invitation or other. And when it did, and Edith came bearing it triumphantly up to my room, where I was being combed, brushed and polished by her maid, and kissed me ecstatically on the brow and whispered, "You little winner, you!" I could have run up a flag for relief and joy.

I kept those invitations stuck into the mirror of my dressing-table as if they were badges of honor. Edith used to make a point of having her luncheon and dinner guests take off their things in my room. I knew it was because of the invitations stuck in the mirror, and I was proud to be able to return something for all the money and effort she had expended.

It appeared incumbent upon me as a kind of holy duty to prove myself a remunerative investment. The long hours spent in the preparation of my toilette; the money paid out for my folderols; the deceptions we had to resort to for the sake of expediency; everything—schemes, plans and devices—all appeared to me as simply necessary parts of a big and difficult contest I had entered and must win. It never occurred to me then that my efforts were unadmirable. When at the end of my first season Edith and I discovered to our delight, when the Summer Colony returned to our hills, that our names had become fixtures on their exclusive list of invitations, I felt as much exaltation as any runner who ever entered a Marathon and crossed the white tape among the first six.

There! That's the kind of New England girl I am. I offer no excuses. I lay no blame upon my sister-in-law. There are many New England girls just like me who have the advantage of mothers—tender and solicitous mothers too. But even mothers cannot keep their children from catching measles if there's an epidemic—not unless they move away. The social fever in my community was simply raging when I was sixteen, and of course I caught it.

Even my education was governed by the demands of society. The boarding-school I went to was selected because of its reputation for wealth and exclusiveness. I practised two hours a day on the piano, had my voice trained, and sat at the conversation-French table at school, because Edith impressed upon me that such accomplishments would be found convenient and convincing. I learned to swim and dive, play tennis and golf, ride horseback, dance and skate, simply because if I was efficient in sports I would prove popular at summer hotels, country clubs and winter resorts. Edith and I attended symphony concerts in Boston every Friday afternoon, and opera occasionally, not because of any special passion for music, but to be able to converse intelligently at dinner parties and teas.

It was not until I had been out two seasons that I met Breckenridge Sewall. When Edith introduced me to society I was younger than the other girls of my set, and to cover up my deficiency in years I affected a veneer of worldly knowledge and sophistication that was misleading. It almost deceived myself. At eighteen I had accepted as a sad truth the wickedness of the world, and especially that of men. I was very blasé, very resigned—at least the two top layers of me were. Down underneath, way down, I know now I was young and innocent and hopeful. I know now that my first meeting with Breckenridge Sewall was simply one of the stratagems that the contest I had entered required of me. I am convinced that there was no thought of anything but harmless sport in my encounter.

Breckenridge Sewall's mother was the owner of Grassmere, the largest and most pretentious estate that crowns our hills. Everybody bowed down to Mrs. Sewall. She was the royalty of the Hilton Summer Colony. Edith's operations had not succeeded in piercing the fifty thousand dollar wrought-iron fence that surrounded the acres of Grassmere. We had never been honored by one of Mrs. F. Rockridge Sewall's heavily crested invitations. We had drunk tea in the same drawing-room with her; we had been formally introduced on one occasion; but that was all. She imported most of her guests from New York and Newport. Even the Summer Colonists considered an invitation from Mrs. Sewall a high mark of distinction.

Her only son Breckenridge was seldom seen in Hilton. He preferred Newport, Aix les Bains, or Paris. It was reported among us girls that he considered Hilton provincial and was distinctly bored at any attempt to inveigle him into its society. Most of us had never met him, but we all knew him by sight. Frequently during the summer months he might be seen speeding along the wide state road that leads out into the region of Grassmere, seated in his great, gray, deep-purring monster, hatless, head ducked down, hair blown straight back and eyes half-closed to combat the wind.

One afternoon Edith and I were invited to a late afternoon tea at Idlewold, the summer residence of Mrs. Leonard Jackson. I was wearing a new gown which Edith had given me. It had been made at an expensive dressmaker's of hers in Boston. I remember my sister-in-law exclaimed as we strolled up the cedar-lined walk together, "My, but you're stunning in that wistaria gown. It's a joy to buy things for you, Ruth. You set them off so. I just wonder who you'll slaughter *this* afternoon."

It was that afternoon that I met Breckenridge Sewall.

It was a week from that afternoon that two dozen American Beauties formed an enormous and fragrant center-piece on the dining-room table at old 240 Main Street. Suspended on a narrow white ribbon above the roses Edith had hung from the center light a tiny square of pasteboard. It bore in engraved letters the name of Breckenridge Sewall.

The family were deeply impressed when they came in for dinner. The twins, Oliver and Malcolm, who were in college at the time, were spending part of their vacation in Hilton; and my sister Lucy was there too. There was quite a tableful. I can hear now the Oh's and Ah's as I sat nonchalantly nibbling a cracker.

"Not too fast, Ruth, not too fast!" anxious Alec had cautioned.

"For the love o' Mike! Hully G!" had ejaculated Oliver and Malcolm, examining the card.

"O Ruth, tell us about it," my sister Lucy in awed tones had exclaimed.

I shrugged. "There's nothing to tell," I said. "I met Mr. Sewall at a tea not long ago, as one is apt to meet people at teas, that's all."

Edith from the head of the table, sparkling, too joyous even to attempt her soup, had sung out, "I'm proud of you, rascal! You're a wonder, you are! Listen, people, little sister here is going to do something splendid one of these days—she is!"

Breckenridge Sewall

WHEN I was a little girl, Idlewold, the estate of Mrs. Leonard Jackson where I first met Breckenridge Sewall, was a region of rough pasture lands. Thither we children used to go forth on Saturday afternoons on marauding expeditions. It was covered in those days with a network of mysteriously winding cow-paths leading from shadow into sunshine, from dark groves through underbrush and berry-bushes to bubbling brooks. Many a thrilling adventure did I pursue with my brothers through those alluring paths, never knowing what treasure or surprise lay around the next curve. Sometimes it would be a cave appearing in the dense growth of wild grape and blackberry vines; sometimes a woodchuck's hole; a snake sunning himself; a branch of black thimble-berries; a baby calf beside its mother, possibly; or perhaps even a wild rabbit or partridge.

Mrs. Leonard Jackson's elaborate brick mansion stood where more than once bands of young vandals were guilty of stealing an ear or two of corn for roasting purposes, to be blackened over a forbidden fire in the corner of an old stone wall; and her famous wistaria-and-grape arbor followed for nearly a quarter of a mile the wandering path laid out years ago by cows on their way to water. What I discovered around one of the curves of that path the day of Mrs. Jackson's garden tea was as thrilling as anything I had ever chanced upon as a little girl. It was Mr. Breckenridge Sewall sitting on the corner of a rustic seat smoking a cigarette!

I had seen Mr. Sewall enter that arbor at the end near the house, a long way off beyond lawns and flower beds. I was standing at the time with a fragrant cup of tea in my hand beside the wistaria arch that forms the entrance of the arbor near the orchard. I happened to be alone for a moment. I finished my tea without haste, and then placing the cup and saucer on a cedar table near-by, I decided it would be pleasant to escape for a little while the chatter and conversation of the two or three dozen women and a handful of men. Unobserved I strolled down underneath the grape-vines.

I walked leisurely along the sun-dappled path, stopped a moment to reach up and pick a solitary, late wistaria blossom, and then went on again smiling a little to myself and wondering just what my plan was. I know now that I intended to waylay Breckenridge Sewall. His attitude toward Hilton had had somewhat the same effect upon me as the No Trespassing and Keep Off signs when I was younger. However, I hadn't gone very far when I lost my superb courage. A little path branching off at the right offered me an opportunity for escape. I took it, and a moment later fell to berating myself for not having been bolder and played my game to a finish. My impulses always fluctuate and flicker for a moment or two before they settle down to a steady resolve.

I did not think that Mr. Sewall had had time to reach the little path, or if so, it did not occur to me that he would select it. It was grass-grown and quite indistinct. So my surprise was not feigned when, coming around a curve, I saw him seated on a rustic bench immediately in front of me. It would have been awkward if I had exclaimed, "Oh!" and turned around and run away. Besides, when I saw Breckenridge Sewall sitting there before me and myself complete mistress of the situation, it appeared almost like a duty to play my cards as well as I knew how. I had been brought up to take advantage of opportunities, remember.

I glanced at the occupied bench impersonally, and then coolly strolled on toward it as if there was no one there. Mr. Sewall got up as I approached.

"Don't rise," I said, and then as if I had dismissed all thought of him, I turned away and fell to contemplating the panorama of stream and meadow. Mr. Sewall could have withdrawn if he had desired. I made it easy for him to pass unheeded behind me while I was contemplating the view. However, he remained standing, looking at me.

"Don't let me disturb you," I repeated after a moment. "I've simply come to see the view of the meadows."

"Oh, no disturbance," he exclaimed, "and say, if it's the view you're keen on, take the seat."

"No, thank you," I replied.

"Go on, I've had enough. Take it. I don't want it."

"Oh, no," I repeated. "It's very kind, but no, thank you."

"Why not? I've had my fill of view. Upon my word, I was just going to clear out anyway."

"Oh, were you?" That altered matters.

"Sure thing."

Then, "Thank you," I said, and went over and sat down.

Often under the cloak of just such innocent and ordinary phrases is carried on a private code of rapid signs and signals as easily understood by those who have been taught as dots and dashes by a telegraphic operator. I couldn't honestly say whether it was Mr. Sewall or I who gave the first signal, but at any rate the eyes of both of us had said what convention would never allow to pass our lips. So I wasn't surprised, as perhaps an outsider will be, when Mr. Sewall didn't raise his hat, excuse himself, and leave me alone on the rustic seat, as he should have done according to all rules of good form and etiquette. Instead he remarked, "I beg your pardon, but haven't I met you before somewhere?"

"Not that I know of," I replied icily, the manner of my glance, however, belying the tone of my voice. "I don't recall you, that is. I'm not in Hilton long at a time, so I doubt it."

"Oh, not in Hilton!" He scoffed at the idea. "Good Lord, no. Perhaps I'm mistaken though. I suppose," he broke off, "you've been having tea up there in the garden."

"I suppose so," I confessed, as if even the thought of it bored me.

He came over toward the bench. I knew it was his cool and audacious intention to sit down. So I laid my parasol lengthwise beside me, leaving the extreme corner vacant, by which I meant to say, "I'm perfectly game, as you see, but I'm perfectly nice too, remember."

He smiled understandingly, and sat down four feet away from me. He leaned back nonchalantly and proceeded to test my gameness by a prolonged and undisguised gaze, which he directed toward me through half-closed lids. I showed no uneasiness. I kept right on looking steadily meadow-ward, as if green fields and winding streams were much more engrossing to me than the presence of a mere stranger. I enjoyed the game I was playing as innocently, upon my word, as I would any contest of endurance. And it was in the same spirit that I took the next dare that was offered me.

I do not know how long it was that Breckenridge Sewall continued to gaze at me, how long I sat undisturbed beneath the fire of his eyes. At any rate it was he who broke the tension first. He leaned forward and drew from his waistcoat pocket a gold cigarette case.

"Do you object?" he asked.

"Certainly not," I replied, with a tiny shrug. And then abruptly, just as he was to return the case to his pocket, he leaned forward again.

"I beg your pardon—won't *you*?" And he offered *me* the cigarettes, his eyes narrowed upon me.

It was not the custom for young girls of my age to smoke cigarettes. It was not considered good form for a débutante to do anything of that sort. I had so far refused all cocktails and wines at dinners. However, I knew how to manage a cigarette. As a lark at boarding-school I had consumed a quarter of an inch of as many as a half-dozen cigarettes. In some amateur theatricals the winter before, in which I took the part of a young man, I had bravely smoked through half of one, and made my speeches too. What this man had said of Hilton and its provincialism was in my mind now. I meant no wickedness, no harm. I took one of the proffered cigarettes with the grand indifference of having done it many times before. Mr. Sewall watched me closely, and when he produced a match, lit it, and stretched it out toward me in the hollow of his hand. I leaned forward and simply played over again my well-learned act of the winter before. Instead of the clapping of many hands and a curtain-call, which had pleased me very much last winter, my applause today came in a less noisy way, but was quite as satisfying.

"Look here," softly exclaimed Breckenridge Sewall. "Say, who are you, anyway?"

Of course I wasn't stupid enough to tell him, and when I saw that he was on the verge of announcing his identity, I exclaimed:

"Oh, don't, please. I'd much rather not know."

"Oh, you don't know then?"

"Are you Mr. Jackson?" I essayed innocently.

"No, I'm not Buck Jackson, but he's a pal of mine. I'm—"

"Oh, please," I exclaimed again. "Don't spoil it!"

"Spoil it!" he repeated a little dazed. "Say, will you talk English?"

"I mean," I explained, carelessly tossing away now into the grass the nasty little thing that was making my throat smart, "I mean, don't spoil my adventure. Life has so few. To walk down a little path for the purpose of looking at a view, and instead to run across a stranger who may be anything from a bandit to an Italian Count is so–so romantic."

"Romantic!" he repeated. He wasn't a bit good at repartee. "Who are you, anyway?"

"Why, I'm any one from a peasant to an heiress."

"You're a darned attractive girl, anyhow!" he ejaculated, and as lacking in subtlety as this speech was, I prized it as sign of my adversary's surrender.

Five minutes later Mr. Sewall suggested that we walk back together to the people gathered on the lawn. But I had no intention of appearing in public with a celebrated person like Breckenridge Sewall, without having first been properly introduced. Besides, my over-eager sister-in-law would be sure to pounce upon us. I remembered my scarf. I had left it by my empty cup on the cedar table. It seemed quite natural for me to suggest to this stranger that before rejoining the party I would appreciate my wrap. It had grown a little chilly. He willingly went to get it. When he returned he discovered that the owner of the bit of lavender silk that he carried in his hand had mysteriously disappeared. Thick, close-growing vines and bushes surrounded the bench, bound in on both sides the shaded path. Through a network of thorns and tangled branches, somehow the owner of that scarf had managed to break her way. The very moment that Mr. Sewall stood blankly surveying the empty bench, she, hidden by a row of young firs, was eagerly skirting the west wall of her hostess's estate.

Episode of a Small Dog

DURING the following week Miss Vars often caught a fleeting glimpse of Mr. Sewall on his way in or out of town. She heard that he attended a Country Club dance the following Saturday night, at which she chanced not to be present. She was told he had actually partaken of refreshment in the dining-room of the Country Club and had allowed himself to be introduced to several of her friends.

It was very assuming of this modest young girl, was it not, to imagine that Mr. Sewall's activities had anything to do with her? It was rather audacious of her to don a smart lavender linen suit one afternoon and stroll out toward the Country Club. Her little dog Dandy might just as well have exercised in the opposite direction, and his mistress avoided certain dangerous possibilities. But fate was on her side. She didn't think so at first when, in the course of his constitutional, Dandy suddenly bristled and growled at a terrier twice his weight and size, and then with a pull and a dash fell to in a mighty encounter, rolling over and over in the dirt and dust. Afterward, with the yelping terrier disappearing down the road, Dandy held up a bleeding paw to his mistress. She didn't have the heart to scold the triumphant little warrior. Besides he was sadly injured. She tied her handkerchief about the paw, gathered the dog up in her arms, turned her back on the Country Club a quarter of a mile further on, and started home. It was just then that a gray, low, deep-purring automobile appeared out of a cloud of dust in the distance. As it approached it slowed down and came to a full stop three feet in front of her. She looked up. The occupant of the car was smiling broadly.

"Well!" he ejaculated. "At last! Where did you drop from?"

"How do you do," she replied loftily.

"Where did you drop from?" he repeated. "I've been hanging around for a week, looking for you."

"For *me*?" She was surprised. "Why, what for?"

"Say," he broke out. "That was a mean trick you played. I was mad clean through at first. What did you run off that way for? What was the game?"

"Previous engagement," she replied primly.

"Previous engagement! Well, you haven't any previous engagement now, have you? Because, if you have, get in, and I'll waft you to it."

"Oh, I wouldn't think of it!" she said. He opened the door to the car and sprang out beside her.

"Come, get in," he urged. "I'll take you anywhere you're going. I'd be delighted."

"Why," she exclaimed, "we haven't been introduced. How do I know who you are?" She was a well brought-up young person, you see.

"I'll tell you who I am fast enough. Glad to. Get in, and we will run up to the Club and get introduced, if that's what you want."

"Oh, it isn't!" she assured him. "I just prefer to walk—that's all. Thank you very much."

"Well, walk then. But you don't give me the slip this time, young lady. Savvy that? Walk, and I'll come along behind on low speed."

She contemplated the situation for a moment, looking away across fields and green pastures. Then she glanced down at Dandy. Her name in full appeared staring at her from the nickel plate of the dog's collar. She smiled.

"I'll tell you what you can do," she said brightly. "I'd be so grateful! My little dog has had an accident, you see, and if you would be so kind—I hate to ask so much of a stranger—it seems a great deal—but if you would leave him at the veterinary's, Dr. Jenkins, just behind the Court House! He's so heavy! I'd be awfully grateful."

"No, you don't," replied Mr. Sewall. "No more of those scarf games on me! Sorry. But I'm not so easy as all that!"

The girl shifted her dog to her other arm.

"He weighs fifteen pounds," she remarked. And then abruptly for no apparent reason Mr. Sewall inquired:

"Is it yours? Your own? The dog, I mean?"

"My own?" she repeated. "Why do you ask?" Innocence was stamped upon her. For nothing in the world would she have glanced down upon the collar.

"Oh, nothing—nice little rat, that's all. And I'm game. Stuff him in, if you want. I'll deliver him to your vet."

"You will? Really? Why, how kind you are! I do appreciate it. You mean it?"

"Of course I do. Stuff him in. Delighted to be of any little service. Come on, Towzer. Make it clear to your little pet, pray, before starting that I'm no abductor. Good-by—and say," he added, as the car began to purr, "Say, please remember you aren't the only clever little guy in the world, Miss Who-ever-you-are!"

"Why, what do you mean?" She looked abused.

"That's all right. Good-by." And off he sped down the road.

Miss "Who-ever-you-are" walked the three miles home slowly, smiling almost all the way. When she arrived, there was a huge box of flowers waiting on the hall-table directed to:

"Miss Ruth Chenery Vars
The Homestead, Hilton, Mass.
License No. 668."

Inside were two dozen American Beauty roses. Tied to the stem of one was an envelope, and inside the envelope was a card which bore the name of Breckenridge Sewall.

*

"So *that's* who he is!" Miss Vars said out loud.

I saw a great deal of the young millionaire during the remainder of the summer. Hardly a day passed but that I heard the approaching purr of his car. And never a week but that flowers and candy, and more flowers and candy, filled the rejoicing Homestead.

I was a canny young person. I allowed Mr. Sewall very little of my time in private. I refused to go off alone with him anywhere, and the result was that he was forced to attend teas and social functions if he wanted to indulge in his latest fancy. The affair, carried on as it was before the eyes of the whole community, soon became the main topic of conversation. I felt myself being pointed out everywhere I went as the girl distinguished by the young millionaire, Breckenridge Sewall. My friends regarded me with wonder.

Before a month had passed a paragraph appeared in a certain periodical in regard to the exciting affair. I burst into flattering notoriety. What had before been slow and difficult sailing for Edith and me now became as swift and easy as if we had added an auxiliary engine to our little boat. We found ourselves receiving invitations from hostesses who before had been impregnable. Extended hands greeted us—kindness, cordiality.

Finally the proud day arrived when I was invited to Grassmere as a guest. One afternoon Breck came rushing in upon me and eagerly explained that his mother sent her apologies, and would I be good enough to fill in a vacancy at a week-end house-party. Of course I would! Proudly I rode away beside Breck in his automobile, out of the gates of the Homestead along the state road a mile or two, and swiftly swerved inside the fifty thousand dollar wrought-iron fence around the cherished grounds of Grassmere. My trunks followed, and Edith's hopes followed too!

It was an exciting three days. I had never spent a night in quite such splendid surroundings; I had never mingled with quite such smart and fashionable people. It was like a play to me. I hoped I would not forget my lines, fail to observe cues, or perform the necessary business awkwardly. I wanted to do credit to my host. And

I believe I did. Within two hours I felt at ease in the grand and luxurious house. The men were older, the women more experienced, but I wasn't uncomfortable. As I wandered through the beautiful rooms, conversed with what to me stood for American aristocracy, basked in the hourly attention of butlers and French maids, it occurred to me that I was peculiarly fitted for such a life as this. It became me. It didn't seem as if I could be the little girl who not so very long ago lived in the old French-roofed house with the cracked walls, stained ceilings and worn Brussels carpets, at 240 Main Street, Hilton, Mass. But the day Breck asked me to marry him I discovered I was that girl, with the same untainted ideal of marriage, too, hidden away safe and sound under my play-acting.

"Why, Breck!" I exclaimed. "Don't be absurd. I wouldn't *marry* you for anything in the world."

And I wouldn't! My marriage was dim and indistinct to me then. I had placed it in a very faraway future. My ideal of love was such, that beside it all my friends' love affairs and many of those in fiction seemed commonplace and mediocre. I prized highly the distinction of Breckenridge Sewall's attentions, but marry him—of course I wouldn't!

Breck's attentions continued spasmodically for over two years. It took some skill to be seen with him frequently, to accept just the right portion of his tokens of regard, to keep him interested, and yet remain absolutely free and uninvolved. I couldn't manage it indefinitely; the time would come when all the finesse in the world would avail nothing. And come it did in the middle of the third summer.

Breck refused to be cool and temperate that third summer. He insisted on all sorts of extravagances. He allowed me to monopolize him to the exclusion of every one else. He wouldn't be civil even to his mother's guests at Grassmere. He deserted them night after night for Edith's sunken garden, and me, though I begged him to be reasonable, urging him to stay away. I didn't blame his mother, midsummer though it was, for closing Grassmere, barring the windows, locking the gates and abruptly packing off with her son to an old English estate of theirs near London. I only hoped Mrs. Sewall didn't think me heartless. I had always been perfectly honest with Breck. I had always, from the first, said I couldn't marry him.

Not until I was convinced that the end must come between Breck and me, did I tell the family that he had ever proposed marriage. There exists, I believe, some sort of unwritten law that once a man proposes and a girl refuses, attentions should cease. I came in on Sunday afternoon from an automobile ride with Breck just before he sailed for England and dramatically announced his proposal to the family—just as if he hadn't been urging the same thing ever since I knew him.

I expected Edith would be displeased when she learned that I wasn't going to marry Breck, so I didn't tell her my decision immediately. I dreaded to undertake to explain to her what a slaughter to my ideals such a marriage would be. Oh, I was young then, you see, young and hopeful. Everything was ahead of me. There was a splendid chance for happiness.

"I can't marry Breck Sewall, Edith," I attempted at last. "I can't marry any one—yet."

"And what do you intend to do with yourself?" she inquired in that cold, unsympathetic way she assumes when she is angry.

"I don't know, yet. There's a chance for all sorts of good things to come true," I replied lightly.

"You've been out three years, you know," she reminded me icily.

The Sewalls occupied their English estate for several seasons. Grassmere remained closed and barred. I did not see my young millionaire again until I was an older girl, and my ideals had undergone extensive alterations.

A Back-Season Débutante

DÉBUTANTES are a good deal like first novels—advertised and introduced at a great expenditure of money and effort, and presented to the public with fear and trembling. But the greatest likeness comes later. The best-sellers of one spring must be put up on the high shelves to make room for new merchandise the next. At the end of several years the once besought and discussed book can be found by the dozens on bargain counters in department stores, marked down to fifty cents a copy.

The first best-seller I happened to observe in this ignominious position was a novel that came out the same fall that I did. It was six years old to the world, and so was I. I stopped a moment at the counter and opened the book. It had been strikingly popular, with scores of reviews and press notices, and hundreds of admirers. It had made a pretty little pile of money for its exploiters. Perhaps, too, it had won a few friends. But its day of intoxicating popularity had passed. And so had mine. And so must every débutante's. By the fourth or fifth season, cards for occasional luncheons and invitations to fill in vacancies at married people's dinner parties must take the place of those feverish all-night balls, preceded by brilliantly lighted tables-full of débutantes, as excited as yourself, with a lot of gay young lords for partners and all the older people looking on, admiring and taking mental notes. Such excitement was all over with me by the time I was twenty-two. I had been a success, too, I suppose. Any girl whom Breckenridge Sewall had launched couldn't help being a success.

During the two or three years that Breck was in Europe I passed through the usual routine of back-season débutantes. They always resort to travel sooner or later; visit boarding-school friends one winter; California, Bermuda or Europe the next; eagerly patronize winter resorts; and fill in various spaces acting as bridesmaids. When they have the chance they take part in pageants and amateur theatricals, periodically devote themselves to some fashionable charity or other, read novels, and attend current event courses if very desperate.

I used to think when I was fifteen that I should like to be an author, more specifically, a poet. I used to write verses that were often read out loud in my English course at the Hilton High School. And I designed book plates, too, and modeled a little in clay. The more important business of establishing ourselves socially interrupted all that sort of thing, however. But I often wish I might have specialized in some line of art. Perhaps now when I have so much time on my hands it would prove my staunchest friend. For a girl who has no established income it might result in an enjoyable means of support.

I have an established income, you see. Father kindly left me a little stock in some mines out West, stock or bonds—I'm not very clear on business terms. Anyhow I have an income of about eight hundred dollars a year, paid over to me by my brother Tom, who has my affairs in charge. It isn't sufficient for me to live on at present, of course. What with the traveling, clothes—one thing and another—Edith has had to help out with generous Christmas and birthday gifts. This she does lavishly. She's enormously rich herself, and very generous. My last Christmas present from her was a set of furs and a luxurious coon-skin motor coat. Perhaps I wouldn't feel quite so hopeless if my father and mother were living, and I felt that my idleness in some way was making them happy. But I haven't such an excuse. I am not necessary to the happiness of any household. I am what is known as a fifth wheel—a useless piece of paraphernalia carried along as necessary impedimenta on other people's journeys.

There are lots of fifth wheels in the world. Some are old and rusty and out of repair, and down in their inmost hubs they long to roll off into the gutter and lie there quiet and undisturbed. These are the old people—silver-haired, self-effacing—who go upstairs to bed early when guests are invited for dinner. Some are emergency fifth wheels, such as are carried on automobiles, always ready to take their place on the road, if one of the regular wheels breaks down and needs to be sent away for repairs. These are the middle-aged, unmarried aunts and cousins—staunch, reliable—who are sent for to take care of the children while mother runs over to Europe for a holiday. And some are fifth wheels like myself—neither old nor self-effacing, neither middle-aged nor useful, but simply expensive to keep painted, and very hungry for the road. It may be only a matter of time, however, when I shall be middle-aged and useful, and later old and self-effacing; when I shall stay and take care of the children, and go upstairs early when the young people are having a party.

A young technical college graduate told me once, to comfort me, I suppose, that a fifth wheel is considered by a carriage-maker a very important part of a wagon. He tried to explain to me just what part of a wagon it was. You can't see it. It's underneath somewhere, and has to be kept well oiled. I am not very mechanical, but it sounded ignominious to me. I told that young man that I wanted to be one of the four wheels that held the coach up and made it speed, not tucked out of sight, smothered in carriage-grease.

It came as a shock to me when I first realized my superfluous position in this world. The result of that shock was what led me to abandon my ideals on love in an attempt to avoid the possibility of going upstairs early and having dinners off a tray.

When my brother Alec married Edith Campbell, and Edith came over to our house and remodeled it, I didn't feel supplanted. There was a room built especially for me with a little bath-room of its own, a big closet, a window-box filled with flowers in the summer, and cretonne hangings that I picked out myself. My sister Lucy had a room too—for she wasn't married then—and the entire attic was finished up as barracks for my brothers, the twins, who were in college at the time. They were invited to bring home all the friends they wanted to. Edith was a big-hearted sister-in-law. To me her coming was like the advent of a fairy godmother. I had chafed terribly under the economies of my earlier years. It wasn't until Alec married Edith that fortune began to smile.

One by one the family left the Homestead—Lucy, when she married Dr. William Maynard and went away to live near the university with which Will was connected, and Oliver and Malcolm when they graduated from college and went into business. I alone was left living with Alec and Edith. I was so busy coming-out and making a social success of myself that it never occurred to me but that I was as important a member in that household as Edith herself. I wasn't far from wrong either. When I was a débutante and admired by Breckenridge Sewall, I was petted and pampered and kept in sight. When I became a back-season number of some four or five years' staleness, any old north room would do for me!

I used to dread Hilton in the winter, with nothing more exciting going on than a few horrible thimble parties with girls who were beginning to discuss how to keep thin, the importance of custom-made corsets, and various other topics of advancing years. I soon acquired the habit of interrupting these long seasons. I was frequently absent two months at a time, visiting boarding-school friends, running out to California, up to Alaska, or down to Mexico with some girl friend or other, with her mother or aunt for a chaperon. Traveling is pleasant enough, but everybody likes to feel a tie pulling gently at his heartstrings when he steps up to a hotel register to write down the name of that little haven that means home. It is like one of those toy return-balls. If the ball is attached by an elastic string to some little girl's middle finger how joyfully it springs forth from her hand, how eagerly returns again! When suddenly on one of its trips the elastic snaps, the ball becomes lifeless and rolls listlessly away in the gutter. When my home ties broke, I, too, abandoned myself.

I had been on a visiting-trip made up of two-week stands in various cities between Massachusetts and the Great Lakes, whither I had set out to visit my oldest brother, Tom, and his wife, Elise, who live on the edge of one of the Lakes in Wisconsin. I had been gone about six weeks and had planned not to return to Hilton until the arrival of Hilton's real society in May.

When I reached Henrietta Morgan's, just outside New York, on the return trip, I fully expected to remain with her for two weeks and stop off another week with the Harts in New Haven. But after about three days at Henrietta's, I suddenly decided I couldn't stand it any longer. My clothes all needed pressing—they had a peculiar trunky odor—even the tissue paper which I used in such abundance in my old-fashioned tray trunk had lost its life and crispness; I had gotten down to my last clean pair of long white gloves; everything I owned needed some sort of attention—I simply must go home!

I woke up possessed with the idea, and after putting on my last really respectable waist and inquiring of myself in the mirror how in the world I expected to visit Henrietta Morgan with such a dreary trunkful of travel-worn articles, anyhow, I went down to the breakfast table with my mind made up.

Henrietta left me after breakfast for a hurried trip to town. I didn't go with her. I had waked up with a kind of cottony feeling in my throat, and as hot coffee and toast didn't seem to help it, I made an examination with a hand-mirror after breakfast. I discovered three white spots! I wasn't alarmed. They never mean anything serious with me, and they offered an excellent excuse for my sudden departure. It didn't come to my mind that the white spots might have been the cause of my sudden longing for my own little pink room. I simply knew I wanted to go home; and wake up in the morning cross and disagreeable; and grumble about the bacon and coffee at the breakfast table if I wanted to.

While Henrietta and her mother were out in the morning, I clinched my decision by engaging a section on the night train and telegraphing Edith. Although I was convinced that my departure wouldn't seriously upset any of the small informal affairs so far planned for my entertainment, I was acquainted with Mrs. Morgan's tenacious form of hospitality. By the time she returned my packing was finished, and I was lying down underneath a down comforter on the couch. I told Mrs. Morgan about the white spots and my decision to return home.

She would scarcely hear me through. She announced emphatically that she wouldn't think of allowing me to travel if I was ill. I was to undress immediately, crawl in between the sheets, and she would call a doctor. I wasn't rude to Mrs. Morgan, simply firm—that was all—quite as persistent in my resolve as she in hers.

When finally she became convinced that nothing under heaven could dissuade me, she flushed slightly and said icily, "Oh, very well, very well. If that is the way you feel about it, very well, my dear," and sailed out of the room, hurt. Even Henrietta, though very solicitous, shared her mother's indignation, and I longed for the comfort and relief of the Pullman, the friendly porters, and my own understanding people at the other end.

So, you see, when in the middle of the afternoon I was summoned to the telephone to receive a telegram from Hilton, I wasn't prepared for the slap in the face that Edith's message was to me.

"Sorry," it was repeated. "Can't conveniently have you until next week. House packed with company. Better stay with the Morgans." Signed, "Edith."

The Unimportant Fifth Wheel

BETTER stay with the Morgans! Who was I to be bandied about in such fashion? Couldn't have me! I wasn't a seamstress who went out by the day. House packed with company! Well—what of that? Hadn't I more right there? Wasn't I Alec's own sister? Wasn't I born under the very roof to which I was now asked not to come? Weren't all my things there—my bed, my bureau, my little old white enameled desk I used when I was a child? Where was I to go, I'd like to ask? Couldn't have me! Very well, then, I wouldn't go!

I called up my brother Malcolm's office in New York. Perhaps he would be kind enough to engage a room in a hospital somewhere, or at least find a bed in a public ward. "Sorry, Miss Vars," came the answer finally to me over the long distance wire, "but Mr. Vars has gone up to Hilton, Massachusetts, for the week-end. Not returning until Monday."

I sat dumbly gazing into the receiver. Where could I go? Lucy, I was sure, would squeeze me in somewhere if I applied to her—she always can—but a letter received from Lucy two days before had contained a glowing description of some celebrated doctor of science and his wife, who were to be her guests during this very week. She has but one guest room. I couldn't turn around and go back to Wisconsin. I couldn't go to Oliver, now married to Madge. They live in a tiny apartment outside Boston. There is nothing for me to sleep on except a lumpy couch in the living-room. Besides there is a baby, and to carry germs into any household with a baby in it is nothing less than criminal.

Never before had I felt so ignominious as when, half an hour later, I meekly passed my telegram to Mrs. Morgan and asked if it would be terribly inconvenient if I did stay after all.

"Not at all. Of course not," she replied coldly. "I shall not turn you out into the street, my dear. But you stated your wish to go so decidedly that I have telephoned Henrietta's friends in Orange to come over to take your place. We had not told you that tickets for the theater tonight and matinée tomorrow had already been bought. The friends are coming this evening. So I shall be obliged to ask you to move your things into the sewing-room."

I moved them. A mean little room it was on the north side of the house. Piles of clothes to be mended, laundry to be put away, a mop and a carpet sweeper greeted me as I went in. The floor was untidy with scraps of cloth pushed into a corner behind the sewing machine. The mantel was decorated with spools of thread, cards of hooks and eyes, and a pin-cushion with threaded needles stuck in it. The bed was uncomfortable. I crawled into it, and lay very still. My heart was filled with bitterness. My eyes rested on the skeleton of a dressmaker's form. A man's shirt ripped up the back hung over a chair. I staid for three days in that room! Mrs. Morgan's family physician called the first night, and announced to Mrs. Morgan that probably I was coming down with a slight attack of tonsilitis. I thought at least it was diphtheria or double pneumonia. There were pains in my back. When I tried to look at the dressmaker's skeleton it jiggled uncomfortably before my eyes.

I didn't see the new guests once. Even Henrietta was allowed to speak to me only from across the hall.

"Tonsilitis *is* catching, you know, my dear," Mrs. Morgan sweetly purred from heights above me, "and I'd never forgive myself if the other two girls caught anything here. I've forbidden Henrietta to see you. She's so susceptible to germs." I felt I was an unholy creature, teeming with microbes.

The room was warm; they fed me; they cared for me; but I begged the doctor for an early deliverance on Monday morning. I longed for home. I cried for it a little. Edith couldn't have known that I was ill; she would have opened her arms wide if she had guessed—of course she would. I ought to have gone in the beginning. I poured out my story into that old doctor's understanding ears, and he opened the way for me finally. He let me escape. Very weak and wobbly I took an early train on Monday morning for Hilton. At the same time I sent the following telegram to my sister-in-law: "Arrive Hilton 6:15 tonight. Have been ill. Still some fever, but doctor finally consents to let me come."

Six fearful hours later I found myself, weak-kneed and trembling, on the old home station platform. I was on the verge of tears. I looked up and down for Edith's anxious face, or for Alec's—they would be disturbed when they heard I had a fever, they might be alarmed—but I couldn't find them. The motor was not at the curb either. I stepped into a telephone-booth and called the house. Edith answered herself. I recognized her quick staccato "Hello."

I replied, "Hello, that you, Edith?"

"Yes. Who is this?" she called.

"Ruth," I answered feebly.

"Ruth! Where in the world are you?" she answered.

"Oh, I'm all right. I'm down here at the station. Just arrived. I'm perfectly all right," I assured her.

"Well, well," she exclaimed. "That's fine. Awfully glad you're back! I do wish I could send the limousine down for you, Ruth. But I just can't. We're going out to dinner—to the Mortimers, and we've just *got* to have it. I'm awfully sorry, but do you mind taking the car, or a carriage? I'm right in the midst of dressing. I've got to hurry like mad. It's almost half-past six now. Jump into a taxi, and we can have a nice little chat before I have to go. Got lots to tell you. It's fine you're back. Good-by. Don't mind if I hurry now, do you?"

I arrived at the house ten minutes later in a hired taxicab. I rang the bell, and after a long wait a maid I had never seen before let me in. Edith resplendent in a brand new bright green satin gown was just coming down the stairs. She had on all her diamonds.

"Hello, Toots," she said. "Did you get homesick, dearie? Welcome. Wish I could kiss you, Honey, but I can't. I've just finished my lips. Why didn't you telegraph, Rascal? It's a shame not to have you met."

"I did," I began.

"Oh, well, our telephone has been out of order all day. It makes me tired the way they persist in telephoning telegrams. We do get the worst service! I had no idea you were coming. Why, I sent off a perfect bunch of mail to you this very morning. You weren't peeved, were you, Toots, about my telegram, I mean? I was right in the midst of the most important house-party I've ever had. As it was I had too many girls, and at the last minute had to telegraph Malcolm to come and help me out. And he did, the lamb! The house-party was a screaming success. I'm going to have a regular series of them all summer. How do you like my gown? Eighty-five, my dear, marked down from a hundred and fifty."

"Stunning," I replied, mingled emotions in my heart.

"There!" exclaimed Edith abruptly. "There's your telegram now. Did you ever? Getting here at this hour!"

A telegraph boy was coming up the steps. I was fortunately near the door, and I opened it before he rang, received my needless message myself, and tore open the envelope.

"You're right," I said. "It is my telegram. It just said I was coming. That's all. It didn't matter much. Guess I'll go up to my room now, if you don't mind."

"Do, dear. Do," said Edith, "and I'll come along too. I want to show you something, anyhow. I've picked up the stunningest high-boy you ever saw in your life. A real old one, worth two hundred and fifty, but I got it for a hundred. I've put it right outside your room, and very carefully—oh, *most* carefully—with my own hands, Honey, I just laid your things in it. I simply couldn't have the bureau drawers in that room filled up, you know, with all the house-parties I'm having, and you not here half the time. I knew *you* wouldn't mind, and the high-boy is so stunning!" We had gone upstairs and were approaching it now. "I put all your underclothes in those long shallow drawers; and your ribbons and gloves and things in these deep, low ones. And then up here in the top I've laid carefully all the truck you had stowed away in that little old white enameled desk of yours. The desk I put up in the store-room. It wasn't decent for guests. I've bought a new one to take its place. I do hope you'll like it. It's a spinet desk, and stunning. Oh, dear—there it is now ten minutes of seven, and I've simply got to go. I promised to pick up Alec at the Club on the way. I don't believe I've told you I've had your room redecorated. I wish I could wait and see if you're pleased. But I can't—simply can't! You understand, don't you, dear? But make yourself comfy."

She kissed me then very lightly on the cheek, and turned and tripped away downstairs. When I caught the purr of the vanishing limousine as it sped away down the winding drive, I opened the door of my room. It was very pretty, very elegant, as perfectly appointed as any hotel room I had ever gazed upon, but mine no more. This one little sacred precinct had been entered in my absence and robbed of every vestige of me. Instead of my single four-poster were two mahogany sleigh beds, spread with expensively embroidered linen. Instead of my magazine cut of Robert Louis Stevenson pinned beside the east window was a signed etching. Instead of my own familiar desk welcoming me with bulging packets of old letters, waiting for some rainy morning to be read and sentimentally destroyed, appeared the spinet desk, furnished with brand new blotters, chaste pens, and a fresh book of two-cent stamps. All but my mere flesh and bones had been conveniently stuffed into a two-hundred and fifty dollar high-boy!

I could have burst into tears if I had dared to fling myself down upon the embroidered spreads. And then suddenly from below I heard the scramble of four little feet on the hardwood floor, the eager, anxious pant of a wheezy little dog hurrying up the stairs. It was Dandy—my Boston terrier. Somehow, down behind the kitchen stove he had sensed me, and his little dog heart was bursting with welcome. Only Dandy had really missed me, sitting long, patient hours at a time at the living-room window, watching for me to come up the drive; and finally starting out on mysterious night searches of his own, as he always does when days pass and I do not return. I heard the thud of his soft body as he slipped and fell, in his haste, on the slippery hall floor. And then a moment later he was upon me—paws and tongue and half-human little yelps and cries pouring out their eloquence.

I held the wriggling, ecstatic little body close to me, and wondered what it would be like if some human being was as glad to see me as Dandy.

Breck Sewall Again

AS I stood there in my devastated room, hugging to me a little scrap of a dog, a desire to conceal my present poverty swept over me, just as I had always wanted to hide the tell-tale economies of our household years ago from my more affluent friends. I did not want pity. I was Ruth, of whom my family had predicted great things—vague great things, I confess. Never had I been quite certain what they were to be—but something rather splendid anyhow.

We become what those nearest to us make us. The family made out of my oldest brother Tom counselor and wise judge; out of my sister Lucy chief cook and general-manager; out of me butterfly and ornament. In the eyes of the family I have always been frivolous and worldly, and though they criticize these qualities of mine, underneath their righteous veneer I discover them marveling. They disparage my extravagance in dressing, and then admire my frocks. In one breath they ridicule social ambition, and in the next inquire into my encounters and triumphs. A desire to remain in my old position I offer now as the least contemptible excuse of any that I can think of for the following events of my life. I didn't want to resign my place like an actress who can no longer take ingénue parts because of wrinkles and gray hairs. When I came home that day and discovered how unimportant I was, how weak had become my applause, instead of trying to play a new part by making myself useful and necessary—helping with the housework, putting away laundry, mending, and so on—I went about concocting ways and methods of filling more dazzlingly my old rôle.

Although my fever had practically disappeared by the time I went to bed that night, I lolled down to the breakfast table the next morning later than ever, making an impression in a shell-pink tea-gown; luxuriously dawdled over a late egg and coffee; and then lazily borrowed a maid about eleven o'clock and allowed her to unpack for me. Meanwhile I lay back on the couch, criticized to Edith the tone of gray of the paper in my room, carelessly suggested that there were too many articles on the shelf from an artistic point of view, and then suffered myself to be consulted on an invitation list for a party Edith was planning to give. The description of my past two months' gaieties, recited in rather a bored and blasé manner, lacked none of the usual color. My references to attentions from various would-be suitors proved to Edith and Alec that I was keeping up my record.

One Saturday afternoon not long after my return to Hilton, Edith and I attended a tea at the Country Club. The terrace, open to the sky and covered with a dozen small round tables, made a pretty sight—girls in light-colored gowns and flowery hats predominating early in the afternoon, but gradually, from mysterious regions of lockers and shower-baths below, joined by men in white flannels and tennis-shoes.

Edith's and my table was popular that day. I had been away from Hilton for so long that a lot of our friends gathered about us to welcome me home. I was chatting away to a half dozen of them, when I saw two men strolling up from the seventeenth green. One of the men was Breckenridge Sewall. I glanced over the rim of my cup the second time to make certain. Yes, it was Breck—the same old blasé, dissipated-looking Breck. I had thought he was still in Europe. To reach the eighteenth tee the men had to pass within ten feet of the terrace. My back would be toward them. I didn't know if a second opportunity would be offered me. Grassmere, the Sewall estate, was not open this year. Breck might be gone by the next day. I happened at the time to be talking about a certain tennis tournament with a man who had been an eye-witness. I rose and put down my cup of tea.

"Come over and tell me about it, please," I said, smiling upon him. "I've finished. Take my chair, Phyllis," I added sweetly to a young girl standing near. "Do, dear. Mr. Call and I are going to decorate the balustrade."

I selected a prominent position beside a huge earthen pot of flowering geraniums. It was a low balustrade with a flat top, designed to sit upon. I leaned back against the earthen jar and proceeded to appear engrossed in tennis. Really, though, I was wondering if Breck would see me after all, and what I should say if he did.

What I did say was conventional enough—simply, "Why, how do you do," to his eager, "Hello, Miss Vars!" while I shook hands with him as he stood beneath me on the ground.

"Saw you on Fifth Avenue a week ago," he went on, "hiking for some place in a taxi. Lost you in the crowd at Forty-second. Thought you might be rounding up here before long. So decided I'd run up and say howdy. Look here, wait for me, will you? I've got only one hole more to play. Do. Wait for me. I'll see that you get home all right."

Edith returned alone in the automobile that afternoon.

"I'll come along later," I explained mysteriously.

She hadn't seen Breck, thank heaven! She would have been sure to have blundered into a dinner invitation, or some such form of effusion. But she surmised that something unusual was in the air, and was watching for me from behind lace curtains in the living-room when I returned two hours later. She saw a foreign-made car whirl into the drive and stop at the door. She saw me get out of it and run up the front steps. The features of the man behind the big mahogany steering-wheel could be discerned easily. When I opened the front door my sister-in-law was in the vestibule. She grasped me by both my arms just above my elbows.

"Breck Sewall!" she ejaculated. "My dear! Breck Sewall again!"

The ecstasy of her voice, the enthusiasm of those hands of hers grasping my arms soothed my hurt feelings of a week ago. I was led tenderly—almost worshipfully—upstairs to my room.

"I believe he is as crazy as ever about you," Edith exclaimed, once behind closed doors. "I honestly think"—she stopped abruptly—"What if—" she began again, then excitedly kissed me. "You little wonder!" she said. "There's no one in the whole family to match you. I'll wager you could become a veritable gateway for us all to pass into New York society if you wanted to. You're a marvel—you are! Tell me about it." Her eyes sparkled as she gazed upon me. I realized in a flash just what the splendid thing was that I might do. Of course! How simple! I might marry Breck!

"Well," I said languidly, gazing at my reflection in the mirror and replacing a stray lock, "I suppose I'd rather be a gateway than a fifth wheel."

The next time that Breck asked me to marry him, I didn't call him absurd. I was older now. I must put away my dolls and air-castles. The time had come, it appeared, for me to assume a woman's burdens, among which often is an expedient marriage. I could no longer offer my tender years as an excuse for side-stepping a big opportunity. I musn't falter. The moment had arrived. I accepted Breck, and down underneath a pile of stockings in the back of my lowest bureau drawer I hid a little velvet-lined jewel-box, inside of which there lay an enormous diamond solitaire—promise of my brilliant return to the footlights.

The Millions Win

SOME people cannot understand how a girl can marry a man she doesn't love. She can do it more easily than she can stay at home, watch half her friends marry, and feel herself slowly ossifying into something worthless and unessential. It takes more courage to sit quietly, wait for what may never come, and observe without misgiving the man you might have had making some other woman's life happy and complete.

I couldn't go on living in guest-rooms forever. I was tired of traveling, and sick to death of leading a life that meant nothing to anybody but Dandy. As a débutante I had had a distinct mission—whether worthy or unworthy isn't the point in question—worked for it hard, schemed, devised, and succeeded. As Mrs. Breckenridge Sewall I could again accomplish results. Many women marry simply because they cannot endure an arid and purposeless future.

Some people think that a girl who marries for position is hard and calculating. Why, I entered into my engagement in the exalted mood of a martyr! I didn't feel hard—I felt self-sacrificing, like a girl in royal circles whose marriage may distinguish herself and her people to such an extent that the mere question of her own personal feelings is of small importance. The more I considered marrying Breck the more convinced I became that it was the best thing I could do. With my position placed upon my brow, like a crown on a king, freed at last from all the mean and besmirching tricks of acquiring social distinction, I could grow and expand. When I looked ahead and saw myself one day mistress of Grassmere, the London house, the grand mansion in New York; wise and careful monitor of the Sewall millions; gracious hostess; kind ruler; I felt as nearly religious as ever before in my life. I meant to do good with my wealth and position and influence. Is that hard and calculating?

I accepted Breck's character and morals as a candidate chosen for the honorable office of governor of a state must accept the condition of politics, whether they are clean or rotten. Clean politics are the exception. So also are clean morals. I knew enough for that. Way back in boarding-school days, we girls had resigned ourselves to the acceptance of the deplorable state of the world's morals. We had statistics. I had dimly hoped that one of the exceptions to the rule might fall to my lot, but if not, I wasn't going to be prudish. Breck's early career could neither surprise nor alarm me. I, like most girls in this frank and open age, had been prepared for it. So when Lucy, who is anything but worldly wise, and Will, her husband, who is a scientist and all brains, came bearing frenzied tales of Breck's indiscretions during his one year at the university where Will is now located, I simply smiled. Some people are so terribly naïve and unsophisticated!

The family's attitude toward my engagement was consistent—deeply impressed, but tainted with disapproval. Tom came way on from Wisconsin to tell me how contemptible it was for a girl to marry for position, even for so amazingly a distinguished one. Elise, his wife, penned me a long letter on the emptiness of power and wealth. Malcolm wrote he hoped I knew what I was getting into, and supposed after I became Mrs. Breckenridge Sewall I'd feel too fine to recognize him, should we meet on Fifth Avenue. Oliver was absolutely "flabbergasted" at first, he wrote, but must confess it would save a lot of expense for the family, if they could stop with Brother Breck when they came down to New York. "How'd you pull it off, Toots?" he added. "Hope little Cupid had something to do with it."

Alec waited until Edith had gone to Boston for a day's shopping, and took me for a long automobile ride. Alec, by the way, is one of this world's saints. He has always been the member of the Vars family who has resigned himself to circumstances. It was Tom who went West and made a brilliant future for himself; Alec who remained in Hilton to stand by father's dying business. It was the twins who were helped to graduate from college in spite of difficulties; Alec who cheerfully gave up his diploma to offer a helping hand at home. When Alec married Edith Campbell it appeared that at last he had come into his own. She was immensely wealthy. Father's business took a new lease of life. At last Alec was prosperous, but he had to go on adapting and resigning just the same. With the arrival of the Summer Colony Edith's ambitions burst into life, and of course he couldn't be a drag on her future—and mine—any more than on Tom's or the twins'. He acquiesced; he fitted in without reproach. Today in regard to my engagement he complained but gently.

"We're simple New England people after all," he said. "A girl is usually happier married to a man of her own sort. You weren't born into the kind of life the Sewalls lead. You weren't born into even the kind of life you're leading now. Edith—Edith's fine, of course, and I've always been glad you two were so congenial—but she does exaggerate the importance of the social game. She plays it too hard. I don't want you to marry Sewall. I'm afraid you won't be happy."

When Edith came home that night I asked her if she knew how Alec felt.

"Of course I do. The dear old fogey! But this is the way I look at it, Ruth. Some people *not* born into a high place get there just the same through sheer nerve and determination, and others spend their whole worthless lives at home on the farm.

It isn't what a person is born into, but what he is equal to, that decides his success. Mercy, child, don't let a dear, silly, older brother bother you. Sweet old Al doesn't know what he's talking about. I'd like to know what he *would* advise doing with his little sister, if, after all the talk there is about her and Breck, he could succeed in breaking off her engagement. She'd be just an old glove kicking around. That's what she'd be. Al is simply crazy. I'll have to talk to him!"

"Don't bother," I said, "I'm safe. I have no intention of becoming an old glove."

Possibly in the privacy of my own bed at night, where so often now I lay wide-awake waiting for the dawn, I did experience a few misgivings. But by the time I was ready to go down to breakfast I had usually persuaded myself into sanity again. I used to reiterate all the desirable points about Breck I could think of and calm my fears by dwelling upon the many demands of my nature that he could supply—influence, power, delight in environment, travel, excitement.

When I was a child I was instructed by my drawing-teacher to sketch with my stick of charcoal a vase, a book, and a red rose, which he arranged in a group on a table before me. I had a great deal of difficulty with the rose; so after struggling for about half an hour I got up and, unobserved, put the rose behind the vase, so that only its stem was visible to me. Then I took a fresh page and began again. The result was a very fair portrayal of the articles as they then appeared. So with my ideal of marriage—when I found its arrangement impossible to portray in my life—I simply slipped out of sight that for which the red rose is sometimes the symbol (I mean love) and went ahead sketching in the other things.

I explained all this to Breck one day. I wanted to be honest with him.

"Say, what are you driving at? Red roses! Drawing lessons! What's that got to do with whether you'll run down to Boston for dinner with me tonight? You do talk the greatest lot of stuff! But have it your own way. I'm satisfied. Just jump in beside me! Will you? Darn it! I haven't the patience of a saint!"

The Horse Show

CONVENTIONS may sometimes appear silly and absurd, but most of them are made for practical purposes. Ignore them and you'll discover yourself in difficulty. Leave your spoon in your cup and your arm will unexpectedly hit it sometime, and over will go everything on to the tablecloth. If I had not ignored certain conventions I wouldn't be crying over spilled milk now.

I allowed myself to become engaged to Breck; accepted his ring and hid it in my lowest bureau drawer; told my family my intentions; let the world see me dining, dancing, theater-ing and motoring like mad with Breck and draw its conclusions; and all this, mind you, before I had received a word of any sort whatsoever from my prospective family-in-law. This, as everybody knows, is irregular, and as bad form as leaving your spoon in your cup. No wonder I got into difficulty!

My prospective family-in-law consisted simply of Breck's mother, Mrs. F. Rockridge Sewall—a very elegant and perfectly poised woman she seemed to me the one time I had seen her at close range, as she sat at the head of the sumptuous table in the tapestry-hung dining-room at Grassmere. I admired Mrs. Sewall. I used to think that I could succeed in living up to her grand manners with better success than the other rather hoidenish young ladies who chanced to be the guests at Grassmere the time I was there. Mrs. Sewall is a small woman, always dressed in black, with a superb string of pearls invariably about her neck, and lots of brilliant diamonds on her slender fingers. Breck with his heavy features, black hair brushed straight back, eyes half-closed as if he was always riding in a fifty-mile gale, deep guffaw of a laugh, and inelegant speech does not resemble his mother. It is strange, but the picture that I most enjoyed dwelling upon, when I contemplated my future life, was one of myself creeping up Fifth Avenue on late afternoons in the Sewalls' crested automobile, seated, not beside Breck, but in intimate conversation beside my aristocratic mother-in-law.

As humiliating as it was to me to continue engaged to a man from whose mother there had been made no sign of welcome or approval, I did so because Breck plead that Mrs. Sewall was on the edge of a nervous break-down, and to announce any startling piece of news to her at such a time would be unwise. I was foolish enough to believe him. I deceived myself into thinking that my course was allowable and self-respecting.

Breck used to run up from New York to Hilton in his car for Sunday; and sometimes during the week, in his absurd eagerness, he would dash up to our door and ring the bell as late as eleven o'clock, simply because he had been seized with a desire to bid me good-night.

When Edith and I went to New York for a week's shopping we were simply deluged with attentions from Breck—theater every night, luncheons, dinners and even breakfasts occasionally squeezed in between. All this, I supposed, was carried on without Mrs. Sewall's knowledge. I ought to have known better than to have excused it. It was my fault. I blame myself. Such an unconventional affair deserved to end in catastrophe. But to Edith it ended not in spilled milk, but in a spilled pint of her life's blood.

One night in midsummer when I was just dropping off to sleep, Edith knocked gently on my door, and then opened it and came in. She was all ready for bed with her hair braided down her back.

"Asleep?"

"No," I replied. "What's the matter?"

"Did you know Grassmere was open?"

"Why?" I demanded.

"Because, just as I was fixing the curtain in my room I happened to look up there. It's all lit up, upstairs and down. Even the ball-room. Did you know about it?"

I had to confess that I didn't. Breck had told me that his mother would remain in the rented palace at Newport for the remainder of the season, under the care of a specialist.

"Looks as if they were having a big affair of some sort up there. I guess Mrs. F. Rockridge has recovered from her nervous break-down! Come, get up and see."

"Oh, I'll take your word for it," I replied indifferently. But I won't say what my next act was after Edith had gone out of the room. You may be sure I didn't immediately drop off to sleep.

I looked for one of Breck's ill-penned letters the next morning, but none came. No wire or telephone message either. Not until five o'clock in the afternoon did I receive any explanation of the lights at Grassmere. Edith had been to her bridge club, and came rushing up on the veranda, eager and excited. There were little bright spots in the center of each cheek. Edith's a handsome woman, thirty-five or eight, I think, and very smart in appearance. She has dark brilliant eyes, and a quality in her voice and manner that makes you feel as if there were about eight cylinders and all in perfect order, too, chugging away underneath her shiny exterior.

"Where's the mail?" she asked of me. I was lying on the wicker couch.

"Oh, inside, I guess, on the hall table. I don't know. Why?"

"Wait a minute," she said, and disappeared. She rejoined me an instant later, with two circulars and a printed post-card.

"Is this all there is?" Edith demanded again, and I could see the red spots on her cheeks grow deeper.

"That's all," I assured her. "Expecting something?"

"Have you had any trouble with Breck?" she flashed out at me next.

"What are you driving at, Edith?" I inquired. "What's the matter?"

"Mrs. Sewall is giving a perfectly enormous ball at Grassmere on the twenty-fourth, and we're left out. That's the matter!" She tossed the mail on the table.

"Oh," I said, "our invitations will come in the morning probably. There are often delays."

"No, sir, I know better. The bridge club girls said their invitations came yesterday afternoon. I can't understand it. We certainly were on Mrs. Sewall's list when she gave that buffet-luncheon three years ago. And now we're not! That's the bald truth of it. It was terribly embarrassing this afternoon—all of them telling about what they were going to wear—it's going to be a masquerade—and I sitting there like a dummy! Héléne McClellan broke the news to me. She blurted right out, 'Oh, do tell us, Edith,' she said to me, 'is Mrs. Sewall's ball to announce your sister's engagement to her son? We're crazy to know!' Of course I didn't let on at first that we weren't even invited, but it had to leak out later. Oh, it is simply humiliating!"

"Is she at Grassmere now—Mrs. Sewall, I mean?" I asked quietly.

"Yes, she is. There's a big house-party going on there this very minute. The club girls knew all about it. Mrs. Sewall has got a niece or somebody or other with her, for the rest of the summer, and the ball is being given in her honor. Gale Oliphant, I believe the girl's name is. But look here, it seems very queer to me that *I'm* the one to be giving you this information instead of Breck. What does it all mean anyhow? Come, confess. You must have had a tiff or something with Breck."

"I don't have tiffs, Edith," I said, annoyed.

"Well, you needn't get mad about it. There must be some reason for our being slighted in this fashion. I'm sure *I've* done nothing. It's not my fault. I wouldn't care if it was small, but everybody who isn't absolutely beyond the pale is invited."

"There's no use losing your nerve, Edith," I said in an exasperatingly calm manner.

"Good heavens!" Edith exclaimed. "You seem to enjoy slights, but if I were in your place I shouldn't enjoy slights from my prospective mother-in-law, anyhow!"

"You needn't be insulting," I remarked, arranging a sofa-pillow with care underneath my head and turning my attention to my magazine.

Edith went into the house. The screen door slammed behind her. I didn't stir, just kept right on staring at the printed page before me and turning a leaf now and again, as if I were really reading.

Gale Oliphant! I knew all about her. I had met her first at the house-party at Grassmere—a silly little thing, I had thought her, rather pretty, and a tremendous flirt. Breck had said she was worth a million in her own name. I remembered that, because he explained that he had been rather keen about her before he met me. "That makes my eight hundred dollars a year look rather sickly, doesn't it?" I replied. "Yes," he said, "it sure does! But let me tell you that *you* make *her* look like a last year's straw hat." However, the last year's straw hat possessed some attraction for Breck, because during the three years that Grassmere was closed and the Sewalls were in Europe, Breck and Gale Oliphant saw a lot of each other. Breck told me that she really was better than nothing, and his mater was terribly keen about having her around.

I tried in every way I could to explain away my fears. I mustn't be hasty. Well-mannered thoughts didn't jump to foolish conclusions. Breck would probably explain the situation to me. I must wait with calmness and composure. And I did, all the next day, and the next, and the third, until finally there arrived one of Breck's infrequent scrawls.

The envelope was post-marked Maine. I opened it, and read:

"Dear Ruth:

"I am crazy to see you. It seems like a week of Sundays. The mater got a notion she wanted me to come up to Bar Harbor and bring down the yacht. I brought three fellows with me. Some spree! But we're good little boys. The captain struck. Waiting for another. Won't round up at your place for another week. I'm yours and don't forget it. It seems like a week of Sundays. Mater popped the news she's going to open up old Grassmere pretty soon. Then it will be like a week of holidays for yours truly, if you're at home to sit in that pergola effect with. Savvy? Showed the fellows the snapshots tonight but didn't tell them. Haven't touched a drop for four weeks and three days. Never did that stunt for any queen before. Good-night, you little fish. Don't worry about that though. I'll warm you up O.K. Trust Willie."

I used to feel apologetic for Breck's letters, and tear them up as quickly as possible, before any one could see how crude and ill-spelled they were. But I wasn't troubled about such details in this letter. It brought immense relief. Breck was so natural and so obviously unaware of trouble brewing at home. Surely, I needn't be alarmed. The invitation for the masquerade might have been misdirected or have slipped down behind something. Accidents do take place. Of course it was most unfortunate, but fate performs unfortunate feats sometimes.

In my eagerness to dispel my fears it never crossed my mind that Breck's absence was planned, so that Mrs. Sewall could start her attack without interference. She was a very clever woman, an old and experienced hand at social maneuvers. I am only a beginner. It was an uneven, one-sided fight—for fight it was after all. She won. She bore away the laurels. I bore away simply the tattered remnants of my self-respect.

*

Every year at the Hilton Country Club a local horse show is held in mid-August, and many of the summer colonists—women as well as men—exhibit and take part in the different events.

Edith always has liked horses, and when she married Alec she rebuilt our run-down stable along with the house, and filled the empty old box stalls with two or three valuable thorough-breds. Edith's Arrow, Pierre, and Blue-grass had won some sort of a ribbon for the last half-dozen years. I usually rode Blue-grass for Edith in the jumping event. I was to do so on the afternoon that Breck's letter arrived.

It was a perfect day. The grand-stand with its temporary boxes that always sell at absurdly high prices was filled with the summer society, dressed in its gayest and best. The brass band was striking up gala airs now and again, and the big bell in the tower clanged at intervals. Between events horses were being led to and fro, and in front of the grand-stand important individuals wearing white badges leaned over the sides of the lowest tier of boxes, chatting familiarly with the ladies above. A lot of outsiders, anybody who could pay a dollar admission, wandered at large, staring openly at the boxes, leveling opera-glasses, and telling each other who the celebrities were.

Alec was West on a business trip, but Edith had a box, of course, as she always does. All around us were gathered in their various stalls our friends and acquaintances. It is the custom to visit back and forth from box to box, and the owner of each box is as much a host in his own reservation as in his own reception-room at home. Our box is usually very popular, but this year there was a marked difference. Of course some of our best friends did stop for a minute or two, but those who sat down and stayed long enough to be observed were only men. I was surprised and unpleasantly disturbed.

Mrs. Sewall's box was not far away. We could see her seated prominently in a corner of it, surrounded by a very smart bevy—strangers mostly, New Yorkers I supposed—with Miss Gale Oliphant, strikingly costumed in scarlet, in their midst. A vigilant group of summer colonists hovered near-by, now and again becoming one of the party. Edith and I sat quite alone in our box for an hour fully; I in my severe black habit, with my elbow on the railing, my chin in my hand, steadily gazing at the track; Edith erect, sharp-eyed, and nervously looking about in search of some one desirable to bow to and invite to join us.

Finally she leaned forward and said to me, "Isn't this simply terrible? I can't stand it. Come, let's get out."

"Where to?" I asked. "My event comes very soon."

"Oh, let's go over and see Mrs. Jackson. I'm sick of sitting here stark alone. Come on—the girls are all over there."

I glanced toward the Jackson box and saw a group of our most intimate friends—Edith's bridge club members and several of the girls in my set, too.

"All right," I said, and we got up and strolled along the aisle.

As we approached I observed one of the women nudge another. I saw Héléne McClellan open her mouth to speak and then close it quickly as she caught sight of us. I felt under Mrs. Jackson's over-effusive greeting the effort it was for her to appear easy and cordial. The group must have been talking about the masquerade, for as we joined it there ensued an uncomfortable silence. I would have withdrawn, but Edith pinched my arm and boldly went over and sat down in one of the empty chairs.

We couldn't have been there five minutes when Mrs. Sewall came strolling along the aisle, accompanied by Miss Oliphant. She, who usually held herself so aloof, was very gracious this afternoon, smiling cordially at left and right, and stopping now and again to present her niece. I saw her recognize Mrs. Jackson and then smilingly approach her. We all rose as our hostess got up and beamingly put her hand into Mrs. Sewall's extended one.

"How do you do, Mrs. Jackson," said Mrs. Sewall. "I've been enjoying your lovely boxful of young ladies all the afternoon. Charming, really! Delightful! I hope you are all planning to come to my masquerade," she went on, addressing the whole group now. "I want it to be a success. I am giving it for my little guest here—and my son also," she added with a significant smile, as if to imply that the coupling of Miss Oliphant's and her son's names was not accidental. "Oh, how do you do, Mrs. McClellan!" she interrupted herself, smiling across the group to Héléne who stood next to me, "I haven't caught your eye before today. I hope you're well—and oh, Miss McDowell!" She bowed to Leslie McDowell on my other side.

It was just about at this juncture that I observed Edith threading her way around back of several chairs toward Mrs. Sewall. I wish I could have stopped her, but it was too late. I heard her clear voice suddenly exclaiming from easy speaking distance,

"How do you do, Mrs. Sewall."

"Ah! how do you do!" the lady condescended to reply. There was chilliness in the voice. Edith continued.

"We're so delighted," she went on bravely, "to have Grassmere occupied again. The lights are very pretty on your hilltop from The Homestead, our place, you know."

"Ah, The Homestead!" The chilliness was frosty now. Edith blushed.

"Perhaps you do not recall me, Mrs. Sewall—I am Mrs. Alexander Vars—you know. My sister——"

"Oh, yes—Mrs. Alexander Vars. I recall you quite well, Mrs. Vars. Perfectly, in fact," she said. Then stopped short. There was a terrible silence. It continued like a long-drawn out note on a violin.

"Oh," nervously piped out some one in the group, at last, "look at that lovely horse! I just adore black ones!"

Mrs. Sewall raised her lorgnette and gazed at the track.

"By the way, Mrs. Jackson," she resumed, as if she had not just slaughtered poor Edith. "By the way, can you tell me the participants in the next event? I've left my program. So careless!" she purred. And afterwards she smilingly accepted a proffered armchair in the midst of the scene of her successful encounter.

It would have been thoughtful, I think, and more humane to have waited until the wounded had been carried away—or crawled away. For there was no one to offer a helping hand to Edith and me. I didn't expect it. In social encounters the vanquished must look out for themselves. With what dignity I could, I advanced towards Mrs. Jackson.

"Well, I must trot along," I said lightly. "My turn at the hurdles will be coming soon. Come, Edith, let's go and have a look at Blue-grass. Good-by." And leisurely, although I longed to cast down my eyes and hasten quickly away from the staring faces, I strolled out of the box, followed by Edith; walked without haste along the aisle, even stopping twice to exchange a word or two with friends; and finally escaped.

Catastrophe

THE incident at the horse show was simply the beginning. I couldn't go anywhere—to a tea, to the Country Club, or even down town for a morning's shopping—and feel sure of escaping a fresh cut or insult of some kind. Mrs. Sewall went out of her way to make occasion to meet and ignore me. It was necessary for her to go out of her way, for we didn't meet often by chance. I was omitted from the many dinners and dances which all the hostesses in Hilton began to give in Miss Oliphant's honor. I was omitted from the more intimate afternoon tea and sewing parties. Gale attended them now, and of course it would have been awkward.

I didn't blame my girl friends for leaving me out. I might have done the same to one of them. It isn't contrary to the rules. In fact the few times I did encounter the old associates it was far from pleasant. There was a feeling of constraint. There was nothing to talk about, either. Even my manicurist and hairdresser, usually so conversational about all the social events of the community, felt embarrassed and ill at ease, with the parties at Grassmere, the costumes for the masquerade, Miss Oliphant, and the Vars scandal barred from the conversation.

I was glad that Alec was away on a western trip. He, at least, was spared the unbeautifying effect of the ordeal upon his wife and sister. Alec hardly ever finds fault or criticizes, but underneath his silence and his kindness I often wonder if there are not hidden, wounded illusions and bleeding ideals. Edith and I were both in the same boat, and we weren't pleasant traveling companions. I had never sailed with Edith under such baffling winds as we now encountered. Squalls, calms, and occasional storms we had experienced, but she had always kept a firm hand on the rudder. Now she seemed to lose her nerve and forget all the rules of successful navigation that she ever had learned. She threw the charts to the winds, and burst into uncontrolled passions of disappointment and rage.

I couldn't believe that Edith was the same woman who but six months ago had nursed her only little daughter, whom she loves passionately, through an alarming sickness. There had been trained nurses, but every night Edith had taken her place in the low chair by the little girl's crib, there to remain hour after hour, waiting, watching, noting with complete control the changes for better or for worse; sleeping scarcely at all; and always smiling quiet encouragement to Alec or to me when we would steal in upon her. Every one said she was marvelous—even the nurses and the doctor. It was as if she actually willed her daughter to pass through her terrific crisis, speaking firmly now and again to the little sufferer, holding her spirit steady as it crossed the yawning abyss. She had seemed superb to me. I had asked myself if I could ever summon to my support such unswerving strength and courage.

I didn't hear from Breck again until he arrived at the front door unexpectedly one night at ten o'clock. I led the way down into the shaded pergola, and there we remained until nearly midnight. When I finally stole back to my room, I found Edith waiting for me, sitting bolt upright on the foot of my bed, wide-awake, alert, eyes bright and hard as steel.

"Well?" she asked the instant I came in, "tell me, is he as keen as ever?"

A wave of something like sickness swept over me.

"Yes," I said shortly.

"Is he *really*?" she pursued. "Oh, isn't that splendid! Really? He still wants you to marry him?"

"Yes," I said.

Edith flung her arm about me and squeezed me hard.

"We'll make that old cat of a mother of his sing another song one of these days," she said. "You're a wonderful little kiddie, after all. You'll save the day! Trust you! You'll pull it off yet! Oh, I have been horrid, Ruth, this last fortnight. Really I have. I was so afraid we were ruined, and we would be if it wasn't for you. Wait a jiffy."

Fifteen minutes later, just as, very wearily, I was putting out my light, Edith pushed open my door again with a cup of something steaming hot in her hand.

"Here," she said. "Malted milk, good and hot, with just a dash of sherry in it. 'Twill make you sleep. You drink it, poor child—wonderful child too! You jump in and drink it! I'll fix the windows and the lights."

I tried to be Edith's idea of wonderful. For a week I endured the ignominy of receiving calls from Breck in secret, late at night when he was able to steal away from the gaieties at Grassmere. For a week I spent long idle days in the garden, in my room, on the veranda—anywhere at all where I could best kill the galling, unoccupied hours until night, and Breck was free to come to me.

I did not annoy him with demands for explanation of a situation already painfully clear to me. I knew that he spoke truth when he assured me he could not alter his mother's opposition at present, and I did not disturb our evening talks by reproaches. I assumed a grand air of indifference toward Mrs. Sewall and her attacks, as if I was some invulnerable creature beyond and above her. I didn't even cheapen myself by appearing to observe that Breck's invitations to appear in public with him had suddenly been replaced by demands for private and stolen interviews.

Of course his duties as host were many and consumed most of his time. His clever mother saw to that. He said that there were twenty guests at Grassmere. Naturally, I told myself, he couldn't take all-day motor trips with me. I was convinced that my strength lay in whatever charm I possessed for him, and I had no intention of injuring it by ill-timed complaints. I was attractive, alluring to him—more so than ever. I tried to be! Oh, I tried to be diplomatic, wise, to bide my time; by quiet and determined endurance to withstand the siege of Mrs. Sewall's disapproval; to hold her son's affection; and to marry him some day, with her sanction, too, just exactly as I had planned. I tried and I failed.

The very fact that I could hold Breck's affection hastened my defeat—that and my lacerated pride.

I met him one day when I was out walking with Dandy, not far from the very spot where once he had begged me to ride with him in his automobile. Today in the seat beside him, which had been of late so often mine, sat Gale Oliphant, her head almost upon his shoulder, and Breck leaning toward her laughing as they sped by.

He saw me, I was sure he saw me, but he did not raise his hat. His signal of recognition had been without Miss Oliphant's knowledge. After they had passed he had stretched out his arm as a sign to turn to the left, and had waved his hand without looking around. My face grew scarlet. What had I become? Why, I might have been a picked-up acquaintance, somebody to be ashamed of! Ruth Chenery Vars—where had disappeared that once proud and self-respecting girl?

Insignificant as the event really was, it stood as a symbol of the whole miserable situation to me. It was just enough to startle me into contempt for myself. That night Breck came stealing down to me along the dark roads in his quiet car about eleven-thirty. I knew he had been to the Jackson dinner and was surprised to find he had changed into street clothes. He was more eager than ever in his greeting.

"Come down into the sunken garden," he pleaded. "I've got something to say to you."

It was light in the garden. There was a full September moon. I stood beside the bird-bath and put a forefinger in it. I could hear Breck breathing hard beside me. I was sure he had broken his pledge and had been drinking.

"Well?" I said at last, calmly, looking up.

He answered me silently, vehemently.

"Don't, please, *here*. It's so fearfully light. Don't, Breck," I said.

"I've got the car," he whispered. "It will take us two hours. I've got it all planned. It's a peach of a night. You've got to come. I'm not for waiting any longer. You've got to marry me tonight, you little fish! I'll wake you up. Do you hear me? Tonight in two hours. I'm not going to hang around any longer. You've got to come!"

I managed to struggle away.

"Don't talk like that to me. It's insulting! Don't!" I said.

"Insulting! Say, ring off on that—will you? Insulting to ask a girl to marry you! Say, that's good! Well, insulting or not, I've made up my mind not to hang around any longer. I'll marry you tonight or not at all! You needn't be afraid. I've got it all fixed up—license and everything." He whipped a paper out of his pocket. "We'll surprise 'em, we will—you and I. I'm mad about you, and always have been. The mater—huh! Be a shock to her—but she'll survive."

"I wouldn't elope with the king of England!" I said hotly. "What do you think I am? Understand this, Breck. I require all the honors and high ceremonies that exist."

"Damn it," he said, "you've been letting me come here without much ceremony every night, late, on the quiet. What have you got to say to that? I'm tired of seeing you pose on that high horse of yours. Come down. You know as well as I you've been leading me along as hard as you could for the last week. Good Lord—what for? Say, what's the game? I don't know. But listen—if you don't marry me *now*, then you never will. There's a limit to a man's endurance. Come, come, you can't do better for yourself. You aren't so much. The mater will never come around. She's got her teeth set. The car's ready. I shan't come again."

"Wait a minute," I said. "I'll be back in a minute." And I went straight into the house and upstairs to my room, knelt down before my bureau and drew out a blue velvet box. Breck's ring was inside.

Just as I was stealing down the stairs again, ever-on-the-guard, Edith appeared in the hall in her nightdress.

"What are you after?" she asked.

For answer I held out the box toward her. She came down two or three of the stairs.

"What you going to do with it?" she demanded.

"Give it back to Breck."

She grasped my wrist. "You little fool!" she exclaimed.

"But he wants me to run off with him. He wants me to elope."

"He does!" she ejaculated, her eyes large. "Well?" she inquired.

I stared up at Edith on the step above me in silence.

"Well?" she repeated.

"You don't mean—" I began.

"His mother is sure to come around in time. They always do. My mother eloped," she said.

"Edith Campbell Vars," I exclaimed, "do you actually mean—" I stopped. Even in the dim light of the hall I saw her flush before my blank astonishment. "Do you mean—"

"Well, if you don't," she interrupted in defense, "everybody will think he threw *you* over. You'll simply become an old glove. There's not much choice."

"But my pride, my own self-respect! Edith Vars, you'd sell your soul for society; and you'd sell me too! But you can't—you can't! Let go my wrist. I'm sick of the whole miserable game. I'm sick of it. Let me go."

"And I'm sick of it too," flung back Edith. "But *I've* got a daughter's future to think about, I'd have you know, as well as yours. I've worked hard to establish ourselves in this place, and I've succeeded too. And now you come along, and look at the mess we're in! Humiliated! Ignored! Insulted! It isn't my fault, is it? If I'd paddled my own canoe, I'd be all right today."

"You can paddle it hereafter," I flashed out. "I shan't trouble you any more."

"Yes, that's pleasant, after you've jabbed it full of holes!"

"Let me go, Edith," I said and pulled away my wrist with a jerk.

"Are you going to give it back to him?"

"Yes, I am!" I retorted and fled down the stairs, out of the door, across the porch, and into the moonlit garden as fast as I could go.

"Here, Breck—here's your ring! Take it. You're free. You don't need to hang around, as you say, any more. And I'm free, too, thank heaven! I would have borne the glory and the honor of your name with pride. Your mother's friendship would have been a happiness, but for no name, and for no woman's favor will I descend to a stolen marriage. You're mistaken in me. Everybody seems to be. I'm mistaken in myself. I don't want to marry you after all. I don't love you, and I don't want to marry you. I'm tired. Please go."

He stared at me. "You little fool!" he exclaimed, just like Edith. Then he slipped the box into his pocket, shrugged his shoulders, and in truly chivalrous fashion added, "Don't imagine I'm going to commit suicide or anything tragic like that, young lady, because I'm not."

"I didn't imagine it," I replied.

"I'm going to marry Gale Oliphant," he informed me coolly. "I'm going to give her a ring in a little box—and she'll wear hers. You'll see." He produced a cigarette and lit it. "She's no fish," he added. "She's a pippin, she is. Good night," he finished, and turned and walked out of the garden.

Three days later I went away from Hilton. Edith's tirades became unendurable. I didn't want even to eat her food. The spinet desk, the bureau, the chiffonier, the closet, I cleared of every trace of me. I stripped the bed of its linen and left the mattress rolled over the foot-board in eloquent abandonment. The waste-basket bulged with discarded odds and ends. One had only to look into that room to feel convinced that its occupant had disappeared, like a spirit from a dead body, never to return.

I went to my sister Lucy's. I did not write her. I simply took a morning train to Boston and called her up on the 'phone in her not far distant university town. She came trotting cheerfully in to meet me. I told her my news; she tenderly gathered what was left of me together, and carried the bits out here to her little white house on the hill.

A University Town

IDID not think I would be seated here on my rustic bench writing so soon again. I finished the history of my catastrophe a week ago. But something almost pleasant has occurred, and I'd like to try my pencil at recording a pleasant story. Scarcely a story yet, though. Just a bit of a conversation—that's all—fragmentary. It refers to this very bench where I am sitting as I write, to the hills I am seeing out beyond the little maple tree stripped now of all its glory. I cannot see a dash of color anywhere. The world is brown. The sky is gray. It is rather chilly for writing out-of-doors.

The conversation I refer to began in an ugly little room in a professor's house. There was a roll-top desk in the room, and a map, yellow with age, hanging on the wall. The conversation ended underneath a lamp-post on a street curbing, and it was rainy and dark and cold. And yet when I think of that conversation, sitting here in the brown chill dusk, I see color, I feel warmth.

When I first came here to Lucy's three weeks ago, she assumed that I was suffering from a broken heart. I had been exposed and showed symptoms—going off alone for long walks and consuming reams of theme paper as if I was half mad. I told Lucy that my heart was too hard to break, but I couldn't convince her. There wasn't a day passed but that she planned some form of amusement or diversion. Even Will, her husband, cooperated and spent long evenings playing rum or three-handed auction, so I might not sit idle. I tried to fall in with Lucy's plans.

"But, please, no men! I don't want to see another man for years. If any man I know finds out I'm here, tell him I won't see him, absolutely," I warned. "I want to be alone. I want to think things out undisturbed. Sometimes I almost wish I could enter a convent."

"Oh, I'm so sorry!" Lucy would exclaim.

"You needn't be. You didn't break my engagement. For heaven's sake, Lucy, *you* needn't take it so hard."

But she did. She simply brooded over me. She read to me, smiled for me, and initiated every sally that I made into public. In conversation she picked her way with me with the precaution of a cat walking across a table covered with delicate china. She made wide detours to avoid a reference or remark that might reflect upon my engagement. Will did likewise. I lived in daily surprise and wonder. As a family we are brutally frank. This was a new phase, and one of the indirect results, I suppose, of my broken engagement.

What I am trying to arrive at is the change of attitude in me toward Lucy. Usually when I visit Lucy I do just about as I please; refuse to attend a lot of stupid student-teas and brain-fagging lectures, or to exert myself to appear engrossed in the conversation of her intellectual dinner guests.

I used to scorn Lucy's dinners. They are very different from Edith's, where, when the last guest in her stunning new gown has arrived and swept into the drawing-room, followed by her husband, a maid enters, balancing on her tray a dozen little glasses, amber filled; everybody takes one, daintily, between a thumb and forefinger and drains it; puts it nonchalantly aside on shelf or table; offers or accepts an arm and floats toward the dining-room. At Edith's dinners the table is long, flower-laden, candle-lighted. Your partner's face smiles at you dimly. His voice is almost drowned by the chatter and the laughter all about, but you hear him—just barely—and you laugh—he is immensely droll—and then reply. And he laughs, too, contagiously, and you know that you are going to get on!

Incidentally at Edith's dinners silent-footed servants pass you things; you take them; you eat a little, too—delicious morsels if you stopped to consider them; but you and your partner are having far too good a time (he is actually audacious, and so, if you please, are you) to bother about the food.

There's a little group of glasses beside your water, and once in a while there appears in your field of vision a hand grasping a white napkin folded like a cornucopia, out of which flows delicious nectar. You sip a little of it occasionally, a very little—you are careful of course—and waves of elation sweep over you because you are alive and happy and good to look upon; waves of keen delight that such a big and splendid life (there are orchids in the center of the table, there are pearls and diamonds everywhere)—that such a life as this is yours to grasp and to enjoy.

At Lucy's dinners the women do not wear diamonds and pearls. Lucy seldom entertains more than six at a time. "Shall we go out?" she says when her Delia mumbles something from the door. You straggle across the hall into the dining-room, where thirteen carnations—you count them later, there's time enough—where thirteen stiff carnations are doing duty in the center of the prim table. At each place there is a soup plate sending forth a cloud of steam. You wait until Lucy points out your place to you, and then sit down at last. There is a terrible pause—you wonder if they say grace—and then finally Lucy picks up her soup-spoon for signal and you're off! The conversation is general. That is because Lucy's guests are usually intellectuals, and whatever any one of them says is supposed to be so important that every one else must keep still and listen. You can't help but notice the food, because there's nothing to soften the effect of it upon your nerves, as it were. There are usually four courses, with chicken or ducks for the main dish, accompanied by potatoes cut in balls, the invariable rubber stamp of a party at Lucy's. Afterward there's coffee in the living-room, and you feel fearfully discouraged when you look at the clock and find it's only eight-thirty. You're surprised after the guests have gone to find that Lucy considers her party a success.

"Why," she exclaims, cheeks aglow, "Dr. Van Breeze gave us the entire résumé of his new book. He seldom thinks anybody clever enough to talk to. It was a perfect combination!"

As I said, I usually visit Lucy in rather a critical state of mind and hold myself aloof from her learned old doctors and professors. On this visit, though, she is so obviously careful of me and my feelings, that I find myself going out of my way to consider hers a little. One day last week when she so brightly suggested that we go to a tea given by the wife of a member of the faculty, instead of exclaiming, "Oh, dear! it would bore me to extinction," I replied sweetly, "All right, if you want to, I'll go."

I wasn't feeling happy. I didn't want to go. I had been roaming the woods and country roads round about for a month in search of an excuse for existence. I had been autobiographing for days in the faint hope that I might run across something worth while in my life. But no. It was hopeless. I had lost all initiative. I couldn't see what reason there was for me to eat three meals a day. It seemed as foolish as stoking the furnaces of an ocean liner when it is in port. In such a mood, and through the drifting mist of a complaining October afternoon, in rubbers and a raincoat, I started out with Lucy for her afternoon tea.

The other guests wore raincoats, too—we met a few on the way—with dull-colored suits underneath, and tailored hats. There wasn't a single bright, frivolous thing about that tea. Even the house was dismal—rows of black walnut bookcases with busts of great men on top, steel engravings framed in oak on the walls, and a Boston fern or two in red pots sitting about on plates. When I looked up from my weak tea, served in a common stock-pattern willow cup, and saw Lucy sparkling with pleasure, talking away for dear life with a white-haired old man who wore a string tie and had had two fingers shot off in the Civil War (I always hated to shake hands with him) a wave of intolerance for age and learning swept over me. I told Lucy if she didn't mind I'd run along home, and stepped across the hall into a little stupid room with a roll-top desk in it, where we had left our raincoats, and rubbers. I put on my things and then stood staring a moment at a picture on the wall. I didn't know what the picture was. I simply looked at it blindly while I fought a sudden desire to cry. I hadn't wept before. But this dreadful house, these dry, drab people were such a contrast to my all-but-realized ambitions that it brought bitter tears to my eyes. Life at Grassmere—*that* was living! This was mere existence.

Just as I was groping for a handkerchief some little fool of a woman exclaimed, "Oh, there she is—in the study! I thought she hadn't gone. O Miss Vars, there's somebody I want you to meet, and meet you. Here she is, Mr. Jennings. Come in. Miss Vars," I was still facing the wall, "Miss Vars, I want to introduce Mr. Jennings." I turned finally, and as I did so she added, "Now, I must go back to Dr. Fuller. I was afraid you'd gone," and out she darted. I could have shot her.

Mr. Jennings came straight across the room. Through a blur I caught an impression of height, breadth and energy. His sudden hand-grasp was firm and decisive. "How do you do?" he said, and then abruptly observed my tears.

"You've caught me with my sails all down," I explained.

"Have I?" he replied pleasantly. "Well, I like sails down."

"Please do not think," I continued, "that I am often guilty of such a thing as this. I'm not. Who was that woman anyhow?"

"Oh, don't blame her," he laughed, and he stepped forward to look at the picture which I had been staring at. I was busy putting away my handkerchief. "Who was that woman?" Mr. Jennings repeated, abruptly turning away from the picture back to me, "Who was she? I'll tell you who she was—a good angel. Why," he went on, "I'd got into the way of thinking that sympathy as expressed by tears had gone out of style with the modern girl. They never shed any at the theater nowadays, I notice. I'm glad to know there is one who hasn't forgotten how."

I stepped forward then to find out what manner of picture it was to cause such a tribute to be paid me. It was called "The Doctor." A crude bare room was depicted. The light from a lamp on an old kitchen table threw its rays on the turned-aside, face of a little girl, who lay asleep—or unconscious—on an improvised bed made of two chairs drawn together. Beyond the narrow confines of the cot the little girl's hand extended, wistfully upturned. Seated beside her, watching, sat the big kind doctor. Anxiety, doubt were in his intelligent face. Near an east window, through which a streak of dawn was creeping, sat a woman, her face buried in the curve of her arms folded on the table. Beside her stood a bearded man, brow furrowed, his pleading eyes upon the doctor, while his hand, big, comforting, rested on the woman's bowed shoulders. A cup with a spoon in it, a collection of bottles near-by—all the poor, human, useless tools of defense were there, eloquent of a long and losing struggle. Every one who recalls the familiar picture knows what a dreary, hopeless scene it is—the room stamped with poverty, the window stark and curtainless, the woman meagerly clad, the man bearing the marks of hardship.

Suddenly in the face of all that, Mr. Jennings softly exclaimed, "That's living."

Only five minutes ago I had said the same thing of life at Grassmere.

"Is it?" I replied. "Is that living? I've been wondering lately. I thought—I thought—it's so poor and sad!" I remonstrated.

"Poor! Oh, no, it's rich," he replied quickly, "rich in everything worth while. Anyhow, only lives that are vacuums are free from sadness."

"Are lives that are vacuums free from happiness, too?" I enquired.

He took my question as if it was a statement. "That's true, too, I suppose," he agreed.

"How hopeless," I murmured, still gazing at the picture, but in reality contemplating my own empty life. He misunderstood.

"See here," he said. "I believe this little girl here is going to pull through after all. Don't worry. I insist she is. That artist ought to paint a sequel—just for you," he added, and abruptly he unfolded his arms and looked at me squarely for the first time. "I didn't in the least get your name," he broke off. "The good angel flew away so soon."

I told him.

"Oh, yes, Miss Vars. Thank you. Mine's Jennings. People mumble names so in introductions." He glanced around at the piles of raincoats and racks of umbrellas. I already had my coat on. "You weren't just going, were you?" he inquired brightly. "For if you were, so was I, too. Perhaps you will let me walk along—unless you're riding."

I forgot just for a minute that I didn't want to see another man for years and years. He wasn't a man just then, but a bright and colorful illumination. He stood before me full of life and vigor. He was tall and straight. His close-cropped hair shone like gold in the pale gas-light, and there was a tan or glow upon his face that made me think of out-of-doors. His smile, his straightforward gaze, his crisp voice, had brightened that dull little room for me. I went with him. Of course I did—out into the rainy darkness of the late October afternoon, drawn as a child towards the glow of red fire.

A Walk in the Rain

ONCE on the side-walk Mr. Jennings said, "I'm glad to know your name, for I know you by sight already. Shall we have any umbrella?"

"Let's not," I replied. "I like the mist. But how do you know me?"

"I thought you would—like the mist, I mean—because you seem to like my woods so well."

"Your woods! Why—what woods?"

"The ones you walk in every day," he cheerfully replied; "they're mine. I discovered them, and to whom else should they belong?"

"I've been trespassing, then."

"Oh, no! I'm delighted to lend my woods to you. If you wear blinders and keep your eyes straight ahead and stuff your ears with cotton so you can't hear the trolleys, you can almost cheat yourself into thinking they're real woods with a mountain to climb at the end of them. Do you like that little rustic seat I made beside the lake?"

"Did you make it?"

"Yes, Saturdays, for recreation last year. I'm afraid it doesn't fit very well." He smiled from out of the light of a sudden lamp-post. "You'll find a birch footstool some day pretty soon. I noticed your feet didn't reach. By the way," he broke off, "pardon me for quoting from you, but *I* don't think back-season débutantes are like out-of-demand best-sellers—not all of them. Anyhow, all best-sellers do not deteriorate. And tell me, is this chap with the deep-purring car the villain or the hero in your novel—the dark one with the hair blown straight back?"

I almost stopped in my amazement. He was quoting from my life history.

"I don't understand," I began. I could feel the color in my cheeks. "I dislike mystery. Tell me. Please. How did you—I dislike mystery," I repeated.

"Are you angry? It's so dark I can't see. Don't be angry. It was written on theme paper, in pencil, and in a university town theme paper is public property. I found them there one day—just two loose leaves behind the seat—and I read them. Afterwards I saw you—not until afterwards," he assured me, "writing there every day. I asked to be introduced to you when I saw you tucked away in a corner there this afternoon drinking tea behind a fern, so that I could return your property."

"Oh, you've kept the leaves! Where are they?" I demanded.

"Right here. Wait a minute." And underneath an arc-light we stopped, and from out of his breast-pocket this surprising man drew a leather case, and from out of that two crumpled pages of my life. "If any one should ask me to guess," he went on, "I should say that the author of these fragments is a student at Shirley" (the girls' college connected with the University) "and that she had strolled out to my woods for inspiration to write a story for an English course. Am I right?" He passed me the leaves. "It sounds promising," he added, "the story, I mean."

I took the leaves and glanced through them. There wasn't a name mentioned on either. "A student at Shirley!" I exclaimed. "How perfectly ridiculous! A school girl! Well, how old do you think I am?" and out of sheer relief I rippled into a laugh.

"I don't know," he replied. "How old are you?" And he laughed, too. The sound of our merriment mixing so rhythmically was music to my ears. I thought I had forgotten how to be foolish, and inconsequential.

"I don't know why it strikes me so funny," I tried to explain—for really I felt fairly elated—"I don't know why, but a story for an English course! A college girl!" And I burst into peals of mirth.

"That's right. Go ahead. I deserve it," urged Mr. Jennings self-depreciatively. "How I blunder! Anyhow I've found you can laugh as well as cry, and that's something. Perhaps now," he continued, "seeing I'm such a failure as a Sherlock Holmes, you will be so kind as to tell me yourself who you are. Do you live here? I never saw you before. I'm sure you're a stranger. Where is your home, Miss Vars?"

"Where is my home?" I repeated, and then paused an instant. Where indeed? "A wardrobe-trunk is my home, Mr. Jennings," I replied.

"Oh!" he took it up. "A wardrobe-trunk. Rather a small house for you to develop your individuality in, very freely, I should say!"

"Yes, but at least nothing hangs within its walls but of my own choosing."

"And it's convenient for house-cleaning, too," he followed it up. "But see here, is there room for two in it, because I was just going to ask to call."

"I usually entertain my callers in the garden," I primly announced.

"How delightful! I much prefer gardens." And we laughed again. "Which way?" he abruptly inquired. "Which way to your garden, please?" We had come to a crossing. I stopped, and he beside me.

"Why, I'm sure I don't know!" Nothing about me looked familiar. "These winding streets of yours! I'm afraid I'm lost," I confessed. "You'll have to put me on a car—a Greene Hill Avenue car. I know my way alone then. At least I believe it's a Greene Hill Avenue car. They've just moved there—my sister. Perhaps you know her—Mrs. William Maynard."

"Lucy Maynard!" he exclaimed. "I should say I did! Are you—why, are you her sister?"

He had heard about me then! Of course. How cruel!

"Yes. Why?" I managed to inquire.

"Oh, nothing. Only I've met you," he brought out triumphantly. "I met you at dinner, two or three years ago—at your sister's house. We're old friends," he said.

"Are we?" I asked in wonder. "Are we old friends?" I wanted to add, "How nice!"

He looked so steady and substantial, standing there—so kind and understanding. Any one would prize him for an old friend. I gazed up at him. The drifting mist had covered his broad chest and shoulders with a glistening veil of white. It shone like frost on the nap of his soft felt hat. It sparkled on his eyebrows and the lashes of his fine eyes. "How nice," I wanted to add. But a desire not to flirt with this man honestly possessed me. Besides I must remember I was tired of men. I wanted nothing of any of them. So instead I said, "Well, then, you know what car I need to take."

He ignored my remark.

"You had on a yellow dress—let's walk along—and wore purple pansies, fresh ones, although it was mid-winter. I remember it distinctly. But a hat and a raincoat today make you look different, and I couldn't get near enough to you in the woods. I remember there was a medical friend of your sister's husband there that night, and Will and he monopolized the conversation. I hardly spoke to you; but tell me, didn't you wear pansies with a yellow dress one night at your sister's?"

"Jennings? Are you Bob Jennings?" (Lucy's Bob Jennings! I remembered now—a teacher of English at the University.) "Of course," I exclaimed, "I recall you now. I remember that night perfectly. When you came into my sister's living-room, looking so—so unprofessor-like—I thought to myself, 'How nice for me; Professor Jennings couldn't come; she's got one of the students to take his place—some one nice and easy and my size.' I wondered if you were on the football team or crew, and it crossed my mind what a perfect shame it was to drag a man like you away from a dance in town, perhaps, to a stupid dinner with one of the faculty. And then you began to talk with Will about—what was it—Chaucer? Anyhow something terrifying, and I knew then that you *were* Professor Jennings after all."

"Oh, but I wasn't. I was just an assistant. I'm not a professor even yet. Never shall be either—the gods willing. I'm trying hard to be a lawyer. Circuitous route, I confess. But you know automobile guide-books often advise the longer and smoother road. Do you mind walking? It isn't far, and the cars are crowded."

We walked.

"I suppose," I remarked a little later, "trying hard to become a lawyer is what keeps your life from being a vacuum."

"Yes, that, and a little white-haired lady I call my mother," he added gallantly.

"Do you want to know what keeps my life from being a vacuum?" I abruptly asked.

"Of course I do!"

"Well, then—a little brown Boston terrier whom I call Dandy," I announced.

He laughed as if it was a joke. "What nonsense! Your sister has told me quite a lot about you, Miss Vars, one time and another; that you write verse a little, for instance. Any one who can create is able to fill all the empty corners of his life. You know that as well as I do."

I considered this new idea in silence for a moment. We turned in at Lucy's street.

"How long shall you be here, Miss Vars?" asked Mr. Jennings. "And, seriously, may I call some evening?"

How could I refuse such a friendly and straightforward request?

"Why, yes," I heard myself saying, man though he was, "I suppose so. I should be glad, only—"

"Only what?"

"Only—well—" We were at Lucy's gate. I stopped beneath the lamp-post. "I don't believe my sister has told you all about me, Mr. Jennings."

"Of course not!" He laughed. "I don't want her to. I don't want to know all that's in a new book I am about to read. It's pleasanter to discover the delights myself."

I felt conscience-stricken. There were no delights left in me. I ought to tell him. However, all I replied was, "How nicely you put things!"

And he: "Do I? Well—when may I come?"

"Why—any night. Only I'm not a very bright book—rather dreary. Truly. I warn you. You found me in tears, remember."

"Don't think again about that," he said to me. "Please. Listen. I always try to take home to the little white-haired lady something pleasant every night—a rose or a couple of pinks, or an incident of some sort to please her, never anything dreary. *You*, looking at the picture of the little sick girl, are to be the gift tonight." And then suddenly embarrassed, he added hastily, "I'm afraid you're awfully wet. I ought to be shot. Perhaps you preferred to ride. You're covered with mist. And perhaps it's spoiled something." He glanced at my hat.

"No, it hasn't," I assured him, "and good night. I can get in all right."

"Oh, let me—"

"No, please," I insisted.

"Very well," he acquiesced. And I gave him my hand and sped up the walk.

He waited until the door was opened to me, and then, "Good night," came his clear, pleasant voice to me from out of the rainy dark.

I went straight upstairs to my room. I felt as if I had just drunk long and deep of pure cold water. Tired and travel-worn I had been, uncertain of my way, disheartened, spent; and then suddenly across my path had appeared an unexpected brook, crystal clear, soul-refreshing. I had rested by it a moment, listened to its cheerful murmur, lifted up a little of its coolness in the hollow of my hand, and drunk. I went up to my room with a lighter heart than I had known for months, walked over to the window, raised it, and let in a little of the precious mistiness that had enshrouded me for the last half hour.

Standing there looking out into the darkness, I was interrupted by a knock on my door.

"I was just turning down the beds, Miss," explained Lucy's Delia, "and so brought up your letter." And she passed me the missive I had not noticed on the table as I came in, so blind a cheerful "good night" called from out of the rain had made me.

"A letter? Thank you, Delia. Isn't it rainy!" I added impulsively.

"It is, Miss. It is indeed, Miss Ruth!"

"Come," I went on, "let me help you turn down the beds. I haven't another thing to do." The letter could wait. Benevolence possessed my soul.

Later alone in my room I opened my note. It was from Edith. I had recognized her handwriting instantly. She seldom harbors ill-feeling for any length of time.

"Three cheers!" the letter jubilantly began. "Run up a flag. We win!" it shouted. "Prepare yourself, Toots. We have been bidden to Grassmere! Also I have received a personal note from the great Mogul herself. You were right, I guess, as always. Let's forgive and forget. Mrs. Sewall writes to know if we will honor her by our presence at a luncheon at Grassmere. What do you say to that? With pleasure, kind lady, say I! I enclose your invitation. You'll be ravishing in a new gown which I want you to go right in and order at Madame's—*on me*, understand, dearie. I'm going to blow myself to a new one, too. Won't the girls be surprised when they hear of this? The joke will be on them, I'm thinking. Probably you and Breck will be patching up your little difference, too. I don't pretend to fathom Mrs. S.'s change of front, but it's changed anyhow! That's all I care about. Good-by. Must hurry to catch mail. Hustle home, rascal. Love, Edith."

Two weeks later on the morning after the luncheon, to which it is unnecessary to say I sent my immediate regrets, the morning paper could not be found at Lucy's house. Will went off to the University berating the paper-boy soundly. After I had finished my coffee and toast and moved over to the front window, Lucy opened the wood-box.

"I stuffed it in here," she said, "just as you and Will were coming downstairs. I thought you'd rather see it first." And she put the lost paper into my hands and left me.

On the front page there appeared the following announcement:

"Breckenridge Sewall Engaged to be Married to Miss Gale Oliphant of New York and Newport. Announcement of Engagement Occasion for Brilliant Luncheon Given by Mrs. F. Rockridge Sewall at her Beautiful Estate in Hilton. Wedding Set for Early December."

I read the announcement two or three times, and afterward the fine print below, containing a long list of the luncheon guests with Edith's name proudly in its midst. The scene of my shame and the actors flashed before me. Ignominy and defeat were no part of the new creature I had become since Lucy's tea. I read the announcement again. It was as if a dark cloud passed high over my head and cast a shadow on the sparkling beauty of the brook beside which I had been lingering for nearly two weeks.

A Dinner Party

ROBERT JENNINGS sees the plainest and commonest things of life through the eyes of an artist. He never goes anywhere without a volume of poetry stuffed into his pocket, and if he runs across anything that no one else has endowed with beauty, then straightway he will endow it himself. Crowded trolleys, railroad stations, a muddy road—all have some hidden appeal. Even greed and discord he manages to ignore as such by looking beneath their exteriors for hidden significance. The simpler a pleasure, the greater to him its joy.

He is tall, broad; of light complexion; vigorous in every movement that he makes. Upon his face there is a perpetual glow, whether due to mere color, or to expression, I cannot make up my mind. He enters the house and brings with him a feeling of out-of-doors. His smile is like sunshine on white snow, his seriousness like a quiet pool hidden among trees, his enthusiasm like mad whitecaps on a lake stirred by a gale, his tenderness like the kind warmth of Indian summer caressing drooping flowers. I have never known any one just like him before. Instead of inviting me in town to luncheon and the matinée, or to dinner and the opera, he takes me out with him to drink draughts of cold November air, and to share the glory of an autumn sunset.

The first time he called he mentioned a course at Shirley offered to special students. I told him if he would use his influence and persuade the authorities to accept me, I believed I should like to take a course in college. I thought it would help to kill time while I was making up my mind how better to dispose of myself. I have therefore become what Mr. Jennings thought I was in the beginning—a student at Shirley; not a full-fledged one but a "special" in English. I attend class twice a week and in between times write compositions that are read out loud in class and criticized. Also in between times I occasionally see Mr. Jennings.

Last week each member of the class was required to submit an original sonnet. Mine is not finished yet. I am trying a rhapsody on the autumn woods. This is the way I work. Pencil, pad, low rocking-chair by the window. First line:

"I see the saffron woods of yesterday!" Then fixedly I gaze at the rubber on the end of my pencil. "I see the saffron woods of yesterday!" (What a young god he looked the day he called for me to go chestnutting! How his eyes laughed and his voice sang, and as we scuffled noisily through the leaf-strewn forest, how his long, easy stride put me in mind of the swinging meter of Longfellow's Hiawatha!)

"I see the saffron woods of yesterday!" (I see, too, the setting sun shining on the yellow leaves, clinging frailly. I see myself standing beneath a tree holding up an overcoat—his overcoat, thrown across my outstretched arms to catch the pelting burrs that he is shaking off. I see his eyes looking down from the tree into mine. Later as we lean over a rock to crack open the prickly burrs, I feel our shoulders touch! Did he feel them, too, I wonder? If he were any other man I would say that he meant that our eyes should meet too long, our shoulders lean too near, and our silence, as we walked home in the dark, continue too tense. But he is different. He is not a lover. He is a friend—a comrade.) "I see the saffron woods of yesterday!"

Abruptly I lay aside my pad and pencil. I put on my coat and hat, pull on my gloves, and in self-defense plunge out into the cold November afternoon. I avoid the country, and try to keep my recreant thoughts on such practical subjects as trolley cars, motor-trucks and delivery wagons, rumbling noisily beside me along the street. A sudden "To Let" card appears in a new apartment. I wonder how much the rent is. I wonder how much the salary of an assistant professor is. Probably something under five thousand a year. The income from the investments left me by my father amounts to almost eight hundred dollars. Clothes alone cost me more than a thousand. Of course one wouldn't need so many, but what with rent, and food, and service, and—what am I thinking of? Why, I've known the man only four weeks, and considering my recent relations with Breckenridge Sewall such mad air-castling is lacking in good taste. Besides, a teacher—a professor! I've always scorned professors. I was predestined to fill a high and influential place. A professor's wife? It is unthinkable! And then abruptly appears a street vender beside me. I smell his roasting chestnuts. And again—again, "I see the saffron woods of yesterday!"

About two days after I went chestnutting with Mr. Jennings, I went picnicking. We built a fire in the corner of two stones and cooked chops and bacon. Two days after that we tramped to an old farm-house, five miles straight-away north, and drank sweet cider—rather warm—from a jelly tumbler with a rough rim. Once we had some tea and thick slabs of bread in a country hotel by the roadside. Often we pillage orchards for apples. Day before yesterday we stopped in a dismantled vegetable garden and pulled a raw turnip from out of the frosty ground. Mr. Jennings scraped the dirt away and pared off a little morsel with his pocket knife. He offered it to me, then took a piece himself.

"Same old taste," I laughed.

"Same old taste," he laughed back. And we looked into each other's eyes in sympathetic appreciation of raw turnip. As he wiped the blade of his knife he added, "If I didn't know it wasn't so, I would swear we played together as children. Most young ladies, of this age, do not care for raw turnips."

A thrill passed through me. I blessed my brothers who had enriched my childhood with the lore of out-of-doors. I blessed even the difficult circumstances of my father's finances, which had forced me as a little girl to seek my pleasures in fields and woods and tilled gardens. Had I once said that my nature required a luxurious environment? I had been mistaken. I gazed upon Robert Jennings standing there before me in the forlorn garden. Bare brown hills were his background. The wind swept down bleakly from the east, bearing with it the dank odor of frostbitten cauliflower. Swift, sharp memories of my childhood swept over me. Smothered traditions stirred in my heart. All the young sweet impulses of my youth took sudden possession of me, and through a mist that blurred my eyes I recognized with a little stab in my breast—that was half joy, half fear—I recognized before me my perfect comrade!

Last night Lucy had one of her dinners and one of the men invited was Robert Jennings. She had increased the usual number of six to eight. "A real party," she explained to me, "with a fish course!"

For no other dinner party in my life did I dress with more care or trembling expectation. Lucy's dinners are always at seven o'clock. I was ready at quarter of, with cold hands and hot cheeks. I knew the very instant that Mr. Jennings entered the room that evening. I was standing at the far end with my back toward the door, talking to the war veteran. At the first sound of Mr. Jennings' greeting as he met Lucy, I became deaf to all else. I heard him speaking to the others near her—such a trained and cultured voice—but I didn't turn around. I kept my eyes riveted on the veteran. It was enough, at that instant, to be in the same room with Robert Jennings. And when Lucy finally said, "Shall we go out?" I wondered if I could bear the ordeal of turning around and meeting his eyes. I needn't have been afraid. He spared me that. There was no greeting of any kind between us until we sat down.

Lucy had placed him at the end of the table farthest away from me, and after the guests were all settled, I dared at last to look up. A swift, sweeping glance I meant it to be, but his eyes were waiting for mine, and secretly, concealed by the noise and chatter all around, somewhere among Lucy's carnations in the center of the table, we met. Only for an instant. He returned immediately to his partner, and I to mine. He answered her, we both selected a piece of silver—and then, abruptly, ran away to each other again. Frequently, during that dinner, as we gained confidence and learned the way, we met among the carnations.

Never before was I so glad of what good looks heaven had bestowed upon me as when I saw this man's eyes examine and approve. Never before did I feel so elated at a dinner, so glad to be alive. My pulse ran high. My spirits fairly danced. And all without cocktails, too! Not only did our eyes meet in stolen interviews, but our voices, too. He couldn't speak but what I heard him, nor did I laugh but what it was meant for him.

During the hour occasions occurred when Mr. Jennings alone did the talking, while the rest listened. I could observe him then without fear of discovery. He sat there opposite me in his perfect evening clothes, as much at home and at ease as in Scotch tweeds in the woods. As he leaned forward a little, one cuffed wrist resting on the table's edge, his fine head held erect, expressing his ideas in clear and well-turned phrases, confident in himself, and listened to with attention, I glowed with pride at the thought of my intimacy with him. A professor's wife? That was a mere name—but *his*, this young aristocrat's—what a privilege!

We didn't speak to each other until late in the evening, when the ladies rose from their chairs about the fire in the living-room and began to talk about the hour. I was standing alone by the mantel when I became conscious that Mr. Jennings had moved away from beside Mrs. Van Breeze, and was making his way toward me. Everybody was saying good night to Lucy. We were quite alone for a minute. He didn't shake hands—just stood before me smiling.

"Well, who are *you*?" he asked.

"Don't you recognize me?" I replied.

He looked me up and down deliberately.

"It is very pretty," he said quietly.

I felt my cheeks grow warm. I blushed. Somebody told me my dress was pretty, and I blushed! I might have been sixteen.

"Your sister said I could stay a little after the others go if I wanted to," Mr. Jennings went on. "Of course I want to. Shall I?"

"Yes," I said, with my cheeks still on fire. "Yes. Stay." And he went away in a moment. I heard him laughing with the others.

I strolled over to the pile of music on the back of Lucy's piano and became engrossed in looking it over. I felt weak and suddenly incompetent. I felt frightened and unprepared. I was still there with the pile of music when, fifteen minutes later, Lucy and Will, with effusive apologies, excused themselves and went upstairs. Mr. Jennings approached me. We were alone at last, and each keenly conscious of it.

"Any music here you know?" he asked indifferently, and drew a sheet towards him.

"Not a great deal."

"It looks pretty much worn," he attempted.

"Doesn't it?" I agreed.

"I hardly know you tonight!" he exclaimed, suddenly personal.

"Don't you? I wore a yellow dress and purple pansies on purpose," I replied as lightly as I could, touching the flowers at my waist.

"Yes, but you didn't wear the same look in your eyes," he remarked.

"No, I didn't," I acknowledged.

A silence enfolded us—sweet, significant.

Mr. Jennings broke it. "I think I had better go," he remarked.

"Had you?" I almost whispered. "Well—" and acquiesced.

"Unless," he added, "you'll sing me something. Do you sing—or play?"

"A little," I confessed.

"Well, *will* you then?"

"Why, yes, if you want me to." And I went over and sat down before the familiar keys.

It was at that moment that I knew at last why I had taken lessons for so many years; why so much money had been put into expensive instruction, and so many hours devoted to daily practise. It was for this—for this particular night—for this particular man. I saw it in a flash. I sang a song in English. "In a Garden," it was called. Softly I played the opening phrases, and then raised my chin a little and began. My voice isn't strong, but it can't help but behave nicely. It can't help but take its high notes truly, like a child who has been taught pretty manners ever since he could walk.

After I had finished Mr. Jennings said nothing for an instant. Then, "Sing something else," he murmured, and afterward he exclaimed, "I didn't know! I had no idea! Your sister never told me *this*!" Then, "I have come to a very lovely part in the beautiful book I discovered," he said to me. "It makes me want never to finish the book. Sing something else." His eyes admired; his voice caressed; his tenderness placed me high in the sacred precincts of his soul.

"Listen, please," I said impulsively. "You mustn't go on thinking well of me. It isn't right. I shall not let you. I'm not what you think. Listen. When I first met you, I had just broken my engagement—just barely. I never said a word about it. I let you go on thinking that I—you see it was this way—my pride was hurt more than my heart. I'm that sort of girl. His mother is Mrs. F. Rockridge Sewall. They have a summer place in Hilton, and—and—"

"Don't bother to go into that. I've known it all from the beginning," Mr. Jennings interrupted gently.

"Oh, have you? You've known then, all along, that I'm just a frivolous society girl who can't do anything but perform a few parlor tricks—and things like that? I was afraid—I was so afraid I had misled you."

"You've misled only yourself," he smiled, and suddenly he put his hand over mine as it rested beside the music rack. I met his steady eyes. Just for an instant. Abruptly he took his hand away, went over to the fireplace, and began poking the logs. When he spoke next he did not turn around.

"This is an evening of confessions," he said. "There are some things about me you might as well know, too. I am an instructor, with a salary of two thousand five hundred dollars a year. I hope to make a lawyer out of myself some day, I don't know when. I've hoped to for a long while. Circumstances made it necessary after I graduated from college to find something to do that was immediately remunerative. I discovered that my mother was entirely dependent upon me. My ambitions had to be postponed for a while. I had tutored enough during my college course to make it evident that I could teach, and I grasped this opportunity as a fortunate one. There are hours each day when I can read law. There are even opportunities to attend lectures. It's a long way around to my goal, I know that, and a steep way. Everything that I can save is laid aside for the time when, finally admitted to the bar, I dare throw off the security of a salary. My mother is quite alone. I must always look out for her. I am all she has. I shall inherit little or nothing. If there is any one who has allowed a possible delusion to continue about himself it is I—not you, Miss Vars. Hello," he interrupted himself, "it's getting late. Quarter of twelve! I ought to be shot." He turned about and came over toward me. "Your sister will be turning me out next," he said glibly. He was quite formal now. We might have been just introduced.

His manner forbade me to speak. He gave me no opportunity to tell him that his circumstances made no difference. Salary or no salary I did not care—nothing made any difference now. He simply wanted me to keep still. He eagerly desired it.

"Good night," he said cheerfully. In matter-of-fact fashion we shook hands. "Forgive me for the disgraceful hour. Good night."

Lucy Takes up the Narrative

IT was an afternoon in late February. A feeling of spring had been in the air all day. In the living-room a lingering sun cast a path of light upon the mahogany surface of a grand piano. In *my* living-room, I should say. For I am Mrs. Maynard, wife of Doctor William Ford Maynard of international guinea-pig fame; sister of Ruth Chenery Vars; one-time confidante of Robert Hopkinson Jennings. I haven't any identity of my own. I'm simply one of the audience, an onlooker—an anxious and worried one, just at present, who wishes somebody would assure me that the play has a happy ending. I don't like sad plays. I don't like being harrowed for nothing. I've taken to paper simply because I'm all of a tremble for fear the play I've been watching for the last month or two won't come out right. Sometimes I feel as if I'd like to dash across the footlights and tell the actors what to say.

Ruth is engaged to be married to Robert Jennings. At first it seemed to me too good to be true. After the sort of bringing up my sister has had, culminating in that miserable affair of hers with Breckenridge Sewall, I was afraid that happiness would slip by her altogether.

Robert Jennings is the salt of the earth. I believe I was as happy as Ruth the first four weeks of her engagement, and then these clouds began to gather. The first time I was conscious of them was the afternoon I have just referred to, in late February.

I went into my living-room that day just to see that it was in order in case of callers. It is difficult to keep a living-room in order when your spoiled young society-sister is visiting you. Today in the middle of one of the large cushions on the sofa appeared an indentation. From beneath one corner of the cushion escaped the edge of a crushed handkerchief. Open, face down, upon the floor lay an abandoned book. I straightened the pillow and then picked up the book.

"Oh!" I exclaimed, actually out loud as my eyes fell on the title. "This!"

It was a modern novel much under discussion, an unpleasant book, reviewers pronounced it, and unnecessarily bold. I opened it. Certain passages were marked with wriggling lines made with a soft pencil. I read a marked paragraph or two, standing just where I was in the middle of the room.

Suddenly the door-bell rang, twice, sharply, and almost immediately afterward I heard some one shove open the front door.

I slipped the book behind the pillow which I had just straightened, walked over to a geranium in the window, and nonchalantly snipped off a leaf.

"Hello!" a man's cheerful voice called out. "Any one at home?"

"Yes, in here, Bob," I called back. "Come in."

Robert Jennings entered. He glowed as if he had just been walking up hill briskly. He shook hands with me.

"Hello," he said, his gray eyes smiling pleasantly. "Been out today? Ought to! Like spring. Where's Ruth?"

"Just gone to the Square. She'll be right back. Run out of cotton for your breakfast-napkins."

"Breakfast-napkins!" he exclaimed, and laughed boyishly. I laughed, too. "It doesn't seem quite possible, does it? Breakfast-napkins, and four months ago I didn't even know her! Mind?" he asked abruptly, holding up a silver case. He selected and lit a cigarette, flipping the charred match straight as an arrow into the fireplace. He smoked in silence a moment, smiling meditatively. "Mother's making some napkins, too!" he broke out. "They're going to get on—Ruth and mother—beautifully. 'She's a dear!' That's what mother says of Ruth half a dozen times a day. 'She's a dear!' And somehow the triteness of the phrase from mother is ridiculously pleasing to me. May I sit down?"

"Of course. Do."

He approached the sofa, but before throwing himself into one of its inviting corners, manlike he placed one of the large sofa pillows rather gingerly on the floor against a table-leg. Behind the pillow appeared the book.

"Hello," he exclaimed, "what's this?" And he held it up.

I put out my hand. "I'll take it, thank you," I said.

"Whose is this, anyhow?" he asked, opening the book instead of passing it over to me. "Looks like Ruth's marks." Then after a pause, "*Is* it Ruth's?"

"I don't know. Perhaps."

"She shouldn't read stuff like this!" pronounced the young judge.

"Oh, Ruth has always read everything she wanted to."

"Yes, I suppose so—more's the pity—best-sellers, anything that's going. But *this—this!* It's not decent for her, for any girl. I don't believe in this modern idea of exposure, anyhow. But here she comes." His face lighted. He put aside the book. "Here Ruth comes!" And he went out into the hall to meet her.

I heard the front door open, the rustle of a greeting, and a moment later my sister and Robert Jennings both came in.

Ruth had become a shining roseate creature. Always beautiful, always exquisite—flawless features, perfect poise, now she pulsated with life. A new brightness glowed in her eyes. Of late across her cheeks color was wont to come and go like the shadow of clouds on a hillside on a windy day. Even her voice, usually steady and controlled, now and again trembled and broke with sudden emotion. She came into the room smiling, very pretty, very lovely (could we really be children of the same parents?), with a pink rose slipped into the opening of her coat. She drew out her rose and came over and passed it to me.

"There," she said, "it's for you, Lucy. I bought it especially!" Such a strange new Ruth! Once so worldly, so selfish; now so sweet and full of queer tenderness. I hardly recognized her. "It's heavenly out-doors," she went on. "I'll be back in a minute." And she went out into the hall to take off her hat and coat.

Robert went over to the book he had laid on the table and picked it up. When Ruth joined us he inquired pleasantly, "Where in the world did you run across this, Ruth?"

"That?" she smiled. "Oh, I bought it. Everybody is talking about it, and I bought it. It isn't so bad. Some parts are really very nice. I've marked a few I liked."

"Why, Ruth," he said solicitously, "it isn't a book for you to read."

"That's very sweet and protective, Bob," she laughed gently, "but after all I'm not—what do you call it—early Victorian. I'm twentieth century, and an American at that. Every book printed is for me to read."

"Oh, no! I should hope not! Too much of this sort of stuff would rob a girl of every illusion she ever had."

"Illusions! Oh, well," she shrugged her shoulders, "who wants illusions? I don't. I want truth, Bob. I want to know everything there is to know in this world, good, bad or indifferent. And you needn't be afraid. It won't hurt me. Truth is good for any one, whether it's pleasant truth or not. It makes one's opinions of more value, if nothing else. And of course you want my opinions to be worth something, don't you?" she wheedled.

"But, my dear," complained Bob, "this book represents more lies than it does truth."

"Do you think so?" she asked earnestly. "Now I thought it was a wonderfully true portrayal of just how a man and woman would feel under those circumstances."

Bob looked actually pained. "O Ruth, how can you judge of such circumstances? Of such feelings? Why, I don't like even to discuss such rottenness with you as *this*."

"How absurd, Bob," Ruth deprecated lightly. "I'm not a Jane Austen sort of girl. I've always read things. I've always read everything I wanted to." Bob was still standing with the book in his hands, looking at it. He didn't reply for a moment. Something especially obnoxious must have met his eyes, for abruptly he threw the book down upon the table.

"Well," he said, "I'm going to ask you not to finish reading *this*."

"You aren't serious!"

"Yes, I am, Ruth," replied Bob. "Let me be the judge about this. Trust it to me. You've read only a little of the book. It's worse later–unpleasant, distorted. There are other avenues to truth–not this one, please. Yes, I am serious."

He smiled disarmingly. For the first time since their engagement I saw Ruth fail to smile back. There was a perceptible pause. Then in a low voice Ruth asked, "Do you mean you ask me to stop reading a book right in the middle of it? Don't ask me to do a childish thing like that, Bob."

"But Ruth," he persisted, "it's to guard you, to protect you."

"But I don't want to be protected, not that way," she protested. Her gray eyes were almost black. Her voice, though low and quiet enough, trembled. They must have forgotten I was in the room.

"Is it such a lot to ask?" pleaded Bob.

"You *do* ask it then?" repeated Ruth uncomprehendingly.

"Why, Ruth, yes, I do. If a doctor told you not to eat a certain thing," Bob began trying to be playful, "that he knew was bad for you and—"

"But you're not my doctor," interrupted Ruth. "That's just it. You're—It seems all wrong somehow," she broke off, "as if I was a child, or an ignorant patient of yours, and I'm not. I'm not. Will you pass it to me, please–the book?"

Bob gave it to her immediately. "You're going to finish it then?" he asked, alarmed.

"I don't know," said Ruth, wide-eyed, a little alarmed herself, I think. "I don't know. I must think it over." She crossed the room to the secretary, opened the glass door, and placed the book on one of the high shelves. "There," she said, "there it is." Then turning around she added, "I'll let you know when I decide, Bob. And now I guess I'll go upstairs, if you don't mind. These walking-shoes are so heavy. Good-by." And she fled, on the verge of what I feared was tears.

Both Bob and Ruth were so surprised at the appearance of this sudden and unlooked-for issue that I felt convinced it was their first difference of opinion. I was worried. I couldn't foretell how it would come out. Their friendship had been brief–perhaps too brief. Their engagement was only four weeks old. They loved–I was sure of that–but they didn't know each other very well. Old friend of Will's and mine as Robert Jennings is, I knew him to be conservative, steeped in traditions since childhood. Robert idealizes everything mellowed by age, from pictures and literature to laws and institutions. Ruth, on the other hand, is a pronounced modernist. It doesn't make much difference whether it's a hat or a novel, if it's new and up to date Ruth delights in it.

I poured out my misgivings to Will that night behind closed doors. Will had never had a high opinion of Ruth.

"Modernism isn't her difficulty, my dear," he remarked. "Selfishness, with a big S. That's the trouble with Ruth. Society too. Big S. And a pinch of stubbornness also. She never would take any advice from any one—self-satisfied little Ruth wouldn't—and poor Bob is the salt of the earth too. It's a shame. Whoever would have thought fine old Bob would have fallen into calculating young Ruth's net anyhow!"

"O Will, please. You do misjudge her," I pleaded. "It isn't so. She isn't calculating. You've said it before, and she isn't—not always. Not this time."

"You ruffle like a protecting mother hen!" laughed Will. "Don't worry that young head of yours too much, dear. It isn't *your* love affair, remember."

It *is* my love affair. That's the difficulty. In all sorts of quiet and covered ways have I tried to help and urge the friendship along. Always, even before Ruth was engaged to Breckenridge Sewall, have I secretly nursed the hope that Robert Jennings and my sister might discover each other some day—each so beautiful to look upon, each so distinguished in poise and speech and manner; Ruth so clever; Bob such a scholar; both of them clean, young New Englanders, born under not dissimilar circumstances, and both much beloved by me. It *is* my love affair, and it simply mustn't have quarrels.

I didn't refer to the book the next day, nor did I let Ruth know by look or word that I noticed her silence at table or her preoccupied manner. I made no observation upon Robert's failure to make his daily call the next afternoon. She may have written and told him to stay away. I did not know. In mute suspense I awaited the announcement of her decision. It was made at last, sweetly, exquisitely, I thought.

On the second afternoon Robert called as usual. I was in the living-room when he came in. When Ruth appeared in the doorway, I got up to go.

"No, please," she said. "Stay, Lucy, you were here before. Hello, Bob," she smiled, then very quietly she added, "I've made my decision."

"Ruth!" Robert began.

"Wait a minute, please," she said.

She went over to the secretary, opened the door and took down the book. Then she crossed to the table, got a match, approached the fireplace, leaned down, and set fire to my cherished selected birch-logs. She held up the book then and smiled radiantly at Robert. "This is my decision!" she said, and laid the book in the flames.

"Good heavens," I wanted to exclaim, "that's worth a dollar thirty-five!"

"I've thought it all over," Ruth said simply, beautiful in the dignity of her new-born self-abnegation. "A book is only paper and print, after all. I was making a mountain out of it. It's as you wish, Bob. I won't finish reading it."

We were very happy that night. Robert stayed to dinner. Will chanced to be absent and there were only the three of us at table. There was a mellow sort of stillness. A softness of voice possessed us all, even when we asked for bread or salt. Our conversation was trivial, unimportant, but kind and gentle. Between Ruth and Robert there glowed adoration for each other, which words and commonplaces could not conceal.

Robert stayed late. Upstairs in Will's study the clock struck eleven-thirty when I heard the front door close, and peeked out and saw Robert walking down over our flag-stones.

A moment later Ruth came upstairs softly. She went straight to her own room. She closed the door without a sound. My sister, I knew, was filled with the kind of exaltation that made her gentle even to stairs and door-knobs.

Next morning she was singing as usual over her initialing. We went into town at eleven-thirty to look up table linen. Edith met us for lunch. One of the summer colonists had told Edith about Robert's "connections" (he has several in Boston in the Back Bay and he himself was born in a house with violet-colored panes) and Edith had become remarkably enthusiastic. She was going to present Ruth with all her lingerie.

"After all," she said one day in way of reassurance to Ruth, "you would have been in a pretty mess if you'd married Breck Sewall. Some gay lady in Breck's dark and shady past sprang up with a spicy little law suit two weeks before he was to be married to that Oliphant girl. Perhaps you saw it in the paper. Wedding all off, and Breck evading the law nobody knows where. This Bob of yours is as poor as Job's turkey, I suppose, but anyhow, he's *decent*. An uncle of his is president of a bank in Boston and belongs to all sorts of exclusive clubs and things. I'm going to give you your wedding, you know, Toots. I've always wanted a good excuse for a hack at Boston."

Bob Turns out a Conservative

BUT Edith didn't give Ruth her wedding. There was no wedding. Ruth didn't marry Robert Jennings!

I cannot feel the pain that is Ruth's, the daily loss of Bob's eyes that worshiped, voice that caressed—no, not that hurt—but I do feel bitterness and disappointment. They loved each other. I thought that love always could rescue. I was mistaken. Love is not the most important thing in marriage. No. They tell me ideals should be considered first. And yet as I sit here in my room and listen to the emptiness of the house—Ruth's song gone out of it, Ruth fled with her wound, I know not where—and see Bob, a new, quiet, subdued Bob, walking along by the house to the University, looking up to my window and smiling (a queer smile that hurts every time), the sparkle and joy gone out like a flame, I whisper to myself fiercely, "It's all wrong. Ideals to the winds. They loved each other, and it is all wrong."

They were engaged about three months in all. They were so jubilant at first that they wanted the engagement announced immediately. The college paper triumphantly blazoned the news, and of course the daily papers too. Everybody was interested. Everybody congratulated them. Ruth has hosts of friends, Robert too. Ruth's mail for a month was enormous. The house was sweet with flowers for days. Her presents rivaled a bride's. And yet she gave it all up—even loving Bob. She chose to face disapproval and distrust. Will called her heartless for it; Tom, fickle; Edith, a fool; but I call her courageous.

There was no doubt of the sincerity of Ruth's love for Robert Jennings. No other man before had got beneath the veneer of her worldliness. Robert laid bare secret expanses of her nature, and then, like warm sunlight on a hillside from which the snow has melted away, persuaded the expanses into bloom and beauty. Timid generosities sprang forth in Ruth. Tolerance, gratitude, appreciation blossomed frailly; and over all there spread, like those hosts of four-petaled flowers we used to call bluets, which grew in such abundance among rarer violets or wild strawberry—there spread through Ruth's awakened nature a thousand and one little kindly impulses that had to do with smiles for servants, kind words for old people, and courtesy to clerks in shops. I don't believe that anything but love could work such a miracle with Ruth. If only she had waited, perhaps it would have performed more wonderful feats.

The book incident was the first indication of trouble. The second was more trivial. It happened one Sunday noon. We had been to church that morning together—Ruth, Will and I—and Robert Jennings was expected for our mid-day dinner at one-thirty. He hadn't arrived when we returned at one, and after Ruth had taken off her church clothes and changed to something soft and filmy, she sat down at the piano and played a little while—five minutes or so—then rose and strolled over toward the front window. She seated herself, humming softly, by a table there. "Bob's late," she remarked and lazily reached across the table, opened my auction-bridge box, selected a pack of cards, and still humming began to play solitaire.

The cards were all laid out before her when Robert finally did arrive. Ruth gave him one of her long, sweet glances, then demurely began laying out more cards. "Good morning, Bob," she said richly.

Bob said good morning, too, but I discerned something forced and peremptory in his voice. I felt that that pack of playing cards laid out before Ruth on the Sabbath-day affected him just as it had me when first Ruth came to live with us. I had been brought up to look upon card-playing on Sunday as forbidden. In Hilton I could remember when policemen searched vacant lots and fields on Sunday for crowds of bad boys engaged in the shocking pastime beneath secreted shade trees. Ruth had traveled so widely and spent so many months visiting in various communities where card-playing on Sunday was the custom that I knew it didn't occur to her as anything out of the ordinary. I tried to listen to what Will was reading out loud to me from the paper, but the fascination of the argument going on behind my back by the window held me.

"But, Bob dear," I heard Ruth's surprised voice expostulate pleasantly, "you play golf occasionally on Sunday. What's the difference? Both a game, one played with sticks and a ball, and the other with black and red cards. I was allowed to play Bible authors when I was a child, and it's terribly narrow, when you look at it squarely, to say that one pack of cards is any more wicked than another."

"It's not a matter of wickedness," Bob replied in a low, disturbed voice. "It's a matter of taste, and reverence for pervading custom."

"But—" put in Ruth.

"Irreverence for pervading custom," went on Bob, "is shown by certain men when they smoke, with no word of apology, in a lady's reception-room, or track mud in on their boots, as if it was a country club. Some people enjoy having their Sundays observed as Sunday, just as they do their reception-rooms as reception-rooms."

"But, Bob—"

"I think of you as such an exquisite person," he pursued, "so fine, so sensitive, I cannot associate you with any form of offense or vulgarity, like this," he must have pointed to the cards, "or extreme fashions, or cigarette smoking. Do you see what I mean?"

"Vulgarity! Cigarette smoking! Why, Bob, some of the most refined women in the world smoke cigarettes—clever, intelligent women, too. And I never could see any justice at all in the idea some people have that it's any worse, or more vulgar, as you say, for women to smoke cigarettes than for men."

"Irreverence for custom again, I suppose," sighed Bob.

"Well, then, if it's a custom that's unjust and based on prejudice, why keep on observing it? It used to be the custom for men to wear satin knickerbockers and lace ruffles over their wrists, but some one was sensible enough—or irreverent enough—" she tucked in good-naturedly, "to object—and you're the gainer. There! How's that for an answer? Doesn't solitaire win?"

"Custom and tradition," replied Bob earnestly, anxiously, "is the work of the conservative and thoughtful majority, and to custom and tradition every civilization must look for a solid foundation. Ignore them and we wouldn't be much of a people."

"Then how shall we ever progress?" eagerly took up Ruth, "if we just keep blindly following old-fogey laws and fashions? It seems to me that the only way people ever get ahead is by breaking traditions. Father broke a few in his generation—he had to to keep up with the game—and so must I."

"Oh, well," said Bob, almost wearily, "let's not argue, you and I."

"Why not?" inquired Ruth, and I heard her dealing out more cards as she went on talking gaily. "I love a good argument. It wakes me up intellectually. My mind's been so lazy. It *needs* to be waked up. It feels good, like the first spring plunge in a pond of cold water to a sleepy old bear who's been rolled up in a ball in some dark hole all winter. That's what it feels like. I never knew what fun it was to think and argue till I began taking the English course at Shirley. We argue by the hour there. It's great fun. But I suppose I'm terribly illogical and no fun to argue with. That's the way with most women. It isn't our fault. Men seem to want to make just nice soft pussy-cats out of us, with ribbons round our necks," she laughed, "and hear us purr. There! wait a minute. I'm going to get this. Come and see." Then abruptly, "Why, Bob, do the cards shock *you*?"

"No, no—not a bit," he assured her.

"They do," she affirmed. "How funny. They do." There was a pause. "Well," she said at last (Will was still reading out loud and I could barely catch her answer).

"Well, I suppose they're only pasteboard, just as the book was only paper and print. I can give them up."

"I don't want you to—not for me. No, don't. Go right ahead. Please," urged Bob. But it was too late.

"Of course not," replied Ruth, and I heard the cards going back into the box. "If I offend—and I see I do—of course not." And she rose and came over and sat on the sofa beside me.

From that time on I noticed a change in Robert and Ruth—nothing very perceptible. Robert came as often, stayed as late—later. That was what disturbed me. Ruth rose in the morning, after some of those protracted sessions, suspiciously quiet and subdued. In place of the radiance that so lately had shone upon her face, often I perceived a puzzled and troubled expression. In place of her almost hilarious joy, a wistfulness stole into her bearing toward Bob.

"Of course," she said to me one day, "I have been living a sort of—well, broad life you might call it for a daughter of father's, I suppose. He was so straightlaced. But all the modes and codes I've been adopting for the last several years I adopted only to be polite, to do as other people did, simply not to offend—as Bob said the other day. I thought if I ever wanted to go back to the strict laws of my childhood again, I could easily enough. In fact I intended to, after I had had my little fling. But I've outgrown them. They don't seem reasonable to me now. I can't go back to them. Convictions stand in my way."

"Women ought not to have convictions," I said shortly.

"Don't you think so?" queried Ruth.

"Men," I replied, "have so much more knowledge and experience of the world. Convictions have foundations with men."

"How unfair somehow," said Ruth, looking away into space.

"Just you take my advice, Ruth," I went on, "and don't you let any convictions you may think you have get in the way of your happiness. Just you let them lie for a while. When you and Bob are hanging up curtains in your new apartment, and pictures and things, you won't care a straw about your convictions, then."

"I don't suppose so," replied Ruth, still meditative. "No, I suppose you're right. I'll let Bob have the convictions for both of us. I'm younger. I can re-adjust easier than he, I guess."

A few days later Ruth went to a suffrage meeting in town; not because she was especially interested, but because a friend she had made in a course she was taking at Shirley College invited her to go.

It was the winter that everybody was discussing suffrage at teas and dinner parties; fairs and balls and parades were being given in various cities in its interest; and anti-organizations being formed to fight it and lend it zest. It was the winter that the term Feminism first reached the United States, and books on the greater freedom of women and their liberalization burst into print and popularity.

On the suffrage question Ruth had always been prettily "on the fence," and "Oh, dear, do let's talk of something else," she would laugh, while her eyes invited. Her dinner partners were always willing.

"On the fence, Kidlet," Edith had once remonstrated to Ruth, "that's stupid!" Edith herself was strongly anti. "Of course I'm anti," she maintained proudly. "Anybody who *is* anybody in Hilton is anti. The suffragists—dear me! Perfect freaks—most of them. People you never heard of! I peeked in at a suffrage tea the other day and mercy, such sights! I wouldn't be one of them for money. We're to give an anti-ball here in Hilton. I'm a patroness. Name to be printed alongside Mrs. ex-Governor Vaile's. How's that? 'On the fence,' Ruth! Why, good heavens, there's simply no two sides to the question. You come along to this anti-ball and you'll see, Kiddie!"

Well, as I said, Ruth went one day to a suffrage meeting in town. She had never heard the question discussed from a platform. When she came into the house about six o'clock, she was so full of enthusiasm that she didn't stop to go upstairs. She came right into the room where Will and I were reading by the cretonne-shaded lamp.

"I've just been to the most wonderful lecture!" she burst out, "on suffrage! I never cared a thing about the vote one way or the other, but I do now. I'm *for* it. Heart and soul, I'm for it! Oh, the most wonderful woman spoke. Every word she said applied straight to me. I didn't know I had such ideas until that woman got up and put them into words for me. They've been growing and ripening in me all these years, and I didn't know it—not until today. That woman said that sacrifices are made again and again to send boys to college and prepare them to earn a living, but that girls are brought up simply to be pretty and attractive, so as to capture a man who will provide them with food and clothes. Why, Lucy, don't you see that that's just what happened in *our* family? We slaved to send Oliver and Malcolm through college—but for *you* and for *me*—what slaving was there done to prepare us to earn a living? Just think what I might be had *I* been prepared for life like Malcolm or Oliver, instead of wasting all my years frivoling. Why, don't you see I could have convictions with a foundation then? I feel so helpless and ignorant with a really educated person now. Oh, dear, I wish this movement had been begun when I was a baby, so I could have profited by it! That woman said that when laws are equal for men and women, *then* advantages will be, and that every step we can make toward equalization is a step in the direction toward a fairer deal for women. Suffrage? Well, I should say I was for it! I think it's wonderful. I went straight up to that woman and said I wanted to join the League; and I did. It cost me a dollar."

"Good heavens, Ruth," exclaimed Will sleepily, from behind his paper. "Don't you go and get rabid on suffrage—Ease up, old girl. Steady."

"I don't see how any one can help but get rabid, Will, as you say, any more than a person could keep calm if he was a slave, when he first heard what Abraham Lincoln was trying to do."

"Steady there, old girl," jibed Will. "Is Bob such a terrific master as all that?"

"That's not the point, Will. Convention is the master–that's what the woman said. It isn't free of men we're trying to be."

"We! we! Come, Ruth. You aren't one of them in an hour, are you? Better wait and consult Bob first."

"Oh, Bob will agree with me. I know he will. It's such a progressive idea. And I *am* one of them. I'm proud to be. I'm going to march in the parade next week."

I came to life at that. "Oh, Ruth, not really–not in Boston!"

"What? Up the center of Washington Street in French heels and a shadow veil?" scoffed Will.

"Up the center of Washington Street in something," announced Ruth, "if that's the line of march. Remember, Will, French heels and shadow veils have been my stock in trade, and not through any choice of mine, either. So don't throw them at me, please."

Will subsided. "Well, well, what next? A raring, tearing little suffragette, in one afternoon, too!"

Ruth went upstairs.

"Poor old Bob," remarked Will to me when we were alone.

Another Catastrophe

I DIDN'T know whether it was more "poor old Bob" or "poor old Ruth." Ruth was so arduous at first, so in earnest—like a child with a new and engrossing plaything for a day or two, and then, I suppose, she showed her new toy to Bob, and he took it away from her. Anyway, she put it by. It seemed rather a shame to me. The new would have worn off after a while.

"And after all, Will," I maintained to my husband, "Robert Jennings is terribly old-school, sweet and chivalrous as can be toward women, but he can't treat Ruth in the way he does that helpless little miniature of a mother of his. He simply lives to protect her from anything practical or disagreeable. She adores it, but Ruth's a different proposition. The trouble with Robert is, he's about ten years behind the times."

"And Ruth," commented Will, "is about ten years ahead of the times."

"That is true of the different members of lots of households, in these times, but they don't need to come to blows because of it. Everybody ought to be patient and wait. Ruth has a pronounced individuality, for all you think she is nothing but a society butterfly. I can see it hurts to cram it into Robert Jennings' ideal of what a woman should be. It makes me feel badly to see Ruth so quiet and resigned, like a little beaten thing, so pitiably anxious to please. Self-confidence became her more. She hasn't mentioned suffrage since Robert called and stayed so late Wednesday, except to say briefly, 'I'm not going to march in the parade.' 'Why not?' I asked. 'Doesn't Bob want you to?' 'Oh, certainly. He leaves it to me,' she pretended proudly. 'But, you see, women in parades do offend some people. It isn't according to tradition, and I think it's only courteous to Bob, just before we are to be married, not to do anything offensive. After all, I must bear in mind,' she said, 'that this parade is only a matter of walking—putting one foot in front of the other. I'm bound to be happy, and I don't intend to allow suffrage to stand in my way either. Even convictions are only a certain condition of gray matter.' Oh, it was just pitiful to hear her trying to convince herself. I'm just afraid, Will, afraid for the future."

Not long after that outburst of mine to Will, my fears came true. One late afternoon, white-faced, wide-eyed, Ruth came in to me. She closed the door behind her. Her outside things were still on. I saw Robert Jennings out the window going slowly down the walk. Before Ruth spoke I knew exactly what she had to say.

"We aren't going to be married," she half whispered to me.

"Oh, Ruth—"

"No. Please. Don't, don't talk about it," she said. "And don't tell Will. Don't tell any one. Promise me. I've tried so hard—so hard. But my life has spoiled me for a man like Bob. Don't talk of it, please."

"I won't, Ruth," I assured her.

"I can do it. I thought I couldn't at first. But I *can*!" she said fiercely, "I *can*! I'll be misunderstood, I know. But I can't help that. We've decided it together. It isn't I alone. Bob has decided it, too. We both prefer to be unhappy alone, rather than unhappy together."

"In every marriage, readjustments are necessary," I commented.

"Don't argue," she burst out at me. "Don't! Don't you suppose Bob and I have thought of every argument that exists to save our happiness? For heaven's sake, Lucy, don't argue. I can't quite bear it." She turned away and went upstairs.

She didn't want any dinner. "I'm going to bed early," she told me an hour later when I knocked at her door. "No, not even toast and tea. Please don't urge me," she begged, and I left her. At ten when I went to bed her room was dark.

At half-past eleven I got up, stole across the hall, and stood listening outside her closed door. At long intervals I could hear her move. She was not sleeping. I waited an hour and stole across the hall again. She was still awake. Poor Ruth—sleepless, tearless (there was no sound of sobbing) hour after hour, there she was lying all night long, staring into the darkness, waiting for the dawn. At three I opened the door gently and went in, carrying something hot to drink on a tray.

"What is the matter?" she asked calmly.

"Nothing, Ruth. Only you must sleep, and here is some hot milk with just a little pinch of salt. It's so flat without. Nobody can sleep on an empty stomach."

"I guess that's the trouble," she said, and sat up and took the milk humbly, like a child. Her fingertips were like ice. I went into the bath-room, filled a hot-water bag, and got out an extra down-comforter. I was tucking it in when she asked, "What time is it?" And I told her. "Only three? Oh, dear—don't go—just yet." So I wrapped myself up in a warm flannel wrapper and sat down on the foot of her bed with my feet drawn up under me.

"I won't," I said, "I'll sit here."

"You're awfully good to me," Ruth remarked. "I *was* cold and hungry, I guess. Oh, Lucy," she exclaimed, "I wish one person could understand, just *one*."

"I do, Ruth. I do understand," I said eagerly.

"It isn't suffrage. It isn't the parade. It isn't any *one* thing. It's just *everything*, Lucy. I'm made up on a wrong pattern for Bob. I hurt him all the time. Isn't it awful—even though he cares for me, and I for him, we hurt each other?"

I kept quite still. I knew that Ruth wanted to talk to some one, and I sat there hugging my knees, thankful that I happened to be the one. Always I had longed for this mysterious sister's confidence, and always I had seemed to her too simple, too obvious, to share and understand.

"You know, Lucy," she went on wistfully, "I was awfully happy at first—so happy—you don't know. Why, I would do anything for Bob. I was glad to give up riches for him. My worldly ambitions shriveled into nothing. Comforts, luxuries—what were they as compared to Bob's love? But, oh, Lucy, it is giving up little things, little independencies of thought, little daily habits, which I can't do. I tried to give up these, too. You know I did. I said that the book was just paper and print and the cards just pasteboard. But all the time they were symbols. I could destroy the symbols easily enough, but I couldn't destroy what they stood for. You see, Bob and I have different ideals. That's at the bottom of all the trouble. We tried for weeks not to admit it, but it had to be faced finally."

"Your ideals aren't very different way down at their roots—both clean, true, sincere, and all that," I said, with a little yawn, so she might not guess how tremblingly concerned I really was.

"You don't know all the differences, Lucy," she said sadly. "There's something the trouble with me—something left out—something that I cannot blame Bob for feeling sorry about. I believe I'll tell you. You see, Bob met me under a misapprehension, and I've been trying to live up to his misapprehension ever since. The first time he ever saw me I was tucked away in a little room by myself looking at the picture of a sick child. I was crying a little. He thought that I was feeling badly out of sympathy for the mother of the child—the mother in me, you see, speaking to the mother in her. I wasn't really. I was crying because the house that the picture happened to hang in was so dull and grimy beside Grassmere. I was crying for the luxuries I had lost. I never told Bob the truth about that picture until last week, and all this time he's been looking upon me as an ideal woman—a kind of madonna, mother of little children, you understand, and all that—and I'm not. Something must be wrong with me. I don't even long to be—yet. Oh, you see how unfitted I am for a man to weave idealistic pictures about—like that. It seemed to hurt Bob when I told him the truth about myself, hurt him terribly, as if I'd tumbled over and broken his image of me—at the cradle, you know. Oh, Lucy, what an unnatural girl I am! I don't admire myself for it. I wish I could be what Bob thinks, but I can't. I can't."

"You aren't unnatural. You're just as human as you can be, Ruth. I felt just the way you do before I was married, and most every girl does as young as you, too. Bob ought to give you chance to grow up."

"Grow up! Oh, Lucy, I feel so old! I feel used up and put by already. I've lived my life and haven't I made a botch of it?" She laughed shortly. "And what shall I do with the botch now? I can't stay here. It would break my heart to stay here where I had hoped to be so happy—everything reminding me, you know. No, I can't stay here."

"Of course you can't, Ruth. We'll think of a way."

"And I simply can't go back to Edith," she went on, "after knowing Bob. I don't want to go out to Michigan with Tom and Elise. I hate Michigan. Dear me! I don't know what I shall do. I'm discouraged. Once I was eager and confident, filled with enthusiasm and self-pride. Like that old hymn, you know. How does it go? 'I loved to choose my path and see, but now lead Thou me on. I loved the garish day, and spite of fears, Pride ruled my will. Remember not past years.' That is what I repeat over and over to myself. 'Lead, kindly light, amidst th' encircling gloom.' The encircling gloom! Oh, dear!" She suddenly broke off, "I wish morning would come." It did finally, and with it, when the approaching sun began to pinken the eastern sky, sleep for my tormented sister.

A Family Conference

WE all were seated about the table at one of Edith's sumptuous Sunday dinners at the Homestead when Ruth broke her news to the family. Tom had come East on a business trip, and was spending Sunday with Alec in Hilton; so Edith telephoned to all of us within motoring distance and invited us up for "Sunday dinner." This was two or three days after Ruth had told me that she and Bob were not to be married.

"Oh, yes, I'll go," she nodded, when I had clapped my hand over the receiver and turned to her questioningly, and afterward she said to me, "Concealing my feelings is one of the accomplishments my education *has* included. I'll go. I shan't tell them about Bob yet. I can't seem to just now."

I was therefore rather surprised when she suddenly abandoned her play-acting. She hadn't figured on the difficult requirements, I suppose, poor child. Bluff and genial Tom, grown rather gray and stout and bald now, had met her with a hearty, "Hello, bride-elect!" Oliver had shouted, "Greetings, Mrs. Prof!" And Madge, his wife, had tucked a tissue-paper-wrapped package under Ruth's arm: "My engagement present," she explained. "Just a half-a-dozen little guest-towels with your initials."

Later at the table Tom had cleared his throat and then remarked, "I like all I hear of this Robert Jennings. He's good stuff, Ruth. You've worried us a good deal, but you've landed on your feet squarely at last. He's a bully chap."

"And he's got a bully girl, too, now that she's got down to brass tacks," said Alec in big-brother style.

"Decided on the date?" cheerfully inquired Tom. "Elise said to be sure and find out. We're coming on in full force, you know."

"Yes, the date's decided," flashed Edith from the head of the table. "June 28th. It'll be hot as mustard, but Hilton will be lovely then, and all the summerites here. You must give me an hour on the lists after dinner, Kidlet. Bob's list, people, is three hundred, and Ruth's four, so I guess there'll be a few little remembrances. The envelopes are half directed already. I want you people to know this wedding is only seven weeks off, so hurry up and order your new gowns and morning coats. Simplicity isn't going to be the keynote of this affair."

"Hello!" exclaimed Tom abruptly, "I haven't inspected the ring yet. Let's see it. Pass it over, Toots."

Ruth glanced down at her hand. It was still there—Bob's unpretentious diamond set in platinum—shining wistfully on Ruth's third finger.

She started to take it off, then stopped and glanced over at me. "I think I'll tell them, Lucy," she said. "I've got something to tell you all," she announced. "I'm wearing the ring still, but—we've broken our engagement. I'm not going to marry Robert Jennings after all."

It sounded harsh, crude. Everybody stared; everybody stopped eating; I saw Tom lay down his fork with a juicy piece of duck on it. It had been within two inches of his mouth.

"Will you repeat that?" he said emphatically.

"Yes," complied Ruth, "I will. I know it seems sudden to you. I meant to write it, but after all I might as well tell you. My engagement to Robert Jennings is broken."

"Is this a joke?" ejaculated Edith.

"No," replied Ruth, still in that calm, composed way of hers. "No, Edith, it isn't a joke."

"Will you explain?" demanded Tom, shoving the piece of duck off his fork and abandoning it for good and all.

Ruth had become pale. "Why, there isn't much to explain, except I found out I wouldn't be happy with Bob. That's all."

"Oh," said Tom, "you found out you wouldn't be happy with Bob! Will you kindly tell us whom you mean to try your happiness on next?"

Ruth's gray eyes darkened. A little pink stole into her cheeks. "There's no good of your using that tone with me, Tom," she said.

"Did you know this?" asked Will of me from across the table.

I nodded.

"Do you mean to say it's *true*?" demanded Edith.

I nodded again.

"You're crazy, Ruth," she burst out, "you're simply stark mad. It would be a public disgrace. You've got to marry him now. You've simply got to. It's worse than a divorce. Why—the invitations are all ordered, even the refreshments. The whole world knows about it. You've *got* to marry him."

"My own disgrace is my own affair, I guess," said Ruth, dangerously low.

"It's *not* your own affair. It's ours; it's the whole family's; it's mine. And I won't stand it—not a second time. Here I have told *everybody*, got my Boston list all made up, too, and all my plans made. Didn't I have new lights put into the ball-room especially, and a lot of repairs made on the house—a new bath-room, and everything? And all my house-party guests invited? Why—we'll be the laughing-stock of this entire town, if you play this game a second time. Good heavens, you'll be getting the habit. No, sir! You *can't* go back on your word in this fashion. You've *got* to marry Robert Jennings *now*."

"I wouldn't marry Breck Sewall to please you, Edith, and I won't marry Robert Jennings to please you either," said Ruth. "She wanted me to elope with Breck!" she announced calmly.

"That isn't true," replied Edith sharply.

"Why don't you call me a liar and have done with it?" demanded Ruth.

"I wanted to save you from disgrace, and you know it. I wanted—" A maid came in.

"Let us wait and continue this conversation later," remarked Tom.

"We don't want *you*," flared Edith at the maid. "I didn't ring. Go out till you're summoned. You're the most ungrateful girl I ever knew, Ruth. You're—"

"Come," interrupted Alec. "This isn't getting anywhere. Let us finish dinner first."

"I'm sure I don't want any more dinner," said Edith.

"Nor I," commented Ruth, with a shrug.

There were a salad fork and a dessert spoon still untouched beside our plates. It would have been thoughtful if Ruth had waited and lit her fuse when the finger-bowls came on. It seemed a shame to me to waste two perfectly good courses, and unnecessarily sensational to interrupt the ceremony of a Sunday dinner. But it was impossible to sit there through two protracted changes of plates.

"I guess we've all had enough," remarked Tom, disgustedly shoving away that innocent piece of duck. We rose stragglingly.

"I don't care to talk about this thing any more," said Ruth, as we passed through the hall. "You can thrash it out by yourselves. Lucy, you can represent me!" And she turned away to go upstairs.

Tom called back, "No, Ruth. This is an occasion that requires your presence, whether you like it or not," he said. "Come back, please. There are a few questions that need to be settled."

Ruth acquiesced condescendingly. "Oh, very well," she replied, and strolled down the stairs and into the library. She walked over to the table and leaned, half sitting, against it, while the rest of us came in and sat down, and some one closed the doors.

"Fire away!" she said flippantly, turning to Tom. She picked up an ivory paper-cutter with a tassel on one end, twisted the cord tight, and then holding the cutter up by the tassel watched it whirl and untwist.

Pretty, graceful, nonchalant, armored in a half smile, Ruth stood before her inquisitors. Bob never would have recognized this composed and unmoved girl as the anxious Ruth who had tried so hard to please and satisfy.

"First," began Tom (he has always held the position of high judge in our family), "first, I should be interested to know if you have any plans for the future, and, if so, will you be kind enough to tell us what they may be."

"I have plans," said Ruth, and began twisting the cord of the paper-cutter again.

"Will you put that down, please," requested Tom.

"Certainly," Ruth smiled over-obligingly and laid the paper-cutter on the table. She folded her arms and began tapping the rug with her toe. She was almost insolent.

"Well, then—what are your plans?" fired Tom at her with an obvious effort to control himself.

"New York," she announced mysteriously.

"Oh, New York!" repeated Tom. It was a scornful voice. "New York! And what do you intend to do in New York?"

"Oh, I don't know. I haven't decided. Something," she said airily.

"Ruth," said Tom, "please listen to me carefully if you can for a minute. We've always given you a pretty loose rein. Haven't we?"

Ruth shrugged her shoulders.

"You've had every advantage; attended one of the most expensive schools in this country; had all the money you required, coming-out party and all that; pleasures, flattery, attention—everything to make a girl contented. You've visited any one you pleased from one end of the United States to the other; traveled in Europe, Florida—anywhere you wanted; come and gone at will. Nothing to handicap you. Nothing hard. Nothing difficult. You'll agree. And what have you done with your advantages? *What*—I want to know?"

Ruth shrugged her shoulders again.

"You can't blame any one but yourself. You haven't been interfered with. I believed in letting you run your own affairs. Thought you were made of the right stuff to do it creditably. I was mistaken. You've had a fair trial at your own management and you've failed to show satisfactory results. Now *I'm* going to step in. *I'm* going to see if *I* can save you from this drifting about and getting nowhere. I don't ask you to go back and anchor with Robert Jennings again. I'm shocked to confess that I don't believe you're worthy of a man like Jennings. It is no small thing to be decided carelessly or frivolously—this matter of marriage. Engaged to two men inside of one year, and now both affairs broken off. It's disgraceful! You've got to learn somehow or other that although you are a woman, you're not especially privileged to go back on decisions."

"I don't want to be especially privileged," said Ruth, and then she added, "special privileges would not be expected by women, if they were given equal rights."

"Oh, Suffrage!!!" exclaimed Tom with three exclamation points. "So that's it! That's at the bottom of all this trouble."

"That's at the bottom of it," suddenly put in my husband, emphatically.

"Oh, I see. Well, first, Ruth, you're to drop all that nonsense. Suffrage indeed! What do *you* know about it? You ought to be married and taking care of your own babies, and you wouldn't be disturbed by all these crazy-headed fads, invented by dissatisfied and unoccupied females. Suffrage! And perhaps you think that this latest exhibition of your changeableness and vacillation is an argument in favor of it."

"You needn't throw women's vacillation in their faces, Tom," replied Ruth calmly. "Stable decisions are matters of training and education. Girls of my acquaintance lack the experience with the business world. They don't come in contact with big transactions. They're guarded from them. A lawyer does the thinking for a woman of property oftentimes, and so, of course, women do not learn the necessity of precise statements, accurate thought, and all that. From the time a girl is old enough to think she knows she is just a girl, who her family hope will grow up to be pretty and attractive and marry well. If her family believed she was to grow up into a responsible citizen who would later control by her vote all sorts of weighty questions that affect taxes and tariffs and things, they would have to devote more thought to making her intelligent, because it would have an effect upon their individual interests. I'm interested in suffrage, Tom, not for the good it is going to do politics, but for the good it's going to do women."

Tom made an exclamation of disgust. He was beside himself with scorn and disapproval.

"Nonsense! Utter rot! Women were made to marry and be mothers. Women were—"

"But we'd be better mothers," Ruth cut in. "Don't you see, if—"

"Oh, I don't want to discuss suffrage," interrupted Tom; "I want to discuss your life. Let's keep to the subject. I want to see you settled and happy some day, and as I'm so much older than you, you must put yourself into my hands, and cheerfully. First, drop suffrage. Drop it. Good Lord, Ruth, don't be a faddist. Then I want you to lay your decision about Jennings on the shelf. Let it rest for a while. Postpone the wedding if you wish—"

"But, Tom," tucked in Edith, "that's impossible. The invitations—"

"Never mind, never mind, Edith," interrupted Tom. Then to Ruth he went on. "Postpone the wedding–oh, say a month or two, and then see how you feel. That's all I ask. Reasonable, isn't it?" he appealed to us all. "I'll have a talk with Jennings in the meanwhile," he went on. "This suffrage tommy-rot is working all sorts of unnecessary havoc. I'm sick of it. I didn't suppose it had caught any one in our family though. You drop it, Ruth, for a while. You wait. I'm going back home next Wednesday. Now I want you to pack up your things and be ready to start with me Wednesday night from New York. We'll see what Elise and the youngsters will do for you."

"I'm sorry, Tom," replied Ruth pleasantly, "but my decision about Bob is final; and as for going out West with you and becoming a fifth wheel in your household–no, I've had enough of that. My mind is made up. I'm going to New York."

"But I shan't allow it," announced Tom.

"Then," replied Ruth, "I shall have to go without your allowing it."

"What do you mean?" demanded Tom.

"Why–just what I say. I'm of age. If I were a man, I wouldn't have to ask my older brother's permission."

"And how do you intend to live?"

"On my income," said Ruth. "I bless father now for that stock he left me. Eight hundred dollars a year has been small for me so far. I have had to have help, I know, but it will support my new life. I never was really grateful to father for that money till now. It makes me independent of you, Tom."

Edith, glaring inimically from her corner, exclaimed, "Grateful to her father! That's good!"

"My dear girl," said Tom, "we've never told you before, because we hoped to spare your feelings, but the time has come now. That stock father left you hasn't paid a dividend for a dozen years. It isn't worth its weight in paper. I have paid four hundred dollars, and Edith has been kind and generous enough to contribute four hundred dollars more, to keep you in carfares, young lady. It isn't much in order to talk of your independence around here."

The color mounted to Ruth's cheeks. She straightened. "What do you mean?" she asked.

"Exactly what I say. You haven't a penny of income. Edith and I are responsible for your living, and I want you to understand clearly that I shall not support a line of conduct which does not meet with my approval. Nor Edith either, I rather imagine."

"No, indeed, I won't," snapped out Edith. "I shan't pay a cent more. It's only rank ingratitude I get for it anyhow."

"Do you mean to say," said Ruth in a low voice—there was no flippancy to her now—"I've been living on Edith's charity, and yours, all these years? That I haven't anything of my own—not even my clothes—not even *this*," she touched a blue enameled watch and chain about her neck, "which I saved and saved so for? Haven't I any income? Haven't I a cent that's mine, Tom?"

"Not a red cent, Ruth—just some papers that we might as well put into the fireplace and burn up."

"Oh," she burst forth, "how unfair—how cruel and unfair!"

"There's gratitude for you," threw in Edith.

"To bring me up," went on Ruth, "under a delusion. To let me go on, year after year, thinking I was provided for, and then suddenly, when it pleases you, to tell me that I'm an absolute dependent, a creature of charity. Oh, how cruel that is! You tell me I ought to be grateful. Well, I'm not—I'm not grateful. You've been false with me. You've brought me up useless and helpless. I'm too old now to develop whatever talent I may have had. I can only drudge now. What is there I can do *now*? Nothing—nothing—except scrub floors or something like that."

"Oh, yes, there is, too," said Edith. "You can marry Robert Jennings and be sensible."

"Marry a man for support, whether I want to or not? I'll die first. You *all* want me to marry him," she burst out at us fiercely, "but I shan't—I shan't. I'm strong and healthy, and I'm just beginning to discover that I've got some brains, too. There's something I can do, surely, some way I can earn money. I shan't go West with you, Tom. Understand that. I can't quite see myself growing old in all your various households—old and useless and dependent like lots of unmarried women in large families. I can't see it without a fight anyhow. I don't care if I haven't any income. I can be a clerk in a store, I guess. Anyhow I shan't go West with you, Tom. I am of age. You can't make me. I know I'm just a woman, but I intend to live my own life just the same, and there's no one in this world who can bind and enslave me either!"

"You go upstairs, Ruth," ordered Tom. "I won't stand for such talk as that. You go upstairs and quiet down, and when you're reasonable, we'll talk again. We're not children."

"No, we're not," replied Ruth, "neither of us, and I shan't be sent upstairs as if I was a child either! You can pauperize me, and you can take away every rag I have on my back, too, if you want to, but I'll tell you one thing, you can't take away my independence. You think, Tom, you can frighten me, and conquer me, perhaps, by bullying. But you can't. Conditions are better for women than they used to be, anyhow, thank heaven, and for the courageous woman there's a chance to escape from just such masters of their fates as *you*—Tom Vars, even though you are my brother. And I shall escape somehow, *sometime*. See if I don't. Oh, I know what you all think of me," she broke off. "You all think I'm hard and heartless. Well—perhaps you're right. I guess I am. Such an experience as this would just about kill any softhearted person, I should think. But *I'm* not killed. Remember that, Tom. You've got money, support, sentiment on your side. I've got nothing but my own determination. But I'm not afraid to fight. And I will, if you force me. You'd better be pretty careful how you handle such an utterly depraved person as you seem to think I am. Why, I didn't know you had such a poor opinion of me."

She gave a short little laugh which ended in a sort of sob. I was afraid she was going to cry before us. But the armor was at hand. She put it on quickly, the cynical smile, the nonchalant air.

"There is no good talking any more, as I see," she was able to go on, thus protected. "This is bordering on a scene, and scenes are such bad taste! I'm going into the living-room."

She crossed the room to the door. "You all can go on maligning me to your hearts' content. I've had about enough, thank you. Only remember supper is at seven, and Edith's maids want to get out early Sundays. Consider the maids at least," she finished, and left us, colors flying.

Ruth Goes to New York

THE next morning when Will and I motored home we were alone. We approached the steeples of our town about noontime. I remember whistles were blowing and bells ringing as we passed through the Square. We saw Robert Jennings coming out of one of the University buildings on his way home from a late morning recitation. We slowed down beside him, and Will sang out to him to pile in behind; which he did, leaning forward and chatting volubly with Will and me for the next ten minutes about a new starter device for an automobile. When Will stopped in front of our walk, Robert hopped out of his back seat and opened the door for me.

It was when Will had motored out of hearing that Robert turned sharply to me and asked, "Did you leave her in Hilton?"

"No, Bob, Ruth isn't in Hilton. She's gone to New York," I told him gently.

"Whom is she staying with in New York? Your brother?" he asked.

"No, not Malcolm. No. But she's all right."

"What do you mean—'she's all right'?"

"Oh, I mean she has money enough—and all that."

"She isn't *alone* in New York!" he exclaimed. "You don't mean to say—"

"Now, Bob, don't *you* go and get excited about it. Ruth's all right. I'm just about worn out persuading my brother Tom that it is perfectly all right for Ruth to go to New York for a little while if she wants to. I can't begin arguing with you, the minute I get home. I'm all worn out on the subject."

"But what is she doing down there? Whom is she visiting? Who is looking out for her? Who went with her? Who met her?"

"Nobody, nobody. Nobody met her; nobody went with her; she isn't visiting anybody. Good heavens, Bob, you'd make a helpless, simpering little idiot out of Ruth if you had your way. She isn't a child. She isn't an inexperienced young girl. She's capable of keeping out of silly difficulties. She can be trusted. Let her use her judgment and good sense a little. It won't hurt her a bit. It will do her good. Don't you worry about Ruth. She's all right."

"But a girl—a pretty young girl like Ruth—you don't mean to say that Ruth—Ruth—"

"Yes, I do, too, Bob! And there are lots of girls just as pretty as Ruth in New York, and just as young, tapping away at typewriters, and balancing accounts in offices, and running shops of their own, too, in perfect safety. You're behind the times, Bob. I don't want to be horrid, but really I'm tired, and if you stay here and talk to me, I warn you I'm going to be cross."

We were in the house now. Bob had followed me in. I was taking off my things. He stared at me as I proceeded.

"I didn't see any sense at all in your breaking off your engagement," I went on. "You both cared for each other. I should have thought—"

"It was inevitable," cut in Bob gravely. "It was inevitable, Lucy."

"Well, then, if it was, Bob, all right. I won't say another word about it. But now that Ruth is nothing to you—"

"Nothing to me!" he exclaimed.

"Yes, that is what I said—nothing to you," I repeated mercilessly, "I beg of you don't come here and show approval or disapproval about what she's up to. Leave her to me now. I'm backing her. I tell you, just as I told Tom and the others, she's all right. Ruth's *all right.*"

But later in my room I wondered—I wondered if Ruth really was all right. Sitting in my little rocking-chair by the window, sheltered and protected by kind, familiar walls, I asked myself what Ruth was doing now. It was nearing the dinner hour. Where would Ruth be eating dinner? It was growing dark slowly. It would be growing dark in New York. Stars would be coming out up above the towering skyscrapers, as they were now above the apple trees in the garden. I thought of Ruth's empty bed across the hall. Where would she sleep tonight? Oh, Ruth—Ruth—poor, little sister Ruth!

I remember when you were a little baby wrapped up in soft, pink, knitted things. The nurse put you in my arms, and I walked very carefully into my mother's room with you and stood staring down at you asleep. I was only a little girl, I was afraid I would drop you, and I didn't realize as I stood there by our mother's bed that she was bidding her two little daughters good-by. She couldn't take one of my hands because they were both busy holding you; but she reached out and touched my shoulder; and she told me always to love you and take care of you and be generous and kind, because you were little and younger. And I said I would, and carried you out very proud and happy.

That was a long while ago. I have never told you about it—we haven't found it easy to talk seriously together—but I have always remembered. I used to love to dress you when you were a baby, and feed you, and take you out in the brown willow baby carriage like the real mothers. But, of course, you had to outgrow the carriage; you had to outgrow the ugly little dresses father and I used to select for you at the department stores in Hilton; you had to outgrow the two little braids I used to plait for you each morning when you were big enough to go to school; you had to outgrow me, too. I am so plain and commonplace.

Yesterday when you put your arms about me there in the smoky train-shed in Hilton, and cried a little as I held you close, with the great noisy train that was to take you away snorting beside us, you became again to me the little helpless sister that mother told me to take care of. All the years between were blotted out. I remembered our mother's room, the black walnut furniture. I saw the white pillows and mother's long, dark braids lying over each of her shoulders. Again I heard her words; again I felt the pride that swelled in my heart as I bore you away.

"I hope you are safe tonight. You can always call on me. I will always come. Don't be afraid. And when you are unhappy, write to me. I shall understand. You are not hard, you are not heartless. You are tender and sensitive. Only your armor is made of flint. You are not changeable and vacillating. They didn't know. You are brave and conscientious." With some such words as these last did I write to Ruth before I slept that night. I believed in her as I never had before. I cherished her with my soul.

This is what had happened in Hilton. After Ruth had left the room the afternoon of her inquisition, the rest of us had sat closeted in serious consultation for two hours or more. It was after five when we emerged.

To Edith's inquiry as to Ruth's whereabouts, a maid explained that Miss Ruth had left word that she was going to walk out to the Country Club, and would return in time for supper at seven. I went upstairs to my room. A feeling of despair possessed me. I sat down and gazed out of the window. A maid knocked lightly as I sat staring and came in with a letter.

"Miss Ruth told me to wait until you were alone and then to give you this," she explained.

I thanked her and she departed. I locked the door, then tore open Ruth's note to me and read it.

"Dear Lucy," it said. "I cannot help but overhear some of the conversation. Obviously, Tom is shouting so I may get the benefit of his remarks without effort. I must get out of this horrible place. How can I endure to meet the disapproval and bitterness and hatred—yes, *hatred*—when they come filing out upon me from that room across the hall. How can I sit down to supper with them all, ask for bread—for water? How can I keep up this farce of polite speech? I can't.

"You are in favor of my going away somewhere. I can hear you urging them. Well, then, if you are, let me go *now*—tonight. I can't go back with you tomorrow. Even though I am hard and heartless, don't ask me to run the risk of seeing Bob by mistake just now. I can't see him now. I can't. I *won't* stay here at Edith's. I won't go with Tom. This isn't the Middle Ages. Then if ultimately I am to go away, alone somewhere, let me go immediately. After I've gone the responsibility of giving me permission will be lifted from Tom's shoulders. Don't you see? You can argue with him to better advantage if the step has been taken.

"I shan't be blindly running away. I've been considering a change in my plans for so long that I've been enquiring. I know of a position I can get in New York, and right off. I wrote about it last week. I heard of it through the Suffrage League. It's a position in the office there in New York. I would have explained all this to Tom if he had been decent, but he wasn't. He is narrow and prejudiced. Oh, Lucy, help me to escape. I've got fifteen dollars, of Tom's and Edith's, and I shall keep it, too! They owe *me* a debt instead of *I*, them. That's the way I feel. But fifteen dollars is not enough to start to New York with. There's a train at 6.20 and another at 8.15. I am going down to the station now, this *minute*, and wait for you to come down there with more money and help me off. If you get out of that room before six, I could take the earlier train. If not, then the 8.15. I will wait for you in the ladies' waiting-room where the couches are. If you think my going suddenly this way is out of the question, then I'll simply turn around and come back with you to the house here, and grin and bear the situation somehow. I'll have to. So meet me anyhow. Don't tell any one where I am. Just stroll out and we'll pretend we've been to the Country Club.

"I know that I've been horrid to you all my life, critical and pharisaic. You can pay me back for it now. You can refuse to help me if you want to. I shan't blame you. But, oh, dear, let me go away alone, just for a little while anyway. Let nature try and heal.

"I have my bag and toilet articles. Money is all I want—money and perhaps just one person in my family to wish me well.

"Ruth."

I glanced at the clock It was just quarter of six. There was no opportunity of laying this question on the table and waiting for the clearing light of morning to help me make a wise decision. This was an occasion when a woman's intuition must be relied upon. As I stood there with Ruth's letter in my hand, swift and sure was the conviction that came to me. I must help Ruth get away. She would surely escape sometime from the kind of bondage Tom was planning to place her under. If not tonight, or next week, then a month hence. Was it not better for her to go, even though suddenly and shockingly, with the God-speed and the trust of some one in her own family?

Is it ever wise to cut the last thread that holds a girl to those who have loved and cherished her? I thought not. Perhaps the slender thread that now existed between Ruth and me might be the means of drawing a stouter cord, which in its turn might haul a cable, strong and reliable. I did not think then of the possible dangers in New York—the difficulties, the risks; there was no time to discuss, no time for doubts and misgivings; there was simply time for me to fill out two blank checks for twenty-five dollars each, put on my hat and coat, and speed with all possible haste to the station.

I found Ruth eagerly awaiting me in the train-shed. There were crowds of people hastening here and there with bags and suit-cases. There were trucks and train-men. There was the roar of an incoming train. Through the confusion Ruth's anxious eyes looked straight into mine.

"Well?"

"Is this your train?" I asked with a nod toward the sweating monster that had just come to a standstill on the first track.

"It's the New York train," said Ruth.

"Well, I've brought some money," I went on quickly. "Fifty dollars. It will last for a while. They don't know about it yet, back there at the house. I shall have to tell them when I go back. I can't predict. Tom may wire Malcolm to meet you and drag you back home. I don't know. But I'll use all the influence I can against it. I'll do my very best, Ruth."

Ruth's hand found mine in a sudden grasp and held it tightly. Another train roared into the train-shed.

"Where shall you stay tonight?" I shrieked at her.

She gave the name of a well-known hotel reserved especially for women. "I shall be all right," she called. "I'll drop you a line tomorrow. You needn't worry about me. I'll let you know if I need anything."

A deep megaphoned voice announced the New York train.

"Your ticket?" I reminded.

"I have it. I was going anyway," she replied.

"Well, then," I said, and opened my bag and produced the two checks. She took them. "Promise me, Ruth, promise *always* to let me know—always if you need anything, or are unhappy."

Her eyes suddenly brimmed with tears. Her under lip quavered. She broke down at last. I held her in my arms.

"Oh, Lucy, Lucy," she cried. "You're so good to me. I miss him so. I left the ring in the corner of your top drawer. You give it to Bob. I can't. You're all I have. I've been so horrid to you all my life. I miss Bob so. I hate Tom. I almost hate Tom. Oh, Lucy, what's to become of me? Whatever is to become of me?"

The train gave a little jerk.

"All aboard, Miss," called a porter.

"Your train, Ruth dear," I said gently and actually pushed her a little toward New York, which even now was beginning to appall me. She kissed me good-by. I looked up and saw her floating away in a cloud of fitful steam.

A Year Later

THAT was nearly a year ago. Until one day last week I have not seen Ruth since, not because of the busy life of a young mother—for such I have become since Ruth went away—no, though busy I have been, and proud and happy and selfish, too, like every other mother of a first son in the world, I suppose—but because Ruth hasn't wished to be seen. That is why I have heard from her only through letters, why I direct my answers in care of a certain woman's club with a request to forward them, and why I have neither sent down Will, nor appointed Malcolm to look her up and find out how she was getting along.

Ruth has requested that I make no endeavor to drag her forth into the light of criticism and comment. She has written every week punctually; she has reported good health; and has invariably assured me that she is congenially employed. I have allowed her her seclusion. In olden days broken-hearted women and distracted men withdrew to the protection of religion, and hid their scars inside the walls of nunneries and monasteries. Why not let Ruth conceal her wounds, too, for a while, without fear of disturbance from commenting friends and an inquisitive family?

However, a fortnight ago, I had a letter from Ruth that set me to planning. It casually referred to the fact that she was going to march in the New York suffrage parade. I knew that she is still deeply interested in suffrage. Any one of her letters bore witness to that. I decided to see that parade. My son was six months old; I hadn't left him for a night since he was born; he was a healthy little animal, gaining ounces every week; and for all I knew the first little baby I had been appointed to take care of was losing ounces. I made up my mind to go down to New York and have a look at Ruth anyway. I told Will about it; he fell in with my scheme; and I began to make arrangements.

When I announced to Robert Jennings that we were going to New York, I tried to be casual about it.

"I haven't been down there for two years," I said one night when he dropped in upon us, as was his occasional custom. "I require a polishing in New York about every six months. Besides I want to begin disciplining myself in leaving that little rascal of mine upstairs, just to prove that he won't swallow a safety-pin or develop pneumonia the moment my back's turned. Don't you think I'm wise?"

"New York?" took up Bob. "Shall you—do you plan to see anybody I know?" he inquired.

He was a different man that falteringly asked me this question from the Robert Jennings of a year ago—the same eyes, the same voice, the same persistent smile, and yet something gone out from them all.

"No, Bob," I replied, "I'm not going to look up Ruth." We seldom spoke of her. When we did it was briefly, and usually when Will happened to be absent.

"There's a suffrage parade in New York, Wednesday," Robert informed me. "While you're there, you know. Had you an idea that she might be in it?"

"Why, I shouldn't be a bit surprised," I allowed.

"Well, then, of course you'll see her," he brought out.

"Well, I might. It's possible. I shall see the parade, I hope. They say they're rather impressive."

"She's well?" asked Bob.

"She writes so," I told him briefly.

"And happy?"

"She seems so."

"What should you think of the idea of my seeing that parade, too?" he asked a little later.

"I shouldn't think very well of it, Bob."

"Should I be in the way?" he smiled, "interrupt yours and Will's *tête-à-tête*?"

"Oh, no, of course not. But—O Bob," I broke off, "why keep on thinking about Ruth? I wish you wouldn't. Life has such a lot else in it." He colored a little at my frankness. "Oh, I know you don't want me to talk about it, but I can't help it. You knew her such a little while, scarcely six months in all, and besides she wasn't suited to you. I see it now myself. She's stark mad about all these suffrage things. You wouldn't have been happy. She's full of theories now. I wish you'd drop all thought of her and go about the next thing. I'm sure Ruth is going about the next thing. *You* ought to."

"Nevertheless," he said, "should I be in the way?"

Of course he went. I could see his mind was made up in spite of what I might say. The three of us—Robert Jennings and Will and I—stood for two hours on the edge of a curbing in New York City waiting for Ruth to walk up Fifth Avenue.

We were a merry little party. A spark of Robert's old fun seemed to have stolen into his eyes, a little of the old crispness into his voice.

"They're going to walk several abreast," he explained. "It will be hard work finding her in such a crowd. She might get by. So this is my plan. I'll take as my responsibility the rows farthest over, you take the middle, Will, and Lucy, you look out for those nearest the curb. See? Now between the three of us we'll see her. Hello! I believe they're coming!"

I looked down Fifth Avenue, lined with a black ribbon of people on each side. It was free from traffic. Clear and uninterrupted lay the way for this peculiar demonstration. I saw in the distance a flag approaching. I heard the stirring strains of a band.

Ruth was very near the front of the parade. One band had passed us and disappeared into dimness and Ruth preceded the second one.

It was a lovely sunny day, with a stiff sharp breeze that made militant every flag that moved. Ruth wore no slogan of any sort. She carried one symbol only—the American flag. She was not walking. Ruth rode, regally, magnificently. We were hunting for her in the rank and file, and then some little urchin called out, "Gee! Look at the peach!"

And there she was—Ruth! Our Ruth, on a black horse, a splendid creature flecked with foam.

"Some girl!" said a man beside me.

"Who's she?" exclaimed somebody else.

Then abruptly the band that she immediately preceded broke into thundering music, and drowned everything but the sight of her.

But oh, such a sight! She was in her black habit and wore the little tri-cornered hat that so became her. She has always ridden horseback. Confidently, easily she sat in her saddle, with one white-gloved hand holding the reins, and the other one the pole of the flag, which waved above her head. In Ruth's eyes there was an expression that was ardent. Neither to left nor right did she look. She seemed oblivious of her surroundings. Straight ahead she gazed; straight ahead she rode; unafraid, eager, hopeful; the flag her only staff. She epitomized for me the hundreds and hundreds of girls that were following after. Where would they all come out? Where, *where* would Ruth come out? She had sought liberty. Well, she had it. Where was it taking her? With a choking throat I watched my sister's stars and stripes vanish up Fifth Avenue. I thought it would satisfy me to see Ruth well and happy—for she looked well, she looked happy—but it didn't satisfy me. I was hungry for more of her.

None of us, Will, Robert or I, had spoken as she rode by. It had been too impressive. I had not looked at Robert. I had observed only his hand as it grasped his coat sleeve as he stood with folded arms. One hand, I thought, had tightened its grasp a little. We all stood perfectly speechless for at least three minutes after Ruth went by. Finally it was Robert who spoke.

"Have you had enough?" he asked of me, leaning down.

"Have you?" I inquired.

"Yes, I have. Let's go. Come on, Will, let's get out," he said. There was a note of impatience in his voice. We wormed our way back to the entrance of a shop.

"What's the rush?" said Will.

Robert replied. I could see his emotion now. "It's this. I'll tell you. I'm going to clear right out of this crowd and look that girl up. You've got that address in Madison Avenue, Lucy. I'm going to look her up—"

"But, Bob," I remonstrated. "She doesn't live there, and she doesn't want to be looked up. She has asked me not to—and besides—"

"I can't help that—I shall be doing the looking up. I'll take the blame," he rather snapped at me.

"Now, look here, Bob, old man," said Will, and he put a hand on one of Robert's shoulders. "What's the good in it *now*? Don't you see she'll be hotter than ever on this thing just now? Wait till she cools off a bit. That's the idea!"

"Oh, it isn't to dissuade her. I don't care about that. It's simply to find out if she's all right. She may need help of some kind or other. She's a proud girl. Good heavens, she isn't going to send for any one. I don't know what we've been thinking of—a whole year down in this place, and no knowledge of what kind of a life she's had to live. That isn't right—no. Lucy, if you'll be kind enough to give me that address, I'll be off."

"I don't believe you can trace her through that."

"I'll see to that end of it." He was really almost sharp with me.

"What do you think, Will?" I inquired.

"Oh, give it to him, give it to him, my dear."

And so I did at last.

Will and I went to the theater that night, and supper afterward. It was after midnight when we strolled into the hotel. Robert Jennings was sitting in one of the big chairs in the corridor with a paper up before his face. Will had gone to the desk to get our key, and I went up and spoke to Bob.

"Well, hello!" I blurted out cheerfully. "What success? Did you see her?"

He stood up, and I saw his face then.

"Yes, I saw her," he replied, then with difficulty added, "Don't ask me about it," and abruptly he turned away, tossed aside the paper, and walked straight out of the hotel. He might have been in a play on the stage.

We had arranged to leave for home the following morning. Will called up Robert's room about nine to find out if he was still planning to return with us. There was no answer. I felt anxious about Bob. Will felt simply irritated.

"Ought to have known more than to have gone pressing his suit on a person in Ruth's frame of mind," he grumbled.

Robert Jennings didn't show up until three minutes before the train pulled out. His reservation hadn't been canceled, but I had little hope of his appearance. My heart gave a bound of relief when I saw him coming into the car at the farther end.

"Oh, here you are!" I said. "I'm so glad you've come. We've been looking for you."

"Hello there," put in Will.

"Have you? That's good of you," said Bob. He had himself well in hand now. I was glad of that. "I went out for breakfast," he explained. "I was sure to show up, however. I have a five o'clock appointment this afternoon," and he took off his overcoat, swung his chair about, and sat down.

For two hours he sat opposite me there without a single reference to the night before. You might have thought I never had seen him cast that newspaper aside and unceremoniously burst out of the hotel. We talked about all sorts of indifferent subjects. Finally I leaned over and asked Will if he didn't want to go into the smoking-car.

"Understand?" I inquired.

"Surely," he replied, "surely, I do, Miss Canny," and left us.

A half-an-hour outside New London Bob began to talk. "Do you want to hear about last night?" he asked me.

"If you want to tell me," I replied.

"Well, I found her. I found Ruth."

"Yes, I know you did, Bob."

"Do you know *where* I found her?"

"Why, no. Of course I don't."

"Well, I'll tell you. After I left you I went first to the Madison Avenue address. It wasn't until I gave the lady at the desk of that club the impression that I came bearing news of some serious nature connected with Ruth's family, that she gave me the address where Ruth's mail is forwarded. She told me it was Ruth's place of business. It was an address up near the region of the Park, no name, just the bare street and number. I called 'information,' and finally the house on the 'phone. I was informed Miss Vars would not be in until after dinner. So I waited, and about half-past eight went up there. I found the house—a big, impressive affair, grilled iron fence close to it in front, very fine, very luxurious; all the windows curtained darkly, with a glow of brightness through the cracks here and there. I hesitated to present myself. I walked up and down twice in front of the house, wondering if it would be wiser to call Ruth by telephone and make an appointment. Then suddenly some one inside opened an upper window—it was a warm night. I saw a man draw aside the laces, raise the shade, and throw up the sash. I saw beyond into the room. I saw Ruth. She was sitting beneath a bright light, on a sofa. She was sewing. She seemed quite at home. I saw the man turn away from the window and go back and sit down on the sofa beside her. I saw him stretch out, put one hand in his pocket, lean back luxuriously, and proceed to smoke. It was all very intimate. A policeman passed me as I stood there staring.

"'Who lives there?' I asked him—and he told me. 'Oh, that's the Sewall place,' he said, 'Young Breckenridge Sewall, you know.' I looked up at the window again. The man was closing it now. Is he dark, quite dark, stoops a little, with a receding forehead?" asked Robert of me.

I nodded. I couldn't speak.

"It was he, it was Sewall without a doubt. What is Ruth doing in that house?" demanded Bob. "What is she doing, sitting there alone with that man at nine o'clock at night—sewing? What does it mean? I didn't go in. I walked back to the hotel and sat there, and then I went out and walked again. What does it mean? For heaven's sake, Lucy—tell me what she's doing there?"

"O Bob," I said tremblingly, "don't think anything awful about Ruth. Whatever she's doing there, it's all right."

"You don't know," he groaned.

"I know Ruth, and that's enough. Of course she's all right. Don't let's get absurd. I can't understand it, of course, but after all——"

"Oh, please," almost shuddered Bob, "don't let's talk about it. I don't want to think about it. She has been such a beautiful memory, and now—please don't talk about it."

"All right," I said and leaned back and gazed out of the window, stunned by his news, frightened more than I dared to show.

We rumbled on in silence for half an hour. I was dimly aware that Bob bought a magazine. Will joined us later, sat down, and fell off to sleep. Bob got up and announced that he was going into the smoking-car. His composure of the early afternoon had left him. He appeared nervous and disturbed. He looked distressed. Just outside Providence he returned to the car with a porter and began gathering up his belongings.

"What is it?" I asked.

"Nothing much," he replied shortly, "only I'm going back to New York. I'm going back now–tonight, that's all."

Ruth Resumes Her Own Story

I HAD no idea what I was undertaking when I went to New York. I had had no experience with the difficulties that exist between announcing you intend to live your own life, and living it. The world is a bewildering place for one unused to it. All the savoir-faire and sophistication acquired in reception-rooms didn't stand me in very good stead when it came to earning my own living in New York City. I was timid, full of fears—imaginary and real. I had been to New York many times before, but the realization that I was in the big city alone, unanchored, afloat, filled me with panic. I was like a young bird, featherless, naked, trembling, knocked out of its nest before it could fly. Every sound, every unknown shape was a monster cat waiting to devour me. I was acutely aware of dangers lurking for young girls in big cities. For two or three days I had all I could do to control myself and keep my nerve steady.

I arrived on a cold, gray, cloudy morning; unaccustomed to reaching destinies unmet; my heart torn and bleeding; nobody to turn to for help and advice; no plan formed in my confused mind; afraid even to trust myself to the care of a taxicab driver. For such a timid pilgrim in quest of freedom, to start out in search of an address she treasures because of the golden apple of immediate employment that it promises, and to learn on arrival that the position already has been filled, is terribly disheartening. To wake up the second morning in a two-dollar hotel room, which she has locked and barred the night before with all the foolish precautions of a young and amateurish traveler, to pay a dollar for a usual breakfast served in her room and a dollar-and-a-half for a luncheon of nothing but a simple soup and chicken-à-la-King, and then to figure out on a piece of paper that at such a rate her fifty dollars will last just about two weeks, is enough to make any young fool of a girl wish she had been taught something else besides setting off expensive gowns. I didn't know what I ought to do. I didn't know how to begin. I was so self-conscious, at first, so fearful that my being at that hotel, alone, unchaperoned, might be questioned and cause unpleasant comment, that I stayed in my room as much as possible. When I look back and see myself those first few days I have to smile out of self-pity. If it hadn't been for my lacerated pride, for the memory of Tom's arrogance and Edith's taunts, I might have persuaded myself to give up my dangerous enterprise, but every time I rehearsed that scene at the Homestead (and, imprisoned as I was, I rehearsed it frequently), something flamed up in me higher and higher each time. I could not go back with self-respect. It was impossible. I concluded that I might as well get singed in New York, as bound in slavery by Tom and Edith.

As soon as I became fully convinced that my lot was cast, I ventured out to look for cheaper accommodations.

Ever since I have been allowed alone on a railroad train, the Y. W. C. A. has been preached to me as a perfectly safe place to ask advice in case of being stranded in a strange city. So I trudged down there one late afternoon and procured a list of several lodging-houses, where my mother's young parlor-maid could stay for a week with safety while we were moving from our summer house. I didn't know whether I could bring myself really to undress and get into the little cot in the room which I finally engaged, but at least the room had a window. I could sit by that. I had been assured that the place was reputable. I moved down there in a taxicab one rainy Saturday afternoon. Lucy had sent me my trunk, and I had to convey it somehow. I didn't sleep at all the first night. There was a fire-escape immediately outside my open window, and there was not a sign of a lock on the door. On Monday I bought a screw-eye and hook for fifteen cents, and put nails in the sash for burglar stops.

At first I used to crawl back to that smelly little hall bedroom at the earliest sign of dusk; at first, if a man on the street spoke to me, I would tremble for five minutes afterward; at first the odor of the continual boiling of mutton bones and onions that met me every time I opened the door of Mrs. Plummet's lodging-house used to make me feel sick to my stomach. I became hardened as time went on, but at first it was rather awful. I don't like to recall those early experiences of mine.

I learned a great deal during my first fortnight at Mrs. Plummet's. I never knew, for instance, that one meal a day, eaten at about four o'clock in the afternoon, takes the place of three, very comfortably, if aided and abetted in the morning by crackers spread with peanut butter, and a glass of milk, a whole bottle of which one could buy for a few cents at the corner grocery store. The girl who roomed next door to me gave me lots of such tips. I had no idea that there were shops on shabby avenues, where one could get an infinitesimal portion of what one paid for a last season's dinner-gown; that furs are a wiser investment than satin and lace; and that my single emerald could be more easily turned into dollars and cents than all the enameled jewelry I owned put together. The feeling of reënforcement that the contents of my trunk gave me did a lot in restoring confidence. The girl next door and I reckoned that their value in secondhand shops would see me through the summer, at least. Surely, I could become established somewhere by fall.

I didn't know how to approach my problem. I didn't know what advertisements in the newspapers were the false ones. I felt shy about applying for work at stores and shops. For whom should I ask? To what department present myself? What should I say first? One day I told a benevolent-looking woman, one of the officers at the Y. W. C. A., the truth about myself, that I, and not my mother's parlor-maid, was occupying the room in the lodging-house. Not until that woman put her hand kindly on my shoulder and advised me to go home—did I realize how determined I had become. New York had not devoured me, the lodging-house had not harmed me. I had found I could sleep, and very well, too, on the lumpy, slumped-in cot with the soiled spread. No one climbed the fire-escape, no one tried my locked door at night. I had pawned my last winter's furs, but my character seemed quite clean and unsmirched. Go home! Of course I wasn't going home. Not yet. The lady gave me a list of reputable employment agencies at last. If Mrs. Plummet's hadn't daunted me, employment offices couldn't either, I said. I was told to provide suitable references.

Now references were just what I couldn't very well provide. I had left home under disagreeable circumstances. I tried to make it clear without too much detail that, except for my sister, my connections with my people were severed, and I couldn't apply to Lucy. I hadn't even given her my actual address. She would be sure to come looking me up, or send some one in her place. Very likely she would ask my brother Malcolm to drop in on me sometime. I was in deadly fear I would run across him on the street, and if Malcolm had ever smelled the inside of the house where I roomed, I fear his nose never would have come down. If Lucy had ever seen the dirt on the stairs she would have pronounced the house disreputable, and dragged me home. Secrecy was my only chance for success, at least for a while. I would have to discover what could be done without references.

It was due to a little new trick I learned of looking on at myself that it was not impossible for me to seek a position through an employment agency. I had become, you see, one of those characters I had read about in short stories dozens of times before—an unemployed girl in New York, even to the hall-bedroom, the handkerchiefs stuck on my window-pane in process of ironing, the water-bugs around the pipes in the bath-room. It was this consciousness of myself that made many of the hardships bearable—this and the grim determination not to give up.

I told the lady in charge of the intelligence office where I first applied that I was willing to try anything, but thought I was best suited as a mother's-helper, or a sort of governess. She shrugged when I told her I had no reference, but occasionally she gave me an opportunity for an interview.

There was something about me that, lacking a reference, impressed my would-be employers unfavorably; possibly it was the modish cut of the hundred-dollar spring suit I wore, or the shape of my hat. Anyhow, they all decided against me. If I had persisted long enough, I might have found some sort of place, but on the fourth or fifth day of my ordeal in intelligence offices, something happened.

I was sitting with the rest of my unemployed sisters in the little inner room provided for us off the main office, when I glanced through the door to see Henrietta Morgan and her mother. I looked hastily away. Here I had been avoiding Fifth Avenue and the region of shops, for fear some of my old friends about New York (and I have many) might run across me, and stupidly I had walked into the very place infested by them. I accomplished my escape easily enough. Naturally Mrs. Morgan wasn't looking for me in such a place, but I didn't take the chance again.

I was lonely and discouraged many times during that first bitter summer of mine in New York. I felt no charity for Edith, no forgiveness for Tom. I hadn't wanted to leave home—not really—I hadn't sought an experience like this. They had forced me to it. If only Tom hadn't treated me like a naughty child! If only Bob—oh if *only* Bob—(no, there were some things I could not dwell upon. It was wiser not to). Some pains are dull and steady. One can endure them and smile. Others recur at intervals, occasioned by some unimportant detail like a man on the street selling roasted chestnuts, which reminds one of saffron woods in late October. Such pain is like the stab of a sharp stiletto.

Mine is the same old story of hope and despair, of periods of courage occasioned by opportunities that flickered for a while and went out. I was not utterly without employment. The first three dollars I earned at directing envelopes in a department store made me happy for a fortnight. It was a distinct triumph. I felt as if I had been initiated into a great society. I had been paid money for the labor of my hands! The girl who roomed next to me had helped me to get the position. I was not without associates. There were twenty-five girls besides myself who carried away in their clothes each morning the odor of Mrs. Plummet's soup-stock. Mrs. Plummet let rooms to girls only, and only rooms. We didn't board with Mrs. Plummet. I wondered how she and old Mr. Plummet ever consumed, alone, so much lamb broth.

For a fortnight I was a model for trying on suits in a down-town wholesale house; several times the Y. W. C. A. found opportunities for me to play accompaniments; in October when the suffrage activities began I was able to pick up a few crumbs of work in the printing office of one of their papers. But such a thing as permanent employment became a veritable will-o'-the-wisp. I was strong and willing, and yet I could not—absolutely *could not*—support myself. I tried writing fiction. I had always yearned to be literary, but the magazines sent all my stuff back. I tried sewing in a dressmaker's shop, but after three days the Madam announced that her shop would be closed during August, the dull season. She had hired me simply to rush a mourning order. From one thing to another I went, becoming more and more disheartened as fall approached, and my stock of clothes and jewelry, on the proceeds of which I was living, became lower and lower. My almost empty trunk stared at me forlornly from its corner; it foretold failure. What should I do when the last little frumpery of my old life had been turned into money to support my new one? To whom turn? I could not ask for help from those who had admonished and criticized. I had written Lucy weekly that I was prospering. I could not acknowledge failure even to her. I bent every nerve to the effort.

One day in a magazine that some one had discarded in a subway train I ran across an advertisement for "a young lady of education and good family, familiar with social obligations, to act as a private secretary to a lady in a private home." I answered that advertisement. I had answered dozens similar before. This, like the others no doubt, would end in failure. But I couldn't sit and fold my hands. I must keep on trying. I answered it—and six others at the same time. Of the seven I had a reply only from the one mentioned above.

It was a unique reply. It was typewritten. "If still interested in the position referred to in attached clipping reply by complying to requirements enclosed—and mail answer by the evening of the day that this communication is received.

"1st. Write a formal acceptance to a formal dinner.

2nd. Write a few words on suffrage appropriate to an older woman who is mildly opposed.

3rd. Write a polite note of refusal to the treasurer of a charitable institution in reply to a request to donate sum of money.

4th. Write a note of condolence to an acquaintance upon the death of a relative.

5th. Write a note of congratulation to a débutante announcing her engagement.

6th. Write an informal invitation to a house-party in the country.

7th. Acknowledge a gift of flowers sent to you during an illness."

I sat down with zest to this task. It was an original way to weed out applicants. I spent the whole afternoon over it. It was late in the evening before I had all my questions answered, neatly copied, sealed, and dropped inside a green letter-box.

A day or two later I received in the same non-committal typewritten form a brief summons to appear the following morning between twelve and one o'clock at a certain uptown hotel, and to inquire at the desk for Miss A. S. Armstrong.

It was a clear starry night. I pinned a towel over my suit, put it on a coat-hanger, and hung it securely to the blind-catch outside my window. I didn't know who Miss A. S. Armstrong was, but at any rate I would offer up to the stars what I possessed of Mrs. Plummet's soup-stock.

The Fifth Wheel Gains Wings

MISS A. S. ARMSTRONG proved to be a thin angular creature with no eyelashes. She saw me come in through the revolving doors of the hotel at sharp twelve o'clock. When I enquired for her at the desk, she was at my elbow. She was not the lady I had come to be interviewed by; she was merely her present private secretary; the lady herself, she explained, was upstairs awaiting me.

"You're younger than we thought," she said, eyeing me critically. She was a very precise person. Her accent was English. My hopes dimmed as I looked upon her. If she had been selected as desirable, then there was little chance for me. My short experience in employment offices had proved to me the undesirability of possessing qualities that impress a would-be employer as too attractive.

"Do you have young men callers?" "Do you like 'to go'?" "Do you want to be out late?" Such inquiries were invariably made when I was trying to obtain a position as a mother's-helper or child's-companion; and though I was able to reply in the negative, my inquisitors would look at me suspiciously, and remain unconvinced. Now, again, I felt sure as we ascended to the apartment above that my appearance (Miss Armstrong had called it my youth) would stand in my way.

I was ushered into a room high up in the air, flooded with New York sunshine. It dazzled me at first. Coming in from the dimness of the corridor, I could not discern the features of the lady sitting in an easy chair.

"I beg your pardon," ejaculated Miss Armstrong at sight of her, "I thought you were in the other room. Shall we come in?"

"Certainly, certainly." There was a note of impatience.

Miss Armstrong turned to me. I was behind her, half hidden. "Come in," she said. "I wish to introduce you to Mrs. Sewall–Mrs. F. Rockridge Sewall. The applicant to your advertisement, Mrs. Sewall."

Miss Armstrong stood aside. I stepped forward (what else could I do?) and stood staring into the eyes of my old enemy. It was she who recovered first from the shock of our meeting. I had seen a slight flush–an angry flush I thought–spread faintly over Mrs. Sewall's features as she first recognized me. But it faded. When she spoke there wasn't a trace of surprise in her voice.

"My applicant, did I understand you to say, Miss Armstrong?"

"Yes," I replied in almost as calm a manner as hers, "I answered your advertisement for a private secretary, and followed it by responding to the test which you sent me, and received word to appear here this morning."

"I see, I see," said Mrs. Sewall, observing me suspiciously.

"But," I went on, "I did not know to whom I was applying. I answered six other advertisements at the same time. I have, of course, heard of Mrs. F. Rockridge Sewall. I doubt if I would be experienced enough for you. Miss Armstrong spoke of my youth downstairs." Mrs. Sewall still continued to observe me. "To save you the trouble of interviewing me," I went on, "I think I had better go. I am not fitted for the position, I am quite sure. I am sorry to have taken any of your time. I would never have answered your advertisement had you given your name." I moved toward the door.

"Wait a minute," said Mrs. Sewall. "Kindly wait a minute, and be seated. Miss Armstrong, your note-book please. Are you ready?"

Miss Armstrong, seated now at a small desk, produced a leather-bound book and fountain-pen. "Quite ready," she replied.

Mrs. Sewall turned to me. "I always finish undertakings. I have undertaken an interview with you. Let us proceed with it, then. Let us see, Miss Armstrong, what did the young lady sign herself?"

"Y–Q–A."

"Yes. 'Y–Q–A.' First then—your name," said Mrs. Sewall.

It was my impulse to escape the grilling that this merciless woman was evidently going to put me to; my first primitive instinct to strike my adversary with some bitterly worded accusation and then turn and fly. But I stood my ground. Without a quiver of obvious embarrassment, or more than a second's hesitation, I replied, looking at Mrs. Sewall squarely.

"My name is Ruth Chenery Vars."

Miss Armstrong scratched it in her book.

"Oh, yes, Ruth Chenery Vars. Your age, please, Miss Vars?" Mrs. Sewall coldly inquired.

I told her briefly.

"Your birthplace?"

And I told her that.

"Your education?" she pursued.

"High-school," I replied, "one year of boarding-school, one year coming out into society, several years stagnating in society, some travel, some hotel life, one summer learning how to live on seven dollars a week."

"Oh, indeed!" I thought I discerned a spark of amusement in Mrs. Sewall's ejaculation. "Indeed! And will you tell me, Miss Vars," she went on, a little more humanely, "why you are seeking a position as private secretary?"

"Why, to earn my living," I replied.

"And why do you wish to earn your living?"

"The instinct to exist, I suppose."

"Come," said Mrs. Sewall, "why are you here in New York, Miss Vars? You appear to be a young lady of good birth and culture, accustomed to the comforts, and I should say, the luxuries of life, if I am a judge. Why are you here in New York seeking employment?"

"To avoid becoming a parasite, Mrs. Sewall," I replied.

"'To avoid becoming a parasite'!" (Yes, there was humor in those eyes. I could see them sparkle.) "Out of the mouths of babes!" she exclaimed, "verily, out of the mouths of babes! You are young to fear parasitism, Miss Vars."

"I suppose so," I acknowledged pleasantly, and looked out of the window.

Beneath Mrs. Sewall's curious gaze I sat, quiet and unperturbed, contemplating miles of roofs and puffing chimneys. I was not embarrassed. I had once feared the shame and mortification that would be mine if I should ever again encounter this woman, but in some miraculous fashion I had opened my own prison doors. It flashed across me that never again could the bogies and false gods of society rule me. I was free! I was independent! I was unafraid! I turned confident eyes back to Mrs. Sewall. She was considering me sharply, interrogatively, tapping an arm of her chair as she sat thinking.

"Well," I said smiling, and stood up as if to go. "If you are through with me—"

"Wait a minute," she interrupted. "Wait a minute. I am not through. Be seated again, please. I sent out about thirty copies of the papers such as you received," she went on. "Some fifteen replies were sent back. Yours proved to be the only possible one among them. That is why I have summoned you here today. The position of my private secretary is a peculiar one, and difficult to fill. Miss Armstrong has been with me some years. She leaves to be married." (Married! This sallow creature.) "She leaves to marry an officer in England. She is obliged to sail tomorrow. Some one to take her place had been engaged, but a death—a sudden death—makes it impossible for the other young lady to keep her contract with me. Now the season is well advanced. I am returning to town late this year. My town house is being prepared for immediate occupancy. The servants are there now. I return to it tomorrow. On Thursday I have a large dinner. My social calendar for the month is very full. You are young—frightfully young—to fill a position of such responsibility as Miss Armstrong's. My private secretary takes care of practically all my correspondence. But many of the letters I asked you to write in the test I sent are letters which actually must be written within the next few days. Your answers pleased me, Miss Vars—yes, pleased me very much, I might say." She got up (I rising too) and procured a fresh handkerchief from a silver box on a table. She touched it, folded, to her nose.

"The salary to begin with is to be a hundred and twenty-five dollars a month," she remarked. She shook out the handkerchief, then she added, coughing slightly first behind the sheer square of linen, "I should like you to start in upon your duties, Miss Vars, as soon as possible—tomorrow morning if it can be arranged."

I was taken unawares. I had not expected this.

"Why—but do you think—I'm sorry," I stumbled, "but on further consideration I feel that I—"

"Wait a minute, please. Before you give me an answer it is fair to explain your position more in detail. It is an official position. Your hours are from ten to four. You are in no sense maid or companion. You live where you think best, are entirely independent, quite free, the mistress of your own affairs. I am a busy woman. The demands upon my time are such that I require a secretary who can do more than add columns of figures, though that she must do too. She must in many cases be my brains, my tact, convey in my correspondence fine shades of feeling. It is a position requiring peculiar talent, Miss Vars, and one, I should say, which would be attractive to you. During the protracted absence of an only son of mine, who is occupying my London house, I shall be alone in my home this winter. You may have until this evening to think over your answer. Don't give it to me now. It is better form, as well as better judgment, never to be hasty. I liked your letters," she smiled graciously upon me now. "After this interview I like them still. I like *you*. I think we would get on."

A hundred and twenty-five dollars a month! The still unmarried Breck safe in England! My almost empty trunk! Why not? Why not accept the position? Was I not free from fear of what people would say? Had I not already broken the confining chains of "what's done," and "what isn't done?" I needed the work; it was respectable; Breck was in England; a hundred and twenty-five dollars a month; my trunk almost empty.

"Well," I said, "I need a position as badly as you seem to need a secretary, Mrs. Sewall. We might try each other anyway. I'll think it over. I won't decide now. I will let you know by five o'clock this afternoon."

I accepted the position. Mrs. Plummet shed real tears when I told her my good news at six o'clock that night; and more tears a fortnight later when I moved out of my little hall bedroom, and my feather-weight trunk, lightsomely balanced on the shoulders of one man, was conveyed to the express-wagon and thence to new lodgings in Irving Place.

It was in the new lodgings that my new life really began. Its birth had been difficult, the pains I had endured for its existence sharp and recurring, but here it was at last—a lovely, interesting thing. I could observe it almost as if it was something I could hold in my two hands. Here it was—mine, to watch grow and develop; mine to tend and nurture and persuade; my life at last, to do with as I pleased.

At the suffrage headquarters I had run across a drab-appearing girl by the name of Esther Claff, and it was with her that I shared the room in Irving Place.

She was writing a book, and used to sit up half the night. She was a college-educated girl, who had been trained to think logically. Social and political questions were keen delights to Esther Claff. She took me to political rallies; we listened to speeches from anarchists and socialists; we attended I. W. W. meetings; we heard discussions on ethical subjects, on religion, on the white-slave traffic, equal suffrage, trusts. Life at all its various points interested Esther Claff. She was a plain, uninteresting girl to look at, but she possessed a rare mind, as beautifully constructed as the inside of a watch, and about as human, sometimes I used to think.

She was very reticent about herself, told me almost nothing of her early life and seemed to feel as little curiosity about mine. I lived with Esther Claff a whole winter with never once an expression from her of regard or affection. I wondered sometimes if she felt any. Esther was an example, it seemed to me, of a woman who had risen above the details of human life, petty annoyances of friendships, eking demands of a community. I had heard her voice tremble with feeling about some reforms she believed in, but evidently she had shaken off all desire for the human touch. I wished sometimes that Esther wasn't quite so emancipated.

My associates were Esther's associates—college friends of hers for the most part, a circle of girls who inspired me with their enthusiasms and star-high aspirations. They were living economically in various places in New York, all keenly interested in what they were doing. There was Flora Bennett, sleeping in a tiny room with a skylight instead of uptown with her family, because her father wouldn't countenance his daughter's becoming a stenographer, making her beg spending money from him every month like a child. There was Anne DeBois who had left a tyrannical parent who didn't believe in educating girls, and worked her way through college. There was a settlement worker or two; there was poor, struggling Rosa who tried to paint; Sidney, an eager little sculptor; Elsie and Lorraine, two would-be journalists, who lived together, and who were so inseparable we called them Alsace and Lorraine; there was able Maria Brown, an investigator who used to spend a fortnight as an employee in various factories and stores and write up the experience afterwards.

There were few or no men in our life. Esther and I frequented our friends' queer little top-story studios in dark alleys for recreation, and got into deep discussions on life and reforms. Sometimes we celebrated to the extent of a sixty-cent table d'hôte dinner in tucked-away restaurants. We occupied fifty-cent seats at the theater occasionally, and often from dizzying heights at the opera would gaze down into the minaret boxes below, while I recalled with a little feeling of triumph that far-distant time when I had sat thus emblazoned and imprisoned.

I had cut loose at last. I was proud of myself. In the secret of my soul I strutted. I was like a boy in his first long trousers. I might not yet show myself off to the family. They would question the propriety of my occupation with Mrs. Sewall, but nevertheless I had not failed. Sometimes lying in my bed at night with all the vague, mysterious roar of New York outside, my beating heart within me seemed actually to swell with pride. I was alone in New York; I was independent; I was self-supporting; I was on the way to success. I used to drop off to sleep on some of those nights with the sweet promise of victory pervading my whole being.

One day I ran across an advertisement in the back of a magazine representing a single wheel with a pair of wings attached to its hub. It was traveling along without the least difficulty in the world. So was I. The fifth wheel had acquired wings!

In the Sewall Mansion

IN spite of Mrs. Sewall's crowded engagement calendar, she was a woman with very few close friends. She was very clever; she could converse ably; she could entertain brilliantly; and yet she had been unable to weave herself into any little circle of loyal companions. She was terribly lonely sometimes.

For the first half-dozen weeks our relations were strictly official. And then one day just as I was leaving to walk back to my rooms as usual, Mrs. Sewall, who was just getting into her automobile, asked me if I would care to ride with her. The lights were all aglow on Fifth Avenue. We joined the parade in luxurious state. This was what I once had dreamed of—to be seated beside Mrs. F. Rockridge Sewall in her automobile, creeping slowly along Fifth Avenue at dusk. Life works out its patterns for people cunningly, I think. I made some such remark as I sat there beside Mrs. Sewall.

"How? Tell me," she said, "how has it worked out its pattern cunningly for you?"

We had never mentioned our former relations. I didn't intend to now.

"Oh," I said, side-stepping what was really in my mind, "cunningly, because here I am, in a last winter's hat and a sweater for warmth underneath my old summer's suit, and yet I'm happy. If life has woven me into such a design as that—I think it's very clever of it."

"*Are* you happy?" questioned Mrs. Sewall.

"Yes, I believe I am," I replied honestly. "That, of course, isn't saying I am not just a little lonely sometimes. But I'm interested. I'm terribly interested, Mrs. Sewall."

"Well, but weren't you interested when you were a débutante? You referred to having been a débutante, you remember, once. Weren't you, as you say, terribly interested *then*?"

"Yes, in a way, I suppose I was. But I believe *then* I was interested in myself, and what was good for my social success, and now—it sounds painfully self-righteous—but now I'm interested in things outside. I'm interested in what's good for the success of the world." I blushed in the dusk. It sounded so affected. "I mean," I said, "I'm interested in reforms and unions, and suffrage, and things like that. I used to be so awfully individualistic."

"Individualistic! Where do you run across these ideas? A girl like you. Parasitism, and suffrage! Is my secretary a suffragette?" she asked me smilingly.

"Well," I replied, "I believe that woman's awakening is one of the greatest forces at work today for human emancipation."

"Well, well," ejaculated Mrs. Sewall. "So my secretary thinks if women vote, all the wrinkles in this old world will be ironed out."

I knew I was being made fun of a little, but I was willing nevertheless.

"The influence suffrage will have on politics will not be so important as the influence it will have on ethics and conventions," I replied, "and I believe it will have such a beneficial influence that it will be worth Uncle Sam's trouble to engage a few more clerks to count the increased number of ballots."

"Well—well. Is that so?" smiled Mrs. Sewall, amused. "Do you think women competent to sit on juries, become just judges, and make unbiased and fair decisions? What have you to say to that, Miss Enthusiast?"

"Women are untrained now, of course, but in time they will learn the manners of positions of trust, as men have, through being ridiculed in print, through bitter experiences of various kinds. If they are given a few years at it, they'll learn that they can't afford to be hasty and pettish in public positions, as they could in their own little narrow spheres at home. A child who first goes to school is awfully new at it. He sulks, cries, wants his own way; he hasn't learned how to work with others. Neither have women yet, but suffrage will help us toward it."

"I had no idea you were such a little enthusiast. Come, don't you want to have tea with me and my friend Mrs. Scot-Williams? I'm to meet her at the Carl. She enjoys a girl with ideas."

"In this?" I indicated my suit. We were drawing up to the lighted restaurant, where costly lace veiled from the street candle-lighted tables.

"In that?" Mrs. Sewall looked at me and smiled. "Talk as you have to me, my dear, and she will not see what your soul goes clothed in."

My enemy—Mrs. Sewall! My almost friend now! She could sting, but she could make honey too. Bittersweet. I went with her to drink some tea.

That was the beginning of our intimate relations. Mrs. Sewall invited me the very next day to lunch with her in the formal dining-room, with the Sewall portraits hanging all around. We talked more suffrage. It seemed to amuse her. She was not particularly interested in the woman's movement. It simply served as an excuse.

One stormy evening not long after the luncheon invitation Mrs. Sewall invited me to stay all night. She was to be alone and had no engagement. She asked me frequently after that. We slipped into relations almost affectionate. I discovered that Mrs. Sewall enjoyed my reading aloud to her. I found out one day, when her maid, who was an hourly irritation to her, was especially slow about arranging her veil, that my fingers pleased and satisfied. Often, annoyed beyond control, she would exclaim, "Come, come, Marie, how clumsy you are! All thumbs! Miss Vars, do you mind? Would you be so kind?" Often I found myself buttoning gloves, untangling knots in platinum chains, and fastening hooks.

As late fall wore into early winter, frequently I presided at the tea-table in Mrs. Sewall's library—the inner holy of holies, upstairs over the drawing-room. "Perkins is so slow" (Perkins was the butler) "and his shoes squeak today. Would you mind, Miss Vars? You're so swift and quiet with cups."

Once she said, in explanation of her friendliness: "I've never had anything but a machine for a private secretary before. Miss Armstrong was hardly a companionable person. No sense of humor. But an excellent machine. Oh, yes—excellent. Better at figures than you, my dear Miss Vars, but oh, her complexion! Really I couldn't drink tea with Miss Armstrong. I never tried it, but I'm sure it would not have been pleasant. You have such pretty coloring, my dear. Shan't I call you Ruth some day?"

Spontaneously it burst out. I had never had the affection of an older woman. I grasped it.

"Do, yes, do call me Ruth," I exclaimed.

I had once believed I could please this difficult woman. I had not been mistaken. It was proved. I did please her. She called me Ruth!

I wrote her letters for her, I kept her expenses, I cut her coupons, I all but signed her generous checks to charitable institutions. Most willingly I advised her in regard to them. She sent five hundred dollars to Esther Claff's settlement house in the Jewish quarter on my suggestion, and bought one of Rosa's paintings, which she gave to me. She wanted me to go with her to her dressmaker's and her milliner's. She consulted me in regard to a room she wanted to redecorate, a bronze that she was considering. She finally confided in me her rheumatism and her diabetes. I was with her every day. Always after her late breakfast served in her room, she sent for me. After all it wasn't surprising. I should have to be very dull and drab indeed not to have become her friend. I was the only one in her whole establishment whom she wasn't obliged to treat as servant and menial.

Of everything we talked, even of Breckenridge—of Breckenridge as a baby, a boy, a college-man. She explained his inheritance, his weaknesses, his virtues. She spoke of Gale Oliphant and the interrupted marriage. Once—once only—she referred to me.

"Oh, dear, oh, dear," she began one day with a sigh, "'the best-laid plans of mice and men'—Oh, dear, oh, dear! Sometimes I think I have made a great many mistakes in my life. For instance, my son—this Breckenridge I talk so much about—he, well, he became very fond of some one I opposed. A nice girl—a girl of high principles. Oh, yes. But not the girl whom his mother had happened to select for him. No. His mother wished him to marry his second cousin—this Gale you've heard me speak of—Gale Oliphant. Breckenridge was fond of her—always had been. She was worth millions, *millions*!

"You see, a short time before Breckenridge formed the attachment for the young lady with the high principles, his mother's lawyer had persuaded her into a most precarious investment. For two years, a large part of her fortune trembled uncertainly on the edge of a precipice. She believed that her son required less a girl with high principles of living, than a girl with principles represented by quarterly dividends. Breckenridge would not make a success as a man without means. But as I said—'the best-laid plans of mice and men!'

"Oh, well, perhaps you read the story. Most unfortunate. It was in the papers. It nearly broke me. A law-suit on the eve of my son's marriage to Miss Gale Oliphant. After I had successfully brought the affair to the desired climax too! Oh, most unfortunate!

"The suit was brought by a creature who had no claims. Put up to it by unscrupulous lawyers of no repute. We paid the money that she asked to hush up the notoriety of the affair, but not before the mischief of breaking off the relations with Miss Oliphant had been nicely accomplished. That was over a year ago. My investments have proved successful. Gale is married to a man twice her age. Breckenridge is still in England."

"And what's become of the girl you didn't approve of?" I asked lightly, threading my needle. I was sewing that day.

"The girl with the high principles?" Mrs. Sewall queried. "I don't know," she said distinctly, slowly. "I don't know, I wish I did. If you should ever run across her, tell her to come and make herself known to me, please. I've something to say."

"I will," I said, carefully drawing the thread through my needle and making a knot. "If I ever run across her. I doubt if I do. I've learned that *that* girl has gone on a long journey to a new and engrossing country."

"Oh? I must send a message to her somehow then. Come here, my dear. Come here. I've got my glasses caught."

I laid down my work and crossed over to Mrs. Sewall. It was true. The chain was in a knot. I untangled it.

"How deft you are!" she exclaimed softly. "Thank you, dear. Thank you." Then she put her cold white fingers on my arm, and patted it a little. She smiled very sweetly upon me.

"My private secretary pleases me better every day!" she said.

The Parade

I DIDN'T tell Lucy that I was with Mrs. Sewall. I had my mail directed to Esther's college club. I rather hated to picture the terrible curses that Edith would call down upon my head when she heard that I was occupying a position which she would certainly term menial. I dreaded to learn what Tom would say of me. Already I had seen Malcolm one day on Fifth Avenue, and bowed to him from the Sewall automobile. Surely, he would report me; but either he didn't recognize me, or else he didn't recognize Mrs. Sewall, for Lucy's letters proved she was still ignorant of my occupation. I accepted kind fate's protection of me; I lived in precious and uninterrupted seclusion.

Of course, I marched in the suffrage parade when it took place in May. I rode on Mrs. Scot-Williams' beautiful, black, blue-ribbon winner. Mrs. Scot-Williams, Mrs. Sewall, and a group of other New York society women tossed me flowers from a prominent balcony as I rode up Fifth Avenue. I carried only the American flag. It was my wish. I wanted no slogan. "Let her have her way," nodded Mrs. Scot-Williams to the other ladies. "The dear child's eyes will tell the rest of the story."

The parade was a tremendous experience to me. Even the long tedious hours of waiting before it started were packed with significance. There we all were, rich and poor; society women and working girls; teachers, stenographers, shirtwaist makers; actresses, mothers, sales-women; Catholic and Protestant; Jew and Gentile; black and white; German, French, Pole and Italian—all there, gathered together by one great common interest. The old sun that shone down upon us that day had never witnessed on this planet such a leveler of fortune, station, country and religion. The petty jealousies and envies had fallen away, for a period, from all us women gathered there that day, and the touch of our joined hands inspired and thrilled. Not far in front of me in the line of march there was a poor, old, half-witted woman, who became the target of gibes and jeers; I felt fierce protection of her. Behind me were dozens of others who were smiled or laughed at by ridiculing spectators; I felt protection of them all.

For hours before the parade started I sat on the curbing of the side-walk with a prominent society woman on one side, and a plain little farmer's wife from up state on the other. We talked, and laughed, and ate sandwiches together that I bought in a grimy lunch-room.

When finally the parade started, and I, mounted on Mrs. Scot-Williams' beautiful Lady F, felt myself moving slowly up Fifth Avenue to the martial music of drums, brass horns, and tambourines; sun shining, banners waving, above me my flag making a sky of stars and stripes, and behind me block upon block of my co-workers; I felt uplifted and at the same time humbled.

"Here we come," I felt like saying. "Here we come a thousand strong—all alike, no one higher than another. Here we come in quest. We come in quest of a broader vision and a bigger life. We come, shoe-strings dragging, skirts impeding, wind disheveling, holding on to inappropriate head-gear, feathers awry, victims of old-time convictions, unadapted to modern conditions, amateur marchers, poorly uniformed—but here we come—just count us—here we come! You'll forget the shoe-strings after you've watched a mile of us. You'll forget the conspicuous fanatics among us (every movement has its lunatic fringe, somebody has said), you'll forget the funny remarks, the jokes of newsboys, and the humorous man you stood beside, after your legs begin to feel stiff and weary, and still we keep on coming, squad upon squad, band upon band, banner upon banner."

As I rode that day with all my sisters I felt for the first time in my life the inspiration of coöperation. It flashed across me that the picture of the wheel with the wings was as untrue as it was impossible. I had made a mistake. I was not that sort of wheel. I wasn't superfluous. I was a tiny little wheel with cogs. I was set in a big and tremendous machine—Life, and beside me were other wheels, which in their turn fitted into other cogs of more and larger wheels. And to make life run smoothly we all must work together, each quietly turning his own big or small circumference as he had been fashioned. Alone nothing could be accomplished. Wings indeed! Fairy-tales. Cog-wheels must mesh. Human beings must coöperate.

That night I had promised to spend with Mrs. Sewall. I didn't want to. I wanted to see Esther Claff. I wanted to hear the tremor of her voice, and watch her faint blue eyes grow bright and black. Tonight she would put on her little ugly brown toque and gray suit, and join the other girls, in somebody's studio or double bedroom. There would be great talk tonight! We had all marched in one company or another. I wanted to hear how the others felt. My feelings were tumultuous, confused. I longed for Esther's fervor and calm eloquence. But I had promised Mrs. Sewall; she had been particularly anxious; I couldn't go back on my word now; she dreaded lonely evenings; and I was glad that I hadn't telephoned and disappointed her when I finally did arrive a little before dinner.

She took my hand in both of hers; she looked straight into my eyes, and if I couldn't hear Esther's voice tremble, then instead I could hear Mrs. Sewall's.

"My dear," she said, "I am very proud of you. You were very beautiful, this afternoon. You will always do me credit."

I leaned and kissed her hand half playfully. "I shall try anyhow," I said lightly.

Mrs. Sewall took out her handkerchief and touched it to her eyes, then slipped one of her arms through mine, and rested her jeweled hand on my wrist, patting it a little.

"What a dear child you are!" she murmured. "I have grown fond of you. I want you to know—tonight, when your eyes are telling me the fervor that is glowing in that arduous soul of yours, how completely you satisfy me. It may be one more little triumph to add to your day's joy. I want you to know that if ever it was in my power to place my wealth and my position on you, dear child, it would be the greatest happiness of my life. I have given myself the liberty of confiding much in you, of taking you into the inner courts, my dear. You are as familiar with my expenditures as with your own; you are acquainted with my notions upon distribution, charitable requests, wise and foolish investments; you appreciate my ideas in regard to handling great fortunes; you agree with me that masters of considerable amounts of money are but temporary keepers of the world's wealth, and must leave their trust for the next steward in clean, healthy, and growing condition; you have been apprenticed to all my dearest hopes and ambitions. Ah, yes, yes, very creditably would you wear my crown. With what grace, intelligence, and appreciation of values would you move among the other monitors of great fortunes, admired by them, praised, and loved, I think. What a factor for good you could become! Your expansive sympathies—what resources they would assume. Ah, well, well, you see I like to paint air-castles. I like to put you into them. This afternoon when I saw you mounted like some inspired goddess on that superb creature of Mrs. Scot-Williams', and caught the murmur that passed over the little company on the balcony as you approached, I thought to myself, 'She's made for something splendid.' And you are, my dear—you are. Something splendid. Who knows, my air-castles may come true."

"O Mrs. Sewall," I said softly, "I'm not worthy of such kind words as those."

"There, there," she interrupted. She had heard the catch in my voice. "There. Think nothing more about it. We won't talk seriously another moment. Dinner will be announced directly. Let us have Perkins light a fire."

An Encounter with Breck

MRS. SEWALL didn't remain long with me in the library after dinner. She excused herself to retire early. I was to read aloud to her later, when Marie called me. I was dawdling over a bit of sewing as I waited. My thoughts were busy, my cheeks hot. The experience of the day, climaxing in Mrs. Sewall's warm words, had excited me, I suppose. I wondered if first nights before footlights on Broadway could be more thrilling than this success of mine. Was it my new feeling of sisterhood that so elated me—or was it, more, Mrs. Sewall's capitulation? Was I still susceptible to flattery?

"Well, hello!" suddenly somebody interrupted.

I recognized the voice. My heart skipped a beat, I think, but my practiced needle managed to finish its stitch.

"Hello, there," the voice repeated, and I looked up and saw Breckenridge Sewall smiling broadly at me from between heavy portières.

"Hello, Breck," I said, and holding my head very high I inquired, "What are you doing *here*?"

"Oh, I'm stopping here," he grinned. "What are *you* doing?"

"You know very well what I'm doing," I replied. "I'm your mother's private secretary. What are you doing around here, Breck?"

He laughed. "You beat 'em all. I swear you do! What am I doing around here! You'd think I didn't have a right in my own house. You'd think it was your house, and I'd broken in. Well, seeing you ask, I'll tell you what I'm doing. I'm observing a darned pretty girl, sitting in the corner of one of my sofas, in my library, and I don't object to it at all—not at all. Make yourself quite at home, my girl. Look here, aren't you glad to see a fellow back again?" He came over to me. "Put your hand there in mine and tell me so then. I've just come from the steamer. Nobody's extended greetings to me yet. I'm hurt."

"Haven't you seen your mother?" I inquired coolly.

"Not yet. The old lady'll keep. You come first on the program, little private secretary. Good Lord—private secretary! What do you know about that? Say, you're clever. Gee!" he broke off, "but it's good to get back. You're the first one I've seen except Perkins. Surprised?" He rested both hands on the table beside me, and leaned toward me. I kept on sewing. "Come, come," he said, "put it down. Don't you recollect I never was much on patience? Come, little private secretary, I'm just about at the end of my rope."

"I think you ought to go upstairs and see your mother," I replied calmly. "Did she expect you?"

"Sure. Sure, my dear. I 'phoned the mater to vanish. Savvy?" He was still leaning toward me. "Come, we're alone. I dropped everything on the spot to come to *you*. Now don't you suppose you can manage to drop that fancy-work stuff to say you're glad to see me?"

"Please, Breck," I said, moving away from him a little. He was very near me. "Don't be in such a hurry. Please. You always had to give me time, you know. Would you mind opening a window? It's so warm in here. And then explain this surprising situation? I'd thank you if you would."

"It is hot in here," he said, leaning still nearer, "hot as hell, or else it's the sight of you that makes my blood boil," he murmured.

I moved away again, reeled off some more thread and threaded my needle.

"You don't fall off!" Breck went on. "You don't lose your looks. By gad, you don't!"

"If you touch the bell by the curtain there," I said, "Perkins will come and open the window for us."

"Good Lord," Breck exclaimed, "you're the coolest proposition I ever ran across. All right. Have your own way, my lady. You always have been able to twist me around your little finger. Here goes." And he strode across to the front window, pulled the hangings back and threw open a sash. I felt the cool air on the back of my neck. Breck came back and stood looking down at me quizzically. I kept on taking stitches. "Keep right at it, industrious little one," he smiled. "Sew as long as you want to. *I* don't mind. I don't have to go out again to get home tonight. I'm satisfied. Stitch away, dear little Busy Bee." He took out a cigarette and lit it; then suddenly sat down on the sofa beside me, leaned back luxuriously, and in silence proceeded to send little rings of smoke ceilingward. "Lovely!" he murmured. "True felicity! I've dreamed of this! This is something like home now, my beauty. This is as it ought to be! I always wear holes in the heels too, my love. And no knots, kindly."

"Breck," I interrupted finally, "is your mother in this?"

"We're all in it, my dear child."

"Will you explain?"

"Sure, delighted. Sit up on my hind legs and beg if you want me to. Anything you say. It was this way. I was in London when mater happened to mention the name of her jewel of a secretary. I was about to start off on a long trip in the yacht—Spain,

Southern France, Algiers. Stocked all up. Supplies, crew, captain—everything all ready. 'I don't care what becomes of 'em,' I said, when I got news where you were. 'I don't care. Throw 'em overboard. Guests too. I don't give a hang. Throw them over—Lady Dunbarton, and the Grand Duke too. Drown 'em! There's somebody back in New York who has hung out her little Come-hither sign for me, and I'm off for the little home-burg in the morning.'"

"Come-hither sign! O Breck, you're mistaken. I—"

"Hold on, my innocent little child, I wasn't born day before yesterday. But let that go. I won't insist. I've come anyhow." He leaned forward. "I'm as crazy about you as ever," he said earnestly. "I never cared a turn of my hand for any one but you. Queer too, but it's so. I'm not much on talking love—the real kind, you know—but I guess it must be what I feel for you. It must be what is keeping me from snatching away that silly stuff there in your hand, and having you in my arms now—whether you'd like it or not. Say," he went on, "I've come home to make this house really yours, and to give you the right of asking what I'm doing around here. You've won all your points—pomp, ceremony, big wedding, all the fuss, mater's blessing. The mater is just daffy about you—ought to see her letters. You're a winner, you're a great little diplomat, and I'm proud of you too. I shall take you everywhere—France, England, India. You'll be a queen in every society you enter—you will. By Jove—you will. Here in New York, too, you'll shine, you little jewel; and up there at Hilton, won't we show them a few things? You bet! Say—I've come to ask you to marry me. Do you get that? That's what I've come for—to make you Mrs. Breckenridge Sewall."

I sat very quietly sewing through this long speech of Breck's. The calm, regular sticking in and pulling out of my needle concealed the tumult of my feelings. I thought I had forever banished my taste for pomp and glory, but I suppose it must be a little like a man who has forsworn alcohol. The old longing returns when he gets a smell of wine, and sees it sparkling within arm's reach.

As I sat contemplating for a moment the bright and brilliant picture of myself as Breck's wife, favored by Mrs. Sewall, envied, admired by my family, homaged by the world, the real mistress of this magnificent house, I asked myself if perhaps fate, now that I had left it to its own resources in regard to Breck, did not come offering this prize as just reward. And then suddenly, borne upon the perfumed breeze that blew through the open window, I felt the sharp keen, stab of a memory of a Spring ago—fields, New England—fields and woods; brooks; hills; a little apartment of seven rooms, bare, unfurnished; and somebody's honest gray eyes looking into mine. It seemed as if the very embodiment of that memory had passed near me. It must have been that some flowering tree outside in the park, bearing its persuasive sweetness through the open window, touched to life in my consciousness a memory imprinted there by the perfume of some sister bloom in New England. I almost felt the presence of him with whom I watched the trees bud and flower a Spring ago. Even though some subtle instinct prompted Breck at this stage to rise and put down the window, the message of the trees had reached me. It made my reply to Breck gentle. When he came back to me I stood up and put aside my needle-work.

"Well?" he questioned,

"I'm so sorry. I can't marry you, Breck. I can't."

"Why not? Why can't you? What's your game? What do you want of me? Don't beat around. I'm serious. What do you mean 'you can't?'"

"I'm sorry, but I don't care enough for you, Breck. I wish I did, but I just don't."

"Oh, you don't! That's it. Well, look here, don't let that worry you. I'll make you care for me. I'll attend to that. Do you understand?" And suddenly he put his arms about me. "I'll marry you and make you care," he murmured. I felt my hot cheek pressed against his rough coat, and smelled again the old familiar smell of tobacco, mixed with the queer eastern perfume which Breck's valet always put a little of on his master's handkerchief. "You've got to marry me. You're helpless to do anything else—as helpless as you are now to get away from me when I want to hold you. I'm crazy about you, and I shall have you some day too. If it's ceremony you want, it's yours. Oh, you're mine—*mine*, little private secretary. Do you hear me? You're mine. Sooner or later you're mine."

He let me go at last.

I went over to a mirror and fixed my hair.

"I wish you hadn't done that," I said, and rang for Perkins. He came creaking in, in his squeaky boots.

"Perkins," I said, "will you call a taxi for me? I'm not staying with Mrs. Sewall now that she has her son here. Please tell her that I am going to Esther's."

"I shall see that you get there safely," warned Breck. "I've rights while you're under this roof."

"It isn't necessary, Breck. I often walk. I'm used to going about alone. But do as you please. However, if you do come, I'm going to ask you not to treat me as if—as if—as you just did. I've given all that to somebody else."

"Somebody else," he echoed.

"Yes," I nodded. "Yes, Breck; yes—somebody else."

"Oh!" he said. "Oh!" and stared at me. I could see it hit him.

"I'll go and put my things on," I explained, and went away.

When I came back he was standing just where I had left him. Something moved me to go up and speak to him. I had never seen Breckenridge Sewall look like this.

"Good-night, Breck," I said. "I'm sorry."

"You! Sorry!" he laughed horribly. Then he added, "This isn't the last chapter—not by a long shot. You can go alone tonight—but remember—this isn't the last chapter."

I rode away feeling a little uneasy. I longed to talk to some one. What did he mean? What did he threaten? If only Esther—but no, we had never been personal. She knew as little about the circumstances of my life as I about hers. She could not help me. Anyway it proved upon my arrival at the rooms in Irving Place that Esther was not there.

I sat down and tried to imagine what Breck could imply by the "last chapter." At any rate I decided that the next one was to resign my position as Mrs. Sewall's secretary. That was clear. I wrote to her in my most careful style. I told her that until she was able to replace me, I would do my best to carry on her correspondence in my rooms in Irving Place. She could send her orders to me by the chauffeur; I was sorry; I hoped she would appreciate my position; she had been very good to me; Breckenridge would explain everything, and I was hers faithfully, Ruth Chenery Vars.

Esther didn't come back all night—nor even the next day. I could have sallied forth and found some of our old associates, I suppose; but I knew that they would all still be discussing the parade, and somehow I wanted no theorizing, no large thinking. I wanted no discussion of the pros and cons of big questions and reforms. I wanted a little practical advice—I wanted somebody's sympathetic hand.

About seven o'clock the next evening, the telephone which Esther and I had indulged in interrupted my lonely contemplations with two abrupt little rings. I got up and answered it weakly. I feared it would be Mrs. Sewall—or Breck, but it wasn't.

"Is that you, Ruth?"

Bob! It was Bob calling me! Bob's dear voice!

"Yes," I managed to reply. "Yes, Bob. Yes, it's I."

"May I see you?"

"Yes, you may see me."

"When? May I see you now?"

"Why, yes. You may see me *now*."

"All right. I'm at the Grand Central. Just in. I called your other number and they gave me this. I don't know where it is. Will you tell me?"

I could feel the foot that my weight wasn't on trembling. "Yes, I'll tell you," I said, "but I'd rather meet *you*—some nicer place. Couldn't I meet you?"

"Yes—if you'd rather. Can you come *now*?"

"Yes, now, Bob, this very minute."

"All right, then." He named a hotel. "The tea-room in half an hour. Good-by."

"Good-by," I managed to finish; and I was glad when I hung up the receiver that Esther wasn't there.

The Open Door

NO one would have guessed who saw a girl in a dark-blue, tailored suit enter the tea-room that evening about seven o'clock, and greet a man, with a brief and ordinary hand-shake, that there was a tremor of knees and hammering of heart underneath her quiet colors; and that the touch of the man's bare hand, even through her glove, sent something zigzagging down through her whole being, like a streak of lightning through a cloud. All she said was: "Hello, Bob. I've come, you see." And he quietly, "Yes, I see. You've come."

He dropped her hand. They looked straight into each other's eyes an instant.

"Anything the matter with anybody at home?" she questioned.

"Oh, no, nothing," he assured her. "Everybody's all right. Are you all right, Ruth?"

"Yes," she smiled. (How good it was to see him. His kind, kind eyes! He looked tired—a little. She remembered that suit. It was new last Spring. What dear, intimate knowledge she still possessed of him.) "Yes," she smiled, "I'm all right."

"Had dinner?" he questioned.

"No, not a bite." She shook her head. (How glowing and fresh he was, even in spite of the tired look. She knew very well what he had done with the half-hour before he met her; he had made himself beautiful for her eyes. How well acquainted she was with all the precious, homely signs, how completely he had been hers once. There was the fountain-pen, with its peculiar patent clasp, in its usual place in his waistcoat pocket. In that same pocket was a pencil, nicely sharpened, and a small note-book with red leather covers. She knew! She had rummaged in that waistcoat pocket often.)

They went into the dining-room together. They sat down at a small table with an electric candle on it, beside a mirror. A waiter stood before them with paper and raised pencil. They ordered, or I suppose they did, for I believe food was brought. The girl didn't eat a great deal. Another thing I noticed—she didn't trust herself to look long at a time into the man's eyes. She contented herself with gazing at his cuffed wrist resting on the table's edge, and at his hands. His familiar hands! The familiar platinum and gold watch chain too! Did it occur to him, when at night he wound his watch, that a little while ago it had been a service she was wont to perform for him? How thrillingly alive the gold case used to seem to her—warmed by its nearness to his body. Oh, dear, oh, dear—what made her so weak and yearning tonight? What made her so in need of this man? What would Esther Claff think? What would Mrs. Scot-Williams say?

"Well, Ruth," the man struck out at last, after the waiter had brought bread and water and butter, and the menu had been put aside, "Well—when you're ready, I am. I am anxious to hear all that's happened—if you're happy—and all that."

The girl dragged her gaze away from him. "Of course, Bob," she said, "of course you want to know, and I am going to tell you from beginning to end. There's a sort of an end tonight, and it happens I need somebody to tell it to, quite badly. I needed an old friend to assure me that I've nothing to be afraid of. I think you're the very one I needed most tonight, Bob." And quite simply, quite frankly, the girl told him her story—there was nothing for her to hide from him—it was a relief to talk freely.

The effect of her story upon the man seemed to act like stimulant. It elated him; she didn't know why. "What a brick you are, Ruth," he broke out. "How glad I am I came down here—what a little brick you are! I guess you're made of the stuff, been dried and baked in a kiln that insures you against danger of crumbling. It's only an unthinking fool who would ever be afraid for you. You need to fear nothing but a splendid last chapter to your life, whoever may threaten. Oh, it's good to see you, Ruth—how good you cannot quite guess. I saw you yesterday in the parade—Lucy and Will too—and I got as near home as Providence, when suddenly I thought I'd turn around and come back here. I was a little disturbed, anxious—I'll acknowledge it—worried a bit—but now, *now*—the relief!"

"You thought I was wasting away in a shirtwaist factory!" she laughed.

He laughed too. "Not quite that. But, never mind, we don't need to go into what I thought, but rather into what I think—what I *think*, Ruth—what I shall always think." Compelling voice! Persuasive gaze! She looked into his eyes. "Ruth!" The man leaned forward. "We've made a mistake. What are you down here for all alone, anyhow? And what am I doing, way up there, longing for you day after day, and missing you every hour? My ambitions have become meaningless since you have dropped out of my future. What is it all for? For what foolish notion, what absurd fear have we sacrificed the most precious thing in the world? Yesterday when I saw you—Oh, my dear, my dear, I need you. Come as you are. I shan't try to make you over. There's only one thing that counts after all, and that is ours."

With some such words as these did Bob frighten me away from the sweet liberties my thoughts had been taking with him. I had been like some hungry little mouse that almost boldly enters human haunts if he thinks he is unobserved, but at the least noise of invitation scampers away into his hole. I scampered now—fast. My problems were not yet solved. I had things I must prove to Lucy, to Edith, to

Tom—things I must test and prove to myself. I could not go to him now. Besides, all the reasons that stood in the way of our happiness existed still, in spite of the fact that our joy of meeting blinded us to them for the moment. I tried to make it clear to Bob.

"You can't have changed in a winter, Bob, and I haven't. We decided so carefully, weighed the consequences of our decision. We were wise and courageous. Let's not go back on it. I don't know what conclusions about life I may reach finally, but I want to be able to grow freely. I'm like a bulb that hasn't been put in the earth till just lately. I don't know what sort of flower or vegetable I am, and you don't either. It's been good to see you, Bob, and I needed some one to tell me that I was all right, but now you must go away and let me grow."

"You wouldn't want to come and grow in my green-house then?" he smiled sadly.

I shook my head. "That's just it, Bob. I don't want to grow in any green-house yet. I want to be blown and tossed by all the winds of the world that blow."

"I'll let you grow as you wish," he persisted.

"Please, Bob," I pleaded. "Please—"

He turned away. I didn't want to hurt him.

"Bob," I said gently, "please understand. It isn't only that I think the reasons for our decision of a year ago still exist, but I've just *got* to stay here now, Bob, even though I don't want to. I've got it firmly fixed in my mind *now* that I'm going to see my undertaking through to a successful end. I'm bound to show Tom and the family what sort of stuff I'm made of. I'm going to prove that women aren't weak and vacillating. Why, I haven't been even a year here yet. I couldn't run to cover the first time I found myself out of a position. Besides the first position wasn't one I could exhibit to the family. I *must* stay. I'm just as anxious to prove myself a success as a young man whose family doesn't think he's got it in him. Please understand, and help me, Bob."

"Shall we see each other sometimes?" he queried.

"It's no use. It doesn't help," I said. "I do care for you, somehow, and seeing you seems to make foggy what was so clear and crystal, as if I were looking at it through a mist. I mean sitting here with you makes me feel—makes me forget what I marched for day before yesterday. I was so full of it—of all it meant and stood for—and now—No, Bob. No. You must let me work these things out alone. I shall never be satisfied now until I do."

He left me at my door. There was a light in the windows upstairs, and I knew that Esther had come home. Bob left me with just an ordinary hand-shake. It hurt somehow—that formal little ceremony from him. It hurt, too, afterward to stand in the doorway and watch him walking away. It hurt to hear the sound of his steady step growing fainter and fainter. O Bob, you might have turned around and waved!

I went upstairs. "Hello," said Esther. "Where have you been?" and I told her to dinner with a man from home. A little later I announced to her that I had resigned my position as private secretary to Mrs. Sewall. She asked no questions but she made her own slow deductions.

I must have impressed her as restless and not very happy that night. I caught her looking at me suspiciously, once or twice, over her gold-bowed reading-glasses. Once she inquired if I was ill, or felt feverish. My cheeks did burn.

"Oh, no," I said, "but I guess I'll go to bed. It's almost midnight."

Esther took off her glasses and rubbed her eyes.

"One gets tired, sometimes, climbing," she observed. I waited. "The trail up the mountain of Self-discovery is not an easy one. One's unaccustomed feet get sore, and one's courage wavers when the trail sometimes creeps along precipices or shoots steeply up over rocks. But I think the greatest test comes when the little hamlets appear—quiet, peaceful little spots, with smoke curling out of the chimneys of nestling houses. They offer such peace and comfort for weary feet. It's then one is tempted to throw away the mountain-staff and accept the invitation of the open door and welcoming hearth."

"Oh, Esther," I exclaimed, "were you afraid I was going to throw away my mountain-staff?"

"Oh, no, no. I was simply speaking figuratively." She would not be personal.

"I'm not such a poor climber as all that," I went on. "I am a bit discouraged tonight. You've guessed it, but I am not for giving up."

"If one ever gets near the top of the mountain of Self-discovery," Esther pursued dreamily, "he becomes master not only of his own little peak, but commands a panorama of hundreds of other peaks. He not only conquers his own difficult trail, but wins, as reward for himself, vision, far-reaching."

I loved Esther when she talked like this.

"Well," I assured her, "I am going to get to the top of my peak, if it takes a lifetime. No hamlets by the wayside for me," I laughed.

"Oh, no," she corrected. "Never to the top, Ruth—not *here*. The top of the mountain of Self-discovery is hidden in the clouds of eternity. We can simply approach it. So then," she broke off, "you aren't deserting me?"

"Of course I'm not, Esther," I assured her.

"What do you mean to do next, then—if you're leaving Mrs. Sewall?"

"I don't know. Don't ask. I'm new at mountain-climbing, and when my trail crawls along precipices, I refuse to look over the edge and get dizzy. Something will turn up."

The next morning's mail brought a letter from Mrs. Sewall. My services would not be needed any longer. Enclosed was a check which paid me up to the day of my departure. In view of the circumstances, it would be wiser to sever our connections immediately. Owing to the unexpected return of her son, they were both starting within a few days for the Pacific coast. Therefore, she would suggest that I return immediately by express all papers and other property of hers which chanced to be in my possession. It was a regret that her confidence had been so misplaced.

I read Mrs. Sewall's displeasure in every sentence of that curt little note. If I had been nursing the hope for understanding from my old employer, it was dead within me now. The letter cut me like a whip.

My feeling for Mrs. Sewall had developed into real affection. Her years, her reserve, her remoteness had simply added romance to the peculiar friendship. I had thrilled beneath the touch of her cold fingertips. There had been moments lately when at the kindness in her eyes as they dwelt upon me, I had longed to put my arms around her and tell her how happy and proud I was to have entered even a little way into the warm region near her heart. I loved to please her. I would do anything for her except marry Breck, and she could write to me like this! She could misunderstand! She could all but call me traitor!

Very well. With bitterness, and with grim determination never to plead or to explain, I sent back by the next express the check-books and papers I was working on evenings in my room, and also by registered mail returned the bar of pearls she had once playfully removed from her own dress and pinned at my throat. "Wear it for me," she had said. "If I had had a daughter I would have spoiled her with pretty things, I fear. Allow an old lady occasionally to indulge her whims on you, my dear."

I lay awake a long time that night, preparing myself for the struggle that awaited me. I had as little chance now to obtain steady employment as when I made my first attempt. I was still untrained, and, stripped of Mrs. Sewall's favor, still unable to provide the necessary letters of reference. I hadn't succeeded in making any tracks into which, on being pushed to the bottom again, I could stick my toes, and mount the way a second time more easily. Lying awake there, flat on my back, I was reminded of a little insect I once watched climbing the slippery surface of a window-pane. It was a stormy day, and he was on the outside of the window, buffeted by winds. I saw that little creature successfully cover more than half his journey four successive times, only to fall wriggling on his back at the bottom again. When he fell the fourth time, righted himself, and, dauntless and determined, began his journey again, I picked him up bodily and placed him at the top. Possibly—how could such a small atom of the universe as I know—possibly my poor attempts were being watched too!

However, I didn't wait to find out. At least I didn't wait to be picked up. The very next day I set forth for employment agencies.

Mountain Climbing

THERE followed a long hot summer. There followed days of hopelessness. There followed a wild desire for crisp muslin curtains, birds to wake me in the morning, a porcelain tub, pretty gowns, tea on somebody's broad veranda. There were days in mid-July when if I had met Bob Jennings, and he had invited me to green fields, or cool woods, I wouldn't have stopped even to pack. There were days in August when a letter from Breck, post-marked Bar Harbor, and returned like three preceding letters unopened, I didn't dare read for fear of the temptation of blue sea, and a yacht with wicker chairs and a servant in white to bring me things.

If it hadn't been for Esther's quiet determination I might have crawled back to Edith any one of those hot stifling nights and begged for admittance to the cool chamber with the spinet desk. My head ached half the time; my feet pained me; food was unattractive. The dead air of the New York subway made me feel ill. In three minutes it could sap me of the little hope I carried down from the surface. I used to dream nights of the bird-like speed of Breckenridge Sewall's powerful automobiles. I used to wake mornings longing for the strong impact of wind against my face.

The big city, the crowds of working people that once inspired, the great mass of congregated humanity had lost its romance. Even my own particular struggle seemed to have no more "punch" in it. The novelty of my undertaking, the adventure had worn away. They had been right at the Y. W. C. A. when they advised me a year ago to go home and give up my enterprise. I had been dauntless then, but now, although toughened and weathered, discouragement and despair possessed me. I allowed myself to sit for days in the room in Irving Place, without even trying for a position.

It was Esther who obtained a steady job for me at last, in a book-binding factory down near the City Hall. From eight in the morning until five at night I folded paper, over and over and over again, with a bone folder; the same process—no change—no variation. The muscles that I used ached like a painful tooth at first. Some nights we worked until nine o'clock. Accuracy and speed were all that was required to be an efficient folder—no brains, no thought—and yet I never became expert. The sameness of my work got on my nerves so at last—the everlasting repetition of sound and motion—that occasionally I lost all sense of time and place. It was like repeating some common word over and over again until it loses all significance except that of a peculiar sound.

It broke me at last. I became ill. What hundreds of other girls were able to do every day the year round, had finished me in three weeks. I was as soft as a baby. It was my nerves that gave way. I got to crying one night over some trivial little thing, and I couldn't stop. They took me to a hospital, I don't remember how or when. I became aware of trained nurses. I drifted back to the consciousness of a queer grating sound near the head of my bed, which they told me was an elevator; I smelled anesthetics. I realized a succession of nights and days. There were flowers. There was a frequent ringing of bells. Heaven couldn't have been more restful. I loved to lie there and watch a breeze blow the sash-curtains at the windows, in and out with a gentle, ship-like motion. Esther visited me often. Sometimes she sat by the window alone, correcting proof (she had secured a position in a publishing house the first of the summer), and sometimes one of the other girls of our little circle was with her. I never talked with them; I never questioned; they came and went; I felt no curiosity. They tell me I lay there like that for nearly three weeks, and then suddenly with no warning and with no sense of shock or surprise the veil lifted.

Esther and the struggling artist we called Rosa were by the window. They had both come from the same little town in Pennsylvania. I'd been watching them for half an hour or more. They had been talking. I had liked the murmur of their low voices. In the most normal fashion in the world I began to listen to their conversation.

"I wouldn't have had the courage," I heard Rosa say.

"Why not?" replied Esther. "Her family could do no more than is being done. If they took her home now, she'd never come back again. Her spirit would be broken. That wouldn't be good for her. Besides *they* don't need her, while I—why, she's the only human being in the world that's ever meant anything in my life, and I am thirty-three. It has been almost like having had a child dependent on me—having had *her*, giving her a new point of view, taking care of her *now*."

"Well, but how long can you stand the expense of this private room, and the doctors?"

"You needn't worry about that," Esther shrugged.

"But it seems a shame, Esther," burst out Rosa, "just when your father's estate begins to pay you enough income to live on, and you could devote the best of yourself to your book—it seems a shame not to be able to take advantage of it. You've always said," she went on, "that a woman can't successfully begin to create after she's thirty-five. This will certainly put you behind a while. And the room rent too! Does she know yet that you didn't tell her the truth about the price of the room in Irving Place?"

"No, Ruth doesn't know," replied Esther. "She's very proud about such matters. When she first came she had only an empty trunk, a new job, and a few dollars. Later, when I was going to explain, she lost her position with Mrs. Sewall. I was thankful I hadn't told her then."

"Well, I must say!" exclaimed Rosa warmly, "I must say!"

"Rosa," said Esther. "You don't understand. If Ruth did pay her full share of the room, she would be obliged to leave me sooner. Don't you see? My motives are selfish. You're the one person who knew me back there at home. You have seen all along how stark and empty my life has been–just my independence, my thoughts, my ambitions. That's all. No one to care, no one to make sacrifices for, no man, no child—Good heavens, if some human being has fallen across my way, don't be surprised if I prize my good fortune."

I lay very still listening to Esther's voice. I closed my eyes for fear she might glance up and meet the tears in them, and sudden understanding. I had never known her till now. I could feel the tears, in spite of me, creeping down my cheeks.

I left the hospital a week later. They sent me back to the room in Irving Place with orders for long walks in the fresh air, two-hour rest periods morning and afternoon, and a diet of eggs, chicken, cream and fresh green vegetables. Ridiculous orders for a working girl in New York! They disturbed Esther. She was very quiet, more uncommunicative than ever. I used to catch her looking at me in a sort of anxious way. It seemed as if I couldn't wait to help her with her too-heavy burden. Although I had brought back from the hospital fifteen pounds less flesh on my bones, there was something in my heart instead that was sure to make me strong and well. My new incentive was the secret knowledge of Esther's devotion. To prove to her that her sacrifices had not been in vain became my ambition. For a few days I idled in the room, as the doctor ordered; strolled about Gramercy Park near-by, feeding my eyes on green grass and trees; indulged in bus rides to the Park occasionally; and walked for the exercise.

It's strange how easily some opportunities turn up, and others can't be dug with spade and shovel. One day, aimlessly strolling along a side street, up among the fifties, a card in a milliner's shop chanced to meet my eye. "Girl Wanted," it said, in large black letters.

It was late in the afternoon. If I had set out in quest of that opportunity, the position would have been filled before I arrived. But this one was still open. They wanted a girl to deliver, and perhaps to help a little in the work-room—sewing in linings, and things like that. The hours were short; the bundles not heavy; I needed exercise; it had been ordered by the hospital.

The work agreed with me perfectly. It was very easy. I liked the varied rides, and the interesting search for streets and numbers. It was just diverting enough for my mending nerves. The pay was not much. I didn't object. I was still convalescing.

Crossing Fifth Avenue one day, rather overloaded with two large bandboxes which, though not heavy, were cumbersome, I saw Mrs. Sewall! A kindly policeman had caught sight of me on the curbing and signaled for the traffic to stop. As I started across, I glanced up at the automobile before which I had to pass. Something familiar about the chauffeur caught my attention. I looked into the open back of the car. Mrs. Sewall's eyes met mine. She didn't smile. There was no sign of recognition. We just stared for a moment, and then I hurried along.

I didn't think she knew me. My illness had disguised me as if I wore a mask.

I was, therefore, surprised the next morning to receive a brief note from Mrs. Sewall asking me to be at my room, if possible, that evening at half-past eight.

The Pot of Gold

ESTHER was out canvassing for suffrage. She canvassed every other evening now. She had not touched the manuscript of her book for weeks.

Esther could earn a dollar an evening at canvassing. One evening's canvassing made a dozen egg-nogs for me. Esther poured them down my throat in place of chicken and fresh vegetables. I couldn't stop her. I wasn't allowed even to say "Thank you."

"I'd do the same for any such bundle of skin and bones as you," she belittled. "Don't be sentimental. You'd do it for me. We'd both do it for a starved cat. It's one of the unwritten laws of humanity—women and children first, and food for the starving."

She was out "egg-nogging," as I used to call it, when Mrs. Sewall called. I had the room to myself. Mrs. Sewall had never visited my quarters before. I lit the lamp on our large table, drew up the Morris-chair near it, straightened our couch-covers, and arranged the screen around the chiffoniers. Mrs. Sewall was not late. I heard her motor draw up to the curbing, scarcely a minute after our alarm clock pointed to the half-hour.

Marie accompanied her mistress up the one flight of stairs to our room. I heard them outside in the dim corridor, searching for my name among the various calling cards tacked upon the half-dozen doors. It was discovered at last. There was a knock. I opened the door.

"That will do," said Mrs. Sewall, addressing herself to Marie, who turned and disappeared, and then briefly to me, "Good evening."

"Good evening, Mrs. Sewall. Come in," I replied. We did not shake hands. I offered her the Morris-chair.

"No," she said, "no, thank you. This will do." And she selected a straight-backed, bedroom chair, as far away as possible from the friendly circle of the lamp-light. "I'm here only for a moment," she went on, "on a matter of business."

I procured a similar straight-backed chair and drew it near enough to converse without too much effort. It was awkward. It was like trying to play an act on a stage with nothing but two straight chairs in the middle—no scenery, nothing to elude or soften. Mrs. Sewall, sitting there before me in her perfect black, a band of white neatly edging her neck and wrists, veil snugly drawn, gloves tightly clasped, was like some hermetically sealed package. Her manner was forbidding, her gaze penetrating.

"So this is where you live!" she remarked.

"Yes, this is where I live," I replied. "It's very quiet, and a most desirable location."

"Oh! Quiet! Desirable! I see." Then after a pause in which my old employer looked so sharply at me that I wanted to exclaim, "I know I'm a little gaunt, but I'm not the least disheartened," she inquired frowning, "Did you remain in this quiet, desirable place all summer, may I ask?"

"Well—not all summer. I was away for three weeks—but my room-mate, Miss Claff, was here. It isn't uncomfortable."

"Where were you then, if not here?"

"Why, resting. I took a vacation," I replied.

"You have been ill," Mrs. Sewall stated with finality, and there was no kindness in her voice; it expressed instead vexation. "That is evident. You have been ill. What was the trouble?"

"Oh, nothing much. Nerves, I suppose."

"Nerves! And why should a girl like you have nerves?"

"I don't know, I'm sure," I smiled. "I went into book-binding. It's quite the fad, you know. Some society women take it up for diversion, but I didn't like it."

"Were you in a hospital? Did your people know? Were you properly cared for?" Each question that she asked came with a little sharper note of irritation.

"Yes. Oh, yes. I was properly cared for. I was in a private room. I have loyal friends here."

"Loyal friends!" scoffed Mrs. Sewall. "Loyal friends indeed! And may I ask what loyal friend allows you to go about in your present distressing condition? You are hardly fit to be seen, Miss Vars."

I flushed. "I'm sorry," I said.

"Disregard of one's health is not admirable."

"I'm being very careful," I assured Mrs. Sewall. "If you could but know the eggs I consume!"

"Miss Vars," inquired Mrs. Sewall, with obvious annoyance in her voice, "was it you that I saw yesterday crossing Fifth Avenue?"

"With the boxes? It was I," I laughed.

She frowned. "I was shocked. Such occupation is unbecoming to you."

"It is a perfectly self-respecting occupation," I maintained.

The frown deepened. "Possibly. Yes, *self-respecting*, but, if I may say so, scarcely respecting your friends, scarcely respecting those who have cared deeply for you—I refer to your family—scarcely respecting your birth, bringing-up, and opportunities.

It was distinctly out of place. The spectacle was not only shocking to me, it was painful. Not that what I think carries any weight with you. I have been made keenly aware of how little my opinions count. But—"

"Oh, please–please, Mrs. Sewall," I interrupted. "Your opinions *do* count. I've wanted to tell you so before. I was sorry to leave you as I did. I've wanted to explain how truly I desired to please you. I would have done anything within my power except—I couldn't do that one special thing, *anything* but that."

Mrs. Sewall raised her hand to silence me. There was displeasure in her eyes. "We will not refer to it, please," she replied. "It is over. I prefer not to discuss it. It is not a matter to be disposed of with a few light words. I have not come here to discuss with you what is beyond your comprehension. Pain caused by a heedless girl, or a steel knife, is not less keen because of the heartlessness of either instrument. I have come purely on business. We will not wander further."

There was a pause. Mrs. Sewall was tapping her bag with a rapid, nervous little motion. I was keeping my hands folded tightly in my lap. We were both making an effort to control our feelings. We sat opposite each other without saying anything for a moment. It was I who spoke at last.

"Very well," I resumed. "What is the business, Mrs. Sewall? Perhaps," I suggested coldly, "I have failed to return something that belongs to you."

"No," replied Mrs. Sewall. "On the contrary, I have something here that belongs to *you*." She held up a package. "Your work-bag. It was found by the butler on the mantel in the library."

"Oh, how careless! I'm sorry. It was of no consequence." My cheeks flamed. It hurt me keenly that Mrs. Sewall should insult the dignity of our relations by a matter so trivial. My work-bag indeed! Behind her, in the desk, were a few sheets of her stationery!

I rose and took the bag. "Thank you," I said briefly.

"Not at all," she replied.

I waited a moment. Then, as she did not move, I inquired, "Shall I call your maid, or will you allow me to take you to your car?"

Mrs. Sewall did not reply. I became aware of something unnatural in her attitude. I noticed her tightly clasped hands.

"Oh, Mrs. Sewall!" I exclaimed. She was ill. I was sure of it now. She was deathly pale. I kneeled down on the floor and took her hands. "You are not well. Let me help–please. You are in pain."

She spoke at last. "Call Marie," she ordered, and drew her hands away.

I sped down to the waiting car. Marie seemed to comprehend before I spoke.

"Oh! Another attack! Mon Dieu! The tablets! I have them. They are here. Make haste. It is the heart. They are coming more often—the attacks. Emotion—and then afterwards the pain. She had one yesterday, late in the afternoon. And now tonight again. Mon Dieu—Mon Dieu! The pain is terrible." All this from Marie as we hastened up the stairs.

Mrs. Sewall sat just where I had left her in the straight-backed chair. She made no outcry, not the slightest moan, but there were tiny beads of perspiration on her usually cool brow, and when she took the glass of water that I offered, her hand shook visibly. She would not lie down. She would have nothing unfastened. She would not allow me to touch her.

"No, no. Marie understands. No. Kindly allow Marie. Come, Marie. Hurry. Stop flying about so. I'm not going to die. Hurry with the tablets. Don't be a fool. Make haste. There! Now I shall be better. Go away—both of you. Leave me. I'll call when I'm ready."

We stepped over to the window and stood looking out, while behind us the heroic sufferer, silently and alone, fought a fresh onslaught of pain. I longed to help her, and she would not let me. I might not even assist her to her automobile. Ten minutes later on her own feet and with head held erect she left my room. The only trace of the struggle was a rip across the back of one of the tight black gloves, caused by desperate clenching of hands. I had heard the cry of the soft kid as I stood by the window with Marie.

I opened my work-bag later. The square of fillet lace was there, the thread and the thimble, the needle threaded just as I had left it when Breck stepped in and interrupted. There was something else in the bag, too—something that had not been there before, a white box, long and thin. It contained the bar of diamonds and pearls, with a note wrapped around it.

"This pin," the note said, "was not a loan as your returning it assumes. My other employees received extra checks at Easter-time when you received this. If you prefer the money, you can, at any time, receive the pin's value at —'s, my jewelers, from my special agent, Mr. Billings. It is my hope that you will make such use of this portion of your earnings with me that I may be spared the possibility of the spectacle you afforded me this afternoon on the Avenue.

"Frances Rockridge Sewall."

The next night when Esther came in from canvassing, there lay upon her desk the neglected manuscript of her book, found in a bottom drawer. Before it stood a chair; beside it a drop-light. A quill pen, brand new, bright green and very gay, perched atop a fresh bottle of ink. Near-by appeared a small flat book showing an account between Esther Claff and Ruth Vars and an uptown bank. Inside, between roseate leaves of thin blotting paper, appeared a deposit to their credit of five hundred dollars.

The tide of my fortune had changed. One good thing followed another. It is always darkest before the storm breaks that clears the sky. My horizon so lately dim and obscure began to clear. As if five hundred dollars, safely deposited in a marble-front bank, wasn't enough for one week to convince me that life had something for me besides misfortune, three days after Mrs. Sewall called I received a summons from Mrs. Scot-Williams, whose horse I rode in the suffrage parade. Out of a sky already cleared of its darkest clouds there shot a shaft of light. I could see nothing at first but the brightness of Mrs. Scot-Williams' proposition. It blinded me to all else. I felt as if some enormous searchlight from heaven had selected poor, battered Ruth Chenery Vars for special illumination.

Mrs. Scot-Williams had observed that my place at Mrs. Sewall's was now filled by another. Therefore it had occurred to her that I might be free to consider another proposition. If so, she wanted to offer me a position in a decorator's shop which she was interested in. I might have heard of it—Van de Vere's, just off Fifth Avenue.

Van de Vere's—good heavens—it was all I could do to keep the tears out of my eyes! Five hundred dollars in the bank—and now kind fate offering me a seat in heaven that I hadn't even stood in line for! What did it mean?

Mrs. Scot-Williams, across a two by four expanse of tablecloth (we were lunching at her club), slowly unfolded her proposition to me, held it up for me to see, turned it about, as it were, so that I could catch the light shining on it from all sides, offered it to me at last to have and to hold. I accepted the precious thing.

"Rainbows really do have pots of gold, then!" I remember I exclaimed.

Van De Vere's

VAN DE VERE'S was a unique shop. It had grown from a single ill-lighted sort of studio into a very smart and beautifully equipped establishment, conveniently located in the shopping district. It looked like a private house, had been, originally. There were no show windows. The door-plate bore simply the sign V. de V's. A maid in black and white met you at the door (you had to ring), and while she went to summon Miss Van de Vere or her assistant, you were asked to be seated in a reception-room, done in black and white stripes.

Virginia Van de Vere was as unique as her shop. She wore long, loose clinging gowns, with heavy, silver chains clanking about her neck or waist. She wore an enormous ring on her forefinger. Her hair, done very low and parted, covered both her ears. It was black, so were her eyes. She hadn't any color. She led a smart and fashionable life outside business hours, going out to dinner a good deal (I had seen her once at Mrs. Sewall's) and making an impression with free and daring speech. She lived in a gorgeous apartment of her own, and for diversion had adopted a little curly-headed Greek boy, for whom she engaged the services of a French nurse. She was very temperamental.

Mrs. Scot-Williams had found Virginia Van de Vere some half dozen years before, languishing in the ill-lighted studio, on the verge of shutting up shop and going home for want of patronage. It was just that kind of talented girl that Mrs. Scot-Williams liked to help and encourage. She established Virginia Van de Vere.

Mrs. Scot-Williams is a philanthropic woman, and enormously wealthy. Her pet charity is what she calls "the little-business woman." New York is filled with small industries run by women, in this loft, or that shop—clever women, too, talented, many of them, and it is to that class that Mrs. Scot-Williams devotes herself. She takes keen delight in studying the tricks and secrets of business success. When some young woman to whom she has lent capital to start a cake and candy shop complains of dull trade, or a little French corsetier finds her customers falling off, Mrs. Scot-Williams likes to investigate the difficulties and suggest remedies—more advertising, a better location, a new superintendent in the workshop, one thing or another—perhaps even a little more capital, which, if she lends and loses it, she simply puts down under the head of charity in her distribution of expenses.

I had occurred to Mrs. Scot-Williams as a possible means for improving conditions at Van de Vere's. Miss Van de Vere possessed so highly a developed artistic temperament that her manner sometimes antagonized. Her assistant's duty, therefore, would be that of a cleverly constructed fly, concealing beneath tact and pretty manners ("and pretty gowns, my dear," added Mrs. Scot-Williams) a hook to catch reluctant customers.

I was fitted for such a position. I had been used as bait before, for other kind of fish. I purchased my fine feathers. Within a fortnight after my interview with Mrs. Scot-Williams, I was cast upon the waters.

There was no jealousy between Virginia Van de Vere and me. Beauty to her was something pulsing and alive. If any one suggested marring it, it tortured her. I was not so sensitive. The result was, I took charge of the customers who mentioned leatherette dens and Moorish libraries, and Virginia's genius was spared injury. She loved me for it. We worked beautifully together.

Van de Vere's was my great chance. It was indeed my pot of gold. I had always loved beautiful things, and here I was in the midst of their creating! Heaven had been kind. The joy of waking in the morning to a day of congenial work, setting forth to labor that was constructing for me a trade of my own, was like a daily tonic. I was very happy, full of ambition. I used to lie awake nights planning how I could make myself able and efficient. I discovered a course I could take evenings in Design and Interior Architecture, and I took advantage of it. I read volumes at the library on period furniture and decorating. I haunted antique shops. I perused articles on good salesmanship. Mornings I was up with the birds (the pigeons, that is) and half-way to my place of business by eight o'clock. It agreed with me. I grew fat on it. I regained the pounds of flesh that I had lost at the hospital with prodigious speed. Color came back to my cheeks, song to my lips.

Esther's book actually towered. It wasn't necessary for her to keep her position in the publishing house any longer. It wasn't necessary for her to conceal from me the price of our room. My salary was generous, and with Esther's little income we were rich indeed. We could drink all the egg-nogs we wanted to. We could even fare on chicken and green vegetables occasionally. We could buy one of Rosa's paintings for twenty-five dollars, and lend fifteen, now and then, if one of the girls was in a tight place. We could afford to canvass for suffrage for nothing. We could engage a bungalow for two or three weeks at the sea next year.

As soon as I felt that my success at Van de Vere's was assured, I wrote to my family and asked them to drop in and see me. The first of the family to arrive was Edith, one day in February. Isabel, the maid, announced Mrs. Alexander Vars to me. I sent down for her to come up.

The second floor of Van de Vere's looks almost like a private house—a dining-room with a fine old sideboard, bedroom hung with English chintz, a living-room with books and low lamps—sample rooms, of course, all of them, but with very little of the atmosphere of shop or warehouse.

I met Edith in the living-room.

"Hello, Edith," I said. She looked just the same, very modish, in some brand-new New York clothes, I suppose.

"Toots!" she exclaimed, and put both arms about me and kissed me. Then to cover up a little sign of mistiness in her eyes that would show, she exclaimed, "You're just as good-looking as ever. I declare you are!"

"So are you, too, Edith!" I said, misty-eyed, too, for some reason. I had fought, bled and died with Edith once.

"Oh, no, I'm not. I've got a streak of gray right up the front."

"Really? Well, it doesn't show one bit," I quavered, and then, "It's terribly good to see some one from home."

Edith got out her handkerchief.

"I, for one, just hate squabbles," she announced.

And "So do I," I agreed.

Later we sat down together on the sofa. She looked around curiously.

"What sort of a place is this, anyhow?" she asked in old, characteristic frankness. "I didn't know what I was getting into. It seems sort of—I don't know—not quite—not quite—I feel as if I might be shut up in here and not let out."

I laughed. Later I took her up to our showrooms on the top floor.

"Good heavens, do you sell people things, Ruth?" she demanded.

"Of course I do," I assured her.

"Just the same as over a counter almost?"

"Yes—not much difference."

"But don't you feel—oh, dear—that seems so queer—what *is* your social position?"

"Oh, I don't know. I've cut loose from all that."

"I know, but still you've got to think about the future. For instance, how would we feel if Malcolm wrote he was going to marry a clerk—or somebody like that—or a manicurist?"

"If she had education to match his—I should think it was very nice."

"Oh, no, you wouldn't. That's talk. Most people wouldn't anyhow. You are awfully queer, Ruth. You aren't a bit like anybody I know. Don't you sometimes feel hungry for relations with people of your own class? Friendly relations, I mean? Something different from the relations of a clerk to a customer? I would. You are just queer." Then suddenly she exclaimed, "Who's that?"

Virginia had passed through the room.

"Oh, that's Virginia. That's Miss Van de Vere."

"My dear," said Edith, impressed, "she was a guest at Mrs. Sewall's once, when you were out West. She's so striking! I saw her at the station when she arrived—Van de Vere—yes, that was the name. It was in the paper. They spoke of her as a talented artist. Everybody was just crazy about her in Hilton. She was at Mrs. Sewall's two weeks. She was reported engaged to a duke Mrs. Sewall had hanging around. I remember distinctly. What is she doing around here?"

"Why, she and I run this establishment," I announced.

"Good heavens! Does she sell people things?"

"Why, of course, Edith, why not?"

"Well—of all things! I don't know what we're coming to. I should think England *would* call us barbarians. Why, in England, even a man who is in trade has a hard time getting into society. But do introduce me to her if there's a chance before I go."

Later Edith exclaimed, "By the way, my dear, you'll be interested to know I've turned suffrage."

"How did that happen?"

"Of course I wouldn't march or anything like that, and I think militancy is simply awful, but you'd be surprised how popular suffrage is getting at home. I gave a bridge in interest of it. Lots of prominent people are taking it up. Look here," she broke off abruptly, "when can you come up for a Sunday? I'm just crazy to get hold of you and have a good old talk."

"Oh, almost any time. I'm anxious to see nice old Hilton again."

"Well, we must plan it. How would you like to bring that Miss Van de Vere? In the spring when the summer people get here. She has quite a number of admirers among them. I'd just love to give you a little tea or something."

Same old Edith! A wave of tenderness swept over me for her—faults and all. "Of course we'll come," I laughed. "I'll arrange it."

I knew in a flash that I should never quarrel with my sister-in-law again. She was no more to blame than a child with a taste for sweets. Why feel bitterness and rancor? She was only a victim of her environment after all. My tenderness—was a revelation. I hadn't realized that tolerance had been part of my soul's growth—tolerance even toward the principles from which I had once fled in righteous indignation.

Tom dropped in at Van de Vere's some time in the spring.

"Looks like a woman's business," he almost sneered, critically surveying the striped walls of the reception-room; and later, "Impractical and affected, I call it," he said. "If I was building a house I'd steer clear of any such place as this."

"Wait a minute," I replied pleasantly. "Come with me," and I took Tom into the well-lighted rooms at the rear, where our workers were engaged, at the time, on a rush order. "Does that look affected, Tom?" I asked. "Every one of those girls is living a decent and self-respecting life, many of them are helping in their family finances; and besides, the few stockholders of Van de Vere's are going to get a ten per cent dividend on their holdings next year. Does that strike you as impractical and affected, too?"

Tom looked at me, shut his mouth very tight, and shook his head. "I suppose all this takes the place of babies in your life. It wouldn't satisfy some women ten minutes. Elise wouldn't give up one of her babies for a business paying thirty per cent."

"But Tom," I replied calmly. "We all can't marry. Some of us—"

"*You* could have. This is not natural. 'Tisn't according to nature. No, sir. Abnormal. Down here in New York living like a man. What do you want to copy men for? Why don't you devote yourself to becoming an ideal woman, Ruth? That's what I want to know. I don't approve of this sort of thing at all."

I felt no anger. I felt no impulse to strike back. I had reached such an elevation on my mountain of Self-discovery, as Esther would have put it, that I commanded vision at last. Tom and his ideas did not obstruct my progress, like the huge blow-down that he had once been in my way, against which I had blindly beaten my fists raw. I had found my way around Tom. I could look down now and see him in correct proportion to other objects in the world about me. I saw from my height that such obstructions as Tom could be circumvented—a path worn around him, as more and more girls pursued the way I had chosen. I looked down and perceived, already, girls trooping after me. There was no use hacking away at Tom any more. Nature herself removes blow-downs on mountain-trails in time, by a process of slow rot and disintegration. When time accomplishes the same with the Toms of the world then we shan't need even to walk around. We can walk over!

So, "I know you don't approve, Tom," I replied almost gently, "and there's truth in what you say—that women are made to run homes and families, instead of businesses, most of them. Of course Elise wouldn't give up one of her babies! She's one of the 'most-of-them.' How are the babies anyway?"

A Call from Bob Jennings

ONE day, however, I realized that I hadn't walked around Tom. I really hadn't circumvented, by persistence and determination, the obstacles that lay in the way to triumph. Some one, like a fairy godmother from Grimm's, had waved a wand and wished the obstacles away. Virginia told me about it. I learned that except for Mrs. Sewall I might still be delivering bandboxes. The searchlight following me about wherever I went for the last six months, making my way bright and easy, came not from heaven. It came instead from a lady in black who chose to conceal her good offices beneath an unforgiving manner, as she hid the five hundred dollars inside a trivial bag.

Mrs. Sewall called one day at the shop. She asked for Miss Van de Vere. She was contemplating redecorating a bed-chamber, it seemed. Virginia came to me in the workshop, and told me about it.

"Your old lady is out there," she said. "You'd better take her order."

"My old lady?"

"Yes, Mrs. Sewall, who landed you in our midst, my dear."

I stared at Virginia.

"Certainly, and pays a portion of your ridiculous salary, baby-mine." She went on pinching my cheek playfully. She delights in patronizing me. "You're an expensive asset, my dear—not but what I am glad. I always urged somebody of your sort to relieve me. Mrs. Scot-Williams never saw it that way, however, until the old lady Sewall came along and crammed you down our throats. I wasn't to tell you, but I see no harm in it. Go on in, and whatever the tiff's about make it up with the old veteran. She's not a bad sort."

I went upstairs. My heart was bursting with gratitude. I had vexed, displeased, cruelly hurt my benefactress—she had likened me to a steel knife—and yet she had bestowed upon me my greatest desire. Much in the same way as I had rescued the little bug, buffeted by winds, Mrs. Sewall had picked me up and placed me at the zenith of my hopes. But for her, no Mrs. Scot-Williams, no Van de Vere's, no trade of my own, no precious business to work for, and make succeed!

"Mrs. Sewall," I began eagerly (I found her alone in the living-room), "Mrs. Sewall—" and then I stopped. There was no encouragement in her expression.

"Ah, Miss Vars," she remarked frostily.

"Mrs. Sewall—please," I begged, "please let me—"

"My time is limited this morning," she cut in. "Doubtless Miss Van de Vere has sent you to me to attend to my order. If so, let us hasten with it. I am hunting for a cretonne with a peacock design for a bed-chamber. I should like to see what you have."

"But Mrs. Sewall—"

"My time is limited," she repeated.

"I know, but I simply *must* speak."

She raised her hand. "I hope," she said, "that you are not going to make me ill again, Miss Vars."

I surrendered at that. "No, no," I assured her. "No, I'm not. I'm thoughtless. I think only of myself. I'll go and call Miss Van de Vere."

"That will not be necessary," said Mrs. Sewall. "You may show me the cretonne, now that you are here."

For half an hour we hunted for peacocks. I had the samples brought down to the living-room, piled on a chair near-by, and then dismissed the attendant. Mrs. Sewall appeared only slightly interested. In fact, I think we both were observing each other more closely than the cretonnes. They acted simply as a screen, through the cracks of which we might surreptitiously gaze.

I noted all the familiar points—the superb string of pearls about Mrs. Sewall's neck; the wealth of diamonds on her slender fingers when she drew off her glove; the band of black on the lower edge of the veil, setting off her small features in a heavy frame. I noted, too, the increased pallor beneath the veil. There was a sort of emaciated appearance just behind the ears, which neither carefully-set earring nor cleverly arranged coiffure could conceal. The veins on Mrs. Sewall's hands, moreover, were prominent and blue.

But for a tangle in the chain of Mrs. Sewall's glasses she would have left me with no sign of friendliness. It was when I passed her a small sample in a book, and she attempted to put on her glasses, that I observed the fine platinum cord was in a knot. I offered my services. I didn't suppose she would accept them. I was surprised at her cool, "Yes, if you will."

Mrs. Sewall was sitting down. I had to kneel to my task. The chain proved to be in a complicated snarl. My fingers trembled. I was very clumsy. I was afraid Mrs. Sewall would become exasperated. "Just a moment," I said, and looked up. Our eyes met. I was so close I could see the tiny network of wrinkles in the face above me. I could see the sudden tenderness in the eyes.

"It seems to be a particularly difficult snarl," I quavered, then bent my head and worked in silence for a moment. We were so near, we could hear each other breathe.

Suddenly in a low voice, almost a whisper, Mrs. Sewall asked, "Are you happy here?"

"Oh, so happy," I replied.

"Are you better? Are you well?" she pursued.

I dropped my hands in her lap, looked up, and nodded. I could not trust myself to speak. I knelt there in silence for a moment.

Finally I said, "Are *you* happy? Are *you* better? Are *you* well, dear Mrs. Sewall?"

"What does it matter? I am an old woman," she replied, in that disparaging little way of hers.

Our old intimacy shone clear and bright in that stolen moment. We were like two lovers forbidden to each other, whispering there together, when the lights suddenly go out, and they are enfolded in the protecting dark. "You are not too old to have created great happiness!" I exclaimed softly.

She shrugged and smiled.

It was a rare moment. I did not mean to spoil it. I ought to have been content. My eagerness was at fault.

"Oh!" I burst out crudely, "if you knew how sorry I am to have done anything to *you*, of all people, that displeased. If—" She recoiled; she drew back. I had ventured where angels feared to tread. The chain was not yet untangled, but she would not let me kneel there any longer. She rose; I too.

"My time is limited, as I said," she reminded me; "I am here on business. Let us endeavor to complete it, Miss Vars."

"Yes," I said, blushing scarlet, "let us, by all means. I'm sorry, excuse me, I'll go upstairs and see what else we have."

*

When Bob finally called at Van de Vere's I hadn't seen him for over a year. While I had been working so hard to establish myself in my new venture, Bob had been starting a brand-new law firm of his own, in a little town I had never heard of in the Middle West. He had severed all connections with the University when his mother had died. I knew as well as if he had told me that when he broke loose from any sort of steady salary he had abandoned all hope of persuading me to come and grow in his green-house, as he had once put it. It had been our original plan that Bob would work gradually into a law firm in Boston, at the same time retaining some small salaried position at the University enabling us to be married before he became established as a lawyer. Bob had been able to lay little by. His mother had required specialists and trained nurses. When I first realized that Bob had gone West and set about planning his life without reference to me I felt peculiarly free and unhampered. When he as much as told me that it was easier for him not to hear from me at all, than in the impersonal way I insisted upon, I was glad. I cared for Bob too much not to feel a little pang in my breast every time I saw my name and address written by his hand. And I wanted nothing to swerve me away from the goal I had my eyes set on—the goal of an acknowledged success as an independent, self-supporting human being.

When Bob first dropped in at Van de Vere's I hardly recognized him as the romantic figure who had wandered over brown hillsides with me, a volume of poetry stuffed into his overcoat pocket. No one would have guessed from this man's enthusiastic interest in the progressive spirit of the West that he had been born on Beacon Hill behind violet-shaded panes of glass. No one would have guessed, when he talked about cleaning out a disreputable school-board by means of the women's vote, that he had once opposed parades for equal suffrage in Massachusetts. When Bob shook hands with me, firmly, shortly, as if scarcely seeing me at all, I wondered if it might have slipped his mind that I was the girl he had once been engaged to marry.

He explained that he was in town on business, leaving the same evening. He could give me only an hour. There was a man he had to meet at his hotel at five. Bob was all nerves and energy that day. He talked about himself a good deal. They wanted to get him into politics out there in that wonderful little city of his. He'd been there only fourteen months, but it was a great place, full of promise—politics in a rather rotten condition—needed cleaning and fumigating. He'd a good mind to get into the job himself—in fact, he might as well confess he was in it to some extent. He was meeting the governor in Chicago the next night, or else he'd stay over and ask me to go to the theater with him.

I don't suppose Bob would have referred to the old days if I hadn't. It was I, who, when at last a lull occurred, said something about that time when he had found me struggling in a mire that threatened to drown, and I had grasped his good, strong arm.

"Wasn't it better, Bob," I asked, "that I should learn to swim myself, and keep my head above water by my own efforts?"

"It certainly seems to be what women are determined to do," he dodged.

"Well, isn't it better?" I insisted.

"I'll say this, Ruth," he generously conceded. "I think there would be less men dragged down if all women learned a few strokes in self-support."

"Oh, Bob!" I exclaimed. "Do you really think that? So do I. Why, *so do I!* We agree! Women would not lose their heads so quickly in times of catastrophe, would they? You see it, too! Women would help carry some of the burden. All they'd need would be one hand on a man's shoulder, while they swam with the other and made progress."

He laughed a little sadly. "Ruth," he said, for the first time becoming the Bob I had known, "I fear you would not need even one hand on a shoulder. It looks to me," he added, as he gazed about the luxuriously furnished living-room of Van de Vere's, "that you can reach the shore quite well alone."

Longings

THE days at Van de Vere's grew gradually into a year, into two years, into nearly three. From assistant to Virginia Van de Vere I became consultant, from consultant, partner finally. Van de Vere's grew, expanded, spread to the house next door. To the two V's upon the door-plate was added at last a third. Van de Vere's became Van de Vere and Vars.

My life, like that of a child's, assumed habits, personality, settled down to characteristics of its own. I remained with Esther in Irving Place, in spite of Virginia's urgent invitation to share her apartment, adding to the room an old Italian chest, a few large pieces of copper and brass, and a strip or two of antique embroidery. I preferred Irving Place. It was simple, quiet, and detached.

I came and went as I pleased; ate where I wanted to and when; wandered here and there at will. Evenings I sometimes went with Esther, when she could leave the book, or with Rosa, or with Alsace and Lorraine, to various favorite haunts; sometimes with Virginia to the luxurious studios of artists who had arrived; sometimes with Mrs. Scot-Williams to suffrage meetings, where occasionally I spoke; sometimes to dinner and opera with stereotyped Malcolm; sometimes simply to bed with a generous book. A beautiful, unhampered sort of existence it was—perfect, I would have called it once.

My relations with the family simmered down to a friendly basis. They accepted my independence as a matter of course. It had been undesired by them, true enough, its birth painful, but like many an unwanted child, once born, once safely here, they became accustomed to it, fond, even proud, as it matured. I spent every Christmas with Edith in Hilton, going up with Malcolm on the same train, and returning with him in time for a following business day. I often ran up for a week-end with Lucy and Will. Once I spent a fortnight with Tom and Elise in Wisconsin. The family seldom came to New York without telephoning to me, and often we dined together and went to the theater. I ought to have been very happy. I had won all I had left home for. I worked; I produced. At Van de Vere's my creative genius had found a soil in which to grow. I, as well as Virginia, conceived dream rooms, sketched them in water-colors, created them in wood, and paint, and drapery. I had escaped the stultifying effects of parasitism, rescued body and brain from sluggishness and inactivity, successfully shaken off the shackles of society. Freedom of act and speech was mine; independence, self-expression—yes, all that, but where—where was the promised joy?

When I look back and observe my life, I see the sharp, difficult ascent that led to my career at Van de Vere's with clearness. As if it was a picture taken on a sunny day I observe the details of the first joyous days of realized ambition. Just when my happiness began to blur I do not know. Less distinct are the events that led to my discontent. Gradual was the tarnishing of the metal I thought was gold within the pot. I closed my eyes to the process, at first refused to recognize it. I wouldn't admit the possibility of lacks and deficiencies in my life. When they became too obvious to ignore, I searched for excuses. I was tired; I had overworked; I needed a change. Never was it because I was a woman, and just plain hungry for a home. The slow disillusion that crept upon me expressed itself at odd and unexpected moments. In the middle of a fine discussion with the girls of the old circle, the "mountain-climbers," as Esther sometimes called us, the ineffectualness of our lives would sweep over me. To my chagrin, immediately after an inspired argument on suffrage a kind of reactionary longing to be petted, and loved, and indulged occasionally would possess me. Sometimes coming home to the room in Irving Place, after a long day at the shop, I would be more impressed by the loneliness of my life than the freedom.

I hid these indications of what I considered weakness, buried them deep in my heart, at first, and covered them over with a bright green patch of exaggerated zest and enthusiasm. One never realizes how many people are suffering with a certain disease until he himself is afflicted. I didn't know, until my little patch of green covered a longing, how many other longings were similarly concealed. As I became more intimately acquainted with the members of our little circle I discovered that there was frequently expressed a desire for human ties. I recalled Esther's confession at the hospital. Her words came back to me with startling significance. "A stark and empty life," she had said, "no man, no child, no one to make sacrifices for—just my thoughts, my hopes and my ambitions—that's all." Virginia, too—successful and brilliant Virginia Van de Vere! For what other reason had Virginia adopted the curly-headed Greek boy except to cover a lack in her life? For what reason than for a desire for some one to love and to be loved by were Alsace and Lorraine so devoted to each other? I read that a philanthropist of world renown, a woman whose splendid service had been praised the country over, was quoted as saying she would give up her public life a second time and choose the seclusion and the joy of a home of her own. At first I stoutly said to myself, "Well, anyhow, *I* shall not run to cover. I needed no one two years ago. Why should I now?" Why, indeed? A nest of gray hairs, discovered not long after, answered me. They set me to thinking in earnest. Gray hairs! Growing old! Creative years slipping by! Good heavens—was there danger that my life would become stark and empty too? I had chosen the mountain trail. Had I lost then the joy and the comfort of the nestling house and curling smoke? There were still interesting contracts of course, engrossing work. There was still the success of Van de Vere's to live for, but the ecstasy had all faded by the time I first realized that I was no longer a young girl.

Mrs. Sewall never came again to the shop after that single call. I was told she was in Europe. I never heard from her. Her son—poor Breck—had died at sea when a huge and luxurious ocean liner had tragically plunged into fathoms of water. I learned that an English girl had become Mrs. Sewall's companion. They were occupying the house in England. No doubt they were very happy together. Sometimes it would sweep over me with distressing reality that nobody really needed me—Breck, or Mrs. Sewall, or self-sufficient Bob in his beloved West. Bob was fast becoming nothing but a memory to me. If I thought of him at all it was as if my mind gazed at him through the wrong end of a pair of opera glasses. He seemed miles away. He must have come to New York occasionally but he didn't look me up. I heard of his activities indirectly through Lucy and Will. With the help of the women voters he had succeeded in cleaning out a board of aldermen, and now the women wanted him to run for mayor. This all interested me, but it didn't make me long for Bob. I wasn't conscious of wanting anything specific. My discontent was simply a vague, empty feeling, a good deal like being hungry, when no food you can call to mind seems to be what you want.

Mrs. Scot-Williams of her own accord suggested a vacation of two months for me. I know she must have observed that my spirits had fallen below normal. Mrs. Scot-Williams said she was afraid I had been working too steadily, and needed a change. I was looking a little tired. She invited me to go to Japan with her, starting in mid-July. We'd pick up some antiques for the shop in the East. It would do me a world of good. Perhaps Mrs. Scot-Williams was right. Such a complete change might help me to regain my old poise. I told her I would go with pleasure.

However, before I ever got started my loneliness culminated one dismal night, two days before the Fourth of July. I had been away for two weeks with Mrs. Scot-Williams on a suffrage campaign, combining a little business en route. Mrs. Scot-Williams had had to return in time to celebrate the holiday with her college-boy son and some friends of his at her summer place on Long Island.

I arrived at the Grand Central alone, hot and tired. It was an exceedingly warm night. I felt forlorn, returning to New York for an uncelebrated holiday. I took the subway down town. The air was stifling. It always manages to rob me of good-cheer. When I reached the room in Irving Place I found Esther writing as usual. Esther had grown pale and anemic of late. Her book had met with success, and it seemed to make her a little more impersonal and remote than ever. I had been away two weeks, but Esther didn't even get up as I came in. That was all right. We're never demonstrative.

"Hello," she said, "you back?" She dipped her pen into the ink-well.

"I'm back," I replied, and went over and raised the shade. A girl all in white and a young man carrying her coat went by, laughing intimately. Oh, well! What of it? I shrugged. I had my career, my affairs, Van de Vere's. "Want to come out somewhere interesting for dinner?" I suggested to Esther.

"Sorry," she said. "Can't possibly. Got to work."

I stared at Esther's back a moment in silence. Her restricted affection was inadequate tonight. I glanced around the room. It was unbeautiful in July. Where was the lure of it? Where had disappeared the charm of my life anyhow? Why should I be standing here, fighting a desire to cry? I could go out and find some one to dine with me. Of course—of course I could. I went to the telephone. Should it be Virginia, Rosa, Alsace and Lorraine, Flora Bennett? None—none of them! My heart cried out for somebody of my own tonight, upon whom I had a claim of some kind or other. I called Malcolm, my own older brother. We had grown a little formal of late. That was true. Never mind. I'd break through the reserve somehow. I'd draw near him. There was the bond of our parents. I wanted bonds tonight.

I got Malcolm's number at last. I was informed by a house-mate of his that my brother had gone to a reunion with his people for over the Fourth of July. His people! What a sound it had for my hungry soul. His people! My people, too, bound in loyalty by identical traditions. I, too, would go to them for a day or two. There would probably be a letter for me.

I went to my desk and glanced through my waiting mail. There was nothing, absolutely nothing. I looked through the pile twice. A family reunion and they had not notified me! I had become as detached as all that! I glanced at Esther again. She was scratching away like mad. I heard the drone of a hurdy-gurdy outside. I would not stay here. The thought of a holiday in Irving Place became suddenly unendurable. I must escape it somehow. There was a train north an hour later. My suitcase was still packed.

"Esther," I said quietly, "I believe I'll go up to Hilton for the holiday. I don't seem to be especially needed here."

"Mind not interrupting?" said Esther, scratching away hard. "I'm right in the midst of an idea."

I picked up my suitcase, and stole out.

Again Lucy Narrates

NO one was more surprised than I on the morning of the Fourth of July, when Ruth unexpectedly arrived from New York.

We Vars were all at Edith's in Hilton, even to Tom and Elise, who had taken a cottage on the Cape for the summer and were able to run up and join us all for the holiday. Will and I had motored up from our university town, and even Malcolm had put in an appearance. I had advised Edith not to bother to write Ruth about the impromptu reunion. I had understood that she was traveling around somewhere with her prominent suffrage leader, Mrs. Scot-Williams. Ruth is a woman of affairs now, and I try not to disturb her with family trivialities. The reunion was not to be a joyful occasion anyhow. A cloud hovered over it. We're a loyal family, and if one of us is in trouble, the others all try to help out. Oliver was the one to be helped just at present. The Fourth of July holiday offered an excellent opportunity for us all to meet and talk over his problem.

Oliver has always been financially unfortunate. In fact, life has dealt out everything in the line of blessings stingily to Oliver, except, possibly, babies. To Oliver and Madge had been born four children. With the last one there had settled upon Madge a persistent little cough. We didn't consider it anything serious. She didn't herself, and when Oliver dropped in one night at Will's and my house, just a week before the Fourth of July, and said something about spots on her lungs, and Colorado immediately, it was a shock. The doctor wanted Madge to start within a week. He was going out to Colorado with another patient and could take her along with him at the same time. He would allow only Marjorie, the oldest little girl, to accompany her mother. The others must positively be left behind. He couldn't predict anything. The lungs were in a serious condition. However, if the climate proved beneficial, Madge would have to stay in Colorado at least six months.

Now Oliver and Madge live very economically. They can't afford governesses and trained nurses. Madge, poor girl, had to go away not knowing what arrangement was to be made for the care of the two little girls and infant son, the first Vars heir, by the way, whom she left behind. Oliver went as far as Hilton with her and got off there with his motherless brood, joining us at Edith's, while Madge and Marjorie were whisked away out West with the doctor and the other patient.

I felt sorry for Oliver. He was anxious and worried, seemed helpless and inadequate. The children hung on him and asked endless questions. He was tired, poor boy, and disheartened. The arrangement we suggested for the children did not please him. Edith had generously offered to assume the care of the little Vars heir.

I had said that I would take. Emily, and to Elise was allotted Becky, aged three. We were all in Edith's living-room talking about it, when Ruth suddenly appeared on the scene.

Now Ruth is an interior decorator. Her shop is one of the most successful and exclusive in New York City. We're all very proud of Ruth. When she appeared that day so unexpectedly at the Homestead, I spied her first coming up the walk to Edith's door.

"Well—look what's coming!" I exclaimed, for Ruth was not alone. She was carrying Oliver's littlest girl, Becky.

"Good gracious!" exclaimed Edith.

"Is it Ruth?" asked Malcolm, staring hard through his thick, near-sighted glasses.

"Has she got Becky?" inquired Oliver.

"Explain yourself," laughed Alec, going to the screen door and letting Ruth in.

We all gathered round her.

"Hello, everybody," she smiled at us over Becky's shoulder. She was warm with walking. "Nothing to explain. Just decided to run up here, that's all, and found this poor little thing crying down by the gate. It's Becky, isn't it, Oliver? I haven't seen her for a year."

"It's just a shame you didn't let us meet you," said Edith. "Walking in this weather! I declare it is. Come, give that child to me, and you go on upstairs and get washed up. She's ruining your skirt. Come, Becky."

Becky is an extremely timid little creature. She hadn't let any one but Oliver touch her since Madge had gone the day before. She had been crying most of the time. Her lip quivered at the sight of Edith's outstretched hands. I saw her plump arm tighten around Ruth's neck.

"Here, come, Becky," said Oliver sternly, and offered to take her himself. She turned away even from him. "She takes fancies," explained Oliver. "You're in for it, I'm afraid, Ruth."

"Am I?" Ruth said, flushing unaccountably. "Well, you see," she went on apologetically, "I came upon her down there by the gate just as she had fallen down and hurt her knee. I was the only one to pick her up, so she had to let me. I put powder on the bruised knee. It interested her. It made her laugh. We had quite a game, and when I came away she insisted upon coming, too."

"You see, Madge has started for Colorado," I explained, "and Becky—"

"Colorado!" exclaimed Ruth. Of course she didn't know.

We told her about it.

"Poor little lonely kiddie," Ruth said softly afterward, giving Becky a strange little caress with the tip of her finger on the end of the child's infinitesimal nose. "Most as forlorn as some one they don't invite to family reunions any more."

"Why, Ruth," I remonstrated. "We thought—you see—"

"Never mind," she interrupted lightly. "I wasn't serious. I'll run upstairs now, and freshen up a bit."

"Come, Becky," ordered Oliver, "get down."

I saw Becky's arm tighten around Ruth's neck again. She's an unaccountable child.

Ruth said quietly, "Let her come upstairs with me, if she wants. I haven't had a welcome like this since the days of poor little Dandy."

An hour later Edith and I found Ruth sitting in a rocking-chair in the room that used to be hers years ago when she was a young girl. She was holding Becky.

"What in the world are you doing?" asked Edith.

"I never held a sleeping child before, and I'm discovering," replied Ruth, softly so as not to disturb Becky. "Aren't the little things limp?"

"Well, put her down now, do," said practical Edith. "We want you downstairs. Luncheon is nearly ready."

"I can't yet," said Ruth. "Every time I start to leave her she cries, and won't let me. Isn't it odd of the little creature? You two go on down. I'll be with you as soon as I can."

Later that afternoon we continued the discussion that Ruth had interrupted. Oliver didn't seem to be any more reconciled to the arrangement than before.

"I hate to break the home all up," he objected. "I want to keep the children together. Madge does, too. I should think there ought to be some one who likes children, and who wants a home, who could come and help me out for six months, who wouldn't cost too much."

"Hired help! No, no. Never works," Tom said, shaking his head.

"You have to be away so much on business, you know, Oliver," I reminded.

Suddenly Ruth spoke, picking up a magazine and opening it. "How would I do, instead of the hired help, Oliver?" she asked, casually glancing at an advertisement. "Becky didn't seem to mind me."

"You!" echoed Malcolm.

"Why, Ruth!" I exclaimed.

"What in the world do you mean?" demanded Edith.

"Oh, thanks," smiled Oliver kindly upon her. "Thanks, Ruth. It is bully of you to offer, but, of course, I wouldn't think of such a thing."

"Why not?" she inquired calmly. "I could give you the entire summer. I'm taking a two months' vacation this year."

"Oh, no, no. No, thanks, Ruth. Our apartment is, no vacation spot. I assure you of that. Hot, noisy, one general housework girl. It certainly is fine of you, but no, thanks, Ruth. Such a sacrifice is not necessary."

"It wouldn't be a sacrifice," remarked Ruth, turning a page of the magazine.

"Oh, come, come, Ruth!" broke in Tom irritably. "Let us not discuss such an impossibility. We're wasting time. You have your duties. This is not one of them. It's a fine impulse, generous. Oliver appreciates it. But it's quite out of the question."

"I don't see why," Ruth pursued. "For an unattached woman to come and take care of her brother's children during her vacation seems to me the most natural thing in the world."

"You know nothing about children," snorted Tom.

"I can learn," Ruth persisted.

Ruth's offer proved to be no passing whim, no sentimental impulse of the moment. Scarcely a week later, and she was actually installed in Oliver's small apartment. The family talked of little else at their various dinner-tables for weeks to come. Of all Ruth's vagaries this seemed the vaguest and most mystifying.

Oliver's apartment is really quite awful, disorderly, crowded, incongruous. It contains a specimen of every kind of furniture since the period of hair-cloth down to mission—cast-offs from the homes of Oliver's more fortunate brothers and sisters. When I first saw Ruth there in the midst of the confusion of unpacking, the room in Irving Place with its old chests and samovars, Esther Claff quietly writing in her corner, the telephone bell muffled to an undisturbing whirr, flashed before me.

The baby was crying. I smelled the odor of steaming clothes, in process of washing in the near-by kitchen. I heard the deep voice of the big Irish wash-woman I had engaged, conversing with the rough Norwegian. Becky was hanging on to Ruth's skirt and begging to be taken up. In the apartment below some one was playing a victrola. I hoped Ruth was not as conscious as I of Van de Vere's at this time in the morning—low bells, subdued voices, velvet-footed attendants, system, order.

"Well, Ruth," I broke out, "I hope you'll be able to stand this. If it's too much you must write and let me know."

She picked up Becky and held her a moment. "I think I shall manage to pull through," she replied.

Ruth Draws Conclusions

WILL and I were buried in a little place in Newfoundland all summer, and Ruth's letters to us, always three days old when they reached me, were few and infrequent. What brief notes she did write were non-committal. They told their facts without comment. I tried to read between the practical lines that announced she had changed the formula for the baby's milk, that she had had to let down Emily's dresses, that she had succeeded in persuading Oliver to spend his three weeks' vacation with Madge in Colorado, finally that Becky had been ill, but was better now. I was unable to draw any conclusions. I knew what sort of service Ruth's new enterprise required—duties performed over and over again, homely tasks, no pay, no praise. I knew the daily wear and tear on good intentions and exalted motives. I used to conjecture by the hour with Will upon what effect the summer would have on Ruth's theories. She has advanced ideas for women. She believes in their emancipation.

Edith and Alec had gone to Alaska. They could not report to me how Ruth was progressing. Elise had been unable to leave her cottage on the Cape for a single trip to Boston. Only Oliver's enthusiastic letters (Oliver who never sees anything but the obvious) assured me that, at least on the surface, Ruth had not regretted her undertaking.

Will and I returned the first of September. Ruth's two months would terminate on September tenth, and I had come back early in order to help close Oliver's apartment and prepare for the distribution of the children, which we had arranged in the early summer. Oliver was still in Colorado when I returned. He was expected within a week, however. I called Ruth up on the telephone as soon as I could, and told her I would be over to see her the next day, or the day after. I couldn't say just when, for Elise and Tom, who were returning to Wisconsin, were to spend the following night with me. Perhaps after dinner we would all get into the automobile and drop in upon her.

We all did. Oliver's apartment is on the other side of Boston from Will and me. We didn't reach there until after eight o'clock. The children, of course, were in bed. Ruth met us in the hall, half-way up the stairs. She was paler than usual. As I saw her it flashed over me how blind we had been to allow this girl—temperamental, exotic, sensitive to surroundings—to plunge herself into the responsibilities that most women acquire gradually. Her first real vacation in years too!

Elise and I kissed her.

"You look a little tired, Ruth," said Elise.

"A woman with children expects to look tired sometimes," Ruth replied, with the sophistication of a mother of three. "I had to be up a few nights with Becky."

I slipped my arm about Ruth as we mounted the stairs. "Has it been an awful summer?" I whispered.

She didn't answer me—simply drew away. I felt my inquiry displeased her. At the top of the landing she ran ahead and opened the door to the apartment, inviting us in. I was unprepared for the sight that awaited us.

"Why, Ruth!" I exclaimed, for I recognized all about me familiar bowl and candlestick from Irving Place, old carved chest, Russian samovar, embroidered strips of peasant's handicraft.

"How lovely!" said Elise, pushing by me into Oliver's living-room.

It really was. I gazed speechless. It made me think of the inside of a peasant's cottage as sometimes prettily portrayed upon the stage. It was very simple, almost bare, and yet there was a charm. At the windows hung yellowish, unbleached cotton. On the sills were red geraniums in bloom. A big clump of southern pine filled an old copper basin on a low tavern table. A queer sort of earthen lamp cast a soft light over all. In the dining-room I caught a glimpse of three sturdy little high chairs painted bright red, picked up in some antique shop, evidently. On the sideboard, a common table covered with a red cloth, I saw the glow of old pewter.

"You've done wonders to this place," commented Tom, gazing about.

"Oliver gave me full permission before he went away," Ruth explained. "I've stored a whole load-full of his things. It *is* rather nice, I think, myself."

"Nice? I should say it was! But did it pay for so short a time?" I inquired.

"Oliver can keep the things as long as he wants them," said Ruth.

"But it must make your room in Irving Place an empty spot to go back to," I replied.

Ruth went over to the lamp and did something to the shade. "Oh," she said carelessly, "haven't I told you? I'm not going back. I've resigned from Van de Vere's. Do all sit down."

Ruth might just as well have set off a cannon-cracker. We were startled to say the least. We stood and stared at her.

"Do sit down," she repeated.

"But, Ruth, why have you done this? Why have you resigned?" I gasped at last. She finished with the lamp-shade before she spoke.

"I insist upon your sitting down," she said. "There. That's better." Then she gave a queer, low laugh and said, "I think it was the sight of the baby's little flannel shirt stretched over the wooden frame hanging in the bath-room that was the last straw that broke me before I wrote to Mrs. Scot-Williams."

"But—"

"There was some one immediately available to take my place at Van de Vere's—another protégée of Mrs. Scot-Williams. I had to decide quickly. Madge is improving every week, Oliver writes, but she has got to stay in Colorado at least during the winter, the doctor says. Becky is still far from strong. She was very ill this summer. She doesn't take to strangers. I think I'm needed here. It seemed necessary for me to stay."

"Perfect nonsense," Tom growled. "There's no more call for you to give up your business than for Malcolm his. Perfectly absurd."

"But oh, how fine—how fine of you, Ruth!" exclaimed Elise.

"You shan't do it. You shan't," I ejaculated.

"Don't all make a mistake, please," said Ruth. "It is no sacrifice. There's no unselfishness about it, no fine altruism. I'm staying because I want to. I'm happier here. Can't any of you understand that?" she asked. There was a quality in her voice that made us all glance at her sharply. There was a look in her eyes which reminded me of her as she had appeared in the suffrage parade. This sister of mine had evidently seen another vision. If it had made her cheeks a little pale, it had more than made up for it in the exalted tone of her voice and expression of her eyes.

"You say you're happier here?" asked Elise. "Weren't you happy then, down there in New York, Ruth?"

"Yes, for a while. But you see my life was like a circle uncompleted. In keeping trimmed the lights of a home even though not my own, even only for a short period, I am tracing in, ever so faintly, the yawning gap."

"Gap! But Ruth, we thought—"

She flushed a little in spite of herself. We were all staring hard at her. "You see," she went on, "I've never been needed before as I have this summer. A home has never depended upon me for its life before. I've liked it. I don't see why you're so surprised. It's natural for a woman to want human ties. Contentment has stolen over me with every little common task I have had to do."

"But, Ruth," I stammered, "we never thought that this—housekeeping—such menial work as this, was meant for *you*."

"Nor love and devotion either, I suppose," she said a little bitterly, "nor the protection of a fireside," she shrugged. "Such rewards are not given without service, I've heard. And service paid by love does not seem menial to me."

Tom laid down his hat upon the table, and leaned forward. He had been observing Ruth keenly. I saw the flash of victory in his eye. Tom had never been in sympathy with Ruth's emancipation ideas, and I saw in her desire for a home and intimate associations the crumbling of her strongest defense against his disapproval. I wished I could come to her aid. Always my sympathies had instinctively gone out to her in the controversies that her theories gave rise to. Would Tom plant at last his flag upon her long-defended fortress?

"This is odd talk for you, Ruth," said Tom.

"Is it?" she inquired innocently. Did she not observe Tom calling together his forces for a last charge?

"Certainly," he replied. "You gave up home, love, devotion—all that, when you might have had it, years ago. You emancipated yourself from the sort of service that is paid by the protection of a fireside."

"Well?" she smiled, unalarmed.

"You see your mistake now," he hurried on. "You make your mad dash for freedom, and now come seeking shelter. That is what most of 'em do. You tried freedom and found it lacking."

"And what is your conclusion, Tom?" asked Ruth, baring herself, it seemed to me, to the onslaught of Tom's opposition.

"My conclusion! Do I need even to state it?" he inquired, as if flourishing the flag before sticking its staff into the pinnacle of Ruth's defense. "Is it not self-evident? If you had married five years ago, today you would have a permanent family of your own instead of a borrowed one for eight months. Your freedom has robbed you of what you imply you desire—a home, I mean. My conclusion is that your own history proves that freedom is a dangerous thing for women."

Ruth answered Tom quietly. I thrilled at her mild and gentle manner. We all listened intently.

"Tom," she said slowly and with conviction, "my own history proves just the opposite. The very fact that I do feel the deficiencies of freedom, is proof that it has not been a dangerous tool. If it had killed in me the home instinct, then I might concede that your fears were justified, but if, as you say, most women do not rove far but come home in answer to their heart's call, then men need not fear to cut the leash." With some such words Ruth pulled Tom's flag from out her fortress where he had planted it. As Tom made no reply she went on talking. "Once I had no excuse for existence unless I married. My efforts were narrowed to that one accomplishment. I sought marriage, desperately, to escape the stigma of becoming a superfluous and unoccupied female. Today if I marry it will be in answer to my great desire, and, whether married or not, a broader outlook and a deeper appreciation are mine. I believe that working hard for something worth while pays dividends to a woman always. If I never have a home of my own," Ruth went on, "and I may not—spinsters," she added playfully, "like the poor must always be with us—at least I have a trade by which I can be self-supporting. I'm better equipped whatever happens. Oh, I don't regret having gone forth. No, Tom, pioneers must expect to pay. I'm so convinced," she burst forth eagerly, "that wider activities and broader outlooks for women generally are a wise thing, that if I had a fortune left me I would spend it in establishing trade-schools in little towns all over the country, like the Carnegie libraries, so that all girls could have easy access to self-support. I'd make it the custom for girls to have a trade as well as an education and athletic and parlor accomplishments. I'd unhamper women in every way I knew how, give them a training to use modern tools, and then I'd give them the tools. They won't tear down homes with them. Don't be afraid of that. Instinct is too strong. They'll build better ones."

My brother shook his head. "I give you up, Ruth, I give you up," he said.

"Don't do that," she replied. "I'm like so many other girls in this age. Don't give us up. We want you. We need your conservatism to balance and steady. We need our new freedom guided and directed. We're the new generation, Tom. We're the new spirit. There are hundreds—thousands—of us. Don't give us up." I seemed to see Ruth's army suddenly swarming about her as she spoke, and Ruth, starry-eyed and victorious, standing on the summit in their midst.

Bob Draws Conclusions Too

IT was Edith who told me the news about Mrs. Sewall. I ought to have been prepared for anything. Ever since Ruth had been employed as secretary to Mrs. Sewall there had been something mysterious about their relations. Ruth had never explained the details of her life in the Sewall household—I had never inquired too particularly—but whenever she referred to Mrs. Sewall there was a troubled and sort of wistful expression in her eyes which made me suspicious. She admired Mrs. Sewall, no doubt of that. She felt deep affection for her. Several times she had said to me during our intimate talks together, of which we had had a good many lately, "Oh, Lucy, I wish the ocean wasn't so wide. I'd run across for over a Sunday." I knew, without asking, that Ruth was thinking of Mrs. Sewall. She was living in London.

Edith called me on the telephone early one Monday morning. She frequently is in Boston, shopping. From the hour, evidently she had just arrived from Hilton.

"Well," she began excitedly, "what have you got to say?"

"Say? What about?"

"Haven't you seen the paper?" she demanded.

"Not yet," I had to confess. "I've been terribly rushed this morning."

"You don't know what has happened, then?"

"No. What has? Out with it," I retorted a little alarmed. Edith's voice was high-pitched and strained.

"The old lady Sewall has died."

"Oh, I'm sorry," I replied, relieved, however.

"In London—a week ago," went on Edith.

"Really? What a shame! Does Ruth know?"

"She ought to. It rather affects her."

"How's that?"

"How's that!" repeated Edith. "Good heavens, if you'd read your paper you'd understand how. The old lady's will is published. It's terribly thrilling."

The color mounted to my face. "What do you mean, Edith?"

"Never you mind. You go along and read for yourself, and then meet me at one o'clock—no, make it twelve. I've got to talk to some one—quick. I never saw the article myself until I was on the train coming down. I'm just about bursting. Good gracious, Lucy, hustle up, and make it eleven o'clock, sharp."

We agreed on a meeting-place and I hung up the receiver, went upstairs to my room, sat down, and opened the paper. I found the article Edith referred to easily enough. It was on the inside of the front page printed underneath large letters. It was appalling! The third sentence of the headlines contained my sister's name. There must be some mistake. Wasn't such news as this borne by a lawyer with proper ceremony and form, or at least delivered by mail, inside an envelope sealed with red wax? Ruth had known nothing of this three days ago when I called to see her. It could not be true. All the way into Boston on the electric car, I felt self-conscious and ill-at-ease. I was afraid some one I knew would meet me, and refer to the newspaper announcement. I would dislike to confess, "I know no more about it than you." I hate newspaper notoriety anyhow.

Edith greeted me as if we hadn't met for years, kissed me ecstatically and grasped both my hands tight in hers. Her sparkling eyes expressed what the publicity of the hotel corridor, where we met, prevented her from proclaiming aloud.

"Where can we go to be alone for half a minute?" she whispered.

"Let's try in here," I said, and we entered a deserted reception-room, and sat down in a bay-window.

"Did you telephone to Ruth?" was Edith's first remark.

I shook my head. "No. I didn't like to," I said.

"Nor I," confessed Edith. "She's always been touchy with me on the subject of Mrs. Sewall since the row. Isn't it too exciting?"

"Can it be legal, Edith?" I inquired.

"Of course, silly. Wills aren't published until they're looked into. Legal? Of course it is. I always said Ruth would do something splendid, one of these days, and she has, she has—the rascal."

"You've got so much money yourself, Edith, why does a little more in the family please you so?" I asked. Edith was extremely excited.

"A little. It isn't a little. It's a *lot*. But it isn't just the money. It's more. It's what the money does. There has always been a kind of pitying attitude toward us in Hilton since that Sewall affair of Ruth's, for all my efforts. This clears it up absolutely. Haven't you read the way the thing's worded? Wait a minute." She opened her folded paper. "Here, I have it." Her eyes knew exactly where to look. Ruth's name appeared in the will at the very end of a long list of bequests to various charitable institutions.

"Listen. 'All the rest, residue, and remainder of my property, wheresoever and whatsoever, including my house in New York City, my house in Hilton, Massachusetts, known as Grassmere; my furniture, books, pictures and jewels, I give, devise, and bequeath to the former fiancée of my son, now deceased, in affectionate memory of our relations. This portion of my estate to be used and to be directed, according to the dictates of her own high discretion, during the term of her natural life and at her death to pass to her lawful issue.' Did you ever hear anything to equal it?" demanded Edith. "Don't you see the old lady recognizes Ruth before the world? Don't you see, however humiliated I was at that distressing affair three or four summers ago, it's all wiped off the slate now, by this? She makes Ruth her heir, Lucy. Don't you see that? And she does it affectionately, too. I can't get over it! I don't know what made the old veteran do such a thing. I don't care much either. All I know is, that we're fixed all right in Hilton society *now*. Grassmere Ruth's! Good heavens—think of it! Think of the power in my hands, if only Ruth behaves, to pay back a few old scores. I only wish Breck was alive. She'd marry him now, I guess, with all this recognition. I wonder whatever she'll do with Grassmere anyhow."

"Turn it into some sort of institution for making women independent human beings, I'll wager." I laughed, recalling Ruth's words of scarcely a fortnight ago.

"If only she hadn't gotten so abnormal, and queer!" Edith sighed. "Perhaps this stroke of good luck will make her a little more like the rest of us. We must all look out and not let Ruth do anything ridiculous with this fortune of hers."

*

Will and I went over to see Ruth that evening.

"Why, hello!" she called down, surprised, through the tube, in answer to my ring. "Will and you! Really? Come right up."

"She doesn't know," I told Will, pushing open the heavy door and beginning to mount.

"Guess not," agreed my husband. "Here's her evening paper in her box, untouched."

We found Ruth just finishing with the dishes. The maid-of-all-work was out, and Ruth was alone. She called to me to come back and help her, and sang out brightly for Will to amuse himself with the paper. He'd probably find it downstairs in the box.

Five minutes later Ruth slipped off her blue-checked apron, and we joined Will by the low lamp in the living-room. My sister looked very pretty in a loose black velvet smock. Her hair was coiled into a simple little knot in the nape of her neck. There were a few slightly waving strands astray about her face. Her hands, still damp from recent dish-washing, were the color of pink coral.

"I'm tired tonight," she said, sighing audibly, and pulling herself up on the top of the high carved chest. She tucked a dull red pillow behind her head, and leaned back in the corner. "There! This is comfort," she went on. "Read the news out loud to me, Will, while I sit here and luxuriate." She closed her eyes.

"All right," Will agreed. "By the way," he broke off, as unconsciously as possible, a minute or so later, "Have you heard anything from Mrs. Sewall lately?"

There was a slight pause. The lady's name invariably clouded my sister's bright spirit. She opened her eyes. They were wistful.

"No," she replied quietly, "I haven't. She's in England. Why do you ask?"

"Oh, I was just wondering," my husband replied, losing his splendid courage. "I suppose you two got to be pretty good friends."

"Yes, we did," Ruth replied shortly. There was another pause. Then in a low, troubled voice Ruth added, "But not now. We're not friends now. Something happened. All her affection for me has died. I have never been forgiven for something."

"Oh, I wouldn't be so sure," belittled Will, making violent signs to me to announce the news we bore.

I had a clipping in my shopping-bag cut from the morning paper. I took it out of the envelope that contained it.

"Ruth," I began, "here's something I ran across today."

The telephone interrupted sharply.

"Just a minute," she said, and slid down off the chest and went out into the hall. "Hello," I heard her say. "Hello," and then in a changed voice, "Oh, you?" A pause and then, "Really? Tonight?" Another pause, and more gently. "Of course you must. Of course I do," and at last very tenderly, "Yes, I'll be right here. I'll be waiting. Good-by."

I looked at Will, and he lifted his eyebrows. Ruth came back and stood in the doorway. There was a peculiar, shining quality about her expression.

"That was Bob," she said quietly.

"Bob?" I exclaimed.

"Bob Jennings?" ejaculated Will.

Ruth nodded and smiled. Standing there before us, dressed simply in the plain black smock, cheeks flushed, eyes like stars, she reminded me of some rare stone in a velvet case. The bareness of the room, with its few genuine articles, set off the jewel-like brightness of my sister in a startling fashion.

"You don't mean to say old Bob's turned up," commented Will.

"Tell us," bluntly I demanded, "what in the world is Robert Jennings doing around here, Ruth?"

"Bob's been in town for several days," she replied. "He has just telephoned that he is called back on business. His train leaves in a little over an hour. He's dropping in here in ten minutes."

"Why, I didn't know you even wrote to each other," I said.

Ruth came over to the table and sat down in a low chair, stretching out her folded hands arms-length along the table's surface, and leaning toward us.

"I'm going to tell you two about it," she announced with finality. "I wrote to Bob," she confessed, half proud, half apologetic. "I wrote to Bob without any excuse at all, except that I wanted to tell him what I'd found out. I wanted to tell him that I had discovered that this sort of thing," she opened her hands, and made a little gesture that included everything that those few small rooms of Oliver's epitomized, "that this sort of thing," she resumed, "was what most women want more than anything else in the world. Any other activity was simply preparation, or courageous makeshift if this was denied. I made it easy for Bob, in my letter, to answer me in the spirit of friendly argument if he chose, but he didn't. He came on instead. We're going to be married," she said, in a voice as casual as if she were announcing that they were going out for dinner.

"You're going to be married?" I repeated.

"Yes," she nodded. "After all these years! Once," she went on in a triumphant voice, "our fields of vision were so small that our differences of opinion loomed up like insurmountable barriers. Now the differences are mere specks on our broadened outlooks. Oh, I know," she went on as if inspired, "I've been a long journey, simply to come back to Bob again. But it hasn't been in vain. There was no short cut to the perfect understanding that is Bob's and mine today."

"And when," timidly I inquired, "do you intend to be married, Ruth?"

My sister's expression clouded. She smiled, and shook her head. "I don't know," she said, "I wish I did. Years are so precious when one is concealing a little nest of gray hairs behind one's left ear. Bob and I have got to wait. You see Bob wasn't planning for this. He had some idea a career would always satisfy me. He hasn't been saving. He has put about all he has been able to earn into fighting for clean politics. I myself haven't been able to lay by but a paltry thousand. Madge comes home in May. I shall then probably have to look up another job for myself somewhere or other, while Bob's establishing himself and making ready for me out there."

Will cleared his throat and coughed. He had simply stared until now. "I suppose," he said, as if in an attempt to lighten the conversation with a little light humor, "I suppose a legacy of some sort wouldn't prove unwelcome to you and Bob just about now."

It must have struck Ruth as a stereotyped attempt at fun. But she smiled and replied in the same vein, "I think we'd know how to make use of a portion of it." Then she rose. The door bell had rung sharply twice. "There he is," she explained. "There's Bob now. I'll let him in."

She went out into the hall and pressed the button that released the lock of the door three floors below.

I knew how fleeting every minute of last hours before train-time can be. I motioned to Will, and when Ruth came back to us I said, "We'll just run down the back way, Ruth."

She flashed me an appreciative glance. "You don't need to," she deprecated.

"Still, we will," I assured her, and then I went over and kissed my radiant sister.

Her face was illumined as it used to be years ago when Robert Jennings was on his way to her. The same old tenderness gleamed in her larger-visioned eyes.

"When he comes read this together," I said, and I slipped the envelope, with the clipping inside it, into her hands.

Then Will and I went out through the kitchen, and down the back stairs.

THE END

Stella Dallas

CHAPTER I

1

Laurel was thirteen years old. Her hair was the color of ripe horse-chestnuts, and had the same gloss. She wore it in a long smooth bang in front, which reached nearly to her eyebrows, and in long smooth curls behind, which reached nearly to her waist. Laurel's mother always placed one of the curls over each shoulder after she had made them perfect by much brushing and smoothing over a dexterous forefinger. Laurel always, with a quiet, almost imperceptible, little motion of her head, placed them behind as soon as her mother turned away.

Laurel's clothes were consistent with the extreme bang and the long curls. There was never anything casual or careless about her costumes. When she appeared for breakfast in the big hotel dining-room dressed in one of her violet ginghams, smocked in seal-brown, with seal-brown stockings, and seal-brown shoes, and a seal-brown hat, she was like an Elsie DeWolfe room in the perfection of her color scheme.

She always changed for luncheon, as did her mother and most of the other smartly dressed women in the hotel, and again for dinner; and always the shoes and stockings, ribbons, hats, sweaters, and what-not harmonized with her various linens, pastel-shaded Japanese crepes, organdies, or hand-embroidered serges for cool days.

"That Dallas woman must spend about all her time over that child's clothes," Laurel had one day overheard from behind the high back of one of the hotel-piazza rocking-chairs.

Laurel was sitting by an open window in an empty cardroom just behind the chairs. Laurel liked to sit and listen to what the women talked about on the other side of that high cane wall of chair-backs. Sometimes, however, she heard things that made her grave, contemplative eyes still graver and still more contemplative. There had been scorn in the voice which had referred to her mother.

"I wonder," she thought, "if we didn't dress quite so well, people mightn't be nicer."

She waited for more enlightening remarks from behind the chair-backs, but none were forthcoming, so she rose, sauntered out of the cardroom, wandered down a long deserted corridor, and drifted into the hotel foyer.

She was tall for thirteen, with long slim legs, long slim arms, and a long slim body. "Nice eyes, kiddie, but you'd make mighty poor eating," one of the habitues of the poolroom had said to Laurel one day, as she stood staring at the clicking balls on the bright green felt, and he had pinched one of Laurel's pipestem arms—bare from the elbow down, and brown now to her finger-tips.

Laurel did have nice eyes. They were gray eyes, set well apart. They had long, well-defined brows—level, almost parallel to the straight bang above which nearly touched them. There was in Laurel's eyes a look of wistful inquiry, an almost spiritual expression sometimes. They were more than nice eyes. They were beautiful eyes. In contemplating them, one forgot her freckles. For Laurel had freckles. In spite of lemon-juice every night—in spite of various concoctions, which so far had not disturbed the line texture of her dark smooth skin, still she had freckles. But beneath the freckles there was a glow, like the glow beneath the flecked tan of a russet apple. This, and the freckles, and the spiritual something in her eyes gave her a sort of woodsy charm, which no amount of garnishing could conceal. She was seldom seen on the floor of the hotel ballroom dancing with the other children. Usually she could be found standing somewhere by herself, quiet and composed; or sitting in a chair with a book. Yet there was something about Laurel, standing or sitting, or walking slowly down the long length of the dining-room behind her mother to their table in a far corner, that recalled certain pictures of young girls dancing in the woods—Isadora Duncan pupils, perhaps—slim, sleek, sylvan creatures in Greek draperies.

Laurel leaned up against one of the pillars in the hotel foyer and gazed about her. The place was wrapped in its usual mid-afternoon lifelessness—a few idle bellboys on the bench at the foot of the broad staircase; a couple of idle elevators; a solitary clerk behind the brass grill over the mahogany desk; dozen upon dozens of empty armchairs; in one of them an old man, with a King Orange nose, sound asleep; in a far corner four women playing silent bridge.

As Laurel gazed at the women, her eyes took on their peculiar contemplative expression. She knew who they were. Three of the players were prominent social leaders in the hotel-world; and the fourth, the poor, pinched-looking, unattractive little creature in black, was Mrs. Tom Lawrence, who had arrived two days ago. Laurel had learned all about Mrs. Tom Lawrence from behind the chair-backs. As she stared, her eyes narrowed. "They Ve being nice to Mrs. Lawrence," she thought, "and Mrs. Lawrence is divorced, while mother is only 'separated.'"

She slid into the deep-seated lap of an enormous leather armchair near by. Through the big front doors she could catch a glimpse of a group of girls about her own age, seated on the piazza railing, swinging their legs, and eating candy. One of the girls was the daughter of the pretty Mrs. Cameron, now playing bridge in the far corner. Laurel did not join the girls. She didn't give mothers at a summer hotel a second opportunity to call, "Come, dear, I think you'd better come in now," to their children when she became one of a group; nor the children themselves to link arms and move away from her.

This year she had scarcely given them a first opportunity. Somehow things had been worse this year than ever before, and right from the start, too.

She looked up at the loud-ticking clock. It was only quarter after four. Her mother had told her that she must amuse herself this afternoon. She always had to do that, whenever her mother was going to be busy in the bedroom they shared, "washing out a few things." There wasn't room for two, when there was laundering going on.

2

Laurel sighed, rose from the big chair and wandered over to the glass-covered case of candies; stared at them for a minute or two; turned away; listlessly observed a rack of picture postcards. Finally she meandered down a long corridor past a series of cardrooms to a little pink parlor at the end. From behind a cushion on a sofa, she drew forth a book, and tucking it under her arm returned to the big chair. She curled herself up in it, child-fashion, and opened the book well towards the middle. She began to read.

The old man woke up and left his chair. The game of bridge came to an end. The four players disappeared. The group of girls on the railing outside drifted apart. But Laurel didn't once glance up. She hardly moved for a whole hour and a half except to turn the pages of the book. The hotel had suddenly ceased to exist for Laurel Dallas. Her heart was bleeding for David Copperfield.

Laurel never read "David Copperfield" when her mother was with her. To-day the book, as usual, would be returned to its hiding-place behind the cushion in the little parlor when she had finished with it. Laurel never carried it with her upstairs for her mother to catch a glimpse of, and make remarks upon. Of course her mother had had to know that she had tucked it, with several other books. into a corner of the bottom of her trunk when they had last packed. But there was no need in flaunting it before her mother's eyes. On the fly-leaf of Laurel's "David Copperfield" was written: "To Laurel, from her father," with Christmas and a date below. There had been a whole boxful of them.

"Books!" her mother had said with an exclamation of disappointment when they had been received the preceding December, "a whole pile of old-fashioned books!"

Laurel knew her mother preferred something more modern, when it came to printed matter—informing literature that kept one up-to-date as to what was going on in the world of clothes, and fashion, and society; photo-play magazines, with some theater-talk in them, and a few snappy short stories. The table in the bedroom which Laurel shared with her mother was always littered with a dog-eared collection of such periodicals.

Laurel took the elevator up to that bedroom now. It was after six o'clock, and by this time, she calculated, the ironing-sheet and forbidden electric-iron would be safely tucked out of sight in the bottom of her mother's trunk.

3

It wasn't an attractive bedroom. It was tucked way up under the eaves, had slanting walls, and a single curtainless window. Its furniture was much too big for it—made it look sick and shrunken, like a child in cast-off clothes many sizes too large. The iron bed, white enamel once but nicked and battered now, extended halfway across the window-pane; and there was a perfectly tremendous stuffed armchair in the room, discarded from some parlor below evidently, a shabby affair which, shut up in this little coop, was like some big ugly animal crammed into a circus cage—a rhinoceros Laurel decided, for it was the same dingy color, and its back and arms were worn bare and napless.

The walls of the room were covered with unpleasant reminders of former occupants—long brown streaks made by the striking of sulphur matches, oil-stains, ink-spots, splotches where flies and mosquitoes had met bloody deaths, and bruises here and there exuding dry plaster. Behind the commode the faded, jaundiced-colored paper bore the whitish, pocked appearance of a face once swept by smallpox; and where the bed was shoved close against the wall the paper was rubbed shiny and amber-colored. Laurel thought it was the worst "cheapest room" that she and her mother had ever occupied for a whole season.

Laurel was experienced in cheapest rooms. They were all more or less alike. That is, there was always something chronic and incurable the matter with them. They were either up very high beneath the eaves, possibly a floor above where the elevator ran, or down very low beside a noisy service-room, or groaning elevator-shaft. Some of them had queer smells. Some developed queer smells. Most of them were furnished with discards, and all of them were equipped with the everlasting commode, bowl-and-pitcher, and unlovely slop-basin.

Laurel used to dread her first glimpse of the latest "cheapest room" her mother had engaged, trailing with a sinking heart after the scornful bellboy who guided them along endless halls and corridors, farther and farther away from the luxury of the office downstairs, to the door of the undesirable little apartment, flinging it open, it seemed to Laurel, with a gesture of disgust. But Laurel's mother told her she ought to be thankful that such things as "cheapest rooms" existed. "It is only by occupying the cheapest room in the house, that you and I can go to nice hotels, where nice people go," Mrs. Dallas explained to her daughter.

The hotels which Mrs. Dallas patronized were always elaborate affairs with expensive, porte-co-chered entrances, big impressive foyers lit by enormous inverted alabaster bowls, and dining-rooms of ballroom dimensions filled with round tables, and mahogany chairs, and during the crowded dinner hour, an army of waiters with huge oval trays rushing about like darting water-bugs.

To Laurel there was something magic in the fact that it was possible under the same roof to eat and sleep in such different surroundings. She used to pretend that, like Cinderella, a wand was waved over her, too, when she emerged from the shabbiness of some "cheapest rooms" and approached the splendor of some ground-floors with their bright lights, bright music, long stretches of soft carpet springy as moss, with women trailing over it on their way to the dining-room for dinner—pretty, rich-looking women with bare necks, and shoulders powdered as white as gardenias.

But their necks and shoulders weren't any barer nor any whiter than Laurel's mother's, nor their cheeks any rosier, nor were they any prettier! Laurel thought that her mother was the very prettiest lady that she had ever seen in any hotel!

4

One morning in late August Laurel woke up very early in the slant-cellinged bedroom under the eaves. She knew it was early, not because the traveling-clock in its worn leather case on the bureau across the room told her so (the clock was turned so she couldn't see its face), but because it was so still, and because she always woke early on the morning of the day set for her yearly visit to her father.

She wished she knew how early it was. A summer hotel, even the service wing, slept so late. The sun could tell Laurel nothing. The sun rose from out the ocean, and of course the "cheapest room" hadn't a glimpse of the ocean.

Laurel didn't dare risk getting up and looking at the clock, for, not for anything, would she have disturbed her mother asleep beside her. Her mother had probably been up until nearly morning to finish her packing. No. She would simply have to wait for the alarm-clocks in the servants' quarters across the alley-way. They usually began to go off about six to six-thirty. in the meanwhile she must lie very quietly and not joggle the bed. Cautiously she folded her hands beneath her head, and proceeded to content herself as best she could, gazing about with slow-moving, wide-awake eyes.

There, opposite her, hanging from the electric-light fixture on the wall, was her traveling-suit carefully arranged upon a stretcher. It was the first real suit with separate coat and skirt that Laurel had ever had I Would her father like it, she wondered? Would he like the close little black velvet hat that went with it, with the bunch of red berries on the side? Her mother had copied the hat from a thirty-dollar model, which she had priced in a shop in Boston. It made her look very grown up. Would her father like to have her look grown up?

Beside the suit stood Laurel's trunk. It was a wardrobe trunk—a beautiful trunk. Laurel thought. Brand-new. It was all ready to be closed. Her dresses, freshly pressed and hanging in order, simply had to be pushed back into the empty space behind. The little drawers beside the dresses were already shut snug and tight. The drawers were filled. Laurel well knew, with various-colored ribbons, bows, and sashes, to match the dresses; shoes and stockings; and piles of soft white underclothes in perfect repair. Her mother had been busy for a fortnight with white thread and darning-cotton. For a missing button or a tiny hole used to disturb Laurel's father years ago.

The beautiful trunk, and its beautiful contents, clashed with its present surroundings. Laurel was aware of it. It flashed over her, with a little stab of joy, that to-morrow morning when she woke up and glanced across the room at her trunk, it would be harmonizing with mahogany and plate-glass and a soft velvet carpet, and a glimpse through an open door of tiles and shining white porcelain. Too bad, oh, too bad, it flashed over her, with another stab that wasn't joy, that to-morrow morning her mother couldn't be waking up with her and glancing across at the trunk. Her mother did love grand rooms sol Her mother did love New York sol To-morrow when Laurel woke up there would be the rumble of New York outside her window hundreds of feet below.

Very carefully Laurel turned her head upon her folded hands and looked at her mother. She wasn't pretty in the early morning in a battered old iron bed, of course. No lady can be pretty with her mouth hanging open, and her hair all mussy and tousled. Laurel's mother's hair looked like straw, now—dry and dead. But when she did it up and put the magic net on it, it seemed to come alive. It was the same with the early-morning ashen look of her skin. It disappeared completely, along with the shadows, and queer greenish hollow places, and tiny wrinkles, when she was ready to step out of the mean little room. It was wonderful what Laurel's mother could do with a little powder and a little rouge, and a bit of chamois skin. It seemed to Laurel there was real magic there—no pretense, as in her Cinderella game.

She turned away from her mother. It wasn't fair to look at a picture till it was finished.

5

It was fully half an hour later when Laurel gazing at the ceiling became aware that her mother was no longer breathing out loud. She knew even without looking that her mother's blue eyes were wide open. She could feel them staring at her!

She turned her head towards her. Her mother was indeed staring at her!

"Hello," said Laurel, smiling tenderly.

"Hello," said her mother, still staring.

"What's the matter? What are you. thinking of?" softly Laurel inquired.

"I was thinking what a burning *shame* you haven't naturally curly hair!" her mother exclaimed. "It makes me about sick to think of you down there for a whole month, with your hair hanging down as straight as a stick."

"Oh, it looks all right."

"I wish now I had had you have a Permanent. Some children are having it, and I don't believe for a minute that it would do good strong hair like yours a mite of harm, the way it's done way down at the ends for long curls, so I'm told. One reason I can keep your hair long like some of the most distinguished children, instead of bobbing it off like an errand girl's in a department store, is because I'm always Johnny-on-the-spot with the curling rags. There's nothing worse than long, straight, Indian hair these days. Oh, I do wish I had had the Permanent, but I simply couldn't afford it and your new trunk, too. It would be pleasant if your father gave you a few things you need once in a while. For goodness' sakes," she broke off, "if your father asks you when you're down there this time, what books you want for Christmas, tell him you can get books for nothing from the Public Library, but there's no public institution where you can get fur coats for nothing, or a wrist-watch, and all the girls you know—or *ought* to know—have fur coats now, and wrist-watches of their own."

"I'll tell him," Laurel said. "Shan't we get up pretty soon?"

"Terribly anxious to get started, aren't you?"

"Oh, no, I'm not anxious a bit," Laurel denied, and she stuck her hands back again under her head as proof; "I'm in no hurry. But it's only three hours to train-time, and I thought—"

"Never mind. That's all right. I don't blame you, kiddie," her mother said, and her eyes suddenly filled with tears. "Funny," she remarked, with her eyes still upon Laurel, "how I can't seem to remember what you look like once you get away." She sniffed. "I'm going to just about die without you, Lollie!" she exclaimed.

"I know it," said Laurel calmly, staring up at the ceiling, but with not a sign of tears herself.

Her mother sniffed again. "And to think," she said, "I didn't want you once. I didn't want you a bit before you were born." Then with a sudden determination she threw back the bedclothes.

"Come," she ejaculated, "let's *do* get up!" and she swung her feet around onto the bare floor.

6

She was a fat, shapeless little ball of a woman in her nightgown. A plain unattractive nightgown it was, made of a crinkly material that didn't require ironing, with a soiled blue ribbon straggling halfway round the neck. She pulled on a cheap cotton-crepe kimono over the nightgown. The kimono had been lavender once, but it had faded to somewhat the same ashen color as her face now. She slipped her feet into some bedroom slippers very much out of repair.

She was the sort of woman whose exterior was never slack or hasty. She was never guilty of substituting a pin for a stitch where it *showed*, but her negligées and night-clothes were always in a state of neglect and shabbiness. Even Laurel had begun to observe that. The first time Laurel had exclaimed, shocked, "Why, mother, there's the same hole in the toe of your stocking that was there yesterday!" Mrs. Dallas had smiled. How like her father it was! Stephen had had the same foolish blind dislike for a hole, or a rip, or a missing button, which nobody was ever going to see.

Wrapped round in her unlovely draperies, Mrs. Dallas now skuffed across the little room to the cheap oak bureau.

"Darn this thing!" she murmured, as she fumbled with the backboneless mirror, which always needed a wad of paper or a hairbrush stuck in its side, to hold it in position. "My! what a sight I am!" she exclaimed, when finally the contrary thing consented to give her back her reflection. "I certainly am some beauty at seven o'clock in the morning," she laughed, and she put both her hands to her head, pushing down the stiff tow-like material, sticking out in a wild ungainly fashion about her face. Then, raising her chin, and frowning a little, she stroked her throat once or twice, where there hung, flabby and inert this morning, an unmistakable double chin.

It was a fitful sort of double chin. Showed much more at times than at others. Seemed to have periods of being sulky and stubborn. Mrs. Dallas was always in a state of indecision as to whether the thing showed less with a low, loose collar, or a high, tight one. This indecision was felt only in connection with daytime costumes, however, for at night in evening-dress she had long ago concluded that the lower the gown the less noticeable the superfluous chin. Once you got below the Dutch neck-line, Mrs. Dallas's skin was as white and firm as a young girl's. She had always had beautiful neck and shoulders, and they didn't grow old and sallow along with her face.

Mrs. Dallas believed that if a woman was clever, and made enough of that feature of hers which chanced to have remained young, whether it was hair, or figure, or complexion, or neck-and-shoulders, defects and blemishes would become less obvious. Unfortunate, of course, that convention deemed that *her* "young" feature could be exhibited only at night. Still, she told herself, she should be thankful that such inventions as powder and paint existed, corsets, and curling-irons, electric massages, and electric needles. For she had a horror of growing old and unattractive—a horror connected with the memories of her own mother.

She could recall that twenty years ago her mother had been gray and shapeless, her face covered with light brown moth-spots, wrinkles, and long hairs here and there—a spiritless creature, who wore loose, mouse-colored wrappers and flat men's shoes. Stella Dallas (Stella Martin she was then) was ashamed to have her young men friends catch a glimpse of her mother when they came to call in the red cottage house in Cataract Village outside the city of Milhampton. Laurel should never be ashamed of *her* mother like that, before *her* young-men friends, Mrs. Dallas decided, not if a little thought and effort could prevent it. Besides, there was another reason for keeping up a young appearance.

Not for eight years had she laid eyes upon her husband, nor he upon her, as far as she knew. It hardly seemed possible, for she had been to New York often, and the hotels where she and Laurel summered were very likely places for automobile parties to spend a day and night. Stephen might walk right into the office or dining-room or parlor any day where she chanced to be seated. If he should, he simply mustn't find her too changed. He mustn't find an old woman in place of the unquestionable belle she had been in their set the fall his business took him to New York.

The elaborate process of her mother's dressing had great interest for Laurel. Sometimes she would watch it from the bed, and other times from a chair near by, sitting, bare-necked and bare-armed in her underclothes with the comb and brush in her hand, waiting for her mother to unroll the eight tight wads around her head, and make them into long loose curls.

She had a long while to wait, for it took her mother a long while to dress. Laurel would pop into *her* clothes in no time, her slim pipe-stem arms and legs simply flashing into the right places, and her quick fingers buttoning and fastening with lightning speed. Laurel worked like a machine, when she dressed. Her mother worked like an artist, whose effects are accomplished by many fine and careful strokes, and many stops, standing away frequently from her work to observe it with a critical and often a dissatisfied eye.

She would not be ready to apply her skill to Laurel until she was complete herself, except for just the finishing touch of her dress. When she would be ready for Laurel, the flabby fleshiness under the nightgown would have become all beautiful firm curves inside the flower-brocaded pink corsets; and the shapeless mop of tow would have become all beautiful firm curves too, like the hair on the wax busts in the show-windows of fashionable hairdressing shops. Her eyes would have become ever so blue, and ever so large beneath transforming eyebrows that arched. The centers of her cheeks would be pink, and her lips red, and her neck and shoulders, bare of course without her dress, would be milky white, with lovely little lavender veins showing faintly here and there, like the guiding lines Laurel used sometimes when she wrote a letter, showing faintly through thick white note-paper.

When Laurel moved over before the mirror and stood in front of her mother for her hair to be done, and caught the reflection of her own freckled face and sunburned neck and arms, bony and hard, and her dark hair with the forbidding bang, it seemed to her that the pink and whiteness above her was like an angel's in comparison.

"When shall you begin to put rouge and powder on *me*, mother?" one day Laurel had asked.

"Not until nice girls your age begin to put it on," her mother replied briefly, with the practicalness that guided all her decisions in regard to Laurel as to what was proper or improper, appropriate or inappropriate.

It was because Mrs. Dallas adhered to models so scrupulously that Laurel's clothes were never cheap or flashy in appearance. Mrs. Dallas was like certain dressmakers, who know how to impart elegance and refinement to the clothes they make for others, while their own costumes are often extreme and unpleasantly conspicuous. Mrs. Dallas wore a good deal of imitation jewelry herself—large imitation pearls around her neck, large imitation pearls in her ears. But Laurel never wore jewelry at all, except a string of tiny gold beads.

The little Holland girl never wore jewelry at all, except a string of tiny gold beads. The little Holland girl was one of Mrs. Dallas's models. In Milhampton the Henry Hollands were one of "the four hundred"—one of the first ten of "the four hundred," in Mrs. Dallas's opinion. Laurel did not attend the same dancing-class which Stephanie Holland attended, but Mrs. Dallas often attended it, looking down from her balcony seat (to occupy which no ticket of admission was required) onto the polished floor below, studying, scrutinizing, and recording in as thorough and business-like a way as a dressmaker at a fashion-show in New York.

7

When Mrs. Dallas and Laurel sat down at their table in the big hotel dining-room an hour later. Laurel was all ready for her long journey to New York, and Mrs. Dallas all ready for her shorter one to Boston, where at the appointed meeting-place in the South Station she was to pass Laurel over as usual to the spectacled Miss Simpson.

The hotel guests seated near Laurel and her mother observed their traveling clothes. One of them later, in the hotel lobby, approached Laurel as she sat, half-hidden in a high-backed armchair, waiting for her mother. Her neat black-enameled suit case stood beside her, and her silver-handled umbrella lay across her knees.

"Are you and your mammar leaving us to-day?" asked the lady.

"*I* am," Laurel replied.

"But not your mammar?"

Laurel wished she wouldn't say "mammar."

"No. Mother isn't."

"Oh, so that's it! You're going alone! And where are you going?"

"To New York."

"To New York! How nice! To visit, I suppose?" Laurel nodded.

"Let's see. I believe I've heard your pappar lives in New York," remarked the lady. Any reference to her father always put Laurel on the defensive. "Doesn't your pappar live there?" the lady persisted.

"I call him father," said Laurel, flushing.

"You funny child! Well, doesn't your father live in New York?"

"My father has business in New York which takes him there frequently," Laurel replied as she had heard her mother reply dozens of times before.

"Oh, I see! And you're going to New York to visit your father. Is that it?" purred the lady.

There were sharp claws behind that purr. Laurel knew. Also she knew that it was not customary for little girls to visit their fathers alone. So now she replied, "No, I'm going to visit a hotel."

"But you'll see your father, of course?" It appeared quite legitimate. Laurel had long ago discovered, for grown-up people to ask questions of a child which they'd never think of asking each other. Therefore, she decided, it was legitimate for children to remain silent when they chose. Of course she wasn't a *little* child who might refuse to speak and not mean to be rude, but if people *would* keep on asking questions as if she were only six, she would keep on being silent. She was silent now. She closed her lips firmly, and from beneath her long bang stared blankly across the lobby. The lady repeated her question.

"You'll see your father, won't you?"

Laurel continued her blank stare. Her eyes took on a vacant, far-away expression, as if she had suddenly fallen to day-dreaming, and was thousands of miles away from the hotel lobby and the lady. In reality she was keenly conscious of the moment and the place, and was keenly suffering, too. Laurel didn't like being rude. She would like to answer every question ever asked her. Only she couldn't always. People nudged, and smiled, and raised their eyebrows sometimes.

"Well," said the lady, less sweetly now, "I'm sure your mother will miss you, whomever you're going to see, for she doesn't seem to have made many intimate friends in the hotel."

How unkind! How cruel! It swept over Laurel that she would like to make up a face at this woman—this hateful, ugly woman. (She *was* ugly. She had a complexion like dough. Beside her mother's rose-petal cheeks, hers were like toadstools. Beside her mother's bright hair, hers was like dull pewter.) Laurel glowered at the lady's retreating back. She had perfectly enormous hips!

"What was Mrs. Lamson saying, kiddie?" asked Laurel's mother a moment later bustling up to her.

"Nothing much."

"Being nice?"

"Oh, yes," said Laurel brightly. Her mother was terribly anxious for people to be "nice," and Laurel almost as anxious that she should believe them so. "She thought my new hat was ever so pretty," she prevaricated smoothly.

"I bet she didn't guess how little it cost," shrugged Mrs. Dallas.

"Well, I didn't tell her," said Laurel.

When Laurel kissed her mother good-bye on the platform at the station, there wasn't a tear in her eyes, although her mother's pretty cheeks were all smeared with them underneath the concealing big-meshed white veil. The arms she put around her mother's neck didn't cling nor clutch, like the arms that held *her* so tightly, and her kiss was cool and brief. But in her throat there was a big lump, and about her mouth there was a drawn, set look that meant she was clenching her teeth together hard, as she stood by the car window, and waved and waved to the lovely pink-and-white figure left behind in the smoke.

CHAPTER II

1

Laurel could always pick out her father in the waiting group behind the gate at the end of the long granolithic walk outside the train in New York, twenty or thirty seconds before he saw her. This was because her eyes were so keen and sharp, while her father was a little near-sighted; and because, too, there was a change in Laurel from year to year, while her father always looked the same.

Laurel and her father were always a little formal and constrained with each other at first. Laurel never could adjust herself quickly to the fact that this distinguished-looking gentleman, with the close-shaven cheeks, little black mustache, and keen gray eyes, was her own father, whom, if he lived at home as other girls' fathers did, she would be familiar enough with to climb over, and tug and pull at, perhaps. It took a little while for him, too, she imagined, to believe that she—freckled, long-banged, and black—was his.

She seemed perfectly calm and quiet when she put her hand in his, and he leaned and kissed her, but really her heart was beating fearfully.

Inside the taxicab on the way to the hotel, where Laurel and Miss Simpson were to stay. Laurel would sit beside Miss Simpson, and her father would occupy the seat opposite them. Most of the conversation, as they rumbled along, would be between Miss Simpson and her father—about the recent journey, the weather in Boston, the weather here, unimportant subjects, with long lapses of silence between; and upon arriving at the hotel. Laurel's father would leave them at the elevator-door, and go away quickly as if he were glad to escape.

Upstairs in the luxurious three-roomed apartment which he had engaged for Laurel, there would be all sorts of surprises—dolls and elaborate toys, when Laurel was younger; candy and flowers, and a dear little fitted work-basket this time, and a pile of brand-new books, lying on the table beside the silk-shaded reading-lamp.

Laurel's father lived in bachelor's apartments not far away from the hotel. It was easy for him to come in every morning and have breakfast alone with Laurel close beside one of the high windows in the private apartment, while Miss Simpson went downstairs to the dining-room. A waiter in black, who treated Laurel as if she were a princess, and her father as if he were a king, would roll in a table with a snowy cloth on it and shining china, with all sorts of delicious smells creeping out from beneath inverted silver bowls.

It would be usually at this first breakfast alone together that the real reunion between Laurel and her father would begin. This time, however, when her father left Laurel at the elevator-door, he had said he would return at seven-thirty, and they would go to dinner somewhere together, if Miss Simpson would pardon his stealing his little girl away the very first night. So on this visit Laurel's and her father's first real words of greeting took place inside the dusky interior of the taxicab that bore them to the restaurant which he had selected. It was the first time in a whole year that they had been alone together.

They sat in silence for a moment or two, after the door had slammed upon them. Then, "Well, here we are," said Laurel's father.

"Yes," murmured Laurel.

"How are you. Laurel?" he asked.

"All right."

"What sort of a year has it been?"

"All right."

Just the shortest, most conventional of question—just the shortest, most non-committal of answers, but full of significance to them both; full of the promise of the dawning of the old sweet intimacy which never failed to steal over Laurel and her father, once they got rid of preliminaries, and to possess them like sunshine a cloudless day, once it breaks through the mists and fogs of early morning.

Laurel's father sat away as far as possible from her and surveyed her from top to toe. The close little toque with the red berries gave her a mature look that was unfamiliar. He sighed.

"You're growing up, Lollie," he said gently.

Whenever Laurel's father called her Lollie, it always brought the vision of her mother sharply before her eyes. Her mother and father were the only two people in the world who had ever called her the silly little baby-name of Lollie—"Lolliepops" once it had been. She shoved the vision away as soon as possible. It hurt somehow. Her mother would have so loved the lights outside the taxicab window, and the taxicab too. She and her mother seldom afforded a taxicab.

"It's my new hat that makes me look grown up," said Laurel with never a reference to the creator of it. Laurel never mentioned her mother to her father. Some fine instinct within her kept her lips as sealed as his. "Don't you like it?" she inquired, a little wistfully, for her father was still gazing at her with a sort of abstracted look which she didn't comprehend.

"What? The hat? Oh, yes. I like the hat very much," he assured her. "It's very nice, and your suit too. I like your suit. Laurel. Only you're growing up, and I don't know that I like that. I don't suppose I shall dare kiss you many years longer in the station before people," he laughed. "Young ladies don't like being kissed in public, I'm told."

Laurel laughed, too—a nervous, pleased little laugh, and moved a little nearer.

"I've finished all the reading," she confided to him proudly.

"You don't mean all of it!"

"Yes, every book you put on the list," she announced, eyes shining.

"Good work, Laurel."

"Oh, it wasn't work. I love to read."

"Do you really?"

"I didn't used to so much. It just seemed to come this year—liking it so, I mean." She turned her face towards him. "When you read a book you like a lot," she went on, "do you try to stop between sentences and look around and think it over, like eating a piece of candy just as slowly as you can, so it will last longer?"

"It used to be like that," he smiled, and he reached over and put his hand over Laurel's. "I'm glad you like to read, Laurel," he said, "for I like to, too. I've hoped you'd like to read when you grew up."

Laurel looked down at her father's hand, and then quickly out of the window, as if not to frighten it away.

"Isn't it funny how many things there are that you like that *I* like too?" she said softly. "I was counting them up coming down on the train."

"Are there? Tell me. What?"

"Well–there's books, and woods, and camping, and dogs, and horses, and fall better than spring, and dark meat better than light, and roast beef better than chicken, and salad better than dessert, and–and–"

"Yes, go on," her father encouraged.

"Well, picture galleries, and Madame Butterfly, and that Mrs. Morrison, and–"

"That Mrs. Morrison!" her father interrupted.

"Yes. Don't you remember last year one afternoon at tea?"

"I supposed you'd forgotten all about Mrs. Morrison."

"I haven't," said Laurel.

"You saw her for only about a half an hour."

"I know it. But you know what you said beforehand?"

"What did I say?"

"Why, for me to notice her, and listen to her nice voice, for she was somebody you'd like me to grow up to be like."

"Did I say that?"

Laurel nodded.

"And you did really like her?"

"Oh, yes! She was ever so nice to me! She gave me a little silver pencil out of her bag."

"And she has invited you to spend a few days with her during this visit of yours, at her summer home on Long Island."

Laurel was silent a moment.

"Will you be there?" she inquired.

"I'm sorry. I can't. I've got to be away. That is why she has invited you, so you won't be lonely here in New York. I must be in Chicago for a few days next week on business. I don't like missing even a day of your visit, but it's necessary."

"I wouldn't mind just staying at the hotel with Miss Simpson."

"Why, I thought you said you liked Mrs. Morrison."

"I do—only—I'm used to hotels. I'm not lonely in them. I don't believe I should like visiting. H as Mrs. Morrison any children?"

"Oh, yes. Several. You'll have a splendid time."

"I think I'd rather stay at the hotel," said Laurel.

"Well, we'll see. Don't have to decide to-night. It's only for a few days anyhow. We're going to have our two weeks together in the woods just the same."

2

Stephen Dallas always tried to arrange his affairs so as to be able to take Laurel off alone with him for two weeks somewhere. The month she spent with him was usually August or September, and he usually took her into the woods.

Stephen had an idea that the farther away from people and conventionalities he could get Laurel, the more susceptible she would be to him, and to his suggestions. However, it seemed sometimes absurd even to hope to be much of a factor in forming the child's tastes and inclinations. He had only thirty short days with her each year, and he knew that during the long lapses between her visits, the influence she lived under was not conducive to the growth of the kind of seeds he planted.

When Laurel was a little girl, seven or eight years old, often Stephen would ask her what form of amusement she would prefer for an afternoon, and almost invariably she replied, when they were in New York, "Oh, the merry-go-round, or the monkeys at the Zoo." He didn't always give her the merry-go-round, nor the monkeys either. He was forever being torn between his inclination to indulge her slightest whim or wish, and thereby win her approval, and a desire to remould those whims and wishes.

When Laurel was ten years old, Stephen began taking her to picture galleries. In an attempt to instill in her some appreciation of beauty in art. Children like colored pictures, he argued. Why not give them good ones? He used to take her to hear good music too. Some of the symphonies, he told her, were just fairy tales told by violins, harps, French horns, and tambourines. Before a concert he took great pains to explain to Laurel the story which the various instruments were going to tell her. She would listen to his explanation fast enough, but more likely than not would fall asleep during the symphony itself.

When she was eleven years old, Stephen arranged to have Laurel visit him during the winter season, and took her for the first time to grand opera; also he took her, that same year, to several Shakespearean plays; to a beautifully staged classic for children; to a lovely fairy-like performance of dancing; all the while trying to place before her beauty in whatever form. When they were in the woods together, following a trail, helping the guides to make camp, cutting balsam boughs, gathering firewood, sitting for long hours in a boat on some lovely lake, listening for bird-calls, watching for a deer to steal down to the water's edge to drink, it was beauty in its natural form, then, that Stephen Dallas was placing before Laurel. He himself bought the clothes that Laurel wore on these trips of theirs into the woods. He took the keenest delight in selecting the rough little flannel shirts, the khaki trousers, and stout boots, visiting sporting-shop after sporting-shop before he was satisfied.

"I never saw so devoted a father as you, Stephen Dallas," one of his women friends said to him one day, during one of Laurel's visits. He had been refusing all his invitations.

Stephen Dallas had smiled and shrugged in reply. Most men, he told himself, weren't obliged to cram a year's fatherhood into one short month. They could spread it along. And most fathers, or many anyhow, in guiding their children were not obliged to exert their strength against another pair of oars, constantly pulling in another direction.

When Laurel came to visit her father for the first time he used every device and scheme he could think of to make her want to come again. It was always a little like that. Surprising, he said to himself, that he was so anxious for her to want to come again. He would think it more normal, wrapped up as he was in his business, and dead as was all desire in connection with the mistaken marriage he had made during the early years of his career in Milhampton, If he had wished to forget and bury everything related to it. Let other people forget and bury it too. If Laurel had been a boy who would grow up to bear his name, he might understand his hopes and ambitions for the child. But a girl—a solemn-eyed, long-banged little girl! He was only forty. His life was full of demands, of interests of the keenest sort, of friends, too, the best in the world. Yet the pleasure that he felt at any expression of affection from Laurel could make his eyes grow misty. And lately—last year, and the year before—a choking wave of pride would sweep over him now and then, as he observed her, or listened to some of her quiet comments.

To hear her exclaim that she loved reading—the sort of reading he had prescribed for her—had obliged him to swallow once or twice before trusting himself to speak. And picture galleries! He had thought her utterly bored by them. She was a polite little creature. She had never said she didn't like them, but after the first half-hour or so in a gallery, she usually made inquiry as to how much longer they were going to stay.

"I didn't know you liked picture galleries. Laurel," he said to her later, seated at a little table beside a trickling fountain with goldfish and twinkling lights—blue and pink and yellow—shining in its depths, and tinkling Hawaiian music sounding from somewhere in the distance. "You never said you did."

"I didn't know it until lately," said Laurel. "It came to me all in a flash. You know how liking things does come in a flash sometimes."

"No. Tell me."

He was fearfully afraid she wouldn't. She was like the gray-tailed squirrels in the park in some ways, at times ready to be friendly and intimate, and at other times shy of him, and as timid as a chipmunk.

"Well, the first time I knew I liked the woods,"—Ah! one of her trustful moods—"wasn't when I was up there *in* them, but right in a city street, looking into an art-store window at a picture of a trail just like lots of trails we've tramped. It flashed over me right there on the crowded city sidewalk, I just love the woods!' And last winter our teacher took our class at school to an art gallery one afternoon, and when I got the first queer smell, and heard the first echo-y sounds that go with art galleries, it came over me what fun *we'd* had picking out our favorite pictures in art galleries here in New York, and going afterwards to get hot chocolate somewhere, and all of a sudden it flashed over me, 'Why, I just love art galleries!'"

"And 'Madame Butterfly'?"

"Yes, the same way," she told him. "I thought I'd forgotten all about it, except the fat woman who sat in front of us, and how she hadn't gotten the powder on even, on the back of her neck; but one day last summer the orchestra at the hotel where mother—where *we*—were staying, played a piece that I knew I'd heard before, and I peeked over the violinist's shoulder, and found out what it was. And all of a sudden I saw that lovely Japanese lady in the beautiful white satin kimono on her porch with the pink sky beyond, singing about her baby. The orchestra played it lots of times after that. I asked them to, and it's my favorite piece of music now."

Laurel's father looked away from her. Some of his seeds, then, had taken root and were growing. Even among thorns! He must plant and plant and plant, then, while it was still the planting season.

3

Later that same night, in Laurel's room at the hotel, Stephen sat down beside her by the reading-lamp, and glanced through the pile of books he had selected for her. "Idyls of the King" was one of the books.

"What do you say we save this one to read out loud in the woods?" he inquired.

Laurel, sunk in a soft deep armchair, the fitted work-basket in her lap, the box of candy open on the table near by, didn't hear him apparently.

"Are there any 'cheapest rooms' in this hotel?" she asked, gazing speculatively at the old-rose draperies at the high windows, and at the expanse of lace beyond.

"Don't you like these rooms, Laurel?"

"Oh, yes! Yes! Only—"

The crystal clock on the mahogany mantel had just struck ten-thirty. The Wednesday night "movies" at the summer hotel would be finishing about now. Laurel's mother, all dressed up in her pretty clothes, would be going upstairs to the horrid little bedroom, very soon, alone.

"Only what?" her father asked.

"Oh, nothing. I've been wondering what it would look like beside this one—that's all."

That wasn't all. Her father felt sure it wasn't all. But many of her thoughts he was unable to follow to their source. A faint suspicion disturbed him. Surely the allowance he sent to Laurel's mother was sufficient. He could vouch that as long as a sure three hundred and fifty dollars was coming to Stella every month, she would live well wherever she was. She delighted in living well.

"Why should you be thinking about cheap rooms?" he asked.

"No reason," Laurel replied shortly.

She was not going to tell him anyhow. That was clear. Useless to coax her.

Before he left her for the night, he said to her, "I really think you'd like it at Mrs. Morrison's, Laurel."

"Do you want me to go?"

"Well, I want you to know Mrs. Morrison," he replied. "I feel that when you are with me I must give you the best of everything I can, Laurel, and when Mrs. Morrison invited you to stay with her I was very happy to give you five whole days of life in her home."

"If it's just for me, then, I think I'd rather stay here, if you don't mind."

Stephen looked down at a book on the table and opened it. He was standing up all ready to go.

"I don't mind," he said, gazing at the printed page, but not seeing it, "only," he went on, "I should feel sorry, I suppose, if you didn't like some little present I'd picked out for you which I thought very nice. And so, too, I suppose I shall feel a little disappointed if you don't wish to go to Mrs. Morrison's." He closed the book. "But of course I don't really mind. You're the one to be pleased."

He did mind. He minded awfully. He always minded when his voice was low and serious, like that.

"I'll go," said Laurel.

"Oh, you don't have to, my dear."

"I'd *like* to go," she assured him brightly, which was true. Laurel would like to do anything to please her father.

CHAPTER III

1

Laurel was to go to Mrs. Morrison's the following Monday. She dreaded the visit. She was suspicious of women, and especially suspicious of mothers. One of the reasons Laurel always looked forward with such joy to the month with her father was that there never were any slights—never any fear of any slights. His presence seemed to prevent the possibility of slights. Everybody to whom he introduced her in his fine proud manner as "my daughter Laurel," treated her with the same kindness—almost deference—with which they treated him. Mrs. Morrison had been kindness itself to her a year ago, at tea in the hotel, but her father had been there then. Ladies had a way of being kind when men were about. Laurel had discovered. It was being left alone with Mrs. Morrison that she dreaded.

Besides, Laurel knew very little about the etiquette of private homes. She was familiar with the ways and customs of a hotel. Knew the proper manner to assume towards waiters, and porters, and clerks; knew, too, the proper fee to pay bellboys and chambermaids, if she asked them to do anything for her, which she seldom did, for dimes and quarters were never freely squandered by Laurel and her mother on ice-water or extra blankets for cool nights. But she was uncertain about the proper manner to assume towards servants in a private home. In the winter-time she and her mother lived in an apartment hotel. How many servants were there usually, anyhow, and what did you call them, and what fee did you give them? And when, and how, and for what? Or didn't you give them a fee at all? And just how, she wondered, should you dress in a private home? Did a girl of thirteen change three times a day, for instance, and put on an organdie for dinner? And who did her hair? Miss Simpson, it appeared, was not to accompany Laurel to Mrs. Morrison's. Miss Simpson wasn't very good at hair. She never even attempted curls. But she could get snarls out, and brush, and divide fairly well, under direction. Laurel was helpless without somebody.

Laurel mentioned none of her perplexities to her father. If she did he might wonder why it was she knew so little about homes. It might reflect upon her mother. For at the private school she attended in the winter-time, she often heard intimate friends talking about spending nights with each other. Laurel had no such intimate friends at the school. That she hadn't was one of the many galling failures of Mrs. Dallas's ambitions for her daughter. Laurel was not unaware of it. No. Her father should know nothing of her ignorance.

On many topics Laurel was as frank and open with her father as any artless child. But she had her reservations. She had great expanses of thought and experience she never let him glimpse at. She never mentioned her mother's name to him. She made as little reference as possible even to her life with her mother. By the time she was thirteen this silence had become like a wall between Laurel and her father. Stephen was aware of it. It loomed high and blank between them, and shut much of Laurel away from him. But it also shut much of Stella, too.

Once the mention of Stella's name, even as "mother" on Laurel's lips, had hurt Stephen. The years had cured him of the hurt, but still he thought it wiser to let the barrier remain. For one reason—it was kinder to Stella. Laurel's silence made it easier for him never to criticize Stella and, therefore, appear to influence the child against her mother. There were many things to criticize, and if they were brought to his attention in detail, he would be sure to wish to alter them. This he could not do without interference with Stella. Interference with Stella would open up new issues, and lead to unpleasant complications. And after all Laurel was Stella's child. Stella had been necessary to Laurel. He could never have been a nurse to a little girl of six. Had he been determined to control Laurel's bringing-up, then he ought to have been willing to have endured Stella. He had made his decision. He had never regretted it.

He took Laurel down to Mrs. Morrison's in his automobile. She talked very little as the car sped over the smooth roads, through pretty settlement after pretty settlement. When finally Stephen announced, "The next town's ours," Laurel murmured miserably, "You'll surely be back for me Saturday, won't you?"

Stephen laughed. "Surely," he said. "Why, you'd think I was putting you in an institution." And a little later he sang out cheerfully, "Here we are at the prison-gates!" and turned the car in between two cement posts, partly ivy-covered, and up a short curving drive.

The house was cement, and partly ivy-covered, too, like the posts. It was set low, seemed to cling to the ground, and the close-cropped lawn ran right up to long French windows on either side of the front door.

The French windows were open, and from out of one of them stepped Mrs. Morrison. She waved her hand at Stephen and Laurel, and called out in a high pretty voice, "Hello!" then walked rapidly towards the approaching car to meet it.

Laurel noticed that she was dressed in an ordinary white skirt and outing waist, and wore tennis shoes. She was at the door of the car when it stopped, and, before Laurel's father had a chance to open it, she had stretched out her arm in front of him—ignoring him completely—grasped one of Laurel's hands, and was saying in the lovely voice Laurel remembered, "Hello, Laurel." She said "Laurel," not "Laurrul"—like most people. Her voice was like a bell. "I'm *ever* so glad to see you. I've been waiting and waiting for you. Get out, dear. Let her out, Stephen." She hadn't paid any attention to Stephen till then. "Your trunk has come," she said, still addressing Laurel, still ignoring her father—or almost, for she flung him only the briefest little "Hello," as he stepped out of the automobile beside her—"and for the last hour I've been thinking you yourself were coming every time I heard a horn blowing outside our drive."

As Laurel stepped off the running-board, Mrs. Morrison put her arm around her and kissed her lightly on the cheek. Afterwards she left her arm there in a casual sort of way as if she forgot to remove it.

"Let's come into the house *this* way," she suggested, and gently drew Laurel across the lawn towards the French windows. "I've tea and cakes all ready," she said in a low tone, as if it was a confidence not meant for Stephen's ears. "And cinnamon toast." She gave Laurel's shoulders the tiniest little bit of squeeze.

Arm in arm with Mrs. Morrison, Laurel stepped across the low threshold of the French window into a big, generous, library-sort of room, with a grand piano at one end, and books all around the dark walls.

It was as easy as that, getting into the house, and all of the way down Laurel had been making herself miserable wondering just how it would be accomplished—whether there would be a butler as in most movies, to answer the bell, or a maid; and if the butler or the maid took your suitcase, like bellboys in hotels, or if you just held onto it yourself. Laurel's father had told her that he must run directly back to New York, after leaving her at Mrs. Morrison's, to catch his train. She had supposed that he had meant he couldn't even see her across the threshold. But no. He followed her into the big room, carrying her suitcase himself, and showed no sign of hurrying away.

There was an Irish setter in the room, lying down by a big chair as Laurel entered it with Mrs. Morrison.

"This is Laurel, Michael," called out Mrs. Morrison to the dog. "Come and tell her how glad we are to see her."

The dog got up, stretched, and wagged his tail languidly, then, with a sudden brightening of expression, a sudden tightening of muscles he barked twice, and shoved past Mrs. Morrison and Laurel towards Stephen, making joyous little whining sounds as he fell to lavishing damp dog-kisses on the hand that held Laurel's suitcase.

"There's no doubt about how glad he is to see your father, is there?" laughed Mrs. Morrison. "Michael adores your father. Laurel, as we all do around here," she added carelessly. "Come, we'll run upstairs, and wash our hands. Give me the suitcase, Stephen."

"Laurel will take the suitcase," said Stephen. "It's not heavy."

"Yes, I'll take it," said Laurel.

"All right. Come along. And, oh, Stephen," Mrs. Morrison called back over her shoulder, in that sort of singing voice of hers, "just light the hot water, will you please?"

There was a tea-table, with a white cloth near one of the windows, with shining silver on it, and shining tea-cups and a plate or two of snowy sandwiches and a basket of frosted cakes. "We'll be down in a minute."

2

Upstairs, inside the most exquisite little bathroom Laurel had ever stepped foot in—creamy tiles clear to the ceiling, creamy floor, creamy fittings, not a scrap of nickel in sight—everything all smooth shining porcelain, like the inside of a beautiful china cup, Laurel thought—Mrs. Morrison said, "Here's the washcloth, and here's the soap, and here's the towel. Use them, and then come into *this* room. It's mine. I'm going to have you in with me. And take off your things. Put them on the bed next to the wall—your bed—then come downstairs. And don't be long. I'll hurry down ahead and get your father started on his tea. He's got to go right back to town." And she left Laurel.

Very carefully Laurel followed her directions, gazing wonderingly about her as she did so, examining various details with investigating nose and fingertips; sniffing the soap; ever so cautiously opening the door of the medicine chest; touching with a gentle forefinger the silk window-hangings in the bedroom; touching with the same gentle forefinger its ivory-colored walls; the shade on the lamp on the table between the beds. It was made of real filet I So, too, were the curious little pillows on the beds. (Laurel had never seen tiny pillows like that on grown-up beds.) So, too, was the bureau-scarf, and the tidy on the back of the big winged-chair by the window. All real filet! And just the simplest little piece of filet cost six-fifty In the neckwear department!

Standing in the center of the bedroom, Laurel drew In a deep breath, and gazed about her. What a lovely bedroom it was! Yellowish—like pale sunshine. She decided that it was lovelier even than her present luxurious apartment at the hotel. It was lovelier than any apartment in any hotel she had ever caught a glimpse of through half-open doors, on her way to and from elevators.

After she had taken off her hat and coat and laid them on the bed next to the wall as directed (*her* bed, she would be sleeping in it to-night!) she opened the door, and went out into the upper hall. She stole noiselessly down the broad staircase—there was a tall, slender, light-mahogany grandfather's clock on the landing, and a high window with pink-and-white petunias making it bright in a window-box outside—and noiselessly approached the door of the big room where she had left her father.

There were others in the room now besides her father and Mrs. Morrison. She could tell from the voices. She stopped when she reached the threshold. Nobody saw her, nobody heard her, and she had a moment to gaze unobserved at the scene before her.

It was like a scene at the "movies," with all those books, and the piano, and the comfortable chairs, and the big portrait hanging over the fireplace, and the pretty lady behind the steaming tea-kettle, and the dog, and the boys (there were three boys in the room. One of them, the littlest one, was seated in her father's lap)—only it was real! There were real bindings on the books, real reading in them, there was real tea in the tea-pot. The people were real, and their feelings for each other were real, too. She, standing on the outside, was the only unreal thing in this home scene.

She looked at her father. Suddenly the room faded, disappeared, and a close-up of his face dawned on the screen before her, as it were. Why, her father was gazing at the lady behind the teakettle, as if—as if—I Laurel had seen too many close-ups of faces not to recognize that look! She drew in her breath sharply. It flashed over Laurel that perhaps this man wasn't really her father after all I She stirred, moved a foot.

Mrs. Morrison glanced over her shoulder.

"Oh! come here, Laurel," she exclaimed at sight of her, and stretched out her arm, and kept it stretched out until Laurel had stepped within its circle.

"This is Laurel, boys," she said briefly. Then, still holding Laurel, not giving her even a chance to go through the agony of a series of curtsies, she went on, "These are your new friends, Laurel. Cornelius, over there by the piano, is the oldest. 'Con' we call him for short. And Dane comes next. 'Great Dane' they call him at school. But *I* call him *little* Dane. And the little boy in your father's lap is Frederick. 'Rick' is his nickname. He's the baby—five years old now. We haven't any little girl for you. Laurel," she sighed. How lucky! No girls! Boys weren't half as cruel.

"And now," Mrs. Morrison broke off, "I wonder would you pass this cup of tea I'm making to your father? And, Con dear, will you pass the sandwiches? Get down, Rickie, and run and get your rabbit and bring it in and show it to Laurel. And, Dane, take Michael out. Michael," she explained to Laurel, "is not fond of Mercedes's society, Mercedes being the rabbit," she smiled.

They were all busy in no time—all but Mrs. Morrison and Stephen, each rushing about on some errand or other. There wasn't a chance for pause or embarrassment. The same rare insight and understanding which made Helen Morrison's dinner parties such a success was quite as reliable with children, or with servants, or with the factory girls at the settlement-house in which she was interested. Not only did everybody with whom Helen Morrison worked and played get on beautifully with *her*, but under her gentle management they got on beautifully with one another, too. And yet she seemed to make no effort at adjusting herself to the various ages, groups, and classes with which she came in contact. That was why she was so successful with Laurel. It was her apparent unawareness that she was saying or doing the diplomatic thing that broke through the barrier of silence and reserve which Laurel hid behind whenever she met strangers.

The women whom Laurel met when visiting her father never by any chance, even indirectly, referred to her mother. It would have been a "break" if they had. Laurel knew that. But Mrs. Morrison made such a break. Mrs. Morrison referred to her mother, and the very first night, too, scarcely an hour after her father had said good-bye.

3

They were upstairs together unpacking. No chambermaid, no lady's-maid assisted at the task. In fact Laurel had begun to wonder if any servants existed in this household. Mrs. Morrison alone helped her, carefully hanging dress after dress in a closet near by, and exclaiming over each one, how pretty she thought it was. What a lovely color! Like jonquils one; like violets another; like a meadow spotted with tiny daisies, a certain English print.

It was when she was hanging up the last dress in the closet that she remarked, ever so naturally, "I think your mother has beautiful taste. Laurel."

Laurel looked up quickly. She had replied so far by only necessary yes-thank-yous and no-thank-yous to Mrs. Morrison, and if-you-pleases—that sort of thing, but now she exclaimed, "My mother has the most beautiful taste in the world!" She didn't know she was going to say just that, nor that her words were going to rush out in such an unfamiliar fashion. She blushed.

But Mrs. Morrison didn't seem to think her reply odd. She didn't even look at her. She said:

"I've always wanted a little girl. It's such fun to dress them. I can see your mother has had great fun getting all your pretty things to match and blend."

Later when Laurel asked her which dress she should put on for dinner, Mrs. Morrison replied, "Why, I don't know, I'm sure. Which dress do you think your mother would have you put on?"

She kept on referring to her mother casually like that right along. "Perhaps," thought Laurel, "she doesn't know there's any reason not to." And yet, being a friend of her father's, how could she help but know that her mother and father didn't live together like other people. Perhaps she didn't know *why* they didn't live together, just as Laurel herseif didn't know why. Whatever the explanation, Mrs. Morrison's frank and open recognition of her mother as a human being, and a human being, too, not unlike her lovely self, warmed Laurel, thawed out her mistrust and fear.

Before twenty-four hours had passed Laurel was worshiping Mrs. Morrison with that admiring kind of worship that a young girl, not quite a child, and yet not quite a woman, often feels for some stranger who stops and smiles.

CHAPTER IV

1

She didn't talk very much at first. She was too engrossed observing unfamiliar surroundings and watching Mrs. Morrison. It was as interesting as reading a new book almost. The ways and habits of a private home were very curious. For instance, you were introduced to the servants. A maid in spic-and-span gray-and-white did appear finally.

"Hannah," Mrs. Morrison said to her familiarly, "this is our guest. Miss Laurel. Laurel, Hannah is the one to ask if there's anything you want. She is a fairy. You've only to make a wish out loud before her, and it comes true."

And the ways and habits of a lady in a private home were curious, too—at least Mrs. Morrison's were curious. Marveling, Laurel observed the lightning speed with which she dressed. It seemed to Laurel that she was a fairy, too, for she had only to wish herself ready for dinner, or breakfast, or lunch, and she *was* ready inside of ten minutes.

It was fascinating to watch her do her hair. She would take out four or five hairpins from it, shake her head till the hair fell soft to her shoulders, brush the shining mass hastily a minute, twist it up, and stick the four or five hairpins back again, hardly looking into the mirror at all.

Laurel had thought Mrs. Morrison lovely to look at the first time she saw her a year ago, at the hotel, but ladies were often lovely to look at when they were dressed up. The amazing thing about Mrs. Morrison was that she was lovely to look at always, even in the early morning, even before she got up! She wasn't young. At least Laurel didn't think she was young. She was old enough to be Con's mother, and Con was older than Laurel. There were besides just a few gray hairs. You didn't see them till she let her hair down.

She had beautiful hair—dark, almost black. At night beneath the strong light of the silk-shaded lamp by the piano, it was like the breast of a dark-feathered pigeon in the sunshine—iridescent. She had long slender fingers—very white, and long slender arms, and a long slender neck. The line of her neck in profile had just the same curve from her throat to the tip of her chin (which was usually lifted) as the lady's in the moon. And she did her hair low, just like the lady in the moon, and it fluffed the same way, too, about her brow and ears, for she wore no net. She was like moonlight in lots of ways. Laurel concluded. Almost no color at all in her cheeks. And the dress she wore the first evening was pale yellow. And she didn't wear a single ornament to brighten it up.

Occupying the same room with Mrs. Morrison, it took much less time than otherwise for Laurel's shyness to wear away. Perhaps Mrs. Morrison was aware with what amazing rapidity the homely processes of dressing build up an intimacy. But, whether or not her motive was to win her way into Laurel's confidence the more quickly, or simply to take every precaution in guarding the child against homesickness, twice the number of hours spent in the drawing-room or garden would not have been sufficient to establish the degree of familiarity which made it possible for Laurel to put into words many of her questions and wonderings before she had been three days a guest of Mrs. Morrison.

"Have you a Permanent?" she asked bluntly the third morning as she sat gazing at Mrs. Morrison, seated before the altar-like dressing-table with nothing on it but two candlesticks and an old silver box and four or five tortoise-shell hairpins.

"Yes," Mrs. Morrison replied, smiling, "but not the kind you mean. I was born with mine."

Still gazing. Laurel inquired a moment later:

"Don't you ever use rouge, or an eyebrow pencil?"

"No"

"Why not?"

"Oh, I don't know. Why do you ask. Laurel?"

"No reason. I was only wondering." Then after a pause Laurel added, "I think you'd be lovely with pink cheeks."

"I would be nicer, wouldn't I?" she agreed, and she stuck in the last hairpin, got up, gathered together a few soft muslin things from a drawer near by (she put on clean clothes every morning: her laundry bill must be terrific), and, wrapped round in a lemon-colored china-silk kimono, passed into one of the little twin bathrooms adjoining, and closed the door.

Laurel heard the click of enamel handles being turned, the violent gush of a stream of water in the marble shower-bath, and a second or two later, or so it seemed, Mrs. Morrison reappeared, as fresh as a pond-lily in her crisp lingerie.

Laurel inquired of her, "If you think you'd be nicer with pink cheeks, then why don't you make them pink?"

"Oh, it takes such a lot of time!" laughed Mrs. Morrison. "And then, besides," she added, "I would always be getting them spoiled. I like to be outdoors so much, digging in the garden, riding horseback, romping with the boys in all sorts of weather. If I did use rouge. Laurel," she went on more seriously, "and an eyebrow pencil, as you suggested, I should want to do it exquisitely, like an artist, so that no one's sense of beauty could possibly be offended."

"Offended?"

"Yes. To some people paint and powder on the human face is distasteful."

"Is it?"

"Like paint and powder on the petals of a flower, I suppose."

"Oh!"

There was a long pause. Laurel broke it at last.

"Is that why you haven't a string of pearls?"

"Is what why. Laurel?"

"Because pearls on your neck would be to some people like pearls on flowers?"

"Oh, no," Helen Morrison replied, managing not even to smile. "I haven't a string of pearls because they're so expensive."

"Imitation pearls aren't very expensive."

"Oh, imitation!"

Laurel considered. Her mother had often told her that her pearls and imitation diamond bar-pin would pass for the genuine articles anywhere.

"They look just like the real ones," she told Mrs. Morrison.

"Oh, no. Laurel, not to a person who knows pearls. They lack inner beauty, just as a wax figure lacks soul. To the really discerning they're as lifeless and unbeautiful as that." Then, with a sudden happy inspiration, as she thought, Helen Morrison added, "Your mother has trimmed several of your pretty dresses with narrow filet lace, but there isn't an inch of imitation filet."

No, of course not, because imitation filet "never fooled anybody," Laurel's mother had often told her. In fact, she had said, and only a short fortnight ago, that there wasn't anything a woman could make more show with, at present, than a lot of splashy real lace, or anything that could kill her socially as surely as the imitation stuff.

Laurel wondered if to the really discerning her mother's imitation pearls were like imitation filet.

2

The next day Laurel asked Mrs. Morrison if she had ever seen her mother. Her mother's name by then was mentioned with perfect ease between them.

"No, I never have. Laurel," said Mrs. Morrison. "Tell me about her." They were walking in the garden. "Is she like you?"

"Oh, no," said Laurel. "She's not the least like me. She hasn't a single freckle. And her hair is yellow. She was born with it yellow, like you with your Permanent." Which was true. Mrs. Dallas had not tampered with the color of her hair as yet. "Her eyes," Laurel went on, "are blue—the color of that little blue pitcher you said was Delft, that you used one morning at breakfast. And her skin is like the cream in it."

"She must be lovely."

"Oh, she is, she is," flashed Laurel.

"Haven't you her picture?"

"No. Not here." After a pause Laurel added gravely, "I never bring her picture to New York when I come to see my father."

It was the first reference she had made to the relation that existed between her mother and father. But Mrs. Morrison made as casual a reply to it, as if it had been a frequent topic of conversation between them.

"Of course you don't. I didn't think for a minute. Naturally it's kinder not to."

Oh, how easy it was to talk to Mrs. Morrison! Questions Laurel had long wanted to know the answers to crowded to her lips. "Why are my mother and father different from other mothers and fathers? Why don't they live together? Why aren't people nice to my mother? And why are they nice to my father?" But she didn't allow one of them to escape. Not yet. Nor did Mrs. Morrison allow a question to escape either. They simply walked on in silence till they came to a turn in the garden path where some late pansies were blooming.

"Let's pick some," said Mrs. Morrison.

"Let's," said Laurel, and they leaned down together over the low-growing flowers.

Laurel's heart was beating fast. She could feel it. Between herself and this lovely lady the gossamer-like bond of sympathy, as delicate at first as a thread of a spider's web, had become now as strong as the silk cable pearls are strung on. It would bear actual spoken words about her father's and mother's separation!

"Is there anything in the world softer than the petal of a pansy!" remarked Mrs. Morrison, pressing one of the flowers against *her* lips, and gently drawing it across them.

Laurel laid a flower against her lips, too, and, closing her eyes, likewise tested its texture.

"The end of a horse's nose is as soft," she said contemplatively, "and," she went on, eyes still closed, "the back of a little tiny baby's head, where they'll let you kiss it."

Mrs. Morrison broke into a laugh.

"Dear delightful Laurel! That's so! That's so!" And suddenly she took hold of one of Laurel's hands and drew the back of that, too, across her lips, and kissed it.

That playful little kiss of Helen Morrison's on the back of Laurel's hand made Laurel's world whirl round her giddily for a moment. No one had ever kissed her on the hand before! It was a caress entirely different from an ordinary kiss upon the lips. She felt exalted, like a young knight in armor before his lady. She wished she dared kneel on the ground and kiss the hem of Mrs. Morrison's dress!

3

Laurel wondered a great deal about Mrs. Morrison's husband, and finally one day concluded to inquire about him.

"Is your husband away on business?" she began politely.

"Why, no. Didn't you know? Didn't your father tell you?"

Laurel shook her head. "No, father has told me nothing."

"He is not living. Laurel," gently Mrs. Morrison announced.

"Oh," said Laurel. "Of course," she went on, "I knew he wasn't really *away* on business, because of the drawers in the chiffonier being perfectly empty, and the closet beside yours, too, where you hung my things. But I didn't see any pictures of him around, so I thought perhaps you were separated."

"The portrait in the big gold frame in the living-room is a picture of him. Laurel, and that's a copy of it, in the silver frame on my dressing-table."

"Is *he* your husband?" exclaimed Laurel.

She had studied the portrait. The man in the portrait looked like a grandfather! He had long drooping mustaches, almost white, and the sockets of his eyes hung down like the eyes of a hunting-hound, Laurel had seen in the Maine woods once.

"Yes. Why?"

"He looks too old for *you!*"

"Does he? Well, he *was* older, but, oh, ever so kind, and the father of my dear boys, and," she added after a pause, "the father of my little girl, too."

"Your little girl?"

"Yes, Laurel, my only little girl. She died, before she was old enough to walk without holding tight onto one of my fingers."

"What was her name?"

"Carol."

"How old would she be?"

"About as old as you, I think."

"Did she have light hair, or dark?"

"Dark."

"Curly?"

"No, straight. Oh, how we did try to make it curl," laughed Mrs. Morrison.

"But I guess she didn't have freckles," said Laurel.

"Not *then*. But I think she would have had, when she grew up. She liked the sun, and out-of-doors. I'd have loved to have had her have ever so freckly a nose!"

"Do you *like* freckles?" Laurel exclaimed, wide-eyed, and amazed.

As easily as that, they wandered into the holy of holies of Helen Morrison's heart, and wandered out again.

4

When Mrs. Morrison had helped Laurel unpack her trunk on the first afternoon, she had been doubtful as to how her athletic young sons would get along with the little spic-and-span, bandbox girl she rather guessed Laurel to be. There were no stout boots, nor rough clothes of any sort among Laurel's things. There was a bathing-suit, but it was an elaborate fragile affair made of black satin, trimmed with orange. Excellent for exhibition on the beach, but it didn't look very appropriate for use in a certain deep black swimming-hole which the boys had discovered between two barnacled rocks. However, she needn't have worried.

The first night after dinner Con had inquired of Laurel, "Do you ride?"

It seemed there was a stable back of the house.

"I ride *some*."

"Can you swim?" Dane had asked.

"I swim a *little*."

To Mrs. Morrison's amazement, to the boys' amazement, too—and to their admiration besides—Laurel's "some" and "little" proved a great deal.

Next morning dressed in an old knickerbocker suit of Dane's (Laurel had never needed her riding-clothes in New York before), after she had ridden four or five times around the paddock back of the stable, she had called out, "Does he jump?" and the next time around she had taken one of the hurdles with perfect ease and familiarity.

It was the same with swimming. It didn't matter if her suit was satin, the swimming-hole didn't daunt her. She could dive better than Con! Laurel had taken swimming-lessons ever since she could remember. She had taken riding-lessons since she was eight. She had taken lessons in every sport which her mother considered fashionable and in which instructions could be bought.

"The funny thing is," said Con to Laurel the second day, "you don't play tennis."

But in games which required partners. Laurel had not had much experience. Solitaire sports were her specialty. However, she was pretty good at golf, she told Con. There had usually been a professional at the links connected with the summer hotels which her mother patronized.

"We'll try it," said Con, "and I'll teach you tennis."

He wouldn't acknowledge that he liked Laurel. None of the boys went as far as that. "But she isn't silly, and she isn't afraid of things!" he told his mother.

"They get along together beautifully, Stephen," said Helen Morrison to Laurel's father the night he came to take Laurel away.

It was after dinner. They were sitting in the garden terrace just outside the big room, where the portrait hung. Through the open windows, uncurtained towards the terrace, they could see Laurel seated with the two older of the boys at a table, busy over some sort of game with cards, with Michael stretched out comfortably at their feet.

"I've enjoyed every moment of her," Helen went on, gazing fondly at the group inside the room. "Only," and there was a sudden change in her voice, "it's brought home to me afresh what I've missed—all these years. Oh, we've had such fun together!" she broke off gaily. "Girls' sort of fun," she laughed; "doing each other's hair, for instance—trying on each other's hats—that sort of thing. Boys—men, couldn't understand. And her questions I Don't you love little girls' blunt questions? Darling things, I think, like awkward little colts and calves—oh. Laurel's a dear child, Stephen. I've kept pretending she was mine," she exclaimed lightly.

"Oh, Helen! if she only were!"

There wasn't a trace of lightness in Stephen's exclamation.

"I couldn't have equipped her any better for the present-day activities of a young girl's life than her own mother has done, Stephen," said Helen. "There doesn't appear to be a muscle or a bone in her body that has been neglected."

"I'm thinking about her soul," Stephen remarked.

"It hasn't lost any of its beauty yet, Stephen," Helen assured him. "She's as unspoiled a little girl as I know—so pleased (so genuinely pleased, too—you can tell by the shine in her eyes) at the least kindness or attention. And the combination in her of sophistication and innocence is a source of constant surprise to me—a source of constant joy, too. Oh, you needn't be afraid. So far the undesirable influences haven't hurt Laurel a bit."

"But she's getting older, Helen. Her youth and innocence cannot protect her always."

"Oh, I know, I know," agreed Helen; "I've thought of that, too. It's a pity. I'm so sorry, Stephen. Let her stay with me often—whenever you can. See them in there—all so happy. Don't take her to a hotel when she comes for the visits. Bring her to me here, or to the town house, if we've moved in."

5

Driving back to New York that night over the almost deserted road (it was late. "Very late for thirteen," Mrs. Morrison had laughed, as she had tucked Laurel into a warm coat of her own), Laurel , sat beside her father like a little stone image for the first ten minutes.

There was something exciting about the beautiful coat that wrapped her round so close. It was a little as if Mrs. Morrison herself held her, wrapped her round in her kindness. Every once in a while Laurel would rub her cheek against the soft fur of the high collar. It felt like Mrs. Morrison's hair the day after it had been washed, and she had let Laurel brush it, and twist it up, and stick the hairpins in. It *smelled* like it, too—fresh, clean like a flower-garden after rain. Laurel drew in great deep breaths of the soft brown sable. "It's Mrs. Morrison," she pretended with all the sentimentality of thirteen.

Gazing up into the sky from out of the fur collar, Laurel could see the full round moon above her. "She's following me to New York," she made-believe. "She's going to follow me wherever I go, always and always, and I can look up at her and see her whenever the moon is full, and tell her how lovely I think she is, and try to be like her. I shan't care so much if people *are* horrid after this."

"Well, Laurel," interrupted Stephen, "how did you get along?"

"All right."

"Was it very terrible?"

"Not very."

"How did you like the boys?"

"All right."

"And how did you like Mrs. Morrison?" Gazing up at the moon. Laurel replied fervently, "I think Mrs. Morrison is the loveliest lady I ever knew."

"Do you?" her father exclaimed; "oh, do you, Lollie, dear?"

Lollie! Suddenly Laurel stiffened inside the long coat. Lollie!

"I mean," she added, with the exaltation all gone out of her voice, "I mean next to—next to—" It had to be. She couldn't avoid the word—"next to my mother."

All the rest of the way back to the hotel Laurel didn't once glance up at the moon. How could she—oh, how could she have become a part of the picture on the screen, while her mother was still in the audience, out there, in the dark, looking on.

CHAPTER V

1

After Mrs. Dallas had said good-bye to Laurel, she retraced her steps along the narrow platform beside the train, and immediately sought refuge in the ladies' public dressing-room in the station. Standing in front of the long horizontal mirror with the row of wash-basins beneath, she removed her hat and veil, and leaning forward drew one of the basins full of steaming water. With her bare hands she bathed her smarting eyes and smeared cheeks. The hot water was as soothing as hot soup to a sore throat. She dried her face and hands on a piece of crepe paper from a roll near by. Afterwards, opening a little red leather case which she always carried with her, she laid it before her on the washstand, first blowing into it, once or twice, to remove a little of the loose pink powder that had shaken out of its container, and was as thick as dust in a carpet-sweeper.

Briskly, in a business-like fashion, Mrs. Dallas proceeded to remedy the damage wrought by her tears, working dexterously with various little sticks and tubes, without any attempt at concealment, apparently without the slightest self-consciousness, although just beside her a prim, school-teacherish-looking little woman, middle-aged, observed her operations with interest. Just when her cheeks presented their customary velvety appearance, her eyes suddenly welled up again with tears. She closed the lids tight. No use. The tears oozed out, streaked her cheeks again.

"Oh, darn it!" she whispered into the hollow of her hands as she pressed her fingers hard against her eyeballs. "Oh, Lollie, Lollie, darn it, darn it!"

Twice she was forced to repeat her operations, and at last gave up the struggle for perfection, satisfying herself with a bit of powder on her nose, trusting that the white veil would suffice to conceal her.

She had planned to spend an hour or two in the shops, take a sandwich and a cup of coffee in a candy-shop a little later, and go to a movie afterwards. It was wholly by accident that she ran across Alfred Munn.

The route she selected to the shops carried her through the outskirts of the wholesale merchandise district of the city. Alfred Munn's present business had something to do with leather or hides—or was it cotton—something of the sort. She ran across Alfred Munn (or rather he ran across her—he saw her before she saw him) at a restaurant.

It had occurred to Stella as she walked away from the station that a cup of coffee would probably help to brace her up better than anything else, and, as it was really time for lunch anyhow, she decided to drop into a certain restaurant she knew about, instead of the candy-shop farther uptown. It was a restaurant where Alfred Munn had taken Laurel and her to lunch one day two years ago. She hadn't seen him since. As she entered it, she observed that men predominated.

She hastened to the dressing-room at the rear. Stella Dallas felt as uncomfortable in the restaurant with her face all red and splotchy, as the school-teacherish little woman would have felt in her stocking-feet. It was with no thought of any man in particular that she set to work again to make herself presentable, now that she had herself under better control or, at least, with no serious thought of any man in particular. She was always playing with the possibility that some old admirer might run across her path at any moment, and always taking necessary precautions.

Prepared as her cheeks may have been, Stella was taken by surprise when somebody leaned across the little table which she had selected beside the wall-mirrors and drawled in a masculine voice, "Well!"

She knew it was Alfred Munn before she looked up. Nobody else in the world could say "Well," like that. All sorts of interesting implications were packed into the single exclamation.

She glanced up and replied briefly, her blue eyes sparkling at him, "Hello!"

She didn't like Ed Munn. Stephen had been right. He *was* cheap. It showed now that he wasn't dressed in his riding-clothes any more. But even if she didn't like him very much, she couldn't be horrid to him. Stella Dallas couldn't be horrid to anybody whose eyes flattered her like that!

"What are you doing here?" he asked in a kind of caressing tone, as irresistible to the lonely Stella as food by whomever offered if she were hungry.

"I'm waiting for *you*." her voice caressed back at him. Oh, a little harmless flirting was the one thing she needed to restore her wilted spirits!

Alfred Munn smiled at her, showing a row of little crooked yellow teeth. His face crackled up into a hundred pleased wrinkles. Attention from the opposite sex was as welcome to him as it was to Stella.

He drew out the chair opposite Stella, thinking, as he did so, "What have I got on for this afternoon anyhow? Only two appointments; I can cancel 'em." What he *said* was, as he sat down, "Where's the offspring?"

Stella thought, "Dear me! How thrilling! He's going to stay!" But out loud she said, "Just shipped her to New York."

"You alone?" Alfred Munn exclaimed. "Unattached? No string tied to you?"

Stella, pouting a little, looking pathetic on purpose, nodded. "All alone. No string. Not a thread."

Alfred Munn drew in a deep breath. Let it out audibly.

"My! This is my lucky day, I guess," he ejaculated. "We're going to have lunch together—you and I, and go to a show afterwards. Did you know it?"

Stella, casting down her eyes, and toying with the silver, shook her head. No. She didn't know it.

"Well," masterfully, "you know it now. Here, pass me that menu."

She obeyed with exaggerated docility. "Have your own way. I'm helpless when you're around. Do with me as you wish," her manner implied.

It pleased Alfred Munn. He summoned a waiter with an arrogant motion of his hand, tossed the menu aside, as wholly beneath his notice, and frowningly ordered cocktails—this was before prohibition—oysters, and soup. Then he leaned across the table and suddenly became all soft suavity. The contrast was effective.

"How've you been?" he asked.

"Oh, pretty well," Stella purred. Any one could make Stella purr who stroked her like that.

"How are things going?" he inquired in his terribly intimate manner.

"Oh, pretty well, I guess," she purred again, and glanced up, her big Delft-blue eyes gazing straight into Alfred Munn's little pig-like spots of brightness, rimmed round with the puffy lids.

"I don't care," Stella thought to herself in defense of the things she was allowing her bold eyes to imply to Alfred Munn. "It's only for to-day, and I'm perfectly aware of what he is—dissipated, rotten old thing, probably. Doesn't hurt me any if he is. I'm beyond hurting now. He's better than nobody."

Stella had almost forgotten what a cocktail tasted like. How it did bring back the good old happy days, when everybody admired and flattered, just as Alfred Munn was doing now. For he was doing *just* that to Stella—over-doing it a little. Well, she could stand a little over-doing in that line. It had been *so* long since any man had found her attractive! Or, at least, since any man had told her so. She had begun to fear that age had got a grip on her at last which she couldn't loosen, however much she strained. Men hated old women. Alfred Munn restored her self-confidence wonderfully. *He* found her pleasing. He found her desirable. He told her the very sight of her made him feel young again. Asked her how in the world she did it. How she managed to keep her wonderful peaches-and-cream appearance. She didn't look to *him* a day over twenty-five!

"Oh," thought Stella, feeling all warm and comforted inside, "if only he could see me in an evening gown!"

As she preceded him out of the restaurant she was as pleased with the present-moment excitement, the present-moment attentions, as a young girl of sixteen on the way to her first matinee with an admiring suitor. Her pleasure was almost as innocent too.

2

Alfred Munn selected for the afternoon's entertainment a popular musical farce. Stella adored a musical farce with all the bold gay costumes. The seats he bought were aisle seats—the best in the house, three rows from the front. As Stella settled herself for the two hours and a half of pleasure in store for her, she was keenly conscious of her nearness to the stage, to the orchestra. How good it did seem to be right down in the midst of things again! When the curtain rolled up on the first act amidst a loud fanfare of trumpets, which Stella could feel tingle inside her, she was filled with gratitude to Alfred Munn. Why, she calculated, already his kindness to her had cost him something like fifteen dollars—twenty possibly. How much were cocktails and wines now, anyhow, and Porterhouse steaks? She mustn't be disappointing to him. She mustn't edge away from Alfred Munn's overlap, ping arm and shoulder. She must remember her age. Nineteen can afford to be as stand-offish as it chooses, but not thirty-nine. Besides, in one way it was gratifying to Stella that Alfred Munn wanted to sit so close. She had been afraid of late that there was nothing but tiny wrinkles and double chins left of her. But there was—there was! Alfred Munn knew women. Alfred Munn made Stella feel that there was lots else left.

She talked and laughed, eyes shining, and cheeks hot and flushed beneath the powder. Occasionally Laurel's serious face, crowned with the unfamiliar toque with the berries on one side, interrupted, shoved itself between her and the stage, between her and Alfred Munn.

The toque made her look frightfully like a young lady. She was growing up. No doubt about that. Stella hadn't seen her cry since—she couldn't remember since when. Funny kid. Just got silent and horribly quiet instead of letting the tears of a year or two ago well up in her eyes and spill over. Of late she, Stella, was the one who did the crying for the two of them. But she mustn't get teary, *here now*, for heaven's sake!

Laurel would be about at New London now, Stella calculated. New Haven, Bridgeport later. New York pretty soon, walking up the long granolithic walk, with the bits of mica in it, sparkling like tiny stars beneath the white artificial light; looking for Stephen; seeing him; greeting him; sitting in a taxicab beside him. They always took a taxicab.

Queer, thought Stella, how the very sight of her present escort used to irritate Stephen. It would be interesting to Alfred Munn, she guessed, and flattering to him, too, if he had a notion how much he used to be discussed between Stephen and herself. Stephen was always making such queer mistakes about her little affairs, picking out somebody she really didn't care a straw about, like Alfred Munn, for instance, to get stuffy over, and remaining undisturbed by the attentions from men who *really* interested her. Alfred Munn, indeed! A riding-teacher! That was what he had been, in Milhampton seven years ago. The smartest women in town took lessons of him. So did Stella. And the smartest women in town were keen about him, or pretended to be. Naturally they weren't any of them seriously keen about Alfred Munn. The other women's husbands understood. But Stephen wouldn't. It was ridiculous, absurd. Stella told Stephen so dozens and dozens of times. But he would persist in making a mountain out of a molehill.

That was how Mrs. Holland described Stephen's attitude. There was no woman in Milhampton more the fashion than Mrs. Holland at that time. Stella had been immensely pleased by her friendship. Every word she uttered was to Stella like the wisdom of an oracle.

"Husbands need a lot of training, my dear," she had told Stella after a burst of confidences from Stella one afternoon. "Don't let yourself become a doormat.

Husbands don't respect doormats, in the long run. Teach him that you can look at another man without wanting to elope with him. And get him used to the idea that you aren't blind to every other masculine creature in the world but himself. Such an attitude keeps them lovers, makes them alert, attentive, my dear."

But it didn't seem to keep Stephen a lover. It didn't make Stephen alert and attentive. It worked just the other way with him.

3

These reflections did not possess Stella in the theater. It was later, alone on the train, returning to her beach hotel that she glanced into her past. She didn't allow herself to do so frequently. It didn't make her any happier. Things had been so rosy, so promising ten years ago—so far beyond her most extravagant girlhood dreams. And now—*now!* Resolutely she turned her thoughts to other things. She was to meet Alfred Munn again the following Saturday for lunch and another matinee. What should she wear? The sudden necessity of a new early-fall hat gave her a little thrill of delight.

There was nothing in the world Stella enjoyed more than a morning spent in Boston at the expensive uptown shops, pricing and trying on hats, followed by an afternoon in the downtown department stores buying buckram, wire, velvet, feathers, ornaments, flowers, and what-not, and the long inspiring day afterwards shut up in her room moulding with her clever fingers a copy of some little gem that a far-away artist in Paris had conceived.

When Stella said good-bye to Laurel, her plan to spend two hours in the shops had not been an exciting prospect to her. It was stupid to shop if you had nothing you had to buy. The chance meeting with Alfred Munn provided Stella with the necessary incentive to start the machinery of her creative genius going. She would have to have a new dress, too. Perhaps she could pick up some summer silk thing marked down, and pep it up with some black bead trimming, at present on an old chiffon evening gown of hers she scarcely ever wore. Bead trimming was being worn again this fall. Possibly it would be a good idea to overhaul her entire wardrobe immediately, even if it was early in the season. Men liked variety, and it looked as if Alfred Munn meant to see her rather often during Laurel's absence.

When he had put her aboard her train, he had told her that if she didn't object to leaving the seashore for the city frequently he was going to keep her from getting lonely, if she'd let him, while the kid was away. She wished he wouldn't call Laurel "the kid" and the "offspring."

She wished his linen collar hadn't been grimy round the top edge. She wished he hadn't chanced to omit shaving that morning. A man who shaved every morning without reference to the day's program, and put on a clean collar without reference to the old one, was one of Stella's tests of a gentleman. Alfred Munn never was guilty of any such offenses when he was the vogue in Milhampton. Yes, yes, Stephen was right. Second-rate—that was the term he used to apply to Alfred Munn. Well, she didn't care. It didn't rob orchestra seats at the most popular shows in town of their attraction for Stella, or luncheon-tables in the most popular restaurant in town of their luxury and joy. Alfred Munn was going to take her for lunch next Saturday to the newest and most expensive hotel in the city.

4

Stella spent that evening packing her trunks (there remained two old-fashioned hump-backed affairs), and again it was early morning before she lay down in the battered white iron bed to go to sleep.

Stella never stayed on at the expensive summer resorts after Laurel went. Fifteen miles nearer Boston, along a sandy beach, there was a stretch of board-walk, with the ocean on one side, and on the other, a row of cheap amusement places. Behind this row of amusement places there was a nest of lodging-houses. By occupying a room in one of these houses, and taking her meals outside, Stella could save enough money over what it cost her to live at the expensive summer hotel, to buy several Permanents for Laurel, and a wrist-watch, and a fur coat, too, if Stephen still persisted in books.

You'd think, perhaps, you wouldn't have to economize on three hundred and fifty dollars a month, if there was only yourself and a child to take care of. But gracious, try it! Try it with a little queen like Laurel to bring up and educate, and give half a chance to. When a twelfth of your yearly income went to the private school your little queen attended, for five days a week; and two-twelfths to a decent hotel roof to put over her head in the summer; and several other twelfths for a decent roof to put over her head in the winter (Laurel couldn't live in a tenement), and a big chunk was eaten out of another twelfth by riding-tickets, at the rate of fifty dollars for twenty rides, and completely gobbled up by private dancing-lessons, and private golf and swimming lessons, and heaven knows what not; I tell you what, you have to stretch every single penny you have left to clothe the child properly, to say nothing of yourself, and your own rags.

"I suppose forty-two hundred dollars a year sounds plenty enough to Stephen," Stella said to her old friend Effie McDavitt. "But Stephen and I have probably got different ideas about how the child should be brought up. Well, I'll never ask him for any more. I'll never go groveling to Stephen Dallas for money as long as I live! I'll tell you that! No, sir-ee! I've got some pride, even though he has acted as if I hadn't any feelings."

The boarding-houses at Belcher's Beach, as the amusement boulevard was called, were not attractive. The people who patronized them were not attractive either. The women were loud-voiced and loud-mannered, and spent a good deal of time walking to and from the beach, in bathrobes and canvas sandals; and the masculine element, if one existed, was likely to be found sitting in his shirt-sleeves on the boarding-house porch, ready to make remarks to the robed ladies as they came trooping up the steps munching peanuts or popcorn cakes.

Stella did not confide this particular economy of hers to Laurel. Laurel mustn't know that her mother mixed up with such society. Stella didn't in fact mix up with it, but Laurel mustn't know that her mother even slept under the same roof with people of that sort.

Laurel, at thirteen, was not a prolific letter-writer, but whatever messages she did send Stella she directed to the summer hotel, where she supposed her mother was to remain. These were forwarded by the clerk at the hotel, according to Stella's instructions, to Milhampton, care of a certain Effie McDavitt. Stella didn't object to Effie's knowing about the cheap lodging-house—poor worn-out, down-at-the-heel Effie. Effie was the only one of her girlhood friends whom Stella hadn't managed to lose. She had tried to lose Effie. Had succeeded for a while, too, during the height of her social success in Milhampton. But Effie hadn't stayed lost. Effie was the sort of woman whom you can grind your heel on in the dirt and it won't kill her loyalty. Like a worm. Cut her feelings of friendship for you in two, and the parts will still wriggle.

Of course Stella might have gone back to the little red cottage house outside Milhampton during Laurel's absence and stayed with her father, if she could have endured the eccentricities of his old age and the lack of any attempt at a self-respecting existence. (He let the hens come right into the kitchen now, and he'd dragged his miserable bed in there, too—all rags, and no sheets.) And Stella *could* endure much to save a little money, but the danger of discovery was great. Ever since her marriage Stella had been struggling to cover up her early connections with the little red cottage house. She had an idea she had succeeded fairly well, too.

At Belcher's Beach Stella never met anybody whom she knew, nor who knew her. It was only fifteen miles away from the big summer hotel where she ana Laurel had spent the season, but it was an entirely different world. The guests from the big summer hotel never left the automobile highway, a half a mile inland, to seek out Belcher's Beach. There was another amusement boulevard of bigger proportions and of less tawdry appearance a few miles farther on.

This wasn't the first time Stella had successfully hidden herself at Belcher's Beach, during Laurel's absence. She had tested its advantages for some three or four years now. It *had* advantages. For one thing, it was near enough to Boston so that when the "dirt-commonness of the hole" got too unbearable she could dress up in her best clothes and escape to the Boylston Street shops without the price of the ticket hurting too much.

It was cheaper than living in Boston itself. Take just the food, for instance. Stella had always liked hot frankforts embedded in a soft biscuit, slimy with mustard. There were several night-lunch-carts at Belcher's Beach. At Belcher's Beach it was not conspicuous, in the least, for a lady to buy a meal at the door of one of the night-lunch-carts, and carry it away, hot, in a damp brown paper, under her arm.

It was not conspicuous to return from Boston at a late hour with Ed Munn after one of his grand parties. It was just as well, Stella supposed, not to be seen with Ed Munn too much, after all the silly talk there had been about him and her in Milhampton years ago. Even if she could have afforded to stay on at the expensive hotel, she would have been obliged to have foregone too many parties with Ed. There were some compensations, and, ostrich-wise, she stuck her head in the sand of Belcher's Beach and proceeded to enjoy them.

One late Saturday night Ed Munn, who had seen Stella decently inside the front door of the boardinghouse at Belcher's Beach, after one of his parties in town, had asked her with an insinuating smile, glancing towards the stairs, "Sure you can unlock your door alone?"

Stella hadn't taken offense. Ed was like that.

"Of course I can, you goose." She flashed back. "Do I look feeble?"

You can just bet she didn't let any masculine escort trail up any inside stairs behind her! Some women in the boarding-house did!

Too bad Ed had that common streak in him. Some men would know when and where it was good taste to spring a joke of that sort.

Stella was blissfully unaware, as she climbed the stairs alone to her room that night, that at the same moment, a touring car, with two excited women in its rear seat, was slipping smoothly away from under the arc light that hung on the tall pole outside Stella's boarding-house.

The automobile had stopped under the light for only a moment. The chauffeur had wanted to find out how much gasoline he had. It was unfortunate for Stella that the car hadn't stopped longer. The two occupants in the back of the car had seen Alfred Munn follow Stella Dallas into the boarding-house, but they hadn't seen him come out!

One of the women in the back of the car was Mrs. Henry Holland. The other was Mrs. Kay Bird. They both lived in Milhampton in the winter. Mrs. Kay Bird occupied rooms directly opposite Stella in the same apartment hotel.

"It was she! I can swear to it!" said Mrs. Henry Holland, as she clutched the arm of her companion.

"It was he. I know him anywhere!" said Mrs. Kay Bird, as she clutched back.

"Only ten more days," said Stella, half an hour later as she knelt in the dark by her bed. "Gosh! how I miss you, Lollie."

CHAPTER VI

1

The red cottage house where Stella had lived as a young girl, and until she married Stephen Dallas, was located in an outlying district of Milhampton. The district was known as Cataract Village. The little settlement of houses was named after the Cataract Mills, and the mills were named after a fall of water hidden inside them somewhere, over which they crouched like some great vampire and sucked the strength that made their wheels go round.

Cataract Village was the home of the Cataract Mill employees. Stella's father had worked in the mills ever since he was a boy. Stella was born in one of the ugly three-deckers, close to the mill gate. She was ten years old when her father bought one of the red cottage-houses on the river-bank. She had been proud of the cottage then, and proud of it, too, as she grew older. On each side of the little porch over the front door, every spring, for years, Stella planted morning-glories and wild-cucumber vine, which climbed a string trellis of her own making.

The first time Stephen went to see Stella at the red cottage her vines were profuse with leaf and blossom. She had trained the docile vines to run all over the picket fence that surrounded the little house, and had shrouded the back porch with them; had shrouded with them, too, a latticed summer-house which stood in the side yard. Stella had copied the summer-house, with much the same genius with which she copied hats or dresses, from a summer-house she had seen in a garden in Milhampton across the river. Stella's summer-house was made of plasterer's laths painted white, and criss-crossed. The summer-house in the garden at Milhampton, designed by a landscape-gardener, had been covered with Dorothy Perkins roses. But sunlight shining through the chinks of Stella's morning-glories and wild-cucumbers, was just as prettily dappled with shadows, as sunshine shining through rose-vines. At night the darkness was just as dense inside Stella's summer-house—a little denser, perhaps. Stella had been particular to plant her seeds thick. Inside Stella's summer-house there hung a Gloucester hammock!

The first night Stephen called on Stella, he had sat in the hammock alone, while Stella had curled herself up on the low step of the summer-house, leaning her head against one of the upright posts, so that the searchlight moon could shine full upon her face, and her caller could observe from the darkness of the hammock how pretty she was.

She was pretty—she was very pretty in those days. But it was not Stella's bright eyes and bright cheeks that Stephen Dallas thought about most, after that first call. It hadn't been quite dark when he arrived. Before he was sure that the red cottage was the house where Stella lived, he had noticed the morning-glories and wild-cucumber vines.

When later that first evening he discovered that Stella had planted the vines herself, had built much of the summer-house, driven all the nails in the diamond lattice-work, done all the painting, it had set him to thinking. Out of a bundle of plasterer's laths and a handful or two of common little seeds, she had created a charming spot. As he leaned back in the Gloucester hammock, and gazed at Stella on the step below him, the simplicity of her setting, the absence from it of everything that required accumulated wealth to possess, had been soothing and comforting to Stephen, suffering as he was—suffering as he had been for the last year and a half.

2

Stephen was young then, barely twenty-three, but for eighteen months he had felt nothing but the resignation of old age, and the bitterness of disappointed old age. It had never occurred to Stephen Dallas that disgrace, disaster, utter and complete ruin, could befall *him*. He had taken it for granted always that he would fulfill, to a greater or less degree, his expectations for himself, and his family's and friend's expectations for him, too. Whether as a doctor or lawyer, or business man of ability, he didn't know which, before he went East to school, but in some capacity he would fill a position of responsibility in his home city. It had always been understood that when Stephen's education was completed, he would return to that home city, where he had been born, and where his father had been born before him, and continue to add honor to the family reputation.

It was a reputation to be proud of. The Dallases of Reddington, Illinois, were a respected and honored family. The Dallas house, built by Stephen's grandfather, was quiet and unostentatious in appearance, but solid, substantial—a big, square brick affair, painted dull brown. There was something so solid and substantial about everything connected with the Dallases, that people in Reddington supposed them to be infallible, as immune to panics and market fluctuations as an oak to the varying antics of the elements.

This attitude of the people toward the Dallases was partly responsible for their ruin. Stephen's father prized and treasured his reputation for indestructibility. To a man of his special brand of pride, it was galling to allow his fellow citizens even to suspect that the roots of the oak tree were not as healthy as the proud and upstanding trunk signified. And so it was not until the great tree fell—was pulled over by its own weight, and lay sprawling on the ground, a mammoth and pitiful wreck, for every curious passer-by to gape at—that the decayed and rotten condition of the roots was discovered by the astonished public.

When the brief telegram from home reached Stephen (he had completed his college course by this time and had nearly completed his post-graduate course—he had decided to follow in his father's steps and become a lawyer) the message gave no details. Simply stated the fact of his father's sudden death and summoned him home immediately.

It was not until he was within a few hours of Reddington that he learned of the manner of his father's death. He read it in a Chicago paper.

His father had committed suicide! He had locked himself up in his office downtown, one night, and shot himself with a revolver!

"For a number of years," the article stated, "Mr. Stephen Dallas, who was a lawyer and one of Reddlngton's most respected citizens, has acted as trustee for various estates, and sole legal and financial advisor for a number of charitable institutions. It is feared that the various funds entrusted to him may have suffered and an investigation of his affairs is now under way."

Stephen learned upon his arrival home that the fears hinted at in the papers were justified. His one desire was to escape, to get away from everybody and everything familiar as soon as possible, after the details of burial were disposed of. He had no forgiveness, no charity, for his father. He told his mother and his older sister Fanny that he wished they could dispose of the ruined thing his father had made of the Dallas reputation as easily as they could dispose of the ruined thing he had made of his body. But no, the reputation they must wear tied round their necks for everybody to see, and stare at, and keep away from. Obliged as he was to bear his father's name (why had his parents handicapped him thus?) he could never hope to succeed in any large way, he said; for who would ever trust a man with the name of Stephen Dallas? It spelled suicide and dishonor now.

His mother tried in a weak, feminine sort of way, Stephen thought, to excuse his father's act. He had never let them even guess at home, she said, that the big house and all the servants, the stable full of expensive cars, and the proportionate demands in way of clothes and entertaining, and contributions to various charitable institutions, were eating into his capital—had been for years.

But why hadn't he? What kindness had it been to them? It was beyond Stephen's young comprehension that his father, like some weak, inexperienced bank clerk, could be tempted into "borrowing" even a portion of the funds entrusted to him.

"Borrowing!" That is what his father's friends and associates called it, when they talked to Stephen. They tried to soften the facts to him, these kind, old, pitying men, who felt sorry to look upon the destruction of so young a man's career, Stephen supposed. Well, there was one satisfaction. Thank heaven, his father hadn't taken liberties with the legacies left to him and Fanny by their grandfather, nor touched the solid securities packed away years ago in his mother's safe-deposit box. By scraping everything together, none of the estates which had been entrusted to his father need to suffer at all. The kind old men told Stephen that he and his mother and sister were under no obligation. Stephen was glad that his mother and Fanny felt, just as he did, that the only thing for them to do was to wipe out his father's dishonesty as far as possible.

Stephen was glad, too, that his mother and Fanny agreed with him that it would be unbearable to continue to live in Reddington. As soon as the big brown house, and the automobiles, and the servants were disposed of, they would disappear as quietly as possible. Fanny and his mother would go to Chicago and conceal themselves there as best they could. There would be little for them to live on. Only the insurance policy. Stephen would, of course, get a job somewhere, as soon as he could. Oh, no, he wouldn't finish at the law school! He couldn't afford the time. He never wanted to see the law school again! He never wanted to see anything again, or anybody that recalled to him his old bright hopes and ambitions, he said.

"Oh, no, least of all Helen Dane," he shuddered, replying to his mother's timid reminder that Helen had sent her card to him, with a message written on it to come and see her.

Stephen was thankful that there had never been anything serious between him and Helen. There might have been. It had seemed last summer as if there probably would have been, but not now–*never* now! There was no girl in Reddington, no girl anywhere, whom he would ever ask to bear the name of Dallas.

3

Stephen first heard of the. Cataract Mills in Milhampton, Massachusetts, through an advertisement in a paper. He answered the advertisement. He had never been to Milhampton. He had no friends, no acquaintances there, that he knew of. It was well removed from Reddington. It would serve his purpose as well as any other place in the United States. His mother had begged him not to put the ocean between himself and her, when he had mentioned Australia or South America.

Upon his arrival in Milhampton, Stephen hunted up a lodging-house in Cataract Village close to the mills,, and hired a room. He worked hard for his eighteen dollars a week. But there was little joy in his work. Even the raise in his position, and pay, at the end of the first three months, gave him no thrill. What was the use of his rising in the world? Wasn't oblivion what he desired more than anything else? Wasn't the feature that he liked best about his new job, the fact that it hid him, covered him up? None of the men who ate breakfast and supper with him–who softened their bread-crusts in their coffee, and prepared their meat and potatoes as Stephen had seen the dog's meat and potatoes prepared at home, chopped all up and covered with gravy–had heard of Stephen Dallas of Reddington. Success, too many raises, would mean exposure finally, opening up the old wound again. Stephen had suffered enough for a while.

Stephen believed he would suffer always. But he didn't take into consideration his youth. There is something about twenty-three that struggles and fights all by itself–never mind how indifferent the soul, how sick the body–and accomplishes its purposes and designs without help. The same month that Stephen's mother's age came to her rescue, Stephen's youth came to *his*. Early in September, before a year had passed since the Dallas oak had fallen, death delivered Mrs. Dallas from her suffering. It was two or three weeks before his mother died that Stephen met Stella.

He met her at a church-sociable, in the vestry of the Congregational Church in Cataract Village. He had gone to the church sociable with the shipping-clerk at the mills, who had told him, with a wink, that he had met some peaches there at the last shindy, and invited him to come along, if he wanted to. Stephen had never in his life before passed a whole year practically void of feminine society.

It so happened that the night before the shipping-clerk invited Stephen to the church sociable, Stephen had drifted into a musical show downtown. The musical show started him to thinking about Helen Dane.

All the way back to Mrs. Bean's lodging-house he had dwelt upon Helen's loveliness, longed, as he didn't suppose he could ever long again, for an hour with her. A wave of despair had swept over him. Helen Dane was miles away, barriered and forbidden now.

Stephen had fallen to sleep in his bare, bleak bedroom very miserable and unhappy. But in reality his state of mind was healthier, more normal than it had been since his father had died, and that night Stephen's youth danced a little delighted jig of triumph on the dingy pillow-case beside him as he slept.

4

Stella Martin was an acknowledged belle in Cataract Village. Her lips were cherry-red, her cheeks peach-blossom pink, and without paint and powder in those days. She had, too, as her girl friends expressed it, "stacks of style." Stella Martin could drape a straight piece of cloth about her hips and shoulders, and it would assume fashionable lines all by itself! She far outshone the other young girls in Cataract Village. She was far better educated than the other girls. Stella had gone all the way through the high school, and graduated in a white dress with ruffles. When Stephen met Stella she was completing a course at the State Normal School on the other side of the river.

Not that Stella meant to make teaching a life-work! By no means! But it happened that next to the State Normal School there was located a technical school for young men. Stella had heard that students at the two institutions of learning sometimes made friendships that led to an interchange of ceremonies that sounded attractive to her.

Stella was ambitious. She couldn't help but see she was different from the girl friends of her childhood. Most of them were content to take a job in the weaving-rooms at the mills, as soon as they had finished the ninth grade, or a year or two in the high school; or else to marry some raw, half-awake young man, from the mills, and live in one of the Cataract Village three-deckers, and have children, and children, and children! Not Stella, however! Nothing like that for Stella Martin!

There was a little brown spot on Stella's neck. It showed when she wore summer dresses cut in a low V in front. She was on the point of having it removed when a certain old woman, a sort of halfwitch, told her it was a sign that some day she would make a brilliant marriage. So Stella kept her little brown spot, and though she laughed and flirted with almost every young man who admired her, and generously let them hold her hand, and take advantage of the dark, she had no notion of marrying in a hurry.

Stella had a streak of common sense in her, and she didn't leave it entirely to the magic power of the brown spot upon her neck to bring about the brilliant marriage. After providing herself with a few possible candidates for the marriage, the enterprising Stella spent long laborious hours making the yard surrounding the red cottage attractive, with morning-glory vines and wild-cucumber; and built herself a little temple that was very becoming to her type of beauty; and when the young men from the technical school came, in their clean collars, and dark suits, with beautiful creases down the front legs of their trousers, to call on Miss Martin, she usually chanced to be sitting in her little shrine. Therefore, during the spring and summer and early fall these young men seldom caught a glimpse of her mother in the ugly mouse-colored wrapper and flat shoes shuffling about in the kitchen, washing dishes, or mixing bread. They never had a chance to discover that the red cottage lacked a diningroom. Later, after Stella's charms had worked their blinding enchantment, it was her theory that the skeletons inside the house were less to be feared.

5

The first night that Stephen Dallas went to see Stella she exerted herself more than usual in behalf of her caller, for though he was one of the spurned Cataract Mill employees, she was aware that he was as far ahead of the technical school students of her acquaintance, as to requirements for a brilliant marriage, as the technical school students were far ahead of the Cataract Village young men.

Stella had an eye for details. This Mr. Dallas, she observed, wasn't too spic-and-span. He didn't look as if he had just stepped out of the barber's shop round the corner, and he didn't smell so. His cheeks didn't shine. His collars didn't shine, and his clothes seemed to have been worn by him long enough to fall naturally into *his* lines, instead of retaining those of the wax dummy's with the black mustache in the gentlemen's furnishing-shop on the corner of Main and Webster Streets downtown. When he leaned forward his waistcoat (but Stella called it vest) clung to him, instead of sticking out and making caves and caverns, in which glimpses of lining and suspenders could be seen; and straight across the vest, rather low-down, where it wrinkles a little (just where it ought to wrinkle when a man leans forward), Stella observed the slender watch-chain made of gold and platinum shafts, linked together.

She observed, too, Mr. Dallas's handkerchief. He had pulled it out of his pocket and offered it to her to sit on, when she insisted upon occupying the low step of the summer-house. She had taken it from him just to feel of it. It was made of finest linen. It had a narrow hemstitched edge, and hand-embroidered letters in the corner.

"What's S stand for, Mr. Dallas?" Stella had asked with the time-worn coyness of her sex when first touching upon so intimate a subject as first names.

"Stephen." Stephen had replied shortly, from the Gloucester hammock.

"Stephen, Stephen," Stella had repeated two or three times—in a dainty, sort of experimental fashion, as if she were tasting some new kind of candy. "Stephen." Then, "It's nice. I like it," she exclaimed and glanced up at Stephen from under her long lashes.

"Really? Do you?" Stephen had laughed, just a little disconcerted.

Stella liked the way he said, "Really?" and "Do you?" and later, "Delightful," and "Int'resting." He spoke like an actor on the stage, she thought.

When Stella discovered that her caller was a college graduate, and a college graduate from the same university which Harold Miller and Spencer Chisholm had attended, as well as a half-dozen other young Milhampton blue-bloods, who lived on the other side of the river, and whom Stella knew by sight and reputation, and by their fine houses on upper Webster Street, she was aware that this Mr. Dallas was the biggest opportunity she had ever had.

You might have thought she would have been a little awed, but Stella had confidence in her personal charms. Experience had convinced her that the same upward glances, intimacies, reservations, shynesses, boldnesses, what-not, were attractive to the genus "young man" whatever his species. When Stephen Dallas bade Stella good-bye that first night, he had held her willing hand a moment longer than is conventional and had asked if he could come again.

Later, when Stella went to bed, she tipped the little high square mirror on her bureau, well forward and gazing up into it, at her bare, fair expanse of gleaming neck and shoulders, she placed her fore-finger on the little brown beauty-spot and pressed it gently.

"I wonder," she whispered.

6

The distance between Mrs. Bean's lodging-house and the little red cottage was only a quarter of a mile. It took Stephen less than ten minutes to walk it. Mrs. Bean's boarding-house was an impossible place in which to spend the evening. The walks around and about the boarding-house had come to seem impossible, too. So also had the bare, white-lighted, white-walled reading-room at the Milhampton Public Library.

Ever since Stephen had come to Milhampton (up to the time he met Stella), each night, when he finished his supper in the boarding-house dining-room, he was faced with the problem of killing two and a half hours somehow till a civilized hour for sleep arrived. But after he met Stella, and found the straight, easy way that led to the red cottage, there was no more problem as to how to spend his evenings—at least as to how he wanted to spend them.

If Stephen's mother hadn't died just when she did; and if, on top of that, Stephen's sister Fanny hadn't received, in reply to an application she had made to teach in a girls' boarding-school in Japan, summons to sail immediately, Stephen's infatuation would probably have burned itself out before he was in a position to consider additional financial burdens of any sort.

Suddenly Stephen found himself free and unfettered. There was no more need to send weekly checks to Chicago. There was no more need to send letters there, or to go there from time to time himself. Stephen was entirely cut off from his old associations, his laboring boat had lost even its dragging anchor, and was touching the shores of a country on the other side of the earth.

CHAPTER VII

1

Stephen married Stella in January, four months after he first saw her. He thought he loved her. Most sincerely he thought he loved her. He desired to be with her—terribly, terrifyingly—more than he had ever desired to be with any girl.

Moreover, he felt very tenderly towards her. He was aware of her limitations, of her little crudities, but what if she did make a few mistakes in grammar, a few mistakes in taste, occasionally. She was wonderfully sweet-tempered, always amiable, always gay, as easily pleased as a child, as easily guided, he believed.

Once, when he corrected her for one of her grammatical offenses (she *would* say "somewheres "; and "would of" for "would have"; and "got *a*" for "got *to*"—"got a-laughing," "got a-going "; and "lay" for "lie"; and "how does it suit," and "how do you like," without an object), she replied good-naturedly, "That's right, Mr. Harvard of Bawston, teach me to talk like you do. I'm crazy to learn."

Stephen thought that he could make her over, rub down the rough edges once they were married, once he had her alone to himself. Alone, to himself! Blinding possibility! Well, well, he must use his head, too!

Of course she was different from the girls he used to know. But he was different from the man he used to be. He required somebody different. Stephen did not want a girl to step down to him. Stephen did not want pity from the woman he married. Stella was not stepping down to him. Stella did not pity him.

When he first told her about his father, she replied, lightly, laughingly, "Mercy, I don't care what your father did, Stephen, nor your great-grandfather either." Then, with disarming honesty, "Gracious, you'd never have looked at poor me unless something had knocked you off your high horse."

No girl who belonged to Stephen's former existence would look upon a hundred and fifty dollars a month as a fortune. Stella did. Nor upon five rooms and a bath in an apartment house in the upper Webster Street district in Milhampton, as a palace. Stella did. Nor upon himself, dethroned, cast out and disgraced, as still a prince. Stella did.

Stephen experienced no crude and sudden awakening. During the first year of their married life, there were surprises for him, gentle shocks almost every day, but nothing shattering. For instance, he was amazed to discover how little education a girl can absorb, and go through a high school and two years of normal school besides. Why, Stella didn't know Thackeray from George Eliot!

"Oh, I suppose I learned about those old fellows once, but you know how things of that sort slip in and out, unless they're dinged in everlastingly."

But didn't normal schools "ding in" such things? Apparently not. Stephen had been counting on the normal-school experience. He had dwelt with emphasis upon it when he had first written his sister Fanny in far-away Japan, about Stella.

It was another shock to Stephen to discover how little interest his precious resurrected library aroused in Stella. Once before they were married she had told him she would simply adore to live in a room with books to the ceiling! But her only passion, as far as books were concerned, seemed to be in their decorative quality. One day she spent three hours changing Stephen's careful arrangement of his books, so that all the bindings of one color should be grouped together, irrespective of subject. One evening, when Stephen started to read out loud to her from one of his favorite authors, in an attempt to lure her inside the books, she told him good-naturedly, for goodness' sake not to spout any more of that dead, old-fashioned, high-brow stuff to her. It gave her the fidgets.

She had no love at all for music, it appeared, although during the short period of their courtship she told Stephen she was "crazy about it," and in fact seemed to him to be. She was a beautiful dancer. "I just can't keep still when there's a tune going on." But after her first real musical concert with Stephen, one Saturday night several weeks after their marriage (Boston artists often came to Milhampton), she frankly confessed herself as horribly bored. A violin made her want to scream. It was so squeaky, like filing finger-nails with a steel file, she thought. Of course if musical concerts, Kneisel quartettes and the like were "the thing," she was game for them. But really a good vaudeville show (movies were then in their infancy) was much more entertaining. And a good play, where you saw modern actors, kept you so much better up-to-date, and rubbed the green moss off you in rolls. The beauty of out-of-doors had no attraction for her, nor flowers either, her morning-glories and wild cucumbers notwithstanding. She spent a good deal of time outdoors, walking; not, however, for the physical exhilaration of it, but simply "to reduce" (even then Stella was inclined to be a little plump) or to save the price of a car-fare, which she usually invested in candy. She was always nibbling at candy.

Often during the first few months of his marriage, grave doubts and misgivings assailed Stephen, but he was able to send them slinking away usually by comparing his present existence with that of a year ago. A year ago his evenings had been awful stretches of loneliness and unloveliness. Now each night there was a very pretty and always good-natured Stella waiting for him in a little sweet-smelling apartment; and after his evening meal there were distant sounds, far from unpleasing to him, of running water and rattling dishes, as he sat smoking and reading in his old Morris chair, wrapped round with his books and his rugs and a few treasured pieces of furniture unburied from a storehouse in Reddington.

Later, there was somebody sitting on the arm of his Morris chair, pressing against his shoulder, somebody soft and warm and alive, and his—all his, to do with as he pleased. No; he was not sorry that he had married Stella.

2

If time had not been steadily at work performing Its gentle cure upon Stephen, he might never have been sorry he had married Stella. But old hopes, old ideals began to reassert themselves. In spite of himself, gradually, slowly, Stephen became interested in his job at the Cataract Mills. More than once that Spring, Stella, coming in from the kitchen of the little apartment after the supper dishes had been put away, found Stephen poring over one of the sheepskin-bound volumes from the bottom shelf of the bookcases he had had built around the living-room, his precious Trollope or Meredith (Lord, what did he find in those old birds?) pushed aside, discarded.

The sheepskin-bound volumes were Stephen's law books. He told Stella he wanted to satisfy a curiosity he had, as to the legal right or wrong of certain affairs at the Cataract Mills. Stephen was in the Complaint Department at the mills at that time. This curiosity of Stephen's percolated through the man immediately above him, and through the next man, and the next, and the next, and so on to the general manager finally. Once the general manager discovered Stephen, it was every night *then* that he pored over the law-books.

Stella did not begrudge the late nights Stephen spent with the big volumes.

"Gracious," she had exclaimed, eyes aglint, when Stephen confided to her that the general manager had suggested that he pass his bar examination, so as to be able to assist in the legal end of the business, if occasion arose. "Gracious, a lawyer! My! Won't I feel just grand? Oh, Stephen, I knew I'd picked a winner. I wouldn't be a bit surprised if I found myself a governor's wife some day, or a president's! Gosh, wouldn't I be thrilled?"

"Oh, Stella. Not 'Gosh!' Please."

"Oh, well—Jiminy then—What's the diff? Lord, I'm excited!"

"Poor Stella," thought Stephen. "Poor Stephen, too!" For it occurred to him suddenly, sickeningly, gazing at Stella, listening to Stella, that there were two reasons now instead of one a year ago why he should avoid the smiles and favors of success.

3

But he didn't. He couldn't. Much in the same way as water seeks its own level, so Stephen had a level he, too, involuntarily sought. He had been born with the love of success running in his veins and it wouldn't be denied.

Mr. Palmer, the general manager of the Cataract Mills, became very much interested in Stephen Dallas. He had no son of his own; he had no protege in whom to feel pride and pleasure. He could well feel pride and pleasure in Stephen. Stephen was by nature very adaptable, very approachable. His father's act had only temporarily crippled his graceful self-confidence. He was tall and slight, more aristocratic than rugged in appearance; forehead high, eyes well-set, chin and mouth strong and distinctive. His dark, close-cut hair grew thick on top of his head, but receded on either side like so many American boys still in their twenties. The mustache, restrained and close-cut, which he had allowed to grow when he first came to Milhampton, in order to make him forget whom he had been before, gave him a foreign look.

"English," delightedly whispered some of the Milhampton women, to whom everything English was desirable.

Mr. Palmer suggested his name for membership at the Milhampton City Club; at the River Country Club; introduced him to a group of young lawyers. Stephen ran across some old college acquaintances, some old law-school contemporaries. Swiftly, with amazing speed old lines of communication were established between himself and the world to which he belonged. The impression he made upon Milhampton was distinctly favorable.

One day Mrs, Palmer invited Stephen and his wife to dinner. Others invited Stephen and his wife to dinner. Stephen became very anxious to feel pride in Stella, now that he had begun to feel pride again in himself. Stella became very anxious that he should feel pride in her. To appear the lady Stephen's wife should have been born became Stella's greatest ambition. On the first few occasions when she appeared with Stephen before the footlights of the social life in Milhampton—a stage she had gazed upon with longing eyes for years—she would do nothing, say nothing, almost think nothing, until it was first approved by Stephen. At first she invited his criticism, responded with eagerness to his constant drilling and grilling, welcomed his slightest suggestion. Of course she made progress. She was a clever mimic. At first Stephen had great hopes for Stella.

4

But success went to Stella's head like wine, even a small amount of success. Stella never became the belle she thought she did in Milhampton society, but she was, for a period, received and accepted by certain of its high prelates and officials, for Stephen's sake. It puffed her all up; it filled her with disastrous self-confidence. Within a period of a few weeks the limelight of recognition made of the soft, pliable clay Stella had been in Stephen's hands, something hard and brittle that would fly to pieces at his slightest touch.

Stella's first dance at the River Club was a bitter occasion for Stephen. She, a stranger, an invited guest of Mrs. Palmer's, had allowed one man to dance with her for the entire last half of the evening. Afterwards in their bedroom, when Stephen spoke to her about it, to his amazement she laughed and scoffed.

"Oh, gracious, Stephen, don't think you can give me pointers on how to treat a man at a dance! There are some things *I* know more about than you, my dear."

It was when Stella began to think that there were some things she knew more than Stephen, and to act upon that superior knowledge, that the seed of the trouble that ended so disastrously for her first began to grow.

"But, Stella, for *you*, a stranger, to dance so much with one man is conspicuous."

"Of course! Of course, it's conspicuous," Stella replied. "Oh, I know what I'm about, stupid! That man was Spencer Chisholm! Gracious, think of it! *The* Chisholms, Stephen! Think of it! An affair between *me* and Spencer Chisholm!" Her eyes sparkled.

Stephen turned away. It was going to be as difficult to stamp out Stella's vulgarity as to rid a lawn of the persistent dandelion once it gets its roots down. Stephen despised kow-towing.

"*The* Chisholms! My dear Stella, I hope you'll avoid that attitude toward people hereafter. You're my wife now."

"And can't look at another man?" she flashed.

"That isn't the point."

"Mercy," she went right on, "I can't help it if a man wants to dance with me. I should think you'd be pleased to have your wife popular. Most men would be. Most men—"

"I'm not pleased to have you talked about. Please don't give any one occasion to again, Stella."

"Good Lord, Stephen, you're not going to turn out to be the jealous kind, I hope, if another man looks at me."

Stephen winced.

"I hate a jealous man," she went on. "I always have!" And she threw down her comb upon the dressing-table. It screeched as it struck the plate-glass protection.

Stephen winced again. Throwing things! His wife! Accusing him of jealousy! Very quietly he went out into the hall, and stood a moment in the darkness, waiting till his jarred nerves stopped tingling.

"I must be patient," he thought. "It isn't her fault. It is only that she has been bred differently. She doesn't know."

5

There were many late-night discussions in the bedroom after that. Stephen hated wrangling, constant argument, constant controversy, but he was willing to endure much if he could prevent Stella from cheapening herself, and him, too, by promiscuous flirtations. But he couldn't. It was a futile attempt. It was as instinctive for Stella's eyes to brighten up, and for her manner to brighten up, too, when a man appeared who might admire her, as for a puppy's tail to wag when a possibly appreciative human being approaches. Stephen might as well have tried to discipline the puppy's tail as Stella's eyes and manner.

Stella's fondness for attention from men was not deep-seated. If her response had aroused any great depth of feeling or desire, red danger-flags would have appeared to warn her. As it was, her very innocence worked to her disadvantage. She could see no reason for not taking a little harmless fun as it came along, especially if it improved her social prospects. Because it was harmless she persisted in it, until Stephen's patience was worn out, and his pride and self-respect torn and tattered.

It was not only in regard to her relations with men that Stella turned deaf ears to Stephen. Under the head-turning effect of attentions paid her by such women as Phyllis Stearns and Myrtle Holland (Myrtle Holland took up Stella Dallas as a sort of fad that Spring, her friends said) she came to consider all Stephen's ideas as old-fashioned, and out-of-date.

She could see nothing but advantage in forming alliances with such women as Phyllis and Myrtle, "They're in everything. They go everywhere." Nothing but distinction in entering into every activity and amusement that they suggested. "Gracious, how little men know how to get on in society." Stephen was harping morning, noon, and night, on the dangers of too intimate friendships, and too rapid progress. "If I followed your advice I wouldn't get anywhere. You'd make out of me just a prim, stupid, little stay-at-home. Myrtle says she'd just die if her husband tried to dictate to her the way you do to me."

Myrtle says, "Oh, Stella, you don't talk over our affairs with your women friends, do you?"

"Oh, no! Of course not. We talk just about the weather!"

"But, Stella, surely your sense of good taste would prevent you from telling any one of our differences of opinion?"

"Our 'squabbles,' you mean? Oh, Stephen, a saint couldn't please you. Finding fault with the things I talk about with my girl friends! Honestly!"

"They'll only ridicule you afterwards. I don't like those women. I wish you'd avoid them. I don't think they're real friends of yours."

"That's right. Run them down. Have friends of your own, you lunch with and play cards with, and golf with, and have a regular good time with, but don't let *me* have anybody! Myrtle says some men are like that—jealous even of their wives' women friends. Oh, Stephen, why *will* you try to take the joy out of everything so? Why don't you let me have a little fun in life without all this argument? I get sick to death of it."

"Oh, very well."

"Yes, you say 'very well,' but you'll be at me again to-morrow. I don't find fault with *you*, do I?"

"No."

"Well—?"

Stephen was silent.

"That's right, now get glum and sulky, and don't say anything to me but stiff formal things for a week. Oh, gracious!"

Stella could forget all about such a discussion as this by the following morning. "I'm blessed with a good disposition," she was fond of boasting. "Dad used to say it was almost impossible to worry me cross when I was a kid. Come on, Stephen, cheer up."

If Stephen didn't, if he couldn't "cheer up," Stella would fling down her comb, or slam a door, and five minutes later be heard humming a song in her bath. Stephen suffered.

6

"Why did you ever marry me, Stella?" once despairingly he inquired.

"Why, because I was crazy about you. I thought you were perfectly great."

"How can a woman be crazy about a man—care for a man, and not be willing to adapt herself somewhat to him, to give up a few things for him?"

"How would it do for *you* to do a little of the adapting, Stephen, a little of the giving up? Why did you ever marry *me?*" she retorted.

CHAPTER VIII

1

It was an ironic coincidence that the same cause that killed the last bit of struggling love Stephen had for Stella (if indeed love it had ever been) should also bind him to her more closely.

Suddenly in the midst of Stella's first year of social success in Milhampton, she found herself facing the dismaying possibility that she might soon become a mother. She didn't want to! Not now! It would be a terrible tragedy just when she was making such headway in Milhampton. It would wipe her off the social map for a whole year, or more! When the possibility became a certainty, it seemed to Stephen that all there was left sweet and fine in Stella disintegrated suddenly and completely into futile and unbeautiful protest.

She fought the frightening fact day after day, night after night, with violent attacks of crying, with uncontrolled fits of rage, self-pity, and despair, as if in frenzied resistance lay possible escape. Her one desire was to escape—somehow, *anyhow*, from the horrible trap that had snapped on her, and held her in its grasp.

She talked in a way during this time that made Stephen want to go into another room and close the door. He did, sometimes. Her complaints were worded in the parlance that came easiest to her tongue. She was in no mood *then* to pick words and choose phrases. All that Stephen held most sacred and precious about marriage went to pieces under the constant fire.

He took many long lonely walks into the open country around Milhampton that fall to escape from Stella, to get out of sight and sound of her and purify himself, if he could, under the open sky. His thoughts were bitter ones as he tramped and tramped. It seemed as if life was determined to grind its heel upon him, and crush him. He didn't believe in fate; he didn't believe ill-fortune or good-fortune was planned and sent to helpless victims. He believed stanchly in the unchanging law of causation. But oh, it did make a man wish there was some other reason than his own fault, for disaster following him, wherever he went, whatever he did. It had been in an attempt to escape the horror of his father's last act that he had come to

Milhampton. And now the horror of finding himself married to a woman he did not love, had never loved (it was to get away from Mrs. Bean's boarding-house that he had married) was his to bear. He wished he might go back to Mrs. Bean's boardinghouse. There are some kinds of unloveliness more difficult to endure than mere dirt and grime. The apartment was no longer a refuge.

Stephen made no effort to reason with Stella. In the beginning he told her briefly, sternly, that she must accept the fact of the coming child, unwelcome as it was to her (unwelcome as it was, therefore, to him). They must both accept it. There was no escape. Absolutely. Having delivered himself of this dictum, he treated her as kindly as he knew how, as he would a sick and unreasonable child—tolerated, indulged, and endured.

Stella's protestations quieted down. Her attacks of crying and abandonment to despair grew less violent, less frequent. They disappeared completely after a month or so. That was nature's way. Stephen knew that no emotion can continue long in intensity, in the consciousness of a human being. It runs a course, like a disease. Mercifully. Recuperation begins its gentle work, once facts are comprehended and accepted. Stephen expected that in time Stella would acquiesce and submit to "her inevitable." But he did not expect her acquiescence and submission to become interest and delight.

One evening in January she showed Stephen a little dress she had been working on in secret, daytimes, when he was absent, she explained. As she held it up by the arms for him to see, she gurgled with amusement and pleased satisfaction.

"Isn't 'he' cute?" she laughed delightedly.

Stephen stared at the little dress, amazed. Why, six weeks ago Stella had declared she wouldn't take a stitch for the baby! He couldn't refrain from reminding her of that.

"Well, what of it?" she shrugged. "I said all sorts of things then, in the beginning, when I was scared, I suppose. Oh, Stephen," she laughed good-naturedly, "you don't know beans about women. Why, I'm getting quite crazy about the baby *now!*"

Stephen looked at her sharply. Did the maternal instinct come alive suddenly in some women, like that?

"Really?"

"Certainly," she assured him lightly. "Of course it will tie me down, terribly, for a while, but Myrtle says" (she was constantly quoting Myrtle to Stephen) , "Myrtle says I'd be awfully out of things in the long run, if I didn't *ever* have a child. All the young married set talk babies—at least the women; and, after all, it is sort of fun to dress the cunning little things up, and send them out rolling, with a nurse-girl. Myrtle has got a baby. She dresses her in darling things, and Phyllis" (Phyllis was often quoted to Stephen, too) "told me something is going to happen to *her* next summer. I'm really quite in the swim."

Stephen turned away, no longer dismayed. Only a little more disillusioned.

2

Laurel was born in June. Stephen named her Laurel—at least it was the name he applied to her the first time he saw her. He had come across some clumps of mountain-laurel in bud a day or two before, when out on one of his long tramps. The buds were clusters of sticky little spurs of deep pink and red. The first morning the trained nurse brought Laurel to Stephen for inspection, the baby was wrapped up in layers upon layers of flannel. Only the tip of her little pink head was showing.

"Hello, you little mountain-laurel bud," Stephen had said to her, at a loss to know what to say.

He never would have called her a laurel-bud again. It was the nurse who insisted upon the term. Every morning when she took the baby to Stephen for inspection (a ceremony she never failed to perform), she remarked, "Here's your little mountain-laurel bud, Mr. Dallas!"

Laurel's real name was Hildegarde—it was as Hildegarde that she was enrolled on the city's records—but she was never called anything but Laurel and "Lollle," and sometimes "Lolliepops." Myrtle Holland had suggested Hildegarde to Stella. It was a name that had style and distinction, she had said. Stella fully intended to adopt it as soon as Lollie was old enough to go to school. But by the time Lollle was old enough to go to school, she had ideas of her own upon the subject. She didn't like Hildegarde.

"It's big and ugly, and has corners," she announced.

3

During the first few weeks of Laurel's existence Stella gloried much more in the pleasing curves her own figure assumed than in the exquisite beauty of Laurel's perfect body. Oh, yes, it was a cute little thing, she acknowledged, but she had wanted a boy—always preferred the opposite sex. She nursed the baby for a week or two, but she warned the doctor, with a gay little nod of her head, she wasn't going to be "a cow" once she got up. How Stephen had cringed when she referred to herself as "a cow." Honestly it was funny how the English language could hurt Stephen.

Laurel was barely five weeks old when Stella donned an evening gown—("Look at me, Stephen," she had exclaimed delightedly; "I'm a perfect sylph.")—and went to an evening dance.

She didn't look pale and tired and wistful, the way most mothers of young babies looked, and go home early. "See," her bright cheeks announced, her ecstatic manner proclaimed, "it hasn't made any difference. I can dance just as well, I can flirt just as well!" She and her partner had been one of the half-dozen couples still dancing on the ballroom floor to the music of a solitary piano at 3 A.M., when the janitor began turning off the lights. Stephen, waiting patiently below, outside the ladles' dressing-room, had been the parent who was wondering—and wondering bitterly too—if the baby had slept through.

Stella returned to the arena of her ambitions with a determination to make up for lost time as quickly and as emphatically as possible. And Stephen returned to the valley of shame and humiliation. During this period the cloak he wore to cover the shivering nakedness of his mortification concealed at the same time much of his natural *camaraderie*. It was impossible for him to participate in mild hilarities of whatever kind, in Milhampton, under the constant ban of his relationship to one whose hilarity was so often overdone. He became extremely subdued in manner, reserved, short of speech, disinclined to respond to friendly approaches. Some people in Milhampton called him glum and ill-humored.

Outside Milhampton, however, there was nothing glum and ill-humored about Stephen Dallas. In another city he met amiability more than half way. His old charm, of which he possessed no small amount, returned to him shining and bright the minute that he escaped his relationship to Stella. He no bore himself with more confidence and effective self-esteem with business associates, too, who were far enough removed from Milhampton to know nothing of his home life. Every week's or two weeks' absence from Stella became oases of refreshment to Stephen. Mr. Palmer, accompanying Stephen on one of his business trips, had witnessed the metamorphosis, and he opened up as many business opportunities out of town for his protégé, as possible. Stephen's reputation for ability in the law spread.

The year Laurel began going to school, a New York law firm asked Stephen to become one of its members. Mr. Palmer advised Stephen to accept the invitation. It would mean, of course, a loss to him, not only a business loss but a personal loss too. Stephen had come to seem to him almost like a son. "But go," he said, "go. It's your big chance, my boy. Go."

It happened that, during the time that Stephen had the New York proposition under consideration, Stella was carrying on a rather more obvious flirtation than usual with a man of a very offensive personality to Stephen. Stephen had told Stella how distasteful this particular man was to him; but Stella had paid no heed to his objections. Stephen was always objecting.

The man's name was Alfred Munn. He was a stranger in Milhampton. There had sprung up in Milhampton an interest in horseback riding the preceding summer. The River Club had filled its stables with a dozen or more Kentucky thoroughbreds obtained from a Southern hostelry. They were somewhat worn-out animals for the most part, but they were safe and steady for beginners, much safer and steadier in fact than their owner—or keeper (It was never definitely known which Alfred Munn was.)

Alfred Munn became almost as much of a craze at the River Club as the sport he taught. It was difficult to get an hour's instruction from him, if you hadn't engaged it weeks in advance. He was busy every day from six in the morning till six at night, instructing women and children mostly. Certain women of the younger married set began paying Alfred Munn ridiculous attention. It was discovered that it was not only on the back of a horse that he was skillful, and the epitome of grace and rhythm; he could also excel on the ballroom floor. One of the younger married women, bolder than her sisters, invited him to a River Club dance. He was soon attending all the River Club dances. He was taken up by a certain set of women in Milhampton like some new exotic food.

In spite of the report that he belonged to an aristocratic Southern family of reduced financial circumstances, most of the women who paid him attention were aware of his lack of breeding. They were simply amusing themselves. But Stella couldn't see why Alfred Munn wasn't a gentleman, she told Stephen. Other women like Edith and Rosamond (it was Edith and Rosamond then, instead of Myrtle and Phyllis) didn't seem to find anything so horribly objectionable about him. Why in the world should Stephen expect *her* to be so particular!

Stephen used to find Alfred Munn sitting with Stella over a kettle and tea-cups, in the living-room, when he came home in the late afternoon. Stephen and Stella had moved from the apartment by then, and were living in a detached house with a lawn and garden.

Afternoon tea was an effort and affectation with most of the young married women in Milhampton, in those days. It was served on low tabourettes, before open fires, in overheated and underlighted living-rooms. It was the Milhampton custom, at that time, for the hostess to dangle a perforated silver ball, filled with tea-leaves in individual cups of hot water, and to inquire, while dangling, as to the cream and lemon and sugar. When Stephen found Stella coquettishly dangling her silver ball for Alfred Munn, as he sat comfortably ensconced in one of the big Dallas arm-chairs, it was more than irritation he felt. It was disgust.

Why, the man left his teaspoon in his cup! He had the habit of drawing air through the spaces between his teeth after eating! And Stella could endure him! When he was not disguised in his riding-clothes, his coarseness was obvious in such details as shirts and waistcoats. He wore conspicuous jewelry too! On his little finger there appeared usually a huge gold ring with red, white, and blue stones in it. Occasionally he wore a gold scarf-pin representing Psyche asleep in a crescent moon. He was that sort of man. Sometimes Stephen found Alfred Munn smoking his cigarettes, handling his precious books. Sometimes he found him fondling Laurel! Laurel didn't seem to object to it. Why should she?—Stephen asked bitterly. Stella was her mother.

4

The reason Laurel didn't seem to object to Alfred Munn's fondling her was for the sake of a marvelous watch he carried. He used to show it to her if she would come and sit in his lap. Laurel never forgot the wonders of that watch. When she grew up she thought of them whenever she thought of Alfred Munn.

It was a gold watch, big and heavy, and very thick. There was a horse's head engraved on the back of it with a diamond eye that twinkled. His bridle was studded with tiny red stones.

Beneath the horse's head on the inside of the back cover (which Mr. Munn had to pry open with his thick thumb-nail) was a picture of another horse. It was a pure white horse with a lady in short skirts standing on tiptoes on his back!

Underneath the white horse, way, way inside, next to the little gold wheels and blue screw-heads, was another picture. It was a colored picture. It was a picture of a lady with long hair. She had no clothes on at all!

5

One day (and it was that day Stephen had decided to go to New York) he had come upon Stella and Alfred Munn in the corridor of the Milhampton City Club. They had been having lunch there in the ladles' dining-room.

The City Club was strictly a man's club. There was a ladles' dining-room, to be sure, but women did not make a practice of lunching there without an escort who was a member. This club had been the one place outside his office where Stephen had felt safe from Stella in Milhampton.

Stephen wasn't alone when he met Stella and Alfred Munn. There was a lawyer from Boston with him, an older man with whom he had been conferring all the morning; and upon whom he was anxious to make just the right impression. Stella had greeted Stephen with enthusiasm when she met him, and he had had to introduce the Boston lawyer to her, to present her impossible escort to him as well.

It was with a sinking heart that Stephen noticed that Stella had probably ordered something in the way of liquor to go with the luncheon she had just been enjoying with Munn. She was particularly vivacious. Stella never drank enough of anything to lose her self-control, but she did like getting her tongue unloosened, once in a while, she said, and her "flirting spirit up." Her "flirting spirit was up" now, Stephen observed. She made an arch attempt to flirt with the Boston lawyer, as she gave him her hand!

Stephen could feel himself grow red with mortification. He hastened the meeting to as speedy an end as possible, but brief as it was, it unpoised him, sapped him of all assurance and self-confidence.

He didn't want to look the Boston lawyer in the eyes after the meeting with Stella and Munn.

That night he wrote to the New York law firm and definitely accepted their proposition. Stephen was in a mood to accept any proposition which offered him relief from Stella.

CHAPTER IX

1

It was only temporary relief he contemplated, then. It was his intention, when he first went to New York, to establish Stella somewhere, sometime, within commuting distance of his business. Not within too easy commuting distance, however. "In New York a man's business-life and his home-life," Mr. Palmer had once said to

Stephen, avoiding his eyes as he did so, "can be made two distinct and separate affairs, which is difficult to accomplish in a place the size of Milhampton."

When Stephen first went to New York, he consulted several real-estate agents, and listened to many confusing arguments, about the desirability of this suburb over that, its commuting advantages, its unexcelled schools, its unusually "nice" set of young people. Stephen fully expected that Stella would join him in the spring in some suburb or other best suited to her peculiar susceptibilities. Or if not in the spring, in the summer. It would be unwise, he concluded, to take Laurel out of school until the end of the year. Laurel had just started in at Miss Fillibrown's in Milhampton, an excellent school for little girls. Stephen had no idea of leaving Stella permanently when he first went to New York.

But until he went to New York, Stephen had no idea what release from Stella would mean to him. He had no idea what possibilities for success, what resources for enjoyment, had been growing in the dark within him, unencouraged, all these years. He went out among people very little the first winter, but he was able to devote himself to work as never before. When he did seek recreation, the freedom to follow whatever whim or fancy his nature dictated was actually exhilarating.

Since October, when he first went to New York, and the New Year, Stephen spent three Sundays with Stella. Each one was an ordeal to him, and each one a more difficult ordeal than the one before. The long periods of absence tended to make him more sensitive to Stella's offenses, he supposed. It seemed to him as if she almost delighted in doing the sort of things he disliked over those week-ends; indulging in all the striking slang of the day; indulging in all the striking styles of the day (she knew how he disliked her in conspicuous clothes); carrying on long giggling conversations over the telephone with "one of the girls," gossiping, tale-bearing; carrying on long giggling flirtations over the telephone with one of her male admirers, going through a series of smiles and smirks, shrugs and arch expressions, as if the man himself were present to see her, ignoring Stephen behind his book at the other end of the room as if he were a plant or piece of furniture; dashing off for her riding-lesson at ten o'clock Sunday morning with Alfred Munn, while Stephen read the paper or went to church or took a walk by himself. Going back on the train after his third week-end with Stella, Stephen asked himself why he persisted in these self-inflicted periods of torture.

To what end? To what purpose? The idea of separation or divorce had always been distasteful to him, but some things were worse—a thousand times worse, after love had turned to contempt, and respect to scorn. Of course there was Laurel. But wasn't it better for Laurel not to grow up beneath the shadow of constant chafing and irritation? He could see Laurel. She could come to New York occasionally. He could have his child alone.

On a certain week-end in January, which Stephen forced himself to spend in Milhampton, he had found upon his arrival some cigarette ashes in a tray upstairs in the little sitting-room off Stella's bedroom. Stella didn't smoke. At that time few of the women in Milhampton smoked. Stephen didn't refer to the cigarette ashes to Stella. He was too listless, too desireless to care who had left the ashes there. He didn't doubt Stella's fidelity. Not then. It was just another offense in taste. She'd be sure to argue, to harangue, to acclaim in a tone, that would become loud and harsh, that she could see no difference between a man's smoking *upstairs* and *down*. And the pity of it was she couldn't see the difference.

A month slipped by. Two months. Stephen wrote only the briefest notes to Stella and they were far between. Oh, how easy it was to drift out of the troubled waters! What a comfort and relief!

2

At first Stephen's periods of absence were a comfort and relief to Stella, too. It was simply wonderful, she told Effie McDavitt, to go about unhampered, when, where, how, and with whom she pleased, and have a little harmless fun in life, without being preached to for hours afterwards. It didn't seriously occur to Stella that Stephen's absences portended anything permanent. When Effie suggested such a possibility, she "pooh-poohed" the idea.

"Oh, goodness, no," she said. "It would just about kill Stephen if his domestic affairs got aired in the newspapers. I know Stephen. I never could even mention divorce, or separation, in our squabbles, even as a joke, without his sort of turning away, as if I'd said something indecent. No. We'll stick—you'll see."

In early March, Stella wrote to Stephen and asked him when he expected to come home next. She'd like to know so as to be there. There was a good deal going on and Rosamond was planning a house-party out at her country place, over some week-end soon.

Stella was unprepared for Stephen's reply. He told her that he had no definite plan as to when he was coming to Milhampton next. She was not to worry about expenses, the letter went on significantly. He would see that she and Laurel were always provided for. Had he known in January that he was not coming back again for so long a while, he would have told her. But after all they had already had their discussions.

"Isn't that the coolest?" Stella exclaimed to Effie. She made frequent trips across the river to Effie's tenement now. She always made frequent trips across the river to Effie's tenement when she had "something on her mind."

"You'd think we'd had a row or something, the last time he was here, but we didn't. In fact, it seemed to me, if anything, he was a little more friendly than usual. I can't imagine what he's got up his sleeve. I think he had a right to kick up a little dust, don't you? Puts me in a pretty position! It wasn't bad, for a while playing around alone, and calling myself a grass-widow, as a joke. But the real thing is an entirely different matter. It's no fun being an extra woman of *any* kind for long, in society. If you don't own a husband, or a brother, or some two-legged article in trousers, you drop out of things—out of *evening* things, anyhow. Of course, there are luncheons, and teas, and women's shindies left, but I get on best with men, and I look best in evening clothes, too. I'm the kind, anyhow, who wants to take in *everything* that's going. The more places you're seen at the more you go to, and it's just *life* to me to keep going! Why, when I don't go out for a week—have a wave and a manicure and a hot bath and get all dressed up in my best clothes, and set out for a real little party of some sort somewheres—I get horribly depressed. Listen here, Effie, I haven't eaten a dinner outside my own house for three weeks now! I haven't been to a River Club dance since Alfred Munn took the horses South in December! I've known for quite a while it was time for Stephen to come back and get Laurel and me."

Effie wanted to know why Stella didn't write to him, and urge him to come back and get her then.

"Urge him to come back!" Stella exclaimed. "Indeed, I won't! I've got a little pride left, I hope. I never urged a man to come back to me yet, and I don't intend to begin. Oh, I'll manage somehow. Don't worry. You'll see."

She herself worried a good deal. What was she to say? She couldn't go on indefinitely, telling people that Stephen had arrived so late on a Saturday and been obliged to go back so early on Sunday, that he hadn't seen any of his friends. Nor could she repeat many times the subterfuge she had successfully carried through once, of stealing across the river, and burying herself for three or four miserable days in the little red cottage with her father, returning with the story that she had been in New York.

It had been necessary to practice involving deceptions in explaining her absence from such generally discussed functions as the River Club costume dance, and the Annual Charity Ball. Once she had pretended a turned ankle, another time a headache. But the truth was that on both these occasions she had stayed at home and had gone to bed at ten o'clock, because no one had invited her to a dinner party beforehand. She couldn't go to a dance without either a man or a party!

She had tried to get up a party of her own before the ball. But everybody's plans seemed to be made. Rosamond might easily have included her in the dinner-party she gave. She had two extra men. Neither Edith nor Rosamond had had her to a single dinner-party since Stephen had gone to New York! And they were her "best friends" in Milhampton now. She had had *them* one night, with two other couples. A real party! Ten in all. She had given them two cocktails apiece and a generous amount of Stephen's champagne. Not one of her guests had reciprocated yet by an invitation of any kind.

The possibility of an empty engagement calendar, the consideration of long stretches of idle days with no climaxes at their ends, filled Stella with alarm. Frightening ghosts of various kinds filtered through the cracks of Stella's bedroom, during this time, woke her up every morning about five, and kept her awake until it was time to get up and dress. The tragic idleness of a certain new gown she had bought in January haunted her day and night. Never had a new dress of hers remained new so long. For three weeks It had hung in the closet, just as it had been lifted from its box. Stella longed to wear the gown. It would make an impression. Now that she could no longer contribute a man to society it was necessary for her to contribute at least an impression. A conspicuous gown could do a lot for a woman at a dance, Stella believed.

"But it can't if it hangs in the closet," she sobbed into her pillow.

3

When Alfred Munn returned from Florida with his horses for another season at the River Club, he put many of Stella's ghosts to flight. He filled her engagement calendar; he provided climaxes to her days; he saw to it that there was never a week when Stella didn't dress up in her best clothes and set out for "a real little party" of some sort somewhere. He broke the back of the worst goblin of all—her fear (her almost conviction now) that when a woman's husband goes out of town for any length of time and people begin to wonder why, all her old admirers turn tail and run, too, to avoid any possible danger of being mentioned in a scandal. Life wouldn't be worth living, Stella felt, if she had no admirers.

Riding was still popular in Milhampton that Spring; Alfred Munn was still popular. Stella grasped at his attentions eagerly, instinctively, as she would at a rope flung to her from the basket of a balloon that offered to rescue her from some unfortunate fate and carry her aloft. But the balloon of Alfred Munn's popularity in Milhampton had already begun to lose its buoyancy. It couldn't carry Stella far. Alfred Munn should have been throwing off ballast instead of taking more on. For a while, though, it lifted Stella out of the valley, and diverted her attention from its shadows. Under the excitement of Alfred Munn's attentions, Stella took heart.

Alfred Munn invited her to every dance there was at the River Club that spring. People began to talk. Women, she told Effie, began to envy. She knew of at least a dozen who would give their eyeteeth if Alfred Munn would ask them to dance with him. He really was as good as a professional. He had asked her to be his partner in one of the new fancy dances last Saturday night. They had been the only two on the floor. Everybody else had sat around and stared, and applauded afterwards! Oh, she was really managing to make quite a splash in Milhampton with Alfred Munn. At the Luncheon Club she belonged to, "the girls" had discussed little else last Friday. Rosamond was simply green with jealousy. Stella could tell she was, because she acted so cool and offish. Lots of people were "jollying" her about him. She got it from all sides. Even that nice old tabby-cat, Mrs. Palmer, had heard the talk. She had stopped her, on the street, one day, and given her a little motherly advice. Too bad nobody ever invited Ed to dinner, or to anything small or private. He would be so much more useful. She couldn't see why they didn't. But never mind, he was convenient just as he was, and oh, *awfully* kind! She was getting a little tired of him, she must confess. But then, she always did, when "the new" wore off, and "they got a little slushy."

Effie wondered if there wasn't danger of Stephen's hearing about the splash Stella was making in Milhampton with Alfred Munn.

"Why, of course," Stella exclaimed to that. "I *want* him to hear about it. I don't intend to give Stephen the satisfaction of thinking I had to go into seclusion the minute he cleared out. He had an idea I couldn't get along in this town without his telling me how to do it. He meant to use his importance to my position here as a kind of gun to point at me and make me do just as he wants, when we get together again. Good gracious, having a good time, being successful all by myself, is the only gun I've got to point at *him*, my dear."

But Stella was inexperienced in the use of firearms. Her gun exploded when she didn't expect it to. And she herself became the victim.

4

It's possible to receive a bullet wound, even a fatal bullet wound, and be unaware of it, until you put your hand to the spot where it tingles a little. You're surprised when your fingers come into contact with something warm and wet. You're shocked when you draw them away, and find them red! Laurel was the messenger who brought the first sign of red to Stella's horrified attention.

Stella sent out a dozen invitations to a party for Laurel in June. All Laurel's schoolmates were having parties this year. Stella intended that Laurel's party should surpass them all. There was going to be a tailless donkey, and a peanut-hunt, and a cobweb contest, and a Jack Horner pie, and creamed chicken, and ice-cream, and paper caps.

Laurel had been told all about the elaborate plans. She had helped select the invitation-cards with the pretty colored pictures in the corner, and the thrilling announcement underneath, "I am going to have a party." She had stood close beside her mother when the blank spaces had been filled in. She had watched the addressing of each one of the little pink envelopes. Afterwards, standing on tiptoes, she had dropped them, one by one, into the green box at the corner.

Laurel mailed the invitations on a Friday night. All day Saturday and Sunday she was full of the exhilarating consciousness that others were sharing the wonderful secret now. When she started to school on Monday there was a sparkle beneath the calm gray surface of her eyes that made them look almost black—like the pools of meadow-brooks in mid-morning sunshine. When Laurel came home at noon her eyes seemed to have faded like the pools when the sun is hidden behind clouds. Instead of the blackness and the sparkle there was a grave, wondering, bewildered look in them.

"Nobody can come to my party, mother," she announced briefly.

All day Sunday the mothers of the recipients of the pink envelopes had been busy at the telephone.

Twice Laurel had to tell her mother that nobody could come to the party before Stella grasped the significance of the announcement. Then fiercely she threw her arms about Laurel, and held her to her tight.

"We don't care. We don't care!" she burst out. "Let them stay away! We'll have our party by ourselves! Don't you mind, Lollie. We'll have the party just the same—you and I and Uncle Ed Munn. Cats! Just because father runs off and leaves us all alone! Well—we've got each other, Lollie, anyhow. I won't ever run off and leave *you, and,* oh, Lollie, *you* won't ever run off and leave *me*, will you—ever, *ever?*" Stella was crying now.

Laurel did not cry. She stood very still, and listened, and afterwards remembered.

CHAPTER X

1

It was several weeks before Stella knew how serious her bullet wound was. She was calm by that time. She could talk over its details with Effie McDavitt with perfect composure and with a touch of brusque humor, too.

"Why," she said, "Ed bores me. He never gave me a thrill in his life. Oh, Milhampton makes me sick! Narrow-minded, evil-minded, nasty-minded, I think. I'll tell you just how it was. I was down there in Boston, for two days, shopping, getting favors and things for Lollie's party. Naturally, when Ed suggested that he run down and take me to the theater in the evening, I was pleased to pieces. Wouldn't you be? I love the theater in Boston. We didn't stay at the same hotel, though for the life of me I don't see why we shouldn't. There were a hundred or so other men staying there. Glory, how I hate all this winking and shoulder-shrugging stuff about hotels and bedrooms! When Ed suggested, after the theater, that he drop around and have breakfast with me, why, I said, 'Sure, Mike,' quick as a wink. It never entered my head but what that was all right. I didn't care if somebody from Milhampton *did* see me. Married woman like me! Breakfast! Right in a public dining-room! What's there so horrible about that, I'd like to know! I didn't want anything of Ed but a little fun, and a little advertising. When Stephen wrote to me in that iceberg-y way of his, and asked if I would like my freedom so as to be able to marry Alfred Munn, I could have screamed! Marry Ed? Why, I'd commit suicide first. I don't want to marry Ed I Hasn't *anybody any* understanding of the human animal? A woman can have other reasons for liking a little attention than just the one the shady stories are all based on. I'm no worn-out old man whose appetite for everything but just indecency has gone dead. I like a little dinner and theater-party just for *fun's* sake. Honestly, Effie, sometimes I think I'm the only one who's got a clean mind in this town."

Stella took rooms, for the season, at a fashionable hotel on the coast of Maine that summer. She had never spent a summer at a hotel. It might prove diverting.

She certainly needed something diverting she thought. But whatever it proved, the arrow of direction pointed her out of Milhampton for a while.

"I'll give the mud-slingers in this town a rest for a month or two," she said to Effie. "By the end of the summer perhaps their muck will have all dried up. Of course, it would be rather nice if I could fall into some harmless, but showy 'little affair' this summer, with some attractive gentleman or other, up there at that fashionable hotel. That would prove there wasn't anything serious in this Alfred Munn business. It would be rather nice, too, if some of the cats in this town could hear that I was having a wonderful time this summer—being taken right into all sorts of inner circles, and select groups. Oh, there are lots of possibilities in this summer hotel scheme of mine, Effie, my dear."

Stella equipped Laurel with a dozen new frocks, replenished her own wardrobe, and, stout-heartedly, set forth to new fields and untried country, in search of fresh laurels with which to cover up the dried and dead ones.

That was the beginning of her summer hotel era. In the fall, not even Effie was told, in detail, of the disheartening experiences of the first experiment.

"You can drill forever for oil in some places, but unless oil is there, it won't do you any good," was how Stella briefly summed it up. "Next summer, I'll try the Cape—or the mountains possibly."

Stella didn't go back to the detached house when she returned from Maine. Instead she took two-rooms-and-a-bath in an apartment hotel that had lately been built in a residential section of Milhampton.

The apartment hotel offered her more companionship than the detached house. There would at least be the necessity of getting out of a kimono when you went down to meals. Besides, she could have people to dinner more safely. The invaluable Hedwig, whom Stephen had engaged six years ago, and taught and trained, had left to be married. Stella was afraid to trust a new servant with all the hard-and-fast rules. In an apartment hotel, all you had to do, if anything went wrong, was to shrug and say, "Oh, dear, isn't the service in this place dreadful?"

Moreover, there were social advantages. The King Arthur (that was the name of the new apartment hotel) was to be patronized by what Stella called "the right people." She needed all the advantages that she could get from close proximity to the right people.

Stella was determined not to let her injury of the preceding spring incapacitate her. It isn't always necessary for a man to go to bed and stay there even if there is a bullet embedded in him somewhere. Stella wasn't going to become a social invalid just because she'd been unfortunate and the target of a little disagreeable gossip.

Alfred Munn had left Milhampton by the time Stella and Laurel returned from Maine. He had gone into another business in another city. Somebody else had taken over the horses. In time people would forget about Ed. Bullet wounds heal. Scars can be covered up. Of course it was a handicap not to have a husband if he was still in the land of the living; at least it was a handicap in Milhampton, Massachusetts. In California single married women were as plentiful as sunshine, and as welcome, Stella had heard—Oh, she did wish it had been in some place in California that she and Stephen had happened to put down their roots. But it couldn't be helped. It was only common sense, of course, to keep on growing in the same place where they'd started. Stella appreciated her own limitations to the extent of realizing that it would be difficult, even in California, to work her way up alone to anything like the position that she had attained with Stephen in Milhampton.

When Stephen's business took him to New York, Laurel was enrolled as a pupil in the exclusive school of the community. She attended the exclusive dancing-class, and she attended the exclusive Sunday-school. Stella belonged to a few helpful organizations herself. Her name was in the Blue Book. She had at least a bowing acquaintance with almost everybody "worth-while." She had lots of men friends. She believed she had quite a few women friends of value. There was, besides, Stephen's membership at the River Club, an asset indeed to her now, since she had no house of her own in which to entertain crowds, and pay back social debts.

It was a very unhappy day for Stella when she first learned that Stephen had resigned from all his Milhampton clubs. She thought it was the cruelest blow he could deal her. At that time Stella was mercifully unaware how many more cruel blows were to follow, not from Stephen alone, but from *everybody*—from *all* sides. They didn't come all at once. If they had, she must have been convinced of the futility of her effort, and given up her fight early.

Her defeat was gradual. She lost ground by degrees. Her various points of vantage and fortresses of strength fell slowly. This season she failed to receive an announcement of the Current Events Class; next season, her name appeared to have been dropped from the Charity Ball list. The season after, the small Luncheon Club she belonged to was reorganized and she was omitted. Every year there were personal slights of various kinds, coolnesses, intentional inattentions from all quarters. Laughingly—bitterly, too—she told herself that the people in Milhampton must be having some sort of chronic eye difficulty. So many old friends and acquaintances failed to recognize her, lately. But Stella didn't lose hope. She didn't, anyhow, show that she lost hope. She managed to keep her eyes bright, and her lips smiling, and her head erect, in spite of repeated rebukes.

"Why, I've got to. For Lollie's sake," she said. "Lollie mustn't know her mother has got anything to look sour-faced over. Oh, we'll be all right after a while—Lollie and me," she told Effie McDavitt.

"We'll come out on top in the end. You watch us."

2

It was always "Lollie and me," always "we," and "us," by that time. Stella didn't even think in the singular number, once her maternal instinct had worked its way up through her vanities and self-interests and appeared in her consciousness. The seed of it must have been planted deep, for it took a period of years to appear. In vain Stephen had looked for it when Laurel was a baby; and later when she was in the helpless, toddling stage.

For the first half-dozen years of Laurel's life, Stella took her lightly. Not that she neglected her in any obvious way. She couldn't. There were certain manners and forms in the modern bringing-up of a child that had to be observed. She had an excellent nurse-girl for Lollie; she spent hours in the selection of Lollie's clothes; she had a Mother-Goose cretonne at Lollie's windows; a Noah's-Ark paper on Lollie's walls. There were low chairs, and low shelves. Stella loved to show Laurel's room to guests, when occasion arose. Laurel benefitted by many an attention from Stella in those days that did not spring from the maternal instinct. However, the maternal instinct must have been growing underneath the surface, and growing according to Nature's own methods—sending down tough wiry roots in the dark, all the while it was sending up its tender arrow-pointed shaft of life, for when it did shoot through into the light, the plant was strong and vigorous.

Perhaps the first time that Stella was aware of the new insistent force within her was the day Laurel came home from school with the news about the party.

"Gosh, Effie," she had said afterwards, "I don't care what people do to me, but to stick hatpins into Lollie—into my baby! Say, that's more than I can stand. I'm ready to use my claws on anybody who hurts Lollie."

3

During the years between Laurel's sixth birthday and her thirteenth there were many times for Stella to use her claws. There were many times that Laurel was hurt and Stella knew it. "Though the funny little kid doesn't think I do. She never lets on to me. I just have to guess at it from the way she acts."

If she came home from school especially quiet and uncommunicative, and was not very hungry at dinner, Stella would begin to be suspicious.

"What's the matter?" she would demand with a piercing look.

"Nothing," Laurel would reply, feigned surprise and wonder in her voice.

"Has anything happened at school?"

"No."

"Who'd you play with at recess?"

"Nobody special."

"Did you play all alone?"

"No."

"Look here, Lollie. Answer me. Has somebody been horrid to you? Has somebody hurt your feelings?"

"No."

If Stella stared at her hard enough, probed long enough. Laurel might reply, "My stomach aches a little bit," and pay the price of two shredded wheat biscuit and no dessert for dinner.

It would never be from Laurel that Stella would get the first wind of a party in prospect from which Laurel was omitted. Laurel would never tell her that the girls in her class were meeting every few days at each other's houses to work for a fair, or to rehearse a play or fete in which she had no part. When information of an event of this sort did reach Stella, she knew then what had been the cause of Laurel's quiet, brown-study day a week ago. And yet she couldn't use her claws after all. It would be the worst policy in the world For the sake of Lollie's future, for that dim, far-away, full-of-promise time when Lollie would "come out" (girls "came out," now, in Milhampton), she must be as nice and purry as she knew how to the women she knew who could help her daughter.

Laurel could see through her mother's little shams and deceits, devised to spare her pain, much quicker than Stella could see through Laurel's. At thirteen Laurel was an odd mixture of artificiality and truthfulness, of craft and naïveté, of grown-up woman and little girl. She could deceive her mother without flickering an eyelash, and could repeat to strangers the little white lies Stella taught her, with the finesse of a woman of the world, but at school in her work and play, she was never anything but strictly honest.

As experienced as Laurel was in certain of the world's cruelties, and as mature in her calm manner of acceptance of whatever befell, she was amazingly young and innocent about many of the facts of life. Another antithesis. Much younger and much more innocent than the group of sophisticated little girls in her class at school. They were constantly spending days and nights with each other. Their intimacies led to easy discussions of all sorts of subjects. By the time they were twelve their activities out of school were closely resembling their mothers'. And their conversations, too. There were already conflicting invitations for every Saturday. Laurel could catch bits of conversation, now and then, as the various competing parties and entertainments were reviewed afterwards, and their details discussed and criticized. Most of these girls became perceiving and canny little critics before they had finished playing dolls.

Laurel had no intimate friends, belonged in no group, joined in no daily gossipings. Her critical faculty went through no such course of training. She was still groping for the whys and wherefores of many of society's verdicts long after her dolls were put away. Why had she no intimate friends? Why was she never asked to lunch, or to spend the night? Why had she been dropped from the Widow's Mite Club which met Saturday mornings at Stephanie Holland's? The worldly-wise little girls at school could have told her.

"It's your mother."

"What's the matter with my mother?" she would have asked, surprised. Laurel thought her mother beautiful. The little girls would have shrugged and said, "Our mothers don't 'know her.'" With just the same shrug and inflection that had silenced them.

But Laurel never asked questions of the little girls. She passed through her childhood blindfolded, picking her way cautiously along, sensitive fingertips stretched out before her to avoid sharp corners and unyielding walls, clinging close to the protection of solitude and isolation.

There were other questions besides those connected with social values to which she didn't know the answers, big questions like, what becomes of dead people, and what God is like, and if He really hears you pray, and knows when a bird falls out of a nest, and where babies come from, and what doctors carry in their mysterious leather bags, and how kittens are born, and if there was ever actually a George Washington, and a Polyphemus, and a Jesus Christ, and a Noah, and a Noah's Ark, with a pair of every kind of animal there is in it, even a pair of mosquitoes, and why there had to be a pair.

Laurel never asked her mother questions about big things. She had discovered that her mother always changed the subject ever so quickly if she did. And once she had exclaimed, "Oh, my! Laurel, nice little girls don't talk about things of that sort!" Until then Laurel had thought that perhaps she might ask her father. He liked talking about big things, about certain big things, that is—like beautiful music, and beautiful sunsets, and how wonderful nature is, and being honest and a good sportsman, and all that. But Laurel was shy with her father during the short periods she spent with him. She usually listened more than she talked. He always introduced the subjects of their conversations. She'd sooner die in ignorance than to ask him a question that wasn't "nice."

CHAPTER XI

1

When Helen Morrison caught the timid, butterfly-like little creature that Laurel was at thirteen, in her soft deft hands, and cautiously lifted one scooped palm from over the other, as it were, and peered into the dark, domed chamber to see what sort of creature was there, her interest was instantly aroused. She had never seen a little-girl specimen of Laurel's sort—so composed and self-possessed in speech and manner, so at home in smart, up-to-date frocks, so skilled in smart, up-to-date sports, so familiar with smart, up-to-date beauty-shop secrets—but underneath like a child who has lived on an island, alone somewhere, untold and untaught.

"She's like a book I bought in Florence once," Helen Morrison told Stephen one day, after Laurel had been visiting her. "It's a beautifully bound book, in full leather, and hand-tooled, in old blue and gold. But its pages are blank. I bought it to write odd bits of poetry in. Yes. Laurel is a little like that—beautifully finished on the outside, but full of pages as white as snow that never have been written on."

2

On a small table beside Helen Morrison's bed there was a picture of a little girl whose pages also had never been written on. Often Helen Morrison would take the lovely little miniature of her dead child close to the strong light, and gaze at it hard and long, in a hungry attempt to recall how the soft cheek used to feel when she brushed her own against it, how the limp little body used to melt into her arms when she held it close.

It was a beautiful baby's face that smiled back at Helen from out of the ivory, but it was always a baby's face. That was the pity of it. What would she have looked like to-day? (Oh, never to know. Never to know!) What strength and confidence and beauty would that weak little body have attained? What strength and confidence and beauty would that spark of fine intelligence, shining so steadily in her baby's face, have kindled under her constant caring and tending? What had they both lost—this little daughter and herself, in way of rare companionship vind human love?

Sometimes as Helen gazed at the picture, it seemed that she caught a wistful expression in the eyes, as if, she sentimentalized, her little girl had become tired of waiting, waiting, waiting, so long to grow up. It hurt, even after years it hurt Helen Morrison, to feel the stab of her uselessness to this child who had so trusted her. Oh, if she could only do something to rescue her from that eternal loveliness of babyhood—give her back the gift of life again, even though it might hurt her sometimes, even as life had hurt her mother.

Helen Morrison had worshiped her gentle, flower-like little daughter. She had been more than just a precious baby to her. She had been a symbol, a manifestation, a gift from heaven. For years and years Helen Morrison had longed for something feminine of her own. She had never had anything feminine of her own. No sister, no mother. Her mother had died when she was born. Her father had never remarried. Helen had been brought up by nurses and governesses, under the strict regime of an elderly and masterful housekeeper.

Helen used to plan by the hour what she would do for a daughter if she ever had one of her own. Even before she thought seriously about marriage, she built air-castles about that little dream-girl of hers. She should have all the joys and delights which her own childhood had lacked. She should be surrounded, day and night, by feminine tenderness and comprehension. She should have a friend always waiting for her at home, to play with her, or to work with her, to walk and talk with her, or to love pretty clothes with her, or pity wounded bugs with her, or to hold hands with her when it "thundered and lightened." Later, when life itself seemed to "thunder and lighten" about her, there would still be somebody holding her hand, reassuring her, making facts lucid and clear, and truth beautiful. Helen had ideas about girls and what made for happiness in their lives. She would have filled the blank pages of her little daughter's book full of inspired and lovely things.

When that little girl was born, Helen Morrison had been married several years. She had already had two boys—fine sturdy specimens—but soldier-material,

American business-man stuff. When a little girl, a little feminine creature of her own, was placed in the curve of Helen Morrison's arm, she could not speak for joy. It seemed as if a bit of heaven itself had slipped through the clouds. Her cup was full and brimming over. That precious relationship that she had lost so long ago, the day she was born when her mother died, had been given back to her again!

She spent two radiantly happy years with her daughter (Carol, she named her. It became the sweetest word in the English language to her), and then suddenly, with the arrow-like directness of a bolt of lightning from the skies, disease struck straight down into the holy of holies of her heart and killed her darling. By a mere accident the realization of her lifelong hope was broken into fragments—disintegrated into a thousand poignant little memories. Her little girl became a dream again, an ideal, a picture on ivory. "There were her boys." That is what people said in way of comfort. Yes, yes. Of course. Thank heaven she had her boys! But, oh, her boys must be made stalwart and bold, strong and tough-muscled. The image she would have modeled out of her bit of little-girl clay was to have been as graceful as poetry, as delicate as violin music, as perfect in detail, as fine and exquisite as an etching.

After Carol died, Helen Morrison offered her services to a certain charitable institution for working-girls in New York City. She was living in New York then. She had been living in New York ever since she married. She thought, perhaps, if something of the young and tender ideals she had had for Carol was given to other girls, then everything about her lovely baby would not remain in that state of undevelopment which hurt her so every time she looked at the miniature.

It was soon discovered at the working-girls' home that Mrs. Morrison possessed rare genius with girls. She knew just how to approach them—just how to talk with them. She could hold the attention of a whole roomful of factory hands reading poetry—Browning and Whitman—out loud to them, and telling them what it meant to her. She could interest a dozen lively little errand girls for an hour at a time, gathered around an ant-hill in operation, at the edge of one of her garden-paths at her summer place on Long Island. Frequently she had groups from the Home come out from the city during the summer, and spend a day with her in her garden, among the illuminating bugs and bees and flowers.

Helen Morrison usually talked with her working-girls in groups. She seldom came in contact with the girls individually. That was probably why they failed to satisfy her, why they remained, always, simply a worthy charity dedicated to the memory of the little girl beside her bed. It wasn't until Laurel came to spend a week with Helen Morrison that she felt the same heart-string, which Carol had pulled so hard once long ago, gently touched again. It hurt a little at first—brought back the old pain. But it also brought back a little timid thrill of the old joy and ecstasy.

There was something of the same pristine beauty about Laurel at thirteen as about her own child's crystallized innocence. There were areas in Laurel's soul, big white expanses, untouched by experience, unsullied by life. It was almost as if those parts of Laurel had disappeared into a picture also, when she, too, was just learning to walk alone.

Laurel was nearly the same age as Carol. She was dark like Carol. Graver than gay, like Carol. She wore the same sort of clothes Carol would have worn. She had slept at night, it occurred to Helen with a little twinge, in the same bed where Carol would have slept, sometimes, now her father was gone. Even her name was something like Carol's.

After Helen Morrison said good-bye to Laurel at the end of her first visit, wrapped her own coat about her, tucked her in beside her father in the automobile, and laughingly, playfully kissed her good-bye, she hurried away quickly to her own room and closed the door. Taking the miniature close to the light, she gazed at it till the slow tears ran down her cheeks.

CHAPTER XII

1

At the same moment that Laurel, high up above the rumbling traffic of New York, was packing her trunk on the last day of her never-to-be-forgotten visit to her father (never to be forgotten because of the wonderful Mrs. Morrison), Stella several hundred miles away, was also packing a trunk.

There was no sound of traffic outside Stella's window, only the distant pound of the surf and a distant glimpse of a deserted board-walk. By the end of September there were only three or four people left at the boarding-house at Belcher's Beach. By the middle of September at least half of the amusement booths on the board-walk had been closed for the season.

Stella had remained until the literal eve of Laurel's return, because she had been very lucky this year, and had found a tenant for her rooms at the King Arthur for the month of September. Laurel could have her fur coat and wrist-watch, too, now! My, though, but Stella was glad her job was over! She did hate horrid places so, and horrid people, and run-down, second-rate boarding-house styles and customs—loud talk and loud laughter and loud women, and flies and dirt, and bathing-suits hanging out all the front windows to dry (that is, when the season was still on), and bathing-corsets, and bathing-garters. (" Honest, Effie, you'd think some people had had no bringing-up.") And all sorts of queer questionable things going on at night—doors opening softly and closing—whispers—giggles. The walls were like paper. Lord, she'd be glad to get away from Belcher's Beach! Thank heaven, the four weeks were at an end.

To-night she'd be sleeping at the King Arthur! To-morrow night Lollie would be sleeping with her at the King Arthur I She hummed deep in her throat as she packed. Nothing gave Stella the blue doldrums like this month of Belcher's Beach. Nothing gave her the spring-song feeling like release from it.

This year Belcher's Beach hadn't been quite so bad as usual, though. At least it ought not to have been. Ed Munn had done his best to brighten it up. Funny, though, Stella would be about as glad to get away from Ed as from the boarding-house. What ailed her? Ed had been ever so generous. Every single Saturday since Laurel had been away, and *one* Sunday, he had planned some diverting form of entertainment. It must have cost him a pretty penny I Stella was filled with remorse that she couldn't work up any real excitement over Ed. He was paying for "all wool," and deserved it, not the imitation stuff she gave him. It was all pretense with her when she returned his various little signs and signals. How pitiful to be so old one isn't even tempted to flirt any more! How amazing to be so crazy about your own child that being crazy about a man loses all interest and excitement in comparison.

Sometimes, looking straight into Ed Munn's little red hippopotamus eyes, trying her utmost to pay for his expensive entertainment in the harmless coin that he liked best, the vision of Laurel would appear back there in the dark cavern behind her eyes, down there in the mysterious cave where her heart beat, like a sudden shaft of light. And the shaft of light would seem to be pointed like a sword, and pierce Stella. Her eyes would become suffused with sudden tears, and tenderness. Dear dear Lollie, with her big gray eyes and her dark hair, and sharp-pointed, little-girl shoulders breaking through the hair as it fell to her waist, over her slim white body when she slipped off her nightgown in the morning. Dear precious little Lollie! in a little while they would be together again! What a zigzagging thrill of joy the thought gave Stella I Good Lord, how she worshiped the kid!

2

Once, when Stella's eyes had become suddenly soft with the thought of Laurel, Ed Munn had mistaken the cause of her emotion, and grasped hold of her hand, of her arm, of as much of her as he could reach across the small table that divided them; and that sort of mouth-watery look which always turned Stella's pleasure in a man's attentions to disgust—if he persisted in it—came into his eyes.

It had been Stella's intention to keep up her masquerade with Ed Munn to the end of the month (she did admire a good sport), but, my goodness, she wasn't a Sarah Bernhardt. Ed got terribly insistent that day she let her mind trail off to Laurel. She simply had to come out with the truth.

"I'm sorry, Ed," she sighed, as she drew away her hand with a little jerk.

At that he simply imprisoned one of her feet under the table between two of his, and leaned towards her, his eyes still gobbling her up.

She drew away her foot, too, and perched it safely on the rung of her chair.

"Nothing doing, Ed," she shrugged.

"What's the matter?" he inquired. She hadn't shown squeamishness before. "What's got into you all of a sudden?"

"I guess it's age, Ed," she confessed, "and it isn't all of a sudden."

He merely laughed at that and tried to grasp her hand again. But she wouldn't let him. He frowned. Flushed a little.

"I don't wonder you're mad, Ed."

"I didn't say I was mad."

"But you aren't pleased, I guess. I know. Ed, listen. I don't blame you a bit. I'm disgusted myself with the way I act, with the way I feel, or the way I *don't* feel. But don't, please, think it's anything personal. There's no man living could get me really going now. It isn't your fault. It's Lollie's. It's that darned little Lollie's fault!" She brought out fiercely. "I'm no good for anything any more Except to be her mother. I'm so crazy about Lollie that she uses up all the emotion I've got, so I'm just sort of dead ashes with everybody else in the world."

"You're alive enough for me."

But Stella was deaf to flattery now. "Ed," she exclaimed, "I simply worship Laurel!" And the expression that forced its way through the make-up on her face had something sublime about it. A tear splashed down her cheeks. "You see!" She shrugged and shamelessly began to wipe her eyes.

"Oh, it makes me so mad!"

Ed Munn leaned over and patted her on the arm, big-brother fashion.

"That's all right. That's all right."

Stella blew her nose. "I'm terribly sorry."

"You needn't be. I'm satisfied. I'm not asking you to get excited over me. I like a woman all the better for being fond of her own kid."

"Oh, Ed, you *are* nice!" She warmed towards him.

"In fact," he went on (he knew *now* what tack to pursue), "the few times I've seen the offspring I've thought to myself, what a peach of a kid she was."

"Oh, she's wonderful, Ed. I'd die without her!" And again the tears welled up in her eyes.

"Sure you would! Well, I've no intention of kidnaping her."

You see, as Stella told Effie McDavitt afterwards, she and Ed had a *perfect understanding*.

3

When Stella paid her bill of indebtedness to the proprietor of the boarding-house at Belcher's Beach, for allowing her to economize for a month on his property, it was with a feeling of triumph and with the comforting sense of a disagreeable job well done. There were those, however, who regarded Stella's sojourn in a different light. Stella was blissfully unaware that any one except Effie and Ed even knew of the sojourn, any one who had any connection with Milhampton.

As the train sped along towards that city, at the end of her ordeal, she was happy with the simple joy of release. She smiled and her heart sang, automatically almost, a little as a kitten purrs when it comes in out of the rain and sees the warm fire on the hearth. She had no premonition of the nest of bombs lying in her letter-box among the other letters and communications that had arrived too near the date of her return to be forwarded. Stella had not seen the automobile standing on the opposite side of the street from the boarding-house at Belcher's Beach the late Saturday night when Ed had brought her back and left her as usual at the foot of the stairs that led up to her room. She had not seen the same automobile the next morning on the Boulevard as she and Ed had started out for lunch in Boston.

The day after Myrtle Holland and Mrs. Kay Bird had seen Alfred Munn follow Stella Dallas into the boarding-house—but had not seen him come out—they had driven to Belcher's Beach again. Myrtle Holland was occupying a summer cottage, that year, thirty miles inland. She had never been to Belcher's Beach before. It was only because the chauffeur had lost the road that she happened to be driving through such a place at all. Myrtle Holland wanted to inspect Stella's boardinghouse by daylight. She told Mrs. Kay Bird she wanted to point it out to her husband so he might look it up and see what sort of a place it was.

It chanced to be over the only week-end of Laurel's absence, when Ed Munn had both a Saturday and Sunday engagement with Stella, that Myrtle Holland and Mrs. Kay Bird made their two visits to Belcher's Beach. On the second visit they had been almost as excited as on their first. They had seen Ed Munn and Stella Dallas again! The pair were leaving the boarding-house this time! It was eleven in the morning! It looked pretty bad, didn't It? It looked still worse when Mrs. Holland called at the fashionable hotel, where Mrs. Kay Bird had heard Stella Dallas was spending the season, and discovered that Mrs. Dallas hadn't been there for three weeks I And that her forwarding address was care of a Mrs. Effie McDavitt, in a very queer part of Mllhampton, way down by the mills somewhere. Obviously Stella Dallas had done her best to cover up her tracks. Oh, wasn't it all too shocking for anything?

"Probably those two have been carrying on their little affair, off and on, ever since the scandal about them when her husband left her. I wouldn't believe then that she'd really gone the limit (I'm always slow at jumping to conclusions of that sort); but now, I do not see that we can very well help thinking the worst. My husband says that Belcher's Beach is full of questionable places. He didn't care to go into an investigation of that particular one, but you could see by looking at it—so dirty, and run-down, and ramshackle—and by observing the women who came out of it, what sort of a place it was. Stella Dallas herself looked a little more common and ordinary than ever—paint just piled on, and that riding-teacher—Munn—has degenerated terribly. Oh, it makes my blood boil to think that the mother of one of the girls, with whom our daughters associate daily at the little private school we've all supporting and protecting to the best of our ability, should be carrying on an affair of that sort with a man of that sort in a place of that sort. As one of the trustees of Miss Fillibrown's School there's only one course open to me. A thing like that cannot be known about a woman, and countenanced, can it?"

"Certainly not," was the general dictum.

"I for one won't countenance it anyhow," announced Mrs. Kay Bird, with emphasis. "Either Mrs. Dallas moves out of the King Arthur or *I* do. I had to play bridge with her twice last winter!"

"And either her child is removed from Miss Fillibrown's or mine is," another voice proclaimed.

This conversation took place in Myrtle Holland's living-room a few days after her return to Milhampton, in late September. There were half a dozen women gathered round the tea-table.

"But," feebly observed one of them, "there's just a possibility that you're mistaken. Myrtle, isn't there?"

"Oh, sweet protector of the innocent, virtuous defender of the maligned," laughed Mrs. Kay Bird.

"My dear Mabel," Myrtle replied, "there's just a possibility a man who frequents corner saloons doesn't drink, but it's rather slight, I fear; and anyhow, whether he drinks or not, the fact that he enjoys the company and atmosphere of corner saloons is sufficient to bar him from certain drawing-rooms. Dear me, Mabel, haven't we all endured Stella Dallas years enough in this town to satisfy you? I, for one, don't enjoy torturing animals even though some of them don't seem to mind it very much. That woman is in for a lot of disappointments when that child of hers she's always using, to boost herself into some sort of prominence, is older. The time has come, for her sake, as well as ours, to put an end to all further suffering."

"The child seems quite a nice little thing."

"But how long will she stay quite a nice little thing with a mother like that? Really, Mabel!"

"And nice little thing or not," spoke up somebody from the other side of the hearth, "I'm sure I don't want my son meeting her at dances, and things, as he grows up, and run the risk of having him fall in love with a girl with such a mother!"

"Oh, isn't it sad?" deplored Phyllis Stearns, with a sanctimonious sigh, "that women exist who care so little for their children as Stella Dallas? I used to know her very slightly, when she was first married, and before her child was ever born she didn't want her. And now she goes off with a man like that! Oh!"

"Such a woman doesn't deserve to have a child," exclaimed Mrs. Kay Bird, who had successfully avoided ever having had one herself.

4

Stella was safely in the haven of her two-rooms-and-a-bath at the King Arthur when she opened her mail. She had just come up from luncheon in the dining-room below, where she had greeted everybody she knew with her usual cordiality. "Be it even an apartment hotel, there's no place like home!" she had laughed to Mrs. Kay Bird. "Gracious, but this place seems good to me!" she had thrown across to the young doctor who ate at the table next to hers; and to the two white-haired old ladies who occasionally asked her of an evening to make a fourth at auction, "All ready for a game, any time," she had exclaimed.

She was still purring as she moved about the three rooms which were hers and Laurel's alone, humming in a low tone to herself, delighting in their luxury and their comfort, as she laid away her hat and veil and gloves, bag and umbrella, in their old familiar nooks and corners.

She sat down on the edge of her bed to open her mail. There was a postcard from Laurel. She read that first. There was a note from Miss Simpson, verifying the hour of Laurel's arrival. She read that next. After Miss Simpson's note there were two announcements of fall openings; a bill; a receipt; then suddenly occurred an explosion of one of the bombs! Miss Fillibrown regretted that, owing to the unexpected increase of pupils in Laurel's class, there would be no place for her next year!

Stella's low humming ceased abruptly. She read the note again. She read it a third time. She was aware of a certain familiar heart-burning sensation which usually followed announcements of this sort. No place for Laurel at Miss Fillibrown's? Oh, that was cruel. There was no other private school in Milhampton. Laurel couldn't go to a public school. Nobody did—except foreigners. No place for Laurel at Miss Fillibrown's! There must be some mistake. But deep in her heart Stella knew there was no mistake. Experience had taught her there never was a mistake in the cruel stabs dealt her.

It was fully ten minutes before the second bomb exploded. The letter immediately underneath Miss Fillibrown's was a note from the proprietor of the King Arthur. The proprietor of the King Arthur regretted that he would be unable to accommodate Stella the following season! He had rented her present apartment, he explained, to a party who had offered almost double what she was paying, and there would be no other space available.

Stella got up and walked over to the window, folded her arms, as if to hold herself under better control, and stood staring out into the street below. What did it mean? What had she done? Why were people so unkind? What was to become of Laurel and herself? It wasn't as if there were other apartment hotels in Milhampton. The King Arthur was unique. The other places were boarding-houses, pure and simple. All sorts of people lived in them. She could no more take Laurel to a boarding-house than send her to a public school. Good heavens, this was a serious situation! Stella had received blows before, but the combination of these two, occurring both at once, and striking such vital parts of the anatomy of her social position in Milhampton, she knew would prove fatal. A wave of physical sickness swept over her.

It was fully half an hour before the last bomb shattered the frail scaffolding of another of Stella's air-castles. The last letter in her pile was from a lawyer in New York. The lawyer stated that he was writing for Mr. Stephen Dallas. Stella's eyes skipped over the introductory sentences. She caught the word "divorce." Stephen wanted to get a divorce!

Hope had never died that sometime she and Stephen might live beneath the same roof again. The possibility that when the golden harvest-time arrived when Laurel was old enough to come out, Stephen, too, would wish to give his child every possible advantage, and resume at least the semblance of a conventional relationship with his wife, had been for years a sort of secret candle Stella would take out and light whenever it seemed dark. But a divorce, a separation would rob her of her candle. Besides, she couldn't say "my husband" any more, could she, to her friends and acquaintances? Nor refer to her husband's absence as temporary. Oh, no one knew what a protection the uncertainty had been to her' all these years.

At one o'clock the next morning Stella lay wide awake in her bed beside Laurel's empty one, tossing and turning in the darkness, reviewing the contents of each of the three cruel notes that had swept so bare her little hill of hopes, and left it bleak and desolate. At two o'clock she was still awake, and again at three she heard the chimes ringing in the Episcopal Church belfry, a half a mile away. At half-past three she got up and went into the bathroom. She poured herself out half a glass of gin, and filled the glass up with hot water from the faucet. She placed two sleeping-tablets on the back of her tongue and washed them down with the strong hot drink.

Laurel was due to arrive the next morning at nine o'clock. Stella simply must pull herself together before Laurel arrived.

CHAPTER XIII

1

"I SHOULDN'T think that Simpson woman earned her salt. She's let your nails get into a terrible condition!" scolded Stella.

"Oh, but Miss Simpson never does my nails, mother," laughed Laurel.

She and Stella were seated opposite each other at a card-table in their bedroom at the King Arthur. There was a bath-towel spread over the table. Laurel held the finger-tips of one hand in a bowl filled with warm water, while her mother worked over the other. It was early afternoon of the first day of Laurel's arrival.

"Gracious, Laurel, this cuticle hasn't been pushed back once since you've been gone, I'll bet. I don't know what will become of you if you don't take more pains with yourself. These nails of yours are all split and broken to pieces."

"But I've been camping, mother."

"I should think you'd been mining, and using your fingers for pick-axes!"

A cat no more vigorously sets herself to work over the deplorable condition of her kitten after a visit to the coal-bin than did Stella over Laurel after her visit to New York and the Maine woods, "where they lived like animals," according to her way of thinking.

Stella was thankful this time, with all her heart, that she could work over Laurel, for when she had anything to conceal it was always easier to talk to the funny little perceiving creature, if she could keep her eyes down close on some sort of fine careful job, like cutting a bit of cuticle, or filing a nail to just the proper arch.

When the manicuring was well under way, Stella inquired, "How is your father?"

She always asked that question before Laurel had been back many hours.

Laurel always replied, "He's all right."

"Didn't seem different any way?"

"No."

"Didn't refer to me, I suppose?"

"No."

Laurel wished he would refer to her sometime, so she might tell her he had.

"Goodness," exclaimed Stella, "I should think he'd ask after my health once in a while!"

Laurel was silent.

Stella applied the blunt end of a steel file to the half-moon just appearing out of the pink flesh of Laurel's thumb.

"I should think he'd have some interest in my Welfare."

Still Laurel was silent.

"I never did anything to have him treat me as if I was dead."

"You hurt, mother."

Stella laid down the file. But it was somewhere inside where Stella was really hurting Laurel. Laurel always suffered when her mother talked like that about her father.

"You'd think from the way he acts such a thing as a marriage ceremony had never taken place between him and me."

"Mother," Laurel interrupted—she must change the subject somehow—"I've learned to use a shotgun."

"I hope, Laurel," Stella went right on, "you have more respect for the promises you make, than your father seems to."

Laurel made another desperate attempt.

"Oh, mother," she exclaimed brightly, "I saw that lovely lady again in New York."

She was successful this time.

"What lovely lady?" asked Stella.

Laurel had been too busy so far answering her mother's questions as to what restaurants and theaters she had visited in New York to tell her about Mrs. Morrison.

"The lovely lady who gave me my silver pencil."

"Oh, yes, you met her at afternoon tea last year. I remember. You said she had on black broadcloth with broad-tail trimming then. What did she wear this time?"

"She isn't wearing black at all this year, but palish colors when she dresses up that you think are white until you see her up against a white wall or something, and then you see they aren't. They're usually pale yellow, or faint blue. She never wears pink."

"Good gracious, how many different rigs did you see this person in?"

"Oh, lots!"

She had not referred to Mrs. Morrison in her letters to her mother. That was not strange. Laurel was not fluent with her pen. Her letters were labored little notes, usually, that mirrored her personality imperfectly. Laurel's father used to say he could scarcely catch a glimpse of Laurel in the stilted notes she wrote to him. Once Laurel had tried to write to her mother about Mrs. Morrison, but Mrs. Morrison was like the Maine woods. There was so much to say that you just didn't know what one or two things to choose to cramp into half a dozen proper little sentences that must begin with a capital, contain a subject and a predicate, and end with a period.

"You'd love her clothes, mother," Laurel now went on. "She's got the loveliest negligée, she's got two or three lovely negligées, but I think my favorite was a yellowish one, made of a most beautiful crêpy stuff, with not a speck of trimming on it anywhere."

"Negligée!" exclaimed Stella. "Did she spend the night with you?"

"Oh, no, I spent the night with her. I spent almost a whole week of nights with her, while father was in Chicago."

"Oh, you did, did you?" said Stella, speaking thickly through an orange-stick which she held between her teeth. Stella often used her mouth to hold small tools, when she sewed or manicured. Lucky for her now! A sudden suspicion had shot up and gripped her in the throat. The orange-stick helped to disguise the tenseness in her voice. "That was a funny arrangement, I should think."

"I didn't want to go a bit, at first," said Laurel.

"I was frightened at the thought of visiting a stranger. But I needn't have been. Mrs. Morrison was perfectly lovely to me!"

"Oh, she was, was she? How?"

"Just every way there is to be lovely. For one thing—she thought I had lovely clothes, and that you had awfully good taste. She said so. *She* talked about you, mother. She thought you must be simply beautiful when I told her what you looked like."

"What does *she* look like?"

"A little like an Indian Pipe," said Laurel reflectively. "That's a sort of flower that grows in dark places up in the Maine woods. It hasn't got any color at all."

"Oh, gracious. I mean is she tall or short, dark or light, fat or thin. I don't care what kind of a flower she looks like."

"Well," Laurel began slowly, methodically. "She's dark—at least her hair is—and tall—at least she looks tall until you see her beside somebody taller like father—and slim, and cool-looking and pale—oh, ever so pale. And the queer thing is, she doesn't use any rouge at all. She does her hair," Laurel went on, "with only five hairpins, and no net. And once I saw her put soap right on her face! And she goes out in the broiling sun and lets it beat down on her without any veil or sunshade, or anything."

"What's her age?"

"She doesn't seem to be any special age. She's like one of those goddesses in my Greek Mythology Book that way."

"Oh, come. You can tell me whether she's twenty or forty, I guess."

"Oh, she's not forty! She can touch her fingers to the floor without bending her knees just as well as I can. We tried it one morning. And she rides horseback, and swims and plays tennis and golf. Father said she could almost beat him at golf. I guess she's about twenty-five."

"Oh, she and your father play golf sometimes."

"Sometimes."

"How in the world did your father become acquainted with this goddess?" Stella inquired, in as light a tone as she could muster. "Happen to know?"

"Yes, and it's like a story. Father found her in Central Park! He saw her there riding horseback one day. He was on a horse, too. She passed him. He didn't like to run after her, and try to catch her, so he went by another path, and cut her off when she came round a curve later on. Con told me about it."

"Who's Con?"

"Con is her oldest son."

"Oh, son! Married is she?"

"She used to be. Her husband is dead now."

"Oh, dead, is he? That's convenient," murmured Stella.

"Oh, no, it isn't. It isn't a bit convenient. Mr. Morrison left a whole lot of money and horses and houses and things, and Mrs. Morrison has to look out for them all alone. She says she wouldn't know what to do without father to help her and advise her."

"Oh, I see, I see." Stella was still polishing, still keeping her voice light and inconsequential with the help of the steadying orange-stick. "A whole lot of money and horses and houses, has she? And what house did you visit her at?"

"I visited her at her house on Long Island. Oh, mother, it's wonderful! It has a beautiful lawn and garden all around it, and on the first floor out of all the rooms there are long windows, like doors, which are always kept open, so you can walk out onto the grass any time, just as easily as walking out from underneath a tree. Upstairs in the house there are the loveliest bedrooms and little tiled bathrooms hidden away like jewels on the inside of a watch. And all the bedroom doors stand open all day. Nobody ever thinks of locking the bedroom door. And in the pantry off the dining-room there's a big tin box with rows of thin cookies on each shelf. You can take one whenever you Ve hungry. Sometimes you can go into the kitchen and make candy! Oh, mother," Laurel broke off, "would it cost too awfully much for us to have a house all of our own somewhere—not a great big expensive one, like Mrs. Morrison's, but a little tiny one with a front door that's just ours, and a dining-room that's just ours, and a warm sleepy-looking kitchen that's just ours, where I could make candy sometimes (Mrs. Morrison and I made fudge one rainy day in the kitchen), and a guest-room so I could ask girls to come and stay all night with me sometimes? Mrs. Morrison asked a girl my age, whose mother she knew, to come and stay with me one night. And she came, and when she went she asked me to come and stay all night with *her!*" (No girl had ever asked Laurel to stay all night with her before.) "But I couldn't because I had to go back to New York the next day. I hated to go back to New York to Miss Simpson. Mother, next to you I think Mrs. Morrison is the loveliest lady I ever saw." Laurel's voice actually trembled.

Stella removed the orange-stick from her mouth and laid it down on the table beside the buffer.

"There," she said, "how do those look?" And she held up Laurel's fingers for her to see. She spoke harshly. She had to or the child might discover the tremble in *her* voice too.

Laurel gave the fingers a hasty glance. "They're all right," she remarked. Then dropping her hands on the bath-towel, and gazing out of the window, she added, and a glow stole into her eyes—into her voice also, "Mrs. Morrison has the most beautiful hands—long and white and slim like the rest of her. I wish I could have hands like hers!"

2

Stella got up and went into the bathroom. She closed the door and locked it, then turned on both faucets, so that Laurel would think she was busy washing up. She stood staring at herself in the mirror over the wash-stand, while the water gushed into the basin.

Laurel had never glowed about a woman before. Stella didn't know what to make of it. It perplexed her. It hurt her. It hurt her more than the possibility that Stephen might be glowing about the same woman. Who was she, anyway—this tall mysterious siren, who was bewitching Lollie with her youth and beauty and prosperity, buying the kiddie's affection, by bestowing luxuries and attentions upon her in a single week which Stella would give her eyeteeth to be able to give Laurel in a lifetime.

Laurel was sensitive to beauty, Stella was aware of it—cruelly aware of it, as she stared at herself in the mirror before her. She saw all the tiny wrinkles. She saw the coarseness and the flabbiness She saw the unmistakable yellow cast of color. It was as definite now as that of a white China silk waist after half a dozen washings. Good gracious, how could she hope to compete with a woman of twenty-five? It seemed lately as if nothing would cover up the defects and blemishes for any length of time. Often within so short a period as half an hour after she had left her bedroom, glancing into some unexpected mirror, she would discover the horrible old look sneaking out of hiding. A wave of discouragement swept over Stella. She had never required youth so much as now.

She pulled open the door to the medicine-closet in the wall beside the wash-stand with a determined jerk. She produced a large jar of cold cream, and began smearing great globs of it over her face. "A cold-cream bath, and a good hot steam is what you need," she announced to her reflection, and with a practiced rotating motion she proceeded to massage cheeks, chin, neck, and forehead vigorously, furiously; admonishing herself the while in the mirror—exhorting, and inciting with fresh courage.

This wasn't the time to lie down and submit. What if the world was treating her like a bunch of cruel boys a dog—kicking her from all sides, all at once? She mustn't put her tail between her legs and yelp and hug the ground. She must stand up and bristle her back, and snarl, and show her teeth, if necessary. And she would, too! Oh, there was a lot of fight left in her yet.

She didn't know exactly how a dog managed to fight so many boys at once. No sooner did she consider lowering her head to offer resistance to one of her tormentors than another hit her from behind. Seemed as if. Really, within the last twenty-four hours it seemed as if everything in the way of sharp-cornered missiles had been thrown in her direction, and struck her somewhere. It was confusing. It was alarming. But she mustn't show she was confused or alarmed. Lollie mustn't guess. Good Lord, no!

Half an hour later Stella emerged from the bathroom, with all her war-paint on. Her cheeks were a little rosier than usual, her eyebrows a little more distinctly emphasized, and her lips a little more definitely bowed.

3

Three days later Stella took the early morning train to Boston, "to do a little fall shopping," she told Laurel, but really to meet Mr. Morley Smith, the lawyer who had written to her from New York about the divorce. Mr. Smith had suggested in his letter that he would like a personal interview with Stella. Stella had replied that she would meet him at the appointed hour, at the office of the Boston law firm which he had mentioned.

You may be sure she had on all her war-paint when she sallied forth that morning, all her war-feathers too. She had selected a costume of wide black-and-white striped foulard in which to combat this particular adversary (the stripes wound sleekly around her. She resembled a zebra somewhat), and she had made herself as formidable as she knew how with all her loudest finery. A hat with sharp futurist angles, a shadow veil that hung unsecured and diaphanous to her shoulders; pearl ear-rings, filbert size; around her neck a long noisy chain of imitation amber beads. Her shoes were French-heeled, and steel-buckled. She carried several dangling articles on her left wrist that clattered every time she moved her hands.

When she was ushered into the private office placed at Mr. Morley Smith's disposal, he had to make an effort not to allow himself to betray his amazement. Stephen had not prepared him for anybody of this sort. The truth is Stephen himself would have been surprised at Stella's appearance. In the days when he had advised plain dark dresses, and no decorations, she had not used rouge, lipsticks, and eyebrow pencils. She hadn't needed to. Stephen didn't take into account that there had been no one to advise Stella since he had given up the enterprise, no friend or protector to care what mistakes she committed during that critical period when her volatile prettiness began to evaporate like ether into air.

As Morley Smith drew up a chair and asked Stella to be seated, he looked at her closely and catalogued her forthwith. Morley Smith had known Stephen Dallas for years. How could he ever have married this woman? How could any man, who was attracted by the gentle, genuine charms of Mrs. Cornelius Morrison (and had been attracted by them, too, according to his story, before he ever met this Stella Martin), have contemplated matrimony with such an absolute antithesis? What a Quixote Stephen Dallas must have been, in spite of his insistence that he had married the pretty Normal-School student of his own free will and in the pursuit of happiness.

"I am glad, Mrs. Dallas," Mr. Morley Smith began from his high place of authority in front of the flat-topped desk, glancing across to Stella in her low place at the side of the desk (three feet and an armchair make all the difference in the world), "that you found it convenient to meet me here to-day. It is so much more satisfactory to talk a matter of this kind over quietly together."

"Oh, that's all right," said Stella. She wished her chair had a deep seat and arms so that she could lean back and assume a position of command.

"It is my hope," Mr. Smith went on suavely, "that I may be performing a service for both you and Mr. Dallas in arranging this affair without publicity, to your mutual satisfaction. I want you to feel, Mrs. Dallas," he smiled, "that I am here, not only as Mr. Dallas's friend and attorney, but as your friend and attorney, too."

"I don't need any attorney," said Stella.

"I agree with you, you do not. This affair should be, and can be settled without contest—between ourselves. That is your husband's wish, too. He and I have gone into the details of this matter and there lies open to us a line of procedure, which, if pursued, will cause almost no unpleasantness, as far as you are concerned."

"And what's that?"

"Why, you are to bring suit against Mr. Dallas for desertion. He will not contest the grounds of your suit, and the divorce will be granted without disagreeable controversy."

"I don't want a divorce," said Stella.

"Really?" Mr. Morley Smith raised his eyebrows in surprise. "Surely, you want your separation of seven years' standing legalized, do you not, and enjoy the advantages thereof?"

"I don't want a divorce," Stella repeated.

"The word has an unpleasant sound for some women, I know," Mr. Smith smiled. "It shouldn't. Let me explain. Perhaps you haven't thought in detail just what the benefits would be of a settlement of the relations existing between you and Mr. Dallas—just what hardships you are inflicting upon yourself, unnecessarily, in allowing them to continue in their present state."

And in the next ten minutes he laid out before Stella, as attractively as he knew how, all the line arguments, moral, social, and financial, for her consideration, that he possessed.

But his display apparently made no impression upon Stella. For when he had finished all she said was, just as if she hadn't been listening, "I don't want a divorce, and," she added, "what's more I don't intend to have one."

Mr. Morley Smith frowned and shrugged. Then, balancing the tips of his elbows on the arms of his chair, and the tips of the fingers of his left hand nicely against the tips of the fingers of his right, he said, "That's a pity."

"I'm sorry to disoblige Stephen, I'm sure," said Stella, shrugging too.

"I meant a pity for you," flashed back Mr. Smith. And the smile and suave manner had disappeared. "Mr. Dallas can obtain his divorce without the least difficulty in the world, by another method. Don't have any doubt on that point. But the other method will not be exactly to your liking, I fear," he announced, fastening his keen shrewd eyes upon Stella. "I always feel sorry for any woman," he went on, "whose mistakes and misdemeanors of a dozen years are dragged out by opposing lawyers from the little hiding-places where she thought they were safe, and held up for the curious public to gape at and glory In. Your husband, Mrs. Dallas, in allowing you to bring suit against him. Instead of the other way round. Is acting chivalrously. He is offering you an avenue of escape."

"I don't want any avenue of escape," Stella retorted. "I tell you I don't want a divorce."

Really it was annoying. Mr. Morley Smith couldn't make the least indentation on her.

"It looks to me, Mrs. Dallas, as if you will be obliged to have a divorce whether you want it or not."

"I don't know why. I don't pretend to know anything about the law, but I've got some common sense, and I never heard of a woman's being forced to get a divorce from her husband because he happens to want to go and get married again. Stephen does want to get married again, doesn't he?"

"That's entirely a side issue in this case, Mrs. Dallas. I am unable to inform you."

"Well, he does. I know he does."

"I should think under the circumstances he would wish to feel free to marry again."

"Well, he can't do it, and that's all there is to it. You can go back to New York and tell him that I refuse, with thanks, his chivalrous offer. Gracious. I don't call it exactly chivalrous for a man to walk off and leave his wife for seven years, and then, when he gets good and ready, give her the privilege of suing him for a divorce, so he can go and marry a rich young widow, and kick the high spots with her."

"You will, then, as I said before, force Mr. Dallas to bring suit against you."

"I never deserted him."

"No, your offense is graver."

"I never knew what my offense was. I've been ransacking my brain for seven years to find some good reason for Stephen's clearing out the way he did."

"Oh, come, Mrs. Dallas," half-laughed, half-sneered Mr. Morley Smith.

"What do you mean by that?"

"Don't try and pretend innocence with me. I've handled too many cases of this nature, dealt with too many women placed in your unenviable position. It won't work."

He looked straight into Stella's eyes, as he spoke, piercingly, drillingly. It was a horrid look. It was a look not to be endured from a man who was your enemy. Stella could feel the blood throbbing up into her throat.

"Are you trying to be insulting to me somehow?"

Mr. Morley Smith's sneer deepened. "That's right. You're acting consistently. It's quite the right tack—surprise, indignation, rage, tears, confession finally. Mrs. Dallas, allow me to spare you further attempt at evasion. I have facts—unalterable, unescapable facts. You were seen." He lowered his voice. "You were seen at Belcher's Beach," he brought out.

"Well, what of that?" flashed Stella.

"You were seen at the boarding-house, with Munn," he added, still keeping his sword-pointed eyes upon Stella.

Oh, so that was it! That was why there was no room for Laurel at Miss Fillibrown's! That was why the proprietor at the King Arthur had rented her apartment.

"Oh, what a rotten, rotten world!" she exclaimed.

Mr. Morley Smith shrugged and looked away. There was a silence. Then, "Well, you understand me, now, I think. You have your choice. Think it over. Either the generous escape Mr. Dallas offers, or the public exposure of acts you have taken such pains heretofore to conceal and cover up."

Stella stared at Mr. Morley Smith speechless, helpless for a moment. Every word he uttered, every glance of his eyes, every pharisaical shrug of his shoulders shamed and degraded her. She would simply have to get out of his presence, or she would do something horribly common and crude to him, like slapping him in the face, or calling him something unladylike, like a cur or a skunk. She stood up.

"I'm going," she said.

He stood up too. He smiled.

"You will cooperate with us, then? You will accept our proposition?"

"Cooperate? Accept your proposition? No, I won't. I'll fight! That's what I'll do. I'll prove to the world whether I'm guilty or not of the filthy things rotten-minded people have said about me. And I'm glad of the chance, too. I hope Stephen *will* sue me for a divorce. I said I didn't need a lawyer, when I first came here, but I need somebody to defend me against such a pack of muck-rakers. Why, Mr. Smith, I have no more done the thing you come here and accuse me of doing than your own wife, or, if you're not married, your own mother, or the woman you honor the most in this world, whoever it is, and I'll get the best lawyer in this country to prove it."

Behind the belying paint and elaborate make-up the white image of this woman's innocence stood out before Morley Smith clear and defined, for an instant, like a white-sailed ship, when the fog lifts a moment—a white-sailed ship in distress. He saw it. He recognized it. He turned away from it.

"You're going through the usual motions, Mrs. Dallas," he commented with another sneer.

CHAPTER XIV

1

The same chaste charm that pervaded Helen Morrison's summer home was even more striking in her New York house. A feeling of space and fresh air is more of a triumph in the city than in the country. In both Helen Morrison's houses there was delicious freedom from deleterious overcrowding of possessions beneath a roof. She knew how to make walls backgrounds, instead of boundaries, as unconfining as the sky behind a mountain, or the sea behind a sail. Yet neither of her houses could be called large. Much as nature conforms itself equally happily to decorating a mountain-side, or a salt-water pool no larger than a baptismal font, so Helen conformed herself instinctively to whatever proportions were offered her. Never for the sake of displaying some beautiful work of art would Helen disturb the nice equilibrium and fine composition of a room. Never were the space and air necessary for the spiritual well-being, as it were, of one rare treasure robbed for another. She possessed a nice sense of harmony, too. She could no more have placed Tiffany glass beside old luster than have mixed people of discordant instincts at her dinner-table. This discernment was not acquired. It was as effortless with her as breathing.

When she married Cornelius Morrison and came as a very young bride to the New York house, filled with its chaotic collection of treasures picked up from all over the globe, not only by her widely traveled husband, but by his father before him, she felt little of the delight which beautiful things had given her before. On the contrary, she was possessed of an incessant desire to escape them, to get outdoors, and breathe deep, and look upon broad spaces.

Finally she asked her husband if he would object if she cleared out just one of the rooms in the house of every single thing that was in it. He told her she could clean out the whole house, for since Cornelius Morrison had obtained *her*, his other treasures had sunk into trivial insignificance. Therefore Helen Morrison had had the entire top floor of the house built into a single room which she called the Museum, and into which she moved the wealth of two generations of collectors.

Cloisonnee no longer rubbed shoulders with Copenhagen in the Morrison drawing-room, nor futurist touched frames with early Italian. Such jarring juxtapositions gave Helen somewhat the same feeling of displeasure that a discord on the piano gives to a sensitively musical child when he is still too young to understand why. Helen Morrison could understand her recoil but imperfectly. She knew little about schools and periods and values in art in its various forms when she married Cornelius Morrison. She warned her husband that she was an expert judge concerning only the merits of table-linen, lingerie, and flat silver. But he soon discovered that if an article was really fine and genuine, the something fine and genuine in his wife recognized it and responded to it. He made her curator of the Museum without hesitation.

Underneath the Museum, Cornelius Morrison's house was like a barn at first. At least so the aunt who had lived with Cornelius before he married told Helen, when she saw it.

Helen had exclaimed, "Isn't it? All beautiful space and shadows, and room enough to dance a spring song in, if you feel like it."

The house didn't remain long like an empty barn, however, though according to the aunt it never seemed "like a really furnished house."

Helen spent hours browsing in the Museum, assimilating it slowly, piece by piece. Gradually various treasures began appearing in the rooms below. When Helen discovered, or believed she had, an affinity between some empty niche downstairs and one of the objects of art in the Museum, she united them with delight. "Trial marriages," she called them humorously to her husband. Many of them proved permanent, but there were certain corners, tables, old chests, and secretaries, "that enjoyed a constant state of polygamy," she laughed, "that adjusted themselves happily to various of the temperamental objects of art in the Museum."

You never could be sure what would be the dominant note in the long room with the old-ivory tinted walls in the front of the house. This room was Helen's own. Here, she changed the ornaments as she would the flowers, with every changing season and mood. Therefore there were few of the objects of value in the Museum that, one time or another, didn't descend to the rooms below.

Cornelius Morrison discovered his collection all over again. As Helen isolated one piece of it after another and placed it in a sympathetic environment, he was constantly finding new beauties in form and line and color, heretofore unseen. He liked to boast that he had never enjoyed his collection until Helen came with her unerring intuitions. She gave it new birth. Helen gave new birth to everything he possessed. He told her that she gave new birth to *him*, too.

2

Helen had known Cornelius Morrison ever since she was a little girl. He was her father's friend—not so old as her father by a decade or so, but a younger brother of the same generation. He used to come occasionally and spend a night in her father's house in Reddington, on his way farther west, or else on his way back to New York from some protracted journey to China or Japan. He was one of the few honored guests for whom the wine-glasses were always produced and the little liqueur set. Helen used to examine his baggage in secret—his umbrella, his overcoat, his toilet articles—for they were permeated with the same vague fascinating cosmopolitanism of which she was aware whenever he opened his mouth to speak. In those days he was "Mr. Morrison" to Helen. He was "Mr. Morrison" to her up to the day she told him she would marry him. One of the hardest things she had to do was to learn to call him Cornelius.

Helen spent the first half-dozen years of her long boarding-school career in a small town in Connecticut. But she finished her education at a boarding-school in New York. Judge Dane wrote to his friend Cornelius Morrison, when Helen went to New York, and asked him if he would look up his little daughter sometime, and see if she seemed happy in her new environment.

Cornelius Morrison was very kind to the little daughter. He became a sort of fairy godfather to Helen and her group of friends at the New York school. He sent them flowers. He sent them candy. He gave them theater-parties, and afternoon-tea-parties, and college football-parties—all properly chaperoned, all properly discussed and arranged with the mistress of such affairs at the school.

Helen was old enough to appreciate that Mr. Cornelius Morrison was something of a personage in New York (her friends left her in no doubt on that point), but she was not old enough to appreciate that the friendship between Mr. Morrison and her father scarcely warranted so much time and thought spent in her entertainment. She accepted his attentions with enthusiasm, and with the simple joy of a child accepting the bounty of a generous Santa Claus. He bestowed them with no more thought of return.

Cornelius Morrison had never married. In spite of the prominence of his name and family in New York, he had always been shy with women. Helen and her friends were an entirely new adventure to him. He became very fond of Helen Dane. At first he believed he was fond of her as he might have been fond of a younger sister, and he mourned the fact that he had been an only child. Later he believed he was fond of her as he might have been fond of a daughter, and he mourned the fact that he had never married. Then suddenly Cornelius Morrison-discovered that he was fond of Helen—that he *loved* Helen—as only a man can love the woman he wants to make his wife. And she was nineteen, and he was fifty-two!

He started for India a few weeks after his discovery. He didn't return for three years. When he came back he stopped off at Reddington as was his custom when returning to New York from the Far East. His old friend, Judge Dane, had died during his absence—he had been dead a year—but he wished to pay respect to his memory and also to find out if the little daughter, who had finished school now, was well and happy.

He was disturbed about the little daughter when he saw her. The death of her father must have cut deep. She had suffered. This tender creature was still suffering, Cornelius Morrison believed. It struck him, as he sat opposite her at dinner in the big ponderous dining-room where he had often sat opposite her father before, that she was like an abandoned kitten in this great empty place, with only paid caretakers to see that she was fed.

After dinner in the drawing-room he said to her, "Helen, I believe you are lonely here."

Calmly, with no tears (Helen had shed all her tears), with no raising of her voice—she might have been a woman of forty who spoke—she replied, "I *am* lonely, Mr. Morrison, and I *am* unhappy, too. I wish I could leave Reddington forever. There's absolutely nothing for me here now."

A wave of tenderness swept over Cornelius Morrison. A wild delirious hope sprang alive within his heart. Could it be that he had anything to offer Helen that she wanted?

3

Cornelius Morrison had arrived in Reddington a few months after the Dallas tragedy. He had reappeared in Helen's life at a time when every waking moment was dull pain to her, and the days and the months and the years stretched ahead of her like a long, dark, drear road with a blind end.

Helen Dane had loved the son of the man whose last act had cast such a shadow upon the boy who bore his name. Helen had loved Stephen from the first time he had come to call on her the night after the dance her father had given her when she returned to be the young mistress of his house. He had danced with her half a dozen times that evening. He had claimed her for "Home, Sweet Home." Well, who had a better right? They had known each other as children, years before they went East to school. Their fathers served on several same boards of directors together. During "Home, Sweet Home" Stephen asked Helen if he might "call." Such was the custom in those days. He was returning to his law school shortly. He asked if he might call the next evening, that is, if she was going to be at home, and if she hadn't too many other bookings. She was going to be at home. If she had other bookings, she cancelled them. Stephen found her alone.

They sat in Judge Dane's big quiet drawing-room, one on each side of the rose-shaded table-lamp and discussed such impersonal subjects as the football game in New Haven last November, and the boat-race on the Thames last June, and the plays they had seen last spring in New York, and the places they had dined and danced there; and Shaw and Ibsen and Arnold Daly and Nazimova. It was a typical call for that era. Helen had carried on conversations of the same sort with many a young man before. But never had her hands been cold, and her face hot, and never had she lain awake afterwards for three hours and a half.

The truth was that Helen, with the same unerring instinct that later guided her in recognizing kinships between objects of art, was aware of something of the sort between Stephen and herself on her first evening alone with him, and it was exciting. It wasn't only that they were both young, with traditions that were not dissimilar, and tastes and ideals that were not antagonistic. For such was the case between Helen and many of the young men she had met. It was something deeper, more vital. Why, even when this Stephen disagreed with her, now and again, as he had that first evening, she had experienced as sharp—as glowing a sense of pleasure, as certain sharp contrasts in color gave her. No. It wasn't that Stephen was like her, any more like her than a cup is like a saucer (but one without the other is incomplete—broken) or the tallow candle like the silver stick to hold it (but one is the perfect complement of the other, even though made of such different stuff).

Stephen also had been awake a good many hours of the night after his first call on Helen. He wouldn't have been, probably, if he had been in his own bed at home, instead of on the train speeding East. (Stephen was less given to contemplation than Helen.) But every time a stop, or jolt, or sudden application of brakes shook him awake, he was conscious of Helen Dane. "By George, she's a pretty girl"—"I'll write to her to-morrow"—"I'll order her some flowers as soon as I reach Boston"—"I'm going to see something more of that girl. She has beautiful eyes—and a brain too"—"I don't know when I've met such a girl"—"I wonder if she'll want to settle down in Reddington."

The world took on a new interest and significance for Helen after that. The sound of the mailman's whistle would often make her heart jump up in the region of her throat. The sight of a certain shaped envelope on the hall table, sometimes bearing two and three stamps in its corner, would fill her with such a choking wave of emotion that she couldn't answer questions coherently until she had closed herself in her room and had devoured the letter's contents. And why not? Wasn't it written by the man she was going to marry (though he might not yet be aware of it), and didn't it discuss thrilling things about religion and philosophy, and art and music, and all sorts of foundation-stones of a life together?

They didn't refer to that life together in their letters, not directly. They didn't refer to it at Easter-time when the discussions continued by the rose-shaded lamp. Of course not. Stephen's education was not finished yet. He had a whole year and a half at the law school still before he could even start upon a self-supporting career. But Helen was not impatient. She liked prolonging the sweet adventure. It couldn't possibly come out but one way. Stephen's eyes had told her over and over that she was the only girl in the world for him, and her eyes had replied, shiningly, mistily, that she knew it—she knew it and was glad! At least she thought that was what his eyes had said. She thought he understood what she had replied.

When his father did that awful thing, Helen's love for Stephen burst into a blinding desire to help and comfort and share. Her own father had died a few months before. She was alone in the world. If Stephen had need of her, she had need of him, too. She must tell him so when his long torturing journey home was over and he came to her.

Helen waited for three days for Stephen to come to her. Finally, convinced that he was waiting for a sign from her, she stole out quietly, one evening, by herself, and called at the Dallas's big brown house, shrouded in its silent and solemn horror. She stood on the doorstep and rang the bell, and without explanation asked for Stephen. He was out. She left her card with a hasty pencil message written on it, "Please come over to-night. Helen." But he didn't come.

4

Helen didn't see Stephen Dallas again until one day, fifteen years later, sauntering along one of the bridle-paths of Central Park, she glanced up and there he was standing before her (on horseback also) with his hat off, smiling and saying, "Do you remember me?"

Her heart had jumped up into her throat in the same old young way it used to at sight of him a lifetime ago.

5

When Helen told Cornelius Morrison that she would marry him, she felt that Stephen was as definitely lost to her as her father. When the doctor had come to her just after her father had died and said, "It is all over," his words were no more final than Stephen's letter, which Helen received a long three weeks after she had called at the Dallas house. The letter was in answer to her note of consolation. For Helen had written to Stephen an outburst of sympathy at the first possible moment.

He thanked her for her note in a formal punctilious manner which she scarcely recognized. He thanked her for the card she had sent over to the house at the time of the funeral. He appreciated her kindness in offering to see him, but it was difficult for him to talk to his friends. He had left Reddington forever. He never wanted to see Reddington again. He was going away—very far away, to Australia, possibly, where he was unknown. He was thankful that Helen's and his friendship was still in its infancy. He was thankful he had formed no business alliances. He was thankful that his father's act cast no sha'dow of shame on any one outside his own immediate household.

Helen read Stephen's letter until every word of it was graven on her heart. Then she put it away and faced the world without him. There was no recalling him. One cannot recall that which one has never had. One cannot pursue that which does not exist. Stephen was aware of no special bond, of no insolubility. That which to her had been one of those rare relationships that occur once in a long, long while in various groups and communities, had been to him but a "friendship in its infancy." He classed it with a dozen others. She was just a girl he had fancied for a season.

6

There was only one small light to relieve the darkness of Helen's solitude that winter. She had always loved children. One of her aunts had a little girl—a baby barely three, who took a fancy to Helen. The baby would clamber up into her arms, and cuddle down contented like a kitten in the sun. When Helen told Cornelius Morrison that she would marry him, it was with the distinct image of a little girl of her own, clambering up into her arms and cuddling down contented.

When he asked her when she would like to be married (he waited a whole week before he broached the question: not for anything would he frighten Helen, would he seem to hasten her), she replied, "I would like to be married soon, within a few weeks."

Her voice did not waver. The pallor of her cheeks was as steady as that of a petal of a white rose. It was Cornelius Morrison who was trembling. He could scarcely trust himself to speak. A few weeks! Did she know what marriage meant? He didn't think so. Well, he would never teach her. It would be more than he had even hoped for, just to have her to be kind to, to take care of for a little while.

"I'll do my very best to make you happy, Helen," he said quietly.

There was something in his voice that struck through the wall of Helen's personal suffering behind which she had shut herself for so long. She leaned toward him. She grasped one of his hands with both of hers.

"I'll do my best to make you happy, too," she said fervently.

Neither of them ever forgot their promise.

CHAPTER XV

1

Although Cornelius Morrison was always aware he was not the perfect mate for Helen, and Helen observed her marriage with wide-open and seeing eyes, they both did much to enrich and beautify the life of the other. All happy marriages are not "made in heaven," Helen discovered. Some are the result of wise human effort, and long steady adaptation.

Cornelius Morrison was thirty years older than Helen. He was never free from the fear that some day a younger man, a more appropriate comrade for his wife, might supplant him in her affections. If a younger man devoted an evening to Helen, if she seemed to respond to his attentions with interest and vivacity, a deep melancholy would take possession of Cornelius Morrison—unreasonable, perhaps, but uncontrollable and terribly painful.

Helen needed no explanations. With her intuition she saw as clearly as through a microscope into the reason for her husband's occasional waves of depression. Not for anything in the world would she hurt him. She might not love him in the romantic way that she had loved Stephen. She knew that she didn't; but there was something fine and untarnished to be preserved about their relations, beside which passing and personal pleasures were trivial and unimportant. She became as careful to spare her husband the secret ignominy of jealousy as to guard her children from groundless fears and premonitions. In spite of her youth, in spite of her natural impulses, she avoided all intimacies that might even indefinitely disturb Cornelius.

With gentle consideration, too, she abandoned all forms of pleasure that emphasized the difference in their ages and placed him at a disadvantage. Cornelius spoke no word of complaint on the several occasions when she danced half the night away on a ballroom floor while he waited for her in a smoky anteroom, but quietly, without comment, Helen gave up dancing after a little while. Cornelius liked to give dinners. Helen learned to like to give them. Cornelius liked to go to the opera. Helen learned to like to go to the opera. Cornelius liked to ride horseback. Helen learned to like to ride horseback. It was when Helen was riding horseback in Central Park one morning alone that she met Stephen Dallas.

2

When Stephen had said, "Do you remember me?" Helen had replied with a little puzzled look, as if she wasn't quite sure, "You're Stephen Dallas, aren't you?"

"You *know* I'm Stephen Dallas," he exclaimed in the old sure way with her he used to have.

There was joy in his eyes. There was gladness in his voice. He had the queer sensation that the intervening years since last he saw this girl were a bad dream, and he had just waked up, as keenly responsive to her as the day he lost consciousness.

He leaned over and they shook hands. The sort of ecstasy swept over Stephen that any victim of a nightmare feels when he returns to the realm of realities and his physical contacts register properly.

They exchanged a commonplace or two—Helen sweetly, but coolly. Stephen with an impetuosity he didn't try to conceal.

"I saw you, half a mile back," he confessed. "You passed me. I didn't think at first it could be really you. Chance isn't usually so kind to me. By the time I had decided it couldn't possibly be anybody else, you had gone too far ahead for me to overtake you with proper park decorum. So I've been contriving ever since how I might head you off. Again chance has favored me. You might have made half a dozen wrong turns. Or, perhaps it wasn't chance at all. Perhaps it was mental telepathy."

To this boyish outburst of Stephen's Helen replied, still sweetly, still coolly (long practice had made her skillful), "I'm delighted we met, but I scarcely think it was due to mental telepathy. I let my horse choose the turns this morning. I usually ride with my husband and we always come this way."

"Oh, I know you're married, Helen," laughed Stephen boldly, as much as to say, "I suppose you think I ought to be told, I seem so glad to see you."

Helen was not to be perturbed by boldness. She was not a young girl to betray a pounding heart which she had reason to wish to conceal.

Politely, calmly, she inquired, "Are you living in New York now?"

He nodded, smiling. (What a beautiful woman she had become!)

"If two rooms in bachelor's apartments is living, yes, I am," he said.

"Have you been here long?"

"Three years."

"Three years? Really!" She raised her lovely brows.

"Oh, people may say the world's a small place, Helen," Stephen exclaimed. "But New York isn't. I've been trying for three years to run across your path, and I haven't succeeded until to-day!" He simply couldn't resist being personal with her at every turn.

Helen replied prosaically, "Well, I'm glad we've met at last. It's always a pleasure to see any one from Reddington."

She was almost convincing. Stephen looked at her sharply. Was it pretense, or was she actually unaware of any special significance in this meeting? "Don't you remember the talks we used to have, Helen?" he asked.

"Why, of course," she answered him, but she managed to sound more tactful than honest.

Stephen looked into her well-remembered eyes. "I've never forgotten them," he told her quietly.

Helen would not give him the slightest sign of response.

"I suppose," she went on serenely, "like most young people of our time we tried to settle all the weighty questions of the day, didn't we?"

Stephen felt a pang of disappointment. The years since last he saw Helen had not been a dream. They were real—every one of them was real, and Helen was as far removed, as beyond recall, as his youth. There she sat opposite him, graceful, lovely, beautifully poised upon her horse (beautifully poised in speech and manner, too), as impervious to him as a picture. She looked at him kindly, graciously, but disinterestedly as if he were a part of the landscape. He turned away from her tranquil face.

"You must come to dinner with us some day," he heard her saying in that cool, smooth, impersonal voice of hers.

"Thank you very much," he replied perfunctorily, not looking back at her. Oh, he, too, could be cool and smooth and impersonal if that was what she really wanted.

3

It was what she really wanted. When he dined for the first time at the Cornelius Morrison's there were half a dozen other guests present. He sat nowhere near his hostess, nor did she give him any chance for conversation after dinner. It was always like that. As time went on, Stephen was frequently in the same drawing-room with Helen, and often one of the same party, but she always contrived to avoid all opportunity for intimate conversation.

Stephen was hungry to talk to Helen. He had no intention of making love to her. She needn't have been afraid. He was scarcely less free than she. He simply wanted to sit occasionally, for short periods, in an outer circle of the warm sunshine of her radiating sympathy. But she wouldn't let him. Her insistence upon a purely impersonal basis of intercourse made anything but the merest superficialities impossible.

When Cornelius Morrison met Stephen Dallas, he took a fancy to the young man. They had several interests in common. Cornelius and Stephen went on a fall fishing-trip together six months after Stephen met Helen in Central Park. Stephen was often at Helen's house after the fishing-trip. Cornelius would bring him home to dinner unannounced. After dinner the two men would play long games of chess in the library, while Helen read to her boys in a room above. Of course Stephen saw Helen alone sometimes, but never for longer than a passing moment or two. Helen always had something to call her away. And during those passing moments or two she was always clothed in her armor.

Stephen made no attempt to pierce that armor. Convinced that it was not only her wish, but her determined resolve to treat him merely as a friend of her husband's, to whom she extended the courtesies of her position, but nothing more, he acquiesced. He even tried to help her. Finally Stephen avoided all chance for intimate conversation with Helen as delicately and adroitly as herself. Through Helen's skillful management Cornelius Morrison never experienced a moment of the cruel suspicion that he was unwelcome in the company of these two creatures so many years younger than himself.

For over half a dozen years Stephen came and went to and from the Morrison home. He was constantly moving before Helen's eyes—vivid and alive, but, as far as she was concerned, apparently divested of all reality.

When Cornelius Morrison died, and suddenly Helen was released from all fear of hurting him. she did not immediately alter her attitude towards Stephen Dallas. Habit was so strong—or was it respect for Cornelius that was so strong?—she contrived to maintain with Stephen for many months the same remote relations which she had established when her husband was alive.

Stephen had a great deal to do in settling Cornelius Morrison's affairs. Cornelius Morrison had concluded that, of all his friends who were members of the bar, Stephen Dallas, who had known Helen as a child, could work with her to the best advantage. He named Stephen as one of his trustees. Therefore Stephen and Helen were necessarily alone together frequently.

At first Stephen treated Helen as she had indicated she wished to be treated. He was almost formal with her unless the children were present as a safeguard. It was difficult to strike a happy medium after Stephen had been alone in Helen's presence for longer than half an hour. For he loved her! He believed he had loved her ever since that day he had met her in Central Park, and his own eagerness and joy at sight of her had so startled and surprised him. No. He believed he had loved her longer. Occasionally a look would pass between Helen and himself—a vague, indefinite look that recalled to Stephen the picture of a girl sitting by a rose-shaded lamp, and a boy opposite her toying with a little bronze which he had picked up from the table near by. Stephen believed he had loved Helen ever since that first night in Judge Dane's drawing-room!

When for the first time Stephen pursued one of those vague illusive looks, gazed straight at Helen in the gray depths of her eyes, and by sheer mind-energy captured that will-o'-the-wisp impulse that had drifted like vapor between them, she had drawn in her breath quickly and her eyelids had flickered and closed for a moment; and color, ever so faint, ever so indefinite, had tinged her cheeks.

It was no picture of a girl that Stephen saw then! It was the girl herself! She was not the wife of Cornelius Morrison. She was his, to love and to win! And again Stephen had the queer sensation of waking up from a bad dream. Again his father's suicide, the black days that had followed, Milhampton, the boarding-house, the little red cottage and Stella, were all parts of a nightmare. Helen alone was real. She was made for him. She was meant for him. All that had happened to prevent nature's plan was a mistake, an abortion.

At the time of Helen's betrayal of her real feelings for Stephen, he made no comment. He seemed not to notice the sharp intaking of her breath, the faint color, the closed lids. He began talking quickly about a certain exchange of property they had been discussing. And he left her very soon. Stephen made up his mind he would not speak a word of love to this beautiful woman until he was free to do 60, with no fear of casting reflection upon her reputation.

Divorce, public acknowledgment of failure in the most sacred department in a man's or a woman's life, had always seemed hideous to Stephen. But wasn't it the failure, after all, that was hideous, rather than the acknowledgment? His and Stella's failure had already been demonstrated. They had already made the slow embittering descent from confidence and hope to doubt and despair. For years their marriage had been absolved. To place the law's decree upon dead hopes is not the saddest part of the experience. It is not the required death notice in the city's records that remains graven forever in the memory of the watcher by the bedside. Thus Stephen reasoned.

4

It was in September, shortly before Laurel's first visit at Mrs. Morrison's, that Stephen called on his friend Morley Smith and started proceedings for a divorce. It was in January when Stephen came to the definite conclusion that there was only one way that he could obtain a divorce; and that one way would defeat the object for it.

Stella was as firm as adamant. Every form of argument that Morley Smith could think of, every variety of persuasion that he could devise, had been brought to bear upon her, but to no avail. Stella would not comply. "If Stephen wants a divorce he will have to fight for it," was her invariable answer.

Stephen's hands were tied. It was unthinkable to expose in court the tawdry and unbeautiful details of his life with Stella before he went to New York, to unbury for the delight of a greedy public her compromising relations with Alfred Munn. He might be granted a divorce (Morley Smith assured him that he would), but of what use would it be to him? Helen's position as Mrs. Cornelius Morrison must be considered. She had always looked upon it as a sort of trust. Besides, there were her boys. They should not be made victims of such a scandal. And there was Laurel. No. A divorce obtained in such a manner was out of the question.

As a last resort Stephen had gone to see Stella himself. It was after that ordeal that he felt convinced that he could never marry Helen Dane. He went to her as soon as possible after he had left the Boston train to tell her of his defeat. He stopped only long enough at his rooms to change, and then hastened directly to her house.

It was nearly twelve o'clock at night before he arrived. As he sat down in the long room two floors above the entrance, he felt a little faint. Helen was not in the room, but it was so peculiarly hers that he could hardly breathe its air lately without feeling her sweet presence. To-night there were fresh logs flaming in the open fireplace. There was a flame-colored porcelain bowl, placed on each of the chests on either side of the hearth. There was a piece of flame-colored brocade, brilliant as a bank of nasturtiums, thrown over one end of the long Sheraton sofa.

When Helen came into the room Stephen was aware that she was in pure white, but there was something as brilliant about her, as flame-colored, as the two bowls, as the brocade, as the fire.

He gazed at her speechless a moment, then went to meet her. He put his arms around her and kissed her.

Afterwards he said quietly, "They're numbered, Helen." And she knew that what she had read in his eyes when first she entered the room was true.

She slipped a firm, steadying arm through his, and guided him to the sofa. They sat down side by side, on the flame-colored brocade. He kissed her again.

In spite of his high resolve to hold himself in restraint, until the law had pronounced him free, he had not done so. As long as there had been hope that he might go to Helen unentangled, some day, he remained silent. But when that hope had grown faint, had all but disappeared, brokenly, despairingly, one day, he had confessed his love to her. That was a month ago. His confession had acted like a lighted match on paper. Once Stephen revealed himself to Helen, her love for him, long concealed, but long realized, flashed into flame, like the combustion of a long-stifled fire once it is given air.

As she sat beside him on the sofa, to-night, her arm thrust through his, she observed with fierce pity his drooping shoulders, his hand lying limp and inert upon his knee. She placed her own on top of it and grasped it hard.

"Never mind, Stephen."

"There's no hope."

"I know. We scarcely expected it so soon."

"Oh, it's final, Helen."

There was a pause.

"Do you care to tell me about it?"

Stephen shook his head. It seemed to him sacrilege to bring even the image he had of Stella in his mind into this room. So long as he remained in Helen's presence, he wished he might erase from his brain the memory of the interview he had just had with the woman who had one day been his wife. (Was it possible that she had one day been his wife?) Stephen closed his eyes an instant. Stella, powdered, painted, perfumed, coarsened in speech and manner as he didn't suppose it possible, her fattened figure covered with cheap trappings from head to toe, flashed into his field of vision. He looked down at Helen's lovely hand. Stella and Helen were as unlike as a wax figure, with highly colored cheeks, glass eyes, and blond hair, is unlike a statue of a beautiful Diana carved in white marble.

"You saw her?"

"Yes, I saw her."

There was another pause.

Gently Helen withdrew her arm and got up. Of course as long as she sat so close to Stephen he could not talk to her. She shoved up her little armchair opposite him and sat down in it.

"Now, Stephen, tell me about it."

Tell her about it? Repeat to her the threat Stella had hurled at him? No! Helen must never surmise that her fair name had been mentioned, even by an unscrupulous lawyer as a correspondent in a divorce case. For such had been the nature of Stella's threat.

It had been torture to Stephen to sit in Stella's presence and listen to her using Helen's name familiarly, daring to refer to her in the same breath that she referred to Alfred Munn. Stephen closed his eyes again an instant. He could hear Stella still. Her speech had grown terribly crude with the years.

"Thank heaven for lawyers, I say *now*. Gracious! I'd never have thought *myself* of getting something on *you*, Stephen, but my lawyer has been right onto his job. He's been down there to New York, and he says that I've got as much grounds to do a little naming as you have. So if you want a divorce, Stephen, go ahead and dig up Ed Munn, and I'll dig up Helen Morrison and we'll give the public something worth reading. Of course, I, myself, don't *want* a divorce. There's nobody *I* want to marry. I'd see myself dead rather than tied up to Ed Munn. And I can't see that it's any advantage to a woman with a daughter she's got to bring out in society to be a grass-widow. I'd just rather have you in New York, on business, the way you've always been. I've taken an apartment in Boston now, and by the time Laurel's old enough to come out, it may strike me as a good idea to have her father in the background somewheres, when we give her a ball at one of the big hotels. Mr. Hinckly, my lawyer, says you'll probably want to do about anything I want you to, just so I don't show up your little affair with that pretty widow down there in New York. My! But I think lawyers are clever. I certainly take off my hat to Mr. Hinckly."

It was Helen's sweet voice saying, "You have had a difficult day, Stephen. I'm so sorry," that called Stephen back to a brief glimpse of heaven again.

He looked at her long and quietly. Then he said, "Helen, I gave you up years ago, because I felt I could bring you nothing but shame. I must give you up again for the same reason."

CHAPTER XVI

1

A NEW venture always acted upon Stella like fresh soil in a garden upon seeds. It brought out renewed effort and vigor. An experiment untried possessed all the possibilities of success. Stella never considered failure until it was demonstrated. Even then she would not accept it as such—invariably searching for some hidden advantage in her various disappointments and rebuffs. Even when she had the daunting situation of a forced exile to face, she kept right on spinning her thread of optimism like a spider rudely ejected from her web, falling dizzily at first, but quickly recovering herself and fastening her slender cable to the first solid support that offered itself.

"You never can tell," she said to Effie McDavitt. "It may be the best thing in the world that ever happened that there wasn't any room for Laurel at Miss Fillibrown's this year, and that I've got to get out of the King Arthur. I'd gotten into the way of thinking that the sun rose and set in Milhampton society. I'm going to take an apartment round Boston somewheres! A housekeeping apartment. Lollie is just crazy to have a home of our own, so she can 'entertain,' and I guess it's high time. Mercy, I just wish I'd had sense enough to get out of Milhampton before. The town has always had it in for Laurel and me, ever since Stephen cleared out."

Stella didn't know anything about apartments in Boston. She didn't know anything about where "the right place was to live," nor "whom the right people were to know," nor which was the "right church," nor the "right school." Her knowledge of Boston was confined to the shopping district.

"But that's where this flare-up with Stephen comes in handy," she told Effie. "Before I had to dig up a lawyer to defend me against that Morley Smith creature,

I didn't have a soul in Boston to ask advice about desirable locations, and desirable schools and things, that you have to know about to start right in any new place."

Mr. Joseph Hinckly, of the firm of Hinckly, Jones and Hinckly, became to Stella more than a mere legal adviser. His knowledge of Boston was somewhat confined too, although not to the same district as Stella's. However, he never hesitated to give her an authoritative opinion on any subject if she asked for it. That was instinctive with him.

When Stella inquired, "Commonwealth Avenue's one of the best residential streets, isn't it?" he had assured her there was nothing to compare with it this side of Riverside Drive.

"Well, I've found an apartment on Commonwealth Avenue, way out beyond the thousands, and its front windows are just flooded with sunshine."

"Snap it up quick," exclaimed Mr. Hinckly. "The sunny side of Commonwealth Avenue! Great Scott! You can't do better than that!"

Mr. Hinckly was fully aware that the distance between one and one thousand in some instances, in some streets, is as great as between one side of the globe and the other. (He himself had been born at the wrong end of a fashionable street, he once said in a political speech.) But he was also fully aware that his client might live in the very heart of the Back Bay and barriers more forbidding than space would prevent her from ever crossing its thresholds.

Stella moved into her five-roomed furnished apartment just before Christmas. She still possessed some of the old knack in copying department-store window effects. But it had been a long time since she had had "her eye out for that sort of thing." With no one to guide her, and the matter of expense a constant argument for the cheaper article, her results were not successful. As Laurel gazed upon the slowly growing tawdriness of the apartment, the joy she thought she would feel in inviting the vague new friends her mother told her she would make in her new environment, once they got settled, began to fade.

The living-room was furnished in Mission of the Roycroft Style—big oak chairs with leather cushions; a rectangular couch, leather-cushioned also; a table that was strong enough to be used for a carpenter's bench. And all in spite of the fact of a two-toned light-green, satin-finished wall-paper of the 1890 "parlor period," and an ivory-tinted mantel, which, mongrel though it was, showed more strain of Adam than of Elbert Hubbard.

Stella put yellow-flowered cretonne at the windows. She told Laurel that she had seen a colored picture of a Mission room, in a magazine with yellow-flowered cretonne for hangings, and it was perfectly stunning! She knew where she could get some yellow-flowered cretonne for only ninety-eight cents a yard as effective as linen at six-fifty. But the hangings did not make the room right. Laurel felt convinced at last that the room would never be right.

One afternoon, when her mother was out shopping, she tried to give it just a little of the same look that Mrs. Morrison gave her rooms. But it was hopeless. Afterwards she wandered through the apartment gazing upon all its details with despairing eyes.

The kitchenette with its piled-up breakfast and dinner dishes, waiting for their nightly washing (Stella kept no maid, and she had her own way of keeping house), suggested to Laurel little of the homeyness of Mrs. Morrison's big roomy kitchen, basking in the afternoon warmth of a great black stove, the table spread with a bright red cloth, and a cheerful, broad-faced clock ticking lazily on the mantel.

The Boston apartment was very little like the "home all of our own" of Laurel's dreams. There was no garden. There was no lawn. There was no front door with a knocker, and a single bell. The only difference, as far as Laurel could see, between an apartment and a hotel was that in an apartment you ate your meals in your own rooms instead of downstairs, and it wasn't against the rules to use the gas for cooking.

2

Laurel didn't like Boston. She didn't know of a single winding river, over which to glide upon skates, in and out among alder bushes; nor of a single bare hillside, white with the first snowfall, down which to fly into the sunset, upon skiis; nor of any stone wall to follow for pussy-willows in March; nor rocky pasture-land nor rough woodland, to steal away to, all alone, in April, in search of trailing arbutus.

She didn't know of any corner store where stationery was sold and pencil boxes and return balls and jackstones, and gumdrops, seven for five cents, and cocoanut cakes, three for two. She didn't know of any hump-backed cobbler, whose tiny shop smelled deliciously of leather and was such a cheery place to visit when school was over and her mother was out. Jake, the hump-backed cobbler, would bow and bob at her like a Rip Van Winkle dwarf, whenever she came into his little box, and sweep off a place with his grimy shirt-sleeve for her to sit down upon, and chuckle and spit, and tell her stories about what his father used to do when he was drunk.

Laurel missed Jake. She missed Tony, too—the black-haired, olive-skinned young Greek, who kept a fruit store, and gave her a plum or a pear, or a banana, not the least bit rotten, whenever she went to see him; and, smiling, showing his beautiful white teeth, told her about the lovely dark girl in Athens, waiting for him to send her a ticket to come to America and marry him.

She missed Mrs. McDavitt, who had so many children, and lived in Cataract Village in the top of a tenement house, whom her mother used to take her to see occasionally of late—but whom she must never refer to, any more than to her grandfather—the queer, glum, ragged old man, who lived all alone in a little reddish house, which her mother called "that hovel," on the edge of the river, whom occasionally, also, of late, her mother used to take her to see. She missed Sadie, the chambermaid at the King Arthur, and Michael Dolan, the policeman; and Jim Doherty, the mailman, who knew her father's handwriting; and "peg-legged Eddy," who sold pencils and shoestrings at the corner of Main and Depot Streets. Laurel missed all her Milhampton friends. For Laurel had friends in Milhampton, although they did not attend Miss Fillibrown's Private School.

Most of all, perhaps, she missed Miss Thomas, the kind, wrinkled-faced, quiet-voiced librarian at the Milhampton Public Library, who let her wander at will, alone, among the book-stalls, and take out and put back any volume she pleased without asking.

She believed she hated the librarian at the public library to which Mr. Hinckly directed her. On her first day there the librarian had spoken harshly to Laurel, and made her blush with shame. Laurel had never used a card catalogue before. It hadn't been necessary with Miss Thomas. In her engrossed interest in the myriads of varying titles she had drawn out and piled on the table beside her at least a dozen of the little drawers that contained the luring cards.

Suddenly somebody at her elbow exclaimed, "You mustn't do that!"

Laurel gave a little startled jump. She had been a thousand miles away.

"It's not necessary to remove but one drawer at a time." There was displeasure in the voice.

Laurel flushed.

The librarian began returning the drawers to their places with emphatic little jerks and shoves. Then, glancing at Laurel sharply, she remarked, "Why, you Ve picked them from A to Z! What book is it you're hunting for, anyway?"

Laurel was forced to answer. "I wasn't hunting for any special book."

"What were you doing, then?"

"I was just looking at the titles for fun," Laurel murmured.

The librarian gave her a withering look. "The card catalogue is not fun. It's for use," she reprimanded. "It's not a toy. It's a tool. Don't ever play with it again."

Once out on the street Laurel said to herself, fighting with tears she could not control, "I'll never go near it again! I'll never go into the building again!"

It was six months before her hunger for books overcame her fear of being recognized, and humiliated a second time.

3

Laurel spent many hours in the trolley-cars in Boston. Her mother decided it was too late in the year to attempt to place her in any private school (of course public schools were no more to be considered in Boston than in Milhampton), but Mr. Hinckly said Boston was full of splendid institutions that specialized in about every subject that existed, and he could arrange for Laurel to take up courses of instruction in almost any of them.

Therefore Laurel traveled from one side of Boston to another, pursuing music in one building, French and German in another. Art in a third. Current Events in a fourth. Filet lace-making in the top loft of a fifth. She chafed beneath the incoherent routine. She longed for Miss Fillibrown's, although she hadn't been very happy there. She thought it was the familiar classrooms and familiar faces she was homesick for, but really it was the coordination and consistency of an organized unit. The pupils in Laurel's classes in Boston were as varied in age, race, sex, and station as are a chance group gathered together in the elevator of a public building.

Night after night Laurel cried softly into her pillow after her mother had fallen safely to sleep. Day after day she struggled with tears that seemed always to be just beneath the thin surface of her smiles.

She tried to reason with herself. She had been away from Milhampton before. Why, almost every summer since she could remember, she had been lonely in some unfamiliar place. But it had been bearable, she supposed, because it had been only for limited periods. And, besides, there had always been bellboys to speak to, elevator-men, and chambermaids. There had always been a game of billiards to watch, or an auction-table of women to listen to.

Once, on the sidewalk outside the apartment, waiting for her mother to return from a shopping-tour, Laurel fell into shy conversation with a dark little girl, a few years younger than herself who lived in the apartment below. The possibility of a friendship with this gentle child filled Laurel with timid happiness for a whole afternoon.

But when she told her mother about the conversation, Stella had exclaimed, "Heavens, we can't know those people. Laurel. They're foreigners! So is the family above us. I've discovered this place is riddled with them. Mr. Hinckly couldn't have known what he was talking about! We've simply got to get out sooner or later."

Until Stella moved to Boston, Laurel had preferred a tramp in the country, or a call on Jake, or Tony, or peg-legged Eddy, to the movies; or a stolen pilgrimage to the little house that used to be red, where the mysterious old man whom she must never tell was her grandfather lived, to a vaudeville or play. But in her new solitude, where there was no place to go and nowhere to call. Laurel looked with interest upon the diverting interior of any amusement place.

She went to the movies with her mother three times a week regularly. They climbed to gallery seats at Keith's every time the bill was changed. On Saturday nights Stella and Laurel usually dressed up in their best clothes, and dined at a fashionable hotel, ordering the lowest-priced entree on the bill, dawdling over their bread and butter, as they observed the gay parties about them, and watched the waiters bear in marvelous planked steaks and Peach Melbas.

It was a bleak and forlorn sort of an existence for both mother and child, and terribly shorn of human contacts. But it needn't have been quite so bleak and forlorn and shorn, Stella said, if Laurel hadn't taken such a dislike to Alfred Munn. Ed tried to be awfully kind. He called at the apartment before they had been in it a week. He tried to be awfully kind to Laurel especially. But the child wouldn't let him.

4

"I can't bear that man, mother," she had said as soon as the door had closed upon him after his first call. "Don't let him come again." There was a red spot in the center of each of her cheeks.

"Mercy, mercy, Lollie," laughed Stella. (Lately Lollie would flare up like a little firebrand every once in a while over the littlest things! Her age, probably, Stella concluded.) "Why, what's the matter with Ed?" she asked lightly, humoringly.

"He's horrid!"

"Horrid? How's he horrid?"

"He tickled me in the ribs and said I was pretty, and kissed me."

"Well, what of that? You're only a little girl. Why shouldn't he tell you you are pretty, and kiss you?"

"His lips were wet, and his breath smelled. Oh, mother!" shuddered Laurel. "Don't let him kiss me again. Don't let him come here again."

"Now don't be silly. Laurel. I can't tell Ed Munn not to come here again. It would be awfully rude and bad-mannered."

"But *he's* rude, *he's* bad-mannered."

"Why, Laurel, how can you talk so about a gentleman who's trying to do so much for us?"

"He isn't a gentleman."

"He's more of a gentleman, I guess, than that dirty old cobbler you like so, who spits and swears, and that Dago who sells fruit, and came over steerage."

"Jake isn't dirty—only on the outside, and Tony is not a Dago. He's a Greek and he comes from a place in Greece where the most beautiful things in the world came from! Besides, Jake and Tony don't kiss me, and Jake and Tony don't say horrid things to me about *you*."

"And what things did Ed say about *me?*"

"When you were out of the room he put his arm around me, and told me he thought you were pretty, too."

"Well?"

"He shouldn't have said that, should he? Not to me? The way he did?"

"Why not? I don't call that horrid."

"Don't you? Really?"

"Certainly not. Why shouldn't he say it, if he thought it?"

Laurel stared at her mother, confused, perplexed. She didn't know how to answer, how to explain. She had never liked Ed Munn, but her dislike of him had never swept over her like this. It was frightening. Her sudden hatred of the man was like a big dense cloud that had rolled upon her unawares and enveloped her completely. She had turned toward her mother for help, for comprehension. She had groped for a steadying hand. But no hand had been held out.

Suddenly Laurel turned and buried her face in the pillow on the couch and burst into violent weeping.

Of late many of her emotions were like enveloping clouds—love and worship, as well as hate and scorn. Her passion for Mrs. Morrison was big, dense, un-understandable. As she lay with her face buried in the dark of the pillow, she could see great masses of red and purple light-dust, shapeless and conglomerate, rolling and shifting senselessly in the dark behind her closed lids. Life was like that.

Oh, if only somebody would show her a straight easy little path leading through the confusion.

"Oh, come, come, Lollie," exclaimed Stella. "Don't do that way. Of course if you feel so badly as all that about poor Ed, why—he needn't come, I suppose. But for the life of me, I don't see what he's done to you."

It was the first time for years Stella had seen Laurel cry like a little girl. It was the last time she ever saw her. After that one outburst. Laurel never again betrayed to her mother her fear of the shifting clouds of the twilight stratum of the dawning of her soul.

Stella was not mistaken in attributing Laurel's sudden aversion to Ed to her age, but she soon discovered it was no whim. In fact. Laurel seemed so terribly set against "poor Ed" that she almost was inclined to believe that Stephen must have "poisoned" her mind somehow. Why, when Ed invited Laurel and her mother to go to the theater with him, and choose their own show, the child refused absolutely to stir an inch. She wouldn't touch a piece of the generous box of candy he sent them. "Oh, how can you bear him?" she remarked quietly (for all the world like Stephen) when she found his name written on the card in the envelope tucked underneath the showy bow of ribbon.

Stella had to tell Ed the truth at last. She hated to give up all the good times he stood ready to shower upon them. She didn't mind giving up Ed himself. She always got sick of him after a little while, anyhow, and she must confess he had run downhill considerably even since last September. He had changed his business again. He was working in some sort of machine-shop now, and his finger-nails were terribly broken and greasy.

CHAPTER XVII

1

Laurel sat on the end of the pier with her feet swinging over the edge. A girl about her own age sat on each side of her. Their arms were thrown lightly around her shoulders, and hers lightly around theirs. All three of the girls were in white, except for their Boutet de Monvel colored sweaters—pale pink, pale yellow, and faintest lavender. The three girls made as pretty a display against the gray-blue of the lake as a fragment of rainbow. Beneath their swinging feet floated a flotilla of canoes, their bright red and green sides flashing in the sun. On the pier behind the girls was a collection of boxes, leather-encased thermos-bottles and jars, and several tea-baskets.

The three girls were waiting for "the crowd" to assemble. "The crowd" was going on a picnic to Stag Island to-day. Laurel was one of "the crowd."

Laurel was seventeen years old now, and this was the first time in all her life she had ever been one of a crowd. The thrilling experience had lasted for ten days. It would be three weeks the day after to-morrow since Laurel and her mother had arrived at this unexpected Paradise.

Laurel was keenly conscious of the careless arms about her shoulders, but she didn't show it. Laurel could conceal joy and pride, she discovered, quite as successfully as disappointment and chagrin. She was keenly conscious, too, of the girl she had always been before on occasions of this sort, as she had strolled by just such intimate little groups as she now miraculously found herself one of, she and her mother taking in what details of exciting preparations as they could, in a glance or two, or covert backward look. Laurel felt sorrier for that girl on this happy morning, she thought, than she ever had before.

Now, down the long pier that stretched out into the lake from the lawn in front of the hotel drifted other fragments of rainbow, other groups of two-and-three girls with arms linked; and among them occasionally a boy or two—tanned, lean, loose-knit, tough-muscled, dressed in light trousers and soft shirts—typical American college boys. There was a whole rollicking bunch of them behind the last trio of girls. By the time "the crowd" had all collected, the pier was as noisy as an ivy-covered wall full of sparrows on the first sunny day of spring.

Laurel and the two girls beside her jumped up and joined the general chatter. Mrs. Adams and Mrs. Grosvenor, the two chaperons for the day's festivities, leisurely approaching the bevy could catch bits and snatches of characteristic conversation.

"Gorgeous day! Good-looking sweater, my dear! One exactly like it in henna. Last one in the dining-room—perfectly stunning! Abso*lute*ly! Crazy about that color."

Laurel didn't contribute much to the staccatoed exclamations, but her eyes shone, and her cheeks were bright.

"Did you ever see any one quite as lovely as Laurel Dallas this morning?" remarked Mrs. Adams to Mrs. Grosvenor.

"She's perfectly exquisite."

"How is your mother, this morning, Laurel, my dear?" Mrs. Adams inquired a moment later.

"Oh, better, thank you, Mrs. Adams," Laurel replied, turning her flushed, pleased face toward the older woman. "The sweet-peas you sent up to her were lovely. She told me to thank you ever and ever so much."

"I left another book at the desk, to be sent up to her later," remarked Mrs. Grosvenor.

"Oh, mother will be so pleased!"

"I hope she likes Wells, and hasn't read his latest."

"I'm sure she hasn't. You're awfully kind, Mrs. Grosvenor."

"Not a bit. I've been ill in a hotel-room myself. Laurel, dear. I know what it is like."

"Oh, Miss Dallas!" suddenly somebody exclaimed, close beside Laurel's other shoulder.

Laurel turned and looked up into the eyes of Mrs. Grosvenor's son Richard—her older son. She had two. Richard was a senior in college. He was one of the oldest boys who played with the "crowd." All the girls were "simply crazy" about Richard Grosvenor.

"But he can't see anybody but *you*, Laurel Dallas," one of the girls who had been sitting on the edge of the pier with Laurel had just told her.

"You're going with me, in *my* canoe, aren't you?" he now said to Laurel, smiling.

Any of the other girls would have known how to respond in the bluff, hearty, good-comradeship style of the day. "Thanks, Dick," or, "Crazy to," or, "Sure I am," but Laurel hadn't acquired all the ways yet. "Am I?" she replied, in the same pleased surprised manner with which she met all attentions shown her.

"Yes, you are," he assured her quietly. He turned away.

"There! What did I *say*! Laurel Dallas?"

"I'll bet he picks a single canoe."

"He was here all last summer and never as much as looked at any of us younger girls."

All the boys were now busy among the canoes, loading them, rearranging the cushions and seat-backs, shoving the dainty little crafts up against the pier, ready for the girls to step into.

"All ready. Miss Dallas."

Laurel turned. Yes, Deborah was right! He had selected a single canoe! He stood up in it now as Laurel approached him. He reached up both hands toward her, the canoe drifting away a little from the wharf as he did so. Laurel placed her hands in his, and he swung her across the widening gap between them into the center of the luxurious nest of cushions he had arranged for her in the bottom of the canoe. She alighted in the frail little boat like a bird on a tender twig. There was something of the same bird-like adroitness in every motion that Laurel made.

Laurel had lost none of the peculiar woodsy quality of her charm in the last four years. Her freckles had disappeared, however. (Stella always maintained it was white vinegar and salt.) Her long curls had disappeared, too. Laurel did her hair up now. Rolled it into a simple knot behind. But the gray eyes with their changing moods from dark to light—like a lake beneath varying skies—were still the same. So was her grave listening manner—like trees on a windless night. She was still slight and sleek in body, too—as un-undulating as a low bas-relief when you draw your hand across its surface, but as possessed of lovely curves, too, and as suggestive of softness and warmth.

"Won't you sit down?" Richard Grosvenor asked her, still holding her hands, though he knew she did not require steadying now, Richard had arranged the pillows so that Laurel would be facing him all the way up to Stag Island.

"Couldn't I paddle, too?"

"Do you want to?"

"I'd like to."

"Oh, all right."

2

They were off ten minutes before the others. Mrs. Adams and Mrs. Grosvenor watched the pretty skiff, with Laurel in the bow and Richard in the stern, disappear like a lazy bird around a clump of trees.

"Richard seems quite taken by her," remarked Mrs. Adams.

Mrs. Grosvenor smiled indulgently. "I can't deny it."

"Well, he certainly shows excellent taste. I think she is a lovely girl."

"Yes, Richard has always been very discerning. I've often told him he's really almost too particular—*too* fastidious about girls. This is his first serious affair since he has been in college as far as I know."

"It really is, then, serious?"

"Oh, I couldn't say that. It is obvious, that's all. Laurel is only seventeen, you know—a mere child, though Richard, absurd boy, says she's more like twenty in many ways than most girls he knows of twenty-two. It's serious enough, you see, for him to want to talk about her to me. He confided to me yesterday he intends inviting her to the game in November and to Class Day next June. She was motoring with us yesterday afternoon and we discovered some mutual friends. It seems she visits at Mrs. Cornelius Morrison's, you know, of New York and Long Island. I am on two charitable boards with Mrs. Morrison. She is a charming woman. Bob, my other son, is at St. Lee's, with Mrs. Morrison's oldest boy, Cornelius. They're delightful people."

3

It was about an hour's paddle to Stag Island, as the bird flies, but Richard guided the canoe along the irregular coastline, gliding through the dappled shadows of the beech and birch, of dogwood, and wild hydrangea, and occasional denser stretches of close-growing spruce and hemlock.

For the first ten or fifteen minutes Laurel didn't say a word. Not a single word! She sat in her perch in the bow, and steadily, rhythmically dipped her paddle into the water, drew it back, raised it, reached forward, dipped it into the water again. Richard, a few feet behind her, followed her slow revolutions. The effect upon him was almost hypnotic. It was awkward to be silent with most girls. He seldom was. Most girls avoided any such lapses as this. But Laurel Dallas would drift into silence as naturally, as unconsciously, as a canary, whose song is interrupted by some simple cause, and out of it in the same unexpected spontaneous fashion.

The crowd had been left far behind—they couldn't even be heard—when Laurel and Richard slipped into a little sequestered cove, almost a cave, with a leaf-covered roof—a lovely spot. Instinctively both the paddles dug deep into the water and held the canoe stationary. Laurel lifted her paddle very gently, and laid it noiselessly across her knees. The only sound in the sylvan sanctuary was the drip—drip—drip of a few drops of water from her paddle's broad end.

Finally Richard said softly from his seat behind Laurel, "Are you there?"

She broke into a low pleased laugh at that. "Every bit of me is here!"

"I wondered. You've been so noisy."

She leaned her head back and gazed up at the blue sky through the low-hanging branches. She drew in her breath deep. "Oh, isn't it too beautiful to be true!"

Richard, gazing only at her, thought it was! He didn't say so, simply smiled and remarked, "You like the woods, don't you?"

"I love them!" Laurel exclaimed.

But it wasn't the woods she was loving so much just then. It was life. Life had never seemed so kind and generous, so good and beautiful to her as now! She sighed, then suddenly lifted her paddle, plunged it into the dark water at her side, and slipped out of the little cave-spot, into the sunshine again. Slipped out into silence again, too,

"You aren't talking to me very much this morning," later Richard informed her.

She made no reply.

"You're a funny girl. I never knew a girl in my life who had silence for a line."

"Do you want me to talk?"

"No."

"When I'm in a canoe, near the shore, like this, I love sneaking around the corners on the birds and animals when they're not expecting you, and see what they're up to."

Some five, ten, fifteen minutes later, the canoe, pushing its nose around a bit of wooded peninsula, came abruptly upon a deer standing upon the shore. Laurel made no exclamation at sight of him, nor did she stop paddling or vary her stroke. She simply gazed in silent admiration for a second or two, then abruptly turned and looked back over her shoulder, to find out if her companion saw the beautiful creature too. Richard thought he had never seen anything so lovely, so blinding as Laurel's eyes as they met his! He smiled, nodded. She turned back satisfied. Not a word was spoken, but sharing the deer that way was—well—"Look here," said Richard a moment later, "haven't you paddled enough? Come, won't you please sit down here on the cushions and talk?" She did finally.

"You're different from any girl I ever knew."

Most girls liked being told they were different. It seemed to distress Laurel.

"I try hard not to be."

"Don't try."

Laurel had never been talked to by any boy like this before. She was at a loss to know how to banter back.

"Are you already booked for the game in November?" asked Richard.

"The game?"

"The big game, I mean. It's in Cambridge this year."

"Oh, no, no, I'm not," Laurel's heart fluttered. He meant the big Harvard-Yale game! Oh, how happy her mother would be!

"I want you to go with me."

"Why, but I—do you think your mother—I mean—we—"

"I know," he interrupted, "that we've known each other only a week, and all the rest of that silly conventional stuff. But I'm not a perfect stranger to you. You can tell your mother that my kid brother knows Con Morrison. He visited him once. Con has been at our house. Anyhow, when your mother is able to come downstairs, she'll know us herself. It will be all right *then*, I simply had to get my word in now for fear you might get booked with somebody else. I want you to go to the game with *me*, if you go with anybody. Will you?"

"Yes, I will," said Laurel, looking off toward the shore, her eyes again suddenly dark and luminous.

Richard looked toward the shore, too. Had she seen another deer?

When they landed at Stag Island half an hour later, "Don't forget you're going to paddle back with me, too," Richard whispered.

4

All day long one happy moment followed another as uninterruptedly as one telegraph-pole another flashing by the window of a railroad train. It had been like that ever since the morning Mrs. Adams had fallen into conversation with Laurel on the hotel veranda. That was ten days ago, yet Laurel was only just beginning to become sufficiently used to the steady succession of kindnesses as to take them for granted, as to forget for an hour or so, occasionally, the phenomenon of their unfailing repetition.

Mrs. Adams had noticed Laurel the first morning she had appeared alone in the hotel dining-room. So, too, had others noticed her. The head-waiter had shown Laurel to a table by a far window. After she had sat there alone during breakfast, lunch, and dinner, Mrs. Adams made inquiries of the clerk. It seemed the new girl's mother was ill upstairs. Tonsillitis. The hotel doctor was taking care of her. Mrs. Adams spoke to Laurel that morning, asked her if there was anything she could do to help, and introduced her to two girls standing, near by, with tennis racquets.

"Do you play?" asked one of the girls.

"*Will* you play?" asked the other.

It was as easy as that. That very morning Laurel played tennis with three girls of "the crowd" that very afternoon played golf with three others; that very evening met the boys and danced until the music stopped, running upstairs between numbers to see if her mother was comfortable, and to let her share what she knew would make her happier than anything else in the world.

"Well, I guess we Ve struck the right place at last, Lollie," Stella exclaimed from her pillow, with a glint of triumph in her eyes. "Don't think of me. Don't come up again, dearie. I'm all right. I'm bound to be. I just knew we'd happen on to gold some day."

It had all been pure luck. Stella had chosen this particular hotel from a circular, on the strength of the fact of its high rates. The start had been anything but propitious. Either she or Laurel had been ill from the first moment of their arrival. Laurel was confined to the bedroom the first twenty-four hours, and Stella had been obliged to wander about the unexplored regions downstairs companionless. Then the moment the fever left Laurel, didn't it go and settle itself upon Stella—settle and stay, too! At the end of two weeks Stella was only just beginning to sit up in a chair by her bed.

5

After lunch under the tall pines on Stag Island, the boys went off to explore the coast; and the girls (after the tea-baskets were repacked and the pine-needle bank made as neat and clean as the inside of a pine chest) grouped themselves in colorful bunches on the soft brown background, and producing gay work-bags, began plying various tools—knitting-needles, crochet-hooks, and tatting-bobbins; conversing the while lazily, meanderingly, breaking into shrill peals of laughter, now and then, or fragment of popular song.

Laurel lay back, flat on the ground, idle, her hands folded under her head, and gazed up at the murmuring tops of the trees. She wished her mother might be hiding up there among the needles, gazing down at her through the gaps, seeing, hearing.

Deborah, seated beside Laurel, was tickling her nose with a spear of field grass. Laurel attempting to catch it in her mouth by occasional puppy-like snaps. Frances on the other side was amusing herself by weaving pine needles through the meshes of Laurel's sweater. "I'll pay you back, somehow," purred Laurel contentedly.

Now they were telling her about the theatricals they gave every year in August, discussing what sort of a role would be best suited to her; now describing the delights of the night she would spend on the top of Spear Mountain before the season was over; now commanding her to make herself useful and sit up and help wind some yarn.

Oh, was it all true? Did they like her a little? Were they her friends? It seemed to Laurel that afternoon, as the shadows grew longer on the western margin of the lake and the hour for the homeward paddle with Richard Grosvenor through those shadows, approached, that her cup of happiness was full to the brim.

6

At the end of the homeward paddle it seemed to her that that cup was overflowing. Richard had asked her to be his partner in the tennis tournament on Saturday; he had asked her to go to lunch at a neighboring hotel with his mother and himself tomorrow noon; he had asked her to come out alone with him, in the canoe, to-night after dinner, when the moon rose; he had asked if he might write to her after he returned to town. He was going back in four days. He had taken a job in his father's office for the rest of the summer.

As they had drawn near to the pier in front of the hotel, he had said to Laurel, interrupting his paddling as he did so, leaning forward, "It doesn't seem possible that I met you only a week ago" (Oh, it was the beginning of the old, old story). "You seem to me like somebody I've known a long while" (told in the old, old way).

Laurel closed her eyes a moment—he didn't see her—then opened them wide. She had a feeling she might wake any moment and find it all a dream.

As she jumped out of the canoe on to the pier beside him, a look passed between them that was like the look when they had shared the deer silently together. For the third or fourth time that day Laurel's heart fluttered and seemed almost to turn over.

Several of "the crowd" were on the pier when Laurel and Richard arrived. Deborah called out brightly to them, "Come along, walk up with us."

She linked a free arm familiarly through Laurel's as she approached, and Richard fell into step on Laurel's other side. Frances and two boys were also with the group. They all moved up the pier together. The girls began singing a popular song. Then suddenly in the midst of the chorus, Deborah stopped singing, stopped walking, too. So did the others.

"Oh, girls! Look!" she exclaimed. "There is that woman!"

Laurel glanced up. Coming down across the lawn in front of the hotel approaching the pier, she saw her mother.

7

Stella was several hundred yards away, but Laurel was familiar with the black-and-white striped foulard which she now wore. Stella had remodeled her foulard this spring. She had given it a lot of fresh "pep," with generous dashes of Kelly green. Deborah seemed familiar with the foulard, too.

"What woman?" Frances inquired.

"Why, my dear, look, look for yourself, and see. Don't you remember that dreadful dress? Of course you do! You were with us. You saw her about two weeks ago. She was around the hotel all one day."

"Good gracious! Of course I do! We wondered how such a person ever got in here, and then decided she must have come, just for the day, from that unspeakable place on the other side of the lake."

"Notice her. Laurel," laughed Deborah, giving Laurel a little squeeze. "I believe she is coming down toward the pier. Take her in. She's a perfect scream. Paint about an inch thick, and plucked eyebrows, and dyed hair, and not a day under forty. Oh, she's a mess. You remember her, Richard, don't you?"

"Yes, I remember her. Awful dame! Horrible creature!"

Behind Laurel lay only water. On either side of her lay only water. She could not turn and run. She watched her mother choose the gravel path that led to the pier. ("She is! She's coming this way, girls!" delightedly ejaculated Deborah.) Then suddenly Laurel exclaimed, "I've lost something."

"Lost something?"

"My watch!" She held up an empty wrist. "It must have dropped off in the canoe."

She turned back immediately. Richard turned back, too.

"Shan't we all come and look?" Deborah offered.

"No, please," Laurel called back.

"You all go along," Richard ordered. "We'll find it."

"I think it must be among the cushions somewhere," said Laurel.

All during the torturing ten or fifteen minutes when she and Richard shook the cushions and pillows, each separate one, and then ran their hands into every possible corner and crevice of the canoe where a watch might lodge, and even searched between the loosely fitted boards of the pier. Laurel kept a constant watch of the shore. She saw her mother walk slowly down the path toward the lake, arrive at the water's edge, hesitate, and then sit down on one of the rustic seats built on either side of the pier, where it joined the bank. She saw the group which she had just left approach the rustic seats, draw nearer to her mother, pass her mother! Thank kind heaven above, they didn't stop! Her mother didn't introduce herself to them after all! Laurel breathed freer. But only for a short time. It soon became evident that her mother was going to wait for her at the rustic seats until her errand at the end of the pier, whatever it was, was finished.

Laurel couldn't keep up the silly search among a half-dozen sofa-pillows and one canoe indefinitely. She must go back along the pier and pass between the rustic seats with Richard Grosvenor beside her, in a minute or two. Would she tell him now—immediately, that the "awful dame" was her mother?

"Well, I guess my watch isn't here, after all," she said with a catch in her voice, with almost a sob. It was over—all over. And so unbeautifully, so hideously.

"If the watch isn't here. It's probably up at Stag Island. If we both paddle hard, we can be there before dark. Jump in, we'll find it."

Laurel gave Richard a look that was like that of a dog to the god who releases his foot from the jaws of a steel trap. "Oh, you are good!" And she jumped into her place in the front of the canoe, he jumped in behind, and they were off, out of sight, out of sound, in three minutes.

They didn't find the watch. They hunted until it was dark on Stag Island and paddled back by the light of a slowly rising July moon. They hardly talked at all. Richard was aware of a high current of feeling that seemed to be coursing through this mysterious girl ever since the first moment that she had noticed that her wrist was bare. It awed and silenced him.

It wasn't until they were returning from Stag Island that he remarked, "You must think a lot of that watch."

She replied, "I'll never forget you're coming to help me find it."

"But we haven't been successful."

"That doesn't matter. I'll never forget it. Never, never, never, never."

A similar high current of feeling coursed through Richard, too, at the sound of her low voice, earnestly repeating the single word to him.

8

It was after nine o'clock when Laurel and Richard reached the pier for the second time that evening. It was deserted. So, too. Laurel observed, with a fresh wave of gratitude for the boy who had saved her, and her mother also, were the rustic seats.

"I'm going in by a side door," Laurel said to Richard, as they walked toward the lighted hotel. "You go in the other way. You see the crowd. I want to go right up to my mother as quickly as I can."

"But you'll be down again?"

"Not to-night."

"You haven't had any dinner."

"I'll have some sent up."

"But—"

"Please."

"Shan't I see you again to-night?"

"Not to-night."

"When shall I see you again?"

(In ten—in *five* minutes, when "the crowd" told him, he wouldn't want to see her *ever* again.)

"To-morrow," she managed to smile.

"Yes. Don't forget. We're going to have lunch together to-morrow."

"I won't."

"I've only four days left," he went on eagerly, "give me the morning before lunch, too, will you? Please. We've so much to talk about, and I've only four days left. We'll go somewhere alone."

They had reached the rear door now. Laurel had one hand on the knob.

"Will you? Please answer. Will you?"

Laurel turned and looked up at him, and nodded.

"Right after breakfast?"

She nodded again.

"Promise?"

For the third time she nodded, then suddenly reached out her free hand and touched Richard Grosvenor on his arm, drew her hand back quickly, and whispered, "Good-night."

Her eyes were as black as the lake beneath the moon.

"Laurel!" Richard moved toward her, but she had turned, she had gone. The big door with its heavy spring closed softly upon him.

CHAPTER XVIII

1

Laurel found her mother propped up in bed.

"Well, of all things! Where have you been?" she exclaimed as Laurel came into the room.

"Didn't any one tell you?"

"Not till just about half an hour ago; then that Mrs. Grosvenor sent a bellboy up with a note, saying not to worry, you had lost something and had gone back to the island with her boy to hunt for it. What did you lose. Laurel?"

"My watch."

"Your watch! Why, don't you remember you said this morning you wouldn't wear it because it might get wet? There it is on the bureau!"

"Why, that is so."

"Gracious! What's the matter with you?"

"I must be losing my memory, I guess," smiled Laurel wanly.

She crossed the room and slipped the watch onto her wrist.

"Had a good time to-day?" Stella inquired.

"Wonderful."

"You must tell me about it. Every word! I'm crazy to hear."

"I will. How have you been, mother?"

"*Where* have I been, you better ask."

"Well, where have you been?"

"Downstairs!" she announced with a triumphant nod of her head.

"Downstairs!"

"It's a wonder you didn't see me. I saw yow. The doctor was here this morning, and said it would do me good to get up and around as soon as possible now. At first I thought I better not till tomorrow morning. Then I said to myself it would be fun to surprise you. So I dressed about four o'clock, and sat around on the veranda for a while. I felt just fine, and when I saw all your party coming down, the lake in the canoes, I walked down to the pier to meet you. I saw you when you went off with that young man, heaven knew where. I supposed you would be right back. I waited for over an hour in that little summer-house at the end of the pier. I thought it would be so nice to meet him like that, offhand, and I was looking rather well."

Laurel, occupied before the mirror—pulling off the lavender sweater over her head, removing the soft felt tam-o'-shanter that matched it, giving her hair gentle little presses and pokes—inquired casually, "Did you stay downstairs to dinner?"

"No, I didn't. Though I felt all right. But I thought *this* way—it would be nicer to meet all your friends when you were around to introduce me. I'll go down to breakfast with you to-morrow morning. I feel just great."

"Then you didn't meet anybody?"

"Not yet."

"Mother," said Laurel, turning toward her from the mirror, "I'm going downstairs just a moment if you're all right. I won't be long."

"Mercy! Don't think about me. Stay as long as you want, and have a good time. Gracious, you deserve it. I'm as contented as a clam, so long as you are happy, Lollie. But you can't go like that, in that wrinkled waist and your hair all mussy."

"Oh, it doesn't matter."

Laurel did not take the elevator downstairs. She walked. The elevator would leave her the whole length of the foyer away from the hotel office. The stairs came down just behind it. Laurel felt fairly sure that none of "the crowd" would be near the office at this time in the evening. She was right. Nobody was near the office. The clerk was alone.

"We're leaving to-morrow," she told him.

"Leaving! I thought your mother—"

"My mother is much better, and something has happened that makes it necessary for us to go home immediately."

"Why, but—"

"Oh, I know we Ve engaged the room for the season. You'll have to charge us for it, if that is the way you do. We've got to go, anyway." There was something very convincing about Laurel. "We're going on the early train," she said.

"Oh, but the early train isn't necessary. The train that connects with the Boston Pullman at the Junction, sixty miles below here, doesn't leave until evening."

That didn't matter to Laurel. If she and her mother preferred leaving on the early train, they could do so, couldn't they, and pick up the Pullman, when it came through the Junction at night?

"Why, of course—but it would be very foolish—nobody ever does it."

"We're going to," Laurel announced.

2

"Mother," she remarked ten minutes later, "you must lie there in bed and watch me pack the trunks."

"Pack the trunks!"

"We're leaving this place to-morrow morning, at half-past seven."

"What are you talking about?"

"We're leaving. We're going."

"What do you mean?"

"What I say. I've just been downstairs and told the clerk."

"Have you lost your mind. Laurel?"

A faint smile drifted across Laurel's features, softened for a moment her firmly set jaw and chin.

"Oh, I'm sorry, mother! I'm ever so sorry."

"What's happened? What's the meaning of this?"

"Oh, I just don't like it here any more," shrugged Laurel. "I just can't stand it here any more."

Stella's eyes narrowed. She nodded her head, slowly up and down. "Humph! Sounds mighty like a quarrel with your young man to *me*."

"Oh, don't say 'my young man,' mother."

"There you go! Just like your father again! Criticizing my language every other minute! Well, then, Richard Grosvenor. Sounds mighty like a quarrel with Richard Grosvenor, to *me*."

"Mother," said Laurel, "I never want to see Richard Grosvenor again as long as I live!"

"I knew it! I knew it! Come, Laurel, don't be a little goose. Mercy, I never saw such a pepper-box! You can't fly out of a hotel like this, on a moment's notice, just because of a little lover's quarrel. Heavens alive! You come to bed and sleep on it. You'll feel entirely different in the morning. So will he. Gracious! I know how those things work. Quarrels make the heart grow fonder. There's a saying something like that. You come to bed, Laurel."

"Not till the packing is finished," said Laurel.

She turned her back upon Stella, crossed the room to the bureau, pulled out a lower drawer, and removed a pile of underclothes.

"You don't mean to say you're going to pack up and clear out of the only place we ever even had a Hook-In' at?"

"Yes, mother."

"Where do you think we're going to at this late date?"

"Why, back to the apartment."

"Back to the apartment in July!"

"Yes, mother."

"Do you mean to say. Laurel, you're thinking of putting me in a train in the condition I'm in?"

"I stopped and asked the doctor. He said it Wouldn't hurt you to travel, he thought."

"And what about the expense of this room?"

"The clerk said we wouldn't have to pay for it. But even if we did, it wouldn't make any difference. Oh, mother, don't talk. Don't argue. We're going, anyway."

Laurel was emptying all the bureau drawers now. Stella, from the bed, stared at her speechless, as helpless, as powerless as if *she* were the child. She recognized that look in Laurel's eyes.

"I've brought you up all wrong," she sighed.

Laurel made no reply to that. Swiftly, effectively, she sorted and piled. Swiftly, effectively began filling the trunks.

"Laurel, you Ve doing a crazy thing," Stella broke out afresh, "and for the life of me, I don't know how to stop you."

"Don't let's go all over it again."

"You're throwing away the best chance you've ever had. Listen to me. Most of these people here come from Philadelphia. I had it all worked out in my mind that if we got the right sort of a start with them this summer, here, we might take an apartment down around Philadelphia somewheres next fall. Then you'd have some of the right kind of friends to play around with, and when the time comes for you to come out, why—"

"Where's the tissue-paper, mother? I think I'll do the dresses next."

Five minutes later Stella became tearful. Laurel brought her a handkerchief.

"I should think," she wailed, after she had vigorously blown her nose and mopped her eyes, "you'd want me to have a little of the good times you've been enjoying these three weeks while I've been cooped up here in bed. *I* like nice people, and things going on myself. You know I do. But just the minute I am able to get out of bed and take in a little of the gayety and excitement, *you* let a silly quarrel with a young fellow you never saw three weeks ago cheat me of it all."

"Where are the trees for your satin slippers? Do you know?" called Laurel from the closet.

3

Laurel and her mother spent all the next day from ten in the morning, until eight at night in the waiting-room at the Junction. The waiting-room at the Junction was hot and dusty. It swarmed with flies, attracted by discarded lunch-boxes and paper bags. It smelled of cinders and hot steel. There were settees built around the edge of the waiting-room. They were painted mop-colored gray, divided by iron arms into spaces, so that no one could lie down upon them. Laurel arranged the suitcases as best she could, for her mother's feet, and rolled up a traveling-coat into a pillow for her head. All day Laurel hovered solicitously about her mother, offering her frequent drinks of water, which she brought in a paper cup; trying to tempt her with crackers and cheese and sweet chocolate, which she procured from a general store, half a mile up the road; asking her from time to time how she felt; showing concern, anxiety, but not the slightest sign of yielding or regret. Stella, resigned now, and stoically submissive, sat silent and unresponsive all day long. At measured intervals she sighed deeply, eloquently.

At eight o'clock in the evening a Pullman car was backed up to the Junction and side-tracked there for an hour or so to await several incoming trains from various points of the compass. Laurel and her mother crawled in between the sheets of a lower berth in the Pullman car a little after nine.

Laurel was on the inside of the berth. Stella's obdurate back was turned toward her. As Laurel stretched her long slim body down beside her mother, she slipped her hand under her mother's arm—around her waist, as she always did when she went to sleep—though she hadn't last night.

"Mother," she whispered, "aren't you going to forgive me pretty soon?"

Stella pressed the precious hand, drew it closely around her.

"Of course I am, you crazy kid," she whispered back. "I don't care what you do, just so I've got you to do it. Gosh, I can't stay mad with you any longer!"

Laurel's arm tightened. That was all right then. Oh, if only Richard—if only he—her arm loosened, grew limp. Laurel fell to sleep almost immediately. So did Stella. They both had been asleep for an hour or more when the hotel train whistled into the Junction at about half-past ten.

4

Laurel was drifting off into unconsciousness for the second time when she became aware of her name being spoken, just outside the heavy curtain of the berth. She had been dimly aware of voices conversing in low tones for five or ten minutes before the sound of her own name prodded her wide awake. The section opposite had not been made up when she and her mother went to bed. Probably, Laurel concluded, some of the people who had come down on the evening train were sitting there and chatting.

"Yes, that very pretty dark girl, who was so popular with the younger set—lovely eyes. Laurel Dallas. Such an odd name."

"But how is it possible? She seemed so very refined, so distinctly nice in every way."

"Well, I asked the clerk. He told me—"

"You mean the woman in the striped dress?"

"Certainly, certainly. She is that lovely child's mother."

"What a handicap to the poor girl."

"I should say so. All those people she's been playing around with had no idea what her mother was like, I suppose. She's been ill ever since she came. I wish I could have stayed a few days longer and seen just what would have happened when that woman appeared on the scene."

"What's the woman's story?"

"I don't know. I never heard of her before. Dallas is her name, from Boston."

"Poor girl. It's like having a ball and chain around her ankle to be obliged to drag a woman like that after her wherever she goes."

"Yes, but those things happen. Once I knew of a young man—charming—such aristocratic manners, and he came from the commonest family—vulgar people. Of course, being a man, he could escape his family, but a girl—a young girl like that"—the train began to move—"perfectly helpless—branded"—it moved faster—"a shame. Such a pity—Richard Grosvenor—" It moved still faster. The voices were drowned in the rumble of flying steel.

5

Oh, had her mother heard? Was her mother awake? No, Laurel thought not. Her breathing was heavy and slightly audible. The hand that had grasped hers so tightly a little while ago was limp and lifeless now. Her whole body was limp and lifeless. It moved slightly with the motion of the train, as unresisting as the curtains.

6

Oh, had Lollie heard? Was she awake? No, Stella thought not. Her soft breathing was as regular as the swinging of a pendulum. The arm that encircled her waist was as consciousless as a sleeping baby's.

7

So that was the story! Oh, what a fool she had been! A handicap to Laurel! And not because of unfair stories, of whispered scandals (these women didn't know who she was, didn't even know she wasn't living with her husband), but just because of *herself*. Was she so awful—so God-awful, then?

Stella had been listening to the voices for ten minutes before Laurel had become aware of them. She had heard herself described in detail, in cruel detail. She didn't suppose anybody knew that she "touched" her hair a little now and then. Why, even Lollie didn't know it. Up to two years ago it hadn't been necessary, but she did so hate the soft-boiled-egg look when yellow hair begins to turn white. Other women kept themselves young and attractive without being criticized. She had tried not to become a perfect sight for Laurel's sake, to keep in the running, as far as appearances went, so the child need never be ashamed of her, as she had been of her mother and the mouse-colored wrappers. But she had failed. Why, it was the same story right over again. Laurel was ashamed of her mother, too. It was as plain as the nose on your face. That was the reason Laurel was leaving the hotel. She would die rather than confess it, of course. That was the way Laurel was—as considerate, as gentle, as delicate with her common, ordinary, vulgar mother (weren't those some of the words the voices had used?) as with the charming Mrs. Grosvenor or the flawless Mrs. Morrison.

Well, what was to be done about it? Now that Stella knew the truth, knew that just her own personality, just her own five senses and the old hulk of a shell they lived in, was like an iron ball tied to Laurel's ankle (pleasant to *learn* that about yourself in the middle of the night, when you so wanted to be wings for your child), well—now that she *had* learned it, what was the next number on the program? Laurel being a girl, the voices had said, couldn't escape, couldn't break the chain to the ball. Well, then (Stella's fingers very gently closed over Laurel's. She still slept—and she really did sleep now)—well, then—It would be pretty awful without her, wouldn't it? Dear little Lollie!—Let's see, let's see. No. No other way.

8

A NARROW ribbon of sunlight was shining into the berth through a crack by the tightly pulled window-shade by Laurel's feet when she stirred and woke. Stella was waiting for her, had been waiting all night.

"Well, honey," she said lightly. "I had a good night?"

Their eyes met.

"Splendid. Have you?"

"Great. Feel lots better."

"No, she didn't hear," thought Laurel.

"No, she didn't hear," thought Stella.

CHAPTER XIX

1

Helen Morrison sat in the big library-sort of room where Laurel had first watched her serve tea. She sat by one of the long windows that looked out upon the willow-shaded avenue that wound up to the front door; by the same window, it chanced, out of which she had run to meet Laurel the first time she had come to visit her four years ago. She was dressed very much as she had been then (it was morning and July), in white skirt and waist and low shoes. She sat in front of a desk, writing, in a dilatory fashion. Every little while she glanced back over her shoulder at the clock upon the mantel, then out the window down the willow-shaded drive, then back again to her pen.

Looking at Helen from the clock as she bent over her writing, she seemed not to have changed at all in the last four years, or in the last fourteen years; the same young-girl slenderness (not the slightest thickening of neck and shoulders, hip or ankle), the same young-girl lightness, as she sat poised on the edge of her chair, which was tilted forward on its two delicate front legs. But, when she raised her head, and looked back at the clock, then one saw without a shadow of doubt that she was no longer a girl. It wasn't only her hair (for in the last four years the few white threads Laurel had discovered had become a definite streak of silver cloud that drifted about the left side of her brow and reached backward to the still dark coil in her neck)—it was something more convincing, something less obvious but deeper-rooted. There was on Helen's face a look of settled calm (or was it settled hopelessness?) that hadn't been there four years ago when she had rushed out of the long window down the lawn to meet Stephen and Laurel. There had been laughter and anticipation in her eyes then. Now there were only quiet smiles and submission.

To-day, again, Helen was awaiting the arrival of an automobile. She had sent the car down to the station to meet the-train due at ten-forty. It was now after eleven. It was only five minutes to the station. The train must be late. She finished her letter, then rose, crossed the room, and stood looking out of another long window that opened out upon the terrace. Helen was awaiting the arrival of Laurel's mother, of Stephen's wife. She had telephoned last night from New York.

"I'm Mrs..Stephen Dallas," the strange voice had announced. "I want to talk with you. Will you be home to-morrow morning if I come out?"

Helen had replied, with no surprise in her voice, that she would be glad to come in town and meet her there if she preferred.

"No. I'd rather come out."

They had arranged the trains. Helen had told her she would have her met.

When finally the bell rang, and the maid announced Mrs. Dallas, Helen crossed the hall to the reception-room with a sensation as near dread as she had ever felt in her life when about to meet a guest.

Stella was standing up. She had on a dark-blue tricolette suit, and wore a summer fur—white fox, fastened behind. The dead animal's head hung halfway down her back. Stella's coat was tightly buttoned, and fitted her generous bust and hips without a ripple. Her hat was large and broad-brimmed, and didn't take a veil well. Therefore she had adjusted her veil over her bare head before putting her hat on. The veil was drawn tightly over her generous cheeks and chin, and it also fitted without a ripple.

2

Helen looked at nothing but Stella's eyes, as she came toward her smiling, with her hand outstretched.

"Good-morning, Mrs. Dallas," she said. "I hope the chauffeur found you."

"No, he didn't. There was quite a crowd. I walked."

"Oh, I'm sorry. It is such a warm morning. Let me send for some water." She made a movement toward the bell.

"I don't want any water." Why, her hair was snow-white on one side! She couldn't be a day under forty!

"Well, do take off your coat and unfasten your fur."

"No, thanks."

"And sit down. Let us come into the other room. It's pleasanter there."

Helen led the way across the hall, shoved a cool, linen-covered armchair in front of one of the terrace windows. "I always like it here better on a warm morning, looking out on the shadows rather than on sunshine. And there's usually a breeze."

Opposite the armchair Helen placed one of the Sheratons for herself. She made a little waving motion toward the armchair. "Sit down, please," she said; "take that chair."

Stella complied—at least partially. She took the extreme edge of the chair. It was one of those low deep affairs. She'd have a frightful time getting out of it if she sat back. Helen sat down, too. There was a pause—a pause that threatened to become awkward.

"Is it very warm in town this morning?" Helen inquired.

Stella ignored the question. Might as well take the bull by the horns.

"I suppose you think it's funny my coming here."

"No, I don't," earnestly Helen assured her, leaning forward, clasping her hands upon her knees. "You and I have a great deal in common. I don't think it's funny at all."

"Well, funny or not, I had to come. I thought of writing at first, but, gracious, if a thing is important enough to you, you'll do it the right way—at least, the way that seems right to you—whatever any one thinks. There are some things I had to know that nobody but you could tell me, so I decided to come right down here myself and ask them."

"That was the right way."

"I've heard a lot about you."

"And so have I—heard a lot about you."

"From Laurel, I mean."

"Yes, I mean from Laurel, too."

"I suppose you know it, but Laurel thinks a lot of you."

Helen smiled. "And I suppose you know it, but Laurel thinks a lot of you."

"Well, I'm her mother. She has to. But she's got what they call a sort of 'crush'—'mash' we called it when I was a girl—on you. She hates to have me call it that. She won't talk about you very much, now. Thinks I might be jealous or something, I guess. Perhaps I was a little at first, though I hardly knew it. Laurel did, though. Trust her. She's the sort of child knows what you feel before you do yourself almost."

"I know. Sensitive, isn't she—oh, so sensitive! I think a great deal of Laurel, Mrs. Dallas. You have a beautiful child, I think."

"She is a nice kiddie," said Stella.

For an instant the two women's eyes met. Was that bright look tears, they both wondered.

3

Stella was the first to look away. She cleared her throat, coughed, made another attempt.

"How's Stephen now?"

"I think he's well."

"I suppose you see him now and then?"

"No. The last few times Laurel has visited me. Miss Simpson has brought her, and taken her away. Stephen and I haven't met for two years."

"Oh, that so?" Stella looked back at Mrs. Morrison. Gracious! What had happened? The shining look had all gone from her eyes and the light from her expression. She looked gray, ashen, and old, terribly old.

"Look here, Mrs. Morrison," Stella went on, "I'm not going to beat about the bush any longer. I've been thinking a good deal lately of the advantages to me if I got things fixed up between Stephen and myself, the way he wanted them fixed up a while ago. But before I do any more thinking I want to find out how things are now between Stephen and you."

Helen's clasped hands tightened upon her knee, but she showed no feeling when she spoke.

"Mrs. Dallas," she said, "I don't want to be unkind, but self-denial, our duty to others, the toll that must be paid for mistakes, separation from each other—nothing will ever destroy that which exists, even though without form or expression, between Stephen and me."

Stella looked puzzled.

"But what I want to know is, if Stephen was free, if I stepped aside, the way he suggested, would you two get married?" Might as well come right out with the nub. After all, it didn't make her jump.

"We would," Helen replied.

"Are you sure?"

"I'm sure."

"But you haven't seen Stephen for two years."

"I know, I know. Oh, I'm sorry, Mrs. Dallas. But the truth is best. I think you want it."

"It's what I came for."

"It's what I shall give you, even though it costs me Stephen himself."

"Well, the next thing I want to get clear is, if you two did marry, what about Laurel?"

"If we did—" Helen drew in her breath quickly, "why, if we did—if we did—"

"Yes, if you did, what about Laurel?"

Helen let her breath out ever so carefully, ever so carefully drew in another.

"Oh, Laurel. Laurel is yours, Mrs. Dallas. A child is always her mother's, I think."

"You mean. Laurel would keep right on making her headquarters with me, the same as she does now?"

"Why, of course. I am a mother, Mrs. Dallas. Once I was the mother of a little girl. My little girl would be just Laurel's age now. As long as I live I shall never be guilty of robbing any woman of her only little daughter."

Stella glanced down at her shoe, out upon the terrace, back to her shoe again, cleared her throat, then boldly raised her eyes to Helen's.

"But if the woman didn't want her daughter. I mean if she couldn't have her very well, if it was inconvenient–"

"Don't you want Laurel, Mrs. Dallas?" Helen exclaimed.

"Oh, of course, I want her, but you see she's a great expense now, and I haven't many maids–no one to leave her with. I'm quite tied down by her, and–"

"Oh," broke out Helen, and again her eyes were shining, "I'd love to have Laurel! I'd love to have Laurel, even if I had her without Stephen."

"No, that wouldn't do," said Stella, hard and practical, her eyes shining, too, but not with tears–with triumph. "If you were married to Stephen your name would be Dallas then, and Laurel's name would be Dallas, too. Don't you see? And everybody would think, who didn't stop to ask, that Laurel was yours. Gracious, she's enough like you–dark and slim as a smokestack, and you've been her model for years, as far as ways and manners go, and when you begin to do things for her–like giving her, well–a coming-out party, or something–you know she's seventeen now–why, then the invitation cards, 'Mr. and Mrs. Dallas, and Miss Dallas,' would read right, don't you see? I've thought it out. And later, if one of the nice young men in your circle fell in love with Laurel, and married her, why, then again, it would read right in the papers and society columns, where those things are printed. And the same way," Stella pursued, warming to her subject, "at hotels and places when you have to register–that is, if you should travel with Laurel in Europe or California. Laurel really ought to travel. It is so expensive, I couldn't manage it myself, what with all the private lessons in riding and skating, and dancing and music, and heaven knows what-not. You'll find she's quite up in those things. Oh, really," earnestly, eagerly she hastened on, unaware of the increasing wonder and surprise in Helen Morrison's wide-open eyes, "really, if you do want a daughter of your own to take the place of that baby you spoke of that died, I'll say this, I don't think you'll ever be *ashamed* of Laurel. She takes after her father, and if you're crazy about her father, why, it popped into my mind that–honestly I can't see a trace of me in Laurel. Nobody can. She's so refined, and sort of elegant in her ways. You know that yourself. Oh, you needn't have a minute's doubt about what sort of a success Laurel will make if you should bring her out in New York society sometime. She makes a wonderful impression upon strangers. Why, If that girl didn't have *me* shackled round one foot everywhere she goes, she'd just *soar*. And another thing I want to make clear to you, don't be afraid I'll be appearing at embarrassing moments. I won't—*ever*. I've got some common sense, thank heaven. I know what sort of an impression *I* make, too."

There was no mistake about the tears in Helen's eyes now. She rose, went quickly over to Stella, sat down on the arm of her chair, and put her arm about her shoulders.

"I see! I understand!" she exclaimed, softly.

4

Stella stiffened. No woman had ever understood before. She had never understood herself. The undercurrent of her life had been flowing beneath the surface waters, unnoticed, unobserved for years, wearing a deeper and deeper channel, gathering strength and power in its hidden course. But not until Mrs. Morrison put her arm around Stella had any one looked down through the flotsam and discovered the crystal waters underneath.

"Everything shall be as you wish," said Helen. "Everything. Travel and parties and friends—everything, that to you means happiness for your child. I'll treat her as my very own, but she will always *be* yours. You will not lose her. You shall see her often. We'll arrange that. Oh, I wonder if I could have done so big a thing for my little girl."

Stella dabbed her eyes with her handkerchief through her veil, struggled to her feet, dabbed her eyes again, bit her lip hard—Good gracious, she mustn't break down and bawl like a baby.

"I'm an awful old fool sometimes lately," she murmured.

"Don't go. Sit down again. Please. We've so much to talk about. I've got so much to learn."

"No, I can't. Laurel thinks I'm in Milhampton, and I must hustle along back to Boston to-night or she'll get suspicious. You've got my idea. There's no need of staying any longer. You tell Stephen I'm ready to get the divorce any day now, and the quicker the better. Only tell him, for goodness' sake, don't put that man Morley Smith on it. I don't believe I could meet that excrescence and be decent to him. Every time I think—but never mind. That's all over. Oh, by the way, one thing more—when Laurel is down here this September visiting you, don't tell her what's up. I can't stand long-drawn-out good-byes. I may mention I'm getting a divorce, but

I shan't tell her what for. Don't let on a word till we're ready to shoot. You and Stephen get married, have Laurel down for a Sunday. I'll send her clothes on afterwards. Something like that. I've thought it out. No soft-music, sob-stuff for me, thank you. is this the living-room?"

"Yes, this is the living-room."

Stella gazed at the high, dignified walls silently a moment. "I can just see her in it, entertaining her young friends; walking around on that terrace with Richard Grosvenor—he's somebody your sons know, a young man that is just crazy about Lollle—walking along in her slow grand way under those big aristocratic-looking trees down there; yes, it will suit her fine. That's why I wanted to come out—to see, what it was like. I walked by your city house last night. It was closed, but I could get an idea. I suppose you think that's funny, but I've picked out Laurel's clothes so much—" she stopped. "I couldn't see some of the other rooms, could I? I'll never be here again, and, well—you know, it's sort of nice to be able to think of a person in a house or a room you've seen yourself, when they write. I thought Laurel and I might write."

"Of course you'll write. Oh, It will only be as If she were away at school or college, having all the things you want her to have. Come out into the dining-room. Come out into the garden. Laurel loves the garden. And then come upstairs. The violet guest-room is Laurel's now. Come and see her pretty valanced bed."

CHAPTER XX

1

Stephen sat in his office, fifteen floors above the sidewalk and street thermometer that registered ninety-five. He sat in the gentle breeze of two silently revolving electric fans, in front of his desk, in a big chair with his elbows on its arm, and his hands folded. He was dictating, gazing out of the high window toward the northeast with a look in his eyes as if he saw a hundred miles away.

To-day, as Stephen sat and gazed, searched, and selected, he was aware of the heat, aware of the rumble of the city outside, aware of the loud insistent pound—pound—pound of a riveter at work near by, aware of his own fatigue, too. He sighed deeply now and then. When Stephen was tired, and gazed out of the high windows in the direction of the green lawns and white beaches of Long Island, there was a Helen between every careful phrase that he spoke.

At a quarter of one that day, or thereabouts, Stephen raised his wrist and glanced at it.

"Time for one more, I think. Miss Mills. Pretty hot, isn't it? Can you stand it? All right. Ready."

He was attacking a difficult second paragraph—twice already had murmured, "No, start again"—when there was a repressed burr at his side. He frowned, turned away from his engrossed contemplation of the illimitable space outside his window, and reached for the telephone, supporting it upon his chest as he leaned back again and spoke into it.

"Who is it?" he asked.

"Long distance. Green Hills, New York, Mrs. Cornelius Morrison," the operator in the outer office announced.

It was as if a current of electricity passed through Stephen. Though he didn't move a hand or foot, Miss Mills observed his sudden alertness, the sudden tightening of the muscles around his jaw and cheek-bones. Discreetly she turned away.

"Connect me," she heard him say. Then he turned to her. His eyes were like spots of phosphorescence. "We'll finish that later. I'll call you." He nodded toward the outer office. She rose. "Please close the door."

Alone, Stephen leaned forward, placed the telephone on the solid foundation of his desk, drew his chair close to it, jerked himself to the edge of the chair, crouched over the telephone eagerly, cupping his hand over the transmitter.

Helen's voice sounded clear and sweet, as if she were in the very room beside him. He hadn't heard her voice for two years.

"Hello."

"Hello, Helen."

"Is it you, Stephen?"

"It's I. Yes. What is it? Are you all right?"

He caught her little laugh.

"Oh, yes, yes. I'm all right. I called you up to find out if you had an engagement for to-night."

"What do you mean?"

"Well, *have* you an engagement?"

"No. Of course I haven't. But—"

"Then could you come down this evening?"

"Helen, what has happened?"

"Nothing awful. Could you?"

"Yes. I could. But–"

"About eight o'clock?"

"Yes, eight o'clock. All right. But, Helen, please–"

"Eight o'clock to-night, then. Good-bye."

She had sent for him! Helen had sent for him to come to her! At one o'clock, at half-past one, at two, Stephen was still sitting in his big chair before his desk, looking far out over the roofs. Miss Mills was still sitting outside the door, waiting to finish the dictation.

2

"I'm sorry to have called you at your office, Stephen," were Helen's first words when she saw him that night, standing ten feet away from him, just inside the threshold of the big room. "I suppose you were having a consultation or doing something important"–she tried to make her voice sound light and careless–"but I wanted to get you, right *straight* off, so that you wouldn't fall down an elevator-shaft, or get killed in an explosion, or something"–she laughed tremulously–"the way they do in novels, sometimes, before I had a chance to tell you that after all our years of waiting, that–that–after–Oh, Stephen–"

3

Stella arrived at the apartment on Commonwealth Avenue at eleven o'clock that night. She telephoned to Laurel from the Back Bay station that she would be out in half an hour, and when she puffed up the last flight of stairs–it grew hotter and hotter as she approached the roof–Laurel, in her thin sleeveless nightgown, with her hair pulled tightly back and braided, was in the hall to meet her.

"I've made some lemonade, mother. It's on the ice. And there's some cold watermelon. Come in and get those horrid hot things off. I've pulled the bed out where it will get the breeze, if there is any, in the early morning. How is Mrs. McDavitt and the children?"

Ten minutes later, Stella, nightgowned and hair pulled back and braided, too, sat on the back porch under the clothes-reel and drank lemonade, and ate cold watermelon, and gazed at Lollie, seated on top of the coal-box with her bare arms locked about her knees, not talking much, looking up at the lop-sided moon that had been full three nights ago on Stag Island.

Funny place, thought Stella, for the lovely Miss Laurel Dallas, who would be staggering New York society one of these days, to be perched in midsummer. Oh, if she could only tell the poor suffering little kiddie (for she was suffering—she had been pretty crazy about that Grosvenor boy, Stella guessed)—if she could only tell her it was only for a short time now; that everything would come out all right in the end. But of course she couldn't. Mum was the word.

"It's simply horrid for you here, honey."

Laurel gave a start, as if she had been a thousand miles away.

"Oh, no, it isn't," she assured Stella lightly. "Really, I like it. Oh, we'll have a good time. See if we don't. There's Revere, and Nantasket, and Norumbega."

"Was it awful lonesome without me?"

"No more awful for me than for you when I'm away, I guess."

"What did you do?"

"Oh, I sat out here."

"Gracious! Seventeen, summer, a moon, and alone, out here."

"About nine o'clock the bell rang. It was that Mr. Munn."

"Oh, Ed! Really?"

"He said he saw the light and thought it was probably you who were here, alone, while I was off visiting somewhere. When he discovered it was I, he said please to excuse him, and went away."

"That sounds real polite of Ed."

"No, it wasn't. He didn't have any right to ring the bell for *you*—a man like that. He knows we don't want him. We've shown him. Oh, I hate that man, mother."

"I know you do. You've told me so enough times. Funny. You're your father right over again, Lollie."

"Did father ever see Ed Munn?"

"Mercy, yes!"

"Did father ever hate Ed Munn?"

"Like fury," laughed Stella; "and there was never any sense in it either—no more than with you—just a whim."

Laurel still gazing at the moon and the few far dim stars that seemed to He beyond was silent. Was Alfred Munn one of the pieces of the puzzle, too?

4

Helen and Stephen were quietly married one afternoon the following spring. The same day Laurel received a note from Mrs. Morrison inviting her to spend a week-end with her, a fortnight later. The invitation did not come as a surprise to Laurel. Mrs. Morrison had told her last September that she hoped to have Laurel stay with her for a few days in the spring. Laurel had told her mother of the possibility. Stella had been working on Laurel's wardrobe, in preparation, for weeks before Mrs. Morrison's note arrived.

Helen was at the station to meet Laurel. She and Mrs. Morrison (she was still Mrs. Morrison to Laurel) were quite alone in the back of the limousine as it threaded its way out of the congestion of Forty-Second Street, and turned north on Fifth Avenue. Laurel sat forward on the edge of the seat beside Helen, cheeks flushed, chin raised, breathing in deep breaths of the intoxicating, Mrs. Morrison-charged air, not saying anything at all.

"Glad to be here?" finally Helen interrupted from her deep corner.

Laurel simply nodded, keeping her starry eyes steadfastly turned away. Her worshipful regard for Mrs. Morrison had not changed in quality in the last four years. The only difference was that she was able to adapt herself a little sooner now than formerly to the dazzling presence of her goddess. Give Laurel an hour and she would find her tongue. Give her several hours and the same emotion which choked, confined—later unloosened, unlocked, threw the gates wide.

"Your father is going to be with us for dinner to-night," briefly Helen announced before the car had left them at the door.

"Oh, I wondered when I'd see father."

Helen and Stephen had decided to tell Laurel together. They waited until after dinner. Con and Dane were away at school, and little Rick, who had been cautioned not to mention the great news, had finally been torn away from Laurel's side (little Rick was devoted to Laurel) and had gone upstairs. Helen and Stephen were alone with Laurel in Helen's lovely ivory-tinted room, seated, all three, before the fire, on the long Sheraton sofa, with Laurel in the middle.

Helen slipped an arm through Laurel's and, smiling across at Stephen, said, "Shall I tell Laurel a story now?"

The story that Helen told was the story of her own life. She told it exquisitely. "And then—and then—and then—" step by step, from the first time when she knew that she loved Stephen when only a little older than Laurel, down through all the years, when their paths diverged, met, diverged again. It was a simple, straightforward statement of facts, with no excuses nor explanations. It sounded to Stephen like some beautiful epic poem. He had to close his eyes frequently to shut out tears. When she reached the end, "And so here we are. Laurel—Stephen and I, together at last."

Laurel whispered softly, "Married?"

"Yes."

"I wondered when you would be," was Laurel's unsurprised reply.

"How long have you wondered that, Laurel?" eagerly Stephen inquired.

"Oh, ever since I saw you together in the big room at Green Hills, when I came down from upstairs that first time, I felt then that you were meant to be married, only—"

"Yes, only?"

"Only you must have taken a wrong turn way back somewhere—you know how it is—a wrong turn or a detour makes all the journey different sometimes."

Stephen slipped his arm through Laurel's, too. "Are you glad?" he asked her.

"Oh, *ever* so glad!" promptly she assured him. "It's like a book, or a play, coming out the way you hoped it would; or a journey ending where it should, even though there was a wrong turn. What shall I call you, Mrs. Morrison?" she broke off. "I've wondered and wondered. Isn't it funny?" she laughed. "You aren't Mrs. Morrison any more!"

What a little girl she was, after all, thought Stephen, and how merciful. It had been easier than he feared to tell her that he had become to another woman what he had one day been to her mother. How simply, how serenely, she accepted that which had been so painfully won.

"Let's call each other by our first names," lightly Helen suggested.

"Oh, I wonder if I ever could! Your name is so—so *special*. Mrs. Morrison is like the word 'America' to me. It *means* things. I couldn't possibly call America anything else."

"You could call it home, couldn't you?" said Helen.

5

Later, placing her hand over Laurel's, and Laurel turning hers palm upwards, and interlacing her fingers with Helen's in impulsive response, Helen said, "There's more to my story. Laurel."

With infinite gentleness she explained to Laurel that she was a part of *this* home now—was a member of *this* family; they were hers and she was theirs. She must have been talking five minutes before Laurel caught the import of her words.

"You mean," suddenly she interrupted, "I'm to live here?"

"Yes, here, and at the place at Green Hills. With us—with your father, with Con and Dane and Rick—they're so happy about it—wherever we are—as one of us. Laurel."

"I never thought of that." Laurel gazed wonderingly around the lovely room. This her home? This beautiful place? A family like other girls? A mother and father who lived together? Mrs. Morrison? "Yes, yes," she gasped, "but what about—what about—"

"What about your mother?" Helen asked for her. "I know, I understand. You shall see your mother often, Laurel."

"You mean"—she still had a manner as if gasping for air—as if groping for light, for comprehension. "You mean mother would still live in Boston?"

"That would seem wisest, wouldn't it?"

"Yes, yes, of course," Laurel nodded. "Yes, that would seem wisest." For a long quarter-minute she was silent, staring straight in front of her, then unlocking her fingers from Helen's, withdrawing her arm linked through her father's, "No," she said quietly, "it wouldn't do."

"You may visit your mother in Boston, Laurel."

Again for a moment Laurel was silent. "No, it wouldn't do," she repeated. The little girl in her had disappeared. The spontaneity, the soft tender impulsiveness had faded, gone. "I'd like to be a member of your family, father," she said, turning toward Stephen, "of yours, too, Mrs. Morrison," turning toward Helen. "Thank you ever and ever so much, but I'm sorry, I couldn't."

"But, Lollie, my dear child—"

"But, Laurel, listen—"

For twenty minutes, for half an hour, both Stephen and Helen labored with Laurel; but to no purpose, to no avail. "I'm sorry. I couldn't," was her unvaried reply.

Finally Stephen exclaimed, "But, Laurel, my dear child, this isn't a matter we are consulting you on. It is a matter that has already been arranged. We are simply telling you about it."

"That makes no difference. I'm sorry. I couldn't," she persisted.

"Why, of course you can, my dear. You don't understand. You are not of age to make your own decisions yet. Laurel."

"Oh, yes, I am, father."

"But you're not. Not on a matter of this sort. Your mother and I have decided this for you."

"Does mother know of it?"

"Certainly, and approves. She is sending your trunks to-morrow."

Two little bright spots appeared in the center of Laurel's cheeks.

"The trunks will have to be sent back then," she announced. "How silly to have tried to force me like that!"

"We didn't think it would be forcing. We believed it would be a plan that would make you very happy. It was your mother's idea, to say nothing about it beforehand, to avoid, I believe, good-byes."

Laurel replied calmly, "I came down here for four days and I am going home in four days, father."

"This is home now," he told her.

"Oh, no, it isn't," she flashed back, "and it never will be home either, as long as my mother is alive." Laurel stood up. "Of course you can lock me up if you want to," she went on, "but I shan't stay any other way. Please understand that."

The bright spots on her cheeks had not disappeared. There were unfamiliar lines and shadows, too, about her chin and jaw. Helen and Stephen stared at her. They had never felt the steel in Laurel before.

"But, Laurel—"

"Oh, don't let's argue about it, father. It won't do the least bit of good."

"Why, this is absurd, impossible. I cannot allow—"

"Just a minute, Stephen," Helen interrupted. There were bright spots in the center of Stephen's cheeks, too. "Laurel, dear," she said, reaching for Laurel's hand, drawing her down on the sofa again. "Listen. Let me explain. It is your mother's wish. It's all your mother's planning. This—all this"—with a wave of her hand she included the whole house and all it stood for in way of happiness for Laurel—"is her gift to you." (The truth was best, Helen concluded.) "She came and saw me about it last summer. We talked it all over in detail, together."

"When last summer?" Laurel exclaimed.

"Last July."

(Oh, then, it flashed across Laurel, her mother had heard! She hadn't been asleep that night on the train! She hadn't been to Milhampton the next day to see Effie McDavitt. She had been to New York to give her Mrs. Morrison!)

"Well, I shan't take her gift," said Laurel. (Her mother! Her wonderful mother! And they had called her "That woman!" "That awful creature!" "That dame!")

CHAPTER XXI

1

"How foolish of you, mother," four days later Laurel scolded Stella, as they stood side by side in front of the sink in the kitchen of the Boston apartment and washed and dried the three-days' collection of dishes Stella had allowed to accumulate. "How foolish to think you could work up any such scheme as that *on* me. You'd think I didn't have any such thing as a will of my own."

"Oh, I know," sighed Stella. "I suppose we did it the wrong way. I ought to have told you, I guess."

"Telling me wouldn't have made any difference. I wouldn't have listened."

"But I don't see *why*. He's your own father, and you've always been crazy about him, and she—"

"I know, I know," Laurel interrupted. "Oh, look here, mother," impatiently she broke off. "Listen to me. I'm never going to leave you as long as you live. Do get that through your head. Do try; and don't talk about it any more." Then, suddenly gentle, "Why, mother," she caressed, "don't you remember you said to me once, way back, when I was a mite of a child, 'I'll never leave you, and you'll never leave me, will you, Lollie?' I've never forgotten that."

"Oh," groaned Stella, "what a fool I was to have talked that way to a little kid!"

"No," Laurel retorted. "Rather, what a fool you were to have worked and slaved for that little kid for seventeen years, and skimped and saved for her all that time, and given her everything under the sun you thought would make her happy—oh, that was an awfully foolish way to treat a child you hoped would trot off and leave you the first chance she got."

"What nonsense," Stella scorned. "Why, I didn't even want you before you were born. I didn't like babies."

"Yes, so you've told me before," laughed Laurel, "and you don't want me now, do you? Poor thing! But you've *got to have me* just as before I was born. *You've got to have me.* You see we happen to belong to each other, mother."

"But you belong to your father, too."

Laurel puckered up her brow, thoughtfully, mopping the plate which she held half in the water, half out, round and round slowly with her dishcloth.

"Yes," she acknowledged, "I suppose I do belong to father, too, but it's different. I'm fond of father. I love to be with him. We always have wonderful times, but father and I have never been through anything long and hard and disagreeable.

We've always had just fun together. Somehow, having fun together doesn't make two people feel as if they belonged the way suffering together does. Besides, father doesn't need me the way you do."

"Pshaw! I don't need you! I get along all right alone."

"So did I last summer, those two days when you left me. I got along all right alone, too. Nobody to wash dishes with, nobody to talk with, nor to eat with, nor to sleep with, nor to do anything with. I know what it is like. No, mother, you can't live like that. It isn't decent."

"Decent! What do you mean?"

"Why, look at the way the apartment looks, for one thing. Not only the kitchen, but all the other rooms, too. I never saw them in such a mess."

"Well, but I didn't know you were coming. If you'd written—"

"Exactly. Without some human being to clean up for, and have a little pride for, this place would look the way grandpa's used to before he died, in a little while. No, mother. You can never live alone. Come, let's change the subject. What show shall we see to-night?"

2

Stella threw down her dish-towel and sat down at the kitchen table, her hands dropping limp into her lap. "But I've gone and given your father his divorce now," she lamented. "I didn't want a divorce! It will be all for nothing, if you won't go and live with him for a while."

"Mother, I've told you, and *told* you, I'm glad you've given father the divorce. It was exactly the right thing to do. Father and Mrs. Morrison cared about each other before you and I ever saw either of them. You've fixed something right that was wrong."

"Yes," sneered Stella, "especially *you*. I've fixed you fine and right! Oh," she sighed, her eyes resting mournfully on Laurel's back as she stood before the sink, "it just almost kills me to see you doing work like that, Lollie."

Laurel was wiping out the large tin dishpan, now, with her dishcloth, which she had just wrung out with several vigorous little twists. Afterwards she hung up the dishpan on a hook underneath the sink and spread out the dishcloth to dry on top of it. Then proceeded to clean the soapstone sink. She used a small rubber-edged shovel for the purpose, scooping up small bits of refuse with it, and emptying it now and then into her free hand.

"I like making things bright and clean," she called out above the loud scraping noise she was making with her shovel, "but if you prefer," she went on cheerfully, "we'll have a servant. You've often said, since the divorce, we could afford several servants if we wanted them."

"Oh, but, Lollie, I don't know how to run a lot of servants. Besides, what's the use of servants when there's nobody to serve? I can't give you a coming-out party. I used to think I could, but I know now I can't. No. It's no use. It's not in me. I've done all I can for you." She lifted her upturned hands, lying idle in her lap, and then let them drop, dead and lifeless. "*She* was going to bring you out in New York society, Lollie," she droned on, "she said she was. You'd be going to dinners, and dances, and balls. You'd be having lovely clothes. You'd be having lovely friends—young ladies in limousines calling mornings for you to go shopping with them; young men in limousines calling evenings for you to go—"

"Mother! Please stop. You've told me all that before."

"I haven't told you *one* thing. I haven't said one word about one *special* thing. Laurel, listen, if you go to New York for a season you'll be almost sure to run across Richard Grosvenor! He knew Mrs. Morrison, and—"

"Oh, don't drag in Richard Grosvenor."

"And if you did—you can't tell. He was crazy about you—"

"Now, mother."

"Well, he was."

"I'm all over Richard Grosvenor, now, mother."

"You're not. No such thing."

"But I am! I am! I never even answered his letters last fall."

"His letters!"

"Yes. He wrote me—twice. Mrs. Morrison forwarded them. I never told you because you were so silly about him."

Stella shoved her chair back from the table with a fierce jerk and stood up.

"I know why you didn't answer his letters. I know mighty well! Of course you couldn't answer his letters! Of course you couldn't, with him in college right across the river, here, likely—no, sure, to look you up in this hole, and find out we didn't know any of his Back Bay friends, not a single one of the young ladies whose dances he's been ushering at! Oh, I've seen his name in the lists in the papers, too. I've got eyes, and I've just suffered for you, Lollie. Of course you couldn't write to him and have him come here, and find out how we live, and what sort of a freak *I* am—"

"Mother!"

"That's all right. *I* know—I'm no fool, Laurel."

"Oh, Lollie, please—*please*, go to your father just for a little while—just for a year or so, just long enough—"

"No, mother. I'm not going."

Stella sank down in her chair. It was useless, futile to beat herself against this soft child's will once she had set it up. Experience had taught Stella that a big buzzing fly is as ineffective in breaking through a plate-glass barrier.

"Well," gloomily, "what are you going to do with yourself, then? You can't hang around a five-roomed apartment all your life, can you, reading two library books a week, and practicing on a piano two hours a day?" (Laurel had not taken any "Courses" this winter.) "What are you going to do to amuse yourself, I'd like to know?"

"I've got a plan," nodded Laurel, smiling.

"Humph."

"I must have something to do, of course. Busy people are always the happiest. I'm going to be very busy. I'm going to be a stenographer, mother."

"A what?" gasped Stella.

"A stenographer. I've thought it all out."

"A stenographer! A stenographer!" Stella repeated, and a third time, "A stenographer!"

If Laurel had said that she was going to be a German spy, Stella couldn't have been more shocked.

"Yes, mother, dear, a stenographer. Don't you see it's the one thing I *can* be, and live along here with you, and keep up our nice times together evenings, at the theater and the movies? And have Sundays with you, and holidays, and nights? I'm going to start right in, next week—this week, if I can—at the very best business college there is in this city, and work *hard*. It's going to be lots of fun!"

"Oh, no, Laurel," Stella broke out. "Not *that!* Not that! Please. Please." Her voice pleaded, her eyes beseeched, implored. "You wouldn't do that. Say you wouldn't. Not *you*. It would break my heart. Say you wouldn't, dearie. Please—please." She grasped hold of Laurel's hand. "Lollie, for my sake! It would kill me, Lollie!"

Laurel drew her hand away. "Oh, come, mother. Don't be silly. Don't be a goose."

3

A stenographer! Laurel, her beautiful Laurel, shut up all day long in an office, reeking with tobacco smoke? Laurel the servant of a lot of men, taking dictation, taking orders? Laurel wearing paper cuffs and elastic bands and pencils in her hair; eating lunch out of a box with a lot of other girls, also wearing paper cuffs and elastic bands and pencils in their hair? No. No. It mustn't be. It simply mustn't be. Why, even she herself wouldn't have been a stenographer.

Stella lay wide awake in the bed beside Laurel. It was nearly two o'clock. Laurel had slept like a baby—sweetly, steadily, all night long so far. She hadn't changed her position. Twice Stella had risen and lit the light to see what time it was, had stopped a moment by the side of the bed, and gazed down upon Laurel.

"Like a lovely Sleeping Beauty, she is. Oh, my God, she can't be a stenographer!" It would be like planting an orchid between the cobblestones at the corner of Washington and Winter Streets to stick Laurel in front of a typewriter, inside of one of the big grimy office-buildings downtown. She'd get all dust and dirt and trampled and spoiled in no time. She mustn't be sacrificed like that! Why, New York would go simply crazy about Lollie. It would exclaim over her, oh-and-ah over her, like the people at the Horticultural Shows over some new amazing flower. "Oh, gracious, what can I do? What can I do to save the kid?"

She must do something, and quick—now. Laurel was all ready to show *now*. Next year, the year after—too late. She'd be touched, handled, brown on the edges. There'd be a story about her—a tale. "She was once a stenographer, you know." People would whisper, "Really! You don't say!" And eyebrows would be raised. That must not occur. Whatever it cost, by whatever means, *that must he avoided*.

About three o'clock in the morning Stella crawled out of bed and, wrapping herself up in a blanket, sat down on the window-seat by the open window. She could always think clearer in a vertical position. "If it wasn't for me. Laurel would go. I'm the reason she's tossing aside her opportunity, dumping her happiness overboard, as if it was so much rubbish, and then scrapping herself—her lovely self, all ready to sail (yes, that's what she's like, too—a ship, beautifully made—beautifully fitted out). Oh, gracious, what can I do? She's ruining her life for *me*—for a big old water-logged hulk like me, (The Lord knows how I happen to be her mother. Talk about miracles!) Oh, why couldn't I have whiffed out last summer at that hotel when I was so sick? She'd have gone to New York then, just as a matter of course. She'd be there, now, to-day. She'd be under steam this minute, admired, desired, flags flying, sun shining. 'As long as you're alive.' Those were her words. Oh, why couldn't I whiff out now? Say, why couldn't I feel a little dizzy and topple over out of the window, down there on the concrete—it's four stories—and clear the job up quick—right now, and no more talk?

"No, I can't. I'm afraid. I haven't the nerve. I haven't the guts. It might only smash me up. Poison would be better, or gas, or a revolver. Poison—what kind? Gas—how long would it take? A revolver—where were they bought? How did you load them? Oh, it would be horrid—horrid! I wonder if I dare."

Stella got down from the window-seat and went over to the bed. The early light of dawn was in the room now, like gray smoke. She stood looking down at Laurel through the thick intangible haze for a long time—for a minute, for two minutes, for three minutes, perhaps.

"Ought I? Oh, gracious, ought I?" she whispered.

The memory of a certain other early morning, when she had stood thus and gazed down upon the sweetly sleeping, defenseless child, recurred to Stella. Then, also, as now, she had whispered, "Ought I? Oh, gracious, ought I?" It was when the doctors were due to arrive in a few hours to perform an operation upon Lollie—years ago, a slight operation, only tonsils—but they were going to make her limp and lifeless, and cut her with a knife.

"Ought I again cut her with a knife?"

It would hurt her, of course—poor kid—at first. Her face would get all white with horror and dismay. "But she'd be rid of me—free, and after a while she'd forget it. She's young, she'd get over it. Or would it also be a story—a tale, to whisper about behind Laurel's back. 'Her mother committed suicide!' 'You don't mean it!' 'And her father's father, too, so I've heard.' 'Really.' 'Runs in the blood on both sides.' 'How shocking!'" Years ago Stella had read in a magazine somewhere that suicidal tendencies were inherited. She recalled it now. Heavens! What if Laurel should grow up and read that, too? Good Lord, it might make her afraid for herself if it was on both sides! She must be saved that horror. A wave of relief swept over Stella.

"I must think of some other way." She went back to the window-seat again. "Oh, how scared I was! What a sniveling coward I am!"

All the next day she submitted compromise after compromise to Laurel. She would keep a servant if only Laurel would go to New York. She would keep two servants, a companion; two companions, return to an apartment hotel, if only—if only—But Laurel simply shrugged her shoulders.

Again and again that day Stella was forced to face the unwelcome consideration of discovering some method of whiffing out that might not arouse suspicion. Slipping down in front of an automobile, making a mistake about sleeping-powders. It might be done. But, oh, she didn't want to die that way. Not that she was much on religion, but she didn't want to take any such chances with immortality. There must be some other way.

It was sometime during the course of the second night, when she was wearied and exhausted almost to the breaking point, that the "some other way" flashed across Stella's mental field of vision. The first consciousness of it made her feel queer and hollow inside for a moment. It was like having a messenger suddenly run onto the scene with your pardon, just when you were settling yourself in the electric chair.

Tremblingly, anxiously, she groped her way across the hall to her desk in the front room. If only she could find the address. It was on a card. She had never thrown the card away. It must be *somewhere.* Oh, what if Laurel in one of her raids upon the cluttered desk had torn it up, tossed it aside? What if it was ashes now? She had no other clue. If the card was lost, *she* was lost. "Help me find it. Help me find it." It was about the size of a calling-card, a little larger, very grimy, because she had carried it about in her shopping-bag for a long while. Here! This looked like it! Yes, this was it! No, it wasn't! Yes, it was. Yes! Yes! She had found it. She held it up close to the electric light.

Alfred Munn,
172 North Blank Street,
Boston, Mass.

She'd go to bed now. She'd go to sleep. "Thanks, oh, thanks," she said on her knees three minutes later. "Do please help me bring this business out all right."

Stella as well as Laurel was sleeping soundly and sweetly at dawn on the second morning.

CHAPTER XXII

1

Stella set forth in quest of 172 North Blank Street the next afternoon. She might have written, of course. If it had been a matter of less importance she would have written. When Ed had given her this address he had meant that she should write.

"Uncle Sam will find me here," he had told her. "Drop me a line sometime when the offspring's away and you're feeling lonesome."

That was over a year ago, when she had chanced to run across Ed one afternoon in the lobby of a moving-picture theater. She hadn't seen him since. She hadn't heard from him since. He might feel entirely different about her now. A year was an awfully long time. Perhaps he wouldn't want to marry her now. Perhaps he'd never really wanted to marry her. He had always laughed when he had suggested it, and she had always laughed back, when she had refused his crazy offers. For years it had been sort of a huge joke on both sides. She guessed Ed would be surprised to be taken seriously all of a sudden. She did hope he hadn't married anybody else. Not that she could imagine such a thing. Ed wasn't a bit the marrying kind, but just hoping so hard made her think of all sorts of catastrophes. Perhaps he'd moved away from Boston entirely. Perhaps he was dead, or perhaps—what if she wasn't attractive to him any more? She was a whole year older, and a whole year after you're forty—well!

He'd find her alimony attractive, anyway, she guessed. Ed hadn't been very successful in his various business ventures. But say—look here, there wouldn't be any alimony, would there, if she married again? Hadn't there been some such clause? She had never given it much thought because she had been so dead sure she never was going to marry again. Gracious, she hadn't thought of that. Well, never mind, she could contribute *something* in the way of funds. She had a savings-bank account amounting to over a thousand dollars. That wasn't to be sneezed at. Last time she had seen Ed, it looked to her as if he hadn't a bank-account amounting to anything.

"I'm sort of out of luck this year," he'd told her apologetically. (The lining of his overcoat had been frayed and ragged round the cuffs. He had caught her looking at it.) "But I can still give you a good time, little girl, just the same. See?" He had opened his overcoat. She had caught a glimpse of a bottle shining. He had patted it tenderly. "More where this comes from, too," he had winked, "but say, it's awful expensive stuff now. Awful! Dearer'n a woman! Prohibition has played the devil and all with my capital, Stella." No. Ed might not scorn her little nest-egg.

She became more and more convinced he might not as she approached the vicinity of the address on the card. She had never been down this way before. Why, it was slums—regular slums! North Blank Street was a narrow, roughly-cobbled sort of alley. There was a row of low brick houses on each side, dilapidated and out of repair. There was a dark damp look to the alley and a dark damp smell, too, that reminded Stella of underground cellar stairs. Unlike most of the other doorways in North Blank Street, 172 still had all three of its digits clinging to the battered brown paint. Stella, standing on the narrow sidewalk, reached up over the two front steps and knocked loudly just below the number. She knocked three times, then receiving no answer, turned the loose knob and walked in.

"Anybody here?" she called up the rickety stairway.

"What yer want?" A young woman of about twenty, with a mop of black bushy hair, cut short, stuck her head out of a door at the rear of the hall.

Stella told her.

"What do you want of *him?*" the young woman demanded eyeing Stella with interest.

"I want to see him on business."

"Ma," called the woman in a powerful voice. "Here's a lady wants to see Munn on business."

"Ma" came to have a look at Stella, too. Both mother and daughter stared at Stella with hard suspicious eyes. It didn't make Stella flush. She didn't blame them. It did look funny.

"He ain't here any more," crisply "Ma" told Stella.

"Oh, ain't he?" groaned Stella.

"No, he ain't. This is a respectable place. This ain't no dope-den."

"Do you know where he has gone?"

"Nope."

"I do, Ma. He's over at Liz Halloran's. She was tellin' me 'bout him."

Eagerly Stella turned toward the younger woman. "Say, take me there. Take me there *now*, I *got* to see him."

But she didn't see him. Not that day. Liz Halloran, a thin haggard old woman with no front teeth had told Stella, standing in her miserable black hole of a doorway (like the opening into the cavity of a decayed tooth, it was), that he wa'n't fit to be seen to-day. "He's just layin' there like dead to-day."

"How often does he get this way?" Stella inquired.

"Oh, off and on, I don't know! I don't keep track. Couldn't get no hooch. That's what done it."

"When do you think I could see him?"

"Oh, he'll be rousin' up to-morrow or the day after. He'll be real bright for a spell, too."

"I'll come day after to-morrow," said Stella.

2

An hour later, as Stella sat gazing out of the window of an electric car that was bearing her back to the apartment and Laurel, she kept saying to herself, grimly, doggedly, "I can stand it. I wasn't brought up in a pink-and-white nursery, thank

God! I shan't mind it after awhile. I'm tough as tripe. Anyhow, it's better than jumping off the Harvard Bridge."

3

Ten days later, nonchalantly to Laurel, Stella remarked one morning, "I shan't be here, most likely, when you get back this afternoon. Laurel." Laurel was attending business college daily now. "I've got an invitation for luncheon and the matinee."

"An invitation? From whom, mother?"

Stella smiled. "I haven't got so many admirers. I guess you can guess."

The color flooded to Laurel's cheeks. "Mother, not Mr. Munn! You haven't accepted an invitation from Mr. Munn!"

"I'd like to know why I haven't!"

"Knowing how I feel about him—how I dislike him."

"Gracious, Lollie! Honestly, it's funny! You act as if you were the mother, and I the child."

"Mother, you haven't been seeing that creature again, have you?"

"That creature! How you talk! Why, Laurel, Ed's a real nice man."

"I don't want to discuss him, mother. I don't want to hear you stand up for him. I don't see why you're bringing him up again. I thought we'd decided we'd drop him long ago."

"You mean *you* decided it. I never did. Mercy, I've got to have a little independence. With you away so much every day. Laurel, and nothing for me to do, I'd be a very foolish woman indeed, to allow a notion of yours to cheat me out of a little harmless entertainment."

Thus did Stella proceed. She mustn't marry Ed immediately, out of a clear sky, on top of the discussion with Laurel following her return from New York. Laurel might smell a rat. There must be no blundering this time. Ed must be slipped onto the field of action naturally, inadvertently. Funny how things worked around. That which Ed had been years ago between herself and her husband, through carelessness and indifference, *now, to-day*, through diligence and effort, she must make him become again, between herself and her child—an issue, a sore point, a bone of contention. Not until then would the time be ripe to marry Ed. Steadily, unswervingly, Stella set herself to her task.

It was easier than she had supposed. Laurel's hostility to Ed was so white-hot that even a reference to him kindled a controversy. Therefore Stella referred to him frequently in a light and inconsequential vein, laughing at Laurel's opposition. Not only did she refer to Ed, but she saw him; she made engagements with him; she kept engagements with him; she stayed out with him until after one o'clock on one occasion; failed to appear for supper, or to telephone, on another. One afternoon, defiantly, she established Ed in an armchair in the living-room of the apartment, and arranged that Laurel, due home from downtown, should find him when she came in. She repeated this a week later. Oh, it was too bad. She hated to watch the slow torture her procedure was to the child. But it couldn't be avoided. Somehow she must make her marriage to Ed seem logical.

Laurel's light laughter faded, disappeared; the soft light in her eyes hardened like a disillusioned lover's. Night after night she lay, on the extreme edge of the bed, beside her mother, silent and unrelenting, and drifted into an unrefreshing sleep. She grew years older.

One afternoon in early June, after a particularly difficult morning of argument with her mother about Alfred Munn (afterwards Stella had called good-bye to Lollie out of the front window, but she wouldn't answer), she returned to the apartment to find it empty. There was a note fastened to the handle of the oven-door on the gas-stove in the kitchen. Laurel discovered it when she went out to get some supper.

Dear Lollie [the note said]

I guess you won't be much surprised. I guess you've sort of seen the way the wind was blowing. Ed has wanted me to marry him for years, and as I hadn't any good reason not to now, I'll be Mrs. Alfred Munn when you read this. I would of told you all about it, but I knew how you felt about poor Ed, and it would only of meant more fuss.

Ed's got a grand job down in South America, and he's crazy to have me go down there with him. You know I never had much of a chance to travel, and it seems a big chance for me. So I'm jumping at it. We may be gone a year or two. I'll send you an address when we get one.

I've had this up my sleeve quite a long while, marrying Ed, I mean. You can't explain everything to a child. That was why I hoped you'd stay with your father. But when you didn't, of course I had to keep my promise to Ed just the same. It wouldn't of been fair if I didn't, and he wouldn't listen to anything else. He's been waiting for me all the time you've been growing up, and I won't say I haven't been waiting, too. I've tried my best to make you see Ed the way I do, these last weeks, but you just won't, so I've given up trying, and gone ahead and done what I think is right.

Ed and I will be back and close up the apartment, sometime before we sail. I guess we all three can fit in somehow. I expect you to be nice to him though, now he's your sort of father.

When you're out, leave the key under the mat, same as usual. Ed and I may be back anytime.

Love from

Your Mother

P.S. It was too bad you wouldn't turn round this morning and wave good-bye.

4

Stephen and Helen, returning late from town the next evening to their summer home on Long Island (they had just moved down), were surprised upon entering the hall to hear a sound in the living-room—a chair suddenly shoved back, soft swift foot-steps. They stepped to the door of the room.

It was Laurel! She still wore her hat. Her suitcase still stood by the chair where she had been sitting.

"Why, Laurel! Why, my dear!" exclaimed Stephen, exclaimed Helen, both hastening toward her.

They met her in the middle of the room. They kissed her—both of them. She returned neither caress.

"What is it. Laurel?"

She was very white. Her eyes had a startled, frightened expression.

"I've come back," she said quietly. "I'll stay now, if you want me—if you'll take me." She made no gesture, her expression did not change. There was fixed calmness about her as hard as adamant.

"What has happened, Laurel?"

"I've been put out. I've no other place to go but here. If you don't want me—if—"

"You know we want you!" exclaimed Helen. "Dear child! Come. Sit down. You're tired. You've had a long journey. Why, you haven't even taken off your hat."

Laurel remarked, not moving, making no sign of response, "Mother has married," and after a pause, "Mother has married." It was like the wailing of a tolling bell.

Stephen said, "Oh!"

Helen said, "I shall take off your hat myself." And quickly, deftly, she removed the small toque and laid it aside on a table. Laurel standing listless and indifferent beneath her administrating hands. "There! That's better. Why, you must have been waiting a long time," lightly she went on. "You ought to have telephoned when you reached New York."

"She's married Alfred Munn, father," said Laurel to Stephen, and after a pause again, "She's married Alfred Munn," as if the tolling bell had changed its note.

Helen touched Laurel gently on her shoulder.

"Come upstairs to your room now," she said.

"We'll talk about it in the morning. I'm going to give you some food and put you to bed now."

"Father, you knew him. You couldn't stand him either. I understand now. I see. Of course you couldn't live with her. I couldn't live with her myself."

"Don't take it so hard, Lollie," said Stephen.

"Don't call me Lollie!"

"Don't suffer so, dear."

"I'm not suffering. I'm not suffering at all."

"Will you bring up Laurel's suitcase, Stephen?" asked Helen. "Come, Laurel." She slipped a steadying arm through Laurel's. "You must go to bed now."

5

They mounted together to the lavender-tinted room, which Helen had told Stella last summer would be Laurel's. ("She'll be sleeping in that, I suppose," Stella had remarked, from the threshold of the room, as she had gazed upon the bed, fresh and crisp with muslin valance and canopy. "I'll be thinking of her in that," and she had wiped her eyes.) Helen recalled the scene, the voice, the tears, as now she set about preparing with her own hands the waiting bed for that absent woman's child.

Behind her Laurel was standing, here, as downstairs, impassive and indifferent, just where Helen had left her when she withdrew her arm that had guided her hither.

"Come. We'll undress now."

"Mother has married a man I hate." Laurel took up the interrupted motif again. "She's married a man she knew I hated. She has chosen him instead of me. She has married Ed Munn. He's awful. He's horrible. An animal is clean beside him. And she likes him. My mother! She's fond of him. She's been waiting for years to marry him."

"Oh, no. Laurel."

"Yes, she has. I know. Read that. Read that."

She drew her mother's letter from the front of her dress, and passed it to Helen.

"Do you want me to?"

Laurel nodded.

Helen sat down on the foot of the bed and opened the folded sheets. The letter had been written by Stella in pencil, carelessly, in haste apparently. It was read by Helen slowly, painstakingly, as if it had been written in blood. She read it twice. Afterwards she looked up at Laurel.

Laurel gave a little shrug. "You see."

"Yes, I think I see," said Helen slowly.

"I thought it was for me she gave father the divorce, so I could come and be with you. And it made me glad. It made me proud. But I was mistaken. It was for *him*. It was to marry him, that creature. He's her kind, down underneath. She is his kind. She chose him. Father's right. The others are right. I'm the one who's been wrong about her all this time. Oh, Mrs. Morrison, she's killed my respect for her, and she knew she would—we have been quarreling about that man for weeks—she knew she would! But she didn't care. She didn't care." Thus pitilessly Laurel sunk her sharp young teeth into the hand that hurt.

Helen murmured, "Greater love hath no woman than this."

Laurel didn't hear her. "I'm very unhappy, Mrs. Morrison," she stated dully.

Helen replied, "You are very tired. You need sleep. Does it fasten behind?"

Very tenderly, as if she were handling a precious body from which life had departed, Helen unfastened Laurel's dress. She slipped it off her shoulders. It fell to the floor. Bare-armed, bare-shouldered, a shiver ran through Laurel—like a breeze rippling a docile sail. Helen put both arms about her shelteringly.

"Oh, Mrs. Morrison! Mrs. Morrison!" Laurel cried out at the touch, and suddenly the storm broke, the long withheld flood burst, the boat tossed, the sail strained and pulled. But Helen's hand was firm and steady on the tiller. She held Laurel close.

"That's right. Cry. You'll feel better. Cry. Cry."

Later in the morning, she would show Laurel the rainbow.

6

When Helen went downstairs half an hour later she found Stephen in the big room waiting for her. He had been smoking ever since she left him—the ash-tray bore witness to that—and walking up and down the room. The two Sheraton armchairs had been carelessly shoved out of their usual places to clear a straight path from the fireplace to the window. As Helen entered the room she replaced one of the chairs, apparently unaware of Stephen's agitation.

"Well?" said Stephen at sight of her.

Helen looked up at him and smiled.

"She's asleep," she said, and started to replace the other chair.

"Poor child. Poor child!" Stephen broke out in a tone that was almost a groan. "It's torture to me to think my own child should have to bear the burden of my mistake like this."

Immediately Helen crossed the room to Stephen. He was standing by the fireplace staring down upon the unlighted logs.

"Why, Stephen," she said gently, reassuringly, "she'll be better in the morning. It's hard to see her suffer, I know, but it's mostly from shock. In a day or two she'll see clearer."

"See clearer!" Stephen exclaimed bitterly.

"Why, Helen, don't you know who the man is whom Stella has married?" he inquired.

"Yes, I know."

"Well!" he shrugged. "Don't you see it justifies our suspicions? For Laurel's sake I hoped they might never be justified. I didn't want the evidence which Morley Smith brought to my attention several years ago forced before me for consideration again. For Laurel's sake I've hoped there was that spark of controlling decency in her mother that wouldn't accept intimate relations with a man like Munn, even though she could endure his society. That hope has gone. This act of hers has destroyed it."

Helen gazed at Stephen and shook her head slowly, wonderingly. "You, too?" she murmured.

He didn't hear her.

"To think," he went on, still bitterly, still despairingly—" to think she chose, of her free will, existence with a man like Munn after Laurel had given up everything to be with her! To think she was willing to allow her child's wonderful love for her, her child's wonderful loyalty to her, to become shame and scorn! To think of it!"

"Yes, to think of it!" repeated Helen, softly, starry-eyed.

"What do you mean?" demanded Stephen, looking at her sharply. Why did she speak like that?

Helen replied slowly, distinctly, looking at Stephen. "Laurel is here. She is here to stay. Who has accomplished it?"

He didn't answer her—just looked at her a moment, then shook his head, and gazed down again into the dead logs in the fireplace.

Helen placed her hand very lightly on one of his folded arms.

"She has always been judged just by appearances," she said in a low earnest tone, "valued just by impressions. Some people go through life with nobody seeing the good in them because of the blurred, unbeautiful reflection they give back. 'Now we see through a glass, darkly.' I think it means in a mirror indistinctly—a dim, dull, imperfect mirror. It seems as if everybody saw Stella 'through a glass, darkly,' Stephen, even her own child to-night."

She withdrew her hand. Stephen replied, still staring into the lifeless fireplace, "I lived with her. I knew her."

"Oh, but, Stephen—"

"My dear, my dear," he interrupted tenderly, fondly. How strange that Helen should be the one to try to show him the good in Stella! "You see with the eyes of an angel."

"No, I don't," said Helen prosaically. "Simply, with the eyes of a mother, Stephen."

CHAPTER XXIII

1

The proof that Helen's rainbow was real—no illusion, no mirage—came in the form of a shadow the following fall. It is dark by five o'clock in the afternoon in New York in November. Returning one late afternoon with Laurel from a tea, where with a dozen other girls of her own age she had been assisting (nominally assisting, but really, like, the others, simply submitting herself to the demands of a crowd of young men blocking the entrance to the room cleared for dancing), Helen observed, as she left the car and crossed the sidewalk to her own door a shadow, a stationary shadow cast upon the sidewalk.

There was an alley ran down to a rear entrance at the spot where the shadow fell. There was a light a few feet down the alley. The light was dim. But in spite of the unrecognizable shape of the blurred outline of the shadow, it had startled Helen into a sudden suspicion.

Once inside the house she had mounted to an upper room, where there was no light, where she would attract no attention, and raising the drawn shade in a bay-window, gazed down into the alley, just back of the spot where the shadow had lain.

There was no one there now.

Quickly she turned and raised the shade of the window opposite. This window looked toward the rear of the house and commanded a view of the narrow, ill-lighted tunnel, along which towered the high, spiked walls of several scores of rear entrances. Proceeding along this tunnel, closely skirting the high spiked walls, Helen could make out the outline of a woman—a short stocky woman. Twice she stopped and looked back at Helen's roof.

Helen's first impulse was to raise the window—to call. She hesitated. It might not be she. The Jolley lights were dim and far away. And if it proved to be, was it wise to establish communication with her when she was taking such pains to avoid it? No. Laurel's mother knew best. The minute she became even a recognized shadow in her child's life she ran the risk of defeating the object of her sacrifice.

Laurel believed her mother was somewhere in South America and submitted without protest to the futility of locating her, submitted, too, without protest to the futility of breaking her determined silence. If she even suspected that her mother was near by in hiding somewhere, watching, looking on in the old eager anxious way, she would not be content till she had found her; and if she found her, and if it proved, indeed, that it was as Helen had persuaded her to hope, that her mother had married Alfred Munn for *her* sake, as likely as not—no, more likely than not—Laurel would insist upon returning to her mother under whatever circumstances. She was capable of it.

Laurel was almost her old self now. She smiled again, laughed again, shone and glowed again over old delights and joys, over new delights and joys. Occasionally the troubled, hurt look would steal across her features. And at such times Helen knew that Laurel was doubting again, suffering again, longing to be brought face to face with actual proof of her mother's high motive. But it was better that the doubts should remain than that her mother's act of self-abnegation should be robbed of its fruit. Helen pulled down the window-shade and went downstairs.

It was not until she was in her own room with her door closed, with the window draperies drawn close, seated before her dressing-table brushing her shining hair, that she thought about the alimony. Stephen had felt just as she had when she first broached the subject to him, that of course Laurel's mother must live as she was accustomed to live whatever had been the terms of the divorce. So far, however, Stephen had failed to establish communication of any sort with Stella. She had left her Boston apartment as a bird a nest, and the route she had taken was as trackless, as scentless as the bird's through the air.

She had left no trace of any kind, an3rwhere—not even with her lawyer, not even with her bank from which she had withdrawn her account. Since her marriage to Alfred Munn not a single check of Stephen's had been cashed by her. Not a single check had even been received by her. They were returned to Stephen unopened, with the recurring announcement "Not known" in the corner of the envelope.

Helen looked into eyes that were troubled as she gazed into the mirror before her. "It might have been she! She might need money! Should I have called, after all?" Usually Helen could depend upon her first instinct in regard to such matters. Her first instinct had said, "No." By the time Helen's hair was rolled again in its soft knot at the back of her head, her eyes had lost their troubled look. Of what importance was money to a woman who was willing to pay for her child's happiness with the child's love if it menaced that happiness? And communication, even secret communication, *would* menace it. It was far safer that she, Helen herself, should remain in doubt as to Stella's hiding-place. It was necessary to be so very honest with Laurel. Helen, too, must not know but that Stella was beyond call in some far country. She mustn't allow herself even to look for the shadow again. She mustn't tell any one about it. Oh, Stella should not be defeated, if Helen could help it.

2

But others were not as protective of the shadow. That same evening, a few hundred miles away, in a dainty and exquisite drawing-room in Milhampton, Massachusetts, four women in dainty and exquisite gowns stood before an open fire, stirring black coffee with tiny gold spoons in tiny porcelain cups. Their motions were as dainty and exquisite as the room, as their gowns. So, too, were their voices and their accents.

They chatted lightly, inconsequently, touching now one subject, now another, like humming-birds passing from one flower to another, whiling the time away in as amusing a manner as possible till the men should join them for bridge.

"Oh, yes," sighed Phyllis, "one sees the name of Laurel Dallas in the New York society columns frequently now. The new Mrs. Dallas is doing her best for the child. I call it awfully decent."

"Oh, it shouldn't be difficult," said Myrtle, "with her social position."

"And the child is really very pretty," Mrs. Kay Bird contributed. "That helps. There isn't a suggestion of her mother in her."

"How fortunate! What has become of that dreadful woman, anyhow?" asked Rosamond.

"Oh! Haven't you heard, my dear?" Mrs. Kay Bird raised slim bare shoulders in surprise. "Myrtle, haven't you told Rosamond you saw the poor thing in New York last time you were down?"

"I haven't seen Rosamond. I returned only night before last."

"Oh, well, tell her. Do. Prepare yourself for a choice bit, Rosamond."

Rosamond placed her empty coffee-cup on the mantel and curled up cozily in a corner of the cushioned divan.

"Tell me first, please, about the divorce. You know I was in Europe all last year. I didn't get a bit of the gossip, and there was no account of it in the papers sent me."

"There was no account of it in any of the papers," Mrs. Kay Bird informed her. "Stephen Dallas obtained his divorce without even a flutter of a struggle, which does not surprise any of us who know the facts. We agree with the former Mrs. Dallas, it would have been very unwise for her to contest her husband's charges."

"Oh, did he make charges?"

"That's the usual proceeding, my dear."

"And what were they?"

"Well, he lives in New York. You know the New York laws, I suppose."

Shrugs. Soft laughter.

"And the child," Phyllis added, "was put immediately into the custody of her father."

"Oh, dear! You never can tell what a woman is at the core, can you?" deplored Rosamond. "Why, when we first knew Stella Dallas she didn't seem really *bad*, though she always was awfully ordinary, of course. Even after that time you saw her at Belcher's Beach, Myrtle, I couldn't believe she'd really fallen as low as that. I thought you must be mistaken."

"Tell Rosamond about New York, Myrtle," said Mrs. Kay Bird.

Myrtle placed her coffee-cup on the mantel; too, and extending a slender hand to a silver box near by, selected a cigarette.

"I saw Stella Dallas in New York, Rosamond," she announced impressively. "I saw her down near Washington Square. I was down that way seeing a friend of mine who has the most fascinating studio in an old stable. I saw Stella Dallas with the Munn man again! They seemed to be on quite familiar terms."

"Did you, really?"

"It was not a pretty sight, I assure you. The Munn man was intoxicated, I think. Anyway, she had to help him walk. I won't say *she* was intoxicated, too, because I don't *know* that she was, but she didn't look *right*. And she has coarsened—oh, terribly, girls! A woman of that sort always does. And has lost her self-respect as to appearances, as is also usual, I believe. Her clothes were really shabby and *his* were in actual rags. City's dregs—that's all I could think of as I looked at them—city's dregs."

"How unpleasant," shuddered Rosamond.

"Disgusting, was my word," said Phyllis.

"Revolting, was mine," laughed Mrs. Kay Bird. Myrtle extended a languid arm. "Please pass me the matches, Phyllis. Thank you, dear. She's a depraved woman, girls," she announced. "Always was, and always will be. Oh, here come the men." She flipped her match into the open fire. "Let's cut for partners."

3

Miss Laurel Dallas was to be formally presented to New York Society at a tea given at the home of her parents, Mr. and Mrs. Stephen Dallas, on the afternoon of November the twenty-first, from four until seven-thirty o'clock. Several luncheons in her honor were scheduled for the week following the tea; also several dinners. The names of Miss Dallas's various hostesses were mentioned. So was the fact that Brightswood, her parents' summer home at Green Hills, Long Island, was to be opened over the Thanksgiving holiday, and filled with a house-party, including a number of this season's debutantes. One of the most anticipated affairs of the season was the ball to be given for Miss Dallas in early January. So the papers said; so the various society columns repeated and repeated again. "Miss Dallas is one of the most popular debutantes of the season, etc., etc." ("oh, she'll like that," thought Helen to herself), "whose picture is printed below" ("she'll cut that out," she smiled).

Helen avoided newspaper notoriety usually. Stephen wondered at her willingness to allow Laurel's name to appear frequently in print, and in conspicuous print.

He wondered at another sudden oddity of Helen's. The servants wondered at it, too. In fact it was one of the servants who brought it to his attention. Twice, lately, upon arriving home in the late afternoon, he had noticed that the shades in the house were not all drawn. He had been able to look into Helen's room on the second floor, and see Laurel seated under the light, at the piano, playing. He spoke to the parlor-maid.

"I know, sir. It hardly seems safe, sir. But it's Mrs. Dallas's orders, sir."

Later to Stephen Helen explained, "But it looks so pretty from the street. Why shut in all our loveliness? I'll run the risk of burglars."

Even on the afternoon of Laurel's tea, Helen ordered the shades raised. She went even further. With her own hands she pulled back the lace curtains in the bay-window where she and Laurel were going to stand to receive their guests.

"It looks out only on the alley," she shrugged.

4

It rained on the morning of Laurel's tea. It rained in torrents.

"Gracious, don't it pour!" exclaimed Stella for the dozenth time to the woman next to her, and for the dozenth time to herself, "'Twon't make any difference, though. They've all got limousines." Then out loud again, "Gracious, don't it pour!"

Every few minutes she looked up from the machine which she had been feeding with coarse white cambric all the morning, and gazed anxiously out of the streaked window beside her toward the building opposite, against the dark background of which she could see the rain sweeping.

About noon she exclaimed, "Say, it looks lights—er! Say, don't it look lighter to you?" Then, "It is letting up. It looks to me as though it was letting up a little." And finally, "Gosh, it's going to clear off!" And it did!

At five o'clock that afternoon, when Stella, with a hundred or so other women, emerged from the big black building through the little opening at the bottom (like the opening cut at the bottom of a big black hogshead; every little while a thin dark stream of humanity would pour out of the building; it housed over a hundred small factories), the air was clear and crisp and cold. Stella stepped out of the little stream, once on the sidewalk, stood still, and gazed straight up. Yes! It was all right! The stars were shining like mad, up there, at the top of the canyon, beyond the dizzy precipices.

CHAPTER XXIV

1

This was Stella's fifth week in the shirt-waist factory. She must be getting used to it, she guessed. She didn't feel a bit tired to-night. If it wasn't so late, she wouldn't have minded walking the whole way. Laurel would be all dressed now. People would be just beginning to arrive. Gracious, she must hustle. But she'd simply got to go over to the room a jiffy first. It wouldn't take long. She had locked the door on Ed, but she always got feeling nervous after a whole day's absence during the times he was bad.

Stella was pretty sure that this landlady guessed what was the matter with Ed, but she could never feel certain how many of the roomers were "on." There are roomers who find it helps to pass away the time to make a fuss over a thing in the house like Ed. Stella didn't want to have to move again. This landlady had been awfully decent about the rent since she had got a job. Gracious, but it hadn't taken that thousand dollars long to fade away. It cost something to keep yourself and a sick man—who has to have a "particular kind of medicine"—going these days, though you didn't buy yourself a single rag, nor spend a cent on theaters, or the movies, or desserts.

Everything was all right at the room, thank heaven! Stella stopped only long enough to light the candle placed upon a chair by the door, hold it aloft a moment, and gaze down upon the double bed. Ed was still there, still harmless, breathing heavily, inert and consciousless.

There wasn't much furniture in the room besides the bed—a commode, a table, and three chairs. One of the chairs was an old Morris chair. It was worth all the rest of the furniture put together to Stella. It was Stella's bed. The back of it was let down so that it extended on the same level as the seat. There was a blanket folded over one arm, and Laurel's old worn-out, out-grown coon coat over the other. There was Ed's cheap suitcase and a pillow piled up on one of the remaining chairs, and this was shoved up close to the end of the makeshift bed to lengthen it. Surprising how well you can sleep on an old Morris chair if you work hard daytimes, or even on the floor if you get cramped. It's all a matter of getting used to it.

The candle spit and sputtered as if it objected to the scene it lighted. Stella didn't blame it. It wasn't especially beautiful. Stella would be busy in the room till midnight "redding it up," when she got back. She did like a neat room to sleep in. It looked like somebody's back yard just at present, with all Ed's clothes and a few of her own hanging up to dry on a cord she'd stretched back and forth from wall to wall. Ed's unwashed breakfast dishes were on the floor beside the bed. He'd roused enough to take the nourishment she'd left for him apparently.

She blew the candle out, put it back upon the chair, closed the door and locked it, descended four flights of bare stairway, and went out again beneath the stars.

2

Stella could have spoken to Laurel if the window had been open. She was as near to her as that! She could see her as clearly as if she had been inside. How lucky the curtains had been forgotten again. How lucky this particular window had been selected in which to stand to meet the guests! Gracious, but the flowers were lovely. Stella had never seen so many in one room in her life. They must smell like a funeral. Those flowers had been sent to Laurel by her friends and admirers. She certainly had a few! The papers hadn't exaggerated any, Stella guessed. Laurel, standing in the midst of her garden, was like a great big flower herself.

Stella had never seen her look more beautiful. Her dress was white, chiffon, she thought, made over something silvery, that made her shine as if there was dew all over her. No dress Stella had ever provided for Laurel could *touch* this. One of those artists, whose address only the few and fortunate possess, had made this fairy gown for Laurel, Stella guessed. My, how she became it! Gosh! She looked like a regular queen to-night!

She carried a sheaf of white orchids on her left arm. Through the chiffon ribbon that tied the flowers Stella caught a glimpse of something that looked like diamonds sparkling on Laurel's wrist! A moment later, as Laurel turned a little, she caught a glimpse of what was clasped about her throat. Pearls! A string of pearls! "Oh, Lollie! Oh, dear, *dear* Lollie!" She had come into her own! She was being crowned in her rightful kingdom at last!

Stella left the window for a moment and stole to the front corner of the house. Yes. There was an awning running from the front door to the street; there was a man in livery at the curbings shouting numbers; there was a long row of automobiles on both sides of the street, reaching far away in both directions. All for Lollie!

Stella glanced up. Every window was faintly aglow. Through one of them that must have been open she could hear music, dance music—piano, violins, saxophone, and drum. All for Lollie! She went back again to her window in the alley.

Everything was as it ought to be. Even Lollle's mother was as *she* ought to be—also wearing a gown made by an artist, also wearing pearls, also beautiful, also queenly. My! Mrs. Morrison was made for the part. As the guests approached her, Stella observed that there was that look of high approval and homage in their eyes that *should* be in the eyes of everybody who shook hands with Laurel's mother. Stella observed, too, that when the guests shook hands with Laurel—with the little queen herself—there was more than high approval in their eyes. There was sudden and spontaneous pleasure, and afterwards murmured words of praise.

For more than an hour Stella stood in the shadow of an electric pole, and feasted and feasted. A policeman finally discovered her and told her to move along.

"All right," she replied cheerfully, "I will. I'm ready now. I've seen enough." For the instant before she had seen straight into Laurel's heart for a fleeting ten seconds!

Laurel didn't know it. Laurel had no idea that her mother's eyes were in the depth of the mirror she had gazed into, at her own reflection.

It had happened like this. Stella had seen it all. She had observed the first faint flush of color creep down the back of Laurel's neck as a young man had rushed up to her, and eagerly taken her hand in his, in greeting. Apparently the young man had asked Laurel to dance with him. As yet she hadn't left her post in the bay-window. She hesitated, glanced around the room—the guests were beginning to thin out—then accepted the invitation.

Still flushed, her neck was still pink beneath her pearls, she looked about her for a place to lay her flowers, spied the window-sill, took three steps toward Stella, and laid her flowers down, almost as if in Stella's lap; paused, raised her eyes. The window was just in front of her. The clear plate-glass with the light behind it was a perfect mirror. Laurel gave herself a long look. Six feet away Stella caught that look, hugged it to her close. She had never seen anything so dazzling, so luminous, in all her life before! It wasn't meant for her. It wasn't meant for any one on earth. It was like catching a bit of shooting star—of shooting heaven.

The young man to whom Laurel gave her hand a moment later—the young god who had made Laurel look at herself like that—was none other than Richard Grosvenor. Stella would have known him anywhere.

"That's all right, then, too," she murmured.

3

"Did not I tell you to get along there?"

"Yes, sir. I'm going. I was only seeing how pretty the young lady was."

www.ingramcontent.com/pod-product-compliance
Lightning Source LLC
Chambersburg PA
CBHW032253020726
47495CB00001B/86

* 9 7 9 8 8 8 0 9 1 8 8 3 6 *